Jonathan Mitchel

The parable of the ten virgins opened & applied

Jonathan Mitchel

The parable of the ten virgins opened & applied

ISBN/EAN: 9783337126414

Printed in Europe, USA, Canada, Australia, Japan

Cover: Foto ©Andreas Hilbeck / pixelio.de

More available books at **www.hansebooks.com**

THE
PARABLE
OF THE
Ten Virgins
OPENED & APPLIED:

Being the Substance of divers

SERMONS

on *Matth.* 25. 1,---13.

Wherein, the Difference between the Sincere Christian and
the most Refined Hypocrite, the Nature and Characters of Saving
and of Common Grace, the Dangers and Diseases incident to
most flourishing Churches or Christians, and other Spiritual
TRUTHS of greatest importance, are clearly
discovered, and practically Improved,

BY
THOMAS SHEPARD
late Worthy and Faithfull Pastor of the Church of Christ at
Cambridge in NEW-ENGLAND.

Now Published from the Authours own Notes, at the desires of
many, for the common Benefit of the Lords people,

By { *Jonathan Mitchell* Minister at *Cambridge*,
Tho. Shepard, Son to the Reverend Author,
now Minister at *Charles-Town* } in NEW-ENGLAND.

LUKE 21. 36.
*Watch ye therefore and pray alwaies, that ye may be accounted worthy to escape all these things
that shall come to passe, and to stand before the Son of man.*

LONDON,
Printed by *J.H.* for *John Rothwell,* at the Fountain in Goldsmiths-Row in Cheap-side,
and *Samuel Thomson* at the Bishops Head in *Pauls* Church-yard. 1660.

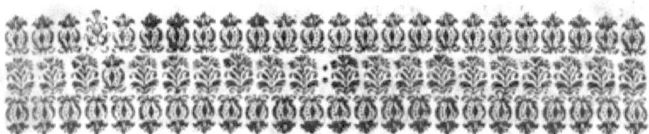

TO THE
READER,
And Especially to the Inhabitants of
CAMBRIDGE
IN
NEW-ENGLAND.

THat to make sure of Life Eternal, is the one necessary Businesse, that we Sons of death have to do in this world, and without which, all our time here is worse than lost, every enlightned mind will easily acknowledge. This present life being by the Rule of it, appointed but to this end, to be preparation-time, spent in a continual care to make ready, that we might have a good meeting with him who shall be seen in this Aire one day. And whether we look up to Heaven, or down to Hell; whether we reflect upon our own immortal souls, or turn our eyes toward the Greatnesse and Goodnesse of that God in Christ with whom we have to do; whether we pace over the time between this and Judgment-day, or send our thoughts to view the Eternity that is to follow after. All things put a Necessity, a Solemnity, a Glory upon this work.

But, *Difficilia quæ Pulchra:* It is one of the Oracles uttered by our Lord with his own mouth, *Strait is the Gate, and narrow is the way that leadeth unto life, and few there be that find it.* It is not so easie a thing to get to Heaven, nor so broad a way thither, as the slight and loose Opinions of some, and Practises of more would make it, nor as the carnal hearts of all would have it. Though that (if it be examined) is the common Scope of all Erroneous Conceits (and how restlesly

have

have the corrupt minds of men laboured therein in all ages, and do in these our daies) to widen the way to Life, to break down the Boundaries of this narrow Path, and make it broader than ever God made it. Mans carnal heart finds it self pinioned and straitned in the way (the good old way of effectual Faith and obedience) that God hath laid out; hence it breaks out on this hand and on that, and will rather pluck up the ancient Land marks of Gods Truth, than not make it broader. The Gospel will not afford men a way broad enough, unlesse the Law be quite removed (not only as a Covenant, but as a commanding Rule of Life too) and laid flat like an old Hedge, that they may go over it at pleasure, and not attend it any further than their spirit listeth. Justification by Faith is too narrow a path, unlesse they may be justified before and without Faith, it is not free enough; they complain of it as if it laid them under a Covenant of works. Conditional Promises are of too straight a size, they must be all absolute, and give us peace without any qualification in us, or else they are not large enough. To be solicitous about Sanctification and inherent Grace, is too troublesom; to seek God diligently in the use of all means, in a daily and hearty performance of holy Duties, in a strict Sanctifying of Sabbaths, in constant watchfulnesse, &c. this must be laid by, as a Legal Businesse. And if the Spirit immediatly will act us and carry us in a Bed of ease to Heaven, without troubling us to act and strive, well and good; otherwise men will shake hands with the power of Godlinesse, and run a drift before their own Corruptions. But when all Stones are turned, the way to Heaven is and will be found to be a straight way: Truth hath said, it is so, God hath laid it out so; and it is not all the Notions of men that will make it otherwise. And hence those solemn Counsels of the Scripture, *Work out your salvation with fear and trembling, Give all diligence to make all sure, Strive to enter in at the Straight Gate, So run that you may obtain,* &c. though they be little attended by the loosenesse of these times, yet they are of endlesse Moment and use, and had need be awfully regarded by all that love their everlasting peace.

He therefore that is in earnest about this great businesse, will be glad of any good help to guide him in this way, this straight way to Life. And though there be many choice helps herein already extant, in the precious Labours of sundry of the Lords Faithful Servants, for which this Age hath cause on bended Knees to blesse the Lord, and which will be such a testimony against the wantonnesse thereof, as it will never be able to answer: Yet of those that do clearly, particularly, livelily and searchingly discover and mark out this straight way, with the several practical turns thereof, and shew where they that miss of the end at last, do turn out of it, although they go far therein; of those that Pilot us, when we come into the narrow Channel, unto the very point of entrance into life, and shew us the Rocks and Shoals on either hand distinctly; of these (I say) there is not too great a number. For to speak any good and useful Truths, is good and commendable;

dable; but yet it is another and a further matter to hold the Candle to the poor people of God (even to the meanest) to light them to Heaven, or to take the soul by the hand, and lead it from step to step through all the difficulties, deceits and turnings at which the closest Hypocrites do misse their way and lose themselves; and to do this so convincingly, throughly and distinctly, as that the secrets of hearts may be made manifest, the secure self-deceiver discovered and awakened, and yet the humble upright Christian confirmed and encouraged.

In this Skill and Work, as the Author of the following Sermons, was known to be among the first Three; so these Lectures of his, up-on *the Parable of the Virgins*, have been esteemed to excel in this kind; having left such a relish upon the Hearers, as that they have not forgotten the Taft of them to this day. It hath therefore been the instant desire of many that heard them, and of some that have but heard of them, that they might be imparted to the Publick. And surely both the Subject and the manner of handling it is such, being wholly upon those things wherein the heart and life of Religion lies, that we cannot disapprove of their Opinions, who have so earnestly desired it. All the Sermons and Books that speak to the heart of Religion are little enough to feed that, and keep life there, especially in this languishing and dying Age; wherein though there wants not common light and outward Profession, yet losse of Love and inward deadnesse are as common. The work being somwhat lengthy, and fitting Scribes not easily attainable in this Wildernesse, it hath occasioned this delay hitherto. But we hope it will now be neither unacceptable nor unseasonable.

These Sermons are now transcribed by industrious and intelligent persons, and have been carefully reviewed and corrected. They are written out of the Authors own Notes, which he prepared for preaching (only about a Sheet himself wrote out in his life-time, having thoughts it seems of yielding to their desires who were earnest for their publishing) by means whereof, though the Reader will often meet with Curtnesse of expression, and though some lively passages that were uttered in preaching may be wanting, yet you will have this benefit to have much in a little room. It may also easily be observed that not curiosity of words, but weight of things was here studied by, and flowed from the heart and pen of the Author, which yet produceth the best and truest, *i. e.* a real Rhetorick. In summe, although many imperfections incident to such post-humous Editions cannot be wanting, yet we doubt not but the work will speak for it self, to the intelligent and serious Reader.

We are not ignorant that there be some who somwhat differ from this our Author in the accommodation of this Parable, and Analysis of some part of the Context, referring it to the times about the expected calling of the *Jews* (and if so, the substance of the work may be accounted to be in a more than ordinary manner proper and seasonable for

these

these times) But therein every man is left free to his own further disquisitions. Neither is it for the sake of the bare exposition (much lesse Chronical Accomodation) of the Text so much, that we publish these things (in that kind the Labours of others do abound) but for the spiritual, practical, lively, soul-searching truths and applications thereof that are therein contained, the substance of which Truths the impartial Reader will easily acknowledge to be clear both from this and from other Scriptures.

These Sermons preached by the Author, in a weekly Lecture, were begun in *June* 1636. and ended in *May* 1640. In which time there was a Leaven of *Antinomian* and *Familistical* opinions stirring in the Country, as the world hath already in Print been informed : By occasion whereof the Reader will meet with sundry passages tending to reprove and refute some of those conceits and to establish the contrary truth ; which we have not expunged, but let them passe mostly as we found them ; seeing it is no more then the world already knows that there were such things then among us ; and though that storm be (as to it's open influence) comfortably blown over with us, yet the like errours are (if not latent among some here) spread elsewhere by the New Lights of these times, whence these helps against them are still needful. And we doubt not but the substance of the Truth here defended by our Author will stand and abide the Trial. Yea I suppose I may freely take liberty to say, that among the many excellencies wherewith the Lord endowed this precious instrument of his, this was none of the least, that God taught him, and helped him to teach others the true middle way of the Gospel between the Legalist on the one hand, and the Antinomian (or loose Gospeller) on the other, with much and sweet clearnesse, as was evident in the whole course and way of his preaching, and may in some measure appear both in his Books formerly printed, and in the following Sermons. Other passages also of special application to this Country and to those first times of it , we willingly permit to passe the Presse, because they may be profitable to others in like cases elsewhere, and of special benefit to the *New-English* Reader. For why should we not desire and hope that the sutable solemn counsels and warnings here given to these Churches by this *Seer in Israel*, in reference to the main matters of life and godlinesse, may now be of living, awakening and soul-instructing use to them (Oh that it may be *!*) unto many Generations *!*

Reader, if thou comest hither to carp and cavil, or to criticise upon each circumstantial imperfection, this work is not for thy turn ; but if thou bringest with thee a serious and humble heart, desirous to have thy soul searched to the quick, the sores thereof lanced, thy spiritual work and way directed, and the interest of thy eternal peace furthered ; if thou desirest to walk with God in good earnest, and escaping all the snares of a flight and flumbring Generation, to stand before the Son of man with comfort in the day of his Glory, then maist thou here find that that will sute thee, and which thou wilt blesse the Lord for, even

words

The Epistle to the Reader.

words that are as Goads and Nails fastned by this Master of Assemblies, given from that one and chief Shepherd. The Lord fix and fasten them in all our hearts, that abiding and being engrafted there, they may be instrumental to further our Salvation, that neither deficiency in the main, nor sloathful security, may hinder us from our desired end; but when that chief Shepherd and that Heavenly Bridegroom, who now sends to us by so many Servants and Messages of his, both in Word and Writing, shall appear himself *in the Glory of his Father, and of all his holy Angels*, we also may *receive a Crown of Glory that fadeth not away*, and (for the last consummation of this happy Marriage) may go home with him to his Fathers House, there to abide in his Rest, in the *Fulnesse of his joy*, and drink down his *Pleasures for evermore.*

And you that somtimes were the Flock of this Shepherd, and have heard these things from the lively voice of this Soul-melting Preacher, whom you never can forget; let it be a welcom Providence to have these Truths thus revived to you, and put into your hands, that he who is dead, may yet speak to you and yours. Get them into your Houses to read, nay, into your Hearts to feed upon, as a choice and precious Treasure. And let them still be a living and continual warning to you to watch and keep alive the power of Godlinesse, the daily practise of working *out your Salvation with fear and trembling*, the love of the Truth, the hatred of every false way, the esteem and improvement of Gods Ordinances, and the true, humble, heavenly Life of Faith in Christ Jesus.

Jonathan Mitchel.

To

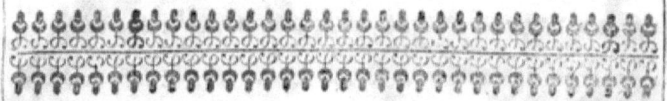

To the READER.

IF thou art one who knowest what 'tis to be serious in the great businesß of providing for Eternity, 'tis very probable thou maist be no stranger to the Name of this Reverend Author, now with God, whose Name in both the Englands is as an oyntment poured forth; and then thou wilt be eagerly desirous to peruse these following Sermons, in tendency to the further increasing thy stock of spiritual oyl, and when thou hast read them, and suckt forth the sweetneß and nourishment contained in them, and by the assistance of the holy Spirit turned them into good and healthfull nutriment to thy soul, we question not but it will inhance the Authors worth in thy thoughts and estimation. But perhaps thou hast never lighted on any of those Flowers which this Holy man hath planted in Gods garden, and then we are confident thou wilt meet with such savoury sweetneß in this Discourse, as will make thee wish Christs Church had longer enjoyed so choice and skilfull a Workman. If thou beest one who hath hitherto little considered of God and thy soul, and the concernments of Eternity, or only now and then had some morning dew thoughts of that which deserves and requires the choicest and most vigorous workings of thy soul, we wish thou wouldst so far comply with Gods goodneß in bringing this Book to thy hand, and gratifie thy self, (we mean thy Soul, thy better self,) as to read over this Treatise, in which thou wilt meet with those serious and soul-piercing Truths, which by Gods blessing may be as poyson to thy lusts, and awaken thee to a serious and hearty engaging in that work which none ever yet repented of. For the occasion of publishing this Piece, we refer thee to the larger Epistle of our Reverend Brother, and only adde, that though a vein of serious, solid and hearty piety run through all this Authors Works, yet he hath reserved the best wine till the last. The Lord help thee and us so to reade and improve these and such like labours of Gods Harvest men, that we may with the Wise Virgins have the Lamps of our souls trimed and furnished with oyl, that when the Bridegroom shall come we may be ready to enter with him into his Kingdom. Which is and shall be the prayer of us, who are hearty well-wishers to thy Soul,

William Greenhill,
Edmund Calamy,
John Jackson,

Simeon Ash,

William Taylor.

Decemb. 14.
1659.

THE

THE
PARABLE
of the
TEN VIRGINS
UNFOLDED;
Out of
MATTH. 25. *from the* 1ˢᵗ *Verſ. to the* 14ᵗʰ.

1. *Then ſhall the Kingdom of heaven be likened unto ten Virgins, which took their Lamps, and went forth to meet the Bridegroom.*

2. *And five of them were wiſe, and five were fooliſh.*

3. *They that were fooliſh took their Lamps, and took no oyl with them.*

4. *But the wiſe took oyl in their veſſels with their Lamps.*

5. *While the Bridegroom tarried, they all ſlumbred and ſlept.*

6. *And at mid-night there was a cry made, Behold the Bridegroom cometh, go ye out to meet him.*

7. *Then all thoſe Virgins aroſe and trimmed their Lamps.*

8. *And the fooliſh ſaid unto the wiſe, Give us of your oyl, for our Lamps are gone out.*

9. *But the wiſe anſwered ſaying, not ſo, leſt there be not enough for us and you, but go ye rather to them that ſell, and buy for your ſelves.*

10. *And while they went to buy, the Bridegroom came, and they that were ready went in with him to the marriage, and the door was ſhut.*

11. *Afterward came alſo the other Virgins, ſaying, Lord, Lord, open to us.*

12. *But he anſwered and ſaid, Verily I ſay unto you, I know you not.*

13. *Watch therefore, for ye know neither the day, nor the hour wherein the Son of man cometh.*

CHAP. I.

SECT. I.

Heſe words are part of our Saviours Anſwer unto two ſolemn queſtions which his Diſciples propounded unto him, *Chap.* 24. *v.* 3. The firſt was concerning the deſtruction of the Temple at *Jeruſalem.* The ſecond concerning the ſign of his coming, and ſo of the end of the world. The firſt ſeems to be occaſioned by our Saviours ſpeech, *c.* 24. *v.* 2. The ſecond from his ſpeech, *c.* 23. *v.* 39. To the firſt therefore he anſwers, from the

B   4th

4th *v.* of the 24th *ch.* to the 23^d *v.* of it. To the fecond he anfwereth from the 23^d *v.* of the fame *chap.* to the end of this 25th *chap.* Wherein he acquaints them,

1. With fome things which fhall be before his coming, *viz.* fubtill and ftrong delufions, mixt with fore tribulations and oppreffions, efpecially in the time of Antichrift's raigne, as alfo great confufions, in all hearts and Churches; if not throughout all the world after the tribulation of thofe daies; *And then* (faith he) *v.*30. *fhall appear the fign of the Son of man*, and he fhall be feen *coming in power and great Glory*; but if you defire farther to know the day and hour when this fhall be, 'tis fuch a fecret as my Father revealeth not to any, no, not to the very Angels in Heaven, and therefore you need not know it, nor yet fhould feek to know it; 'tis fufficient for you to know that before my coming there fhall be lamentable and fad times, and that when they are at their worft, that the Sun and the Moon (through the horrours of mens hearts, and the univerfal confufions in the world) fhall feem to be darkned, *&c.* that then it is time for me to come, and fet all in order again, then the time of my coming drawes nigh: Now this Chrift doth from *v.* 23. of the 24th *chap.* to *v.*37.

2. Having thus fpoken concerning his coming, he breaks off his fpeech in defcribing his coming, and fals to difcovering the ftate of the times toward, and about the days of his coming, and this he doth from *c.* 24. *v.*37. to *c.* 25.*v.*31. by the confideration of which he perfwades to watchfulneffe againft his coming. 1.Either (faith he) the times will be very fenfuall and degenerate, as in the daies of *Noah*, in fome places of the world, *c.* 24.*v.*38. which he illuftrates from two Parables, perfwading therefore to watchfulneffe, to the end of the 24th *chap.* 2. Or there will be great fecurity in other places, and among other perfons (not given up to fenfuality as in the daies of *Noah*, but) who are the chaft, Virgin, pure Churches of the world, not defiled with the whoredoms in the world; and this our Saviour unfolds in this Parable. 3. Or if any be awakened (as fome fhall) to look for Chrift's coming, yet among thefe, fome through hard conceits of the Lord Jefus, fhall be wilfully careleffe, and nor improve their Talents for the fake and ufe of the Lord Jefus, and this is fet down in the next Parable of the ten Talents, from *v.*14. to *v.* 31. You fee therefore where this Parable ftands, and to what purpofe it is brought in. In which are two things.

SECT. II.

1. THe Parable it felf, concerning the ten Virgins, from *v.*1. to *v.*13.
2. The fcope of the Parable, *v.*13. which is to perfwade not fimply to watchfulneffe, but to continuance and perfeverance in it from a prudent forefight of the coming of Chrift.

1. The Parable it felf is fet down, agreeable to the cuftom of thofe times wherein our Saviour lived, wherein their Marriages were ufually celebrated in the night time, fhe that was the Bride was attended with fundry Virgins to meet the Bridegroom; thefe Virgins (it being night feafon) took therefore their Lamps with them; thofe that were ready, and met the Bridegroom, were admitted to the Marriage-Room and Supper; thofe that came after that time, if once the doors were fhut, were furely kept out, though they knockt hard to come in. All this, thofe who are acquainted with *Jewifh* Hiftories and cuftoms know to be true, which we are to attend, becaufe it gives not a little light to the true and genuine explication of this Parable.

In which Parable note thefe two parts.
1. The Churches preparation to meet with Chrift (called here the Bridegroom) from the 1 to the 5 *verf.*   2.The

2. The Bridegroom's coming forth to meet them, from the 5 to the 12 *verf.*

SECT. III.

The firſt part of the Parable.

Irſt, I ſhall ſpeak of the preparation made by the Church to meet with Chriſt Jeſus. Wherein alſo note theſe three things.

1. The place where this preparation is made, *viz.* in the *Kingdom of Heaven*, *verf.* 1.

2. The time when it ſhall be made, ſet down in the firſt word, *Then*, v. 1.

3. The perſons that ſhall make this preparation, they ſhall not be corrupted Members of degenerate Churches, where mens profeſſion is grown foul through length of wearing ; but they are Profeſſors of ſome eminent ſtrain, ſome whereof are truly ſincere, others ſecretly unſound. And there is a double deſcription of them. 1. From ſome things wherein they all agree. 2. From ſome other particulars wherein they manifeſtly differ ;

Firſt, Thoſe things wherein they all agree are three.

1. They are all Virgins, Virgin-Profeſſors.

2. They were all awake and watchful for ſome time, ready to meet the Bridegroom , and hence it is ſaid , *They took their Lamps.*

3. They all had ſo much Faith as to go out to meet the Bridegroom.

Secondly, Thoſe things wherein they did differ, are,

1. Generally, *five were wiſe*, and *five were fooliſh*, v. 2.

2. Specially, the fooliſh *took Lamps* but no Oyl , the wiſe did both, v. 3, 4.

This is the rude draught of this firſt part of the Parable, the ſum whereof is this, That the ſtate of the Members of ſome Churches about the time of Chriſt's coming, ſhall be this, they ſhall not be openly prophane, corrupt and ſcandalous , but Virgin-Profeſſors , awakened (for ſome ſeaſon) out of carnal ſecurity, ſtirring, lively Chriſtians, not preſerving their Chaſtity and Purity meerly in a way of works, but waiting for Chriſt in a Covenant of Grace, only ſome of theſe, and a good part of theſe, ſhall be indeed wiſe, ſtored with ſpiritual wiſdom, fill'd with the power of Grace; but others of them, and a great part of them too, ſhall be found fooliſh at the coming of the Lord Jeſus.

I come therefore to handle the firſt Particular in this firſt Part, *viz.*

CHAP. II.

Of the Visible Church of God.

SECT. I.

1. HE place where this preparation to meet Chriſt ſhall be made, and that is not in the Kingdoms of this world (earthly Kingdoms) but in the Kingdom of Heaven, and therefore 'tis ſaid, *The Kingdom of Heaven ſhall be like*, &c.

I will not trouble you with telling you how many waies the Kingdom of Heaven is taken in Scripture ; by Kingdom of Heaven here, is not meant the Kingdom of Glory in the third Heaven, for there ſhall be no fooliſh Virgins at all there, no unclean thing ſhall enter thither; nor by it is meant the head of this Kingdom, *viz.*

Chriſt

Chrift Jefus, for how can he be like to ten Virgins; nor by it is meant the Gofpel of the Kingdom, (which *Mat.*13. is call'd the *Kingdom of Heaven*, and compared to a draw-net) for how can it be like unto ten Virgins? nor yet the internal Kingdom of grace fet up in the heart of every believer (which is called a grain of Muftard-feed, *Mat.*13.) for how can any foolifh Virgins be there? or what fhare have they in that? Therefore I conceive 'tis clear, that by the Kingdom of Heaven here, is meant the external Kingdom of Chrift in this world: that is, the vifible Church, or the eftate of the vifible Church, which is frequently called in Scripture, *the Kingdoms of Heaven*, as, *Mat.* 8. 12. & 21. 43. In which Kingdom fome are wife, fome foolifh, all profeffe Chrift, look for the coming of Chrift, for falvation from Chrift, the eftate of this vifible Church fhall be like ten Virgins.

SECT. II.

Doct. 1.

A ND hence I fhall note this one thing.
That the vifible Church of God on earth, efpecially in the times of the Gofpel, is the Kingdom of Heaven upon earth.

For look upon the face of the whole earth, there you may fee the Kingdoms of men, and the Kingdom of Satan, fin and death, which the Apoftle faith, *Rom.* 5. reig-eth over all men; here is only the Kingdom of Heaven, upon earth, *viz.* in the vifible Church; 'tis not the place only which makes either Heaven or Hell, (though there is a place for both) but the ftate principally makes both, one may be in Hell upon earth, as Chrift was in his bitter agony, and a man may be in a kind of Heaven upon earth, as Chrift tels his hearers, that *the Kingdom of Heaven was at hand*; a man may be under the Kingdom of Satan and darkneffe upon earth, *Col.* 1. 13. which is a kind of Hell, and why not as well under the Kingdom of God on earth, which is a kind of Heaven, efpecially (I fay) now under the Gofpel, wherein the Lord hath begun to fulfil, that which was but only promifed under the Old Teftament to be fulfilled in the fourth and laft Monarchy, (*Dan.* 2. 44.) in the time of the New: In the ftate of Chrift's vifible Church, which fhould by little and little beat down all other Kingdoms of the world.

SECT. III.

Reaf. 1.

1. B Ecaufe the fame King that is reigning in Heaven, is reigning here, is pre-fent here, *Pfa.* 2. 6. And here the Saints are commanded to rejoyce, to fhout, and to be glad with all their hearts, becaufe of the prefence of this their King a-mong them, *Zeph.* 3. 14, 15. 'Tis true indeed he is King over all the world; the immediate execution of all Gods common, as well as fpecial providence, is put into the hand of this King, the Lord Jefus. But as for his Enemies, and other creatures, he reignes over them as a King of power, but he reignes not for them alfo as a King of Grace and love, for thus he reignes among his people in his Church, *Deut.* 33. 26, 27. The Lord is prefent with every one of his people, feve-rally, but much more joyntly, when two or three of them are met together in his Name.

Reaf. 2.

2. Becaufe here are the Lawes of Heaven, *Heb.* 12. 25. Take heed (fpeaking of the Miniftry of the Gofpel in the Churches) that ye refufe not to hear him who fpeaketh from Heaven, which Lawes are not only here promulgated (as they be among the enemies of this Kingdom) but accepted and received alfo, without which Lawes what Kingdom could there be? Chrift's Kingdom in this world is neither tyrannical, nor arbitrary, to govern without Law; no, no, but if he be

our

our King, he is our Law-giver also, *Isa.33.22.* Nay the same Laws by which we shall be ruled in Heaven, we have here, and we are now under : That as our Divines say against the Papists, though before *Moses* his time, there was not *scriptio verbi*, yet there was *verbum scriptum*, which the Patriarchs had before the Floud, and afterward until *Moses* his time : So I say here, though in Heaven the external Letter and scription both of Law and Gospel, shall be abolished, because they need them not when the day-star is risen, *2 Pet.1.19.* Yet the living Rules of both for substance, shall remain ; the end of the Ministry is to bring us to the unity of Faith in a perfect estate, *Eph.4.13.* Therefore Faith shall not cease, when Ministers shall, and that perfect man shall come. Our Faith indeed shall not then by such glasses see Christ, nor adhere unto Christ, by such means of Promises and Ordinances as we do now, but without them we shall both see, and for ever adhere to him who is our King at that day; and though indeed the Law is now abolished, as a Covenant of life, yet it shall ever remain as a Rule of life ; perfect subjection to it, is the happinesse of Saints in Heaven, *1 Joh.1.* as a heart contrary to it is the greatest misery of the Saints on earth, *Rom.7.24.*

3. Because here are the Subjects of Heaven, *Eph.2.19.* Fellow-Citizens of the Saints, not only on earth, but as *Paul* speaketh, *Phil.3.20. Our conversation* (or, as it may be rendred, our free Burgess-ship) *is in Heaven.* God, himself hath canonized all the true Members of visible Churches with the name of Saints, throughout the whole new Testament, here are the great heirs of Heaven, nay, possessours of Heaven by Faith, as others are by feeling, as near and dear to God (in some respect) as those that be in Heaven already ; because the same motive which makes him love them, makes him love these, though poor abjects, and out-casts of the world ; there is but a paper-wall of their bodies between them and Heaven, only here is the difference, they there, are Subjects in their own countrey ; these here, are the same Countreymen, only strangers for a time here upon earth : Some define a Kingdom to be *dominatus regis in populum subjectum.* If Christ (the King) was present, and his Laws publishe, but there were no people to be subject to him, there could be no Kingdom ; but when the King, Laws, and Subjects of Heaven are here met together in the visible Church, here is now the Kingdom of Heaven. *Reason 3.*

4. Because here is the very Glory of Heaven begun, that look as the same Sun which fils the Stars with Glory, the very same beams touch the earth also; so the same Glory which shines in Heaven, shines into the poor Church here, *1 Pet. 5.10.* God hath called his people into his eternal Glory. And *Rom.8.30. whom* Christ *hath justified, them he hath glorified,* i.e. he hath begun it here ; here in a special manner is the presence of the Angels in Heaven, *Eph.3.10.* Here the pure in heart see God, and that after another manner, than many times they can in their solitary condition, *Psal.63.1,2,3.* And what is this but Heaven ? *Reason 4.*

SECT. IV.

1. SEE therefore hence their happinesse and honour, whom God hath called out of the world, and planted in his Church : What hath the Lord done, but opened the way to the Tree of life, and let you into Paradise again ? Nay (which is more) What hath he done but taken you up into the very Kingdom of Heaven it self ? where you have the Lord of glory to be your King, the Laws of Heaven made known, his heart opened, where you have the heirs of Heaven your companions, and the Angels of Heaven your guard, desiring to look into those things which your eyes see, and your hearts feel, *1 Pet. 1.12.* Where you have the love of a Father appearing, the Son of God inhabiting, and the Spirit of Heaven comforting. *Lord what is man that thou art thus mindful of him!* That when the Lord seeth it unmeet to take you out of this world up unto Heaven, that *Use 1.*

Heaven should come down into this world unto you, who were once enemies to this Kingdom, shut up under the Kingdom of death and darknesse, strangers to the Common-wealth of *Israel*, without God and Christ in the world, without promise, without hope. I do not cry the Temple of the Lord, nor Idolize Order and Churches, but I tell you what your priviledge is, and thereby what Gods goodnesse is: I know the world neither seeth nor seeketh any such Heaven on earth, but soon grow despisers secretly of all Ordinances, who if they were in Heaven it self with their carnal hearts, they would not abide there with much contentment, yet verily Heaven hath been, and is found here by Gods hidden ones, even such things which eye hath not seen, nor ear heard, and if it be not thus with thee, blame thy self, and mourn the more, who in the midst of light art in utter darknesse, and in the place where Heaven is begun to some, it should be made a little Hell to thee.

Use 2.

* Some think from thence that the lapsed Angels did not fall in the third Heaven, but in some place in the earth, or that is an inheritance undefiled.

2. Take heed of defiling secretly the Church of God: For what do you do thereby, but pollute the Kingdom of Heaven it self? And the better any thing is, the greater is the defilement cast upon it. It is said, 1 *Pet.*1.4. that the Kingdom of Heaven above is *an inheritance undefiled* *, never yet the subject place where any sin was committed, and this is one part of the Glory of it. Take you heed of coming into Church-fellowship with defiled hearts, and so defiling Gods holy things, for do you know where you are? I know it is not in that Heaven where you cannot sin, but yet 'tis in such a Heaven where you should not sin, much lesse defile the Church of God. It was one of Gods heavy indictements against the Church of the *Jews*, that when the Lord had brought them out of a land of pits, into a plentiful countrey, yet they defiled his Land, neither Priests nor people said, *Where is the Lord*? *Jer.*2.7,8. It will be much more heavy another day with you, that walking in the fellowship of Gods people, shall be found guilty of defiling the Kingdom of Heaven it self, which you should be careful to keep as an undefiled inheritance, which defile ments whether spiritual or sensual, as they stain the very glory of Heaven it self, so they keep you from seeing the Truth of this Doctrine, even of this Heaven upon earth in your own experience.

Use 3.

3. Let all Members of Churches hence learn to have their conversation in Heaven, and walk as men come down from Heaven, and returning thither again, and that are as it were already in Heaven. *Paul* did thus, and wept to see so many that did not thus, but did *mind earthly things*, *Phil.*3.19,20. Do not only forsake, but even *forget your Countrey, and your Fathers house, so shall the King* of Glory *desire your beauty, Psal.* 45.10,11, Let the reproach of earthly-mindednesse cast upon the face of Christians, be wiped off by your carriage, being heavenly, holy, loosened from things below. Art thou in Heaven with an earthly heart? Is not Heaven good enough for thee? Cannot that content thee which many have desired to see, and could not see, even the Lord Jesus, the King of Glory in his beauty, in the assemblies of his Saints?

Use 4.

4. Take heed of pulling down this Kingdom. Loyal Subjects will rather lose their lives, than their Prince shall lose his Kingdom. Fear not enemies without, but your selves at home. The enemies of the Church, did never yet hurt the Church, but the Church's sins, *Zach.*7.14. Oh consider what mercy the Lord hath betrusted us withal, that unlesse the Lord should carry us to Heaven it self, immediatly on the wings of Angels, he can shew us no greater outward favour, in this world, than to bring us into this his Kingdom of Heaven on earth. I professe one daies fellowship here with a number of broken-hearted Christians, either mourning together, or rejoycing in their God and King together, it out-bids the many years Glory of the whole world, (howsoever 'tis hidden from the world) And will you betray this Kingdom?

SECT.

SECT. V.

Quest. VVHat are those things that may pull down this Kingdom?
Answ. 1. Ignorance of those sins which may hurt and ruine it. There
are common infirmities which all the faithful have in common, for which the
Lord pities his, but there are some that are proper and personal to some particular
persons, *Psal.*18.23. for which the Lord is angry even with his own; so there are
some sins which are common Church-infirmities, for which the Lord will not
cast off his people, but there are sometimes in several Churches proper Church-
sins. Now the Rule here is, if these be not seen and lamented and removed, if
the Lord be angry for these (as verily he will) and yet they do not so much as
know all this while what it is that hurts them, these sins will canker the roots,
and blast the most flourishing Churches. *Ephesus, Rev.*1.4. had her sin;
*Sardis, Rev.*2.1. had her sin. *Laodicea* had her sins, *Rev.*3.16. Now what if
they never know these, nor repent of these, you know then *Ephesus* Candlestick
must be removed, and *Laodicea* shall be spued out of Christs mouth. Oh this
hath been the bane of Churches, while they enjoyed their liberties, they could
not, nay (in truth) would not know their aile, in the day of Christs visitation of
them, and hence came their ruine, the cause of which they saw not; only it may
be the remnant that escaped, to whom the Lord shewed mercy, could read their
sins in their plagues. It is a lamentable spectacle to behold the ruines of *Germany*, and that after such great slaughter and effusion of blood, they cannot tell
the thing that hath hurt, and doth still wast them.

2. Self-seeking, a Spirit of self. Look as it is in a Kingdom, if there be a common enemy, and the body of the Army which should encounter with them, be
every man taken up, and taking thought how he may preserve his own Tent,
and do not joyn their forces together for common safety, it must perish, and the
Kingdom will be easily conquered: Or as it is with the body, if every member
seeks to preserve it self alone, and not that which preserves them all, (*viz.* the
Head) the body will drop down and die shortly. Christ Jesus is the Head of
this Body [his Church] Now 'tis certain if ye seek to preserve your own
name more than Christ's, to give more content to your own lusts, then to the
will and heart of Christ, if more careful of fetching feathers to your own nests,
and to shift for your selves, and not to attend (every man in his place) the
publick good of the Church, and Christ in it; 'tis certain God will forsake you,
and all will to ruine quickly, 2 *Chron.*15.1,2.

Church-members of publick spirits, are ever prosperous men. *They shall prosper that love thee, Psal.*122.6. That say in their hearts out of sense of Christ's
love, Lord, what shall I doe for thee? How may I be useful to thy people? But
if back and belly, mine and thine, be chief in request, this will ruine you.

3. League and Amity with the enemies of Christ's Kingdom, or peace with
our lusts; it is not sin, but a privy peace with sin, and a secret quietnesse in sin, which
overthrowes Christ's Kingdom: The Canaanites that were left alive, because
('tis said) they could not drive them out, how often did they vex, and prick,
and yoke the *Israel* of God? Those sins which you say, you cannot part with,
and hence yield unto them, and mourn not under them, those will ruine Churches: Some sins you have forsaken, and could forsake, the danger lies not here.
Wrath goeth out against *Jehosaphat* because he loved him who hated the Lord,
2 *Chron.*19.2.

4. When the Church laies by her weapons. No Kingdom can be kept safe
in an ordinary way, where all their weapons are taken from them, or not used by
them, when their enemies are upon their borders: When the Church hang by,
and lay aside Faith (the shield whereby we defend our selves) and prayer
(whereby

(whereby we offend our enemies) what safety is to be expected now in Churches? Only be strong (saith the Lord to *Joshuah*) when he went out upon that great service of the Lord, *Josh.1.7. Eph.6.13.* There is no more fearful sign of ruine to a Church, than where the Spirit of prayer begins to fail; and verily if any people under Heaven are ready to miscarry herein, we (that have our fill of peace, and our yokes broken off from our shoulders) are in most danger; but if it be so, look for such shakings of all hearts, and Churches also, as shall make you find your tongues, and knees, and eares, and hearts again, if the Lord means to dwell with you.

5. Not bringing forth the fruits of the Kingdom, *Mat.21.43.* Cut that Church down that cumbers the ground, after many years pruning and wetting. That Kingdom where there is Church-trading, but no considerable gain coming in, will consume quickly, and die of it self. Fruit is the last end of the tree: All duties you do, wherein you attain not, or (at least) aim not at your last and utmost end, but make your selves your own end, that is not fruit; Fruit refresheth others that tast it; when a Christian walketh so as that another is not the better, [not much refreshed] by him, but it may be hardned rather, by a saplesse example, here is no fruit, and this cals for the axe to cut down the tree.

6. Divisions: This puls down Kingdoms without help of forreign enemies. If a Kingdom thrusts swords into each others bellies, this will soon dispatch them. It's the Jesuits plot to subdue by private divisions, whom they cannot conquer by force of Armes: It was most pleasing to Satan to prevail with Christ to cast himself down headlong from the Pinacle, rather than to fling him down himself. It is the delight of Hell to set & see Churches at variance among themselves, this is the first thing he attempts in the best Churches, and it is commonly prosperous, if the Lord leaves the watchmen to slumber, and not to be watchful, and fearful, and sudddenly sensible of the least beginnings herein. It is a wonderful thing to see what a small occasion of offence will do; a word, a gesture, a garment, a matter of indifferency, 'tis strange to see, how such small matters will gore, if Satans head be in them, and his Horns be set upon them, especially in Churches where men are set at liberty, and enjoy it, one must have liberty to speak one thing, and another, another thing, I am of this mind saith one, I am not of that mind (Brother) saith another: 'Tis wonderful to see what a fire, a secret smother, and smoak of suspition will do. But oh take heed here, *Gal.5.15.* Love the Truth, receive no opinion differing from the most approved in the Church suddenly, but weep, and pray, and ask councel, and tremble to entertain a thought of contention: The first sin which brake out in the first Christian Church, was murmurings, *Acts 6.1.* What followes? *Stephen* an earthly Angel, full of the holy Ghost, suffers, and is taken from them, *Acts 7.* And after this the whole Church is scattered, *Acts 8.* Oh keep the peace of the Church, and rend it not for small matters, love one another sincerely, and you cannot but live together quietly.

CHAP. III.

Concerning the Coming of Christ, and the security of Professors.

SECT. I.

Quest.
Answ.

THus much of the place ; now let us consider of the time when, this preparation is made, set down in that word *Then*, which word hath reference to the 37th *v.* of the 24th *ch.* *viz.* to the daies of the coming of the Son of man.

Now when are these daies ?

We shall read both in Prophetical and Apostolical writings, that all the time from the Ascension to the second coming of Christ, is called the last daies, *Acts* 2.16,17. Hence the Primitive Churches did (long since) and all the Churches at this day ought, to live in a daily expectation of his coming again, as these Virgins here did. And hence some think, that all this time may be the daie of the coming of Christ, wherein all the Churches either do, or should look out for the coming of Christ. Now although I dare not exclude these daies (in a large sense) from being the daies of Christ's coming, as being the last daies, and it being the duty of all to wait for this coming of Christ, as well as those who lived long before us, 1 *Thes.*1.10. 1 *Cor.*1.7. Yet I believe here is meant more particularly the latter part of those last daies : For our Saviour having foretold of many things which shall fall out before his second coming, yet he seems to single out some particular time in these last daies ; to which he doth annexe this [*then*] and that is evident to all that view well the Text, that they are the daies of his coming, for though all the daies of the Gospel may be called the daies of the Son of man, and some daies especially wherein there is some kind of coming of the Son of man, as when he comes to hear prayers, *Luke* 18.8. yet to speak properly , they are not the daies of the coming of the Son of man. And look as the daies of *Noah* were not all the daies from the Creation to the Deluge, but those particular years before the Flood, so 'tis here, some special times before his coming, are *the daies of his coming.*

SECT. II.

Quest.
Answ.

BUt what is this *Coming of Christ ?*
There is a double coming of Christ.

1. His coming to call the *Jews*, and to gather in the fulnesse of the *Gentiles* with them, which is called the *brightnesse of his coming*, 2 *Thes.*2.8. When there shall be such a brightnesse of the Truth shining forth in the world, armed with such Instruments as shall utterly destroy Antichrist, long before his second coming, *Rev.*19.19,20.

2. His coming to Judgement, *Heb.*9.28. 1 *Cor.* 15.23,24. When there shall be an universal resurrection of good and bad, 1 *Thes.*4.15,16,17. Now although it be true, that at the time of the coming of Christ, to call the *Jews*, the Churches like chast Virgins shall wait and make themselves ready for the marriage of the Lamb, *Rev.*19.7. Yet the second coming of Christ seems to be the

C   time

time which is here directly pointed at. Then shall those Churches be Virgin-Churches, waiting for Christ's coming, both to their particular judgment, but especially to the general judgment, when he shall appear as a glorious Bridegroom to the consolation and salvation of those who in truth have waited for him the second time: For this coming of Christ spoken of in these two chapters, is that coming which is *in power and great Glory* (not in the Churches spiritually) but *in the clouds of Heaven*, chap.24.30. Wherein he shall separate the sheep from the goats, the one to lie among Devils, the other to possesse (not an earthly Kingdom here for a thousand years, as some from mistaking the meaning of the 20th ch. of the *Revel.* imagine) but to inherit *the Kingdom prepared for them from the foundation of the world*, *Mat.* 25.34. which cannot be any better, nor any other, than the third Heaven, where the face of God is seen, and where he hath had an innumerable Host of glorious Angels, his Subjects to serve him, not only since the first time of mans creation, but the first foundation of the world, *Gen.*1.1. Which also Christ himself *is gone to prepare for us*, *John* 14.2,3. And which *Abrahams* Faith only expected, even a City which was not earthly, but heavenly, *which hath foundations, whose builder and maker is God*, *Heb.*11.10,11. So that although this Parable looks most directly unto those times which are yet to come, yet as all examples registred in holy Scripture for time past, are applicable and useful for us, so these that are yet to come, are alike instructive to us, especially in these times and places, wherein the Lord (according to his manner of working great things usually) gives among us some small, yet lively resemblance of those daies.

Doct.

SECT. V.

That in those daies of Christ's coming, wherein the Churches of Christ, and Professors of the Gospel shall grow Virgin-Churches, all visible Saints, when all Members, seem to be espoused to Christ, yet there will be found desperate folly in some, and in time great security will fall upon all.

Some there are who think the daies we live in now, are not only the daies of the Son of man, but part of the daies of the coming of the Son of man, wherein the Churches (especially in these places) grow to be Virgin-Professours: Our judgments hold it, our practise maintaines it, all Church-members are and must be visible Saints, visible Believers, Virgins espoused to Christ, escaping the pollutions of Idolatry and the world: Take heed the Lord find not many of you foolish, take heed you that are not so, that in time you grow not secure; you have the pillow of peace to lie on, and the cares of the world to make you dream away your time, and you have no pinching persecutions to awaken you, and if no wrestlings within, look for security there. Folly will be the death and bane of some, hence boast not. Security, a sleeping sicknesse will be the disease of others, if the Lord prevent not: But I intend not to anchor here, only to set up markes at these Flats, that you may avoid them and come not near them.

CHAP. IV.

*Sheweth that the Soul that will enjoy Communi-
on with Christ, must be divorced from all other
Lords, particularly from Lusts, and from the
Law. The manner of its Espousals unto Christ.*

SECT. I.

Now therefore to come to the Third thing; the persons that make this preparation are set forth, 1. In what they all agree in, and that is, first in that they are all Virgins; What are these? *Ans.* To omit the Popish Interpretation of their Nuns, and mock-Virgins.

I shall rather make use of Scripture to give light to interpret this place: for opening of it, know, the whole Church may be called the Spouse of Christ, and take every member alone, a Virgin attending on this Spouse, *Psal.* 45. nay the Apostle, 2 *Cor.* 11. 2. calls the whole Church a *Virgin*, so that by Virgins are meant whole particular Churches of Christ, together with the several Members thereof. Now Virgins are such as are fit for marriage, and not defiled with any man, as it's said of *Rebecca*: so by Virgins are meant those that are not polluted within, or without with the evils of the world, *Rev.* 14. 4. but more is to be understood here, 2 *Cor.* 11. 2. when once marriage is come, they cease to be Virgins, and are Wives; yet when espoused to Christ, now they are spiritually Virgins; hence these here are only like to Virgins: so that the meaning of Virgins is this; by Virgins is meant such Churches, or members of Churches as are divorced from all other Lovers, and match'd only to Jesus Christ: these only look for the coming of Christ, and communion with him, these only are received into communion.

SECT. II.

WHoever look for everlasting Communion with the Bridegroom of the Church, *Jesus Christ, must be Virgins Divorced from all others, and Espoused only to Jesus Christ.*   *Obs.* 1.

Here were indeed foolish ones among these, yet as foolish and blind as they were, they saw that this was the way, to be like the wise, to be Virgins as well as they, *Psal.* 45. 10, 11. *Jer.* 3. 19, 20. as a Wife departs, so ye; *but how shall I put thee among the Children, &c. you shall call me my Father, i. e.* one instead of all other things, *and shall not turn aside from me,* Hos. 2. 23. there is their communion; Hence the Lord will, 1. take away the names of *Baalim*; 2. Betroth them to himself.

SECT. III.

WHat is it to be divorced from all other Lovers?   *Quest.* 1.
Idolatry is called Whoredom in Scripture, and this is one thing, the   *Ans.*

Soul muſt be Divorced from, before it can be match'd to the Lord, *Hoſ.* 2. 2. I ſhall not need to preſs this here ; but there are two other things which I ſhall ſhew, for there are two things that every man doth before he is eſpouſed to the Lord Jeſus ; either firſt he departs and goes a whoring by unlawfully luſting after the creature, *Pſal.* 73. 27. *James* 4. 4. Or 2. He is lawfully married as he thinks unto the Law, *Rom.* 7. 3, 4. the Law is there compared to a Husband, from which Chriſt indeed delivers his, yet ſome will ſtick to it : either the Soul takes content in ſome creature more than in Chriſt, or in ſome righteouſneſſe more than in the Lord Jeſus ; Now to be divorced from all other things, is for the heart to be taken off from all worldly contentments. Secondly, from comforting it ſelf in the boſom of its own work and righteouſneſs, and this muſt be found in all them that ſeek for communion with the Lord Jeſus.

SECT. IV.

1 THE heart muſt be divorced from Luſts after, and pleaſures in any creature; for proof, we muſt know this :

1. The ſoul of every man muſt have ſomething to quiet and comfort it like the ſtomack, it's death and hell to want it (as the *Iſraelites* in the wilderneſſe :) hence it muſt have it.

2. That there is nothing that can comfort the thirſty heart, but 'tis either in the ſpring, or ciſtern, fountain, or bottles, either in God, or in the creature.

3. Hence man having loſt God, and all good there, ſeeks for it in the creature, and becauſe he finds not enough in one, digs for it in another, *Pſal.* 4. *Who will ſhew us any good ?* and hence the Soul becauſe it never found that infinite ſweetneſſe in God himſelf, hence luſts after, and delights in the creature for it ſelf, loves pleaſure for pleaſure, delights in creature for the creature, not for God, why ſhould he, ſeeing he never found content there ? and here the ſoul of man cleaves night and day, committing ſpiritual whoredom before the face of God ; now if ever any ſoul hath communion with Chriſt, it muſt be divorced from all creatures thus, for Luſt is a deſire after, and content in the creature for the creatures ſake.

Reaſ. 1.   1 Becauſe while the heart is in league with any creature beſides the Lord, 'tis at deadly enmity with the Lord, *James* 4. 4. If a man hath a rich commodity, and one comes and offers half the worth of it, he takes it as a contempt ; if it be not worth this, it is worth nothing ; ſo the Lord is worthy of all our love, our lives, our ſouls though we had a thouſand of them, and will a man not part with his luſts for him ? I tell you the Lord takes himſelf ſleighted, contemned, and loathed ; if not worth all a mans love, he is worth nothing; now the creature is made a God, becauſe made a mans laſt end, which is as proper to God, as to make him the *Alpha* of all. Here the greateſt wrath is to give a man his fill of the creature.

Reaſ. 2.   2 Becauſe ſo long the ſoul cannot ſee, nor come by the eye and feet of Faith to the Lord Jeſus, *John* 5. 44. and think Chriſt better than all ; as Birds in a ſtring may fly high, but when they come to the end of the line, fall down there ; and ſo though the ſoul flies to Chriſt, yet when indeed it comes to the end of parting withall, it falls down, and falls off from Chriſt. Whole men have no heart nor deſire after Phyſicians; when all limbs are whole and ſtrong, no deſire after Plaiſters : ſo while any thing eaſeth and contenteth the heart, there is no deſire after Chriſt, *Hoſ.* 4. 11. *Whoredom and wine have taken away the heart.*

Reaſon 3.   3 Becauſe ſo long the heart if it do come, cannot ſtay with Chriſt to do any thing for Chriſt, *Mat.* 6. 24. *You cannot ſerve God and riches,* i. e. two Maſters, who have conſtant employment, and Chriſt hath ſet us ſuch employment. Hence men on ſick-beds are tame as may be, promiſe any thing, becauſe their joy in the

the creature is gone : Hence on the other side many men after many springings of heart are choaked by thorns of the world.

4 From the abundant love that the Lord Jesus shews to them that ever have, or look for communion with him. Those to whom we shew much love, from those we expect much again. As a man if taken or cast out to be servant, one looks not for love from him; but when a man hath given himself, and made over all his estate to another, now all love is too little. So 'tis with the Lord Jesus, *John* 6. *Will you also depart* ?

SECT. V.

2 THE soul must be divorced from the Law , *i.e.* from comforting it self with the righteousnesse thereof : For explication of which we must consider these things.

1. That the Lord doth not ever give a man content in his sins and lusts, but wounds Conscience for the same.

2. That so long as the Lord wounds a mans Conscience for sin, no creature can give a man comfort or content. *A wounded spirit who can bear* ? *Judas* casts away his silver pieces; and *Belshazzar* quakes, who was but even now quaffing in his cups. As a man that hath an aking tooth , or broken bones, What can comfort him now ?

3. Hereupon the Law fals upon a man, or a man meets with the Law ; for as all a mans sorrow is upon him because the Law is broken , all a mans care is how he may keep it again. What shall I do ? As a man cast in prison for debt, there all is opened ; and the Law like an earnest suitor, 1. Pleadeth hard for love and obedience. 2. Promiseth a rich portion, eternal life , if he can keep it; If not you must be damned ; therefore now forsake your sins, &c.

4. Hence the soul not knowing a better Husband, consents and resolves to cleave to it, *Rom.*10.3. *Deut.*5. *Whatever the Lord will have us do, we will do it*; and here it stayes, and is comforted , here it rests ; as in *Asa* his time she rejoyced for the Oath , 2 *Chro.* 15. *Isai.* 58. 1, 2. and if it find not perfect comfort because of imperfect work, it then closeth with Christ for to make up and piece up all , *Gal.* 5. 1. And now I say 'tis comforted in what it hath, and doth, and here it rests ; now from hence it must be divorced : What need I prove it, when the Apostle hath so fully, *Galat. per totum* , and consider the young man , *Mat.* 19. Divorced, I say, the soul must be from this.

1. Because he that doth thus, sets up another Christ, and makes himself his own Saviour ; can the Lord Jesus take such a soul into communion with him ? Suppose a Prince be pulled by his people from his Throne , and they set up another pious vertuous Prince to Rule, will this serve the turn to say he is an honest Prince ? so though duties be never so good, yet not to advance Christ, is to pull down Christ.

2. Because such persons do commonly most oppose the Lord Jesus in a way of believing, though not in a way of doing ; the Lord hath more ado if any of these be brought home, to bring them in , they have somewhat to say for themselves, they have stronger forts, &c. The Scribes and Pharisees rejected the counsel of God against themselves , and hence no people left to such deep desertions as these; if the Lord intend mercy to them, for they have more need than others.

3. Because hereby a man doth but make a conspiracy against Gods greatest plot that ever he had a foot, *viz.* to advance his free Grace, *Gal.* 5. 4. you are fallen from Grace, for nothing makes a man more fit to boast than works, and resting in them ; sin makes a man ashamed, and therefore if they come to Heaven , they have laid a foundation to thank themselves for somewhat ; hence no communion

with

with Jesus Christ in this frame; no the Lord will tear down this foundation, and make the soul cry guilty, and make this Husband, the Law, to be judge, to examine, and condemn, and now come and ask, what have you to plead for your life and peace, it hath no plea to shew but mercy, &c. it hath its duties evidencing against it.

SECT. VI.

Answ. 1.

2 THe soul now comes to be Espoused to the Lord Jesus. *Quest. How?*

The soul beholding the glory of the Lord Jesus, makes choice of him, as in all Marriage bonds there is a choice made, and if love be great, there is little standing on terms: let me have him though I begg with him; so the soul sees such a suitableness in the Lord Jesus, as that it stands not on terms, let me have him though in prison with him, though in the Garden in Agonies with him, though in the Cross in desertions with him, he is enough; as *Peter* when he saw Christ on the Sea, desired he might come to him there, *Heb.* 11. 26. *Chusing the reproach of Christ,* &c. And look as Christ chuseth the soul, 1. The whole soul. 2. Everlastingly. 3. Above all others: so it makes choice of Christ, whole Christ, *Phil.* 3. 9. 2. Everlastingly. *The Lord is my portion for ever*. *Psalm* 73. 26. And before ever you can look for communion with him, you must make this choice of him, and glad too you may have him on any terms, nay put it to any soul the Lord hath done good to, and ask it, will you have him? 'tis such a mercy I cannot conceive how one so vile as I should have it: have him, the Lord of glory, the Prince of life and peace; O yes; Hence *Peter* said, *Master, What shall we have that have forsaken all, and followed thee?* you shall sit with me on Thrones; and look as Christ now chuseth the soul above others, as well as in Heaven, *John* 15. 16. so it now chuseth Christ, *Whom have I in Heaven or earth*; many when they think of death, or are dying, then chuse him, but not now; or chuse him for outward blessings, not spiritual favour and life, *John* 6. 26, 27.

2. The soul hence gives it self like one espoused to her Husband to the Lord Jesus, *Cant.* 2. 16. *I am my beloveds*; servants give work for their wages, and masters give wages for their work, but Husbands and Wives give themselves one unto another; Suitors also give Tokens to draw on love, not themselves; so servants in the Church, they do for God in hope of wages, and the Lord blesseth them it may be outwardly; but he that is espoused to Christ, gives himself, Lord I can do nothing for thee, give nothing to thee, but I give my self to thee, that thou wouldst work in me, and by me, *Rom.* 6. 13. So the Lord is a suitor to many a man that never gives himself to him: he gives them some comforts, some winning, drawing, melting mercies, but not himself; they give him some entertainment, and good words, a thousand wishes as *Capernaum* did, but not themselves; but this must be, if ever you look for communion with him: hence *David* saith, *I am thine, save me*; hence some made shipwrack of Faith, they were not the Lords; hence the Lord saith, he knows who are his, 2 *Tim.* 2. 18, 19. his send their tokens again: for look as 'tis an evidence of much love when a man gives the dearest thing he hath, *viz.* his whole self to the Lord Jesus, so 'tis also an evidence of little love, when he will not give, especially anothers own: thou art none of thine own, thou hast but little love if thou give not thy self to him, without which never look for life and communion with the Lord.

3. The soul hence takes full contentment in the Lord Jesus, as a Spouse hath enough, would not change for all the world, as *Peter* when he had a glimpse of Christs glory, Lord, *let us be here*: or as *Simeon* that had been waiting for the consolation of *Israel*, when once he had Christ in his arms, *Now let thy servant depart in peace*: I have enough, now let me dye, and not live to sin more; and 'tis certain

tain as there is somewhat in creatures that contents the heart without Christ in an unregenerate man, so contrary-wise in a regenerate, *John 3. 29.* if hearing the Bridegroom is joy, what is having him? indeed they take content in other things, but as coming from the Husband; and this you must do if ever you look for communion with him; cannot you be content with the Lord alone in Heaven? you shall never come there then, let you quarrel for want of something. Men make nothing of this, to bathe their hearts in the sun, and joy in what they have, and hope to have, but the Lord may be gone, and you grieve not; why? because other things ease your hearts; there can be no communion hereafter if you despise it now.

SECT. VII.

THis serves to discover the great error, most common and dangerous of the whole christian world, who think that they may love and embrace the world and the Lord Jesus too, and be saved at last by him too, *i. e.* they may not be Virgins, but go a whoring from Christ, and yet partake of Christ, and mercy from him: that look as it was in those sad dayes, *Isai. 4. 1.* so in these dayes many lay hold on Jesus Christ, they will eat their own bread, live on their own suits, and wear their own apparel, their own rags, only let us be called by thy name [*Believers*] to take away our reproach, for that is an open shame not to believe in Christ, for this is the proceeded thought of some; every one is a sinner, and I am one, and a great one too, and who can say his heart is clean, none can free himself from sin in this life, and I cannot do it if I would: and hence look on Christ to save them, though sin sleeps in them: you cannot have both; I would but enquire, hath not every man something that contents him? what is it? is it the love, the fellowship of Jesus? yes, it may be at a Sacrament, and it may be not, for thou mayst say, the Lord never yet revealed his love and self unto me, never yet assured me, yet somewhat joyes thy heart. What think you, can you have the Lord, and content your selves thus with other things? why? I trust to him I hope so; it cannot be so. If the Lord Jesus was a Patron of Brothel-houses, a protector of Steews, you might think so; some say they cannot pray to him, nor prize him; why? something else contents them besides him; but know it cannot be so: I know a Saint may be taken aside, as *David* with envy at others prosperity; but when he considers of it, O what a Beast! he returns again. The Raven and the Dove were sent forth, the one came again and again, the other not; therefore as *Joshua 24.* brought the people to these thoughts, *you cannot serve the Lord, and other gods,* as *Junius* notes, so bring thy self to that strait: O that the Lord would set on this one thing this day; when I sadly weigh it, it confounds me, and makes me say, Lord who then can be saved! I know with God all things are possible, but this is rare.

SECT. VIII.

HEnce we may learn who they are that never shall have everlasting communion with the Lord Jesus, *viz.* those that never were espoused to him, and you may know this, if never yet divorced from all others beside him, *Psal. 73. 25, 26.* I shall stay awhile here, because there is never an unsound heart in the world, but as they say of witches, they have some Familiar that sucks them, so they have some Lust that is beloved of them, some beloved, there is they have given a promise to, never to forsake; and also because most men do seem and think they are Virgins espoused to Christ, and look for communion with him, and yet

not

not divorced from all other befides him. I fhall fhew hence,

  1. When the foul is in league with the creature.

  2. When married to the Law. I fhould account it happy if any be found out.

CHAP. V.

Sheweth the Markes and Signes whereby the Soul may know whether he be in league or love with any luſt or creature, or married to the Law.

SECT. I.

1   **T**Hofe that never were in bitterneffe and forrow of heart for the loffe of God. For thefe two things are as clear as the Sun. 1. That the loffe of God is the greateſt loffe ; for 'tis the utmoſt and laſt plague upon the damned in Hell : My Comforts, my Friends, Means, Heaven is gone, but if God were mine, I could be comforted ; No, God is gone : Hence no forrow for any loffe fo much as for this. *Saul,* 1 Sam. 28.15. *God is departed from me.* Hence *fore diſtreſſed.* Nay, the Lord Jefus when the Father departed for a time, and he knew he would return and viſit him, cried out, *My God why haſt thou forſaken me ?* 2. That all men living have loſt God, *Iſa.*59.1,2. *Pſal.* 58.3. *The wicked go aſtray from their womb.* Now I would demand why men either feel no loffe at all, or if they do, have not fo much Grace as the damned in Hell, to mourn bitterly for it, fo as nothing can comfort them, or if they do, they are foon eafed and quieted before the Lord returns ? Why furely here is the great caufe of it, they have fome other thing to eafe their hearts in the want and loffe of God, *Jer.*2.13,14. Men muſt have water to drink, why do men live from the fountain, go not to it, nay not know it ? Becaufe they have broken pits, and wels at their own doors : So here. And hence the damned that have lived at eafe here all their life time, affoon as ever dead, then they cry out of the loffe of God, when 'tis too late, becaufe while they lived, they had fomwhat to eafe themfelves withall. And hence many that have lived long with convinced Spirits and guilty Confciences, when they come to die, then they are in perplexities of mind, agonies of heart, infomuch as their fweat trickles like water from them, and their doleful outcries for loffe of time, ſtrike to the hearts of all that come near them. Oh ! God is gone, becaufe now all comforts which were their Gods, and in ſtead of God before, have taken their final leave of them. Search your hearts therefore all you that hear me this day. Waſt never troubled yet ? Yes, I have loſt my health, my child, my husband, my goods, and this hath troubled me : But tell me, Did'ſt never feel a loffe of God bleſſed for ever ? lofs of his light, his fweetneffe, his love, his fellowſhip, his prefence, &c. and this hath been thy intollerable load ? Or if thou haſt felt it, haſt thou fought and found him ? No, but art jocund in that eſtate, and now and then it troubles thee a little, then 'tis certain and as clear as the Sun, there is fome creature or content that thy heart is in league withal, which eafeth thee in the want of God, and which is in ſtead of God to thee, and which therefore is thy God. It may be thy

                                         apparel,

apparel, thy wife, child, &c. and if thou die in this estate, never shalt thou have communion with Jesus Christ, *The mouth of the Lord hath spoken it.*

2. Dost find the Lord a stranger to thee in all his Ordinances, wherein it may be the Lord sweetly and wonderfully and mightily, yet not alway, but seasonably reveals himself to others. Oh but thy heart dries and parches away, and that without much trouble under them all. If so, suspect it, beleeve it that there is some league with a lust. For there is a double life of a Christian. 1. An outward life, which others see: Men see he comes to Church, prayes in the Family, &c. 2. There is a secret inward life; according to that of *Mat.6.6. Thy Father which sees in secret*, which none knowes but himself, and the Lord; and this is an ineffable communion with God, vision of God, delight in God, &c. *Psal.45. The Kings daughter is all glorious within.* There is an open life of prayer, and hearing, and fasting, and there is an inward, secret life in all these, wherein the Lord acquaints himself with his people, *Psal.63.1,2,3. To see thee as I have seen thee.* Now there be divers have this open life, yet wanting the secret life. As we love not to live among Tombes, nor to have communion with dead men; so the Lord is a stranger to them. He may secretly sweeten an Ordinance to them, and move them, and shake and trouble them, but himself is a stranger, spiritual miseries not removed, spiritual mercies not coveyed, *Isa.58.1,2,3,4. Why have we fasted, and thou regardest not? You took pleasure saith the Lord, and break the bonds of wickednesse,* &c. I know Saints may be thus denied, and it may be for some space of time, yet they quarrel not with God for denying them, but are more taken off from pleasures thereby. *Thou hidst thy face, and I was troubled,* though the Mount stood still. But some there be whom neither good day mends them, nor bad day pairs them: Surely there is some content thy heart is bewitched withal. That look as 'tis with a suitor to another, let him while he comes to her, professe never so much love, and desire love, yet if when he goes from her, commits lewdnesse with every one, she will lock him out. So 'tis here; never did I know any lockt out from the power and sweetnesse of Ordinances, but because they went a whoring from God out of them. The Lord knowes (though others do not) whether 'tis so with you. Look therefore upon thy self, you enjoy great means every where in this place. Is it enough to have Ordinances? the Ark? No, Do you find the Lord in them? Blessed be God. But tell me truly, Do you find no want of God? Yes. Do you find him? I find more knowledge, strength, &c. But do you find no God usually? No. Then either some creature contents thee, or if the Lord should refresh thee, thou would'st be content without him. Man and wife will (if they love) meet at Meals, *John* 14. But when no meeting, dead prayers, dry Sermons, saplesse Sacraments, worse then before. If thou beest the Lord's, he will by afflictions purge, &c. But if thou continuest so, look for no communion in Heaven.

3. Dost thou find no rest in any thing that thou hast? For this is clear, nothing can give rest to a mans soul but God: He is big enough only to fill it, and then a man hath it, *Isa.26.3.* Now if no rest, 'tis a sign thy heart sticks to the creature, yet thou saist I would fain have the Lord: It may be so; but thou wouldst have creatures too. And hence God will not, and creatures cannot give the fulnesse of rest. Thus it was with *Solomon, Ecclef.2.3.* So 'tis with thee, thou findest thy soul delighting it self in all things; yet *vanity and vexation*, and withal giving thy self to wisdom too. 'Tis true, a Saint feels an emptinesse in these things, yet he feels a fulnesse in something else. (He hath better meat which you know not of) which *Solomon* did not for a time, yet afterward he did. But thou findest a vanity and trouble, and art never at peace when all is done; weary of world, But hath the Lord swallowed thee up into himself, in the cloud of his Glory, so that in his favour and presence thou findest life? No, Then there is

some luft thou loveft, and dying thus, fhalt never fee the face of Chrift. Yea, this will come as a heavy endictment againft thee, that God hath fo wearied thee in thy way. Yet *Jer.2.25. There is no hope, after thy Lovers thou wilt go.* You fhall fcarce find any but feel the creature vain, and yet get not to reft in God.

SECT. II.

II. **D**Ifcoveries whether we are married to the Law or not. And here I fhall ftay longer. Where I premife,

1. When I fpeak of not being married to the Law in ftead of Chrift, I do not hereby exempt your felves from obedience to the Law, after you are in Chrift.

2. Do not think I fpeak againft all evidencing your eftates from conformity to the Law; though I do from fome fubjection and obedience performed to the Law.

1. If the Law was never dead in thee, thou art married to the Law, *Rom.7.2.* Now look as tis with a husband, if the wife be fick, and he be at home, whoever forfakes her, he will comfort her, and fupport and chear her; fo that if he chear her not, its a fign he is dead; if he doth, its a fign he is alive; for the life of the Law, is the comfort and fupport that the Law doth give for a time. So that if thou wert never brought to that fore ftraight, that thou haft not felt any one duty to cheer or revive thee, and comfort thee, but haft found fome little thing or other to do it, its certain you are yet married to the Law. *Ex. gr.* It may be thou haft been troubled in mind for thy fins, What hath cheared thee? I have forfaken them, and caft out *Jonah*, and there hath been a calm: Why this forfaking thy fins (which hath not been all but fome) is not Chrift, but an act of the Law. Oh but I have fallen again into fins, this hath troubled thee: What hath cheared thee? I have repented and been forry for them, and purpofed to do fo no more. This is the life of the Law ftill. Oh but you find fins prevailing againft you, and you cannot part with them; and hence dare not refolve againft them. Oh but my defire is good though, my will hath ever been againft them. Oh ignorance! This defire is but a work of the Law, 'tis not Chrift. Oh but I have found no defire fometime: What hath quieted you now? I have trufted to Chrift: You have done it. The Lord never made you feel a need of the Lord, to draw you to truft; though to be affured of Chrift's love. Is this a legal Act? *Anf.* As obedience to the Law done by the power of Chrift, is an Evangelical work, fo to perform any Evangelical work from a mans felf, is a Legal work; and you are under the life of the Law. So that thou haft not been fo oft troubled, but the Law hath fupported thee; thou haft not been brought to that paffe as the Church, the Spoufe was, *Ifa.54.5,6.* And as one of my beft friends, and beft men that lives this day in the world, after many wreftlings to find fomwhat in himfelf to chear him, and could not; Now faith he, *if the Lord out of his good Nature*, &c. *do not help me, I am undone for ever; for I have a heart and a nature againft him, and the more I do, the worfe I am. And therefore thither I look.* Surely you are under the life of the Law, and are far enough off from Chrift, if not fenfible of this. Not that a man is alway thus, for he that cannot feel afterward the Lord Jefus by the power of his Grace working in his heart, I would conclude, he never had any at all. But at firft 'tis fo. For thefe two things man naturally feeks,

1. To have a righteoufnefle in himfelf that will eafe him.

2. To have it from himfelf: Kitchin Phyfick is not far to fetch.

Now the Lords plot in faving his, is, 1. To make them feek it out of themfelves in another: *Look unto me and be faved, all the ends of the earth.* 2. To have all

all from another, that so, *no flesh might glory before him.* And to doubt of this, is to doubt whether God hath plotted the Glory of his Grace or no. Hence the Lord empties the soul of both, that the soul saith, *Ashur shall not save us,* Hof.14. 3, 4. None durst, none can comfort it. And now to the wonderment of Heaven, and everlasting joy of a poor cast-away, and the eternal honour of his free Grace, now, and never till now, doth he begin to make the match between the Lord Jesus and this poor soul : And as the Lord never comes to him till now, so he never will come to the Lord, while he hath the least good ; as it was with the Prodigal, while any husks, or as it was with the woman with her bloody issue, while any mony to spend on other Physitians, never will try what Christ can do. And therefore those that never yet knew of the death of the Law, they are yet married to it, *Rom.*2.17. I know many a soul grieves for the death of this husband, and now thinks 'tis undone, I cannot do this and that, though formerly I could indeed ; I say if there be any love of Christ, now is the time of it. Only understand Gods scope here in it.

2. If a man complains more or chiefly for want of grace or righteousnesse, to remove sin, and not so much for want of Jesus Christ : Then in this case 'tis as it is with a woman, that man for whose absence she mourns most, that is her husband : She faith the other is, no but he is not. So this is the estate of many a soul, they have neither Christ nor righteousnesse : Now they complain so much that their hearts sink and dye away quite within them : And what is it for ? I cannot do this, nor I do not find nor feel such signs and affections within me. Such a vile heart, I know not the like, such rising in my heart to sin and thoughts of it ; why if you had Christ, all this would be mended. *I can do all through Christ.* But you complain not for want of Christ, nor need of him from these two Arguments.

1. Because the feeling of your sins, does not make you feel a greater need of Christ, as *John, I have need to be baptized,* &c. but drive you further from Christ, and reason it out against him, And why ? Because you would have a righteousnes without him which you stand in need of.

2. Because he that feels a need of the Lord Jesus, shall not when he is offered, need intreating to take him ; as you shall not need intreat hungry men to eat their bread, you shall not need to intreat *Zacheus* to receive Christ joyfuly. But no commands, no intreaties can prevail with you to take him when he is offered, you have no heart to it. Like women that love their own husbands, grieve so for their absence, that they have no heart to any other offer. Is it thus with thee ? Then 'tis with thee, as it was with that young man, that askt Christ what he should do to inhe it eternal life ; he liked Christ well, but he did not feel a need of Christ himself so much, as of some more knowledge of the Law, and ability to do it. Its the great plot of Arminians, to make Christ a means only, to make every man a first *Adam* ; setting men to work for their living again ; for they grant all Grace is lost, all comes from Christ, Christ gives all, and to Christ we must look for all ; and then when we have it, use it well, thus you shall have life, else look for death : So 'tis a misery many a soul is in. Men will trade in small wares, rather than live on anothers Almes. Do you think the Lord takes it well to make him a Merchant for your ends ? Oh no, never look to have communion with him in this way !

3. Those that close with, but rejoyce more in a little Grace they receive from Christ, than in all the fulnesse in Christ, more in a little they do, than in all the Lord Jesus hath done, *Phil.*3.3. That is a womans husband, in whom she rejoyceth most. Do you rejoyce more in what you have, and do, than in what the Lord Jesus hath, and hath done ? more in what you receive from him (for a hypocrite may receive from Christ, *John* 15.2.) than in what there is in him ? It argues a whorish heart. I know a man may rejoyce in what Christ works in

him, but 1. not more in this than in Christ himself. 2. A child of God may while he knows not whether Christ is his do so: but you think the Lord is yours; well, when you feel affections and life, then you are glad, when that is lost then sad; why is there no life when thou art dead, no glory when thou art base, no wisdom, no communion with God when thou hast none? Yes, why dost thou not rejoyce in this which is here most fully, which Saints presenting, please the Lord more by, than by giving the glory of Angels infinite millions of years: Oh thy heart is not in love with Christ, but somewhat else, for here is the joy of all Saints, *In thy seed shall all Nations account themselves blessed*: all Nations, one and another, *Isai*.45.24,25. *shall all the seed of Israel be justified, and shall glory*. Consider therefore this, thou art sometime joyed; why? O I find my heart thus and thus, and is this all? yes, for when this is gone, all joy dies; and should I not do thus? yes, else you never felt comfort of it: but not only rejoyce here, but when the beam is gone, the Lord is not gone, *Rom*. 7. *ult*. when the bottles are spent, the spring is full.

Sign 4.

4. He that performs any duty ultimately to ease his conscience, he is married yet unto the Law, for there are two sorts of duties to the Law.

1. Some are directed to give Christ content to ease his heart, by seeing Gods love in Christ, then love being shed, the heart sheds it on Christ again: and thus saith the Apostle, *I through the Law am dead to it, that I might live to God*, *Gal*. 2. 19.

2. Some are to give the soul ease, it sees sin, and fears it must dye, and the Devil appears, and when it lies down, it fears it shall never awaken again; and when it hears, thinks no mercy, but only threats belong to it: and hence having no peace of conscience to think God will love it, it loves duties, doth duties, and now takes these for good tokens and signs of love, and if it feels a need of Christ, 'tis only to ease it. Now a man is married to the Law, when he crouds for ease into the bosome of it, *Deut*. 5. 27. they were in great fear, *Whatever God will have us do, we will do it*: is it not thus with many? How shall we know this?

Answ. Dost find this while fears and terrors of conscience are on thee, so long thou dost seek, and pray, and hear, and call on God, and when they are worn away by time, or blown over with feeling some good things, and hopes from them, then thy heart is careless again; 'tis certain you are yet married to the Law: as many a man exceeding forward while prest under sense of sin for a year or two. Lord! how many hundreds drop away by little and little afterwards? *Deut*. 5. 29. Oh that there were such a heart alway. *Mat*.3.7. to 13. they saw a wrath to come, hence feared, and hence came to *Johns* Baptism to repent and confesse him.

Sign 5.

5. No man that is married to the Law, but his fig-leaves ever cover some nakedness; all the duties ever brood some lust: there is some one sin or other the man lives in, which either the Lord discovers, and he will not part with, as the young man, or else is so spiritual he cannot see all his life-time; read through the strictest of all, and see this, *Mat*. 23. *Painted Sepulchres*: *Paul* that was blameless, yet *Eph*. 2. 3. *Tit*. 3.3. served divers *lusts and pleasures*, and the reason is, the Law is not the ministration of the Spirit, 2 *Cor*.3.8,9. which breaks off from every sin, there is no law that can give life, *Gal*. 3. 21. And hence many men have strong resolutions, and break all again; hence men sin, and sorrow, and pray again, and then go with more ease in their sin; examine thy self, is there any living lust with thy righteousnesse, 'tis sure 'tis a righteousnesse thou art married to, and never wert yet match'd to Christ; hence note thy self, it may be thou hast rested in duties, and since more light came, saw it; and seeing this, thinking that here is all thy errour, thou hast laboured to see the emptinesse of thy own Righteousnesse, and the fulnesse of Christ, and now thou art come to both, and now well. So then thou hast not found out any lust thou livest in all that time; nor the venom

Isai. 1. 11

of

of thy old nature: no; why then I pronounce thou art yet married to the Law, take and trust never so much to Christs righteousnesse, if under the power of a proud heart, an unclean heart still, never speak of Christ.

6. They that are fearful to be troubled at their estate to have it prove ill, which a Saint may do, yet brings it out to the light at last, *John* 3. 20. When a Woman is married to a condemned man, guilt being upon him, he loves not to be seen abroad in the sight of others; thou hearest a Sermon, and art loath it should be found out, loath to be troubled; he that hath righteousnesse in Christ will not only bring it to tryal, before men, but God himself. Now is it thus with any of you? what shall I say? shall I say that Christ is or may be thine in this estate? truly if I durst I should; bless thy self thou maist: but remember that the Lord will take thee to do for it; and what is it to lose communion with Christ, I cannot express it. The Disciples were sad when he went away from them in his abasement, but for the Lord to leave thee, when in his glory, to stand afar off and see him go, never to see him more, when no tears shall ever prevail again; Therefore if thou hast been found out this day, confess and give glory to God, and let thine eyes be tears, that Christ would overcome and draw thy soul with love, and espouse thee to himself for ever. *Sign* 6.

CHAP. VI.

Containing Motives and Arguments to perswade us unto the Love of Christ, and to be Espoused to him.

IS there no communion to be had with the Lord Jesus, unlesse Virgins? unlesse espoused to him? Oh therefore here is a match for you, chuse him, get your affections, if entangled, to come off if ensnared to any other thing, and set your hearts, bestow your love upon him. For 'tis not a dead Faith, (but such a faith as is animated by love) that doth espouse you to him, *Gal.* 5.6. *Faith which works by love.* And therefore as the love of other things (not worth looking after) hath got the soveraignty and royalty of thy heart, so this is a conjugal love, when it bears rule in the heart; let Christ have this love. And as you have loved creatures for themselves, now love the Lord Jesus for himself. And as they have easily enticed you to set your hearts upon them, now be perswaded to set your dearest affections on him. Its said of *John* Baptist, he was the *Bride-groom's Friend,* to speak for him, *John* 3.29. And truly 'tis the main work of the Ministry, to wooe for Christ; and so to present chast Virgins to Christ. This shall be my work now, which may be seasonable in this decaying time. Therefore I shall chiefly bend my speech to three sorts. *Use* 3.

1. To them that never yet loved the Lord Jesus, unlesse it be from the teeth outward.

2. Those that have been striving for this, yet cannot to their own feeling come to this.

3. Those that have so, but their affections are dried up, and love is parched away, *iniquity abounds,* &c. And my Motives shall be these four,

1. Consider the Glory of the person, whom I shall be a spokes-man for this day.

2. Con-

2. Confider he makes love to thee.

3. Confider that all he feeks for is love.

4. Confider what he will do for thee, how he will love thee, if thou wilt love him.

SECT. I.

1. CONfider the Glory of the perfon, for whom I plead for love. What can you love befides him? Where can you find any like unto him? I know the Glory of the Lord is not revealed, becaufe the graffe withers not, the flower fades not, the creature appears not in his withering vanity, *Ifa*.40. But if the Lord would but open your eyes, to fee him, this would win your hearts alone to him.

Now I fhall fingle out only thefe five things, to give you a glimpfe of his Glory. Lift up thy heart, and fay, *Lord hide not now thy face from me.*

1. He is the Prince of the Kings of the earth, *Rev*.1.5. The glory of the world is a Kingdom, the glorious Diamond of that Kingdom is a Prince in his Glory; now for a poor Beggar to have an offer of love from the greateft Prince in the world, would it not tempt her? Would fhe not forfake her lovers, and fet her heart on him? Why look what a diftance there is between the pooreft Peafant and the higheft Prince, fo bafe, and a thoufand times more are all the Princes of the world to Chrift, whofe Dominion is from fea to fea, from Sun to Sun, who fets up and puls down Kings like Counters, who rule: their Courts, their Kingdoms, their hearts, and they do not do, they cannot do, but what he will. Other Kings are Princes, are Rulers of men, Chrift Prince of Kings. Now who would not be glad of his love? who having tafted death, is fet down on the right hand of God, on high, cloathed with endleffe Glory, who hath Kings in his chaines, whofe breath is not in his noftrils, whofe favour is not for a day, but he lives and reignes for ever. Now doth Chrift reign? Is he a Lord, and in Glory upon his Throne? Methinks I fee Jefus at the right hand of God, your foolifh affections have undone you if you love him not.

2. He is appointed by the Father to be Judge of quick and dead, at the laft day, *John* 5.22,23. as well as to rule all now. So that if you do maintain enmity againft him, he may let you alone, you may live in health, and die in peace, in the eye of man, and in thine own eyes too: Yet there is a day coming he will break out of Heaven *with a fhout*, and appear in the clouds in the amazing Glory of his Father, *with all his mighty Angels, and all the dead fhall hear his voice*, and you fhall appear before him with this body, when the Heavens fhall burn round about him, and the earth fhall tremble under him, and all guilty eyes mourning and wayling becaufe of him. Then you fhall know what 'tis to defpife him, and wifh, oh that I had loved him, *Rev*.1.7. You that fay you love him, yet by an impenitent heart pierce him, you fhall wayl, even fo, *Amen*. Men do not fee an end of thefe things, nor the Glory of the Lord another day. Hence creatures are loved, and the Lord of Glory is loathed. A great Prince may not be fo highly efteemed, untill he appears in his ftate. Prifoners would give any mony, much more love, for the Judges Favour.

3. He only is the procurer and author of all the good that ever thou didft fuck out here, though thou haft neither known him, nor been thankful to him. For look as it was with Angels, fo it fhould have been with man; the wrath of God fhould have been poured out upon him, and on all the world, and creatures fhould have been tormentors of him, but that the Lord Jefus begged and bought the world. And hence, 1 *Tim*.4.10. called *Saviour of all, but chiefly of the Elect.* Micah 4.4. *In his daies, men fhall fit under Vines and Fig-trees*: So

that

that if ever any creature did thee good, it was Jesus that put that sweetnesse in it, out of his fulnesse, and set it awork, sent it to thee, gave it thee to do thee good. Thou shouldst never have had wink of sleep, never restrained from one sin, but lived in blaspheming God, never have heard of a Gospel but for Christ: And will you not love him? Oh ungrateful world! unnatural generation of men! Why dost love any creature? 'Tis for the paint of it and good in it. If there be so much in it, what is there in Christ that gave it, that drops it into it? Never love him if there be any thing good that is not by him, *Psal.* 116.1. *The Lord hath heard my prayer, I will call on him as long as I live.* Much more when the Lord hath delivered, and thou didst never seek to him.

4. He is the everlasting wonderment of Saints in Heaven; the Queen of *Sheba* heard of *Solomon*, which made her come to see him, but she before imagined but that which now she saw with her own eyes, and that wrapt her out of her self. Here we hear of the Lord Jesus, of his beauty and glory, and this draws Saints to him, and when come, they see that which they never saw before, especially when in Heaven: then fall down in everlasting admiration at this mystery, for the blessednesse of Saints is to see Christ in his glory, *John* 17. 24. Now this lies in an infinite good, this cannot be seen in a finite time: hence Saints shall be piercing their eyes deeper and deeper into this mystery, and shall ever see more and more, but never see all, and this is their joy and glory in Heaven; Is it so? what think you, is Christ worthy of your love or no? look upon all the glory of the field of this world, you may see an end of all perfection, but never here.

5. He is the delights and bosome love of God himself, *Prov.* 8. 30. Hence *John* when he came to set Christ out, *John* 3. 35. *The Father loveth the Son.* Now is it so, surely though you see not, taste not this good, yet there is; now tell me if this person do not challenge love! would you not be glad to have him? you will say, can he look upon such a VVretch, embrace such a Leper as I? no surely he will never do it.

SECT. II.

2. COnsider he makes love to thee, not one soul that hears me this day, but the Lord Jesus is a Suitor unto, that now you would be espoused to him: *He came unto his own, and they received him not.* Whatever the secret purpose of Christ is, I regard not: In this Evangelical dispensation of Grace, he makes love to all, *John* 1. 12. 'Tis clear, *Mat.* 22.2,3. If there be a Gospel in the world, there is this love of Christ yearning towards all; especially all that have this Gospel of peace sent to them, *Luke* 2. 10. *'Tis tidings of great joy to all people,* as Law is tidings of great sorrow to all people, *Luke* 2. 14. Angels from Heaven preacht this *good will towards men.* For if the challenge of love from men should be founded on his actual love to some, having died for some, then the offer would be particular. But 'tis grounded, 1. On his own worth and Glory, and hence he challengeth love. 2. On this, for ought I know he hath loved me. So that thou art not so vile, but the Lord Jesus his heart is toward thee, and his eye is upon thee for love. But 'tis not all love, but only some that overcomes. 1. Now 'tis real love. 2. Fervent love, 3. Constant. 4. Pure love he makes to thee.

1. 'Tis real love, when the Gospel and Ministers seek for love, the Lord is real in his desires, there is no collusion or dissembling, 2 *Cor.* 5. 20. in Christs stead, *He that receiveth you, receiveth me;* thou thinkest the Lord cares not for thee, nor doth not desire thee though he doth others: but

1. Either the Lord would have thee loath him, or love him; what think you?
2. If the Lord did not really make love to thee, he would not be really angry
for

for rejecting of this love, but the Lord is really angry for rejecting it , and wroth with nothing so much as that, *Psal.* 2. 12. here he swears in his wrath , *Psal.* 95. 11. when he opens his bosom for thee to rest in, and thou wilt not.

3. Look but upon the dealings of God with thee: 1. Hast not oft thought some in Hell better than thee ? why the ruine of millions of men is to win love from thee, *Jer.* 3. 8, 9, 10. 2. Hath not the Lord sent many a mercy to thee, not one but was to win thee, *Psal.* 81. 10, 11, 12. 3. Hath not the Lord with-held many from thee, as here in this wildernesse, *Jer.* 3. 3, 4. 4. Hath not the Lord sent many sorrows, terrors, fears, cares, wearisome businesses that thou hast wished an end of life ? this is love, *Hos.* 2. 6. 5. Hath not the Lord moved thy heart many a time toward him by perswasions , arguments which have a power to move the heart, this is love, *Hos.* 11. 4. *Cords of a man.* 6. Hath not the Lord oft melted thy heart for mercies, as *David* when he might have killed *Saul*; truly you may feel his love which is much towards you ; that which keeps off thy heart from love, is the Lord intends it not to me, he is not plain with me. But he sends to thee his plain Gospel which thou art to attend unto ; and he takes fittest seasons to speak to thee now in the time of thy health : and doth he not oft visit thy heart when thou art alone ?

2. 'Tis fervent, vehement, earnest love: sometimes a *Suitor* is real , but he is not earnest; now thus the Lord is: 1. The Lord longs for this, *Deut.* 5. 29. 2. Pleads for this, *Jer.* 2. 5. *What iniquity*, &c. 3. Thinks long for this time, *Jer.* 13. 27. *Jerusalem will not be made clean, when shall it once be ?* 4. Mourns when he hath not this, *Ezek.* 6. 9. *Broken with their whorish heart.* 5. Content to give away any thing for it, all the love of Christ is founded on this. 6. If thou comest not presently, he is content to wait that he may be gracious.

3. 'Tis constant and continual , there is not a moment , thou dost not so oft breath, as thou maist see and taste love, *Isai.* 27. 3. *Isai.* 65. 2. 1. After all thy whorish departing from God , that if man should do so, no man would own, yet he saith, *Return to me*: thou seest never a creature but thou hast loved more than Christ, yet return. 2. When God threatens most terribly, and sets his fury on record, yet then there he minds nothing but love, *Jer.* 36. 2, 3. 3. When none else will own and pitty thee thou art so vile, yet *Ezek.* 16. 2, 3. the Lord saith *live*, *then is a time of love.* 4. Nay when thou hast cast away thy self as a forlorn creature, yet *Hos.* 14. 3. *In thee the Fatherless find mercy.* 5. When he hath thee in his arms, ready to give thee up , yet then, *How shall I give thee up O Ephraim*, *Hos.* 11. 8. I tell thee if one sparkle of his eternal blasting displeasure should fall upon thee, it would be so intollerable that it would sink thee; his love is as strong as death, no water can quench it; oh 'tis not so with man, or great men , once repulsed is enough : why should the Lord do so here ? many think time is past, 'tis not so , 'tis the temptation of them that have time, not of them that want it ; take heed this make thee not despise him.

4. 'Tis a pure love, others make love for their own ends, but the Lord hath no need of thee, or of thy love: he could raise up of stones children of praise , he could have gone to others, he could have and can fetch his glory out of thy ruine: he was blessed before all worlds ; and by all thy sins thou dost but throw stones against the wind, or snow-balls against the Sun : why doth he do it ? O 'tis thy good, he pitties thee as once *Jerusalem*, to look upon thy destruction and desolation : as 'tis with the Elect, they have wrath before their eyes, and hence perswade others, so the Lord Jesus.

SECT. III.

3. COnsider 'tis nothing else but love the Lord looks for, or cares for. Love looks for nothing but love, *Prov.* 8. 17. and this is the end of all Election,

to be holy before him in love: and mark it, if it be a stayed love, that constrains thee to him, you cannot wrong him: As if thou come and perswade one to murder his Child, he cannot; so if perswaded to despise, oh bowels of heart-breaking love, 2 *Cor.* 5. And surely 'tis admirable love; What if it were thy Goods, thy *Isaac* to be sacrificed, thy body to be burned, it was nothing, but the desires only love, only thy heart which hath forged so much villany against him: let him never be called upon, or professed, if not worthy of this. After all, is this all? yes, no Portion he cares for, and when he hath this he hath all. Wonder at this O Angels!

SECT. IV.

4. COnsider what he will do for thee, how he will love thee, if thou wilt thus love him.

1. He will set thee next himself in honour, *Psalm* 45. 9. that as the Lord Jesus is next to God, sits at his right hand; so here, which is an honour that the Angels have not, who are no where called Chrifts Spouse: hence never had such an union, hence never shall partake of that honour of Saints.

2. He will enrich thee, as 'tis with Man and Wife, all that he hath is hers: so himself, and all his glory, his God, his Father, his Kingdom is thine, *Prov.* 8. 21. they that love me inherit something, others nothing: no, nothing indeed, only shews of good, and they find it so when they awake, nothing their own, nothing long: that let thy outward man, yea thy inward be never so poor, thou shalt by him be heir of all.

3. He will counsel thee: hence *David*, *Psal.* 73. made choice of God, *Thou wilt guide me by thy counsel*; no greater curse than to be left to the guidance of a mans own counsel but here there shall not be any strait, but the Lord will shew thee a way out of it, either by his prudence or providence; there shall not be any secret of Christ that thou desirest to know, but as Christ told them, *You are my Friends*, so you are my Spouse: hence all his secrets shall be opened to thee: there shall not be one act of thy life, but ordered by infinite prudence, and wisdom, and love; sometimes we are befooled in our own counsels, and left to them to teach us to depend on the Lord the more, yet thereby shall come out such good, that it shall be among us as with *Josephs* Brethren.

4. He will dwell with thee as a man must dwell with his Wife, *John* 14. 23. that the great Mediator that passeth by Kings and Princes, and will not look on them, should come and dwell with thee: this is better than to have the presence of Kings, the guard of Angels, better than Heaven it self, that he should dwel where is nothing worthy to entertain him, only something to grieve him. Now this is,

1. A constant assistance of the Spirit, that let the Soul go where he will, be brought to never so low an ebb, yet Christ will not out, but some stirrings, sighings, lookings, pantings after Christ; when heart and strength fail, yet God, &c. when ready to give all for lost, then consider as *Psal.* 73. 2. If he doth depart, he will not be long but return again: and those that know his affection, know it so to be, *Isai.* 54. *for a little moment*, &c. so the Lord may depart, and when his presence is a little more esteemed, come again with everlasting mercies: as a man may know many weaknesses by his Wife, yet she having not bestowed her heart on any other, he will return: so if thou canst say, yet I am the Lords, he will return.

5. He will rejoyce in thee and over thee, *Zeph.* 3. 17. as a Bridegroom doth over the Bride: Not because of any beauty in thee, for there is none, but because given in marriage of the Father, and for his own sake. This day thou shalt no sooner set thy heart on Christ, but he falls in love with thee, and will take thee with joy; thou thinkest he will be angry if thou closest with him and love him, no, it will be the joy of Heaven, of Jesus Christ himself.

E   6. He

6. He will exceedingly comfort thee; and look as 'tis with tender husbands, then they comfort most when most sorrowes betide them, for who could endure his wife should be alway drooping? So even then when nothing doth or can comfort thee, the Lord will, *Isa.*54.5. For the Lord doth not alway comfort, but when in need, as it was with the Patriarchs, Then God appeared, when they were at worst; and these are abundant comforts, 2 *Cor.*1.3,4,5. You shall not need to scramble for it as many do, whose hearts do not love Christ in truth as yet.

7. He will put up all wrongs, and bear exceedingly with thee. Many think even when God hath sealed love to them, if any little sin be committed, then they are cast off; no, if under the Law so indeed, but when espoused to him, 'tis not weaknesses, nor wilfulnesse can make the Lord cast thee away, but he will heal the one, and afflict thee for (yet not cast thee off) for the other, *Psal.*89. 33. *My loving kindnesse will I never take away.* Yea, he will forgive both, *Luke* 7.47. *Much forgiven because she loved much.* Nay, thy wrongs shall be an occasion to make him love thee more, *Rom.*5. *Where sin abounds, Grace abounds.*

8. He will never part with thee, *Hos.*2.19. Once love him, and he will never lose thee.

1. No sin shall part thee and him; for Christ when he enters into marriage covenant, doth not suspend his love on our Grace or Holinesse, then he might leave quickly, but on his own. Grace to wash away our filthinesse, *Eph.*5.25,26. If a husband marries a woman only for so long as she is in health, then when sicknesse comes he may depart. But *è contra*, if to take away her sicknesses, then they cannot hinder: Nothing but Adultery can part; Now that they cannot do, for nothing breaks, till covenant is broken: And the covenant here is everlasting, and so undertaken for by the Lord that it can never be broken.

2. No miseries can, *Rom.*8.35,36,37. *Can tribulation?* It makes man leave us, but this is peculiar to Christ, he will not leave.

3. Death cannot, it must part man and wife, though loved never so dearly before, but here not; but then he will come himself and fetch thee, *John* 14.1, 2,3. Take thy soul to the Bride-chamber, there to be with him for ever and ever, and he will keep the dust of thy blessed body, and not lose one dust of it, and at the last day raise it; and then when others shall cry out Yonder is him whom I have grieved, then shalt thou lift up thy head, Yonder comes my husband to comfort me, to crown me, that I may dwell with him. It shall be the blessed day to thee. And when judgement is done, thou shalt go with thy beloved from the air up to Heaven with a shout, and live in his love and dearest embracings of thee, and this he will do for thee so poor and vile in thine own eyes? Now will you have him? and that now, or no?

SECT. V.

*Object.*1.
Answ.

1. IF the Lord be so desirous of me, why doth he not overcome me?
If the Lord doth it, 'tis by these cords of love, and if not, the brand of a reprobate is upon thee.

*Object.*2.
Answ.

2. But I do love him already.
Is it with such a love as makes you unable to resist him? to wrong him? as the Apostle said, *We cannot speak against the Truth, but for it*; for if not 'tis naught. There is a natural love to Christ, as to one that doth thee good, and for thine own ends; and spiritually for himself, whereby the Lord only is exalted: Hast thou this?

*Object.*3.
Answ.
*Object.*4.
Answ.

3. But I do not have Christ.
If any man do not love him with a positive love, let him be *Anathema.*

4. I cannot love him.
1. What canst thou love else? 2. Thou canst not love him so well as thou
ouldst)

shouldst, therefore close with him, and love will follow. 3. Get the Lord to overcome thy heart, *Jer.*3.19.

How shall I do it?

1. Set him before thee? Who will commit lewdnesse while her husband looks on? *Psal.*16.8.

2. See what content thou givest Christ by love: Smallest duties coming from love are accepted. What makes thee wrong him to please thy self? Let a thing crosse thee, yet it contents Christ Jesus.

3. Get him, and wait by Faith on him to overcome thy heart, and the work is done then. Now will you do this or no? If not say then you have had a fair offer, and tell the Devils so, when thou goest down to Hell, as it may be thou maiest ere long. Men talk of terrible Sermons, but these sink deepest. Tell me, dost thou love the lord only? Wil't keep lusts or Christ alone? If so, then look to it. In this Countrey a woman killed her child, and she said, when she did it, her child smiled upon her. Wilt thou kick Christs love now when he smiles upon thee. Afterward shee repented, but it was too late. Women when they have a mind to some other, murder their husbands, but if known, burnt they must be. But wilt have him and love him alone? Oh if perswaded to this, then happy for ever. Let this day be the beginning of eternal Glory to thy soul, and the God of peace be with thee.

CHAP. VII.

Sheweth that a man hath no power in himself to do any spiritual work, but that he must receive all from Christ.

4. HEnce we see a necessity, if ever we look to have communion with Christ, to do all spiritual work, all we do (*Theologice*) from the mighty power of Christ, from the life and Spirit of Christ. To bring forth no Spirituall Act but from Christ, and for Christ, (I shall put both in one, and the latter into the first; for none act truly from him but it is for him) for you know if a woman bring forth children to any other but her own husband, that woman hath lost her chastity: So when men shall bring forth the fruits of obedience to any other, from any other, but from Christ, they lose their virginity, their chastity, without which no communion with Christ. For I have ever made two parts or degrees of Christian chastity, (as 'tis in outward chastity.)

1. The soul sets its chief affections on Christ alone, that look as 'tis with a woman, though she cannot do much, nor deserve his love, yet her heart is with him, her self is his, *Cant.*6.3. *I am my Beloveds.*

2. The soul brings forth fruits of love only unto Christ, *i. e.* from Christ and for Christ, as in marriage the woman brings forth fruit of her womb to her Husband; and this is set down plainly, *Rom.*7.4. The first we have handled. Now a little of this. And that I may presse this which is of much use to you, give me leave to expresse my self in these Conclusions.

SECT.

SECT. I.

THat all men living nakedly considered in themselves, have lost all power to do any thing that is good, *Rom.* 3. 12. *None that doth good,* 1. His light is quite extinct, and his eyes quite out: hence said to *sit in darknesse, and the shadow of death, Mat.* 4. 16. now a shadow is a privation of some light, this of all light, hence called darknesse it self; take the blindest *Indian*, he is a witnesse of this truth, and a right picture of a soul fallen from God: hence because he cannot see, he cannot do, 1 *Cor.* 2. 14. 2. All that life he had to act well is lost too, *Eph.* 2. 1. he is dead in trespasses and sins: he cannot breath, nor speak, nor think, nor do one thing that is good: I say nakedly considered in himself. And hence look upon a man quite forsaken of God in Hell, there you may see as in a lively looking-glass what every man living is when the Lord leaves him: he can blaspheme him, he cannot love him, he can contemn God, he cannot esteem him: he can wish there were no God to punish him: he cannot submit unto God, though he leaves the most heavy load upon him, and you see not your selves untill you see your selves here, and see your selves thus.

SECT. II.

THat unto some men especially, nay unto all men almost, though vile, yet more or lesse the Lord gives a power to act, and live, and move, and to do many spiritual duties, or good duties from themselves For as there is a bredth in the wayes of Grace, that every Christian hath not the like measure of Grace, so there is a bredth or latitude in the wayes of sin: every sinner breaks not forth into the like measure of sin, but some are far better than others; as the three grounds that were bad, yet one better than another. Now how comes this about? why, the Lord gives that power to act (as all the knowledg of a God) by the light of Nature (falsly so called) this is the work of God, *Rom.* 1. 19. Hence all terrors, and comforts, and duties of Conscience are all from God: so the Historical Faith of the Gospel which many have, and so to confesse and professe no salvation but by Christ, together with a readinesse to dye in defence of this truth and Religion, and joy from this, and reformation of life upon this, none of these are natural to this soyl of a mans soul, but all are planted there by God, 1 *Cor.* 12. 2, 3. and so that man can act according to the Law, be strict in Sabbaths, frequent in Fastings and Prayers, &c. 'tis from God, *Rom.* 10. 2. And why doth the Lord work this? 'tis else no living in the world among men, and because Christ is the *politicum caput*, and hath bought all men in the world to be his servants, hence gives them gifts which he turns for the good of his people: but yet this is the nature of all these abilities, that a man acts from the strength and power of them, not from Christ, *Mic.* 4. 5. Other Nations *will walk in the name, &c.* and the reason is,

1. Because every man is under the guidance either of the first or second Covenant, and power of either: now as the power of the second Covenant is to draw a man out of himself to another, and so to make him act from another: so the power of the First is to drive a man into himself by terrors, and fears, and hopes, and rewards, and so to enable him to act from himself; hence 'tis impossible but they must act ever from themselves.

And 2. Because though many good Gifts, and moral vertues may be said to be supernatural, *i.e.* above the power of Nature to work, yet never above the improvement of nature: for let God work never so many good things in men, nature, i.e an ill stomack when diseased, is strongest, there Nature turns all into the
humor,

humor, and so a man dyes at last; so the power of sin in Nature being more powerful than any Grace which by common work is given it, ever turns that Grace into it self, and leads it into captivity, bondage, and service of it self; so that there is never a Grace but 'tis made to serve some lust, as in _Jehu_, in _Judas_, &c. and God complains, _Isai._ 43. 24. So this I say is the case of thousands unregenerate, who can do many good things, but from themselves, which God hath wrought to: and hence many a child of God hath been long hindred from conversion, and others not converted at all, because they have thought wicked men whom God minds to damn, are such as have no good, nor do no good, or if they do, they have it not from God; but 'tis not so with me, for I have and do many good things, which I acknowledg come from God, and I thank God I am not as other men. Now mark, 'tis true, nakedly considered no good could come from unregenerate men, but yet the Lord gives power to many to do, so the Lord hath done to thee, and thou hast been thankful for it. And this is common, many account themselves great sinners, but yet they can believe: many say they can do little, but their desire and will at worst is to do: tell them these are not right, unlesse they come from the Lord, they will say the Lord doth all, and they acknowledg it, and so I believe, and 'tis true, but 'tis not such a work of the Lord as is peculiar to the Elect, because when the Lord hath wrought these, you act only from then, and hence never feel a want of these, for the Lord never yet wrought any Grace in his people, but after they have had it, and tasted of it, he hath more or lesse deserted them, and so hath made them feel a want of it, and made them fetch it again with sighs, and groans, and tears; now it hath never been so with thee.

SECT. III.

THat it's _most pleasing to man, and agreeable to his nature to act only from himself_: As it was with the Prodigal, he desired his Stock in his own hands, and while any thing lasted, he would never come home; and hence those, _John 6._ 28. _What shall we do to work the works of God_: and when Christ spake of Faith, they were stumbled there, insomuch that divers did forsake him.

1. Because mans acting from himself is best able to attain his own ends, to which you know a man is gently and necessarily carried: for no man out of Christ, but his own ends draw him; now Christ crosseth a mans own ends, and to live on him is to live on him that will confound then of their own ends, or else no life there: Hence they live from themselves. As 'tis with a Crafts-man, or Artificer, propounding the gain or credit they may get by being excellent in their Trade, may by their own study and frequency of acts, grow dexterous, and very skilful at last, and hence delight in it, so here, profession and practise of Religion may be a mans trade which he may drive for his own ends and gain, and hence may desire to be excellent, and by endeavour be excellent, and profit exceedingly in many excellent endowments: hence he acts and works for himself, _Rom._ 1. 14.

2. Because a man naturally knows not how to fetch it from Christ from Heaven, _Rom._ 10. 3. Hence 'tis with them as with a Child cast off by the Father, and put to some hard Master, because they have no Father to maintain them, they must live as they are, and do as well as they can. A man comes to pray, knows not how to fetch strength from Christ, and he must pray, and hence prayes as well as he can.

3 Because it's so hard a thing to live upon another, it's easie and sweet to a spiritual heart, but most difficult to any carnal heart, _John 6._ Christ tells them they must eat his flesh, they say, _who then can be saved_, and many departed. Men had rather make holes, and keep water in their own house, than have it far to

E 3　　　　fetch,

Concl. 3.

fetch, and when they come to fetch it, to beftow fuch ftrength in drawing of it.

4. Becaufe every man thinks he loves and cares for himfelf beft, and fees no God nor Chrift caring for or loving of him more than himfelf; Hence a man plots for himfelf, and lives for himfelf, and all from himfelf. As when *Jofephs* Brethren faw their Brother, then they came down and lived upon him, before they came to him indeed, but with their mony, to live of themfelves. And thus it was with the young man, *Sell all and have riches in Heaven*: No, he loved himfelf, and cared for himfelf better than fo; hence would not commit and give away all to Chrift.

5. Becaufe whatever a man doth from himfelf, either 'tis good, or he thinks it fo, or hopes if not, God will accept it. Some evil in it perhaps, but he hath his allowances which will make it go, fome good defires or Faith in Chrift, and hence hopes if not thinks God will accept of what comes from himfelf. As, *Prov. 21. 2. All a mans waies are right in his own eyes.* And truly Nature and Satan have ever been Imitators and Apes of God, to forge and make Grace like true Grace, hence deceived. This being pleafing to men, is the practice of moft men, yea, all men out of Chrift. And this is one great part of the inward, fecret, fubtil, fpiritual whoredom of the foul. Thus men may force forrow, when yet there is little true forrow, and fo in other cafes.

SECT. VII.

Concl. 4.

THat all thefe works though good in themfelves, yet are moft vile before the Lord; as Chrift fpeaks of the Pharifees, Its abomination in the fight of God, which is glorious before man, *Luke* 16.15.

1. Becaufe hereby the foul deprives Chrift of the end of his coming; for all men having loft the ftock and power to live, the Lord hence will truft no man with it again; hence puts it into a furer and better hand, that thither poor, blind, dead creatures might fly for life, & when they are there, live there like bees on their hony, *John* 6.27. & 17.23. He might never have looked after you, and will you defpife him now? What folly and unkindneffe is this, that when your pits are dry, and bottles empty, and fouls miferable here, you will not (I do not fay fip) when water runs by your door, but not live.

2. Becaufe whatever comes from felf, its ever for felf. A man can do nothing from himfelf, but his laft end is felf. As 'tis with water-works, they rife no higher than the fpring, *Gen.*11.4. *This Babel I have built*, *Dan.*4.30. And a man that hath but common Grace, look as by vertue of that Grace, or gift of God, he may act for God, becaufe it came from God; fo nature and fin being more powerful than that Grace, hence he never fo acts for God, but in the laft place acts for it felf, as in *Jehu*: And fo a man makes himfelf his own God.

3. Becaufe whatever a man doth from himfelf, he will grow proud of it, *Rom.* 4. *Not of works, left any man fhould boaft.* Hence *Joab* fent to *David* to take the City that he might have the Crown. This robs Chrift of the Glory.

4. Becaufe whatever work is not done by vertue of the Lord Jefus, is a dead work, which a living God, and a living Chrift, and a living Spirit loath, *Heb.*9.14. *Sprinkle your Confciences from dead works.* Deadly works are fins, dead works are good works done, but not from the principle of the life of Faith, but life of Nature. Now as Confcience is the principle of the life of Nature, fo Chrift is the principle of a Chriftian life, *Col.*3. 1 *John* 5.10,11,12. For 'tis not fanctification that is the principle of life, but the life it felf that flows from it, as from union of foul and body, the foul is not the life but the principle of it, hence as foon as its out, the body is dead: So, &c. And do you not find it thus, whenas you do many duties, how tedious, wearifom are they? yet muft be done, this

this is a dead work. What comfort, what peace is there, when you have done them? because not from life.

5. Because what comes from self, comes from all sin, 'tis dipt and dyed, and tainted and poysoned with all sin in a manner. *Who can bring a clean thing out of an unclean?*

6. Because when a man will act from himself, and not suffer Christ to act for him, he will not have Christ to reign over him, he puts down the Kingdom of God that should be within him. For when a man professeth Christ is King of his Church, he is now a King in name: When a man feels an impossibility to rule himself, and hence desireth and chuseth Christ to rule, now Christ is a King by choice: When the soul after this choice, depends on Christ for what he chose him for, and the Lord works, now Christ is a King indeed. Now if you will not have the Lord to reign over you, you will be found enemies to the Lords Kingdom.

SECT. V.

HEnce it will follow, *The soul is to act wholly and only from the Lord Jesus Christ, and whatever fruits of love it shews to Christ, to bring them forth from Christ.* Which doth not only concern them that never yet knew Christ, and yet pride up themselves in what they have and do, but those that be in Christ in a special manner. For *John* 15.2. *Every Branch in me that brings not forth fruit.* 'Tis not meant of one indeed in Christ, for he shall bring forth fruit, but every branch, *i.e.* by outward profession, so that it brings not forth fruit, but appears fair, and deceives man, God will cast away: *And without me, even ye Disciples can do nothing.* *Concl. 5.*

1. How is the soul to act from Christ only, when it hath life, especially the elect? *Quest. 1.*
2. By what means may this be done, to get and keep this chastity? *Quest. 2.*
First, How is the soul to act from Christ alone when there is sanctification within? *Quest. 1.*

1. If the soul feel no power to act from Grace received, as Saints somtimes do, either after Gods deserting them, or their forsaking God long, or after some hardning sin; then 'tis clear the soul in this case is (though not in a way of carelesness) to depend upon the Lord Jesus, that he would quicken and help. As *David* after his grosse fall, *Lord create in me a clean heart.* And *Isa.* 63.17. *Why hast thou hardned our hearts from thy fear? Oh return!* In this case the soul is not to bring the soul to God, but God to the soul. As many a Christian cannot prize nor love the Lord nor his waies, he is not to say, I will bring my soul and offer it to him; but look to the Lord that he would raise up my dead affections again. As the Centurion of his Servant, *Speak the word,* &c. Christ *marveiled at his Faith.* Men think when they feel nothing, that they must and can work it out; and hence comes one of these three things. *Answ. 1.*

1. Either the soul cannot love Christ when it sees such Lawes it cannot submit to. And hence a Christian once said to me, If the least thing was left for me to do of my self, I could not love Christ; but now that when brought low and can do nothing, he brings all the help we need. This makes the Spouse go to the bosom of her Husband, *Psal.* 116.6,7. Or else,

2. It cannot do it, for corruption in a Saint is too hard for his Grace, *I am but a child, and thy people many,* 1 Kings 3.7. Hence he must be strong in the Lord.

Or 3. If it do, it never hath any peace in what it doth, the duties never so well done. Whereas otherwise the poorest duty done from Christ, witnesse *Heb.* 11. 4,5. as a child begot of the Father, he will own, but other children not. If any poor tired heart that hears me this day, thou hast been making thy Brick, and promises and vowes will not help, now away to the Lord, if ever help now 'tis when most helplesse.

2. If

2. If you can do any thing favingly good, the foul is bound now (by the powe: of Faith) to ftir up it felf to act, though not to truft to it alone, for fomtimes the foul hath the regenerate part uppermoft, and the prevailing Spirit of God, *Pfal.* 21.3. which comes to him, and gives it power to act before the foul come to it. Now a man is bound to act, becaufe 'tis from Chrift now. Hence *Timo-thy* was to *ftir up the gift*, 2 Tim.1.6. Hence complained of them *Ifa.*64.8. *None ftirs up himfelf to take hold on the Lord.* A man muft ftir up himfelf to be-lieve, as well as other Graces, hence *the Kingdom of Heaven is taken with violence,* and though corruption is ftronger than Grace, yet Grace affifted with the Spirit, is ftronger than it, which is never quite out of the foul, but 'tis in the foul, 1 *John* 4.4. *Stronger is he that is in you.* And 'tis faid profeffedly, *He purgeth himfelf, and keepeth himfelf, the evil one toucheth him not*, 1 John 5.18. But mark, truft not barely to this, but when you do this, withall remember, Lord I cannot hold out in this unleffe thou doft help me : But know, *Ifa.* 26. *The Lord is the rock of my ftrength.* And *if you by the Spirit mortifie*, &c. Rom.8.13. Therefore ever hold up failes, but look for a wind. And if a man be not to do this, then when any finful temptation comes , if a man do not find the Spirit and ftrength ready at hand to help, if he be not to ftir up himfelf againft it, he is to fuffer himfelf to be carried down by it. Hence a man may neglect all duties a long time, if he do not find the Spirit affifting, if fo be a man muft not ftir himfelf up, and fo (will fome fay) a man may. May ? What fhall I fay to fuch fluggifh foul, but fleep on ? But know it, the Lord will awaken thee, when you fhall fay, Oh that I had improved the Ta-lent I had ! And if you do find Chrift in fuch a condition, know it they be but the laft vifits of Chrift before he departs. You can do more than you do, and the Lord will have you do it.

But I cannot do it for good ends without Chrift.

Yet do the thing as far as you can, elfe if you owe another a debt, and will not pay, becaufe not for a good end, that excufe will not ferve : So you owe the Lord your lives, your fpirits, your abilities ; lay them out for the Lord, though evil be in them, be humbled for that. Is this good requital to fay you find your hearts dead in prayer, and God muft do all, and there leave it ?

3. You are to expect and look for power from the Lord Jefus in the ufe of means, all known means : For Faith fetcheth all from Chrift, hence we muft go thither where Chrift is to be found, and he dwells in his Houfe, in his Ordi-nances : Therefore there you muft depend upon him. As 'tis with a Merchant, he wades not over the Sea for Pearls, but gets into his fhip, and there he fits ftill, fo here, *Mat.*13. *The Kingdom of Heaven is like a Merchant man.* Hence you that know you can do nothing, being under a fpirit of conviction, and hence do nothing, under a fpirit of floth and neglect of means, by vertue of a fpirit of pre-fumption, and fay Chrift muft do all, I fay you take not the right courfe for the Lord to help you in. The Lord will never be a flave to thy floth, but thou fhalt be like a fhrub, never to fee good when it comes, and fhalt die in horrour with this, Oh I might have done more ! Hence you are worfe than the other, that think if a man fafts, prayes, watches againft his diftempers, mourns for want of Chrift and Grace, and followes God hard here, he is a Legal Chriftian : Why, thefe are but his own works , and this is not living on Chrift. I confefie bare ufing them, or trufting to them is not, but he that lives not on Chrift in ufe of means (thefe and all other means) to find Chrift, er enjoy more of Chrift, fhall never have him. Neither do I know what turning Gods Grace into wantonneffe is, if this be not ; and under a conceit of liberty to be a fervant of corruption. I know not whether it be thus with any, but if I did, I would pity them.

4. If the foul cannot every moment live on Chrift, *i. e.* for every particular act, have a diftinct act of Faith, for this cannot be, yet every fit feafon that it can, it ought to look up to the Lord for life and frefh ftrength. Pray as 'tis πάντη χαιρᾶ, every

ry fit season. And as he brings forth fruit, so he goes for fruit in season, *Psal.1.3.*
And when the soul doth this, the Spirit of the Lord helps, when the act is ceased.

Now the fit seasons are,

1. At beginning of any action, as prayer, hearing, reading : All the time a
man is in his journey, or in his work, he is carried on by the act of Faith at first
setting out : The reach of Faith is long, and continues all prayers, all the duty
throughout, the act of faith is short : Now the Lord looks to his people according to the first.

2. When our act begins to die ; as *Moses lifted up his hands, and when they were
heavy, Aaron and Hur* supported them again.

3. When a man feels himself strong, now apt to be self-confident ; now Lord
for an humble heart ! And thus you are to live on Christ, which if done, would
make a Christians life glorious, and give infinite content to the heart of Christ.
But here is the misery, either hearts are full, and need not, or slothful, and care
not for living so. That truly I do not wonder to hear and see so many withering
trees, as though blasted by wrath, because you fetch not all out of this stock ;
and Christ is such a stranger, because you are so seldom with him to act, and bring
forth fruit to him.

SECT. VI.

2 COnsider of the means to act from Christ Jesus, and indeed herein lies the
skill and life of a Christian, and this is the complaint of many a Soul,
Christ is full, and he is not for himself, but for those that want, and I come to
him when I want it, and yet I find no help ; and hence many are brought to
think either it's in vain to come to Christ, or else I have no Faith in Christ ; I will
therefore premise these three things.

1. That a false, double, treacherous, disloyal heart to Christ cannot expect to
receive any thing it comes for unto Christ. As 'tis with a Woman, that
though others do not, yet her Husband knows she is fallen in league with some o-
ther man, he will be strange to her, and will not do any thing for her. *John 2. ult.
He knew what was in man* ; as 'tis in grafts, *James 1. 7, 8.* Let not a double-minded man think to receive any thing at the hands of the Lord. For that is the nature
of man under the power of any lust, it makes all serve it, even Christ himself,
which he will never do, *I am weary of your new Moons*, saith the Lord, and you
fast, and pray, and have no answer, for you fast for Debate: and therefore I take
a man considered as broken off from the power of his lusts, not one that feels himself under the power of it, for such an one may be delivered from it, such a soul
as can say, much ado have I had to feel my sin, and to be willing to part with it,
but now I am ; here is the Soul I speak of.

2. That the Lord in the dispensation of Grace to his people, is wholly free to
give it when he will : for a man that works for his wages, must in justice have his
wages when his work is done: but he that begs for his living must be content to stay:
We live by Faith, and free gift, not by works and deserts, and hence must wait and
stay, *Mic. 7. 7.* Hence let not any man think sensibly to receive what he goes for
to the Lord Jesus presently, as many feel a want of Grace, and think the Lord
hath promised to help, and now how would it make for his honour to give, but
find it not, and hence grow sad or discouraged, and think it is in vain to seek ? no,
no, Christs hour is not yet come, when you think it is, *John 2. My hour is not yet come*;
and hence many get nothing because they lie out of the way of the Covenant, *viz.*
to think, oh the Lord owes me nothing, and I deserve the contrary.

3. That no man is to look to receive all that which he comes to the Lord for,
but

but only so much as is fit for him : a man feels much straitnesse, and he would
have many enlargements ; he finds much deadnesse, and he would have deep and
over-flowing affections, and he comes to the Lord for it, and the Lord gives some,
Doth he or ? do you no: find it ? can you say you seek the Lord, and attend on
the Lord in vain with these Hypocrites, *Mat.* 3. 14.   True, but yet me thinks
more would be better.   How do you know that ? I think so, that it would be more
for his honour: you think so, then it seems you have one eye more than Christ, and
that he is very carelesse and foolish in raising his own honour : Oh abhor those
thoughts, he gives you such a coat as is fit for you, such a sail as fits your boat, such
shoes as fit your feet, *Psal.* 21. 5. *Honour and Majesty hast thou sitted for him* :
therefore do not loo, to receive any more than is fit for you, and know it, that is
best for you. The Physitian prescribes that which is fit, not that which is most
desired of the Patients : if they will not accept of this, he will not look after
them, 1 *Cor.* 12. 7, 8.

4. I think not to get any thing from the Lord Jesus with ease, I mean to the
fleshly part : it hath been an old complaint, I go to Christ, and fish all night, and
can catch nothing : and why ? here is the cause, they cannot get it easily, and
therefore they cannot get it at all, yea there 'tis. *Heb.* 11. 6. This is one of the
two main handles of Faith, *he is a rewarder of all them that diligently seek him,*
not negligently : and hence at their first conversion how doth Christs Fruits overflow, and his *Jordan* rise above the banks : and what a deal doth a christian gain, yet
not afterward : so in time of great trouble, oh 'tis because you seek him diligently : Therefore in prescribing means, do not say this is hard, and so depart as those
did upon the very same ground, *John* 6. 60.

SECT. VII.
The Meanes are these.

1. LAbour for a comprehending knowledge, what is the love of Christ to thee :
there is a double knowledg of Christs love.

1. That he loves me, and this very apprehension fetcheth in warmth and life
into the heart, *In thy favour is life.*

2. What that love is, and that in all the dimensions of it : and beloved this is
that which fills a man, *Eph.* 3. 18, 19. that as 'tis with Women when the fulnesse
of the Husbands love is seen, it knits the heart invincibly to him, and makes her do
any thing for him, so here.   And as we say of Trees, if the Tree begins to wither
and dye, the only way is not to cast water on the branches, or to pray for water and
dews from Heaven on them, but water the root.   Love is the next root of all
Grace, love Christ, and you will never be weary of doing for Christ, love him, and
he will love you, *Prov.* 8. 17.   Now what kindles love so much as this comprehending knowledg of the Lord Jesus, and his love, this will make a man a burning Beacon of love, make a man melt into love, which is as strong as death, much water
cannot quench it, 2 *Cor.* 5. 14. *Love of Christ constrains,* *Gal.* 5. 6. *Faith works by
love* : Faith is our feet whereby we come to Christ, Love is our hand whereby we
work for Christ: now let any Chirurgeons servant come to a Chirurgeon with a broken arm, and tell him he can do no work for him, therefore desire him to give him
strength to do it, come saith he, let me heal your arm first : no by no means ; let
me first do your work, that so you may heal, and I may feel my arm to be whole : It
can never be : So 'tis many a Christians course, Lord let me do thy work, and
hence he cries, Lord give me strength, and then falls to do it, and cannot without
pain, because his love is broken.   Many say, I will go to Christ, and act for
Christ, and then I will think the Lord loves me, but never find it : first see and comprehend the love of the Lord: And truly this is the reason why no heart, no
                                                                        strength

strength to act for God, unlesse it be in a-wearisom manner, and why? oh love is out, and why is that out? why 'tis not comprehended by the eye of Faith, it's despised by some, other things are sweet to them, or it's forgotten by others; men remember not what once they were, and what the Lord hath done, 'tis seen a little, and hence a little life and strength, but 'tis comprehended by few. O sinful times! O unkind world! never was my heart so dead faith one, never so straitned and shut up faith another, never so feeble in all duties faith another: why, you see, and taste, and sip of this love, but you feed not heartily, abundantly on it. Never didst thou think so little of this love; for though Christ will conveigh rich Grace to his people, yet it shall be by love. Christians will come to Christ, and when they receive and feel the good they come for, they will think of Christs love and that he loves them, no first come unto the Lord Jesus, being once come, know he will not cast thee away, *John* 6. 37. then think of this love; stay here, first feed here and you may act, and then the Lord will conveigh strength and power, and inable you hereunto: For though when a man trusts to his love as *Peter* without Faith, a man will fall because he trusts to an arm of flesh: yet when Faith imploies love, the work is very great. As a Father hath a child who must keep at home with him, but he hath never a Steward to lay out that estate for him that he means to give him, but when an able Steward, now he gives his Son richly. So here:

Quest. *How shall I comprehend it?*

Answ. First, the Apostle prayes for it. Secondly, see what 'tis by his description, and meditate on it.

1. The bredth, *i.e.* the same love wherewith the Lord comprehends all Saints, as *Abrahams*, &c. thou art as dear to the Lord as he or any in Heaven, nay it may be did cost more: not a crosse, not a mercy, but it's common (for substance) unto all Saints.

2. The length, from eternity to eternity, nothing can part, nothing shall part; all other things are but Summer Swallows that build with us for a time.

3. The depth, that the Lord should look upon thee when in thy Pest-house, when no eye pittied thee, when as low as the Grave, nay as low as Hell, nay lower, for they in Hell would come out, thou wouldst not. Never think to see what infinite love is, till thou feest infinite wrath.

4. The height, to be as happy as Angels, and more to, nay to be all one with Christ, and in Christ, and loved with the same love Christ is, *John* 17. 23, 26.

5. When thou seest it thus, yet it's the love of Christ that passeth knowledg: As children cannot tell how Parents love them, Will you do this? 'Tis with many Christians as 'tis with many Trees, the Tree is good, and the soil is good, and rain, dews, sun, Husband-man good, yet it begins to dye, then now nothing is wanting, but only to be set a little deeper, that it may take more root of the soyl. And so here, there is nothing wanting in many a Christian, but to be set a little deeper, and to take more rooting in the Lords love. Faith roots it self in Gods love, and now prospers by love. The eye is but little, yet can comprehend a mighty world quickly: mans mind is but little, yet can comprehend, though not the infinitenesse, yet an infinite love. If there be this light of glory, see by it all your poor sad hearts that conceive nothing but terror and holinesse in God; if you see it not, know it here is your work now; for the first work is to get Faith, then to get love, then to act from Faith by love. Now the Lord hath wrought the first, and thou art busie a doing the third work, not remembring the second.

2. Content not thy self with feeling a want of supply, but labour to feel a need of supply from the Lord Jesus, for many a Christian feels a want of Grace from Christ, brokennesse, &c. sees he hath nothing, and is sometime by fits troubled for the want of it: but he can be well content though he have no supply, having some- **Means 2.**
what

what elſe to eaſe and content him, he feels no need of ſupply, ſo as he cannot be without it, that his Spirit fails unleſſe the Lord Jeſus in mercy give it, and therefore muſt have it, there is a neceſſity of it. Hence he never finds ſupply, and wonders at it why 'tis ſo · and here 'tis, here is his wound, and ſo brings up an ill report of the Lord, ſaying he is loath to give, and of the Ordinances of the Lord, 'tis in vain to ſeek, and truly ſo it is to ſeek ſo: for let thy condition be never ſo miſerable, if thou ſee'eſt a need of ſupply, the Lord will make bare his arm, and work wonders, bring Heaven out of Hell, joy out of ſorrow, and light out of the thickeſt darkneſſe, and floods out of dry ground, *Iſai.* 41. 17, 18. when the ground is dry and perched away, no moiſture left; now the Lord pours out water on this ſoul, *Iſai.* 44. 3. *Heb.* 4. *ult.* Many come to the Lord for Grace, and find it not, methinks I hear the Lord ſpeaking thus to his people, I love you dearly, and I am content to give you any thing you need, but you do not need my Grace, my Spirit, my preſence, *i. e.* you feel not a need of it, for if you had it now, you would not prize it much, nor keep it long: my precious Grace muſt not be ſpilt. Many know their wants and diſtempers, and know there is no help in themſelves, and ſee all fulneſſe in Chriſt, and hence come to him, but find none, becauſe they can be content though the Lord deny: no nor never ſhall unleſſe you feel the woe of your wants, that your Spirit fails if the Lord ſend not in ſupply, *Iſai.* 57. 16. *I will not contend, leſt the Spirit fail.* Hence there God promiſeth to dwell, to ſend and create peace and comfort: for what is the reaſon that Chriſtians at firſt beginnings ſeek peace and mercy, and have abundantly then? why truly I was long time before I had any thing, but when my ſpirit began to fail, and I gave all for gone, and could hold out no more, now the Lord helped and pittied me; but where are thoſe comforts, and that preſence of the Lord now? Truly now you think the worſt is paſt, and would be glad of the life of Chriſt, and Grace from Chriſt, but if not, you have a little, your ſtate is ſafe, and ſo can lie without putting your ſelf to a neceſſity of it. Is it not thus? is not this your very wound? if it be, for the Lords ſake then get it healed, and do as people in Chriſts time, thoſe that were well, and had not deſperate Diſeaſes, commonly came not to him, but when the Diſeaſe was deſperate, you know the Fame of Chriſt being ſpread abroad, then they brought their ſick and laid them before his merciful eyes, then they looked for the laying on of his hand, or a word of his mouth, and all were healed: ſo do you, you have heard of the Fame of Chriſt, and ſeen others humbled, others pardoned, lay thy ſick Soul (but look that it be ſick) before his eyes, and ſo look for one word of his mouth, as the Woman of *Canaan*, he may deny for a time, yet ſhe muſt have it, and the Lord will ſay, *Be it unto thee according to thy Faith*, not according to thy deſerts, thou wilt have it, I muſt give it, thou dyeſt without it, behold I live to revive thee, and therefore to give it. You come to Prayer, and Word, and want many things, but find them not. Oh come therefore, Lord I muſt have, I cannot go without ſupply. Not but that a Chriſtian muſt wait, and be content humbly, but not careleſly: Therefore think within thy ſelf,

1. What is there that I need but this, the preſence of God, the life of God, *&c.* Is it not enough in Heaven, where's no wealth nor comforts elſe? and is it not ſufficient now?

2. May I have it on this condition, [I muſt have it, I am reſolved not to go without it] *Rev.* 22. 17. if you will come, take it. Are the termes ſo ſweet?

3. Do wicked men thirſt more and more after their luſts, and is Chriſt, and his Grace, and his Preſence no better, that I have enough of them quickly? God forbid there ſhould be ſuch a heart.

4. Doth the leaſt ſin ſo exceedingly go to the heart of my God, and ſhall I ſuffer it not only to act here, and tempt here, but remain alive here?

5. Is not the Lord after all love ſhewn me, worthy of infinite (not a little) honour from me? and doth he deſerve all, and muſt I not, ſhall I not give it him before

fore I dye? it muſt, it ſhall be ſo. Now when here you feel a need, know it that you are at the very door of relief: I conceive this is the great door at which Chriſt enters into the ſoul. The root of Faith (*i. e.* the author, object, and foundation of Faith) is out of a mans ſelf, the door of Faith which opens to all treaſures is in a mans ſelf: This door is not any good in us, for then we ſhould have ſomewhat to boaſt of, nor ſin in us, for that ſhuts out God from us; nor knowledg of want, for that the Devils have, but ſenſe of want, which when the Saints have, now the door is opened for the Lord Jeſus in all his fulneſſe to come in. Now *if you know theſe things, bleſſed are you if you do them.*

SECT. VIII.

uſe 5.

TO all the Churches of the Lord Jeſus here planted in theſe Weſtern parts of the World, to maintain your Church-chaſtity and Virginity, you have a name of it abroad, pure chaſte Virgin-churches, not polluted with the mixtures of mens inventions, not defiled with the company of evill men: pure Ordinances, pure People, pure Churches, which is the cauſe of the ſcoffs and enmity of ſome, but of the deſire and joy of others. O if there, how happy I? and how bleſſed they? Take heed you do not defile your ſelves again. Open whoredoom is too groſſ, too ſhameful, to yeild to mans inventions, to open the door for all comers into the Church: but take heed of ſecret whoredoms and departings from Chriſt, for think of this ſpeech when you ſee me dead, that of all Churches in the World, the Lord Jeſus carries a moſt jealous eye over theſe for whom he hath done ſuch great things; and I know it, he takes exceeding ill your ſecret wantonneſſe and whoredoms of heart; the Lord hath kept you hitherto, look you maintain it, for you may be ſoon deſſoured again, few Churches retain their purity long, aged, gray-haired purity is ſeldom ſeen. I will tell you of the ſeveral Temptations (ſome at leaſt) that may prevail to the defilement of you.

Firſt, Spiritual defilement is forſaking of the Husband, a total ſecret forſaking of Chriſt; for here is the temptation to it, *viz.* Gods withdrawing himſelf in his Ordinances from his Ordinances. For three ſorts of Temptations make men fall back.

1. By Perſecution, and there many fall (though ſome hold out) as in the ſtony land.

2. By Peace, and here many fall like the thorny ground; like Saylors that in a ſtorm at Sea, every man is ready, and will be pulling his rope, but when a calm, then go to their Cabbins, and there fall aſleep, and here many fall in this place, and others ſtand it out.

3. By the Lords withdrawing from them, as thoſe, *Mal.* 3. 14. and here the great ones fall. Many come to enjoy Ordinances, and perſecution vext them not, world it's baſe, it troubles them not, and they think to find much, but do not, but the Lord withdraws, and they can get no good, hereupon their falſe hearts diſcover themſelves, they draw back from God, and lie ſtill, whereas Saints cry the more after him, and look the more into themſelves, and find out the cauſe of it, and then the Lord helps them, *Iſai.* 63. 17. Oh take heed of this.

1. Shall I forſake the Lord that hath done theſe great things for my Soul?

2. Shall I now do it after I am ſo near Heaven?

3. Shall I forſake him when he departs from me but for a time it may be, when as he followed me when I departed long from him?

4. Is it not Hell to dye without him, and ſhall it not be Death to live without him?

5. Doth he depart without a cauſe, he hath no cauſe to follow me, I have all reaſon to follow him, the Lord grant you may do ſo.

Secondly,

Secondly, Secret defilement is by neglect of private communion with him: this is whorish in a Wife. Here is stronger Temptation to neglect private Prayer and Meditation, partly by want of room, partly by multitudes of businesses, and work, and cares hereabout, that being weary in the day, sleepy at night, busie in the morning, Prayer, Meditation, daily examination are sent away as *Paul* from *Felix*, we will speak with these at some more convenient season; and hence straitnesse of heart toward Christ, and no means do good. Oh Beloved, have you such a Husband as Christ in Heaven that loves thy looks, thy company, thy sighs, thy speeches, and will you neglect him thus? what no love? 2. Is he not broken with this whorish heart? 3. Is that speech worth any thing with you, *We shall ever be with the Lord,* doth it comfort you to think of being ever with him, and now neglect him? where are your hearts?

Thirdly, Secret defilement is by bringing other lovers into the same bed, the same heart with him: and here the Temptation to this is strong, for most men have lost and sunk in their Estates, and it's hard to live lower than we did, and this is a grief, and here 'tis possible to recover estate again, and here grief for losse hath a vent by greedinesse and pursuit after more. In other places men hid a very comfortable estate, hence rejoyced in what they had, and did not greedily desire more; but now want makes men hungry and greedy: and now when a man hath thought and lookt about him, and seen what he may gain by his labours of many acres, by his Goats and Cattel in so many year; now he casts himself into the world, and also will not forsake Christ utterly, but bring both into the same heart, Christ shall have some love, some desire, but the world as much, and so the heart is divided: and hence some set high prizes on their corn, commodities, cattel, others look for large wages, *&c.* and yet Christ too. Hence men cry out of the world because it hinders them from Christ, and yet bring it into, and hugg it in their hearts, because they must have it in the bed with Christ. It was the speech of one, that he never heard of any Saint in Scripture given to covetousnesse, some to one sin, some to another, but none to that; I have read of *Lot*, but God fired him out of his estate at last: and that is all I would say to this.

Fourthly, Secret defilement is by decaying in love to those whom Christ loves, and those are his Saints, and Temptation is strong in this place to this: 1. Because we have multitudes of them; Even Gold it self being so common as to pave our streets, is despised. 2. Because there wants a common enemy to drive them together. Take several men that never knew one another, yet in time of War they will love abundantly, and then encourage one another, and can with joy lie together: so 'tis here, hence arise your petty Duels and jars in Churches, surmisings, censurings, *&c.* and the reason is this, there is little love to Saints, and for want of this, men shall not know whether you be Christs Disciples or no. Be thy Brethren Saints or not? bear they the Image of Christ or no? if they do not, why dost not convince them, admonish them? and if they will not be better, away with them: If they be, Oh bear, Oh love, Oh tender them, as thou lookest the Lord Jesus should tender thee. And therefore let the Image of Christ appear, and then see it, and then love, and then no more breaches will follow: if not, the Lord can and will soon send Wolves to make Sheep run more together.

Fifthly, Letting a new Generation of Harlots into Christs bosom, I mean, not greatly caring for Posterity, that they may know and serve this God, for after this Generation is past, our children are to follow, and 'tis very rare that they prove right, yet it may be so. Hearken therefore you Parents, if God brought them over for this end, and if they never know God, what a sad thing would it be? or if they be brought forth to pull down the Temple of God. Oh therefore, 1. Be careful of a pious education of them in Schools, in private, and take some course for that end before others come over, this will draw them. 2. Oh make many Prayers for them. 3. Set Faith awork in Gods promise; as he said, he would not abate the

Lord

Lord, (though he gave it him in 99) of that one. Leave in record what the Lord hath done for you, that the Lord may be with them, and that all these Churches may be the glory of Christ, and then you shall enter into the Bride-chamber of the Lamb at last.

CHAP. VII.

Concerning a Christians Duty of being constantly and continually ready to meet Christ, and to enjoy Communion with him.

2. *Took their Lamps.*

SECT. I.

MUch dust is raised, and much Dispute is made, especially by Popish Interpreters, What the Lamps, what the Oyl, what the Vessels should be? The general conceit of most of them is: that by Oyl is meant good works, and by Lamps Faith; answerable to their own conceit, that not Faith but good works chiefly save: Whereas if we consider the thing rather *e contra*, that by lighted Lamps are meant good works, or external shining profession, according to that of Christ, *Mat.* 5. *Let your light so shine before men*, &c. and that by Oyl should be meant Faith, because 'tis inward, and is th nourishment of works and outward profession. And in this sense some of our Divines do take this Scripture; and the *Rhemists* likewise, who understand by Lamps lighted, good works; by Oyl a good intention: To which 'tis answered by *Cartwright*, (that burning and shining light of our Times) that rather by Lamps lighted is to be understood, *watchful minds alway lifted up in attending for the coming of Christ*, according as 'tis *ver.* 13. And I doubt not but this is one thing aimed at, that they *took their Lamps*, i. e. were watchful for Christs coming. But when I weigh other circumstances, methinks there is somewhat else more plainly and principally intended, of which I scarce read any Divine, but he gives a hint of, *viz.* that by lighted Lamps, and taking of them, is meant nothing else but the readinesse of the Churches to meet and to have fellowship with the Lord Jesus. And my Reasons are these:

1. Because the Lord Jesus to teach his people watchfulnesse, and to put them to a narrow search of themselves, borrows a similitude from the custom of those Times, wherein their Marriages were celebrated in the Night, and hence the Virgins (the only children of the Bride-chamber, and some think their number never exceeded Ten) being to walk out in the Night, took their Lamps: and when they had kindled their Lamps, (usually the last thing that is done) now they are ready to go out, and this is that which Christ aims at.

2. From *Luke* 12. 35. *Let your loyns be girt, and lamps burning*; it's evident that thereby is meant nothing else but readinesse to meet the Lord when-ever he comes; for when loyns are girt, then one is fit for travail, but seeing 'tis in the Night, hence lamps must be burning too.

3. Because 'tis said plainly, *ver.* 10. when their lamps were kindled again, *they that were ready went in*; I know the Word is called a lamp for our feet, *Psal.* 119. and

and so by lamps may be meant minds enlightned and kindled by the word. The eminent profession and excellencies of the Church is like a lamp, *Isai.* 62. 1. and more particularly may be here included and aimed at : but in this *verse* lamps are spoken of in general , including light, Oyl, Vessels ; and hence I give this general Interpretation here, intending Particulars if need be afterward : So that now I shall only raise this Point.

SECT. II.

Doct. **T**Hat all those that are Espoused unto Christ , ought to be in a constant or continual readinesse to meet Christ , and to have immediate communion with Christ.

A Woman may be Espoused to another , and yet she may be sometimes not ready to meet him, her soul apparel is on.   So here , therefore 'tis not enough to be espoused unto Christ, but being espoused , now you ought to be in a continual readinesse to claspe the Lord in your arms , and to lay your heads in his bosome in Heaven : this is commanded by Christ , *Mat.* 24. 44. This was the mighty power of Gods Grace in *Paul*, when others were weeping to think of his Bonds, *Why do you break my heart, I am ready not only to be bound, but to dye for Christ* , and so doubtlesse to be with Christ ; much more ready to meet Christ when ever he shall come, ready to welcome Death, much more ready to welcome Christ, *Acts* 21. 13. This also is the end of *Johns* Ministry, *Luke* 1. 17. To make ready a people prepared for the Lord, to meet with Christ on earth ; Now he is gone, our work is to prepare a people to meet the Lord in Heaven. Hence this is put in as the difference between Vessels of wrath, and Vessels of Glory : the one are fitted for destruction , the others are fitted , prepared, or made ready for Glory , and the glory of a christian is chiefly to enjoy fellowship immediatly with Jesus Christ.   There is many a soul dear unto Christ, and espoused to him, and hath his heart affected to think of the good time that is coming, when we shall ever be with the Lord : but ask , are you ready yet for to go to him, though it be through fires, waters, thorns, sorrows , death it self ? who can say yes ? but (say mens hearts) shut the Lord out a little longer , let not the door stand open yet ; yet this must be : And therefore for explications sake, let me, 1. shew you when the Soul is in a readinesse for the Lord Jesus. 2. The reasons why there must be a continual readinesse.

SECT. III.

Quest.
Answ.

VVHen is the Soul in a readinesse to enjoy Christ ?
As there are four things which make a christian unready, so this readinesse consists in Four things contrary.

1. That which makes a christian unready for him, are those strong fears , and jealousies, and damping doubts of the love of Christ to him. The soul happly hath made choice of him, is content with him, melts into wonderment and love to think that he should love him : what me ? and Christ hath writ him on his heart, and on the palms of his hands ; *but Israel saith , my God hath forsaken me, my God hath forgotten me, Isai.* 49. 14. Is it possible? is it credible? one that hath been so vile, one that still hath such a heart, for him to set his heart on me ? surely no : hence the Soul is afraid to dye, and desires too much to live still : and the more he thinks of that time, and blessednesse of following the Lamb where-ever he goes; the more he sees and fears this may possibly never be my portion : there may be some falseness in my heart towards him that I never yet saw , some secret

knot

knot that was never yet unlofed: and hence not yet ready. Hence many a chriftian faith, if I had a little more affurance, let him come when he will: Thus fome think it was with *Hezekiah*, who though he had walked before God with a *perfect heart*, yet bitterly complained that he was cut off, *Ifai.* 38. *per totum*. So therefore then the foul is prepared & ready for him, when he hath fome comfortable affurance of the love of Chrift towards him, that it can fay, if I live he loves me, though he kils me by Death, yet I know that he loves me: nay, then he loves me moft, when he puts an end to my fins, and to my forrows too? And therefore now faith as one ready to receive a Prince, now let him come to me, or fend for me when he will: why fo? *Who can feparate me from the love of Chrift? Rom.* 8. 35. That look as 'tis with a Souldier that is to go to war, where many bullets and arrows are like to fall about him, and hit him while he hath no armour on; call him to the Captain, and he will fay he is not ready yet, but when he hath his armour on of proof, and fuch armour that he knows let him receive never fo many wounds, yet he fhall efcape with his life, and triumph with his Captain afterward: Now give him but his watch-word he is ready, though never fo weak, yet I am fure I fhall efcape with my life, nay not fo much as hurt. So a chriftian wanting his affurance, wants his armour; he is weak, and powers of darkneffe will affault him, and he is flain by them, now he is unready: but if affured, though weak and feeble, he is now at Chrifts watch-word, I know I fhall live, I may fall, but I fhall rife again, this puts courage and fpirit into a chriftian, *Dan.* 3. 17, 18. *Heb.* 11. 35. Others were tormented, (and fo ready) *not accepting deliverance*; why fo? to *obtain a better Refurrection*, which they are faid to fee by the eye of Faith, and this was by poor weak Women; therefore labour for this, elfe not prepared. The Lord would have his people look death and dangers in the face, and triumph in forrows, and not faint-hearted, (which cannot be done without this) that the world may fee that there is more than men in them, 2 *Cor.* 4. 16, 17, 18. and 5. 1. who would be without this? yet may we not complain, as Chrift of his Difciples; *Oh foolifh and flow of heart to believe all that is written*, fo many promifes yet not affured, fo many experiences yet not eftablifhed, and therefore not yet prepared and ready for the coming of the Lord. A man that hath a fair eftate and houfe befallen him, fo long as he is in Suit for it, dares not dwell in it, but makes a fhift where he is: but then he is ready when quiet poffeffion is given him. So get the Lord to paffe fentence for affurance of your everlafting habitation, then are you ready to dwell therein.

2. Then a man is unprepared for the Lord Jefus his coming, while he wants affections fuitable to the Majefty, and according to the worth and love of the Lord Jefus: Suppofe a Woman knows her Husbands love, yet if fhe have loft her love to him, or if fhe love him, 'tis only as fhe loves another man, not according to the worth of her Husbands perfon, or the greatneffe of his love: Is fhe fit now to appear before him, when no heart to receive him? fo although you queftion not Chrifts love to you, & thank God you doubt little of it, yet where is your heart? your love to him? have you not loft your love, your firft love, or fecond love? if you have love, is it not divided to other things, as Wife, Child, Friends, hopes of provifion for them, and too much care hereupon for that? or if you do love him, 'tis with a carnal love, he hath no more than a luft hath had, and it may be not fo much, 'tis with a cold love; now you are unfit for him: hence the Lord, *Luke* 21. 34. *Take heed your hearts be not overcharged*, 1 *Pet.* 4. 7. Now therefore then the foul is prepared to meet Chrift, when if the foul hath loft its affections, it recovers them out of the hands of all creatures that ftole them away from Chrift; and hence *David* prayes, *Oh fpare that I may recover my ftrength*: and when it breaks out with fuch love unto Chrift as is fitting for him, 2 *Tim.* 4. 8. There is the righteous Judge ready to give the Crown, when Chrifts appearing is loved, *i. e.* they are fo taken with him, as that they love the looks of him, it would rejoyce

my heart to see, which thall make others tremble to behold him ; Oh it must be a dear love, a spring of running love without measure, for this is the difference between affections of Saints and Hypocrites to Christ, the one ariseth like a morning dew which is soon lickt up by the Sun, *Hos.* 6. 4. the heat of affection: after other things licks it up; but the love of Saints to Christ is like a spring which riseth to everlasting life : a spring is but little, but yet the farther it goes, the wider 'tis, till at last swallowed up in the Sun, and there is no measure of water : so Saints have but a little love, but the longer they live, the more enlarged for Christ, and there is no measure, but all is too little, they never can, never do love enough, so that look as 'tis said in another case, *Psalm* 102. 13, 14. *'Tis time for thee to build up Jerusalem*, *i. e.* to return to thy people in thy Ordinances, for *they love the stones*; so then it's time for Christ to come, and then the set and fit time is come for a people to meet with Christ out of Ordinances, when the set time is come when they love Ordinances, and love Christ much more. When a man is gone beyond Sea, and all his Friends and estate are at home, they long for him, and he is left among enemies : why comes he not to them ? why send not they for him ? why they know he is sickly, and cannot live on the dyer of the country ; hence he is unfit to come, but when that is once come to passe that he can live only on it, then he is ready when-ever they send: so when men can live with, and be content alone with Christ and his love, now they are fit. With what face can a man appear before Christ, when he requires nothing but love, and he hath not that.

3. Then a man is unready for Christ, whiles he neglects the work of Christ, for suppose a man hath some inward love to Christ, yet neglects & hath no heart to do the work of Christ : he is as yet no more fit to meet Christ, than a Steward who hath had much betrusted him, to improve for his Lords use, and he hath let all seasons go wherein he might have traded for him, and gained somewhat to him. How can he appear before him when no fair accounts to be seen ; so the Lord hath betrusted thee with many Talents, times, strength, means, &c. & you are not Lords, but Stewards of all these. Now do you not let many fair seasons and winds blow by, you have (if espoused to Christ) every man some work. Now how can you stand before Christ if that be neglected. Oh thus 'tis with many christians ; hence those sad alarums of conscience, and shakings of Gods Spirit, after many loose dayes dipt in some good duties. What dost thou that others do not that never shall see Gods face in Heaven ?

Now therefore then the soul is ready for the Lord, when 'tis daily at it, finishing Gods work: hence *John* 17. 5. *I have finished my work, now glorifie me* : Christ hath given us our lives, work, dayes-work, every hours work, for Christ hath ever employment ; now though a soul may live long, and cannot finish its lives work, yet if it finish its dayes work, or hours work, it may have comfort then if the Lord should come. That look as 'tis with a Marriner when he hath his Fraight, now let the wind come to drive him out of the Haven, he is ready to depart : so here, 2 *Pet.* 1. 8, 9, 10, 11. *If ye do these things, and abound, an open entrance shall be ministred unto you*, *i. e.* when a christian is ever acting for Christ, and adding one Grace to another in his course, then he is so ready that an open entrance is made for him : Therefore look after this. 'Tis with most Professors commonly, as 'tis with a Woman that loves her Husband, and begins to dresse her self, but so much businesse to do, that she doth it but by starts ; hence call her never so late, she will say she is not yet ready, she hath so much to do she cannot ; so 'tis here : Or as 'tis in a house where all things are in a lumber, and many things wrapt up and put into holes, so long as all things be in a lumber, there is no readinesse. So many a soul hath a heart fit to receive Christ, but all things are in a lumber, in a confusion, out of place and order, and hence not yet ready to entertain Christ, but when this work is done, then ready. Oh betimes do this work, set things to rights in your souls.   4. Then

4. Then a man is unready, when having done his work he grows puft up with it : for let all the three former be wrought in the soul, if now the soul be puft up, thinks highly of it self, attributes any thing to it self : as he said in another case, *they are too many for the Lord* ; so he is too big for the Lord. And truly this we shall find it's pretty easie to be mean in our own eyes, after we have been indeed carelesse and vile before the Lord ; but when the Lord hath mightily assisted, enlarged, assured, enabled, comforted, quickened, now to be as nothing, this is difficult. Hence *Knox* on his death-bed had this Temptation of Meriting. When *Hezekiah* was sick, he was cast down, but when well, and God gave him great Treasures, his heart was lifted up ; now he was unfit. Now therefore when a christian is ready to give all to free Grace, and to adore that, now he is ready for the Lord, *Psalm* 108. 1. *My heart is prepared, I will sing and give praise*. Gods last end is to bring the soul to the praise of the riches of his Grace, not only to enjoy God as *Adam*. Now the great reason why Christ comes not to his people presently after they are espoused to him, 'tis to make them ready to attain that end. Hence he leaves sins, temptations, sorrows, desertions, on purpose that they may at conclusion look back, and see if ever saved, pardoned, it's Grace. Now therefore when the soul is brought to do this, when he hath this rent in his hand, now the Lord is ready to receive him, and it too, and he is prepared for the Lord : he that hath not his Rent ready, himself is not as yet at all ready to meet with, and see his Landlord. So that you think you boast not, Oh the Lord sees you do, or have not hearts so enlarged towards Grace as you should, it's certain you are yet unready then, but when empty, and poor, and cast down, and makest an infinite matter of a small sin, and settest a high price on a little love much more on infinite, now you are prepared : Hence *David* falls a praising when near to death, and the Lord near to come to him.

SECT. IV.

1. THe law of Respect and Love requires this of us : when *Peter* would expresse his love unto Christ, *Luke* 22. 33. he professeth he was *not only ready to go to prison, but to dye with him*. Christ hath poor respect and love if men will not so much as be alway ready to receive him : it certainly argues a carelesse heart that sleights Christ, that is not ever prepared to receive Christ. *Reasons.*

2. Because the time of Christs coming is then when we least look for him, *vers.* 13. Hence a christian ought to be ever ready to receive him. Many of eminent parts, when the Church had most need of them, then are cut down : Many at their first conversion, before they or others almost could tell what to make of them, the Lord hath cropt them in the bud. Men find their hearts unfit and unready, they think hereupon that hereafter they shall get their hearts into better order and tune, when these businesses are over ; but yet will live at liberty a little while : why then it's most likely is the Lords time of coming, even now when they think least of it, *Luke* 12. 40.

3. Because the Lord hath set apart every one that is espoused to the Lord Jesus, only for the fruition of Christ, and use of Christ, 1 *Cor*. 3. *ult. You are Christs, and Christ is Gods*. A Woman that is not chosen, nor set apart for the fellowship of a Prince, she may go how she will, and do what she will, any base drudgery work ; but she that is chosen to be next unto him, and only to behold and love him, she is not to plead she hath so much businesse to do, and so many Friends to speak with, that she cannot make her self ready : she is set apart for a better person, and for more noble employment. So here men of the world not loved of God, nor chosen and set apart for him, may do what they will ; but when the Lord hath chosen and set you apart of purpose for this end, *Ephes*. 1. 4. *Chosen to be holy*

before

before him in love, i. e. to stand ever in his presence before him, with a spirit of dearest love unto him. Hence the Lord hath taken the care of all things else, 1 *Pet.* 5. 7. that we might mind and do this thing ; If in danger, he will deliver, if in want, he will provide, if weak, he will strengthen, only now be ready for the Lord, *Psalm* 45. 10. *Forget thy Country, and thy Fathers house, so shall the Lord desire thy beauty.* You are not now free to love and follow whom you please, the Lord hath bound you to himself by love, and you have bound your self by promise to the Lord again : Therefore now a christian after once espoused to Christ, is better than all the world, being the Bride of the Lamb ; and he hath a better and greater good for to enjoy : therefore he should scorn and abhor to match himself to, or to do any thing for any other creature ; and therefore methinks should sit as one upon a watch-tower, looking out, and telling the clock now day is near, waiting only for Christ, Oh let it be so : If in Heaven, you shall have only Christ, Oh prepare for him much more now. As a Woman that is Matcht to a rich man, all the servants attend on her, and follow her, she is wholly and only for her Husband : so it should be here.

4. Because he hath prepared and made all things else ready for the soul, it's hard if he hath prepared a place in Heaven, and Grace in Heaven, not to prepare an heart, and make it ready for him, *John* 14. 1, 2, 3. his Kingdom was ready long ago, and his Father ready to accept and entertain thee, and his heart loves and desires, all are ready after thee : hence be ready to meet with him. *I am my Beloveds.*

SECT. V.

Use 1.

Hence see the great unkindnesse of many a soul immediatly after his espousing to Jesus Christ, who having once given himself to Christ, and received comfort thereby, presently grows more carelesse than before he was matcht unto the Lord Jesus, who should now stand in a holy watchfulnesse and readinesse to receive Christ, as 'tis *Psalm* 85. 8. *Let them not turn again to folly,* because they are very apt so to do. Many say when in some distresse, and after long waiting, if the Lord would pitty once, then happy I; I would give away any thing, all I have unto him : well, the Lord pitties the soul when in its low estate, and then it blesseth God, but like the *Israelites*, soon forgets his works, his love, and after great peace from God, comes greatest carelesnesse : can this stand with Grace, and Christ ? very hardly ; but yet it may, for there are Two things that make for it.

1. Because at first conversion there is much seeking of Christ, for healing the horrour and smart of sin, as well as for the curing of the wound and scar of sin : hence when espoused, and horrour being past, that wheel being broken, a man draws more heavily now, and neglects seeking ; now the Knife is out of his heart he cries not so earnestly.

2. Because when espoused, and much affected, commonly a man trusts to his affections, when he hath a fulnesse of them : hence the Lord lets Satan prevail, *Luke* 22. 31, 33. *Satan hath desired to winnow thee as wheat,* and *I* (saith *Peter*) *am ready to dye with thee* ; but you see he fell, and then when the Lord looked upon him, he *went out and wept bitterly* : How shamefully hast thou fallen, should any love him more than you if ever he pitty ? well, for his Name-sake he hath done it. But how oft hast thou broken Covenant ? how forgetful of the Lords kindnesse ? The Lord looks upon thee this day, why hast thou so soon forgot me, and forsaken me ? have I not took thee from the Dung-hill, nay from Hell ? and whereas I had so many thousands to set my love on, I chose thee ; and whereas thou couldest not love me when I offered my self, thou couldest not return me
                                                                                    love

love again, I gave it therefore to thee, yea and have given my self to thee for ever: Hast thou thus forgotten me, when as I take little wrongs from thee more heavily than great ones from others? Oh that this might make you go out and mourn bitterly: so if ever you have tasted that love as *Peter* did, Christs looks will humble you.

Hence see the reason why some Godly People dye so uncomfortably, and with such distresse of spirit; why they have not lived in an expectation of Christ, and hence they cry out of themselves, not knowing whither they go, insomuch as some have not been comforted by all former experiences, and by all present consolations of Ministers: Oh no, 'tis now too late to speak, they thank them for their love, but God hath otherwise thought of them; yet if any hope be given them 'tis ever pickt out from some word, and they cry, Oh I thirst for a little mercy, and then dye; and what is the reason of it? what need I speak? Themselves will tell you, and have done it, Oh I have lived thus and thus before you, but my heart in secret hath gone after the world, &c. I have neglected the Lord secretly, I have seldom thought of, or prepared for Death, and I had thought to have been better, but the Lord hath met with me: I know violence of Disease may do it sometime, but I speak how 'tis many times; whereas otherwise an open entrance should be made, 2 *Pet.* 1.8,9,10,11. And as it hath been with some, so take warning lest it be so with you; you may be saved alive, yet to suffer wrack on the shoar is uncomfortable, and know it if your conscience be awake, it cannot but be so. Therefore do not conclude they were damned without Christ, but they were not made ready for Christ; and it may be your time draws nigh, and what have you to say? now a world for half an hour will a dying distressed man say.   *Use 2.*

Is of a Four-fold exhortation, to all those especially that the Lord hath espoused to himself.   *Use 3.*

CHAP. VIII.

A Four-fold Exhortation to Believers.

SECT. I.

TO quicken up all those doubting, drooping, yet sincere hearts, that much question the love of Christ to them, Now to use all diligence to make their Calling, and Election, and the love of Christ sure to them, not but that it's sure on Christs part, but make it sure on your part too; else how can you be in a readinesse to meet the Lord Jesus; while the strong man keeps the Palace, the Goods be in peace; but when Christ hath once driven Satan out of his Throne, then nothing sometimes but war, but doubts and fears; Satan told God to his face, *Job* served him for nought, much more will he accuse the Soul it self: and some Divines think the very first ingredient of Satans poyson, and the first assault on Christ himself, *Mat.* 4. was by seeking to make him doubt of his Sonship, *If thou be the Son of God, &c.* And his wiles are here very great, that hence very few living christians have any setled comfortable evidence of Gods eternal love to them in his Son: and hence many sad events follow. How can any blesse the Lord for that love which he knows not of? many times 'tis with a mans doubts drooping from his mind, as 'tis with his continual dropping on his Lungs, there is a daily consuming of what once was; that many a christian doubts away his life, his heart, his strength, and when all is wasted, glad now to return to that where   *Exhort. 1.*

he should at first have begun. And hence in one word, he is made every day un-ready for Christ. Oh therefore quiet not your selves in that estate as I fear too many do (at least for a time) it's one of the most dangerous estates that can be, to be troubled with weak fears, and yet rest in uncertain hopes; but bring it to a conclusion, Is the Lord Jesus mine or no? and if he be yours, and his love yours, see it, that you may trample on the neck of death, and triumph over hell, and the grave, and long to be with the Lord, and love the appearing of the Lord, and go away with joy unspeakable and full of glory out of this world, as to your Wedding, and if there be any hope of getting it, who would be without it? Some of you it may be have a long time been carelesse in seeking for it, hence want it, some of you have been traders with the Lord long, and yet doubt; some of you have not clear evidence, but content your selves without being thankful to the Lord for what he hath done for you, hence still doubt. Others have gray hairs on your head, or at least are near your Graves, the battel is near, your armour is not on, you are not yet ready, and so still doubt. I remember what Christ said of *Maries* Box, *she prepared that for his burial*, it may be that these Truths may be prepared for your approaching departure; and therefore light your Lamps at this fire, and light of the Lords love to you, and see that indeed he loves thee.

Object. But why do you perswade to this, till the Spirit comes and speaks it? How can I see it?

Answ. 1. 'Tis true the Spirit only can do it, but yet the same Spirit that seals the Elect, the same Spirit commands the Elect not to sit Idle, and dream of the Spirit, but to use all diligence to make it sure; and you shall never have it (unlesse you lay hold on a Fancy for it) on those terms.

2. Though there is an immediate witnesse of the Spirit, of the love of Christ, yet it doth most usually and firstly witnesse by means. And hence I shall give you means looking only to the Spirit of Christ to set them on. Evangelical Precepts have a power: For Gospel-ministration of the Spirit consists not only of stories and promises, but commands, and the Elect feel them: Hence carnal men under the Law, yet pretending Gospel, will professe the Law is preached when they are pressed to any Evangelical duty, because they feel not the power of the Gospel, being not yet under it. And the means I shall mention, are only general to establish the hearts of some.

Means 1. Make a sad enquiry first of this, Whether the Lord hath loved thee for his own everlasting Names-sake or no, for if the Lord hath loved Thee for this cause, then thy great Objection will be answered, and that deep valley will be filled. How can the Lord love me that am thus vile before God, and fallen from God? why if the Lord for his own sake hath loved thee, then as no good in thee moved him to love thee, so no sin which he did know was and would be in thee can quench that love; and if he hath manifested his love to be grounded on this, though but once, that same Name when thou changest is not changed, but is still as dear to him, and ever before him to move him to love thee still, *Rom.* 11. 2. The Apostle answers a Cavil, *will God cast away his people*? no saith he, none that he foreknew; and who are these? *verf.* 5. *A remnant according to Grace as with us*, i.e. God hath for his Grace-sake chosen and called without respect of any thing else: Hence that is to be understood, 1 *Sam.* 12. 21, 22. For there are two sorts of people in the Church; 1. Servants. 2. Sons, *John* 8. 35. Hence there is a double love the Lord manifests to men.

1. Some he loves as servants, that as we hire some men to do our work, and give them meat and wages, and then turn them out of doors, or let them go: so God hath work to be done, for his Son and Saints, and for many reasons hires wicked men to it, either by giving them reward in this life, or hopes of reward hereafter, and when the work is done, and use made of their Gifts, Graces, Spirits, then turns them out of doors.

But

But 2. Some he love: as Sons, even the most foolish and weak in the world sometimes: hence not for any service they can do, but for his own sake he will give them an Inheritance, and love them as sons, because he will; these abide ever in the Lords love: *Hagar* and *Ishmael* cast out, *Sarah* and *Isaac* stay in the Family. *How shall I know that?*

Quest.
Answ.

1. If the Lord loves thee for his Name-sake, it will draw thee to that fellowship with it self, that what-ever thou wantest, thou wilt seek for it hence, by presenting that Name of God, that for his own sake he would supply: I know the Lord loves for Christs sake, but why should Christ help? for his Name-sake: For thus many hypocrites think when they see Gods anger against them for their sin, they seek to remove that sin, and when that is done, think God is at peace, and now all is well. They see the Lord is delighted with the obedience of his people, hence fall to that work, and now think the Lord is pleased with them. But if ever the Lord loves any man, he will first stop his mouth, whether Jew or Gentile, *Rom.* 3. 19. and make him on his Knees know there is no reason for it, nay all reason against it. Now hath not the Lord brought thee to this? and hence having nothing to quench Gods anger, but Christ, hast held up him before God, and having nothing to move Christ, hast held up his Name before him, and here hast rested thy wearied heart looking to him, if any Grace be begun in thee, that he would perfect it; if none, that he would begin it; if unfit and unworthy, to prepare thee for it, only for his own good pleasure: this is one evidence of it. As 'tis in some Seals, you can hardly perceive in the Seal what is engraven there, but set it on Wax, you may see it evidently: so here, hardly can you see the Lords love, look on thy heart if it loves him; his choice, see if thou chusest him, his love for his own sake; if thou cleavest with dearest affection to this love for its own sake, there thou art safe, *Prov.* 18. 10. *The name of the Lord is a strong Tower*, &c. and this not only at first conversion, but ever after all duties, all enlargements, *Ezek.* 16. ult. And this doth evidence love.

1. Because if thou had'st the righteousnesse of Angels thou would'st think it a good evidence, but this of Christ is a thousand times dearer.

2. This is a setting of God against himself, *i. e.* to answer himself, and hence Saints in all their straights and sorrows, hither had recourse; I speak not now of Temporal Blessings, but of Everlasting love, and all the Fruits of it, that here it hangs. Now I say you are built in a Rock higher than all powers of Darkness; now a Key is put into thy hand to unlock all Gods Treasure; now thou art in the very lap of love wrapt up in it, when here thy heart rests: and if not Beloved, the Lord would never let thee lean thus in his bosom: and therefore if this be thus, see it, and wonder his Name hath moved him to love me.

2. You shall find this, if the Lord for his Name-sake loves thee, there is not any carriage or passage of Providence of him to thee, but he gets himself a Name first or last by it: for if this be Gods end, every passage of Providence is but a means to this end: hence he will attain this end by every act of his Providence towards thee: hence you shall find that those very sins that dishonour his Name, he will even by them (and if by them, by all things else) get himself a Name: he will be so far from casting thee out of his love, that he will do thee good by them. Those very sins that God damns others for, he will make to humble thee, empty thee. Pharisees persecuted Christ, and lost all for it, *Paul* was so, and it humbled him all his life, *Not worthy to be called an Apostle, because I persecuted the Church of God*, and it made him lay up all his wealth in mercy, *I was received to mercy*, 1 *Tim.* 1. *Mary* sins much, and God forgives much, and she loves much; others sinned much, and God hardened much; *Judas* bettaies Christ, and repents, and hangs himself, and flies from him; *Peter* denies him, and weeps, and hence he is the first that Preacheth him. And this is certain, in the best Hypocrite, sins left in him, either never make him better, but

blind

blind and harden him, and he hath his distinctions of infirmity, &c. that he sleights them day by day, till all his dayes are run out, or if any good, 'tis no more than *Judas*, or *Cain*, some legal terrors, or other light flashes of comfort, but to be more humble indeed, &c. this he findeth not. Now is it not so with thee? Doth not thy weaknesse strengthen thee with *Paul* ? Doth not thy blindnesse make thee cry for light? and those cries have been heard, out of darknesse, God hath brought light. Thou hast felt venome and risings of heart against Christ, and do they not make thee loath thy self more? that thou thinkest never any so beholding to Grace? do not thy falls into sin make thee more weary of it, watchful against it, long to be rid of it? and so sin abounds, but Grace abounds: Why should this be so ? for his Names-sake, because he will love thee; hence 'tis so great and unmatchable, that he will make thy poyson thy Food, thy Death thy Life, thy Damnation Salvation, thy very greatest Enemies thy greater Friends. And hence Mr. *Fox* said, he thanked God for his sins more than for his good works. I have marvailed at Gods dealings with his people, they depart, and stay long, and care not for returning again; in that time a mighty power teacheth, humbleth, brings back, when they never thought of it. Oh the reason is, God will have his Name : now if thus, your assurance will be strong and constant, but if you build thus, I have done this, &c. I have that, your assurance will not stand; therefore look and see if it be not thus with you.

Means 2.

Take heed you do not build your assurance from a mingled Covenant of Works and Grace, for this is the frame of divers when they lye under the first Covenant only of doing, they will not take this as any evidence, as they have no reason so to do, *Rom.* 9. 31. Nor when a man lies under the Second Covenant of Believing barely, and if it be a dead Faith, they have no evidence or reason so to do. Hence they mingle the Covenants, and think thus. If I can believe in Christ, and perform universal obedience to all the commands of God, I shall be safe ; hence set upon the observance of both, and finding they can never do them, especially the latter, hence are ever troubled, and never have any setled peace. Hence those *Galatians Paul* writes to, perverting and mingling the Covenants, were troubled, *Gal.* 1. 7. & 5. 12. Not (beloved) but that whoever beleeves and performs universal obedience Evangelically to the whole Law, he cannot but do well ; and he that doth it not, but lives in any one sin, let him evidence his Faith if he can. But I speak when a man submits to it, *sub forma fæderis*, if I can do it, and because I cannot do it, hence doubt. Hence gather your evidence of Gods love primarily and chiefly from your subjection to the Second Covenant, *Gal.* 6. 16. *Peace on them that walk according to this rule* ; for *Adams* righteousnesse that did tye him to God, it brake ; hence no life, nor evidence from that, but Faith is an everlasting invincible Grace, upheld by the mighty power of God, and hence here will be everlasting evidence and peace, 1 *Pet.* 1. 8. *Whom though we see not, yet believing we rejoyce*. Objection. *Is a Christian then free from the Law ?* Ans. Yes, he is free from it as from a Covenant: hence though it be broken by him, he is not cast out of Covenant, or favour, but he is not free from it as a Rule, from which if he swerves he is to call himself, not Gods love into question : Why? because it hath pleased the Father in another Covenant to offer life, give life, and hence only to evidence life. What-ever the Law requires I have, at that instant I did believe, I performed it in a Saviour by Faith : and that I my self may do every tittle of it, I come unto a Saviour for it by Faith ; so that when Satan objects you have no Christ, nor love of a Christ, because no Faith, and no Faith because you cannot do this or that. Answer, I cannot do it indeed, I never undertook it to have life or love thus, but I have done it in another, and I can do all things by Christ, if he will help me, under whose Grace I lie, and hence will be so far from doubting, that I will rejoyce in mine infirmities, that I am a fit subject for the power and Grace of Christ to shew it self upon. Thus retire to the Second Covenant ever if ever you would get any setled peace. And from neglect of this flows a world of unpeaceablenesse in many a spirit, ever complaining, and why? I cannot do this or that, never peace now; but cannot you lye under the Lord that he would help? keep here, and keep your peace here.

But many a Christian that retires hither hath no peace, and so have I done, yet find now. *Object.*

It's then upon a double ground which you are to avoid: either, 1. Because you have Faith, but you imprison your Faith, you put out the eyes, and shackle the feet of Faith, for Faith will conquer and triumph over all sins, and fears of the world, if at liberty, 1 *John* 5. 4. like a Master in a Ship, if he cannot save the Ship one way, let him have liberty, he will by another. As if it be Objected, You have departed from Christ, what have you to do with him? I'le return faith Faith to my first Husband. *Ob.* But he is angry with you. *Anf.* If he be angry for my departure from him, I will not provoke him more by staying here, who knows but he may repent? *Ob.* But you cannot go to him with all your heart. *Answ.* True, yet I'le look to him to draw me. *Ob.* But you feel nothing. *Anf.* Yet I will wait. *Ob.* But you will wait in vain. *Anf.* Still I'le look he would keep me from that. Now stop at any of these, trouble comes, suffer it to shift it will find rest. As 'tis with the Anchor, let it down but little, the ship drives, but let it down at full length, it will ride in storms; then, 'tis wrestling of Faith that gets the Blessing, where opposition makes the Soul take faster hold; as it was with *Jacob.* The Woman of *Canaan* got it thus. *Anfw.*

Or 2. 'Tis because they look for another kind of Faith, and hence own not this, as the *Jews* the *Messiah*, they made account to have received him in state, and he came low; so men look for a superlative Faith, but want it. But thus the Soul espoused to Christ, so long as Marriage-Covenant lasts, she may conclude of love.

Do not fear the love of Christ is not toward you, because he hides his face, and departs some times from you; Husbands remain so when they depart, and leave the house for many a day, and 'tis simple to say he is not my Husband now. So here the Lord loves his people, yet departs, *Isai.* 54. 1, 2, 3, 4, 5, 6, 7. and truly 'tis very hard when inward blows, and sad desertions, and outward miseries, and no Christ found, though sought for. But how shall I then know and discern his love? *Answ.* Many things might be said this way, only one thing observe, whether thy love remains still to him for himself; for it's a rule that most commonly a christians purest and dearest love appears in Christs absence from him. As 'tis with Friends, while with us we love them, but when gone, we feel that love more quick than before. *Jerusalem* lies in the dust, and now the very dust is beloved, *Pfal.* 102. 13, 14. and if it be so, it's certain we love him because he loved us, and we continue to love him, because he continues to love us; now look then if thy love do not appear, 1. In mourning for his absence. 2. In longing for his presence. 3. In blessing him for a little that is left of himself, as seeing such want of him; and is not this for himself to have his company again, that though God gives thee all other things, yet when thou comest to consider the Lord is gone, this strikes near, as when Christ departed away, *John* 16. 5, 6. But because love may be benummed, and lye dead, therefore try it a time of parting, and put thy heart thus to it; if he be none of thine, then take thy fill in thy sin, and forsake him: no Beloved, here you shall see the heart will yeild and melt, *John* 13. 3, 4, 5, 6, &c. and it will say, Lord let me never sin more against thee, though never saved by thee. And take it for a rule, do not think the Lord hath left off his love to you when you depart from him, and he from you: but lying in your Departures, Oh that is sad; but return again, it comforts the Lords heart, especially when 'tis for himself, not for peace and salvation, but though he never saves me, Oh yet I will look after him. *Means* 3.

H

Look

Means 4.   Look to the tender-heartednesse of the Lord Jesus, for (Beloved) all the doubts of Christians arise chiefly from this head, from a hard opinion of Christ, which Satan suggests, as at first, *Gen.* 3. 5. that so they might take in his wares. Gods people do not know the tender-heartednesse of the Lord Jesus; Satan presents him only in wrath, when any threats are spoken, all these are mine saith the soul, *&c.* And now if any Woman lives with a man that is of a hoggish churlish disposition, she will be ever doubting of his love. Men do not know it I say, and hence when any misery or trouble comes, they grow jealous of him, which the Lord takes exceeding ill, *Deut.* 1. 27.

Quest. *How shall I know that tender-heartednesse of Christ?*

Answ. By his carriage towards men when he was here on earth, for now he is in Heaven in Glory, and we know not what his disposition is: therefore his life on earth was the living looking-glasse of his heart for ever. In Four Things.

1. Never any came to him that he cast away, whatever their sorrows or sins were, but healed them every one if they came to him with their miseries: for in healing their miseries, he did but shew his readinesse to heal them of their sin; hence *Matthew* applies that, *Mat.* 8. 17. *He bare our infirmities.*

2. When men came to him for by-ends, not for himself chiefly, he rebukes them for it, and shews he was more ready to give himself, than bread to them, *John* 6. 27.

3. Those that were lost, and sick, and miserable, and came not to him, he went up and down to seek and save them, the *lost Sheep, Luke* 19. 10.

4. Those that would none of his love, he pittied and had compassion on their misery and sin; as on them that were sheep without a shepheard; he mourned for the hardnesse of their hearts: he wept over *Jerusalem.* Now look upon Christ the same still: thou comest to him in secret to take away all iniquity, to give thee himself; tell me, dost think the Lord if here would reject thee ever. 2. But I dare not receive him. *Auf.* Thou wilt take Bread from him daily, and he is more willing to give himself. 3. Thou canst not come to him, nor find him, but only sometimes, nor see him; well, but then he will seek thee out. 4. Oh but I oft reject: yet he pitties thee still. O think of this compassion of Christ, and make him as if present; 'tis a speciall means to establish the heart in Believing.

Means 5.   Learn to know when you are bound not to give way to your fear of Gods love; for sometime it is the case of many a precious soul, that he hath clear evidence of Gods love to him: and what is there against it? nothing but a fear, what if I should be deceived when all is done? and hence the heart sinks exceedingly. As some Women that have speciall love, if once they take a jealousie of their Husbands love, it's never removed; So here.

Quest.
Answ.   *How shall I know this?*

First, If those fears thou hast drive thee farther from Christ, it's clear you are then to cast them off: those fears that cause sin are sinfull, but to be driven from Christ is sinfull, *Luke* 5. 9, 10. *Lord depart from me, I am sinfull:* fear not saith Christ, 1 *Sam.* 12. 20. they were ready to cast off all, *Fear not,* saith he; think of this, what 'tis you get by nursing up those fears, they hinder your joy in, and your love to Christ, your blessing of Christ, cause a dead discouraged heart: nay though they drive you to Christ one way, if they drive you from Christ another way by questioning his care, concluding against his Truth, never doubt they are vile, *Mat.* 8. 26. *Why did ye fear O ye of little Faith.* So far therefore as fear drives us to Christ, 'tis good, otherwise to be cut off.

2. If the Lord hath drawn thy heart to come to Christ, and when undone, every way secretly perswaded thy heart that thou shalt have help if thou come, and by coming hast received healing Vertues of thy lusts and vile affections from the Lord Jesus, fear not now, 'tis a sin to fear I shall not have help, as *Mark* 5. 33. the Woman with the Bloody-issue, she was afraid she had presumed, hence came
trembling,

trembling; but the Lord told her, *Now fear not , be it unto thee according to thy Faith : only thy Issue is but begun to heal.* What say you , have you never come to him , never received any healing from him ? that is hard. Surely 'tis so , that I would not be in my lust again for a world.

If none of these prevail, but the Lord follows thee with fears on fears , as wave on wave, then see if there be not some guile of spirit in thee, *i.e.* some sin you have or would give way to if you had assurance of Gods love. It was the speech of one to me, next to the Donation of Christ, no mercy like this, to deny assurance long ; and why ? for if the Lord had not, I should have given way to a loose heart and life, but, *&c.* so if the Lord should deal so with thee , it may be thou would'st lye in thy sins, if thou had'st peace there, and it may be you have had it,but sinned, and not confessed, not lamented, not opposed : Thus it was with *David* , *Psalm* 32. 1,2,3,4. Hence when he confessed, the Lord forgave in his Conscience his sin. Men will withdraw their love from their Wives if it make them wanton, and deal sharply with them : so one that never restored , could never get peace; some ever complaining, never setled , because they have their Truces with sin, and would have peace with Christ, and it cannot be. And this is a rule I have long held, in them that have clear light of the Gospel, long denial of assurance is like fire to burn out some sin , and then the Lord will speak peace , *Judg.* 10. 16. And therefore take this counsel, and God will tell thee thy sin, if thou art desirous that he should find it out , but get this mercy from him , *Zach.* 13. 9.

Bring thy heart to a straight , either to reject or receive him to be thine , he is offered to be King, and Saviour, and Lord, and Husband ; now thou shalt have his heart, his hand, his Spirit, his Father, his Kingdom, his Ordinances, his Angels, himself if you receive him,or else if not, you shall lose him , and then woe to thee when any mercy, any misery, any Ordinance befalls thee , for all shall suck thy Blood, consume thee, and fit thee for eternal ruine : and then wish , Oh that I had taken him , but then too late ; therefore receive him or reject him : Oh I cannot ; that's another matter : However we propound these Evangelical commands that may come with power, and therefore know, that if they do not now, they shall arise again in time.

SECT. II.

THis is not all that which makes you ready for Christ, unlesse your love is set and fixed on him : and therefore look that it be ready. I doubt not but that there is glowing in your hearts, some love to the Lord , it cannot be that all should be quenched , that all his kindnesse should be forgotten , but remembred many times with some affliction : but know it , if it be so , your lamp is not yet in your hand, nor your Souls ready to meet the Lord : For look as 'tis with a mighty Prince that shall set his heart on some poor servant , and he requires no portion but to love him the more , and she cannot bring her heart to love him more than other mean Fellows , is she fit or ready to be Matcht unto him ? So here : hence *Mat.* 10. 37. *He that loves Father or Mother, &c.* then you are ready when your love is fit for such an Husband ; and therefore though you feel some love under the ashes (when you stir up your hearts) to the Lord Jesus , yet if it be not a fit love beseeming his Excellency , and the Glory of his Person , when you can draw out buckets of love, and pour it upon other things , but scarce fetch out a drop for Christ, and yet you hope that will serve the turn ; I tell you no , you are yet unfit and unready for him. Look as it was with their offering the Testimonies of love and thankfulnesse , *Mal.* 1. 14. so it's here. And therefore my Exhortation shall be as 'tis said in that Psalm, *Give unto the Lord the kingdoms of*

H 2

the

Means 6.

Means 7.

Exhort. 2.

Psal. 86. 7, 8.

the earth. Give unto the Lord the honour due unto his Name: So give to the Lord the love that is due unto him, that love that is fit for him.

What is that love the Lord would have, which is fit for him?

1.Beloved, I hope if you think not your Blood too dear for Christ, you will not think any love too much for Christ: Yet because I would not have you aim at an uncertain mark, and shoot at a venture, I shall single out that love which I hope your own Consciences cannot but say is fit. And,

1. I had thought to have sought for this from you, *viz.* Give the Lord Jesus but that love, no more love than thou hast given to thy lusts, the Lord will be contented with it, *Rom.* 6. 19. *As ye have yeilded,* &c. so now; but that it may be you may think this love too base for him, yet give him but this, and the Lord would be contented with it, and accept of it; and those that shall not, it shall be their Torment in Hell to think of this word: Oh that I had given the Lord Jesus that love I gave to my base lusts, I had had him, and been in Heaven with him. But I wholly presse a Second.

2. Do but love him as he loveth thee, *i. e.* you cannot answer the greatnesse of his love, but do it for your measure: If you cannot pay him in pounds, yet pay him in pence, and this is fit for him: For 1. He is worthy of love, there is beauty in him why thou shouldest desire him; there is none in thee. 2. Thy love shall have a recompence, 2 *Tim.* 4. 8. he never can have recompence from thee. 3. He loves thee first with his own love, now that is unreasonable not to reflect his beams, and return him his own again in similitude, if not in parity.

Wherein appears the love of the Lord to me, that so I may see how to manifest the like love to him?

He hath loved thee more than himself, more than his own honour, for *he made himself of no reputation*, *Phil.* 2. 7. more than his own comforts, he left the bosom of a Father, and bore the wrath of a Father for thee; more than his own life, he saw thy neck upon the block, and Gods Axe up to give the Bloody Fatal stroke; and he came in thy room, and loved thy life more than his own, lost his own before one hair of thy head should perish, though he knew thee a Traytor to God, and an enemy to himself, *Rom.* 5. 10. *Rev.* 1. 5, 6. if this be not thus, woe to thee living, woe to thee dying. What art thou but a sad spectacle hung up in thy chains in this world for Angels in Heaven to see and tremble at, and for Devils, Sins, and eternal Sorrows, like Fouls of Heaven to Prey upon. Now is it not fit that thou shouldst love him more than thy self? his honour more than thine, his consolations more than thine own, his Person more than thine own, nay more than thy life? *Rev.* 12. 11. I have known them whom the Lord hath revealed this love to, that have thought it too little to do, and hence have wish'd they had been born in those Times that they might have laid down their lives for him: VVhere is now this love? Doth not self-love swallow up all? Lord, what self-seeking, self-serving, self-minding, self-honouring, self-pleasing, and the Lord himself and his love forgot, as if there were no Christ, or in him no love.

2. He hath loved thee when he might have passed by thee, and loved others that might have wone the Lord towards them (I speak after the manner of men) rather than thee; men of greater place, greater gifts and parts, greater pomp in the world, but *Rom.* 9. *Jacob* shall be loved, *Esau* hated: he hath passed by Kings with their Crowns, and now set his heart on thee a Babe, when wise ones know him not; foolish, when prudent ones see him not; weak, when strong and mighty receive him not. Yea, as the Apostle speaketh, 1 *Cor.* 1. 28. *Base things, and things which are not.* God hath made thee nothing in thine own eies. Behold his love, and now do the like for him. It may be somtime thy carnal eye sees more Glory in the creature, than in Christ; more in the honour of man, than in the honour of a Christ, &c. And hence might'st set thy heart on them

rather

rather than on Chrift, becaufe ftrongly tempted fo to do, and it may after fome fcourges be faved at laft, yet paffe by them, and fet thy heart only on him. We judge of a Friend by the times of triall, and of a Chriftian, by a time of temptation. Now a *Balaam*, a Witch may not dare in time of temptation, to fall into it. Oh get one ftrain higher, and go one ftep farther than a Witch, though I might let my heart loofe after the world, I will not love it, the love of the Lord deferves it, the love of the Lord conftrains me to give my love to him and not to the world, though I might hide it, and have pardon for it.

3. He loves thee although thou wrongeft him, *Ifa.* 43. 22. to 26. when he is fo wronged that he is ready to give thee up, yet *Hof.* 11. 8, 9. *He is God and not man*, nay, which is more wonderful, where fin there Grace abounds. Hence *David* makes this an Argument, *Pfal.* 25. 11. *Forgive becaufe 'tis great.* And hence *Mofes*, *Deut.* 33. 9. *Becaufe 'tis a ftiffnecked people.* Oh therefore love him, though he fmites thee, though he forfakes thee, wherein he may feem, but indeed doth no wrong to thee, but love thee ; for chaftifement is part of the portion of fons, not of Baftards, *Heb.* 12. 6, 8. But do as that woman when fhe came to the ftake, gave away her cloaths, fome to one, fome to another, *Now farewell friends, and world, welcome Love, welcome Chrift.* So if the Lord comes to take away all from thee, the child of thy body, the husband of thy youth, the wife of thy bofom, the comforts of thy life, provifions from thy family, bread from thy mouth, bid farewel to them, give them into the Lords hands, and now fay, welcome Chrift. Its ufual for Chriftians at firft converfion and efpoufing, the Lord loves them dearly, and tenders them, fhews nothing but love to them, and then their love is frefh ; afterward come hard Frofts, and Winter-ftorms, and cold blafts of difpleafure : Chrift departs from the Soul, withdraws himfelf, hides his face, and fends fad afflictions ; now the Soul apprehending anger, and nothing elfe, it grows difcouraged, and fo dies : when if it could ftay and wait, it fhould fee all from love, and doing it the greateft good. Oh remember this : he doth afflict me, he doth depart from me, he doth fear me with Hell, yet I'le love him never a whit the leffe : Though the Lord buries all the Bleffings he gives me, yet my love fhall live, and if it do fall it fhall arife.

4. He loved thee when in thy low eftate, *Pfal.* 136. 23. even when as no eye pittied thee, *Ezek.* 16. nay when thou wert vileft, at the height of thy fin, under deepeft depths of mifery, and ftraighteft captivity, after Friends had almoft ceafed to counfel, Word and Spirit could do no good, after Confcience had warned thee. Oh love him when he is in his loweft eftate, when his enemies perfecute him, and his feeming Friends forfake him. Before you came to this Land, you thought Chrift and perfecution, Chrift and the meaneft condition, nay Chrift and death would be fweet : the Lord it may be doth or will try your love ; and here you find Chrift and loffes in Eftate, Chrift and croffes in your Family, Chrift and many fears, and toils, and cares. Do you love him now as well as ever you did for all this ? Oh never was my heart worfe ? I doubt not but a difcerning Chriftian may fee how all the world is againft Chrift, nay many Traytors in his own Family, who love the bagg more than Chrift. Many foolifh Virgins who love their fleep and floth more than Chrift ; nay the hearts and Spirits of his own Friends declining, that there is not that life of Chrift, that prefence, and favour, and power of Chrift in Hearts, in Prayers, in Lives, and no complaints of this : Now is the fitteft time of love, when no eye fees, when no heart loves him, or cares for him, *Pfalm* 119. 126, 127. *Therefore I love thy commands*, when he is fhut out of every heart, when none to receive him, if any love it will appear now.

5. He doth love thee conftantly every moment, *John* 13. 1. 2. He hath thee every moment in his own bofom, every moment thou art finning, and he is pardoning. Sin, and Satan, and Hell, and wrath are every moment waiting to hurt

thee, and he is every moment watching over thee, redeeming of thee. Every moment fin and juſtice cry againſt thee, and yet he is continually *making interceſ-ſion for thee*, Iſai. 27. 2, 3. Every moment he is bleſſing when thou art ſinning. Oh the unknown love of the Lord Jeſus! Oh theſe fits of love are not fit for him. Love him every moment, delight in him every moment. When a man hath a fire every moment warming him, but ſtill is cold, it's a ſad ſign that Death is near: You can love him ſometimes in a Sermon, but ſoon after cold again, or in a Sacrament, and preſently heart-dead again: or after anſwer to Prayers, and ſome ſpecial deliverances, and then the heart is un-affected again, and ſo a little pang of love muſt content Chriſt: if he ceaſeth one moment to love thee, and to mani-feſt it to thee, then ceaſe to love him; if he ceaſeth not to love thee dearly, never to leave thee, Oh then ever love him.

Objeſt.
Anſw.

But we have ſuch diſtractions and cares?

Men in love will follow their work, and Women will do the Huſwifry of the houſe, and yet love is at no time to ſeek to their Husbands, and ſhall the Lord have leſſe?

6. He loves thee with an unmeaſurable love, *Rom.* 5. 20. *Where ſin, there Grace hath abounded*: hence Eph. 2. 3, 4. *Love*, and *great love*, *verſ.* 7. *Exceeding riches of his Grace*: For there is in Chriſt.

1. A created love. One man loves another exceedingly, as *Jonathan* did *David*. Now he hath the perfection of all humane or Angelical love towards his people put in him.

2. Increaſed love, infinite love of a God, and hence 'tis immeaſurable. He thinks nothing he doth too much, nothing he gives too dear: hence when world is ſlain, Satan caſt out, when he is out ſin muſt out; when ſome ſins removed, the reſt muſt; when they are out, then death muſt; when Death, then Hell. And when there is no life, no Grace, he works it; it decaies, he reſtores it; it cannot act, he quickens it; it cannot, doth not grow, he waters it. He hath given thee the earth, and the dayes of peace and patience; thoſe are too little: he calls thee, and when thou canſt not come, draws thee, and gives thee pardon: that is too little: he gives earth to thee, that is too little: (world is theirs) he gives Hea-ven to thee, that's too little (for they are made Co-heirs:) he gives promiſe to thee, that is too little: he gives himſelf, and Spirit, and can he do more? Yes, we cannot drink in all that goodneſſe and love; hence he gives eternity to thee, and he ſhall more and more enlighten thee: not only let thy Soul live to bleſſe him, but thy poor body, and every duſt of it to be raiſed up, to Glory with him. What the Lord promiſed to *Abraham*, *In bleſſing I will bleſſe*, that portion is thine. Oh now love him without meaſure. *Oh how I love thy law!* how did *David* love it? I cannot tell; but if he loved the word of Chriſt, then much more the perſon of Chriſt, the preſence of Chriſt, everlaſting fellowſhip with Chriſt. Oh take heed of giving Chriſt, and meaſuring out unto Chriſt his portion, his allowance, that when the Lord comes to you for more love (as he doth daily) you give him that anſwer which many do in their practice, you have let him have as much as you can: ſo that you cannot ſpare any more from your ſelves, from a baſe world, from Wife, and Child, and Creature, from a ſlothful courſe: you hope the Lord will accept of that little he hath. I confeſſe a little water in a Spring is bet-ter than much that comes by Land-floods, but be ſure it be a Spring, elſe not ac-cepted. Beloved, time was you lived without Chriſt, did nothing for him: now you do; and what thou doſt this year, did'ſt laſt year, and no more: what love Chriſt had yeſterday, the ſame he hath to day and no more: Will you thus ſtint the Lord? Either do more, give more, or mourn you cannot: Oh one lfe, one heart is too little for him. It hath put me to ſad fears of many mens eſtates to ſee this frame, a world of ſin without meaſure every day: where is the Chriſtian that loves the Lord the more every day? how can any then ſay much is forgiven, when they do not love much.   7. He

7. He loves thee now in Glory, there hath prepared a place for thee, *John* 14. 1, 2, 3. where he longs for thee, *John* 17. 24. You know *Pharaoh's* Butler when exalted to his place, forgot poor *Joseph*. One would think now the Lord Jesus is in Glory, and hath God, and Angels, and his Kingdom to content him, he should never look after such a worm, such a poor helpleſſe creature as thee. But as the High Prieſt carried the Names on his breaſt, and precious ſtones, ſo the Lord Jeſus hath thy Name writ upon his very heart. Oh now love him when he exalts thee to Glory, to give thee the Kingdom of Heaven on earth, with peace and quietneſſe. When *Germany* lies in blood, and Eaſtern Churches ſlain by the Dragon, devoured by the *Turk*, when *Englands* lights and lamps are going out, no people have ſuch peace, ſuch glory in ſo ſmall a time. Beloved, now where is love? The Churches of Chriſt never loſt their love ſo much as when they had their peace, and have been 1600 years a learning by Afflictions and Perſecutions, how to enjoy their peace, and to have their love ſmell as ſweet then, as when beaten moſt, and yet have not, but like the Globe without the Croſſe in the Emblem rolling and running farther and farther from God, *In Cruce quies*. Oh unreaſonable to love him leaſt whom he tenders moſt. Doth not Prayer grow cold for the Name of Chriſt, for the Churches of Chriſt? then love grows cold. Doth not plenty of means make thy ſoul ſleight means : when you went many miles to hear, and had ſcarce bread at home, Oh you thought if once you had ſuch liberties! but when they are made yours, now what fruit. Doſt not fall in affections to Saints? Oh love dies, Chriſt deals not ſo with thee, and who knows but in Rocks and Mountains of the Wilderneſſe thou maiſt lament theſe evils which peace breed now?

8. He loves thee ſo as when any evil toucheth thee, he hath a feeling of it, and is grieved at it, *Jud.* 10. 16. *Iſai.* 63. 9. nay he then comforts thee moſt, both in them, and by them, *John* 14. 27. *Not as the world gives peace, ſo give I it to you* : Oh then grieve thou for thoſe evils that betide him, the wrongs that others offer him, but eſpecially the unkindneſſe thy own Soul ſhews him, *Mark* 5. 3. He *mourned for the hardneſſe of their heart*, *Eph.* 4. 29, 30. *Let no corrupt communication proceed out of your mouth, and grieve not the Holy Ghoſt*, *Heb.* 3. 10. *Forty years long was I grieved becauſe they erred*; I confeſſe you will wrong him, but will you, muſt you be impenitent too? Did his enemies grieve him on earth, and ſhall his Friends grieve him in Heaven, and no ſorrows, no ſecret tears? he hath ſhed his Blood for thy ſin, it ſhall never condemn, and wilt not thou ſhed tears? Is there no good Nature? But what is there no ſpirit of mourning? It may be many a day and week haſt thou grieved him, and not a ſigh to any purpoſe to eaſe thee of thy ſin, but what hath eaſed thee in thy ſin. Oh now comfort his heart again after thou haſt moſt grieved him; comfort his Spirit that is dying ſighing in thee; as he comforts thee by thy troubles, comfort him by making a right uſe of all thy ſins to be more humble, more vile, to love him the more, and love thy ſelf the leſſe, as the Prodigal Son, *Luke* 15. 18, 20, 24.

9. He loves thee ſo, that though he departs, he will not, doth not ſtay long from thee, though you may think it long, *Iſai.* 54. 7. Hence it's wonder to ſee when heart gone, love loſt, life loſt, yet ſuddenly thou art brought down on thy knees : Oh 'tis the Lord that doth it : Thou waſt in ſorrow of heart, he did not ſtay long, but came and comforted thee; thou waſt in thy ſins, it was not long but he delivered thee; thou waſt in want of knowledg of him, it hath not been long but that he hath revealed the Lord to thee; thou haſt been in afflictions and troubles, it hath not been long but he hath heard thee : So give him the like love. I know you will fall from him in love, in delight, in care; but do not ſtay long from him. Sometime the baits of the world will draw thee from him when thou haſt thy eaſe and peace, Oh think it was better with me once than now; when fears drive thee from him, yet return, 1 *Sam.* 12. 21, 22. Oh here is that which hardens

dens hearts, breaks your peace, and grieves the Lord so as he is forced to send many sad afflictions, because you lie in your falls: Oh be not long, nor far from him.   He returns to thee when thou art most unkind to him: return when he is ever kind.   He returns to thee though he hath no need of thee, thou hast of him; *He will not leave thee:* Oh leave not him !

10. He hath from before all worlds loved thee, when no reason for it, *Jer.* 31. 1, 2, 3. Thou hast neglected to love him long, all thy youth, nay it may be all thy life; Oh you beloved of the Lord begin to do it now, when there is all reason for it, when Heaven calls for it, Earth calls for it, Ordinance; plead for it, Spirit faith come, and calls for it too.   It may be thy life is not long.   What not yet ?

Quest.
Answ.
But how shall I come to do this, thus to love the Lord?

The Lord only can plant, can water this Grace, yet because the Lord doth it by meanes, I will give you some now.

I. Labour to find out the true sweetnesse, and to taste the bitternesse of the deceitful sweetnesse of all Creatures, for this is a rule in reason, a mans affections like streams must run some way: and 'tis a rule in Theology, stop the affections from running to the Creature, and in a sincere heart it will run unto Christ, *Hos.* 2. 6, 7. if it be from all creatures: Now then the affection is turned from the Creature, when it finds the bitternesse of the deceiving sweetnesse of it: and Secondly finds out the real sweetnesse of it; for make it as a rule, when a mans heart cannot love Christ (unlesse it be when it is benummed) 'tis because he hath somewhat else to joy his heart; now let the Creature yeild you no more joy, and Christ hath your love: indeed you may and must joy in the real sweetnesse of it, and this will encrease, and not diminish your love.

Quest.   What is the real sweetnesse of the Creature?

Answ.   Christs love: Oh see this, if Christ should not love thee, would not thy life be death, thy Salvation from many dangers be Damnation, thy Friends miserable comforters, thy joyes sorrows? what good would any thing do thee if thou hadst these thoughts, all these I have, but wrath with them? What comfort can a man take in his Feast, if news were then brought that after 'tis done, you must go to the stake to be burnt? You that joy in your pastimes, one frown of Christ would blast all.   Oh see this, *Psalm* 63. *Thy loving-kindnesse is better than life, in thy favour is life.* Now joy for this, and this will knit your heart nearer to him.   For Jesus sake ponder this Point.

Now 2. Taste the bitternesse of the sweetnesse remaining now 'tis distilled; and Satan shews a Three-fold sweetnes, before, in, and after the enjoying of it.

Now 1. Before, remember how they have drawn away and held thy heart from God, done thee more hurt than all afflictions, many a sweet smile hadst thou had from God, but for them.

2. In the enjoying of it 'tis sweet, but when 'tis sweet to thee, 'tis then most bitter to the heart of God; when thy joy is kindled, the Lords sorrow is stirred up and provoked.

3. After. 1. It will draw thy heart from God: and 2. It will be bitter in thy belly at last.   Whatever sweetnesse draws thee from the love of Christ, Oh it will be bitter. *Rom.* 6. 21. Chew upon this, and see if any thing here be worthy of your joy, and if not, then return to your first Husband.

II. Taste the allsufficiency of the love of Christ: a Woman that is not content with her Husbands love, she will not love him as 'tis fit.   So when other things make love to us, and the Lords love is not enough, *Cant.* 1. 4. *More than wine:* hence *the upright love thee.* Do but sit down and think what this is: If once he loves thee, what-ever he can he will do for thee, he will order all thy life, not one thing shall hurt thee, every thing in providence shall work for thy glory, sins, sorrows, &c. so as thou shalt say his denyals are better than his gifts, his blows better

than

than smiles, his withdrawings better than his presence, these evils better than joyes, and when once he loves me, he will never leave me, that come life, come death, I am safe. Oh taste this!

III. See the Lord Jesus now as he is, and in truth this were enough to make any prophane heart love him, much more a Saint espoused to him, but the Lord hath hid himself from their eyes, shall he be so, is he to from yours? 1 *Pet.* 1. 8. *When seeing not with bodily eyes, but with Faith, ye love him,* 1 *John* 3. 1, 2, 3. *We shall see him as he is.* VVhy suppose the day of doom was come, Christ in the clouds, and all creatures before him, all Angels ministring to him, in all the Glory of his Father; Oh then the love of Christ, Oh one smile, one word of Christ would be precious. Lord that men should be in a Dream! See Christ a little higher set in his Throne, a place more glorious, though lesse seen, in all the Glory of his Father, all mighty Angels ministring to him, all the world put into his hand, doing what he will, and all he will; why will you not love him now? Is the Gospel a Fable? say so if it be, then love him not if you can. VVhen *Simeon* and the VVise men saw him, though but in his abasement, they honoured him, much more now if see him in glory. It's a question whether the beams of the Sun are fire: Some demonstrate it thus, Take a Glasse and gather together the beams, it burns. Therefore so if you would see so as to be affected, gather together the beams of his glory and love; Thus you see the e means to get fit love, and if it be lost, Oh now get it again, left the Lord strain for it, else you are not fit, and if it be not any love that sufficeth, much lesse no love, as in many of you: but consider 1 *Cor.* 16. 22. *He that loves not Christ, let him be accursed*: Oh that this might be won from you, O little love goes out to Christ, who sees it not? Ordinances of Christ, men are weary of them, the truths of Christ, despise them, the Servants of Christ, they quarrel with them. Now recover your Love, the Lord help you so to do.

SECT. III.

TO do the work of Christ, to be daily at it, and finishing of it; for look as it   *Exhort.* 3. was with the Head, 'tis so with all the Members that are to remain a while in this life, they have some work to do for the Lord; some common, some special work, and when that is done, now they are ready to return home again. Hence *John* 17. 4, 5. *I have finished the work*, and now he stands at the door and knocks, and is ready for entrance, *Now glorifie me with thy self*, and you shall find a faithful heart will neither be willing nor ready to go till this is done.

What is this work I am to do?   *Quest.*

I have answered this else-where at large, yet these two things I would say.   *Answ.*

1. That a mans chief work lies not in facile duties, for though Grace and Christs Spirit makes duties easie, his yoke easie; yet there is a contrary Spirit that will make them hard and difficult at first.

2. Least I should leave you unsatisfied altogether, we shall find a christian life is carried with a double motion: 1. In seeking of God in his Ordinances. 2. Or in walking with God out of his Ordinances, these are joyned together, *Gen.* 6.8, 9. *Noah* found Grace, hence sought it, though not in the eyes of the world: and hence *Noah* walked with God. Hence we see Christ was sometime in the Mount alone, Sometime abroad going up and down doing good. *Moses* in the Mount and in the Camp too. Now look as before a man is justified, his chief work then is to seek God in his Ordinances for a principle: so a soul now espoused to Christ is to walk with Christ: now walking implies constant following of another, or a continual work; so Christ hath work for you every moment. Hence in every company, time, place, temptation, enquire thus, Am I not like to lose my time,

my heart, Chrifts honour? What work hath Chrift for me to do? hold here, for here lies your work. Look as an ambitious man asks, how ferves this for my honour, and Satan how he may difhonour Chrift; fo do you ask, how you may honour him, *Rom.* 6. 19. *As you have given your felves inftruments of iniquity*, &c. And now becaufe we live in times and places wherein men have fo much work of their own to do, that Chrift is neglected, wherein very few walk with God. Hence men taking mens examples for patterns and copies of their courfe, content themfelves to do as others do: And this being a clofe act, mainly confifting in what is unfeen; and becaufe men are apt to put off Chrift with defires, and ferve Satan indeed, and becaufe apt to refolve all Religion into fome two or three duties or Graces, and becaufe mens hearts are catching at comforts and promifes, but commands tedious and burdenfome; I fhall preffe this upon thefe Motives; only here let me premife when I preffe you to this, 'tis not to a Covenant of Works, as though you could act your felves, but we look to Chrifts Blood and Spirit to fet on things; I fpeak to them under Grace, who have the Spirit without, and Faith within to act and carry them here. But

Mot. 1.

    1. Whofe work will you do? you cannot ceafe to do Chrifts work, but you muft do your own work, (I fpeak not for idleneffe) *i. e.* you muft ferve your luft; now confider what good did thy felf ever do thee, nay Satan never fuch an eneny as thy own felf: and will you fall down to fuch an Image? Shall thy lufts have content more and rather than Chrift?

    2. Confider the Lord will take care and charge of thee, to do thy work, to bring about thy ends for thee, do but thou do his. *Martha* was cumbred about many things, hence forfook the better part: fo men neglect, forget Chrifts work, becaufe of fo many diftractions of their own. What will become of my hundred Talents? what will become of my Wife; Child? Now do you take care of the Lords work, take that for your charge, and the Lord will take charge of you. The beft, readieft, and only way to have your own ends, is to feek the Lords, and forget your own. As in *Solomon*, his great work and care was to rule a State well, and the Lord gave all the reft. Set thy face to the Sun, and thefe fhadows will follow you. The Servant takes charge of his Mafters work, and he need not trouble himfelf for meat and drink, and *è contra*.

    Firft, there fhall not any evill hurt thee, whereas elfe thy good things fhall, *Ifai.* 27. 3.

    Secondly, All Creatures in Heaven and Earth fhall ferve that man that ferves his God, *Hof.* 2. 21, 23. whereas elfe they groan under thee.

    Thirdly, Angels fhall come out of Heaven to guard thee.

    Fourthly, Nay the Lord Jefus himfelf fhall ftand at the top of the ladder, that when every thing elfe fhall leave thee, he fhall then bring the beft wine at the laft, he will be a portion to thee, *Pfalm* 16. *Phil.* 3. 8.

    3. Confider that the more difficult any duty is, the more fweetneffe fhall you receive if you break through it: Men plead difficulty, I plead gain. Hence he that overcomes fhall eat of the hidden Manna: Hence never any fo comforted, honoured as Chrift, becaufe never any went through fo hot a work for the Father as Chrift, *Phil.* 2. You plead the difficulty of a chriftian life, and tafte not the fweetneffe of that life: if you can do no more than what is eafie, and pleafeth felf, the Lord will never let you tafte the fweetneffe of pleafing him. Have you not fometimes found your hearts dead to Prayer, yet you fell to it, and then would not but have took the feafon for a world.

    4. Confider, let the duty be to Nature impoffible, yet the Lord is at hand to help, even when no ftrength, *Ifai.* 40. 29. Nay *Heb.* 11. 34. *Out of weakneffe were made ftrong.* If you had no Chrift, no Spirit, no Promifes to affure you of help, you might then ceafe acting, and fay 'tis impoffible I fhould ever overcome fuch evils, attain to that meafure: but when Promifes to affure, and Chrift and

Spirit

Spirit at hand, now to plead impossibility, is to reproach the Lord; to think he will set his people to make Brick, and give them no straw: nay to war against God and to make the Lord war against you, *Numb.* 14. You know how they cried out of impossibilities, and now the Lords anger rose when they were ready to enter *Canaan*: So when men are ready to enter upon possession of Christ, and Promises, then impossibilities appear. Consider therefore what the Lord hath done for *David, Gideon, Samson*, who went out in the name and Spirit of the Lord, and were helped: If you were under the Law, you might plead this, but under Grace 'tis horrible to make this excuse.

5. Consider if the Lord do not help (as he will be free) yet he will accept thy will, I know he will not accept the wishes of servants, yet he will accept the will of Sons; neither will he accept the will of Sons in a work they might have strength from him to do, and go not to him for it; but in that case he will, as 2 *Cor.* 12. 9. *i.e.* 'tis enough, I accept thee: and this is very sweet, that for his own sake he should be pleased as well with the will as with the work, for this is that which troubles, I would have help, the Lord gives none; why the Lord accepts of it as if thou didst it, as in *Davids* building a Temple: For a Christians work is done two wayes.

First, Sometimes by feeling, when we feel help.

Secondly, Sometimes by Faith, by going to another for it: and this the Lord accepts most mercifully, for this is his Victory over all sin, even his Faith. When we see a duty hard, and do not go to the Lord for help, then we are overcome properly: For out of the abundance of the heart the person acts for Christ.

6. Consider the Lord will honour thee (though the work doth not) *John* 12. 26. *Him will my Father honour*, both in this life, *Rom.* 2. 29. and in that to come. Now as 'tis in acting parts, 'tis no matter what Fellow-acters think, God is the great Spectator, God will esteem of thee, and Conscience shall witnesse as much when no eye sees, or when men see and judge amisse, yet the Lord approves, and at the great Day before Men and Angels, and all the world, 1 *Cor.* 4. 5. *Then shall every man have praise of God*: and hence *Mat.* 25. Christs judgement is made according to the works of his people: because then they shall not be compared with themselves and their sins, but with the wicked: and hence to set out their glory, he reckons up all they have done. All men in all their acts seek to avoid shame, and attain honour: now if you did know a way for all men in the world to honour you, would you not attend it? what is their Dreams to Gods honour? Hence not one act but is now chronicled, *Mal.* 3. 16. and afterward rewarded, 1 *Cor.* 15. 58. Oh then give content to the Lord.

7. Consider the peace you shall have by this means, both while you live, and when you dye: what's the cause of so many doleful clamours of Conscience, but a loose carelesse heart, the Lord is neglected; that when one pleads Faith, it will be replyed, the true Faith is the *Faith of the Son of God*. Now is the Faith of God a carelesse Faith, a secure, worldly, impenitent, dead Faith? you may sit down, and rise again, and say true, yet I'le believe, so you may, but it will be with such a trembling spirit as you will find no peace: Neither do I know how any can keep his peace otherwise, for there are children but Still-born; if born a living Son, thou wilt live to God, necessarily I must do it: But by this means, Oh there is unspeakable peace, *Mat.* 11. 29, 30. Hence *Paul, I have finished my work*, &c. *John* 14. 21. to 24. you live without God, and walk without God, and Pray without God, but there is a day approaching that you shall appear before the Lord Jesus, you shall wish then, Oh that I had lived so and so: Oh do that now.

8. Consider the Lord will have it done, it must be done, hence *Paul* said, *Necessity lies upon me, and woe to me*, &c. the Lord should be forsworn if he should not bring you to it, *Luke* 1. 73, 74, 75. *According to the Oath*, &c. Belo-

I 2

Beloved you think lafie defires will ferve: no, it muft be done: you fay I cannot, it muft be better with you. And hence look for a rod, and that the Lord
will bring you into great affliction till all is removed, and fo purge you; and if one
affliction will not do it, then worfe fhall come, he loves you better than fo. And
remember you have had warning this day: you came hither for the Lords work,
and now your own juftles it out: look that God will take away the Kingdom from
you, or fet oppreffors over you, or fend fome ftings among you: and then fay,
Oh I may thank my walking unworthy of God and Gofpel for this.

9. Confider elfe you fhall make the Blood of Chrift fhed of no effect, 2 *Cor.*
5. 14, 15. Now wicked men need not fear this, no Blood fhed for them. Will
you do fo? God forbid: The Jews have killed him, will you drag him up and
down the ftreets, trample on his Blood, and put him to open fhame.

10. Confider your time is but fhort, and you have done but little work, and 'tis
not long but that your Crown fhall be put upon your head. It's noted of *Enoch
Gen.* 5. that he walked with God three hundred years, (and that having Sons
and Daughters, having Family-contentments, and incumbrances,) and he lived
the fhorteft time. I am fure Angels are content to come out of Heaven to do
the work of God: what not do it here? *Paul* thought himfelf born too foon becaufe for a time he lived without Chrift. Oh but now make tryal, and you will
find it the fweeteft life, that you will fay, why have I neglected this fo long?
and if thou doft not find feven times more peace therein than in all the world, never fet foot here.

Queft.
Anfw. *How fhall I thus do the work of* Chrift?

1. *Without* Chrift *you can do nothing*, John 15. 5. The Sun runs ftill becaufe it's
light of it felf; fo when the Lord is in you, you will do fo. Hence go not out
to any duty in your own ftrength, for then you will either not do it, or nor hold
out in it: No man can hold out at his work that feeds not abundantly on his meat,
fo here; and here note but thefe two things.

1. Do not only in Ordinances do thus, but out of Ordinances then, as in particular times of tryal (for the Lord will not give you in an Ordinance as much Grace
as fhall ferve you out of it) lift up your hearts to Chrift, and fay as Chrift, *Father
the hour is come, now glorifie thy Name*, John 12. 28. So Lord, here is work to do,
but a dead heart is upon me, Lord glorifie thy Name. I have feldom feen but the
Lord either helped then, or at fome other time when thou didft come, and then
the Lord puts thee in remembrance that 'tis out of refpect to that.

2. Thus coming and feeding on the Lord Jefus, believe that he will help, and
that fhall be fo; fome have never got ftrength againft fin till then, but this hath
conquered difficulties, *Rom.* 8. 37, 38. *In all thefe things we overcome, for I am
perfwaded, &c.* So you coming helplefle to a Chrift, all his ftrength is yours by
covenant. Be perfwaded he cannot go from his word: but yet we muft ufe o-
ther means fanctified by Chrift, for Chrift worketh by meanes. And therefore,

II. Find out where the caufe of all your negligence and floth lies in not doing
the Lords work, nay of your doing Satans work. It may be you will fay you cannot, I know there is that in Saints in part, but this is not the main, therefore I
will tell you thus.

1. Before converfion the main wound of men is their Will, *Video meliora
proboq; dexteriora fequor*: Hence John 8. 44. *His lufts ye will do.* Hence Mat. 23. 37.
You would not: they fay hence we have a Will, I fay no. And hence we anfwer
that great Objection for Poffibilities to keep all Laws by univerfal Grace, which tis
unjuft to punifh for not doing that a man cannot do. VVe anfwer, There is a
double impotency, *Ex infirmitate*, or *Ex malignitate*, when men will not,
Prov. 11, 12, 13.

2. Hence

2. Hence it follows after conversion, though the Will is changed, so that a man would but cannot do many things, *Ex infirmitate*, yet the great cause why he cannot do more is from the remnant of malignity not yet removed. A man will sleep, he loves it, and secretly loaths the wayes of the Lord: Hence the Church, *Isai.* 63. 17. complains of this. A man shall find his heart wills the end exceedingly, but when he comes to will the means, there his heart is weary of them, and loaths them; a man will be carelesse, and this being not seen, is not fought against. Sin is vilified, and hence the enemy to all good remains still. It's an old Rule, *Tantum possumus, quantum volumus.* Get Christ to help here.

3. Make this your last end, to live unto Christ, and to do his worke: Hence *Paul* did not account his life dear; this is your last end, for the end of being born by Faith, nay of being redeemed by Blood, 'tis to live unto Christ, *Tit.* 2. 11. When you cry for Faith, and Peace, and Assurance, that is not your end, for he that doth so is a very Hypocrite, and hath a false heart, but 'tis to live to Christ: Hence *Paul, Phil.* 3. 9, 10, 12, 13. fought to be found in him, but further to know him, *&c.* The Father is glorified in our bringing forth much Fruit. Hence make it your last end, and then your happinesse will lie in acting thus, and that that is a mans happinesse he is carried to with most infinite delight. For presse people to do Chrifts work, their hearts are dead, tell them the Lord Jesus shall have a Name by what they do for him, yet dead, because though they see it good, yet they place not their happinesse there, because that is not their last end. But come to this, now it will do; a man cannot bear a crosse, yet let him consider, the Lord shall gain though I do not; so for Faith, so for any other duty. Men think it good, but not their greatest good. Hence see Christ better than thy self, and his honour better than thy glory for ever. Hence the Lord denies us help, because we ask it for our Lusts, not for himself, *James* 4. 3.

4. Keep those glorious apprehensions of the Lord and his wayes, which you have sometimes in an Ordinance: You are sometimes near the Lord, and you then see a beauty in Christ, in his wayes, and then thinkest shall I ever wrong him more? then you come out and lose your light, and so you ever lose your strength and life. Hence *Eph.* 5. 11. 'tis as with a man that eats, but he looseth and spends his spirits, he can do no more work, but faints away: see 2 *Pet.* 2. 9. *Steven* can be content to have stones about his ears, when he can say, *I see Jesus.* And hence when those glorious apprehensions come into your minds, stamp them there, for set up other Images of other things in your minds, and your hearts will bow down every moment to them. Doth not Chrifts Spirit do all? yes, but by this *medium*, 2 *Cor.* 3. 18. *As by the Spirit of the Lord.*

SECT. IV.

Use 4. *Of Exhort.*

AFter you have done your work be ever humble, and be ready to give the Lord the honour of his Grace, that ever he gave any thing to you, that ever he did any thing by you; for the last end of all the Elect, 'tis to admire and honour the riches of Gods Grace, *Eph.* 1. 5, 6. Hence the Fall was permitted, never should Grace have been seen, if sin and misery had not come in. Now if this be our last end in Glory, then the heart is ready to have immediate fellowship with Christ there, when 'tis ready to set for its last end. Hence it's frequent in the *Psalms*, when *David* was in any strait, wanted any mercy, nay the presence of the Lord here, this is the last end he pursues, the last word he speaks before the Lord, *My soul shall blesse thee*, as *Psalm* 63. 3, 4. and hence when all his enemies were subdued, and he ready to lay all in the dust, he gives the Lord all, 2 *Sam.* 22. *per totum.* and 23. 5. Beloved, this is Heavens work, Oh learn this Song before you go there, which none can learn but the Redeemed and Sealed of the Lord,)

Rev. 14. 3. *John* 1. 14. It's writ of Christ, he was *full of Grace and Truth* : Do you ever think to meet with him , that get not your hearts full of the sense of it ?

Before I come therefore to presse this, I shall premise these two things.

First ; That the Lord in all his dealings with his people , sees lastly to bring about the glory of his Grace : he regards nothing men do , if at last they deny him this ; He respects not what sins and evils men have, if at last he gets this, for this is his last end : hence all he doth to his people, for his people , by his people , 'tis for this. And hence

1. He leaves them a long time in their Graves and Sins, that they live like other men, which is strange that he that hath loved them so long , should leave them so long to be as bad as any , yet th's he doth , because it makes for the praise of his Grace, *Ephes.* 2. 4,7, 8. *Dead in sin, that in ages to come,* &c. And this doth so confound Gods people, that they wish not only Heaven , but Earth , and Ages to come may record this love.

2. Hence out of men fallen , he picks out usually the poorest and vilest , the younger Brother lesse loved out of a Family , leaves elder , *Rom.* 9. 11. and *the foolish, and weak things, and things that are not , that no flesh might glory, but in the Lord*, 1 Cor. 1. 26, 31. and this is strange that the Lord should chuse thus , but this he doth to blur the glory of all the world.

3. Hence the Lord saves by Faith, and justifies by Faith , and seals by Faith, *Eph.* 1. 13. and sanctifies by Faith, and glorifies by Faith , 1 *Pet.* 1. 3. So that all a Christians life is a Beggars life , and 'tis strange the Lord should chuse the basest, poorest Grace to save by ; and the end is the glory of his Grace , *Rom.* 4. 16. 'Tis of Faith that it might be of Grace.

4. The Lord leaves many wants in his people , under which they sit sighing, and that sometime very long, refuseth to hear their Prayers, that they may repair to the Throne of Grace, and so in conclusion blesse Grace, *Heb.* 4. 16.

5. Hence the Lord takes away sometimes those feelings, those enlargements they had, and baits them with most vexing sins , and pricking distempers, 2 *Cor.* 12. 7, 9. and it is to advance Grace.

6. Hence the Lord is sometimes angry with his people , and hides his face from them, that if ever he returns in love, his Grace may be the sweeter, and last the longer, *Isai.* 54. 7. Nay hence sometimes strips them so of all that they have had , or can do , that if you ask what have you now to say for your selves ? nothing but Grace, their mouths are stopt. Hence *Psalm* 6. *Lord save me for thy mercies sake* , *Psalm* 51. 11. *According to the multitude of thy mercies,* &c.

7. Hence the Lord speaks peace to his people, that they may say, I was so vile, and yet loved ; Oh Grace! Oh love! *Ezek.* 16.63. When they see nothing but shame, and shame covers them , and afraid to appear before God, it is for this end. I'le name no more. Do you not observe it ? Sometime you shall find the Lord so strangely carrying matters, as if he did not love nor care for his people, against the hair and grain of their desires, and when all co res to winding up, 'tis to advance Grace. All a mans good dayes, and bad dayes , all Gods frowns and smiles, all the Lords Food and Physick, all God cares for, works, plots for , 'tis to do his people no more hurt than this, to advance his Grace in them, and by them. All his hewings and hammerings of you, nay his knocking you a pieces, and new melting, and new casting of you, 'tis that you may be Vessels of his glorious Grace, that you may be able to live in the air of Gods Grace, to suck in, and breath out Grace, and let all the power of Hell seek to blur it , yet Grace shall conquer. VVho would not be under Grace ? Oh poor creature, Satan is tempting , sin vexing, yet Grace must reign.

Secondly , This I say, that Gods own people do by strange wayes and courses deny the Lord, and deprive the Lord of the Glory of his rich Grace, for that being the Diamond in Gods Crown, and the beloved Attribute which God intends to advance; all the policy of Hell is against this; this is the reason why Satans enmity is so bitter against Faith, as in *Peter*; and observe, however there be many Temptations, his end is to crush Faith: the reason is, as 'tis with an enemy, if the Besieged hath water brought to the City by Pipes, he cuts off them and stops them, so Faith fetching all from Grace, and returning all to Grace, hence Faith is opposed most; and hence the unregenerate part will take Satans part, and doth strangely rob the Lord of the glory of this, though I confesse the Lord will have it for all that they seek to scatter it, *Isai.* 43. 21, 22. It's strange to see how few plot for the praise of Grace; hence how many are straitned, nay do crosse Christ in this. As

1. If the Lord give them not what Grace they would, then they sleight what little he bestows; and if he gives them much, then they solace themselves in it, and grow puft up and proud. It's the temper of Gods own people to set up such a measure of Gods Grace and Spirit which they would have, and therein they do well: *Paul, Phil.* 3. 11. lookt to the Resurrection of the dead; but if the Lord denies them that, (as he will make his people live from hand to mouth) they sleight what they have, either as if all were but hypocrisie, or because it is but little, not so much as they would have, and herein they do ill, for here the Lord loseth the glory of some Grace, for it's Grace that you have the least desires after it; nay that you do but know what it is, and see the want of it, and yet ever complaining, and never rejoycing, for every degree of Grace in Saints, is vertually saving, though formally common. But suppose the Lord fills the bottle full, and gives as much peace, affections, enlargements of heart, as it hath almost required, (for there are Spring-tides, and over-flowing times of Gods Spirit, now they are ready to swell, and be puft up above measure, as *Paul*, 2 *Cor.* 12. 7. *Lest I should be exalted above measure*, for there is self-love in Saints. Hence they desire an excellency in themselves: hence when they find none of their own, they are apt to deck and set out themselves with what the Lord hath done, and so to joy in this, and now to think themselves better than others of Gods Saints, whereas they should be more vile, and advance Grace the more, *Eph.* 3. 8. *To me the least of Saints*. And hence the Lord after greatest deliverances and mercies sends great sorrows, as to them in the Wildernesse. Hence the Lord takes away affections, and they dye, that Grace might be the more advanced.

2. If the sins of their hearts are common, and cannot be removed, and so seem little, then they passe them by, and never take notice of them, God will pardon them, and hence the Lord hath sad times of reckoning (with a rod in his hand) with his own people, *Ezek.* 6. 9. That those loose times are heavy times, this is for my neglect, &c. but hereby Grace loseth Glory; for how can they see how deeply they are indebted to the Lord, if they see not their Debt? on the other side, if their sins be very violent, and their distempers so strong, that they think none like me, now their hearts sink, and dye away, and grow discouraged, and all the use they make is this, I think it will never be better with me, and can there be life for me so dead, deliverance, redemption for me in such bondage, love for one that cannot but loath my self, and if others did know me, they would do so too. Can the Lord love me now? Yes Beloved, that he can and will, *Isai.* 63. 16. *Though Abraham know us not, yet*, &c. But here is your sin, when you should make this use of all, to feel the more need of Grace to pity, and say, the more precious shall Grace be to me for ever: your hearts now sink. The Lord brings his people into very low condition to humble them, and to shew them more of his Grace, *Psalm* 78. 19. *Can God prepare a Table?* they spake therein against God: so 'tis here; for herein the Lords Grace is seen, to love them when Lepers.

3. Grace that hath been shewen, for times past they forget it, 2 *Pet.* 1. 9. And

what

what is this but deſtroying Gods Grace? for why is Grace ſo precious at firſt converſion, that Heaven and Earth are too little to hold praiſes enough for it? And afterward, the Lord hath little love; Oh you forget what once you were, and what the Lord hath done, hence 1 *Tim.* 1. 13,14. I was ſo and ſo, &c. but now have received abundant Grace.   You have had many meetings with God, many anſwers from God, many conſolations and times of refreſhing and reviving, and theſe forgotten and buried, the life of them after a year or two expired.   And what is this but eclipſing Gods Grace? On the other ſide, as for Grace for time to come, they fear it, eſpecially when worms and no men in their own eyes.   Hence ſaith God, *Fear not worm Jacob, Iſai.* 41. 14. There is a certain Divining Spirit (as one once told me) that untill that was pulled out, no honour can the Lord get.   Before you come to Word or Prayer, thou wilt fear thou ſhalt never get any good; and when the Lord gives any, thou wilt fear thou ſhalt never hold out; and what Promiſe ſoever is made, thou wilt fear thou ſhalt never find it.   And what doth this but eclipſe Grace? we ſhould go with boldneſs to the Throne of Grace; nay hence let the Lord ſend never ſo much Mercy for the Preſent, a Fear will cut off all, that all this will riſe up in Judgement againſt me.

4. When they are moſt fit to honour Gods Grace by Faith, now they will not believe, not then above any other time: for then a man is moſt fit to honour Grace, when he feels moſt need of it: and when hath he moſt need, but when he feels moſt emptineſſe? why now above any other time a man will not come in, but will have ſomewhat in himſeif firſt, and then he will, when his heart is ſo and ſo ſweetly ſetled, &c. Hence *Luke* 14. Poor, and blind, and lame, and halt compelled to come in: one would think there needed not that; but now when fitteſt, now they will not: for let any man obſerve what would endear his heart ſo much to Grace as this: to think if it be the Lords mind to ſave a poor dead damned creature, then happy I? This is wonderful, this hath quickened dead love, and dead Faith, and a dead heart.   And on the other ſide, if the Lord delay, if it comes not at their own time, then they diſtruſt it; Grace! alas I feel my ſelf never a whit better: For there be two things in Faith,

Firſt, A coming to Chriſt, which is our work, *i. e.* Gods work in us.

Secondly, Receiving what I come for from Chriſt, which is the Lords work; Now the firſt gives evidence he ſhall have it, *John* 6. 35, 37. Hence the Lord will have them rejoyce in what Chriſt hath, as *my Grace is ſufficient*; but if it comes not preſently, then they caſt off Faith, and ſo caſt away Grace, I feel no good: hence *John* 4. 48. &c. I know there is a ſeeming coming to Chriſt, to have the Grace of Chriſt and ſin too, and this you may well caſt off: and a coming for his Grace and Spirit only, and you deſpiſe Grace, and diſtruſt the Lord if you caſt off this, or you ſeek to put the Lord out of his working by a covenant of Grace, (where he takes his times as he pleaſes) and give a flat lie to all promiſes of Grace, and refuſe to be contented with Chriſts Grace, that thou mighteſt have the more attributed to thy ſelf, and the Lord the leſſe.

5. Either they think not of the exceeding greatneſſe of the Lords love and free Grace to them, and hence *Paul* bowes to Heaven for this, *Eph.* 3. 16, 17. And hence it comes to paſſe, that look as 'tis with ſweet things, ſwallow them down in the lump, you never taſte the ſweetneſſe to purpoſe, nor never commend them; ſo 'tis when men ſwallow down Gods love, and chew not upon it, whereas if they did but think of it, Oh how ſweet would it be! *Pſalm* 63. 5, 6. Lord, how many dayes and weeks are ſpent thus? It's apparent you have the profeſſion of a Chriſtian life; but do you taſte the ſweetneſs of a Chriſtian courſe? No: why if you did think, you would; But you are weary at Night, ſleepy in the morning, buſie in the day, dead on the Sabbath: hence think not, hence give not God the glory of Grace: or if they do think of it, and the greatneſs of it, then they cannot think ſo great things ſhould be given unto them, or done for them: that God ſhould love

me as his Son, make me an Heir of all he hath with him, redeem me that have despised his Blood: 'tis too good News to be true. Hence the Disciple believed not for joy, *Luke* 24. 41. Hence when delivered out of *Babel*, we were in a Dream; this robs the Lord of Grace, for the greater the love is, and the more you take, the more love shall the Lord have, it cannot be otherwise, if you come to say this is mine.

6. Either they will pore only on their sins, and distempers, and miseries, and never look unto Christ the brazen Serpent, and search for a righteousness of their own, and cannot find it, and hence pore still. As when men have wounds, they only think on them, that when awakened out of sleep, they complain in their beds like the *Israelites, Exod.* 6. 9. that would not hear *Moses* because of anguish. As the impotent man answered Christ, *John* 5. 5, 6, 7. *Wilt be made whole?* he turns his eyes upon his misery, *I have none else to help me at the time*; here is but this means, and when I come my self, others step in before me, &c. Now so do men, and never look beyond means, the Lord can, the Lord will, and so eye not him: or on the other side, if they get healing of their wounds, then they eye Christ only, *Eph.* 2. 6. They were exalted in Heavenly places, yet remember, as *verf.* 11, 12. For let any Christian see that he is poor and miserable, but he is not much affected with it, nor afflicted with it, and so eye Christ, and trust to Christ, and ease himself here, & say we must look only to Christ, either you will hear of his fall (yea and himself shall find a decay) or he will grow very proud, unfit to give all to Christ. Is there Grace here?

7. Either if the Lord gives him any thing, himself and mercy, he will now add something of his own to Christ, and pull the vail of the Law over the face of the glory of Christ, *Gal.* 1. 6. or else do nothing at all for him, unless it be when the good fit takes him, under a pretence Christ must do all; as here the five wise Virgins that fell asleep: and thus you see how Grace is opposed by the children of Grace. Now therefore my Exhortation is, to take heed of this, and be ever ready to attribute all to the Lord, as they cryed when the Second Temple was building from beginning to the end, *Zec.* 4. 6, 7. so that thou wast spared so long, that called by means that the Lord should by Faith accept, that he should speak peace, this is Grace, that though vile, yet he will save me: 'tis Grace, that though I can do nothing, yet he will help me, and afterwards Crown me: Oh this is wonderful Grace! And

First, Do not only give the Lord the glory of Grace to redeem you from misery, for this you may do, and be full ready to give it, yet perish at last, as the *Israelites* that sang Gods praises did, but that he will save thee from greater, *i.e.* from sin. And

Secondly, Not only when you feel nothing, but when you feel most, Oh to honour Grace! And

Thirdly, Not to do it coldly, but with a heart enflamed with sense of it, that I live, I have, I do, I am what I am: Oh 'tis Grace. So that now if the Lord shall come and ask you, what will you say if I'le deliver you from all misery, subdue all sins, passe by all wrong, hear all Prayers, do all good to thee, do much good by thee, love thee every moment, give a Kingdom when thy work is done to thee, and my self better than all? say, Lord I can never recompence this, I shall be I hope the more vile in my own eyes for ever, and give all to Grace. Oh sing that Song, or get that Song by heart now, for *Rev.* 7. 10. there is a Song, *Salvation to the Lamb*, which none else could sing. This is our work, and a great work indeed.

How shall I do this?

1. Get a new light from the Lord to shew you clearly the infinite, endless, unknown evill of the least sin; *Paul* was a proud Pharisee until he saw sin, and *Jer.* 3. 24, 25. for if sin be seen, one smile, one day, nay a moments breathing-time in

this world will be matter of amazement to thee after all thou haft, and haft done: much more when thou feeft fo many fins, and that in every thing: Intreat the Lord to do this. We walk up and down the world, and fay we fin and grieve the Lord; but Oh 'tis not known, happy art thou if the Lord hath difcovered it; then thou wilt fay, why doth the Lord do any thing for me? could not he pick out ftones, nay Toads that never finned againft him, rather than me to enjoy him, efpecially is fin vile in thee, fo near God, and fo near Heaven too. Angels were hurled down for one fin.

2. Set a high price upon a little Grace; a man will be exceeding humbly thankful for the giving a little of that which he highly efteems, much more for giving much of what we value. The poor Woman of *Canaan*, *Mat.* 15. was glad of crumbs. How thankful do you think fhe was for loaves? that made her ready to receive all; *Be it as thou wilt*; fo it fhall be with you, for if you prize a little, Oh when all fhall be given, this will fwallow you up into Grace. And it's certain, there is never a mercy but 'tis great, if you confider him that gives it, who receives it, him that bought it. But the moft of Gods Grace in us appears to be but fmall; hence we prize it not, and hence never ready to give all to the Lord again.

3. Learn to put a difference between your double being: for every Chriftian hath a double being: 1. In himfelf. 2. He hath a fubfiftence in Chrift. Now look upon your felves as in your felves, you will ever complain there, ever dead, and never have your hearts ready to blefs the Lord. If you only look on your felves in Chrift, you will be proud, and never give the Lord honour. I fay therefore, put a difference between thefe two, for men appropriating to themfelves what is Chrifts, they rob Chrift of his glory. Hence *Paul* fo humble, 1 *Cor.* 15. 10, 11. For if you look upon your felf, I am dead, guilty, damned, weak, here will be fhame; if any life, or Grace, this is Chrifts. As a man on a Mount is the fame man, no taller, only the Mountain makes him fo: fo think of thy felf. Or as a mud wall, the fun fhines on it, but in it felf it is a mud-wall ftill; all the warmth and luftre is from the Sun.

4. Learn to love Grace; what we love we will feek the good of more than our own, and commend it.

Firft, It's the only firft mover of all our good: thou fhouldft never have had a dram of peace or mercy. Why haft it? the Lord will have it fo, Grace pleads it may be fo; this is the only Petitioner at Court againft the cry of fin, againft the cry of Juftice.

Secondly, 'Tis the only fupport under the heavieft evills; fometime God frowns, and Hell fmokes, and Satan tempts, and fin rageth, and it may be no feeling of Grace, no reafon to fhew there fhall ever be any; now what have you done, what will you do? Fly for refuge to the Promife of Grace, *Heb.* 6. 18. It is fuch a Friend as holds up the head when finking, when dying holds that, when all fails, and againft which the gates of Hell cannot prevail. To him that laies hold on Grace, this is wonderful, *Paul* was a man taken with Grace: hence he every where commends it, *I was received to mercy, &c.* 1 *Tim.* 1. 13, 14.

5. See how the Lord loves that thou fhouldeft honour it, for the greateft honour Grace hath is by Faith; hence they are put for one, *Rom.* 4. 16. and the great caufe why Faith ftirs not, is becaufe he fees not how the Lord fhall have by it the praife of his rich Grace, nor how the Lord loves it fhould do fo. For if a man did fee how by Faith he fhall honour Grace, and how the Lord is pleafed with it, it would draw the heart to be affured, and to blefs Grace; for when the Soul fee's it felf at worft, why doth it not believe? I fhall prefume: True, if you have this only in your eye to fave your felf; but if the Spirit prefents the glory of Grace, and this draws your will that you will glorifie Grace, then you will fay 'tis no prefumption fo to do, and fo to believe, for the Lord loves his Grace, and all means for the glory of Grace. Hence he will ufe Faith for that end, to ho-

nour

nour Grace. Oh therefore see how the Lord loves to have thee honour it. This gives Gods heart full rest; this is that which he desires most, because 'tis his end: This is that which all the business of the world is for: Oh see how he loves it! and then you will love to act thus. Now set upon this last work: look over all your life, and like Bees gather honey from every flower, and then come loaden home; so do you, and look over all the Lords love, turn over all the leaves of it: The Lord hath now called me; why? it's because Christ hath redeemed; and why that? because the Father hath chosen; and why me? to glorifie his Grace: And why me rather than another? No reason, but he would. This I doubt not will be the work of Heaven, I am glorified because called, because redeemed, because elected, for none other reason why, and here astonished. You have not christian hearts in you, that will now have no care to do this work there before you are turned off the stage: you poor doubting Spirits, that see so much vileness, and cannot be perswaded; be not discouraged. Wait for the Lord, and say, if he shall save, I shall for ever love him the more. Now hold here, and be ready to do so, and it's certain thou art a vessel of Glory, ready to sing the Song of the Lamb, and shalt follow him where-ever he goes.

CHAP. IX.

Concerning the Souls immediate closing with the Person of Christ, as the proper Object of Saving-Faith.

3. *Went forth to meet the Bride-Groom.*

SECT. I.

Here needs the Explication of Three Things.

I. VV Ho is the Bride-groom?
Answ. The conclusion of this Parable is the Explication of this, *viz.* the Son of Man, the Lord Jesus Christ, who according to the several conditions, or dispositions the Church is in, appears to his Church under several relations and titles. The Church is oppressed by her enemies, he appears now to her as her Prince and King: the Church wants wisdom, light, and life, he appears now unto her as an head. The Church hath been seeking of his love, and yielding her self to the obedience of him as her Lord: at last he appears more fully to her as an Husband, or as a Bride-groom with whom she is to have her nearest and everlasting fellowship and communion, and so here. And when Christ comes to shew most special love, and to have most special fellowship with his people, he thus stiles himself, *Isai.* 54. 5, 6. So *John* 3. 29. And when the Church hath tasted that love, she calls him so.

II. *What it is to meet the Bride-groom?*
Answ. To enjoy fellowship and familiarity with him.

III. *What is it [to go forth to meet] the Bride-groom?*
Answ. There are but three wayes of going forth to meet with Christ in Scripture.

1. When Soul and Body at the last Day meet the Lord in the clouds of the air, 1 *Thes.* 4. 17. Thus the whole Church, the Bride shall appear in glory to meet the Bride-groom. K 2 2. When

2. When the Soul only goeth out of the Body by the ministry of Angels to meet the Lord in Heaven , as *Paul* that knew not whether in or out of the body, 2 *Cor.* 12. 3. *We know it here shall go out of the body* : as Christ is said when he went to Heaven, *I go to my Father* , *and your Father* : so it goes forth then to Christ, *Eccles.* 12. 7. and neither of these can be meant here ; for

First, this shews the state of the Jewish Church long before Christs coming, at least among many of them.

Secondly , Because the shutting out, *verf.* 10. is by and at Death : hence letting in is so too. Now this was before.

3. When the Soul goes out of it self by Faith: hence *John* 6. 3 5. 'tis called coming to Christ ; and this not any Physical natural departing of the Soul out of the body, but Ethical, supernatural, by the operations of the Soul out of it self. And look as the whole Soul by unbelief departs from God in Christ , so the whole Soul by Faith comes again unto God by Christ. The mind sees , affections make after him , will fasten on him, and there depends. This is the first work of Faith, or the first Faith , the coming (as in all motions there are two extreams) of the Soul from a nothingness, emptiness in it self , to an allness and fulness in Christ : And as 'tis in other motions , if there was a *vacuum* , there would be *motus in instanti* ; so if there was an emptiness seen in the world, and all the works of it , and in all fears that all mountains were cast down , Faith then would suddenly come by the Spirit to the Lord Jesus , and this coming to Christ is not meant here : For

First, These Virgins were espoused to Christ by Faith already.

Secondly , At the first coming to Christ it goes to the Lord for life in him, and from him ; but here having life already, they go forth to live with him : there the Soul goes out to meet him in the Gospel , in the Promise ; here the Virgins go forth to meet him in Glory. There the Soul goes to be justified by him, here the Virgins go to be glorified with him: and therefore 'tis meant of a second going out of the Soul by some special acts of Faith, after that it doth believe , and after 'tis ready for him. And for Explication.

From whence doth the Soul go?

It's chiefly going out of this world by trampling this Moon under her feet , by forgetting this her Fathers house, by a holy contempt of it , and a holy dying to it, and all the glory of it. For 'tis a thousand to one if Satan doth not intangle here, if *Lot* be not taken with *Sodom* though burnt out there ; and if this going out is to enjoy the Lord in another world chiefly , then going out is from the opposite terme, from this world. Hence *Paul* singles out this mercy , *Gal.* 1. 4. Christ gave himself to deliver us from this present evil world. Oh say men, 'tis a good world, and good being here. 'Tis an evil world : 'tis so when Death comes, but for present 'tis best. No, 'tis a *present evil world.*

By what acts of Faith doth it go forth?

There be two affections of the Soul that chiefly look to a good absent , yet loving that good, go forth to meet it , and those are Hope and Desire ; like the blind man and the lame, both together can make a shift to go. Hope like the eye goes out and looks ; Desire like the feet runs out and longs. The going forth therefore to meet Christ, is : 1. By a real expectation of him. 2. By a longing desire to be with him. Hope gets on the top of the world , and cries , Oh I see him, Desire stands by and longs for him, Oh come Lord. A careless blind world look not for him, nor after him, the Saints do. *Heb.* 9. 28. An earthly-minded world longs not for him, the Bride doth, *Rev.* 22. 17, 20. *Oh come Lord Jesus , come quickly* ; by love and joy we imbrace and entertain the Bride-groom, by hope and desire we go forth to meet the Bridegroom. Hence many things are to be observed, and yet not all I might.

SECT.

SECT. II.

THat the object to which Faith chiefly looks, and closeth with, is the Person of the Lord Jesus.

'Tis the Bride-groom himself that the Virgins chiefly have to do withall; they are espoused to him, as in Marriage; there is a giving of themselves one unto another; they make themselves ready for him, they go out to meet him: 'Tis him they love, 'tis him they want, 'tis him they look for, 'tis him they close withall. Whorish lovers look not after him, but his: his peace to comfort them when in horror and fear, his mercy to save them from eternal flames; but Virgins look to him, they look to [His] indeed, but 'tis himself chiefly they care for, John 1. 12. to so many as received him, he gave power to be Sons, John 6. 27. when the people followed him, but it was for loaves: Labour not for bread that perisheth, but, &c. for him hath the Father sealed, Mat. 13. 44. The man did not buy the Treasure, but bought the field: 'tis him Faith seeks for, Jer. 50. 4. They shall seek the Lord weeping; 'tis him Faith chuseth, and is contented with, Whom have I in Heaven but thee? Psal. 73. 25. 'Tis him Faith glories in, Isai. 45. 25. In him shall all the Seed of Israel glory.

SECT. III.

'TIs chiefly and firstly the Person of Christ that the Father gives unto the Soul, Isai. 9. 6. hence Faith laies hold on him: 'Tis not seemly to keep a Portion from any, much less Orphans Portion. Faith empties a man so as it makes him the poorest Orphan in the world; now the Father cannot, will not keep back his Portion, but gives it him: Wicked men have their Portion in this world, Psalm 17. 14. and they think the Lord loves them because he blesseth them: they have many moral excellencies given them, which makes them honoured and lovely in the eyes of men, and they have honour, and that is their reward; they have bread, but not the staff of bread, they have Ordinances, but not the Lord in them: the Lord gives them answer to many Prayers, but never gives them himself, nor his Son; this is highest love. But 'tis his Son himself he gives to Orphan, fatherless, helpless creatures, for the Lord is their Portion, Lam. 3. 24. The portion of Jacob, Jer. 10. 16. hence 'tis him that Faith receives, and pitcheth upon; so that the Lord may deny them many outward, many inward Blessings, yet they have himself that's better than all, better as he said than Ten Sons. Children may be Prodigals for a time, but when in want, they will then sue for their Portion. Saints for a time may misspend all Times, Talents, Ordinances the Lord gives, but the Lord will bring them to want, and then they will sue for their Portion, and the Lord will give, and they will receive that.

Because there is no satisfying of the Father without him; bring Benjamin with you, or never look to see my face. The conscience of a man can never be pacified until God is satisfied for all wrongs. Now the Lord Jesus hath satisfied, nay perfected for ever them that are sanctified, by once offering up of himself to God, Heb. 10. 14. Now the soul never comes to have setled peace in his own conscience (though peace was purchased before) but by offering up of the Lord Jesus by Faith, even Christ himself: the Soul wants him, the Father shews a Ram in the bush, gives Christ; and that the Soul gives him for satisfaction, and offers him to God again. As the Priests in the Old law, when the Sacrifice was slain, then it was offered. God offers the Soul a crucified Son, Faith takes him and offers him, Lord behold thy Son, Rom. 3. 25. And hence comes Propitiation and

K 3   peace,

peace, peace to see that God is satisfied. Now if by Faith we come to have the peace of the Fathers satisfaction with us, then it must needs pitch upon the person of the Son first. Hence many never have peace, because 'tis not a Son himself they look for, but somewhat from him : they are blind, and dead, and hard, and these things they would have helped, but close not with Christ himself.

Reason 3. Because the Soul can neither actually receive, nor expect to receive any thing from Christ, unless it hath first pitcht upon the person of Christ. A man may hope he shall, and presume and think he shall, and it may be receive somewhat out of the common courtesie Christ shews to them that look towards him, but never shall receive any saving-good thing till now, *John* 6. 53. *Unlesse ye eat the flesh of the Son of God, and drink his Blood, ye have no life.* Look as 'tis in our eating, as if a man should seek to get nourishment out of meat or drink, not by feeding on it it self; so 'tis here : Some said this was a hard saying, and so 'tis to a carnal heart, *Rom.* 8. 32. And hence observe when the Lord promiseth any great thing to his people, *Isai.* 7. 14. he ever brings in the Lord Jesus, that if he shall be given, then all things also.

Reason 4. Because true Faith ever closeth with Christ by love to Christ, as false Faith closeth with him out of self-love, *Cant.* 1. 2, 3. *The Virgins love thee* : that's love indeed which is set upon the person. The Lord never puts his Pearl, nor sets it in a swinish faith that contemns the Son : no, 'tis a precious Faith that loves the Lord. Hence it carries the soul to the Beloved.

SECT. IV.

Use 1. HEnce see the reason why the Lord keeps his people hungry, and empty, and cuts them short of many spiritual Blessings : 'tis that they might close with, and be contented with the Person of the Son. There are three things some of Gods people seek for, and find not, if the Lord intends good to them.

1. They desire the comforts, and conveniencies, and peace of this World, Oh rest is sweet ! and the Lord will give them none of these, or keep them at short commons with these : and why ? that they might lay up their peace, and find all in himself, *Gen.* 15. 1, 2. *Abraham* after the slaughter of the Kings was in fear that he might make the Lord his shield, *Hos.* 2. 6, 7. *She shall seek her Lovers, but shall not overtake them.*

2. They seek for some good to themselves, in themselves, from themselves ; I would fain believe and cannot ; I would fain do (sayes a man) but alass he grows worse and worse ; the commandment comes, you will do, there is your task, do it, yet they languish and dye, and why so ? *Jer.* 3. 23. that they might look for help and righteousness in another, *In the Lord our God is the salvation of Israel* ; not from the Mountains the strongest helps and means ; in the Lord 'tis alone.

3. They seek for Grace, and strength, and peace from the Lord Jesus very importunately, and many times very impatiently, and so sinfully too, and the Lord denies them ; it hath been better with them than now, therefore they wonder the Lord should be so full, and they so empty, and think sometimes to seek no more, and the Lord denies a dole at this door to, that they might content themselves, and lay up their joyes in the Lord Jesus Christ, 2 *Cor.* 12. 9. *My Grace is sufficient* ; It's strange that Christ so able, so ready to help, yet denies : I confess 'tis sometimes some lust and stumbling-block the Lord Jesus sees, Oh but against that they seek, and truly here is the cause, that having no good from him, they might place all their happiness and felicity in him. Look as it was with *Jacob*, a great Famine comes, and all the sacks are spent, and they are used roughly, though not hardly nor wrongfully, and all was to bring them to the sight and embrace-

ings

ings of *Joseph*: all the time of Famine was for this. So the famine of Spirit is to last long, and the Lord denies supply, to bring the Soul to see, embrace, and rejoyce in the Lord Jesus: the most flourishing Trees in Gods House shall have their winter seasons, and cast their coat, that they might preserve themselves in their root. This is the great wound of many a believing soul for a time, to rest more contented with what he receives from the Lord, than to quiet himself and his heart with what is in the Lord: Man would have his lost happiness in his own hand, and this the Lord will not suffer his people to lye in long, *Gen.* 26. 4. and the best and surest course that can be taken, is to cut them short of all: for Faith is an unconquerable Grace, that whatever it loseth out of its own hand, it will find it and enjoy it in another. And therefore see Gods end, and meet the Lord in this end of his. See all in the Lord, and seeing your blessedness there in all your wants, lay it up there, that if you will boast, here you may do it all the day long: for this is Gods greatest plot to pull all men down that his Son may be set up, to wither all the grass and beauty of all the flowers of the field, that the glory of the Lord might be revealed. I must here give you a taste, for it doth me good to think, and it will do you more good to enjoy the sweetnesse of this Truth. There are four Things you desire all, which are chiefly laid up in Christ, to that end that you might in all wants quiet your hearts with unspeakable peace there.

1. The free Grace and love of the Father, this is that I hope which you prize most, pray for most, fear the loss of most, would rejoyce in the having of most, without which thy life is death, and blessings curses, and death the beginning of Hell. Would you see this love better than life to thee? Oh I cannot see it, or but very little of it. 'Tis true, look upon your selves you can see but little, many fears, many tears, many heart-sorrows, many temptations, many desertions, many vexing sins, many denyals to your Prayers; but Oh look up to that Ointment which is poured upon this blessed head, that love that is shed abundantly upon the Son from before all worlds, and look what love, what Grace the Father shews to him, that love is thine; that love in him is shewn to thee, 2 *Tim.* 1. 9, 10. Here stand amazed all ye people of the Lord, you have heard the Lord loves you, and sometime believe it, but being under water, cannot conceive of it, nor see how he loves you, how dearly, how abundantly; Oh look now upon the love of God the Father in the Son, as he loves him, so he loves thee a worm, a Devil, notwithstanding all thy want, all thy sins, all thy miseries, *John* 17. 23, 26.

2. Life: Oh Death is terrible, and a dead heart is woful, 'tis the great plague that lies upon men without Christ, that are strangers to the life of God, *Eph.* 4. 18. Is thy heart ever so joyed as when it's most enlarged for God, and hath most delight and liberty in the wayes of God: alas thy life is but a lingering sickness, a poor life to that which thou hast in Christ. Oh look up there, *Col.* 3. 3. You think when your hearts are affected, and warmed, and quickened in Prayer by word, or by Divine thoughts, &c. Oh if it might be ever so, how happy! Oh but it dyes presently, and thou knowest not how. Look up to the Lord Jesus, he is alive when thou art dead, and his life is thine, and 'tis ever thine in him, even eternal life, 1 *John* 5. 10, 11, 12. *This is the record, that he hath given us eternal life*; alas I find none: Oh 'tis in his Son, in whom thou livest a better life than Men, than Kings, than Angels. And I doubt not but the Lord suffers Temptations to rob you of your life, that you might find it when 'tis lost here, and rejoyce that when you have none, yet here it is: blessed be God, he will keep our lives as the life of *Jacob* was knit up, and bound up in the life of the child; nay that life is ours.

3. Conquest and Victory over all Enemies; it may be you say often, the Lord hath commanded me to seek for help, and he will help, he hath promised so to do, but I find my Distempers still raging, Satan still buffeting, and winnowing, and

and vexing, and foiling: and as I feel many, so I fear more sorrows before I dye, and then Death and delusion, that at last I may be deceived: Nay the agonies of Hell many times assault me, and then I am put to a loss, that is it possible I should escape? why Beloved, the Lord Jesus conquered Death, and Sin, and Hell, and the Grave, and Satan, with all the strength of darkness and delusion, and hath spoiled them, *Col.* 2. 14, 15. And now he is in Heaven in his Kingdom triumphing over them, that they cannot hurt him. I but what is that to me? Why this very Victory is thine: hence we are said to be dead with him, *Rom.*6.8. and risen with him, *Col.* 3. 1. Nay to sit in *Heavenly places* as it were triumphing in him, in glory with him, *Eph.* 2.6. Nay *Heb.* 10. 14. *He hath by one offering perfected his people for ever that are sanctified*: 'Tis true, you may rejoyce in that you shall conquer, but Oh remember this, 'tis done already in thy Head, and in thy Husband.

4. Immutability and certainty of standing in a happy estate, for this is that which sads the heart, I shall fall at last. How is it possible but I should be so? no Beloved, look upon the Lord Jesus, in him thou art, if he can fall, if he can dye, if he can be cast from the Fathers face, then thou maist; believe *that I live, you shall live also*, *John* 14. 19. *Adam* indeed was chosen to be head of Mankind, and as when he stood perfect we stood, so (though mutably) he falling we fall: so we are chosen in Christ, and as he stands unchangeably, so we stand, and as he was tempted every way, yet did not, could not fall, no more canst thou: so that Oh that the Lord would give you hearts to learn this lesson, when there is nothing but want in thee; Do not shift so much for a little from the Lord, but see Gods end and reach it. Oh rejoyce, glory in, and bless the Lord. This was *Paul's* life, and the life of the Churches first planted. Oh bless the Lord for all spiritual blessings in Christ; this will be joy in sorrow, life in death, this is golden Faith, this will answer all fears; when Satan saith thou hast not this or that, nor canst not do this nor that, and to Hell therefore thou must go: Reply again, 'tis true, I have little, I am dead, but Christ lives for ever; I am under miseries, Christ is triumphing in Heaven for ever: I may fall in my self, I never can fall in him; that which he hath is mine.

Object.
'Tis true they may do this that know the Lord Jesus is theirs, but alas I know not that.

Answ.
If you do not you must wait then untill the Lord make himself known unto you: but tell me, will you do this, if you did thus know it? It may be some of you have not done so, unless by force sometimes, and you will find it one of the toughest works of Faith that is: What is a poor man better for anothers wealth? and a sick man for anothers health, and a naked man when others are cloathed? Yet Beloved, by vertue of the power of Faith, and our union to the Lord Jesus, a man is the better. A Woman that is matcht to a Prince may have never a penny in her purse, and yet she rejoyceth in that her Husband hath it. It's the secret nature of Faith to make a man all one with Christ, in Christ, in that manner that I cannot find such an union in the world; and hence his health, his cloaths, his Grace, his life may be matter of as much joy as if a man had all this in himself. And because many a soul hath Christ, but feeling such emptiness in himself, as that he cannot think so, and it may be would do so if he saw whether he might do so or no: I shall therefore express my thoughts to them thus in these particulars.

1. That all that fulness that is in the Lord Jesus, 'tis not for himself, but for them that want it, *John* 17. 19. he might have been blessed in his Fathers bosom without thee; why should he therefore live, and do, and suffer, and rise, and glorifie his blessed Nature, but for them that wanted this. He is filled with wisdom, life, strength, because men are blind, dead, weak.

2. But

2. But you will say, all the world want it, and yet few in the world shall ever have any share there, therefore all them in the world that hunger after all that good that is in him, they may now in the absence of it content themselves with it, that there 'tis in him for them, for the Lord fills the hungry, and so hungry as 'tis not something or other that they pick out, but all Christ, and all of that that is in Christ: now is the season to eat, if bread and hunger meet, now satisfie your self. 2 *Cor.* 12. 9. *Paul* prayed, and the Lord denyed, yet now the Lord bid him feed on his Grace: so that when thy heart asks what hast thou to do with him when so vile? answer, Yet the Lord hath all, and I want him, and hunger after him. Take heed of despising his Grace; if thou hast no hunger, the Lord be merciful to thee!

3. If you have so contented your selves with him, as now you place all your felicity in him, to this end, to receive life from him, as a man satisfies himself with bread that he may have life: for as I would not damp the Faith of the Elect, no more would I patronize the sloth of the wicked. Many a man it may be may say, I have nothing in my self, and all is in Christ, and comfort himself there, and so fall asleep; hands off and touch not this Ark, left the Lord slay thee: a christ of clouts would serve your turn as well. Run not to this Temple to make it a Denn of your thievish heart; no, do you so content, or will you so content your selves with him, as to account your selves happy here, that all the world is Dung in respect of this; and this you do to suck and receive more from Christ, and so to be like him: now hold here, and live here, and rejoyce here for ever, *Phil.* 3. 9, 10, 11. *Isai.* 12. 2, 3. First, *The Lord is my Song and Salvation*; therefore we, will draw hence: if the Lord gives nothing, yet I have it in him; if he gives any thing, the honour shall be given to him. Oh take this course: 1. Left you lose Christ and all too. 2. Left the Lord ever keep you short in a complaining condition. 3. That you may be every day and moment in Heaven, and win the Crown from every Hypocrite who knows not what this life in Christ means. 4. That the Lord may be your glory, for he is not only the glory of God, but of his people *Israel* too. 5. That you may love your selves the lesse, and the Lord the more.

SECT. V.

Use 2.

HEnce see a necessity of seeing & knowing Christ, before a man can believe, or if ever the soul believe; for if Faith closeth with the person of the Lord Jesus, the same Faith must first see that person: If it takes the Bride-groom himself, it must see and know him first. Did you ever see any espoused together that did not first see and know each other? the eye must first see, my meaning is, there must precede this act of the understanding to see Christ, before a man can close with Christ by his will: for I aim not at this, whether it goes before in time, but in order of nature it does precede, and absolutely necessary it is: hence *John* 6.40. *He that seeth and believeth in the Son hath eternal life*: this is so necessary to Faith, that Faith it self puts on this name, *Isai.* 53. 11. *By his knowledg, Luke* 19. 41. *Oh that thou hadst known. Isai.* 46. 22. *Look unto me and be saved.* And hence unbelief in Scripture is exprest by being blinded, *Rom.* 11. 7, 8. for though Christ be absent from us on earth, yet that's the excellency of faith, it makes things absent present, and sees unseen things, *Heb.* 11. 1. *John* 8. 56. *Abraham saw my day*; and that's the wonderment of Saints; there is light in *Goshen* when all *Egypt* is dark, when others are blind they see, *Isai.* 60. 1, 2.

Quest.
Answ.

What is this knowledg or seeing of the Lord?

I make this question, partly because this is the first chief Evangelical work, as it appears to us, nay indeed 'tis in a manner all; hence *Mat.* 11. 27. *I thank thee thou hast hid these things*, &c. If this be right, Faith is right, &c. And if this be not, a mans Faith is but a Fancy, and a mans Sanctification and Reformation, hopes, desires, are but the works of death and darknesse, if this Sun be not risen, And partly also because all the policy and power of Satan is to blind the eye here, for then he knowes men will stumble at every step, 2 *Cor.*4.4. He will help to beleeve, and joy in beleeving, and reformation after than joy, that a man might content himself with this joy and Faith, and look not after the sight of Christ. And if I was to leave the world, I should leave this to be thought of, as Christ told the woman of *Samaria*, *Ye worship whom ye know not*, so men beleeve in whom they know not, and pray to one whom they know not, and depend on whom they see not, and hence do not wonder at an adulterous generation rising up that deny all evidencing of a mans justification from his sanctification, and that 'tis but a fading thing, because they never felt what it meant, because they never knew what the Lord Jesus meant, and therefore listen to it. I say therefore first what this knowledge is not, for every man hath some knowledge.

1. There is a knowledge of the Lord Jesus by report, the fame of a man may come where himself is not seen, so of Christ, there may be a fame spread of him and of some excellencies in him, where he is not savingly known, and this is not seeing of Christ, for a man may live and die a damned creature with this knowledge. The *Samaritans* had some knowledge by report of the Messiah, *John* 4.25. *When he is come he will tell us all things*; so many among us hear that Christ is come and risen, and glorified, and the Saviour of the world and of sinners, &c. But how come they to know this? By way of tradition and report only. I confesse this knowledge may be a means in the Elect to bring them to saving knowledge, as in the Queen of *Sheba*, that heard *Solomons* fame, and the Disciples *John* 1. *Come and see*. But Reprobates are not drawn by it, as *Herod*, *Luke* 23.8. *heard many things of Christ*, but never saw him till he came to judge him. So here, because they can live well without Christ, hence rest content with the bare report. Whereas they that had diseases, heard of his fame, and came to see Jesus.

2. There is a knowledg of Christ from his works, as we know what Trade and what Artificers many men be because these are external things, yet know not the man: so there is a knowledg of Christ by his works, that by him the worlds were made, *Heb.* 1. and all creatures governed, and a man may see him in his trading with others, and himself, all comes from him, that a man may say, the Lord hath done all this and that for me, and yet strangers to Christ. And if men be ignorant of him here, he may do such wonderful things before their eyes, that they cannot but wonder and say, this is the Lords work, and yet know him not, *Mat.* 11.20. He upbraided the Cities where most of his mighty works were done, but they saw him not, *John* 15.24. *If I had not done*, &c. the Lord may work strange temporal deliverances, that you may know all power is in Christs hand to save and pardon, *Mat.* 8.27. so as to marvail and not envy; *What manner of man is this that winds and seas obey him*? 'Tis true the Saints do know the Lord here, but they are not idle spectators and receivers of them, but Oh that I might see and have that Christ himself, they do him no good, give him no content without him; as he said, *What givest thou me if I go childlesse*? *John* 9. Christ had opened the blind mans eyes, and yet he cries, *Lord, who is he*? *verf.* 36,37,38. whereas others see the works of Christ, and vanish, or if affected, an evill spirit comes on them, as on *Saul* when he saw *Davids* love.

3. There is a litteral knowledg of the Lord Jesus by the bare letter only of the Word, and 'tis wrought in this manner. A man doth not only take up the knowledg of Christ by report, not from his works, but he hears, reads, is well Catechiz'd concerning Christ, and all his Offices, and Benefits, that there is much light let in; hence his mind having those litteral relations, guesseth at them, and conceives

ceives of the n, and because the mind is carnal, it apprehends them in a carnal manner (though it thinks it sees Christ truly.) Hence a man having a form of this knowledg in his head, he may be able to expreſs much, and make a large confeſsion of his Faith, diſcourſe of points of controverſie, in matters that concern Chriſt, and juſtification by Chriſt, &c. and inſtruct others, and yet having no more, know not all thi while what the Lord Jeſus is.

First, Becauſe as he was a carnal Jew that had but the form of Knowledg in the Law, *Rom. 7. 20.* ſo he is but a carnal Chriſtian that hath but a form of Knowledg in the Goſpel. The Jews were exceedingly verſed in Scripture, and boaſted they heard God, and ſaw Chriſt tells them, they never heard his voice, nor ſaw his face, *John 5. 37. i. e.* they only ſaw it litterally, not ſavingly.

Secondly, This is but a carnal knowledg which letter and fancy beget, *1 Cor. 2. 14. He cannot know them becauſe they are ſpiritually diſcerned.*

Thirdly, 'Tis a dead Knowledg, or will be dead and unſavory; and hence many that know much of Chriſt, feed on their luſts and Dunghill delights, becauſe their Knowledg feeds them not, fills them not, as fancies do not feed.

Fourthly, 'Tis a falſe Knowledg, for give a blind man a deſcription of the Sun, or a taſteleſs man of honey, he may ſet up a falſe Image and deceive himſelf, and ſo doth this. Many ſet up a falſe Image of Chriſt, and truſt to that. Or as in the deſcription of another Country, when he ſees it, then he ſees he was deceived: ſo Saints ſee they were deceived, and ſaw not Chriſt, nor Sin, nor God; and ſo ſhall men in Hell ſee; hence *Iſai. 6. 9. In ſeeing they ſee not:* how came that to paſs? they did ſee, but ſaw not really.

Fifthly, 'Tis ſuch a Knowledg as hinders from ſaving-knowledg of Chriſt, *John 9. 39. I came that they that ſee might be made blind.* The wiſe learned *Corinthians* muſt become fooliſhneſs, and the light that is in thee is darkneſs. This light ſtands in your light: and yet this is the Knowledg that thouſand thouſands content themſelves withall, and hence catch hold on Chriſt, and think they have him, when in truth 'tis but the Image and fancy of him.

What then is this knowledg or ſeeing of Chriſt? Queſt. Anſw.

There is a ſeeing of Chriſt after a man believes, which is Chriſt in his love, &c. but I ſpeak of that firſt ſight of him that precedes the ſecond act of Faith, and 'tis an intuitive or real ſight of him as he is in his Glory. Chriſt reveals his wonderful glory to the ſoul really, as *ex gr.* A man hears ſin to be the greateſt evil, and ſometime conceives by argument how, but ſees not the thing ſin, though he ſees the word ſin: ſo a man that never travailed into forraign parts, may hear, and read, and ſpeak of Countries: or as Herbaliſts read of the nature of Plants and Trees, yet never ſaw the things, nay trample upon them when they ſee them: ſo it is one thing to read of the Sun in a Book, or to know it by relation, another thing to know it by ſight. This is therefore the ſaving-knowledg of Chriſt, to ſee the Lord in his Glory as he is: not perfectly, for that is in Heaven; hence we ſhall there ſee him, and be like unto him, but imperfectly, and in part, *2 Cor. 3. 18. Changed here into the ſame Image.* And this appears from theſe four Grounds.

1. That Knowledg the Saints have of Chriſt, 'tis not by bare word only, but alſo by the Spirit. The word relates Chriſt, but the Spirit is the interpreter of the Word: the Interpreter of Heaven muſt interpret the language of Heaven. Now the Spirit ever ſhews us things as they are, even though they be deep things, and myſteries, it makes them plain, *1 Cor. 2. 9, 10. As the Sun when it ariſeth it ſcatters all darkneſſe, ſo when this day-ſtar ariſeth:* Not that theſe things are revealed without the Word: for *2 Cor. 2. 14.* and *2 Cor. 4. 4.* leſt the light of the Goſpel ſhould ſhine: 'tis by the Word that the Spirit doth enlighten.

2. Becauſe the ſight of the Knowledg of Chriſt, 'tis as the knowledg of a thing in a glaſs, *1 Cor. 13. 12.* Now though you ſee not the man face to face, yet if

you

you see him in a glasse, there you see him as he is: *Quod videtur in speculo, non est imago*, as some think. A man may know another by relation, or by some picture, but in a glasse that is more full. The Jews they saw Christ, but it was under Vails and Types, and Pictures of him, this was obscure: under the Gospel the vail is pulled off, aud *with open face we see as in a glasse the glory of the Lord.* In Heaven the glasse is taken away, and then we see as we are seen.

3. Because that estate the Saints are translated into is a state of Glory. Hence when justified, then glorified. Hence as that sanctification that is in the will is the beginning of the life of Glory, so that light God puts into their mind, is the beginning of the light of Glory. Hence as in Heaven the soul sees Christ by the full light of Glory perfectly, face to face, so in this life the soul sees Christ really as he is, yet as in a glasse imperfectly. Hence we are said to *see in part.*

4. In regard of that abundant goodnesse and love of Christ to his people. Love cannot lock up secrets, *Joseph* hid himself from his Brethren for a time, but his bowels melt, he must tell them that he is *Joseph*. Christ may do so, but his love even constrains him afterward, to let them see whom he is, *John* 14.21. I confesse its admirable love to reveal Christ in the Word and letter of the Gospel, to hear of him is happinesse, and if the Lord saves you, you will think so too: But this is common to wicked men; there is a manifestation of himself as he is unto his people. And now he is in Glory, hence reveals himself in his inconceiveable, Glory, that now a mans eye sees the Lord, and such things he never thought of before, which eye never saw, 1 *Cor.*2.9.

How doth the soul see him as he is?

I in this case, rather desire to learn than teach, even from the meanest; yet what is obvious I shall suggest, in this weighty businesse.

This seeing of him appears in three particulars.

1. True saving knowledge and sight of Christ consists in the sight of the glory of his person, especially now *caught up to Heaven, and sitting at the right hand of God, in all the Glory of the Father.* Look as at the Judgment-day the Lord shall break out of Heaven in such Glory as shall amaze all the world, and all eyes shall see him, that he shall not only be admired in himself, but in all his Saints, by all that are round about him: just so doth the soul see him now (though not by the eye of sense, yet by the eye of Faith) though not come to judge the world, yet now ruling of the world; though not in the clouds, yet in Heaven; though his Humanity only in Heaven, yet his God-heads beams filling Heaven and Earth; though not yet coming in the Fathers Glory, yet sitting clothed with the Fathers Glory: for if a man looks on Creatures, he sees Gods foot-steps of power; if on Angels and Saints, Gods Image of Holinesse; if in Christ, there God himself, 2 *Cor.* 4.4, 5, 6, 7. 'Tis true then Christs Glory shall be seen by the Wicked, but that's by sense, not by Faith, that is only in their minds, but there is no shining into the heart, to the kindling of an infinite esteem of him: and this the god of this World hides from people; Christ the Lord of another world in spight of Satan reveals to his people. Before a man sees Christ, there is nothing more base than Christ, even to the Elect, and then the wayes and work of Christ, *Jer.*2.11. *Have any Heathen changed their gods? these change their glory for that which doth not profit:* now the Lord will be, must be esteemed of his people; hence will and doth reveal this Glory of his to his Saints, whereas here others are blind.

2. In the beholding of the Lord as he comes and appears in the Glory of his Covenant, for when the Lord reveals himself so as to cause the soul to believe, and thereby to make it one of his people, he never makes any a people, but by entring into Covenant with them. Hence he ever appears in his Covenant first, *Isai.* 49.*ult.* Look as when the Lord made him a people at *Mount Sinai*, *Moses* came

Quest.
Answ.

came down from God, and appears with Tables in his hands, &c. So when Christ comes to make any his people, he comes as Mediator of a better Testament, Heb. 7. 22. On Mount Sion, Heb. 12. 22, 24. Now look as it was with the Israelites, 2 Cor. 3. they had the Covenant of Christ, and Christ revealed; but as Moses face was covered, so theirs was, and Christ there was vailed over with the Law, even the Moral Law written in stone. Hence there was a vail on their hearts too, they could not see Christ, the end of the Law, but only the Vail, viz. the Law, and hence looked for life by that, and hence were hardened against Christ, Rom. 9. 31, 32. So 'tis the misery and blindnesse of many people at this day, they see the Lord Jesus, but with his vail on: for people being not able to see and prize the glory of Christ immediatly, the Lord appears with the law first, requiring this and that, and they endeavour to do it; and hence if they cannot, they comfort themselves with this, the Lord accepts my endeavours, not seeing the hypocrisie of them, or else they are never at peace, or very seldom; and why? because they see not to the end of that which is abolished, never saw the end, the Lord Jesus Christ. Now therefore when the Lord reveals himself, the Lord makes himself known without the vail, so that when conscience cries you must do what ever is commanded, or dye, the Lord Jesus now comes and appears, and saith, therefore see what need thou hast of me, who have fulfilled all Righteousnes, and done all. Receive me that have done it, and thou shalt live. Oh but may I now live as I list? Am I now free from the Law? No, 'tis to be thy Rule and life in Heaven, but *I will write my Laws in thy heart, and cause thee to walk in my wayes.* Hence the soul sees all done for him; 1. In Christ. 2. All that he is to do for Christ; he sees it not in means, nor in himself, but in the Lords promise, and here Faith hangs, and hath peace. For two things trouble,

First, I have broke the first Covenant of the Law, Christ appears not as one that exacts the Debt, but as one that comes to enrich him when poor.

Secondly, I cannot walk after it as a Rule, Christ appears in this Covenant, and promiseth to cause him to do it; and hence after all departings from the Lord, he will not depart further by unbelief, but sees the end of the Law, which is Christ, that in him he may perform the Covenant, and by him be strengthned to walk with him as after a Rule: For the Covenant of Grace is not, Christ will be righteousnesse to thee if thou wilt walk after the Law as a Rule, but Christ will do both: and this the soul sees in it's Glory, else it's no sight. Hence 2 Cor. 3. Gospel is called *The ministration of Glory,* which no carnal heart can see, for the vail is taken away when it turns to the Lord, and sees him. The Saints only with open face behold this: 'Tis true for a time they may make of Christ a Moses, as Peter, Luke 5. 8. *Lord depart from me, I am a sinful man.* And the Lord may deal roughly with them to humble them, as *Joseph* did to his Brethren, but it will not ever hold; and the Lord appearing thus to them that have been stung by the Law, and that killing letter, now the Lord appears in ineffable Beauty and Glory; To others there is nothing in it, they may see this, yet not believe.

3. In seeing the Lord in the Glory of his Grace, or fitnesse for him, and this is the main: for look as 'tis in Marriage, there is a respect to Beauty and feature, and that draws. Now a Woman sometimes appears to one so, that though Portion be great, &c. yet he cannot like, another can because God hath a hand in it, and what fits the fancy, that's beauty: there is a suitablenesse every way. So Christ is presented with a rich portion to many, and yet they cannot like, cannot see a Beauty, because they cannot see a fitnesse and suitablenesse to them, and for them: another man can, because he sees a fitnesse and suitablenesse in the Lord Jesus for him, in respect of his misery and sin, and his gracious disposition, *John* 1. 14. *But we saw his glory full of Grace and truth. Psalm* 45. 2. *Thou art fairer than the*

children

children of men, *full of Grace are thy lips*: which is so beautiful in the Lords eyes, that the Father hence exalts the Son, for all the Grace he shews to his Elect. Now what makes Christ appear fit? *Answ.* The knowledg of a mans self, and sense of vileness; hence *Luke* 7. 29, 30. *The Pharisees despised the counsel of God against themselves, when Publicans justified God*, &c. And 'tis a Rule, that the saving-knowledg of Christ is dependant upon the sensible knowledg of a mans self. Let a Christian in Christ lye in his sins, and comfort himself in Remission of them without repentance, he may talk of Christ, but no beauty will appear in Christ: So 'tis at first, first the Soul feels sin, and that God is holy, and will hate him : then the Lord shews Christ; come to call such. Yea but I have no good, and cannot help my self ; Christ appears fit to seek out such. Oh but I cannot see, nor believe, nor be affected ; Christ appears one fit to do all, full of wisdom to perform the Second Covenant. Oh but I want all things ; Christ appears all-sufficient. Oh but I shall fall ; Christ appears constant in his love. Oh but he is far to seek ; Christ appears present. Oh but I shall sin ; Christ appears merciful to bear with, and heal infirmities. Oh but I shall believe too soon ; he is fit to prepare and dispose. Oh but all the world will be against me ; Christ therefore appears fit to rule all for me. Oh but Death and Grave may hurt me; Christ appears fit who hath conquered all : and this is ever in the Saints. Now least you should think you have this when you have not ; and know it not, see the evidences hereof.

1. If ever the Lord hath thus revealed himself to thee, he hath brought this light out of darkness, and made thee sensible of it, 2 *Cor.* 4. 5, 6. Oh you that have been a little troubled, and then hear of Christ, and then depend on him, and wait for comfort from him, and now you are well: you never yet saw him. Nay if truly enlightened, you will go mourning to your Graves for your ignorance of him, *Prov.* 30. 2. and seldom is your darkness seen and felt, but there is some beam let in.

2. It damps the glory of all the world, that a man laies down all at Christs feet, as the Wise-men *Mat.* 2. As glow-worm-stars go out when the light of the Sun ariseth, so all the comforts, and all the miseries of the world are nothing now, *Acts* 7. I see Jesus.

3. It makes a man very vile in his own eyes, *Isai.* 6. 5. Nay his excellency vile as *Isaiah* his tongue, and wonders that the Lord should look upon him a Worm who is so glorious. *What am I that the Mother of my Lord should come to me, &c.* He sees Christ fit, and then sees his Glory, and then saith, *What me Lord ?* me to stand before thee ? Lord depart, I am a sinful man !

4. It necessitates the heart to believe, not with assurance, but with a clinging to him : Hypocrites have knowledg of Christ, but it never heats the heart ; this as fire necessarily heats, and that which is put to it is heated ; so here, for the sight of the last end doth necessitate when 'tis seen, *Isai.* 55. 4, 5. *They shall run to thee, because God hath glorified thee,* Rom. 1. 16, 17. 'tis the power of God, for there is righteousness revealed : that though the Lord bids depart, yet he cannot be gone, nay when he concludes, yet as *Jonah* 2. 4. so he can see to a Temple through the belly of a Whale. Many say, may I believe ? or I cannot prize him! I tell you when the Lord appears as he is, you cannot resist that light, but you must cling to him.

5. Where this is, a man rests not here, but sees more and more of him, *John* 1. 49, 50. A man sees now his Glory, but after he shall see his love, and after that he shall know his mind, 1 *Cor.* 2. 9. *Eph.* 1. 9. *The mystery of his will.* And then his constant presence, and all his walkings with him and towards him, so as to be familiar with him, that in time of old Age he shall be an Acquaintance of Christs, 2 *Cor.* 3. 18. *From glory to glory* ; whereas an hypocrites light goes out or grows not. Hence many ancient standers take all their comfort from the first

work,

work, and droop when in old age. I know the Saints light is obscured, and the Lord hides his face, but then they are troubled, and it shall break out *with healing in his wings.* Nay all their life time they may think they know him not, because they have not those measures. Oh therefore see a necessity of it.

1. You that are vile, and ignorant of Christ, no Faith yet, no Christ yet: And what then? Thy sins are upon thee now, and wo to thee, for *the wrath to come.* Oh poor creature! thou dost not see, nor canst not see, if thou didst, thou wouldst not crucifie the Lord of Glory,

2. You that be Professours of the Church. Oh deceive not your selves, if the Lord hath enlightened you, Oh blesse him. If Christ were here, he would blesse you, *Mat.*13.16. Nay when he was here, he did it, he doth it in Heaven. *I thank thee Father*, &c. *Mat.* 11. 25. *Luke* 10.21. But if not, all is unsound, that ever you had. Oh therefore look you be not deceived here, and therefore wait upon the Lord to manifest himself, Who knows but the Lord may help? Nay when you are feeling of the infinite need of it, and of your own woful blindnesse, 'tis begun.

SECT. VI.

SEE the happinesse of Saints (all you standers by) and of all Believers. You think what are they? What have they, that I have not? What get they by seeking, by mourning? They have the Lord himself, not Kingdoms, nor Heaven, not guard of Angels, not pardon, nor comfort or Grace only, but which is greater, and than which there can be no greater, the Lord of Glory himself. Is there any thing that is good there? 'tis theirs. I doubt not but Angels stand amazed at this. What hast thou? Thou hast peace, and ease, and duties, and friends, but no Christ, then poor and cursed thou art. *Use 3.*

SECT. VII.

HEnce learn to judge of your Faith, whether it be of the right make or no? whether it be such a Faith as will never fail you, but shall in deepest miseries, in sorest agonies, and most furious temptations; nay in greatest sins and desertions, be indeed a friend unto you? Is it such a Faith as pitcheth on, and closeth with the person of Christ himself, and him alone? So that all the delights in creatures quiet thee not, unlesse thou canst find him through them; Nay no Ordinances chear thee, unlesse thou canst see him in them? Nay, Heaven it self will not content thee, but him in Heaven, *Psal.*73.25. And hence 'tis him thou seekest, 'tis him thou seest, 'tis him thou approvest thy self unto, and servest: So that 'tis this *Rock of ages* thou trustest to, *Isa.*26.3,4. 'Tis his strength thou art strong by, 'tis his life thou livest by, 'tis the Lord himself that thy Faith fadoms. This is right, 1 *Pet.*2.7. For now what good can the Father deny thee, when he hath given a Son to thee? What hurt can Satan do thee by all his shakings, when thou hast the Son himself, this corner-stone, this horn of salvation to support thee? What hurt can the Law do thee; when thou hast righteousnesse in a Son? What hurt can delusion do thee, when thou hast wisdom ever plotting for thy good, in such a glorious Head as the Son? What hurt can death do thee, or sin do thee, when thy life is in the Son? *Oh lead me to the Rock*, saith *David*, *that is higher than I.* Oh here is a rock higher than death, than grave, than sin, than Satan; Who can hurt thee now? But oh Beloved, how many fall short of *entring into this rest*? and closing with this person? And *Use 4.*

there

there are four sorts of them, that spin the finest thread of deceit to themselves, that think they believe when yet they have not the Son.

1. Those that do not close with himself, but only come to him for some righteousness out of himself (for I shall not speak of then that forsake all, and follow Christ for the bagg and for the loaves) for 'tis with all men living naturally, as 'tis with men that have been rich shop-keepers, but now they are broke, and cast into great want; steal they will not, digg they cannot, begg they know not how; turn Prentice to another they must not, they have not been used to that life; hence they resolve to set up their Trade again, though they sell but Pins, and Points, and small Wares; and because they cannot set up for themselves, they go unto Merchants to help them, and run into their Books on trust, and desire day and patience, and they will pay them all again: now 'tis not the man that they respect, but to make up their markets out of him, but alass they cannot pay their Debts, and hence to Prison they go: so 'tis here, God set up *Adam* with a stock in his own hand, now he is broken and cast into great want, and fears the arrest of Gods displeasure, now sin men dare not, digg and help themselves they cannot, and to begg and live upon the Lord and his Alms they know not how, indeed they will not, they are not used to this life; hence seek to set up their Trade again, though in never so small duties; and because they cannot help themselves, hence they go to Christ, not as to an Husband for himself, but as to a Merchant to set them up again: and truly Christ for many ends, and to shew his freeness to his own, gives many Talents to such, which they receiving hope to please the Lord by; when I can get the Lord to give me some more knowledg, brokenness, affections, enlargements, abilities to do, then I hope I shall please him: but either they spend all and fall away to nothing before they dye, or else Death comes and carries them captive to the judgement-seat of God, and there they see they are run but the deeper in Debt, and not able to pay. Thus it is with Papists who profess that none of their own Works save, but his works in us, and his Blood meriting, that these shall save. Hence they trust not to what they do, but to what the Lord does, against which very Faith the Apostle disputes, *Rom.* 4. 5. Thus it was with the Jews, divers despised Christ, and sought a righteousness of their own; others cryed *Lord, Lord*: Lord there be these sins that wring my Conscience, else me of them, here be these duties I must do, else never saved, and my heart is dead, Oh affect me, and help me to do them: there be such works I am to perform, and have no strength to Pray, to Prophesie, Lord assist me, *Mat.* 7. 21, 22. *Depart, I know you not*, never accepted of you, you thought these things would please me, you closed not with me, Oh now depart from me, from my fellowship, my bosom, my presence: for this is ever their frame, they think to pacifie God by what they do, and though they think his justice cannot, yet they hope there is such indulgence in his mercy that he will accept. Thus it was, *Isai.* 58. 2. for this is their temper, they are not wounded with the want of Christ himself, but with some jarrings against the Law, for which they fear they must dye. Hence not seeing into the spiritual nature of the Law, they are wounded, not slain by the Law: they hope they shall live if they can leave such sins, perform such duties, feel such abilities. Now having made tryal at home, they go to Christ, and see him with delight for to work this or that, and then they are well: now if they do not receive at present, then they hope by seeking to find in time, if he doth not help them, then they shall be well. Hence they ever live in some sin, and know it not, as these did, and as the young man, *Mat.* 19. And thus 'tis, as 'tis with two Princes, one is in trouble by inroders, he sends for aid to another, but doth not cast down his Crown, and put himself in subjection to the other. So men will be Kings, and hence send for aid against the inrodes of some sin that stings Conscience, but put not themselves under the Lord Jesus. Bring those mine enemies hither, *Luke* 19. 27. In one word; as the Wound is, so is my closing with

Christ.

Christ, if one be in outward trouble, now to Christ he goes to deliver; if pressed with inward trouble for some sins, now to Christ to remove them, and so to pacifie conscience; it with want of Christ himself, now he goes for himself.

2. Those that close with Promises without Christ himself, and divide between them two, that strip Christ of these his Swadling-clouts, make their gain of these, and let himself go. I confesse all a Christians wealth is laid up in Promises, not in words and syllables, for they are dead things, but Christ in them, and Gods faithfulnesse in them, 2 Sam. 23. 4, 5. This is all my salvation, for all fulnesse is in Christ, he is rich, but what am I the better? nay the more miserable, for all emptinesse is in me; therefore in the promise lies my peace. And this is a Christians support in all troubles, and hence he casts anchor here; but here is his frame, he layes not hold on them without Christ, but by them goes to Christ, and there rests, *John* 6. 45. *He that hath heard of the Father cometh unto me.* Give children milk in the dish, they cry still, they must have it from the Mother, and there suck: so 2 Pet. 1. 2, 3. Now there are others that finding some work in themselves without Christ, and thinking that it's saving, and so a good signe; hence are mistaken, and close with it without Christ, and now they think it's well. I doubt not but the Jews that be devout comforted themselves with that promise, *He that confesseth, &c. Prov.* 28. 13. not understanding of it, *Mat.* 3. *Say not within your selves we have Abraham to our Father*, that promise kept them off from Christ, *Mat.* 22. Some came not to the Feast, some came but without a Wedding Garment. 'Tis with these men as 'tis with men that come to buy Wines, they taste them, and content themselves with a taste, another buyes the thing: a Saint doth so; another tastes the sweet, and after falls to the impardonible sin, *Heb.* 6. Or as 'tis with a man that sees corn on the ground, he buyes the field, another he gleans somewhat, and contents himself with that. There is in one word a double error.

First, When a man shall close with Christ without Promises; and hence seek to be setled without a Promise. Hence say some, you must not gather any evidence from any qualification you feel in your self.

Secondly, When men shall snatch and nibble at Promises, and misapply them, not closing with Christ in them and by them; I have confessed my sin, and repented, and run away with this without Christ. Oh time will come the Lord will say, how camest thou in hither? what hast thou to do to take my Promises into thy mouth? to arm thy self against Christ by Promises to make a spoyl of Christs grants, and let him be crucified. When *Saul* rent off *Samuels* garment, he said, *The Lord shall rend, &c.* 1 Sam. 15. 27, 28. The letter kills, all Promises without Christ slay, because they keep the famishing Soul from Bread it self.

3. Those that close not with Promises only, but with Christ himself, but it's only with the Image and fancy of him, which they think is himself. In true Faith the Father reveals the Son as he is, the Son reveals himself as he is, and Faith hence closeth with him as he is, *John* 6. 40. But some there be that heir of him, hence think what he is. Hence a carnal mind imagines of him as it imagines of a King in a far Country, and falls down to his Image, and trusts to it, and depends on it, and joyes in it, untill a man comes to be converted, or to dye: and then he sees the deceit. Or if he did see him, yet he can see no beauty in him to desire him. There is many a man in this case that trusts to, and joyes in Christ, whom if he did know he would loath. *John* came preaching the Gospel to shew them Christ, they all came to him, and rejoyced in his light, but it was but for a season: for when he came to shew them *there he is*, *John* 1. 29. not one man stirs when he shews them Christ, and *verf.* 35. only two: and *chap.* 3. 32. No man received his testimony. This is (Beloved) the great sin and cause of all the rest, if they had known they would not have crucified the Lord of Glory. Christ is not seen, hence not thought of, hence not esteemed; hence men boast not in him:

M   Nay,

Nay 'tis the great plague under meanes, that in seeing they see not. *Lord how long:* You say Christ never so clearly seen, true, but thou in seeing maist not see ; and it it be thus, then look for ruine , *Isai.* 6. 9, 10, 11, 12. We say Christians want not light, but life and affections. Oh begg for light that will bring affections, else all affections will dry up if not fed with this Spring , *John* 5. 37. What people had such means as they, yet they not eyes to see ?

4. Those that do not close with the bare fancy of Christ, but with himself ; but 'tis not for himself, and for his holinesse, but only for his peace, and consolations, and joyes. Like a sick woman that comes to the Physitian, not to marry her, but to heal her, cure her, and so comfort her. Or if she doth come to marry him, 'tis only to satisfie her lust, or to save her from trouble, *&c.* In a word, they receive Christ, that he may give contentment to them, and not that hereby they may also give contentment unto him. They close with Christ to make them happy, not to make them holy ; But they thus closing with him, think they have him, and hence rejoyce exceedingly, and hence have a love to him, and hence some kind of communion with him, and hence think they are espoused to him, and more familiar with him than others, and hence verily look with these *five foolish Virgins* to embrace the Bride-groom : That look as a Saint from a false apprehension of Christ, to be none of his, may be very sad, lose his joy, nay his very love, in the act of it, nay his communion and boldnesse to go to him, nay his expectation of him ; so from a false conceit that Christ is mine, è *contra.* Thus a man is grievously troubled with the sight of Gods anger, and with horror, and useth all means, at last he sees only Christ can do it , and hence seeks for and prizeth his love (for his one ease) for as horror may be his greatest evil, so love to ease him , may be his greatest good : At last he is fully perswaded. How ? By any work or word ? No, but God hath perswaded, and its now sealed, hence joy. But now there is matter of more trouble, holinesse, and close walking with Christ, this is troublesome, he cares not for Christ, to help him here ; but deviseth how to keep Christ and joy without holinesse. Hence let a world of sin lie upon them, they be not troubled with that, they look up to Christ ; or if they see and be troubled at it, they take it as a burden, not as the greatest burden. Hence (say men) you must not judge of your estate by any thing or qualification you feel in your self, for these may fail , our eye-sight in misty times (But we must follow it then, and not rest till we see and find it , for *without holinesse no man shall see God*) Hence also let there be never so many falls, yet say they, never call your state into question, hence they professe, we cannot move till we be moved, and if I do not, it is not my fault. Hence if Ministers do preach any things which are not about the person of Christ, or the excellency of a Christian in Christ, or the emptinesse of the creature to prepare for Christ, (which are indeed of great use) and presse to any work or service of Christ, they are Legal Preachers, and bring people under a Covenant of works. Whereas if we preach duties, and leave them as signs, before being in Christ, they are so, but here to preach any duty of the Law, is part of the sweet will of Christ. Tell us (say they) what we should do. What can a man do ? *He can do all things through Christ* : True, but Christ must come to act it. Yea, But he hath a Faith to fetch it , 1 *John* 1. 6. many said they had communion with him, 1 *John* 2. 3, 4. It seems , they said *they had no sin* , as now some say, God sees no sin in justified people, God looks to the new creature only , 'tis not I but sin : if the Spirit help not , 'tis not my fault. Not many dayes since it did lye upon the spirit of one, who seeing Christ hath undertaken all , closed with him, rejoyced in him, not for this end , nor from the beauty they saw in holiness, nor bitternesse of sinfulness, but because they should be eased of the work. I have known them that have lived in some sin , and promised the Lord shall be blessed if he save them in their sin, and conceiting he would, have loved him ; thus

these.

these. In a word, the soul of man desires rest and peace, seeks for it in Creatures, seeks to satisfie it self there, there it cannot ; hence seeks for it (as many dying men do) in Christ, not in the Grace, but in the joy of Christ ; not in Christs holy presence, but in his comforting presence ; seeking the utmost perfection of a Christian in the seale of the Spirit , not in the mighty actings of the Spirit for God. Hence he is deluded, and fancies he hath Christ, and hence joy. Sin is the great evil , hence the end of Christs coming is to take it away. Hence if a man close with Christ, to remove horror, not sin , and so hath not closed with him for his holiness, you never closed with Christ for the end of his coming, nor for his , but on to your own ends, and so 'tis not him, but his, 2 *Cor.* 2. 15. The Gospel is a savour *to them that perish,* if of Death to death. Oh consider of these things if it be not thus. 1 *John* 5. 11, 12. Hast the Son for thy portion ? Dost see his Glory of Grace to accept and sanctifie thee, thou hast life : if not the Son , but only something from him , Oh death and not life ! the bonds of Death (not life) are upon thee, which no creature can unloose unlesse the Lord come to thy Grave-side and unloose thee.

SECT. VIII.

Use 5.
Of Exhort.

TO close with the Person of the Lord Jesus : you will think this is not a right course thus to do. We cannot do it. *Answ.* Yet the Gospel hath commands and entreaties wherewith Christs Spirit goes to the Elect ; and if you could see Christ in the ministry of man, you should feel it ; And hence we look it should be so : and besides, Saints that have Faith and power , are quickened by the voice of the Son of God. Consider therefore,

1. All men are fallen into a bottomless gulf of misery and sin , though once righteous. Hence Gods truth having said, *he that sins shall dye* : hence justice comes out to do execution , and when the neck of all men thus lies on the block, yet mercy pities , and faith , Oh spare, save ! Satisfie me saith justice, then I will : hence mercy sends forth a Son, when no men nor Angels could help, and he takes flesh, takes all their sin , fulfills all righteousnes, bears their sorrows , and by *one offering perfects for ever them that are sanctified* ; and having done this, is now at the right hand of God in the Glory of his Father , all creatures subject to him, all excellencies being met together in him : so that now he is the delight of God, the joy of Heaven ; so that whatsoever thou canst want , or losest , if thou hadst him, thou shalt find it in him : and also whatever he can do for thee , in his time thou shalt receive it from him, *Deut.* 33. 26, 29. *Who is like the God of Jesurun.*

2. Now there is a universal offer to all people where the Gospel comes ; enemies are entreated to be reconciled ; for though he hath not dyed for all , yet now being King, such is his excellency, that he is worthy of all : Hence commands all to receive him : and if this be a condemning sin to reject him , 'tis then a command lies upon you to receive him, and the foundation of this offer is your wants and miseries. You are dead, Oh come to him therefore for life ; weak, guilty, blind, Oh therefore come to him for pardon, peace, and life. Not fulness, nothing but emptiness is the ground of this offer, *Jer.* 3. 22.

3. Hence there is nothing on Gods part , nor yet on your part that can keep you from him. No sins, no wants, unless it be your will, *Mat.* 23. 37. Therefore now who-ever will shall have him , let him take him , *Rev.* 22. 17. There be two acts of the Will, Election and Resolution , I must have him , which if you will , nothing that ever thou didst or canst do can please the Father so much : so that he will I. Adopt thee to be his Son , *John* 1. 12. As è contra. 2. Thou shalt enrich thy self with a greater blessing than if Heaven, and Earth, and all glory

was put into thy hand, as the Lord himself is better than all; and hence once thine, ever thine, none shall pull thee out of his hand, 2 *Pet.* 1. 5. And it shall rejoyce the heart of Christ himself in Heaven, when as his Bride thou givest to him thy good will, *Isai.* 62. 5. And if you do not kiss the Son he will be angry, *Psalm* 2. And God knows whether now the last word, the last offer is to be made to thee.

Object. 1.
Answ.

But I find such sins in me, that till they are gone I dare not.

Then you will first remove sin, and after receive Christ: first be your own saviours, and then make him another: you shall never do it. Oh close with him to take sin away, because sick, therefore receive him.

Object. 2.
Answ.

But I have no will, my heart is endeared to my sin.

Therefore resign up thy self to him to give thee a will, (put it into his hand as bad as it is, this is Spouse-like) and to take away that will to sin, so thou shalt have him, *I am my Beloveds, he is mine:* For the Father looks to the Law, and saith, Sinner if thou believe thou shalt be saved; now lie under the Spirit, and you are where you should be; resist here, you resist the Holy Ghost. Oh but sin is dear. Consider, 1. What good did it ever do thee. 2. Hath Christ shed his Blood or no, if not, Oh the wrath of God is to come; if he hath, Oh wilt thou offer this wrong to his Blood, that a Lust shall be dearer than it, thy bloody Knives dearer than the life, and death, and mercy of a Son: Oh therefore if any Soul hath any lust dear, I beseech you by all the bitter sorrows of Christ, not to reject so great salvation.

Object. 3.
Answ.

But must I receive Christ with my own strength?

No, you cannot, nor ought not, but if the Lord puts strength in thee, put it forth. Many followed Christ for loaves, but none that ever came to him for himself that ever he put away, *Psalm* 81. 11, 12, 13. *I shewed much love, but they would none of me; Oh that they had hearkened.* At this instant God may give thee a heart.

Object. 4.

But I fear I shall never get my sins removed that I feel, which I think cannot stand with Grace.

Answ.

Gods Promise and Reason is cross to thy fears; if a Son, all things also though many years hence, *Rom.* 8. 32. If not by receiving, is it by rejecting that thou shalt attain thy end? 'Tis true, thou hast fallen off by thy sin from Christ, because thy falls have made thee fall off by unbelief from him, and made thee say, either I do not believe, or the Lord intends no good to me: you have had no strength, because not satisfied with meat.

Object. 5.
Answ.

But I may presume.

Is it presumption to honour Christ, and to have him honoured in thee? No, Dost think if the Lord shall after all thy sins, and in the midst of all thy miseries give thee Christ, shall he not be honoured by this? yes, who can ever have such cause to love him as I? Shall not thy receiving of him by Faith honour him? yes, *Rom.* 4. 20. Canst dishonour him so much as by rejecting him? when he hath laid down his life, shewed his love, offers himself: now to reject him, 'tis to offer greatest contempt to him and his love that can be: hence can you honour him so much as by this? Do never so much without him, he is unsatisfied: do this, he is well-pleased. Nay after all thy sins, yet he saith, *Return to me:* Nay, nothing else is such a means to honour him, by doing for him. If so, grant thou art vile, unworthy, poor, yet for the honour of the Lord Jesus do it, who is but little honoured in the world, and stand out no longer: thus receive him, and then know it you are Sons, and rejoyce in it, and do it now while the Spirit is upon thee, and remember now not to change, *Jer.* 2. 11. As Women, Oh I would not change; see how happy is thy choice: But Lord who hath believed our Report!

Quest.
Answ.

How may the Soul come to close with the person of the Lord Jesus?

1. Before any man can close, i.e. see and say he doth close with the Lord as

his

his own , he muſt feel a want of the Lord and his preſence, not only of his comforting, but of his holy preſence, for ſome people there be that neve felt a
want of Chriſt at all, they are great and grievous ſinners, but they truſt to Chriſt,
and though he kill them, yet they will truſt to him : others are in miſery, and
they feel a want of redemption, and hence cloſe with Chriſt for that, *Pſalm* 78.
35. Others are in horror, and know not what to do, and they feel a want of the
comforts of Chriſt, and hence cloſe with Chriſt for that, and if they find it they
depart from Chriſt by looſeneſs of life, if not by deſpair of heart, as *Saul*, 1 *Sam.*
28. *God anſwers me not by Urim, &c.* Others feel a want of ſome righteouſneſs
from Chriſt, the having of which ſupports and ſuſtains them without Chriſt,
till with the Prodigal, when all is ſpent, then they think of Bread at home, and
the want of which makes them to have leſſe eſteem of, and deſire after Chriſt, but
they are full of Objections againſt the thoughts of cloſing with him, but hence
they cloſe with Chriſt for that. Others there are that feel a want of the Lord
himſelf, and hence cloſe with him for himſelf ; ſo that let a man have all bleſſings
in the world, the purity of Ordinances, never ſo many illapſes, and droppings of
divine light, and life, and comfort in theſe Ordinances, that he wonders the Lord
ſhould be ſo good to him, yet he ſhall find (if right) his ſoul ſecretly unquiet and
unſatisfied till he hath the Lord himſelf. As the favour of meat makes a man
that wants it, cry the more after it, long the more for it ; ſo the favour and
ſweet of all creatures, all Ordinances, all Duties, do not ſtay, but ſtir up the
ſoul to ſeek Chriſt, when he is himſelf, *Jer.*50.4. *They ſhall ſeek the Lord weeping.*
Hence firſt they felt a want of him. *The full ſoul loaths the honey-comb.* Let the
Lord be never ſo ſweet, let him do them never ſo much good, the more good he
doth then, the leſſe they regard him, *Jer.* 2.6. *They ſaid not where is the Lord ?*
Therefore that ſoul that truly cloſeth with the Lord, muſt firſt feel a want of the
Lord, and ſay theſe Ordinances are not bread, theſe creatures are not bread, all
theſe parts, gifts, duties are not bread, bran, not bread. All this favour, this
ſweetneſſe 'tis not bread. Hence I periſh for want of bread, I have creatures,
Ordinances, Affections, comforts, Duties, but Oh no Chriſt. Like the Prodi-
gall, *Luke* 15.17. Oh therefore do not only ſee, but feel the want of the Lord
Jeſus, you that never had him yet ; nay you that have him, you cannot have
more of him, but by feeling more the want of him. Oh it was a marvellous expreſſion of *Moſes*, when the Lord began to grow weary of their company, *Exod.*
33.15. *If thou goeſt not with us, carry us not up hence,* i.e. Let us rather die than
live without thee. *Mary* when Chriſt was crucified, the carcaſe of the Lord
was gone, ſhe ſate there weeping : Oh much more for the Lord himſelf. Its
obſerved by ſome for the ſaddeſt ſpectacle, to ſee a deſert Town : Oh what is
it to ſee a deſert heart, where no Chriſt inhabits ? Or a city, and no Inhabitants. And hence its *Romes* curſe, to be made *an habitation of devils* ; ſo here.
What is Hell, but this, to ſee not *Abraham*, but to ſee Chriſt afar off ? and thy ſelf
ſhut out. It may be 'tis no ſorrow now, but it will be. Its a ſad thing to ſee a
man *riſe up early, go to bed late, eat the bread of carefulneſſe,* and yet gain nothing,
*Phil.*1.21. This is very ſad. Chriſt is our gain, all the creatures you have,
means you uſe, duties you do, comforts you receive, they are not gain, nay, the
more God doth for thee, the more thou loſeſt, if no Chriſt, becauſe now thou
art full by this means. Oh therefore get a heart ſenſible of the want of the Lord.
Think there is a Chriſt, whoſe Glory is the amazement of Heaven, but Oh I ſee
him not. Happy for ever are they that have him, but Oh I have him not. Your
hungry bellies cannot want bread, if they do, they are never quiet till they have
it. Is the Lord no better ? Lord grant this contempt be not revenged with
ſpirituall plagues ! Some of you know not your want, others feel it not, you can
live without him ; worſe than *Saul*, he went to Urim, and lamented in great diſtreſſe, *He anſwers me not !* Oh you feel no diſtreſſe, becauſe of this, I have him
not !

not! Nay worse than *Dives*, that begg'd, Oh a drop of *water to cool my tongue!*
Why cry not you, Oh the Lord Christ to comfort my heart! Why is not all
this fulnesse longed for? Oh therefore let nothing else comfort, and let nothing
discourage, but make this use of all, Oh I want him!

2. To the right closing with his person, this is also required, to tast the bitternesse of sin, as the greatest evil: Else a man will never close with Christ, for
his holinesse in him, and from him as the greatest good. For we told you that
that's the right closing with Christ for himself, when it is for his holinesse. For
ask a whorish heart what beauty he sees in the person of Christ, he will after he
hath looked over his Kingdom, his Righteousnesse, all his works, see a beauty
in them, because they do serve his turn to comfort him only. Ask a Virgin, he
will see his happinesse in all; but that which makes the Lord amiable, is his Holinesse, which is in him, to make him holy too; as in marriage, it is personal
beauty draws the heart. And hence I have thought it reason that he that loves
Brethren for a little Grace, will love Christ much more. Hence if a man feels
not the want of Christ, the bitternesse of sin, as his greatest evil, he will never
see nor admire Christs beauty, much lesse close with it. Hence *John* 16.9. *Con-*
vinceth the world of sin, because they believe not in me, i.e. of that chiefly. Oh
their wrongs done against the Lord! Why not of wrath and Hell! Oh
sin is the evil, and then it appears exceeding evil, when not against God simply,
but against a Son. *Paul why persecutest thou me? Acts* 9. Why? Did he not
live in lusts and self-confidence? Yes, but in all these he saw he persecuted
Christ. And after saddest search, I have feared the want of this, is the great
cause of all a mans closing amisse with Christ. I would but ask where was *Judas*
wound? Was it resting in a Pharisaical righteousness without Christ? Without Christ,
no, for he forsook all and followed Christ. Was it want of profession of him,
preaching for him? No. Was it for want of communion with him? No: one
sin he lived in, he had his bagg. And hence when many went from him,
he stuck to him, *John* 6. *Judas* still cleaves to him: yet even then Christ calls him
a Devil, which if ever he had tasted the bitternesse of, he would not have lived in,
nor dyed desperately, some think impardonably without Christ, and so sin more
against him. Let any man living shew me how he can close with Christ, and yet
love one sin: I'le be his bond-man, that can say, I close with Christ as
my Husband, and yet I love my Whore too. Let any man living close with
Christ, and keep his sin, or hide his sin, or let it be hid, his closing with
Christ shall harden him in his sin, and so he shall dye without Christ in his
sins, as it is writ, *Exod.* 21.14. As it was with *Joab*, who fled to the Horns of
the Altar, so 'tis with many men, they sin, and confess and sin under all Laws:
why? they fly to Christ, and this imboldens them, hardens them, why? because
they never tasted the bitterness of sin. I know a mans sin may be crucified before
'tis mortified, as it may be buried after 'tis dead. Oh therefore I beseech you
look to this, you faii not here. Many of you are troubled, Oh take heed of
being comforted until you get the Lord to do this for you, or unlesse you depend
upon the Lord for this in his time. Some apply comfort when they see no good:
I dare not to my self or others: Oh therefore imagine thou didst hear the Lord
speaking, Why dost thou persecute me? why is a man so grieved at any thing that
crosseth himself because a man loves himself, because he thinks his good lies there
most: Oh see thy good more in Christ than in thy self, *Acts* 9. 4. Oh me, me in
whom all good is, oh to persecute him! Two men hear, and one is in horror, and
the other not; oh 'tis because God sets it on: so here.

3. Make the Lord Jesus present with you, and set him really before you, and see
him willing to give himself unto you, even to thee in particular. Those that give
themselves in Marriage, separate themselves from all company, and get alone together, and give themselves one unto another: so sever thy self from all the
world,

world, and set the Lord really before thee, as *David*, *Psalm* 16.8. and so close one with another. For two things keep from Christ. Either

First, they care not for him, and the cause is, they make him not present, only have a notion and report of him.

Secondly, They dare not close with him, because they fear he is not willing to close with them, with others, not with me; so that all the Scriptures they read, all the Promises they hear are very sweet, but they look on them as spoken to others. Hence *Acts* 2.39. *For the Promise is made to you, and to them afar off*; be thou never so far off, if thou received him, he will receive thee, *Luke* 2.14. *Good will to men*: Oh see this good-will in the Lord to have thee receive him, though thou hast no money, nay because dead and vile, nay because not sensible, *Rev.* 3. 17,18. Oh wonderful because senseless of misery, therefore close with him. 1. Is it not his command it should be so? 2. Is it not a sin to reject him? will he not be angry with thee to reject him? 3. Are not his conditions easie, so as he hath undertaken to do all that which thou saist thou canst not? Why wilt not? 1. Oh if I were a child, a son in Covenant I would, but because otherwise, hence I dare not. *Ans.* *Joh.*1.12. Receive him, he will make thee a Son. 2. Oh but my wants are many. *Ans.* Receive him he will make thee rich, *Isai.* 55.1, 2, 3. Oh but I find my heart endeared to creatures. *Ans.* 1 *John* 5.4. *This is the Victory that overcometh the world, even your Faith.* 4. Oh but I shall fall back. No, *Jer.*3.22. *Return, and he will heal thy back-sliding.* 5. Oh but I shall never be able to do any thing. *Ans.* Yes, close with him and thou shalt. 6. Oh but I am very vile before the Lord after all I do. *Ans.* Yet *Eph.* 5.25, 26, 27. He shall make thee amiable, only receive him, set thy heart on him alone. Now do you think he bears a good will toward you? can you deny it? Shall not this overcome thee, that the Lord of Glory should fall in love with thee, and bear good will to thee a Leper, and that canst do nothing for him, and yet for all this, Oh this will draw thee, *Psal.* 36.6, 7. Oh *how great is thy loving-kindness*; this makes a heart of steel to yield, *Jer.* 31.1, 2, 3. Oh this will out you in Hell, Oh hard hearts that despised such Grace!

4. If the serious thoughts of this do not draw thee, at least not so fully; look up to the Lord to reveal himself unto thee to be thine. For as no man can take Christ until God gives him, so no man can say he is his, untill the Lord shews him that he is his. And as the creature cannot resist, but take when the Lord gives: so it cannot but see the Lord when he reveals himself as indeed he is. And look to see him to be yours by some Promise; for there is a seeing Christ mine in great *fulgor* without the light of a Promise, and Spirit in it. Is Christ yours? Yes, I see it. How? by any word or promise? No, this is a delusion. The other is by promise, & that opened in the Gospel, *Eph.* 1.13, 14. He saith not in whom after ye were sealed you believed, but *è contra*. And how believed? by hearing the Gospel. Hence Saints return to this, *Psalm* 51.8. *Let me hear the voice*, 1 *Pet.* 2.1, 2, 3. And this is that which hath knit the hearts of Saints to Christ for ever, *Oh thou hast the words of life*: For there is a voice of love to the Saints engraven in all mercies, in all afflictions, in all Gods leadings of them, though it be in a Wilderness; but Beloved, only the Word can tell me the meaning of these words of love. So there is love of Christ revealed according to a Promise, not by it, and love spoken in mercies, but the Word interprets them and clears them to be no delusions; I mean the Spirit there: This is judged to be a good answer to Papists, who shall be judge of controversies? We answer that which shall be judge at the last Day, must be judge now: but so, *Rom.* 2.16. *John* 12.48. So whether doth Gods Spirit seal, or the Devil delude? It's a great controversie if you have not a word to see Gods love by, but think you have a way to see it without, this Word shall judge you. Oh look therefore for the Lord by a word to do it, and say *Speak Lord*; and if by word, look not for it without a work on your own heart. Some Christians have rested with a work without Christ, which is abominable; but after a man is in

Christ,

Christ not to judge by the work, is first not to judge from a word. For though there is a word which may give a man dependance on Christ, without feeling any work, nay when he feels none, as absolute promises, yet no word giving assurance, but that which is made to some work, *He that believeth*, *or is poor in spirit, &c.* till that work is seen, hath no assurance from that Promise. Tell him God hath promised to pour *clean water*, *Ezek.* 36. Yes for some, not for me. Secondly, 'tis not to judge by the Spirit, for the Apostle makes the earnest of the Spirit to be the Seal ; now earnest is part of the money bargained for, the beginning of Heaven, of the light and life of it : He that sees not the Lord is his by that, sees no God his at all : Oh therefore do not look for a Spirit without a word to reveal, nor a word to reveal without seeing and feeling of some work first, I thank the Lord I do but pitty those that think otherwise: if a sheep of Christ, Oh wander not. *Ob.* But I have waited long for this. *Ans.* True, therefore more need to wait still, it may be now 'tis not far off. *Ob.* Oh but it may be he will not, if I knew that I could be quiet. *Answ.* Down proud heart, Oh take heed of that pride : art' not worthy never to hear a voice from God ? Be silent then, and humble, and now hear what the Lord will say, he speaks in a still voice, *Psalm* 85.8. do as they in that Psalm did ; Thou hast done thus and thus, Oh hear us, turn us, and then lie still and listen : Oh do thus, else you make God a lyar if the word comes, 1 *John* 5. 10, 11. and now when thou hast him, Oh change him not.

First, What dost want, and where wilt go to find it but there ? any creatures, and all the excellencies of them are there, and in time of trouble he will be instead of all, and also blesse all.

Secondly, Dost want Grace to honour a God ? it is in him the fulnesse of it. Dost want God and his love ? thou hast him, and now all his love, his care, his wisdom is thine. Oh wonder at thy lot and portion, and say, Lord I have enough. Thus much of the first Doctrine.

CHAP. X.

Shewing that True Believers do with hope expect the Second Coming of Christ.

SECT. I.

Now they go forth by $\left\{ \begin{matrix} \text{Hope} \\ \text{Desire} \end{matrix} \right\}$ Of Him and his Coming.

Observ. 2.

THat the Church and People of God after they are truly Espoused to Christ, and made in any measure ready for Christ, they now are no more of this world, but look out of it, and verily expect the Second Coming, and Glorious Appearing of Christ.

'Tis true, they look for his coming and company at the last period of their life, but this they look upon but as their welcome in the way, until the last Trump shall blow, and that they shall meet the Lord in the clouds of the Aire, 1 *Thes.* 4. 18. which is the last and chief time of his Coming they look out for. The Five Wise Virgins did here verily look for him ; the Five Foolish seemingly did so too: That look as it was before the first Coming of Christ, all their thoughts and searchings of heart were after the day, and time, and glory of it, 1 *Pet.* 1. 10, 11. And the nearer His Coming was, the more ardently was he expected : Hence such flocking to *Johns* Ministry. Hence *Simeon* waited long for the *consolation of Israel*. So the Espoused and Beloved of the Lord looks out for his coming now. He hath left them as Orphans in this world, he hath divers of his Elect yet to bring

home,

hone, and enemies to put under his feet, and then they know he will come, and this day they look for. As Christ expects it, *Heb.*10.13. By the same Spirit they look for it.

This is that which Christ so oft presseth on his Disciples, foreseeing the slumbers of the world, to be ever watching for his second coming ; and hence these alone are accounted blessed, *Luke* 12.37,38. That let Christ come at any watch , Oh blessed. The duration of the world from the first to the second coming, is but as it were a night divided into several watches ; the Saints are the watchmen of the world, who you know look for day-light, though it be long, 'tis but a night ; it will be morning : All the rest are like birds at their chirse. And hence he tells them the reason of the uncertainty of his coming, makes this the end of it. They are Evangelical commands with which there goes a power. Look through all the Primitive Church in the Golden Age, they had all this stamp, 1 *Cor.*1.7. *Waiting.* 1 *Thes.*1.10. *To wait for Christ from Heaven.* Nay, *Heb.*9. 28. He professeth those only may know the fruit of his first coming, that *now look for him.*

SECT. II.

Reas. 1.

1 **B**Ecause they really foresee, and see such a day, 2 *Pet.*3.3,4. *In the last days shall come Scoffers, saying, where is the promise of his coming ? all things are as they were,* and hence live in their lusts, die in their own dung, and never look for it. But these foresee it really, and hence look for it. Men that live on land, and love the smoak of their own chimneys, never look out to other coasts and countreys, or to a strange Land, but Sea-men that are bound for a Voyage, and have a Pilot with them that hath seen the coast, that's it they look for ; so men that live in this world, and are well here, look not after Christ nor his coming, but they that have a Pilot , a Spirit to shew them, this day, this coast, and are bound for another world, they look out for this ; they see it two waies ;

1. By the eye of Faith in the promise, 2 *Pet.*3.13. And this makes the soul see it, when all things seem to be against it, and hence expects it ; for that is the difference between Faith and hope : Faith closeth with Christ, and all the Glory of Christ, in the promise as present, hope hence steps forth and laies hold upon the performance it self as absent. Faith entertains the promise as a faithful messenger, and sees that his message is true. Hope runs out of doors and leaves it with Faith, and looks for the Lord himself, *Heb.*11.1.

2. By the Light of Glory in the thing it self ; for Saints do not only see things in Letters and Syllables, and words, but see things as they are in themselves. The wicked see the word, sin, and Christ, and Heaven (and in seeing see not) but not the things themselves. Now the Glorious coming of Christ being a thing to come, yet to be done, how do they see it but by report ? Yes, they have the Spirit of Glory, which Spirit *shews them things to come,* John 16.13. *Which eye hath not seen.* That look as their Head Christ sees this day as it shall be, and his apprehensions are not false, but as he conceives of this day , so shall it be : so the Saints by the same Spirit see it before it comes, and are not mistaken about it, though it be very darkly, yet sometimes when the Spirit of God is not overclouded, they see it more evidently. For this is the great plague of the wicked, they see nothing as 'tis, and in Hell they see how they have been deceived. So this is the happinesse of Saints, that though they see things darkly, yet they see things truly, the Spirit creating glorious impressions on the mind of things as they are. They know things that the eye sees not, as they are. That look as *Abraham* John 8.56. *saw Christs day, and was glad,* though afar off ; so the Saints by the same Spirit. Now why did *Noah* make his Ark, and look for a Flood ? Because he saw it really.

Did

Did not others? No, 'tis said, *They knew not*, Mat. 24. 38,39. Never knew *till the Floud came*: The Lord made it not known. *Noah* did, the other did not. Hence the Saints cannot but look for it.

2. Because they see nothing else in this world worth looking after, no, not for the present. For if a man sees the day of the Lord, yet hath some prey in his eye, in this world, and his game before him, he will follow his hunting to catch his venison, though he comes too late for the blessing. But the Lord makes his people to see nothing in the world worth the hawking or catching.

1. They see the Glory of another day, another world, and this puts out the Glory of this, and hence makes them look for that; and hence when Christ would comfort his Disciples, he promiseth nothing here, but tels them, *In my Fathers House are many Mansions. I go to prepare a place, and Ile come to you again*, *John* 14. 1, 2,3. And hence they seeing this to be enough, look for this.

2. They see an end of all these things, of all the Glory of them, and that these summer swallows will take their wings, and fly away in greatest extremities. Hence they look to eternal things, the Lord, and his coming, 2 *Cor.*4.18: *We look not at temporal things.*

3. They find the Lord crossing them of what they look for in this world, somtimes of outward comforts, somtimes of the performance of spiritual promises, And when God thus *hedgeth their way with thorns*, then they *think of their first Husband*. Look as it was with *Abraham*, Heb.11.13. You know strangers when their way is uncomfortable, ever and anon look for their home. *Abraham* was heir of the world, yet he sojourns as a stranger in it, in Tents, *because he looks for a City*, *v.*10. So here, Saints the heirs of all creatures, yet the Lord makes them strangers here, and hence they look for somthing else. The things God hath promised to his people are very great, but not accomplished. Why? Because full accomplishment is left till the last day, that hope may wait, and that we may live by Faith. God hath promised to *take away all tears*, Oh welcome that day! This world cannot do it, and the Lord here will not, 1 *Cor.*15.19. *If our hope were only here, we were most miserable.*

3. Because they see and are sensible of their deliverance from wrath to come: There hath been much wrath in the world seen, but yet the great wrath is to come, what that is they see. What their escape from it is they see. Hence they look for Christ, when he shall appear like the rising Sun, and like a Bridegroom from his chamber to comfort them, 1 *Thes.*1.10. For the Devils look for this day, and natural men, but seeing wrath, wish themselves under rocks and mountains, and seek to smother it: But Saints seeing themselves delivered, hence calmly look for it. The sense of this love makes them say, Oh when will he come, that I may *see him with these eyes*! They fear not (for why should they) the terrour of this day.

4. Because the Lord hath given unto them the first-fruits of Glory, and of that day of Glory, hence they look and wait for it. You know the first fruits were part of the whole vintage, hence they gave thanks for all, because they then looked for all, *Exod.*23. *Rom.*8.23. *We having the first-fruits of the Spirit, wait for the adoption.* That look as 'tis with the wicked, that have rejected Christ, and counted his Blood a common thing, and *done despite* to Gods Spirit, there remains nothing *but a fearful looking for of vengeance*, so here *è contra*. Rom.5.1,2,3,4,5. *Being justified by Faith*, now 1. *Peace with God.* 2. Accesse by Christ to God. 3. Standing in that Grace. 4. Shedding of love, hence not only hope, but *Glory in hope of the Glory of God*. There is none espoused to Christ, but tast this love, feel the warmth of his fellowship, feel the abundance of his love, but 'tis but in a little measure, in the first-fruits, hence they look for and expect the rest

at

at his coming. They are somtime full of fears, what if shut out at last? But when they feel the first-fruits of Glory at that day, now they verily look for his coming. Christ dies we know, but it was not possible for him to be held long, and hence rose again, and then looked for Glory, and then was taken up to Glory: So here, the Saints lie dead in the grave of sins and fears, but its not possible for them ever to be held here; hence when *risen with Christ*, they look upon *things above*, and are waiting for Glory, and at last are taken to Glory with himself. That look as *Jacob*, Gen.49.18. said, *My soul waiteth for thy salvation*, when the stakes and pins of this fleshly Tabernacle are loosing, and so the Lord is loosing him from the excellency of this world; though he minds other things, yet he recalls himself, *My soul waiteth for thy salvation Oh Lord.*

SECT. III.

Use. 1.

HEnce let all flesh take notice that there is such a time, and day, and coming of the Lord Jesus. This was the Apostles Argument to prove a resurrection, *Christ is risen*, and to prove this, and so the resurrection from the dead at Christs coming, *else is your Faith vain, i.e.* Expectation of him vain, 1 *Cor.*15. 14, & 17. Men think it easie to believe a resurrection, and a second coming of Christ for that end; but an hoverly sleight work is quickly done, and an hoverly Faith is quickly wrought. But when a man comes to look considerately, Is there such a day indeed? Is there one now in the third Heavens that will fire this whole world, and gather his Saints to his Glory? Now its very hard. Its usual with Satan to pierce with extremities, that when they do begin indeed to close with Christ, and receive comfort from him, to smite them with thoughts: Is there a Christ, and is there such a time of coming? Now of all the Arguments to convince and perswade, me-thinks none like this, *viz.* That there be a Generation of men in the world, that verily look for this day and see it, and have the first-fruits and beginnings of it already in their souls. A number of people that once never minded it, heard of it, but looked not for it, now to see it; flesh and blood could not, Satan would not reveal it, hence God that cannot lie, hath shewn it unto them, so as they are in a manner eye-witnesses of it. Men will believe eye-witnesses of any thing, especially if many. Such are the espoused of the Lord in all ages. *The things which we have heard and seen we speak.*

Object.
Answ.

But may they not be deceived, and conceit that which is not?

True, but Divine revelation of any Truth that cannot deceive, for that is no fancy of the head, nor delusion of Satan. Now this is a secret the Spirit makes known.

1. In that it fils the mind and feeds the heart with it, that it carries unto God with wonderment of blessing him that ever he saw this. Fancies cannot feed, especially in greatest agonies: Now they chuse misery on this ground, rather than present peace here, Heb.11.35. *Not accepting deliverance.*

2. In that it works effects crosse to Nature, nay to all a mans lusts in them. *Noah* foresaw a Flood nigh, but he might be deceived. No, 'tis said *he feared*, kept close to God and it came, so here.

3. This Light whereby they see, it is not only sweet and Glorious, and cross to heart and lusts, but its sudden, that as with *Paul*, when going to persecute, *suddenly there fell a great Light*, and so he saw Christ. So when a man goes on in his sin, and suddenly the Lord reveals this and that by a word (else 'tis a deceit) which all Angels could not do before, so as to see it, and that none can reveal it as he sees it, especially to bring this light out of darknesse, this must be miraculous power, and no dream. But what do I speak of seeing? they feel the beginnings of it in the first-fruits of it.

N 2   For

For two great things shall be at that day.

First, Then all the Elect shall have their fill of love.

Secondly, Triumph in Christ when in the clouds with him. Have they not the first here? *Rom.5.5.* The feeling of which love cannot be a Fancy, for it cannot conceive of it nor hold it. This is an infinite love, and that in the midst of the sence of sin and death. That many times they are even fain to say, Lord hold. 2, Triumph, *Rom. 5.3.* and that in afflictions, which make them by experience so to feel God in part, that they triumph for time to come. 'Tis true at times they look down the Tower, and so tremble, but while they look up here, then they triumph, having accesse to the Grace wherein they stand, So then look for it, there shall be such a day, and such a coming of Christ, *Rev.1.7.* The Father hath exalted the Son to ineffable Glory. But Lord! Who sees him as these, in his Glory, or to come forth out of his Glory? 'Tis but Table-talk. *But behold he comes, and every eye shall see him.* The Lord pities you, and holds out bowels of love, and Faith; Oh receive me, Oh cast away those bloody knives that have pierced me; and sends his good Spirit like his hand to draw you. But Oh do you not kick his bowels, do you not pierce his hands and feet daily? And when you have done no tears! But he cometh, and you that pierce him shall see him, *&c.* Consider of it therefore you that doubt of this, you that think not of this, and hence live and lie in your lusts, and despise him. Behold he cometh!

SECT. IV.

Use 2.

HEnce behold the happinesse of all them that be espoused to the Lord Jesus, in that their hopes are laid up in another world, at the day of the coming of the Lord Jesus, 1 *Cor.*15.19. *If we had hope only in this life, we were of all men most miserable.* Because none so foolish, or so sensible of misery as they, but our hopes stretch to another life, to the second coming of the Lord Jesus Christ. Suppose a man had all the Crowns of the world cast at his feet, but at last to be dragged before the judgment-seat of Christ, and there to stand quaking, What should he be the better? What though Saints have all the miseries in this world, but at last *with these eyes they shall see the Lord,* and stand triumphing before him, and have a real sight and certain expectation of this. What people in the world so great as these?

Quest.
Answ.

What do they wait and expect for?

Great things which may astonish the whole Creation.

This was preached about the time of the Pequot wars.

1. They look for him *to change their vile bodies,* that this their Husband at the marriage day should take away these rags, *& make them like unto his Glorious body,* brighter than the Sun; so that burn them, cut them to peices, (as some by the *Indians* have been, Lord help!) they see Christ loves both, and hence holds sword and soul in one hand, and scabberd in another, *&c.*

2. They expect he should take away all their sins, and make them like unto himself, engrave on their souls perfectly his own Image, that their enemies they feel now, they look they *shall never see them more.* 1 *John* 3.2. And as no evil like it, no mercy like this; and no evil to Saints like this, that yet they should grieve the heart of such a Husband.

3. They look he should take away all sorrows and tears from them, for this the Lord promiseth, and begins to execute now, but it shall be perfected then, *Isa.* 25.8,9. And hence called *the times of refreshing,* Acts 3.19,20. 'Tis true the Spouse and Church is now sorrowful to the very heart many times, but there is a time coming that they shall never sorrow more.

4. They look he should take away all shame from them. For no people in the world loaden with more calumnies and reproaches by the wicked and by hypocrites,

cries, and hard speeches from the Godly, and they doubt whether they be Sons or no. Now then the whole world shall see they are Sons, and shall stand amazed at them, and shall not doubt of it, nor themselves, for the Lord shall proclaim it, and they shall hear, these are my Jewels. And this they look for, 1 *John* 3.1,2.

5. They then look for recompence to all their *labour of love* to him and his. Hence 1 Cor.15.58. *Knowing your labour is not in vain in the Lord.* Hence the Apostle oft defers men for that recompence till now. *The Lord shew mercy to the House of Onesephorus in that day,* 2 Tim.1.18. So that some Hereticks have thought souls sleep till then. They may pray and no answer, seek to do good, and do none. Oh but the Lord will recompence then abundantly.

6. They look then to *be ever with the Lord,* 1 Thes.4.17. Never to be parted from him, never to live without him, nay never to go away from under his wing, out of his bleeding bosom of love and endlesse and unspeakable compassions any more: And being with him to see his Glory, and never see the depth of it, and to have the Lord to serve them, *Luke* 12.37,38. and giving whatever they call for, and all this when thousand thousands shall at this time be crying for a drop of water, and cannot get it. Now all this they look for, and more too: Which is, 1. Certain. For *hope maketh not ashamed.* 2. Which fills their hearts with Glory, and unspeakable Glory too: for it makes it so clear and certain, that they have it all already, for though absent, hope makes it as present, *Rom.*8.24. He doth not say we shall be, but *we are saved by hope.* Faith takes hold on the beginning, hope on the end. Oh the heavy wrath of God upon a world of poor, blind, ignorant men that have no hope, no hope of Christ, no hope of Glory, unlesse a flattering, dead hope. What a sad thing is it to think of a number of men that are buried in the world, and never to awaken until they see Christ in the clouds of Heaven, coming to be revenged on them. Oh me-thinks I see them falling down before the Judgment-seat, and crying out, Oh that we had known of this day! Oh alas that I had hope, but not such an hope, but am now deceived. Oh 'tis otherwise with Saints, they shall find what they hoped for, and infinitely more. What hurt can any do them? Let all the world come against them, their husband will come, and will kick them under his feet. Let them load them with reproaches, fill their hearts with sorrows, and their eyes with tears, their Lords coming will comfort them. Let Satan tempt, and a Father hide his face, behold the Lord cometh, that shall deliver and redeem them! Oh see their blessednesse, and let it draw you to make up the match with Christ, that never did it yet! He hath bin wooing of you, longing for you, and you wooing of him again, Lord take me! What hinders you then from striking the march, and concluding it? To give thy self this day to him, and take him only, rejoyce in him only, when nothing thou dost can be so pleasing to him. And now you may look and believe what one day you shall to your comfort feel. And account your selves most wretched creatures until the Lord be pleased to espouse you to himself.

SECT. V.

OR hence learn what to judge of those that never look for the coming and company of the Lord Jesus, but 'tis with them, as it was with the *Israelites,* when *Moses* was gone into the Mount, and stayed there long, the people made their Calf, and went to their feasting and rejoycing: So the Lord Jesus being gone for the Spirit of life, and to prepare a place of Glory, it being now long since, they make Idols of their Jewels, and of their own excellencies, and of whatsoever is glorious in their eyes in this world. Or as Christ compares the se-

Use 3. Of Exam.

cure world, *as it was in the daies of Noah, so shall it be*, or as in the daies of *Lot*, when they never knew nor look't for it, though told of it ; so 'tis with them. Do you think these are espoused to Christ ? or made ready for Christ ? whose glorious appearing is never , or seldom, or the least thing in their thoughts , and are far from seeing and setting it before their eyes.

Now because if you ask most men, Do you look for such a time to see the world consumed, and the Lord revealed, and your Glory with him ? Every one will say, yes, because indeed they have a dead hope. I shall therefore give discoveries of it.

Sign I.

I. Those whose hearts prize (though their heads do not) and whose eyes are dazeled with the withering Glory of this world. When men lie under (not for a fit, for Christ's Disciples wondred at the Beauty of the Temple) a great mistake of all things here, and put that good in them which is not, and that worth upon them which they ought not. For he on whose eyes the Sun of Glory hath risen, and looks for the Glory which shall be revealed ; looks upon a Dunghill world as strangers upon their Inne, and as Travellers do on their Tents, make a shift to rub it out there for a time, but Oh home. Oh *that Glory that shall be revealed, Heb.* 11. 13. They were strangers , because *they looked for a City* : Nay they look upon these things, as God and Christ judge of them (for they have Christ's mind) 1 *Cor.* 2. 15. Which stand for Cyphers in the Lords Book : Nay they look upon the very miseries of this world for Christ , greater treasures than the happinesse of it , and hence chuse it and account their scars their Crown, their shame their Glory, their losses their gain, their sorrows their joys, as *Heb.* 11. 25, 26. *Moses* chose to suffer, and esteemed Christs reproach his Glory. And why ? *He had an eye to the recompence of reward,* and saw the God invisible. And 2 *Cor.* 4. 17. *It works an exceeding weight of Glory.* That look as 'tis with a man that is born to great hopes of a Crown and Kingdom, and therefore brought up not in the Countrey, but in the Court ; let a poor man offer him his thatcht house, and promise him if he will come and live with him, and serve him in his patcht cloaths, What will he say ? No, be gone to your friends, I am a greater man than you can make me, so here ; A man that is born and begotten to a lively hope of a Crown now by the resurrection of Christ, and brought up under the wings and care of Christ, to the hopes of a better world, offer never so much, promise never so fair, I am greater than all the world can make me, I must not have, if I love Christ, and I cannot have, if he loves me, both ; and hence looks to honour then, and peace and glory then, *Col.* 3. 1, 2, 3. Its clear then thou lookest upon the things of the world as great things ; Oh to have such honour, such an estate, so many Cowes and Goats, so much ground paled in, so many ploughs, lands and oxen fit to labour, so much gain to come in every year, and such parts, & gifts and duties to get me a name, to live before the best men, and to be good signs (to comfort me) of the favour of God : This is a goodly thing, the very hopes heat and warm the heart.

1. If you do not find pangs in parting with a friend, a bosom-blessing so dear, you are not dead yet to it, nor risen to a lively hope of better things.

2. He that doth not prize the evils of the world, more than the good in it, his eyes are dazeled with it : If the life of the world be not death to thee, the comfort of the world sorrow to thee, Oh they draw thy heart from God : Hence called *lying vanities.* Look as 'tis with a King or Master that gives Talents to use, they cast them by, and fish for themselves, they look not for the coming of their Masters : So the Lord gives you his Ordinances, and Word to use for him, and you scramble for your selves, to enrich, and honour, and comfort your selves, you look not for the Lord. Factors that go far for wealth, they will not bring home stones and rubbish, which they know will not go in their own Countrey, hence other things that are of more price he spends his time for : So here. What do

do you do? You that eat the bread of carefulnesse, sell your commodities dear, and set your buyers on Tainter-hooks? I look to be rich. You that can speak well, and have parts, and professe fairly; but go into your Closets, God is neglected in your hearts, your constant union to Christ, dependance on Christ, approving your selves to Christ, is not maintained. I would fain be honoured. You are come far from your own Countrey: Why did you depart thence? To be free from trouble. And now here, what stay you for? Oh for ease. Will these Coynes go, and be taken at the last day? No, you look not for that.

II. They that say they look for Christ, but do not rejoyce abundantly in hope of this time. Sometimes the hopes of Gods people begin to die, and then comfortlesse, but when their hopes are up, and stirring, and not wounded by some sin or sleeping, there is a double joy that now they have. _Sign 2._

1. This alone comforts them and fils them, _John_ 14.1,2,3. So that they wonder at God, though they have never so little here, to have these blessings now, and everlasting Glory, endlesse compassions and mercy at that day, _John_ 16.22.

2. This joy is Glorious joy, highest comfort, _Rom._ 5.3. _We Glory in hope of the glory of God._ Disgraced, but then honoured; hated of men, but then loved of Christ; poor, but then enriched; miserable, but then blessed; empty, but then filled; fatherlesse, friendlesse, but then glorified. Oh I tell you miseries thus considered, are sweet! Can it be otherwise? Now you say you hope and look for this day. Where is your comfort of it? Where is your glory in it? _Acts_ 1.11,12. Compared with _Luke_ 24.52. So thou wilt be in the Temple, nay in the fields rejoycing and blessing the Lord, that ever he should intend to set thee at his right hand, at that great day of his coming. No man but hath something to joy his heart. Is it _Corn, and wine and Oyl,_ and not _the Light of Gods countenance_ at this day? Its a sign they never look for it. Do the world rejoyce in their hopes, and not Saints?

III. They that content themselves with any measure of holinesse and Grace; they look not for Christs coming and company. For Saints that do look for him, though they have not that Holinesse and Grace they would have, yet they rest not satisfied with any measure, 1 _John_ 3.3. _He that hath this hope purifieth himself as he is pure._ Christ finds us not lovely, but makes us lovely, by putting on his own garments, imprinting his own Image. Hence Saints content not themselves with any dressings, till made glorious, and so fit for fellowship with that Spouse. And when the Soul sees this Love to be a Son, and then to be proclaimed Heir, Oh this makes them set Christ himself as the pattern to walk by. Now therefore, _Sign 3._

1. When men shall think this way is bad, & another way of some Saints is good, and so take a Copy of his course from them, and now is well, this only is to be pure as man is pure.

2. When a man leaves not till he gets such a measure of Faith and Grace, and now when he hath got this, contents himself with this as a good sign he shall be saved, he looks not for Christ. Or

3. When men are heavily loaden with sin, then close with Christ, and then are comforted, sealed, and have joy that fils them, and now the work is done, and they are past Grace, and past Repentance, and daily cleansing, now they study not what to do for Christ, that neither Family nor Church where they live, are the better for them.

4. When men shall not content themselves with any measure, but wish they had more, if Grace would grow, while they tell Clocks, and sit idle, and so God must do all, but do not purge themselves, and make work of it (Indeed Saints purge not themselves of themselves, for dirty hands will never wash a foul face) but by a daily dependance on, and importunity of Faith sigh after the Lord

to

to do it ; verily if not thus, you look not for Chrift, 2 *Pet.*3.11,12,14. For if
you did, you would fay and think, if to be like him be my Glory, Oh then that
I might then have it now. Sons that are born to their hopes in the Court, will
go in the Court-fashion : Beggars that are born and brought up under hedges,
content themselves with their rags, fo here : Lord where is this Spirit ? especially even among us. There is fcarce any but either would be honeft, and then hopes
God accepts of his will, or will be fo, & then 'tis only fo much as will credit or comfort him. Lord where is the man that mourns for this, how far fhort he falls of
Chrift, of Chrifts thoughts, Chrifts prayers, Chrifts fpeeches, Chrifts meeknefs,
but only patches up his comforts with fome ends of Gold and Silver, and fhreds
of Honefty : He hath heard others teach and preach, and gets fome fhreds of
knowledge, thence he fees what others are, and do, and gets fomewhat to be
like them. Have we not cryed out, men are too good to be better in our own
Land ? And unleffe a few under Affliction or Temptation, who is ? I pray
God fuch a race come not over hither, where God looks you fhould get a higher
pitch ; put off your wildernesse-fhoes, get thofe fins removed that provoked God
there ; or elfe befides the mifery of a heart-brand upon thee, thou doft not look
for Chrift, and therefore are either not efpoufed, or afleep ; and fhalt if not by
the Word, by the terrour of God be dreadfully awakened. Oh *New-England,*
New-England, that art now making a conqueft of the world, and feekeft for the
fpoyl of it to enrich thy felf, to recover thy loffes, and therefore makeft a truce
with thy diftempers for a time, and doft not purge thy felf as Chrift is pure, I dare
not yet tell thee what Chrift Jefus hath to fay unto thee ! Therefore think of this,
if not thus, you have no hope, 'tis but talk and notion in thy head. And you
that do not, he fhall come in a time when thou lookeft not for him : And haft
not fo much Grace as the five foolifh Virgins had ? This is the frame of men
and Profeffors, what are they ? They were troubled, humiliation is paft, they
have looked for falvation by Chrift, that is paft ; they have been comforted,
that is paft ; What Holineffe ? They will pray in Families, keep company with
Saints, get into Chrift, receive Sacraments, that is paft. What lack they yet ?
Many wants, but God accepts their defires for what they want, and that is their
Circle of Honefty now, and there reft. Is it not thus ? Is this to purge like
Chrift ? If any have more, Oh wonder at the Lord for it. But if not , Oh thy
doom !

SECT. VI.

OH you efpoufed and beloved of the Lord, look for his coming, look for his
company ; the world looks not for him, becaufe they care not for him. *Will*
you alfo depart ? Hath he called thee as a Virgin forfaken, and not comforted, as
a wife of youth, and given himfelf to thee, and given thee a heart to give content
to him, and thy felf to him in lieu of his love, life and all, if it might do him any
good ? Oh are you born to fo great hopes, and are they not worth the looking after ? God forbid. Do this therefore efpecially in thefe five Cafes.

1. In cafe of ftrangeneffe felt between thy foul and Chrift : It may be thou
thinkeft, Oh he that hath faved, preferved me, called me, when I never lookt
after him, redeemed me when a captive, every moment pardons me , a daily
friend unto me, that hath given me Ordinances, given me the comfort of them :
But Oh yet to be a ftranger to him, this cuts : Oh look now for this time, 1 *Th.*
4.17,18. When thou fhalt fee that bleeding heart, that hath loved thee above
all Princes and Angels, that body in the Glory of the Father, and be as familiar
with him as thou art with any friend, and fee his Glory, and the Father in him, and
know as thou art known. Oh look for this, for it fhall be fo.

2. In

2. In case Gods promises are not made good to thee. For at that instant a man beleeves he gives Christ and all things, all Grace, all consolation, all Glory, but 'tis in the promise, because he would have them live by Faith a while here, as by sence in Heaven; and being wrapt up in the promise, they feel it not, only plead with God: Hast not said Lord, thou wilt subdue iniquities, purge me as Gold is tried? Why then do I go childlesse, gracelesse? No more Grace, no more Spirit, no better heart for thee? Oh now the heart calls in question Gods promise or sinks! Oh now remember this day, for the perfect restitution of all things, perfect accomplishment of all promises is reserved for this time, *Isa.*25.9. Thou prayest for many things, but they come not; Christ reserves the payment till this day. What a comfort is this? What a sweet speech was it of *Joshua*, Josh.23.14. *One thing hath not failed*, when he had conquered the Land. So then when the conquest is made, to see all the promises made good to thee.

3. In case of Gods absence or withdrawing, or when thou feelest but little of his presence here in his Providences or in his Ordinances, private, publick, and that in *New-England* too. Thou hast found one half hours time with the Lord, alone, sweeter and better than a thousand worlds. Oh but this holds not! Thou maist it may be wait on the Lord in his Ordinances, and go away with a sad heart, Oh I cannot see him, and canst not find out the cause why so heavy, and vile, and so loathest thy self, Oh now think of this day, 1 *Cor.*15.28. Then God shall be *all in all*, then thou shalt have thy fill of love, and fill of God.

4. In case of sorrow for the uproar of the world against God and Christ, and the wrongs done to Christ and his people; to see Christ crucified, and crying spare my life, and saying, *If you seek me, let these little ones depart*, yet they are abused, and every one against Christ, as this day the world is coming to the last fit of madnesse against the Lord of Glory. Oh now, remember and look for this day, 1 *Cor.*15.25. *He must reign.* Lord what a comfort will it be to see Christ King then? Men come to see him King here, but Oh what will it be when he shall come himself? To see all secrets open, and the Lord glorified in himself and people, of all creatures. Look for this, to see the great and last plot of God brought to perfection. Oh think that is our day, that is our victory!

5. When you come to die, and to think of leaving thy carcase to rot in the dust a long time; Oh think and look upon this day! *They that hear shall live.* Why do I die? John 5.28,29. *They shall then come out of their graves*, &c. Thus look for this.

Motives.

1. All creatures look for this in a manner, *Rom.* 8. 22, 23. Nay Christ and Saints in Heaven look for this day, *Heb.*10.13. *From thence expecting till his enemies*, &c. Nay Devils look for it, but tremble: Only a secure world rockt asleep to their eternal wo, look not for it.

2. This will help you to ride all storms, bear all knocks chearfully. Our Hope is our Helmet. Our Hope is our Anchor, *Heb.*6.19. *Eph.*6.17. You will meet with them here it may be before you die.

3. The Lord hath called you out of this world, he might have left you in it, and given you your hope, your portion here, and then wo to thee, but he hath called thee to this hope, that if Princes of the world knew, they would lay down, my crt away their Crowns at thy feet for it, and say, Oh that I were in that mans case! *Eph.*1.18. *Hope of his calling.*

4. Hope and expectation of all other things shall fail, if God loves thee, he will make you know what 'tis to forsake your portion. If not, they shall fail you when you die, this shall not; it *makes not ashamed.*

5. Me-thinks this is the Glory of a Christian, that he turns his back upon the world, and lives and waits for the coming of the Lord.

6. Oh this will give Christs heart full content, when he shall come, *Luke* 12.37.

O

He

He will make thee sit down to eat, and serve thee. The Lord Jesus himself shall only then poure out to thee and give thee whatever thou callest for, honour thee as it were above himself. When thou art at rest in Heaven, he will be at work for thee.

7. If not, *he may come in an hour thou lookest not for him.* Christ may say to thee, from henceforth sleep on.

*Quest.
Answ.*

What Means are there to make me look for him?

1. Get some promise that thou maist beleeve the Lord is thine, else thou wilt never look for him; or if you do, you will be deceived, for *hope is of things not seen.* Nay, commonly when the Lord brings any man to his hopes, having given him a promise, and Faith to beleeve it, the Lord in the mid-way seems to cross his promise. When the Lord promiseth life, glory, peace, honour, joy, fulness, Heaven, they shall then and never so much before feel darkness, death, shame, trouble, sorrow, Hell. For the Lord tries them by this, and *tribulation breeds experience, and experience hope.* Hence you must first get a promise of Christ and Glory, before you can hope for it, or expect Glory, and then you may, *Heb.6.18.* For the promise will support hope, when heart, and strength and all shall fail: Nay it will expect contraries out of contraries, *Gen. 22.5. I'le come again to you.* Compared with *Heb.11.18,19.* So that soul that hath a promise, may say when he considers Gods power, and what Glory he gives to God by beleeving it, God hath said he will comfort me, he will cleanse me, he will give me Glory, I will have all these out of my sorrow, my sin, my Hell.

Take heed therefore of two extreams.

First, Of hoping without a promise, for that is but Faith scared out of its wits, when it comes to be examined; I hope so, and I have had joy and perswasion of it.

Secondly, Of not expecting when God gives a promise. Can you live one day without it? It may be you have no feeling yet: But *Isa.25.8,9,10.* Dost wait for the Lord? *i. e.* From a sense of emptinesse, for all fulnesse thou shalt find it in part here, and fully then, and say, *Lo, this is our God, we have waited for him!* When a mans anchor is strong, and in good ground, he will look for safety, when at anchor in the Harbour. Oh thou afflicted, tossed with tempests, the Lord hath brought thee at last to Christ, after many drivings to and fro, and it clasps about him according to a promise; if God changeth then thy comfort may not be. If revelations come, I know they may deceive, but a promise cannot.

2. Fear the terrour of the Lord at this day, fear parting from him: I speak not of doubting, but the holy fear of Saints, for that is the nature of fear, it makes a man eye the thing feared: As *Jacob* when *Esau* was meeting of him. *Noah* he fears and looks to safety in and by an Arke, *Heb.11.7. Lots* children took not his counsel, they feared not, but *he seemed as one that mocked to them.* Paul *2 Cor.5.10,11. knew the terrour of the Lord,* hence looked for him, sought to approve himself unto him. Men that fear not parting with Christ, will never look nor care for him. And let it be a strong fear, else it will never carry you above your cares and surfettings of the world.

How shall I fear thus?

*Quest.
Answ.*

1. Unlesse the Lord put it into your heart, none can; for the security of the world is not sleepy, but deadly: Men are bound up as strong as with chains of death; that till they feel the misery, they cannot fear it strongly. Oh look up to the Lord to unchain those chains of death.

2. Know the happinesse of them that shall ever be with Christ, what is the sweetnesse of Christs love, and worth of it. Imagine the last day come, and all the dead raised, Christ with flaming fire, all the wicked on the left hand, and then sent away with *depart ye cursed*; all the Saints on the right hand, and then

Oh

Oh come! and when all is difpatched, then to go up to Heaven, and when gone, there to be for ever rejoycing, triumphing in the prefence of God Almighty; and now what it will be to be far off from Chrift, weeping, never to be pitied more. Oh he that was fo full of pity, no heart then to pity, no hand to help? I can but only paint this fire. Oh that the Lord would help you here, that fo you might look out for him. Saylors fleep in calms, and fo it may be have many here in this place of reft. Others of you take heed, Ile tell you your bar, It may be moft eftates are brought low and funk; when you fee that, now you either look back, or look for Lots accomodations, and fuch an eftate as is loft, it may be you will fpy fome hope of it, and then follow the game, and never look out till you die. The Lord keep you from it! You then will not look up for Chrifts coming at the laft day, or in his Ordinances here: If thou doft fo, had it not been better thou hadft been buried in the Sea, or left in forrow on the Shore? Oh take heed therefore, look for the coming and company of Chrift, and let this be enough, and becaufe you cannot look for him in the the clouds now, Oh look and wait for him in his Ordinances; and confider if efpoufed ones look for his coming then, and for perfect knowledge of him, and communion with him, then think, Lord what a heart have I that look not for him here! But Lord who will believe our report?

Thus they went out by hope and expectation of his coming: Now the Second thing follows, they went forth with longing defires after his coming.

CHAP. XI.

That Believers do long and defire for the appearance and Second Coming of Chrift.

SECT. I.

Doct. 3.

THat all thofe that are efpoufed to Chrift, and beloved of Chrift, they ought not only to look, but to long for the coming of, and their everlafting communion with the Lord Chrift Jefus. For the confummation of their marriage with him, that though he be gone, our hearts may be with him, before our fouls be, or before our fouls and bodies be; that though we may die, and lie down in the duft, our defires may live and lie in Heaven, and cry come Lord. Now do not think this point true, and fo far good if we could reach it, but this is a high pitch, for you muft long for it. God forbid a Chriftian efpoufed to Chrift, fhould plead that work too much, which Hypocrites, the five foolifh Virgins in their kind attained to. See Prefidents for this in all ages: Abraham, and thofe in his time, who was Father of the Faithful, Heb. 11. 15, 16. A better Countrey, where they might have fellowfhip with the Lord, and hence God is not afhamed, &c. As if the Lord were afhamed of all them to be his people, that profeffe themfelves fo, but defire not this. In Chrift's time, Simeon, Luke 2. 29. with 25. Where he waited for the confolation of Ifrael, &c. to enjoy more of him. In the Apoftles time, 'tis alfo that which they all felt, 2 Cor. 5. 2. In this we groan earneftly, &c. But you will fay, It may be this was becaufe of miferies, and want of Ordinances, &c. Therefore fee in the laft age of the Church, when the new Jerufalem was built, and when peace, and when Chrift's face was feen in his Houfe, yet then the Spirit and the Bride fay come, Rev. 22. 17. They are the laft breathings of *John* and the Spirit in him. *Lord Jesus come quickly.* But *Cant.8. 14.* The Church there intreats her Beloved to *fly away to the Mountains of Spices,* that she might enjoy him out of this world.

SECT. II.

Reaf. 1.

1 BEcause they are bound to love Christ and his appearing: to love his looks when he shall appear to the world, 2 *Tim.4.8.* The *Crown of Glory* comes as it were by succession, not only to me, but to *all them that love his appearing.* Now can there be any love of him and his appearing; and not so much as any desire after him and after it? Certainly there is no love, or if there be any, it lies languishing: For answerable to our love to any thing, is our desire, what we love only, we desire only; what we love not at all, or but little, we desire not at all, or but little: so here. Now therefore to question, May a Christian desire it? is to question whether a Christian ought to love the Lord Jesus or no. We are bound not to love earth, hence bound to love Christ and his fellowship in Heaven. *Let him be Anathema* that doth not so.

Reaf. 2.

2. Because the Lord Jesus longs for them, *John 17.24.* Throughout which Chapter he prays as if in Heaven already. *Hence I am no more in this world, and where I am, let them be also.* He was on earth, but looks on himself as in Heaven. That as it was with the High Priest, he carries the Names of the twelve Tribes on his heart, *beset with precious Stones*; very dear to him, *into the Holy of Holies,* so Christ. Not that he sees any beauty in them of their own, why he should desire them, but because he freely loves them, and dearly loves them, as being given him of the Father, and as having cost him dear; and hence if he loves them, he longs for them: Now if he longs for them, ought not they much more to long for him? Psal.27.8. *Thou saidst seek my face, thy face Lord will I seek.*

1. He longs for thee now in Glory, when one would think his thoughts and heart should be swallowed up with it, and shall not we long for him here in the valley of Myrtle trees, in misery, on the dunghill?

2. He longs for thee when thou hast nothing to make him desire thee, he hath all that thy heart can desire, being the very bosom-delight of God himself, *Rev. 22. penult.* He did but say he would come, and *John* desires, Oh come. But doth he long for thee? Now not to long for him. If this love be not worth longing for, truly 'tis worth nothing.

Reaf. 3.

3. Because this is our last and ultimate end that we are made for, chosen for, bought for, called for, sealed for, that at last we might be with the Lord, and be made perfect in one, 2 Cor. 5.5. *He that hath made us for this is God,* &c. For the whole Trinity enjoying infinite sweet fellowship with himself, hence desire it might be communicated, in Christ 'tis so, and now the last end is attained. Now if this be our last end, ought we not to desire it? Then we ought not to desire to be blessed, nor to desire the Lord may be glorified. Nay you know that whatever we make our last end, it will swallow up all our desires after any other thing. This is the Center and rest and journeys end of our tired weary spirits. And the truth is, when we make it our last end, we cannot but desire it.

SECT.

SECT. III.

BUT ought not a man to defire to live here in this world as *David* and *Hezekiah* did. May not one fin in this defire?

1. 'Tis true, *precious in the fight of the Lord is the death of his Saints*, not only in regard that they are as precious to him when they come to die, as while they live, as Gold when 'tis melting is as precious to the Goldfinith, as when whole, and it may be more too, becaufe 'tis then made better; but alfo becaufe he will not lightly caft away their lives. He that bottles their tears, and will not let them be loft, will not eafily let go their lives, and if God will not, they ought not upon every flight occafion to defire their death, and loffe of their lives to be with the Lord.

Now there are two cafes Gods own people may not defire to remove hence, where though there be fome fire I confeffe, yet there is more fmoak than fire, more fin than Grace.

1. In cafe they meet with much unkindneffe from, and many forrows in the world, and behold the fins of it. Thus it was with *Elias*, 1 *Kings* 19.4. Who when *Jezabel* threatned his life, fled, and would needs fet fail prefently and be gone; fo 'tis with Gods people, when they fee enemies without, the univerfal rot of Profeffion, that they think they are almoft left alone; when God hath begun to do good by them, as by *Elijah*, but they think their beft daies are paft, there is all they fhall do, and God himfelf it may be meeting them with fome croffes in this world; now prefently they grow weary of their lives, and defire to die, which is nothing elfe but a pang of difcontent, truly God will not fuffer it, nor you ought not to defire it, to die away in fuch a fnuffe: No, the Lord hath work for them to do, and a journey to go. This defire is naught, and 'tis but a weed, and to be pulled up, that growes out of fuch a root as a difcontented heart for croffes. I confeffe God ufeth forrows as means to fmoak us out of our Hive, and we may ufe them for that end, but not only or chiefly them, nor from a pang or moody fit of difcontent.

2. In cafe they defire death, and not life, before they be ripe for death. Husbandmen defire their Corn in, but 'tis follyto defire it before it be ripe, and then they may. I confeffe 'tis the commendation of fome trees, if not only good, but if ripe betimes, and 'tis the honour of a Chriftian, to be ripe for death betimes; yet ftill before he is ripe he is not to defire it.

Now when is this?

1. While the Lord hides his face and denies full affurance of his love, in this cafe as a Chriftian cannot, fo he ought not (if it were the Lords will) defire to be gone as yet, and this is one reafon why *David* and *Hezekiah* defired life, not death as yet, God had broken their bones, and his arrowes were yet in their hearts; now a man is to defire he may ftay a little while longer, that he may *fing the Song of the Lamb*, and tell the world *what the Lord hath done for him*, and that he may not fet in a cloud and die in horrour. Mariners long to be on fhore, but before they come there, they would not venture in a mift, but fee Land firft, fo fhould we defire to fee the Lord in the Land of the living. Nay though the Lord gives his people a promife, which ftaies their hearts and is a twig to keep them from finking, nay when he gives them fome joy, yet ftill God hath promifed to reveal more of himfelf and his Chrift in the promife, feeing him but darkly now: Now they ought not to defire but wait, as in *Simeons* cafe, *now let thy Servant depart in peace*, having long *waited for the confolation of Ifrael*. Children that will be up before 'tis day muft be whipt, a rod is moft fit for them, ftay till 'tis day.

2. While their work remains unfinifhed, and the Lord hath got little or no

Glory from them, though they may have clear evidence of the Lords love. Chrift himself defired it not till now, *John* 17.5. If thou couldeft fcale Heaven before thy work was done, the Lord would fend thee down from thence again, as he did the foul of *Lazarus*, and truly to do the work of Chrift one moment here, is better than to have a thoufand years felicity in Heaven, nakedly confidered in it felf, in as much as the Honour of Chrift is a thoufand times better than our own good. It may be there is much work within doors, many odd diftempers to be cafhierd, fpirituall decaies, *&c.* It may be there is work without, Chrift hath many enemies in the world, many prayers are yet to be fpent againft them, much good to do for his Church, many tears to be fhed for them, for praying trade is paft in Heaven. It may be fome friends yet to be converted, thou haft been a fcandal to them, it may be as yet few have been, or can fay they be the warmer or better for thee ; that work is yet to be done : It may be God hath fome fecrets to reveal by thee before thou dieft, ftay therefore a while, while your work is done ; 'Tis true, thou haft but one Talent, but little thou haft or canft do ; yet God looks you fhould improve it whilft he is gone. A man that will needs to bed at noon-day, before night comes, what deferves he but a cudgel ? So he that will die before his night comes, and while 'tis light to fee and work by. When therefore you apprehend your work even done, then as not only Chrift, but *Paul*, not only *Paul*, but Gods watchful fervants have fecret warnings of death. And as Mariners when they can fee no Land, yet by their foundings can tell they are near Land or Sands, then you may defire it, for then you are ripe, but its fin to do it otherwife. And verily happy is that man that accounts not his life dear, but only the finifhing of his courfe with joy. To conclude all, we are to defire our fellowfhip with Chrift, as a man defires his laft end, which defire doth not exclude but include defire after all the means and the means firft, before the end. Now many things are to be done by God upon us, and by us for the Lord again, before we appear before Chrift, which we may defire firftly for this our laft end.

SECT. IV.

HEnce we fee the vilenefle of the great, yet hidden fecret fin of the whole world, which may be in part alfo in Gods deareft Saints, *viz.* in their hungry luftings and dropfie defires after the fweet of the things of this world. You fhall have many a man that amends his life, reformes his courfe, forfakes his own righteoufnefle, no mans tongue can tell him, his own Confcience cannot bear witnefle againft him that he lives in any unlawful courfe ; and I believe it is fo, and may be and will be fo. Shall I tell you therefore what hurts them? They are inordinate luftings after lawful things in themfelves, and thefe they ferve, *Tit.*3. 3. Partly they grieve them if they do not fatisfie and ferve them, partly becaufe they pay them with pleafures and delights if they do. Hence *ferving lufts and pleafures* too, thefe like tops of mountains are feen, now when floods of wickednefle begin to abate, thefe will continue while the life lafts.

I intend not to fhew you at large, but according to my Text the vilenefle of them.

1. They eat out all defire after the Lord Jefus and his fellowfhip, that he cannot long for the Lord Jefus. For a man can lay out no more than he hath, now when his defires are lavifht and let out to other things, How can he lay out any on Chrift? And thus the Lord of Glory comes to bear moft horrible contempt, that he is not worth defiring in fuch a mans Books. Thus it was with them, *Luke* 14.18. *Every one refufed.* Why? Becaufe of their Oxen, and Wives, and Farms; Lawful things, but they lufted too much after thefe. When a Harlot

feeks

seeks to satisfie her lusts, she cares not how far her Husband be off, never desires his coming home; so here: Many a one complains he cannot desire the Lord Jesus, which I confesse is in mercy to some. But where is the cause of it? Oh they are running in another channel, and spent on other things: What a heavy curse is this? Some never think of death once in a Moon, much lesse long for Christ; desire not his fellowship here, much lesse there. And why? Because of their lusts that eat out all.

2. Suppose they do not thus, but your heart is divided, so that you long for these things now, and preserve your longing for him against you come to die; yet these will make you lose his sweet fellowship. For a mans affections are precious things, and 'tis pity any else should have them, they are all little enough for Christ, and Christ is worth desiring and longing for, and he stands upon it, and will make them know that have him, that all is too little for him, and they shall give him all before he give himself to their comfort. Hence deny him these, and never think to have himself, and his fellowship, Psal.73.25,26. *Its good for me to draw nigh.* How? By desiring, not Earth nor Heaven, but him. Hence he saith, *Thou destroyest all them that go a whoring from thee,* v.27.

3. Suppose thou shouldst have him at last, yet he will never desire thee, never take any delight in thee, until that you come to get your affections unloosed here, *Psal.*45.10,11. Dost not find a strangenesse between Christ and thy soul? Doth he not hide his face? Doth he not soon depart from thee, though he appears somtimes to thee? Doth he not let thee lie like a Broom behind the door? And doth little by thee either within or without. And is not this a sad and heavy thing? Why saist thou, doth the Lord deal thus with me? Oh thy heart is yet after thy Fathers house, if thou didst forget it, then he would *take pleasure in thy beauty.* What pleasure can earth give thee, when the Lord takes no pleasure in thee?

But may not a man desire these things? If we may, how far? *Object. Answ.*

I. A man may lawfully desire them, provided his desires are not swallowed up in them, but run through them to Christ himself. For 'tis not lust properly to desire a creature, or any pleasure in it; but to desire it for it self, and for pleasures sake. For now a man makes a god of it. Thus it was with the *Israelites,* Exod.17. *Give us water that we may drink*; so give me sleep that I may rest, give me cloaths that I may be warm, give me estate that I may be rich, &c. Now when a heart desires them, but his desires end not there, but run through them to Christ, that he flings down all comforts, and saith what is this to fellowship with Christ: Thus far a man may desire and rejoyce in them, and 'tis a sin to do otherwise. *Nehem. 9. 35.* A man may be content to have a Spring run through his ground to the Sea, to be swallowed up there, but to swell, and rise, and overflow his ground and house, that's not safe, he may be drowned so: So men come to be drowned in their lusts, that let them swell within doors.

II. A man may desire them, if he doth not spend more desire upon them than they be worth. A man may desire them for a good end as he thinks, but then he laies out too much upon them. A man may spend too much in his Inne, when he takes it up only as a way to his home.

1. They are perishing things, therefore let them have perishing desires. *The world passeth away.* They are passengers by us, that stay to rest with us for a time, let them have passengers welcome.

2. They are not necessary things, let them have therefore indifferent desires: I must have Christ, and his Spirit, &c. not these things: They are to be sought not in the first, but in the second place. Therefore say first Christ, now let me have Christ: Men say now these things, then Christ. I say now the Lord Jesus, whether ever you have them or no.

III. Now all superfluity of evil desires are to be crucified, Gal.5.24. *They that are*

are in Christ , have crucified , &c. Chriſt was not a dead, but firſt a crucified Chriſt before : So no Saint living, but he hath ſome ſuperfluous deſires, but though they live, they do crucifie them, ſo ought you. There is two things in crucify-ing.

1. There is extream pain upon the Croſs.
2. A looking for death : So then luſts are crucified,
1. When you taſt the bitterneſſe of your luſts, by putting them on Chriſts Croſſe. Oh the wrong ; they have done the Son of God ! And do this with vio-lence, ſay, you ſhall to the Croſſe, he that looks to Chriſt with a frolick heart to kill his luſts, ſhall never find him.

2. Now looking and longing for their death, by holding them there. Unleſs the Blood of Chriſt ſlay theſe, I will never have any death for them. For all the reaſon in the world will never kill a luſt, no more than all the reaſon will per-ſwade the Stomach not to hunger. The Belly hath no ears.

Thus you are to moderate your deſires after theſe things : Which I ſpeak of,

First, Becauſe 'tis a wilderneſs-ſin, *Pſal.*106.14,15. Which it may be you feel brings leanneſſe on your ſoul. And

Secondly, Becauſe 'tis the ſin of proſperity and peace which God hath given us, which will grow up and choak the Word, that all Ordinances and Truths will in time be ſapieſſe, ſavourleſſe things unto us.

Thirdly, Becauſe I have had ſtrong fears lately of ſome unexpected trials among us, and I ſhould be glad if it might not be, if the freedom from them might make us better, elſe I ſay let them come. But

Fourthly, Becauſe 'tis a rare thing among us to ſee ſuch burning Lamps as look and long for Chriſts coming, which when I conſider, though there be other cauſes, yet one great one is this, Oh the heart is gone away by violent luſts after theſe things here ! Oh therefore take heed of them ! And therefore conſider,

1. You ſhall have Chriſt and his fellowſhip, if indeed you long for him, *John* 4. 10. That's his love, you are not ſo deſirous, but he is a thouſand times more Thou maiſt deſire theſe things, and if God loves thee miſſe of them. God will make thee poor when thou wouldſt be rich, baſe when thou wilt be honoured, and when you would have honey, he will give you ſtings ; and cauſe you have to thank the Lord too, that he will not give you your portion here.

2. If thou haſt them, and doſt deſire them, and God gives them, and thou letteſt Chriſt go, thou hadſt better a thouſand times be without them, Pſal.78.30, 31. *The meat was in their mouths, and the wrath of God came upon them.* If the Lord gives thee Chriſt, happy for ever ; if theſe things when thou doſt ſo deſire them, oh wo for ever !

3. The Fellowſhip of the Lord Jeſus thou ſhalt never loſe. Death ſhall not part thee from that, nothing ſhall rob thee of that ; but look after and long for theſe things, they will periſh and die away. *All fleſh is graſſe, the Word of the Lord,* and the Lord himſelf much more *endureth for ever.*

4. Why doſt deſire theſe things ? For ſome ſweet in them. Why is not all that in the preſence of the Lord Jeſus , and enjoying him ? *It pleaſeth the Father that in him ſhould all fulneſſe dwell,* ſo that thou ſhalt drink as out of a pure Foun-tain all that is there. If there be any ſweetneſſe here , he gave it, 'tis much more eminently in himſelf, Exod. 24. 11. *They ſaw the God of Iſrael , and eat and drank.* Had they meat up with them ? Oh no. But the ſight of him was meat and drink and all unto them. As therefore you deſire Chriſts fellowſhip, Oh long no more after theſe things here !

Uſe 2. Hence ſee death is not to be feared, but deſired of all Saints. It was an odd ſpeech of a Heathen, *'Tis ill to deſire death, and worſe to fear it* ; he meant not be-cauſe of any good in it, but becauſe we muſt die : But death brings us into eter-nal

nal Fellowship with the Lord Jesus. It doth Saints more good than all Ordinances, all afflictions, (wherein we complain we can get no good) than all means. It brings us into his Fellowship, 1. Quickly, as Christ was caught up, so the Soul by Christ to himself. 2. Immediately, for the next thing we shall see is Christ himself, our Husband himself, and then see the Kingdom, and then wonder at the Lord. 3. Everlastingly, never to part more. Oh fear it not therefore, Christ hath sweetned it to you.

SECT. V.

use 3.

HEnce see a clear foundation and ground-work of longing for fellowship with the Lord Jesus in his Ordinances here. This is that I shall exhort to. For

1. You cannot, shall not, must not now go to him in Heaven, nor enjoy fellowship with him, nor meet him in the clouds though you do long for that day; but in his Ordinances you may meet with him now. And truly those whom we love and long for, if we cannot go to their house, or find them at home, we are glad to meet with them abroad. As with those who stand before Princes, if we cannot be with them on the Throne, or at Court, we will desire to be with them in the Countrey, Nay on the Dunghil. Oh the Spirit of *David!* Psal. 27.4. *One thing have I desired, and that I will seek for,* though I never have it. What is that *David?* Is it to wear the Crown in *Jerusalem?* Is it to have all thine enemies lick the dust of thy feet? Is it to have thy Name spread, and thine Honour great through all the Kingdomes of the world? No, but *that I may dwell in the Courts of the Lords House all the daies of my life,* and that seeing I cannot, shall not die presently, and so go to see his Glory in Heaven, therefore that I may see his Beauty here, enjoy him here, and that not for some years, but all the daies of my life.

2. Ought you not to long to taste and passe through the sorrows of death, that you may be with him? And are Christs Ordinances more bitter than death, that you are loath to break through the difficulty of them, that in them you may enjoy him? The truth is so 'tis with many a man, that such is the strength of his hidden contempt of Christ, and his love to his sloath, that he had rather die than pray, and be damned eternally than to follow the Lord in an Ordinance till he hath found him graciously. How come Gods own people to lament this, if there were not this?

3. I remember a sweet speech of one with God, *That a Christian ought to prepare for a Sacrament as he would prepare to die, for,* saith he, *there is but this difference, when we die we then go to Christ, in a Sacrament Christ comes to us.* What he said of a Sacrament, I say of every Ordinance, in every Ordinance Christ comes to us, when we die we go to him. Now ought you to long when you are absent from him to be with him, and will you not care for him, nor long to see him and enjoy him when he comes to you? And so be worse than poor naked *Indians,* Christ comes not to them, no dews fall down on their *Gilboahs,* no Manna at their Tent doors, and hence they live without him, and desire him not; and when he comes to you, do you see no beauty in him now why you should desire him? Will you thus require him for his love, *oh foolish* children *and unwise?*

4. Truly Beloved, you can have but little evidence you do desire the Lord Jesus company in Heaven at the last day, that long not vehemently after him in his Ordinances now. *You have followed me in the regeneration,* saith Christ, *Mat.19. 28.* therefore *you shall sit with me upon Thrones.* If Christs presence here, a little of himself be burdensom, What will it be in Heaven then? *Depart from me,* saith Christ, *I was in prison and you visited me not.* Shall you depart for not visiting an imprisoned, persecuted, sick, sorrowful Christ in midst of miseries, and shall

not you depart for not visiting a comforting Christ, a teaching Christ, an intreating, embracing Christ in the midst of his Ordinances. If the Lord tries you with water, with a little of himself here, and you care not for him, long not after him, and hence let all leak out again, How shall the Lord trust you with wine? with full fruition of himself in Heaven?

5. Oh Beloved have you ever found him in his Ordinances? If not, Oh the heavy wrath of the Lord Jesus upon thee: If you have, if ever he hath comforted thee when sad and sorrowful, if ever quickned thee when death and darknesse did lie upon thee, if ever he did deliver thee when distressed, Oh then take heed of despising him in his Ordinances now, but long for him again, *That I may see thee as I have seen thee*, Psal.63.2. Let them that never found him, deal so with him. *Peter* when he saw Christs Glory on the Mount, *Lord* saith he, *'tis good for us to be here*. Hath the Lord ever transfigured himself before thee, so as he hath appeared in another manner to thee in his Ordinances than ever thou sawest before? Then say, seeing Lord I cannot come to Heaven to thee, 'tis good being in the Mount, in thy Ordinances with thee, its good being here, 1 *Pet*.2.2,3,4. I know Brethren you have many employments in the world, and are called away to them, and cannot ever be with the Lord, yet let your longings be there, nay though cast out of Gods sight, yet look to the Temple; this will give you peace.

6. This if I may have leave to speak plainly, is the great sin, one of them, of *New-England*. Men come over hither for Ordinances, and when they have them neglect them; or if it be too horrible to live in a grosse neglect of them, yet who maintains his Fellowship with Christ? or longing after the Fellowship of Christ in them? And therefore I shall stay a while on this point. Men that are sick of consumptions have somtimes a mighty stomach after meat, and when 'tis brought them, they are weary of the very smell of it, and then say, truly I had thought I could have eaten so much; so men loath Ordinances, nay the Cooks that dresse, and the Dish that brings, and the Ministry of Christ Jesus that provides the meat, because consuming and pining away in their iniquities. I know many use Ordinances, but are they not indifferent whether they find him therein or no? Now,

1. When men had enough by them to live comfortably upon, then God and his Ordinances were desired by them, but here mens removing begetting want, want of the creature joyned with fear and distrust of Gods Providence to provide for them and theirs, either sink their hearts, that Ordinances are not sweet, no more than *Moses* message to a people in anguish, or meat to a wounded man; or else makes them hungry after the creature, and hence lavishing out their desires, that they have none after the Lord himself.

2. When men are persecuted by enemies, driven into corners, or to Townes six miles off to find a Sacrament, or hear a Sermon, then the Gospel of peace, and them that brought the glad tidings of peace, their feet were beautiful, and then men thought if one Sabbath here so sweet where Ordinances are much corrupted, if some of them be so comfortable in the midst of enemies, Oh how sweet to enjoy them all among Saints, among Friends? And so I know they be to some, and I hope to more than I know; but *New-Englands* peace and plenty of means breeds strange security; and hence prayer is neglected here: There are no enemies to hunt you to Heaven, nor no chains to make you cry; hence the Gospel and Christ in it is sleighted. Why? Here are no soure herbs to make the Lamb sweet. And if I get no good this Sabbath, this Sermon, this Sacrament, this Prayer, I hope I shall some other time, when my heart is better, and my businesse is over: Not considering that the daies of trouble may be near, or Gods final farewel may be quickly taken.

3. It was a sad speech of a Brother lately, which hath oft affected me, *that a*

man

men may pray out, hear out all the Grace of his heart: Meaning this, when God begins to work upon a mans heart at first, then prayer and Word is sweet, stay a while they hear out their hearing, and pray out their praying, so as in praying, they pray not ; and in hearing, they hear not ! Would to God there were not a generation of those men among us, that having been so oft Sermon-trod and Prayer-beaten, that now their hearts are hardned, and being used to Ordinances, and being so long ridden under them, I wish they were not tired, and jaded under them before they come half way home, that they had rather lie & die in the high way, than get up and with mighty groans and invincible wrastlings of heart seek after, and so find the Lord in them.

4. There is no place in all the world, where there is such expectation to find the Lord, as here , and hence men blesse the Lord for our rising Sun, when 'tis setting every where else : Here therefore they come and find it not, hence not considering the great and last temptation of this place, whereby God tries his friends before he will trust them with more of himself, _viz._ deep and frequent desertions , they give in , and therefore care not for , nor desire after those plaisters which they feel heal them not, nor that food which they find nourisheth them not. 'Tis strange to see what a Faith some men have that can close with Christ as their end, and comfort themselves there; 'tis not means (say they) but Christ, not duties but Christ, and by this Faith can comfort and quiet themselves in the neglect and contempt of Christ in means, as infallible a brand of Gods eternal reprobation of such a soul as any I know. So that this is _New-Englands_ sin. Is not Prayer neglected, wanting place and heart? if not in family, is it not in secret ? so that you have none, nor poor servants have none. If any Prayer in secret, yet doth it not die? Didst ever find thy Spirit so straitned ? Where are the mighty groans ? What is become of meditation ? Dost not let Sabbaths, Sermons passe over, which shall be preacht over again at the last day, and find no Christ, no Spirit in them ; and thus lie famishing, and yet not cry for bread ? If it be not so, I am glad, God, Angels, Saints, and all the world shall call you blessed : If it be so, I dare be bold to prophesie ruine to this place and people, and that you or your posterity shall either in woods, or in the Land, or hands of your enemies in this place lament with tears the contempt of means ; and you even Disciples of Christ _shall desire to see one of the daies of the Son of man , and shall not see them._ Jer.8.13,14. _Let us go into strong holds,_ &c. I know there are many that do meet the Lord , but are you not apt to fall asleep again ? Oh therefore let me entreat you, if the Lord hath espoused you to himself, if you have any longings after him in Heaven, seeing those desires cannot be fulfilled presently, Oh long to meet him here, and so long to meet him, as that you may indeed meet with him and with more and more of him.

SECT. VI.

WHat is it to meet Christ , and to have Fellowship with him in an Ordinance ? _Quest._

I have been oft asked this, and for the sake of them that be weak, I shall give you a tast of it. _Answ._

1. Therefore look as 'tis with a man that receives any common mercy from God, from Christ, if he sees not the Lord Jesus really giving it, he enjoyes it, but not Christ in it, though he get some good out of the thing : So let a man receive more knowledge of Truths, and more Truth be discovered , more Promises revealed, more affections and life dropt into the heart, which may do a man some good, yet if he sees them as separated from Christ, if he sees not the Truth as it is in Jesus, if he sees not Promises spoken from Heaven by Jesus, if

he

he looks not on all Commands as part of the secret of Jesus, if he receive affections, and by them behold not the Lord Jesus, he doth not at that time enjoy the Lord Jesus. For he now indeed enjoyes his gifts, but by these he doth not enjoy him: And therefore then a man may be said to have fellowship with Christ in an Ordinance, when by all the light and life and comfort there, he comes to see him, and sees them all in him, and seeing a transcendent Glory in him, sees and beholds a hidden Glory in them. This Command is a secret of Jesus, this Promise the sweet voice of Jesus, these Consolations the comforts of Jesus, these Messengers the Ministers of Jesus, these Ordinances the Kingdom of Jesus. And therefore look throughout all the Scriptures, you shall see our Fellowship with Christ both in Heaven and here, 'tis exprest by *seeing of the Lord*, *John* 17.24. *Psal.*63.2. & 27.4. I have oft said to my friends, the great sin of Christians is to see Scriptures, Ordinances, Truths, Commands, Blowes, Kindnesses, as not flowing from and abiding in the Lord Jesus, to see them separate from Christ, and not Christ and them together. And hence Promises comfort not, because you receive them not as spoken by Jesus: Commands awe not, because not as the voice of Jesus: Every Truth is not dear, because you see it not as the Bridegrooms voice. Parents that have had rude children, have turned them out of doors, they themselves have sent them money and cloaths in pity, but themselves have not been seen, that they might seek for a Fathers face at last: So when God is angry with some of his people, he doth send to them in his Providences and Ordinances, because he pities them, but himself is not seen. Why? That at last they might come home, and seek to see his face again, and say, What good does all this do me, if I see no God? I confesse he that receives gifts from another, ought to be thankful; but a heart that loves and longs after the Lord, will say, here is Blessing, Means, Truth, Warmth, but Lord when wilt thou come thy self? Oh labour for this!

2. When a man feels the power of the Lord Jesus in his Ordinances; this is the second part of *Davids* desire, Psal.63.2,3. *That I may see* not only thy Glory, but *thy power*, for there is never a child of God but feels a strong party within him against Christ, so that he cannot seek Christ, cleave to Christ, live to Christ, now you will find in some Ordinances your hearts shaken and troubled for sin, and some desires and consolations stirred up, and hopes never to be as you have been: But Beloved all dies and falls down again: Now I confesse there is somwhat of Christ in all this; but yet content not your selves with this, because you want a power, or until you find a mighty power of Christ by little and little subduing sin, for when Christ comes into the heart indeed, he comes with his power, Psal.24.7,8. *The Lord of Hosts mighty in Battel. His flesh is meat indeed*, Col.1.29. Christs power works in a man mightily. If you enjoy never such comfort, but find not a power pulling down thy lusts, there is no Christ. If a man be sick, and he eats his meat, and great care be had to tend him, but the disease is stronger than the strength of nature and food; ask him, Do you eat? Yes, but it doth me no good; So here: Such comfort, such a Christ doth you no good, unlesse you feel a power. Oh long to meet Christ, and enjoy Christ thus!

Quest. How shall I do this?

Answ. 1. Mourn bitterly for the Lords absence as for one of the greatest evils that can befall thee. For Christs presence will never be sweet to him that can live without him, and can you look for him then? John 16.22. *You have now sorrow, which* he said, *filled their hearts, but I will see you again*, visit you, come down to you by my Spirit again, and you shall rejoyce, and none shall take it away: And therefore its noted, the first that had comfort was *Mary*, when she sate at the Sepulcher weeping, *John* 20.11, &c. And therefore do but observe your own hearts, when your hearts have been soaked in grief, for want of or for the absence of Christ, Oh I have lived without him, and prayed without him, and heard

without

without him, and spoke without him, him that hath pitied me, spared me, over-come me, laid down his life, sent his Spirit to me? that then you shall more or lesse see the Lord, and feel the power and presence of the Lord. Oh Beloved, shall not Heaven be sweet to you without him, and shall earth be sweeter than Heaven, that you can live here without him? Beloved, whatever you account of it now, in Hell the sting of all sorrows shall be this, Oh Christ hides his face? One frown shall be more bitter than death, than a thousand deaths, and shall it be so in Hell, and shall not many frowns, many daies be more bitter than death? Shall it be so to Devils, and not to Saints? Shall the hiding of Christs face from enemies be heavy, and shall not his friends take it to heart? If you do not, then think not to meet him, but that Word and Prayer shall be dead drink to thee; but if you do, I tell thee if he manifests himself to any, he will reveal himself to thee.

2. Prize and love his presence, his face, the lifting up of the light of his coun-tenance. Princes will not come, or if they do, not stay, if they perceive their company is a burden, and is not esteemed; no more will the Lord Jesus. They that are fallen in love together will find out each other though it be at midnight; prize Christs company, and you will not complain for want of time, and say you cannot, but you will find him out in Word, in prayers, though others be fast a-sleep, *Mat.*13.44. When the man *sells all*, now he *buyes the field*, hath it, and enjoyes it. You would have the Lords company and fellowship, I believe you; But what will you give for it? I will tell you. It may be you will give him the hearing for it, and give him a few good wishes, and a few good words, and a lit-tle leisure. But will you turn the whole world behind your back, and whatever you have out of doors, that he may come in: That now 'tis not honour, nor wealth, nor life, nor ease, nor Heaven, but him, and that not only in Heaven, but in his Swadling-clouts, his Ordinances here, beleeve it salvation is at your doors. *Zacheus* being a low man of stature, gets out of the crowd, stands in the way, and the Lord bids him come down. Do thus when you come to any Ordi-nance, I tell you 'tis better than an host of Angels compassing thee about with praises. Oh that you had the life of experience! Hast not found him better than friends, than means, than thy self? Oh that you would believe expe-rience!

3. Make it not your task but your trade to seek for him, that you may enjoy him here. Make this your businesse. Men make it not their main businesse to seek out Christ, but only some work they must dispatch by the by. They make it not their Trade but their Task which must be done. *Esau* would have the bles-sing, but 'tis his hunting that he delights in. You shall have a man that is a close worldling, come and hear, and joy therein, but his trade his heart is after that, *Ezek.*33.31. Look but on a Christian at his first conversion, what great gains gets he then? Oh 'tis his trade to follow the Lord, afterward he is idle, and then feels little, *Mat.*13.46. Like a merchant, he ventures all, and then finds. Now you shall find him, *Heb.*11.6. *He is the rewarder,* not *of them that seek him* sluggishly, but *diligently.* What do you else seek for? *Why spend you your money for that which is not bread?* Or if there be ought else that is necessary, let thy care be for him, and his care shall be for thee.

4. Look before thou comest to an Ordinance, if there be no lust, no stumbling block of iniquity that thou harbourest in thy heart, or sufferest to remain in the sight of God, *Isa.*59.1,2. I have known in experience, and seen it in Scripture, many of Gods people and others have taken on that God hides his face, &c. And this hath been found to be the cause, either some sin not yet subdued or mortified, or some sin that they have not gone for pardon of to the Blood of Christ, and so unpardoned. When both these have been removed, the Lord hath appeared, *Exod.*24.10. After the Covenant made by Blood, *they saw the God of Israel.*

Ezek.

*Ezek.14.3. Should I be enquired of by them that set the stumbling block of their iniqui-
ties? &c.* Come therefore to an Ordinance that the Lord would take away thy sin,
do not come to it that you may be comforted in your sin, so that though there be
sin in your heart, yet the Lord will not cast that in thy dish, when thou comest to
him to take it away. It may be you know none. *You know not what Spirit you are
of.* Get the Lord to discover it to thee.

5. Oh be thankful, and cleave the closer to Christ for a little : For that's the
infinite mercy and love of Christ to his people, he lets them see their end, the
height of Grace and Glory the Lord will bring them to, but makes them feel the
want of it, and tast but a little, but the first-fruits. Now there is Satans policy to
make them sleight what they have, because they have not what they would have.
Hence Christ estrangeth himself greatly ; Do you thus despise my love ; Oh
therefore cleave close to him for that little, and then see, *John* 1.50. *Thou
shalt see greater things than these, the Son of God, and Angels ascending and descending
on him.* Think that I feel or have the sense of any want of Grace, and peace,
and mercy, and Christ, Oh 'tis mercy ! That I have the Star, oh this is mercy, this
brought them to Christ himself afterward. Oh unthankfulnesse stops Gods heart !
God will never cease pouring out on thee, that art pouring out praises on him ;
for else mans kindnesse should exceed the Lords.

Thus you see the Means, now use them, and long for the Lord Jesus in them,
and so long as that you may meet him ; and do it presently, else you may seek and
not find him, and *die in your sins, John* 8.21. A sad and heavy speech. Hath
God singled you out of all people in the world to enjoy him, and will you now
forsake him, and be eaten up with your Lots, and buried in the bellies of your
Beasts, or sit grieving that your estates are sunk ? It may be Hypocrites will forsake the Lord Jesus, but *will you also depart ?* Others care not for him, others
long not after him, others give him no meeting, will you depart ? *Lord to whom
shall we go ?* Oh and long for more of him, *forget what is behind,* and hear, and
pray as if thou never didst so before, as if but new to begin. There is a plot a-
foot to make you loath Ordinances, that so God may loath you : Men that are
sick and like to die, can eat no common wholsom meat, but are now nourished by
conserves, and Alchermies, and Spirits of Gold : So when wholsom Truths of
God are despised, men are deadly sick, when any new-fangled device shall feed
their fancy. The Lord keep you from it. Oh do you love and long for the Lord
in them the more, for his Spirit, his love, his Truth, his Christ, his company,
his Grace, his consolations, and then when death comes, you shall not need to
fear it, but make it welcome, and when Conscience shall ask , Do you think to
be with the Lord ? Oh it shall be peace in thy bosom ! Lord thee have I longed
for, thee have I sought for, wept for here, because I could not come to thee presently in Heaven. Now Lord let me come to thee, and so go triumphing to Glory.

SECT. VII.

Hence we see no Christian ought to content himself with any measure of
knowledge or fellowship with the Lord Jesus here. For if full, perfect and
immediate fellowship with him in Heaven and at last day ought to be the mark he
aimes at , and journies end of all his desires, then he is not to sit down in the
mid-way, but to breath, and aspire after still more and more of him. Thus *Paul,*
though fully sealed with the Spirit , yet he makes this his mark, *Phil.*3.14,15,
16. 1 *Pet.*1.10,11,12,13. The Apostle tels them the Prophets looked after
*the Grace given in their times, therefore gird up your loyns , and hope perfectly for
Grace to be given you at the revelation of Christ Jesus.* Men that have preferment in
their

their eye, and are to come on by degrees to it, never content themselves with any (though they will not sleight what they have) until they come to their highest: You are born to great hopes, sleight not what you have, but look after more, 2 *Pet.*3.18.

Hence three sorts are to be greatly blamed. For as 'tis with sinful lusts, so 'tis with spiritual, they are endlesse, infinite, and unsatiable, if they want, they are not satisfied; if they have, they are whet on in their appetites after more. Oh let it be so here!

1. Some there be that are so far from thirsting after more of him, that they have forsaken his fellowship, and lie still content it should be so. Time was while horrour was upon their Consciences, trouble in their minds, and heat of affection lasted, that their prayers were many, their tears abundant, they could not take their rest in the night, but pray they must, they could not hear of a Sermon, but through wet and dry to it; and it may be the Lord *drew them with the cords of a man,* and laid meat before them, and sweetned their labours with great hopes to them; but the Father not having drawn them with an invincible power, and knit them by an indissolluble union to Christ, they are now fallen off from Christ, *John* 6.66. And if you observe it, he looks not after them, speaks not one word to them, because content to be without him. Would to God this were not the temper of Saints that know it was better with you once than now, and God *hedgeth your way with thorns,* and gives you no rest. But Oh the grievous wracks of Professours! One can see some Boards and Planks at low water, but that's all, *Jer.*2.13,14. The Lord will fetch you home if he loves you, by weeping Crosse.

2. Some there are that fall not to forsake the Lord, but like the door on the hinge, and wheel on the pin, hang and turn about where they did. This Gods own people are very apt to do, and hence the Apostle wisheth them to take heed of it, from a dreadful Argument, *Heb.*6.4, 5,6,7.

First, Because the Lord at first conversion drawes his people sweetly, drives them gently; being weak and young Infants, as yet keeps them in his armes, that they may find a greater good in him than in the world: But afterward he suffers Satan to tempt, himself deserts them, leads through a wildernesse of sinnes and miseries, that they may know what is in their own hearts. Hence now if they will have mercy, they must fetch it, fight for it, and overcome, now hence sloath is apt to prevail for a time, as with the Disciples.

Secondly, Because before they have Christ, they feel a total want, afterward but a partial, & hence apt to be ful & self-confident in what they have, their stomachs are staid by some bits,& hence the Lord is fain to withdraw the feeling of all that which they had before, that they feeling how soon that vanisheth, might hunger after more; as the Disciples could have been content with Christs being upon earth with them, *then* saith he, *the Spirit will not come*, hence away he goes, that they might have more of him in the Spirit. But this is too common with many Hypocrites.

1. When men serve their turn of Christ. There is never a Hypocrite living but closeth with Christ for his own ends, for he cannot work beyond his Principle. Now when men have served their own turns out of another man, away they go, and keep that which they have. An Hypocrite closeth with Christ as a man with a rich shop; he will not be at cost to buy all the shop, but so much as serves his turn. Commonly men in horrour seek for so much of Christ as will ease them, and hence professe and hence seek for so much of Christ as will credit them, and hence their desires after Christ are soon satisfied. *Appetitus finis est infinitus.*

2. No Hypocrite though he closeth with Christ, and for a time grow up in knowledge of, and communion with Christ, but he hath at that time hidden lusts,

lusts, and thorns that overgrow his growings, and choakall at last ; and in conclusion mediates a League between Christ and his lusts, and seeks to reconcile them
together : Christ saith out with every Lust , and let more of my self come in ; no
faith sin, let me stay here, remember what ease, what honour I bring you, I cannot leave you : Now a man moderates , I'le keep my Lust because I love it , but
I'le keep it as my burden, that I may have Christ with it. Christ calls to seek for
more of him, Lust saith no, the work is hard, and duties are difficult. And 'tis it
may be to no purpose to seek, you have other irons in the fire , many worldly businesses : Now here men moderate ; Do not say thou wilt seek no more after him,
nor indeed use means diligently for more of him ; be sure only you give him some
desires to be better, and this will serve the turn. The Lord Jesus wooes many a
soul whom he never matcheth himself unto ; one comes and wins the heart afterward, and makes the match : so here, The lusts of a mans heart grow sweeter than
Christ and his Ordinances, and hence there is no heart to seek after more of Christ,
when the Match is once made with the world, and affections won, 2 *Tim.*4. 10.

3. Some seek for more of Christ , but 'tis of an idol christ, not as manifesting
himself in and by a Word : for look as any act of obedience is an act of will-
worship and imagery, that we have not a particular command for, or is not directly
deducted from some rule in the Word ; so that act of Faith is an act of will-
worship, which sees and chuseth Christ as his own, when he hath not a particular
promise for it, 'Tis an imagination of Christ, not Christ ; and you have more of
your own imagination, not more of the Lord Jesus, 1 *Pet.* 1. 25. Monks had
sublime contemplations of God , *Luther* calls them such as looked upon a *Deus
& Christus absolutus,*---- not beholding the beams of his love , and glory in the
word. Oh therefore labour for more of such a Christ, as the word holds forth. And
look as in Heaven,

First, They are all one with him in fellowship, the Father in him, and he in
them, and they in him, and so made perfect in one.

Secondly , They have his fellowship only : so do you long for more of his fellowship, so as to be made more one with him, and him with you , so as he may be
your strength, and life, and peace, and for his fellowship only , otherwise you may
go without him at last, *Luke* 13. 26, 27. *Have we not eat and drank in thy presence,&c.*
The Jews before Christs coming had Christs presence then , but a greater measure
of it is given to the Church since his Resurrection and Glorification , for it was reserved to honour Christ in his first coming. But how many be there that see not
the Lord Jesus so as they did under vails ? either get more , or say Christ is not
risen, *John* 14. 16. Christ promiseth to send his Disciples another comforter : who
was that ? the spirit of truth whom the world could not receive , because it knew
him not : Why had the Disciples no spirit now ? yes, he was in them, but not that
full measure, with which though they were not as yet sealed , yet they knew they
had him , and that Christ was theirs too. So, hast thou the Spirit of the Lord Jesus, Oh begg for more of it, not miraculous gifts, for that is in vain, but more of the
special powerful presence and fulnesse of it , for 'tis this that the world cannot receive. I have oft feared it's the great sin of this last age to comfort and settle christians in their weak beginnings, as though there was no more of Gods Spirit to be
poured down in times of the Gospel. But consider,

First , What came you into this wildernesse to see, Reeds shaken with the wind?
No, for more of the Lord Jesus , and will you now forget the end for which you
come ? it may be you never found lesse , no but God is emptying of you that you
might seek for more. *Herod* a long time desired to see Jesus , and then despised
him.

Secondly , You have here more means to have fellowship with the Lord , and
will you content your self with what you have had. If you do what can you look
for , but that the Lord should take away Ordinances , if they do you no more
                                                                                      good

good, and eafe you of the burden of the Lord of Hofts ; or fend fad and heavy tryals It's that I have oft thought of, why are the wicked exalted, and Saints deba-
fed? the worft are not bad enough to receive their plagues, nor the beft good
enough to partake of bleffings. You have had fome means do you fome good,
here you have more, that you may receive more good, more life, more of Chrift
Jefus ; if not, then look for fire to purge you if you be Gold, or flames to devour
you if you be but rottenneffe and ftubble. But is this thus? the Jews did long for
Chrift, and when he came they crucified him, they loved the Prophets, they fhall
have Prophets and their blood too, to flay them; you love the Meffengers of Chrift,
and you would have more of Chrift, &c. they have them Lord, but defpife them,
they have them, but condemn them, they have them, and though they will not
caft them out of their places, yet they will fo weary their fpirits, and grieve thy
Spirit in them, that they will make them glad to bury themfelves, and leave their
places. You fhall have Prophets, and their Blood too, and their tears and forrows
too. But why do I complain? Let me perfwade : oh labour for more of Chrift in
his Servants, in his Ordinances, in his Providences, in his Saints, until at laft thy
defires break thy veffel, and carry thee up to behold the Lord in Heaven. If there
were never faving work of Grace wrought, but thou haft only refted in Duties
without Chrift, now fell thy felf out of all for him. If there be any that the Lord
hath fetled there on his promife which never can be fhaken, hold your ftedfaftnefs,
but yet ftill grow in Grace, and in the knowledg of the Lord Jefus.

SECT. VIII.

OH long to be with the Lord Jefus. Before a man hath Chrift, now his defires fhould be to have him; when he hath Chrift, now his longings fhould be
to be with him. Do thus in this place, especially in this Age. I have oft thought
one great end of Gods bringing his own people into this place is to learn them to
die, and be with Chrift. Men have heard of Chrift, and paffed through the
waves of death, and ftood many a week within fix inches of Death to fee Chrift
here ; well, when you come here, God vifits you with troubles, temptations, loffes,
defertions, fears for future times ; here it may be you fee (as fome fee) an *end of all
perfection*, Church-builders, Church-ordinances, Church-profeffors, &c. or if
they find the Lord, 'tis foon gone ; why all is that you might long to be at
home.

    The Lord when he called *Abraham* out of his own Country to his Friends, he
followed the Lord he knew not whither. You live now out of your Fathers houfe,
and from all your Friends that long to fee you, nay are left among enemies, and you
know whither you are to go, *to God the Judge of all, and to an innumerable company
of Angels, and to the Spirits of juft men made perfect.*

    Look but upon the men of this world, they long for things here, though but
temporal, though they have no Chrift. Oh long for this though thou haft no
world.

    When Chrift would needs go to *Jerufalem*, *John* 11. 16. faith *Thomas, Let us
go and die with him*, and fhall not we go to live with him ?

    Did *Mofes* forfake *Egypt* honours, treafures, and embraced the reproach of
Chrift as far better. Oh if God fhould fet thee up in a Throne, Oh depart from
it to enjoy the glory of Chrift himfelf in Glory !

    Grant Death be dreadful, yet when Soldiers fee their Captain upon the walls
among the enemies, they will preffe hard after to follow, though they die in the
breach. To part with fin is bitter, or to part with Chrift, but to part with the
body for a time, and caft off the clothes, this will be found to be exceeding
fweet.

*Use 5.
Of Exhort.*

Motive 1.

Motive 2.

Motive 3.

Motive 4.

Motive 5.

Friends

Motive 6.

Friends that send to us, and provide for us in a desart place, we long to see them. Now who hath clothed thee, comforted, pardoned, revived, found thee, kept thee that nothing hath hurt thee? nay that thy sins have humbled thee, and done thee good: Oh 'tis Christ! Wilt not say, who and where is he that doth all this?

Motive 7.

Oh consider how glad the Lord Jesus will be of thee, though the world and thou art weary of thy self, *Zeph.* 3. 17. *Luke* 10. 21. *I thank thee O Father* : so will the Lord say then.

Means 1.

Labour for assurance that Christ is thine, else you will fear Death and Hell that follows it, and such an assurance as doth not only chase away vexation and anguish of spirit, but fears, at least in the power of them ; for there is many a christian can find the Proposition true in the word, *He that comes to Christ he will not cast away* ; the Spirit clears Gods work, and his own experience, and faith, *Thou comest unto Christ*, now when he comes to make the conclusion, though he dares not sin against clear light and evidence of the Spirit, and conclude, *yet I shall be cast away* : yet he dares not, nor cannot for a time conclude fully ; why? because of some fears, what if I should be mistaken, and when I die all prove naught? and while this fear lasts you will not long (till needs must) to be with Christ ; for while you fear or suspect Christ as an enemy, you will not heartily love him, nor long to be with him, therefore get these fears removed.

Quest.
Answ.

How may this be?

Rom. 8. 15, 16. By the Spirit of Adoption only ; for though I do not exclude the work of sanctified reason from the witnesse of the Spirit, yet this I say, that all the men in the world, nor all the wisdom and reason of man can never chase away all fears, scatter all mists, till the Spirit it self saith peace and be still, and puts its hand and seal to the Evidence ; till the Spirit not by an audible, but powerful voice shews and perswades, *Acts* 12. 13, 14, 15, 16. They had been praying for *Peter*, *Peter* knocks, the Damsel saith, *Peter* is there ; now see their unbelief after such a mighty Spirit of Prayer, *'Tis his Angel*, say they, and could not be perswaded till he came in and shewed himself. So the soul is praying, a mans own Spirit goes out and sees there is more unbelief and fear, say no 'tis a delusion: well the Spirit still knocks, and the soul opens, and then he comes in, and the soul is astonished. And that you may have it,

1. See there be no guilt upon thy conscience, no reservation, love, liking to some lust, *Heb.* 10. 22. For these fears are commonly the fruit of guilt which is not washed away, but *by the blood of sprinkling*.

2. Pray for the Spirit, *Psalm* 8 5. from 4. to 9. say they, 1. *Turn us from sin*, 2. *Turn from thy wrath*, when the Father is angry, then no good word. 3. The end, *That our hearts may rejoyce in thee.* 4. *Shew us mercy.* 5. Then they come to listen after it, for many times a Friend speaks not because he hath us not alone.

Means 2.

3. Mourn heavily for want of it, *Psal.* 51. 8. and so look for it in a word.

Labour to partake of the fellowship of Christs Resurrection, else no desires can be raised up, *Col.* 3. 1, 2.

Quest. What is that?

Ans. Look as we then have fellowship with Christ, and with the Church in miseries, when we from the serious apprehension of their sorrows, condole and suffer with them, so with Christ in Glory, when from serious deep apprehensions of his Glory, we reign with him, we are risen with him ; for let a man be assured Christ is not his, if he knows not what the worth and glory of his fellowship is, a man will then never long to be with him : Oh therefore labour to comprehend this glory of the Lord Jesus, and that by the spirit of Revelation, *Ephes.* 1. 17, 18. The word reveals the Glory of Saints, that there is a kingdom, that they shall be

perfect

Perfect in one, that they shall have that Glory the Father hath given to Christ, _John_ 17.22. Oh get the Spirit to shew thee the thing what this means, what this is ; else somthing in the world will make you look back. There are false Spies that vilifie Gods Kingdom to his Saints, Oh say 'tis a good God, and countrey, and Christ, and Mercy, and love ; _let me go up and possesse it._ Oh get the Lord to give thee but one glimpse of this !

Thus much of the first verse.

CHAP. XII.

Shewing that there are Hypocrites in the best and purest Churches.

V.2. _And five of them were wise, and five were foolish._

SECT. I.

FRom this Second verse to the Fifth there is set down the difference appearing between the Virgins, wherein the Lord the searcher of hearts, makes an open discovery of the particular estates of these Virgins, for all the best Churches especially to take notice of, to the second coming of the Lord Jesus. This difference is set down,

1, Generally, in this second verse.
2, Particularly, in the 3ᵈ and 4ᵗʰ verses.

I. Generally in this verse.

1. That some of them were sincere and wise-hearted to the number of five.
2. Others of them were foolish and false-hearted to the number of five more. So that the summe is this, one half of them were indeed Virgins, another half were in appearance Virgins ; the one part were Virgins in the sight of God, who saith they are wise ; the other were so in the judgment of man, and hence called foolish ones. In this general description therefore of them, we may note,

First, Their description from the number of each sort, _viz._ five.

Secondly, From their different qualities or qualifications, holy wisdom or prudence in the one, sinful folly in the other. He doth not say five were holy and five prophane ; five were friends to the Bridegroom, five were persecutors of him, but _five were wise_ and _five were foolish_ : Why the Virgins are described by the number of ten, Ispake before, either because it was a perfect number, and so signifies the estate of all Virgin-Churches ; or because it was the custom not to exceed the number of Ten, to honour them at their Marriage. Now why five of them were wise, and five foolish, as though the one half of them only were sincere, the other false, this seems to carry the face of Truth ; but I am fearful to rack & torment Parables, wherein I chiefly look unto the scope, and that is this, that not one or two but a great part of them were sincere, and a great part of them false. And hence the Observations out of these words are these, omitting all the rest.

1. _That when the Churches of Christ Jesus prove Virgin-Churches, and are most pure, yet even then there will be some secret Hypocrites that shall mingle themselves with them._ Or, _There will be a number of Hypocrites, mingling themselves with the purest Churches._ Observ.1.

Q 2   2. That

2. *That when the Churches are Virgin-Churches, the Hypocrites in these times will be Evangelical. Or, The secret Hypocrites of pure Churches are Evangelical.*

3. *That there are certain special, saving qualifications of heart, whereby ariseth a great internal difference between sincere-hearted Virgins and the closest Hypocrites.*

4. *That the Spring or one main principle of Evangelical sincerity or hypocrisie it lies in the understanding or mind of man.*

SECT. II.

THat there is and will be a mixture of close *Hypocrites* with the *wise-hearted Virgins* in the purest *Churches.*

This I might manifest out of several Scriptures, from several times. Look but upon *Josias* time, where there was as great a reformation as under any King before him, 2 *King.23.25.* Yet *Jer.3.10.* & 4.3,4. Look on the Apostles time, and what apostacy afterward. The Apostle complained of it, *Every one seeks their own,* Phil.2.21. *Many walk,* &c. Phil.3.18,19. Whom he could not think on *without tears.* The mystery of iniquity began to work even then. Christ manifests this by divers Parables, *Mat.22.14. Many are called,* and so called as to come in, and so fit and not to be known, till the Lord looks on them. And here the wise-hearted could not discern and keep out, but opened the door for the five foolish. Look as 'tis said, Job 1.6. *There was a day the Sons of God presented themselves before the Lord, and Satan came in also,* so here. I shall not, do not speak of every particular Church, but of the state of the Churches in general. For its possible there may be a *Philadelphia,* a new *Jerusalem which comes down from Heaven,* a *Golden Foundation,* and for a time *no hay nor stubble built upon it:* But this is rare, and not usuall nor general.

SECT. III.

FRom Satan, the ancient enemy of the purity of the Church; he being an unclean creature himself, if he could he would make Heaven it self unclean; but that is beyond his reach; hence he seeks to make Heaven on earth unclean; hence he will get into Paradise, and if he cannot come in the shape of a man, yet in that of a Serpent to beguile and pollute innocency there: He will follow Christ into the wildernesse, and tempt him there, and hence will seek to get into Churches, to pollute them. And if he cannot pollute the Church by unclean Ordinances, he will then seek to defile it by unclean persons, *Mat.13.25.* The Tares be in *Judea* like the Wheat, yet indeed annoy the Wheat: And how come they there? They are sown there, *i. e.* hid for a time, and mingled, and die there too. Who doth this? Why the enemy did it, so that Satan will do it. If there be a Devil in the Church, he will sow his tares.

Obj. But we see him not.

Ans. No, 'tis therefore said *he went away,* his care is over now they are sown. Look as 'tis the Jesuits policy at this day, the end of their Order is to raise up the collapsed ruines of *Rome,* and to bring all Christendom (and if it be possible all the world) to the Hellish bondage and blind obedience of the See of *Rome.* Hence some Kingdomes, because they cannot conquer them by power, they seek to do it by craft; hence they seek to lay their Leaven and make their party within, from whom they may have intelligence, and hence they shall do well enough with them: So Satan seeking the ruine of the Church, seeks to make his party within the Church, for one of these three ends chiefly.

1. Either

1. Either that he may divide the Church, that when any Errour shall be hatched, he may have his party to maintain it, and his faction to plead for it. Or

2. That he may corrupt it, if he cannot divide it, that the Tares may suck out the heart and life and power of Godlinesse in the hearts of the Elect; for you know 'tis not the Briar but the Ivy that sucks out the life and sap of the tree, and 'tis not prophane pricking persecutors, but seeming friends to the Church, that suck out the heart and life of it. It was not *Jeroboams* greatnesse, but the old Prophets gravity and seeming Piety that suckt out the Spirit and Sap of the young Prophet, 1 *Kings* 13. That so by this little Leaven he may defile the whole lump, and so provoke wrath against them all.

3. If he cannot do either, yet that he may blur and stain the Glory of the Church : For the greatest Glory in the world is to see a Temple built, not of stones of Gold or Pearl, but of living precious Saints, holy to the Lord only and his Son, and the sight of which in Heaven shall be one part of the Glory in Heaven. Hence Satan will do what he can to blur it; that though the greatest Glory God hath, shines in his Church, yet that he may blur it: And hence *Jude* saith, *Some that crept in unawares, were Spots in their Feasts.* And 2 *Pet.*2.2. *By reason of whom the way of Truth shall be evil spoken of.*

2. From the Officers chiefly of a Church, who when they should be full of *Reas.* 2. eyes, as they are described, *Rev.* 4. And these eyes should be ever watching, they are then sleeping, *Mat.* 13.25. For 'tis not the having, so much as the acting of Grace that helps men to read and understand the Book of the Scriptures, and the Book of mens hearts and lives, 2 *Pet.* 1.9. Hence in affliction and temptation we know the Lord, and his mind, and our own hearts, and the world best : When *Jonathan* eats the honey, *his eyes are open :* Now sometime the watchmen are not acting or watching, but sleeping, and hence those are taken for wheat, that indeed are but Tares. The Book hath a fair Superscription or Frontispiece, and they so sleepy they do not read it through, and so either see no fault at all, or if any, they be but *Errata* in the Printing, and weaknesses to be born with ; or if they do, yet the man is commended, and hath a Name to live when indeed he is dead, and so this serves the turn, and though he comes in, yet they shall do well enough with him, though indeed they herein have but a wolf by the ears.

3. In regard of Hypocrites themselves, who must be like themselves, ever to *Reas.* 3. act for their own ends, for they ever have an evil eye ; now it makes for their ends, to joyn themselves to the purest Churches of the Lord Jesus.

1. Sometimes it makes for their honour : Hence you know the Church of *Sardis* lost her power of life, for that is a burden, yet kept their name to live, for that is an honour. For if men live out of Church-Fellowship, that is a great shame, and now they have little love from Saints; Indeed the wicked may honour them, but what is that to the honour of the whole Church ? Who would think *Saul* should have cared for *Samuel*, that dealt so plainly and sharply with him ? Yet Oh *honour me before this people* ; that's the businesse. There are many excellent gifts Christ poures down upon his Church: *Simon believes also, Acts* 8. and would give any money for those gifts, that he might be wondred at, as he was before. A man seeing others gifts, and the love they have thereby, even a *Simon* may desire such gifts, and a mighty power of Grace to animate those gifts, and would give any money for this, that he may be wondred at. Some refined, polished Spirits scorn honour of base men ; and hence fish for it else-where.

2. Their gain, 'tis strange that *Judas* follows Christ for the bagg, that was so poor, yet he did, until he saw after three years and a half waiting, so little came in. So 'tis strange men should seek to joyn to poor Churches for that, yet they do and will so long as they have any lots to give, or purses to lend , or hearts to take care and provide for those that are joyned to them. You shall have many poor Christian

men, that be but kind and bountiful to them, you may lead them into any errors, catch them at your pleasure with a silver hook, until they see their gain grows little and respect lesse, and then they fall off.

3. Their comfort for union to the Church of God, 1. Covers their sin, and hides it from the eyes of the world. Theeves walk without suspicion in true mens companies, and thus they make the *House of Prayer* a *Den of Theeves*, and this is some comfort. For Hypocrites if they can carry it cleverly that none see, though God see 'tis no matter. It will not be thought that a Member of a Church dares do such a wickednesse, yet so it is sometimes. 2. Comforts their conscience in their sin; men love their lusts, but what, no respect to Ordinances of Christ? yet, and so conscience is quiet, and sin lives too, *Jer.* 7. 3. Because there is much comfort in Gods Ordinances, and in attending on God there, not only verbal, but the visible Gospel is sweet, the Sacraments: hence they joyn themselves as in *Johns* Ministry, *You rejoyced for a season*, not only in Christ, but in communion of Saints, especially in dangerous times, that a man fears the judgements of God will come in those places where ever they live without them. And now they are quiet when got into the Cities of the Levites, from the pursuer of blood.

Reas. 4.

4. In regard of the Saints themselves.

First, There is seen many times a Divine Majesty and excellency in them, which hath a drawing vertue with it, that many out of respect to that, close with them, as *Gen.* 26, 27, 28. God makes *Balaam* to see *Israels* glory in his Tents, and he cannot curse (if he might have all the world) but must bless them.

Secondly, There is much charity which thinks no evil, that where they see evils, they cover them; where there is but little good appearing, they hope there is more than they see, the *Kings Daughter* being *all glorious within.*

Thirdly, There is a spirit of humility in them, to think others that appear fair better than themselves, until God discovers them, especially if they are yet unsetled.

Fourthly, A spirit of desire to have all as near the Lord as they can, and though there be evils in them, yet they hope that will make them better.

Reas. 5.

5. From the Lord himself: who hath,

First, Reserved this exact separation as one part of his own glory at his Second coming: Then he shall separate sheep and Goats.

Secondly, Because some are very serviceable to his Church, and so to Christ, as *Caput politicum*, both in regard of outward means of subsistance, and also with edifying gifts: hence into his Family he will let them come, being servants, and like Carriers that carry anothers money and wealth to him, and then turns them out of doors.

Thirdly, Because of a certain real, yet not thorow work of the Lord, whereby he draws them to some fellowship with the Church, the Members, and some kind of fellowship with his Son; yet it not being a thorow effectual Almighty drawing, they prove unsound, *John* 6. 65.

Fourthly, That the Lord might manifest the exceeding greatness of his wrath in some, for Gods last end in all the wicked is to shew the greatnesse of it, *Rom.* 9. 21, 22. yet in some more than others: and hence raiseth them up in the Church to great eminency of profession, and parts, and honour, that all the Saints also may admire Gods Grace to themselves the more, that when *Two in the field, one should be taken, another left*, that they should sit in the same seats, and yet some called, others left, and of them that are called to leave many, and love me, and that men of great parts, and I a poor simple one to chuse such a base thing, to confound the wise, the mighty. But as it's said of *Pharaoh*, what meant all the miracles? all the humblings of heart? and yet he would not let them go: *For this cause have I raised thee up*, *Exod.* 9. 16. *Of all that thou hast given me* (saith Christ) *not one is lost, but the Son of Perdition, that the Scripture might be fulfilled.* So here.

SECT.

SECT. IV.

THis serves to clear us in this Country from a foul aspersion that is cast out of the mouths of Pulpits upon us, that we hold the Churches of Christ to have no Hypocrites in them. We answer, that though if Hypocrites could be openly and Ecclesiastically discerned, they should not be received in, nor kept in, because matter fit to ruine a Church are not fit to make a Church: yet we say there will be Tares and Wheat, there will be chaff and corn, there will be wise and foolish Virgins, there will be good and bad mingled together in the Churches until the worlds end.

To the Watch-men of the Churches: nay to all that professe themselves to be their Brethrens keepers; to all that are wise-hearted Virgins, not to lavish your charity too far, it's a precious Grace, and you have little enough for them that are sincere, but to bear a jealous heart, and to labour for a quick discerning eye to find out them that will mingle themselves among you. This was the commendation and honour of the Ephesians, Rev. 2. 2. I confesse it's a sinful extream to cry down all the Virgins as foolish, when there be Five wise. Satan will seek to break he bond of Brotherly-love by sowing false reports, and horrible suspicions: and 'tis a hard thing for a Paul after the Lord hath wrapt him up to the Third Heaven in Revelations, not to be puft up, and in seeing himself at a distance from other men, not to despise and condemn them that have not risen so high as he, especially in a discontented spirit nothing will please them. A false heart when he sees more than others as he thinks, now thinks highly of himself, as some great reformer of Churches and world, especially if men of shallow heads; and hence such do censure and condemn all that do not magnifie them, and reverence their Judgements, and the dust of their feet. And yet 'tis another sinful extream to swallow down all flies that be in the cup, and to think too charitably of every one that doth professe. Children that have no children themselves, will make children of clouts, and then love them; and hence many a soul lies bleeding to death because they have such tender Friends as will not lsearch them. And I doubt not but many in Hell may say, Oh that I should live among such and such, and they never deal faithfully with me.

If a man walk fairly, should I censure him?

No, but yet maintain a holy jealousie over them, as Paul did over the Galatians: This stands with love, as it was with Job ch. 1. 5. As 'tis with Chirurgions, 'tis love to cut to the quick. Love them because they appear to be Christs, and are so to thee, and this shall have a reward; but yet be jealous in love, because there may be that hid which was never yet seen.

1. It may be thou maist save a soul, and they will love thee; or else thou shalt clear justice by being a witnesse against them.

2. 'Tis the chief work for Christ here, there being no prophane ones among us, to overthrow the kingdom of hypocrisie, as well as of civility and prophanenesse.

3. You will save the Lord a purging and cleansing time, for when Christ purgeth not with the Holy Ghost in his Saints and Ordinances, he will with fire. Here I might give rules for discerning mens spirits, as

First, Mark their speech, for by thy words thou shalt be justified, and many times one word will give a light to see all, as in Simon Magus: as with men in a labyrinth found out by one thread.

Secondly, Mark them that you see not grapling with Sin and Temptation, for if we see them without that, they are not yet tryed, therefore observe them here, here is their trial, when time of Temptation comes.

Thirdly, Get thy self to stand at a distance from sinful men, from all the world;

We know we are of God, 1 *John* 5. 19. As men that are in the water look only to themselves, but standing safe on shore, they see others drowning: I speak this because I fear the Churches are so busie about their own things, that their watch is not kept: if they see no grosse sin then all is well.

Hence be not offended, if you see great Cedars fall, stars fall from Heaven, great Professors die and decay: 1. Do not think they be all such. 2. Do not think the Elect shall fall. Truly some are such, that when they fall, one would think a man truly sanctified might fall away, as the *Arminians* think, 1 *John* 2. 19. *They were not of us*; I speak this because the Lord is shaking, and I look for great Apostacies towards, for God is trying all his Friends through all the christian world: in *Germany* what profession was there? who would have thought it? The Lord who delights to manifest that openly which was hid secretly, sends a sword, and they fall; others in other places receive the Word with joy, the Lord sends Persecution, and fearing men more than the filth of sin, and anger of Christ, they fall: others stand it out there, and suffer and venture hither, and *Issachar*-like see rest is good, and crouch under their burdens, and so they fall. Others have had sweetnesse in Ordinances, the Lord departs, and so they fall. Others have corrupt hearts, and received the truth in the form, not in love, and stood in defence of the truth, not love of the truth, the Lord lets errour loose, and they fall. Well, never be offended at this, I am not, because I never knew man fall but he loved some lust, and was never broken from sin, and although this is not seen when they do fall, it offends not me.

Oh therefore search your own hearts: when Christ said to the Disciples *one shall betray me: Lord is it I?* say they: so when not one, but many, Lord is it I? Oh many a christian lies fast asleep, never comes to a thorow search, a strict watch. Do but consider this: 1. That in Churches, nay purest Churches many may lye hid not discerned. 2. Thou maist be one. 3. If thou beest, that of all men living none shall so deeply sink in Hell. 4. That all Ordinances shall tend to this end, and all thy joyes, all thy afflictions: and therefore Oh search before the Lord search, and say, Lord, as no mans punishments and plagues can be like mine, not sins, if I perish, so if pardoned, loved, never any shall have such cause to blesse thee; and therefore take not up with weak and groundlesse hopes, but love that hand that smites and wounds thee, for this discovery is to awaken thee: but you have so much businesse you will not, cannot, &c. Consider what a fearful thing 'tis to be hung up as for a gazing-stock to Saints, so an everlasting terror to the damned themselves.

CHAP.

CHAP. XIII.

Containing a Discovery of Gospel-Hypocrites.

SECT. I.

Observ. 2.

That the most hidden hypocrites of the purest Churches under the Gospel are Evangelical, or Gospel Hypocrites.

For these that were foolish were not such as in appearance rested in the Law, or in a Covenant of Works, but they had escaped those intanglements, and now were Virgins that plead their interest in, and their communion and fellowship, and love-knot with Christ, they had now their Lamps ready, and made much preparation for him, and they did wait for him, and verily looked to have eternal fellowship with him their Beloved, insomuch that they took their flight so high towards Heaven and Christ, that they passed for a time the discerning of the wise: for you must know that where the Gospel comes, there are two sorts of enemies against it.

1. Open, and those are your Justiciaries, that seeking to establish their own righteousnesse, and being puffed up with it, can with pretended good consciences in doing God service, oppose the righteousnesse of God.

2. Secret and subtil enemies, yet seeming Friends, and these are your carnal Gospellers that cry down all their own righteousnesse, and cry up Christ, and see nothing in themselves, as there is good cause so to think, and look for all from Christ, and yet these when the Lord comes to search are found false; and these are the worms that grow in this wood, in this building, in these Churches. Thus it was in Christs time, the Church of the Jews had left their grosse idolatries, yet this was their stumbling-stone, they sought to establish their own righteousnesse, and hence he came to his own, and his own received him not, and hence were cut off for this their unbelief, but others (divers sorts of them) did receive him, beleeved in him, *John* 2. 23. Many took hold on Christ, and he took no hold on them, wondred at him, and entertained him when others did reject him, as *Capernaums* did, yet under his woe. And these are the spots of Evangelical purity, wenns in the best bodies of the best constituted Churches. Look but upon Christs own Family: *John* 6. 69, 70. The Disciples professed when others departed, *Lord, to whom should we go? thou hast words of life*; yet saith he, *I have chosen you indeed to be for me, but one is a devil*, viz. *Judas* the Deacon stood not on his own righteousnesse, but was for Christ, and followed him, and yet in this Evangelical Angel without, is a Devil within, because he still harboured his lusts within. This the Apostle *Paul* fore-saw, *Acts* 20. 29, 30. Some Wolves without should come, and also some cankers within should fret, that should draw many Disciples after them (in a Church bought by Christs own blood) *speaking perverse things*, pretending to draw Disciples after Christ, but 'tis indeed after themselves; and *Paul* laments this, *Many walk*, i.e. professe Christ and his Crosse, *yet enemies to it*, *Phil.* 3. 19. This Christ foretels, *Luke* 13. 25, 26. Many seek, many knock, and at last cry *Lord, Lord open*, and in their life-time they pleaded communion with Christ, yet *Depart ye workers of iniquity. Jude* 4. Certain men are crept in turning Grace into Lasciviousnesse; for that is the very form of an Evangelical hypocrite, in denying his own righteousnesse, to establish his sin, 'tis advancing Christ to advance his Lust. The Epistles

R of

of *James* and *John* are antidotes againſt this kind of poyſon, and I look on them as lamps hung up to diſcover theſe men, not but that theſe men are indeed under a covenant of Works, for there be but two ſorts of men, and two ends of all men, hence but Two Covenants; hence thoſe that are not indeed under Grace, are under the Law, and under the Curſe; but becauſe the moſt ſubtil hypocrites ap. ear or ſeem to be under Grace, and their external operations are chiefly Evangelical, hence I call them Evangelical Hypocrites.

SECT. II.

Reaſ. 1

IN regard of the power of the Word and Goſpel of life and ſpirit in ſuch Churches: For the Goſpel where it comes, as it advanceth the glorious and everlaſting righteouſneſſe of Chriſt, ſo it knocks under-foot all mans, as a means ſubſervient to that end, and it coming with power and light, it would be too groſſe for Hypocrites to maintain life by Works: hence Chriſt is that which they look unto; for Chriſt when he preached, not only many *believed becauſe of his Miracles*, but *when they heard his Word*, *John* 8. 30. *Mat.* 13. In the Parable of the Sower, the Word came with much power, that they received it with joy, and did believe, but fell by their Luſts. And look as 'tis with the Sun, there comes light and heat with it, ſo there comes

1. Truth to the mind, and conquers the judgements of Hypocrites, that there is no life, good, righteouſneſſe, but in Chriſt, nor ſalvation but by Chriſt.

2. There comes ſome goodneſſe of the Goſpel to the heart, that men hearing and ſeeing Salvation wrapt up there, Oh that is ſweet and good! and hence their affections and hearts are in ſome meaſure conquered by the power of the over-dazeling truth, and hence Hypocrites being thus conquered, partly being of this opinion, partly taſting ſome good of it, deſire it out of ſelf-love, expect it out of ſelf-deluſion, and profeſſe themſelves Virgins out of theſe Principles.

Reaſ. 2.

In regard of the power of Evangelical examples in the five wiſe Virgins: for look as 'tis with living men when the Sun ſhines upon their heads, they caſt their ſhadows that follow them; ſo when the Lord Jeſus ſhines upon the ſouls of his own people, almoſt every honeſt ſincere-hearted man will caſt his ſhadow that will be like him; hence Hypocrites in thoſe Churches which are commonly rather led by example than by rule, will be very like them, and imitate them: if they ſhould not, what communion could they have with them, or what love could they receive from them? for there is a mighty power in eminent examples to over-bear Hypocrites, that if they will turn themſelves into any form, they muſt into theirs, as in *Joaſh*: for there are two things in the carriage of the Saints.

1. There is a condemning power in it; hence men fear to live unlike them.

2. There is a winning vertue in it, an attractive vertue; hence men endeavour to be and live like them, to be of the ſame mind, the ſame heart with them: and hence others take them, and they take themſelves to be ſincere, and hence they are Evangelical Goſpel Hypocrites that lye hid in theſe Churches: Hence *Zach.* 8. 23. *Many ſhall take hold of a Jews skirt* (I doubt not but ſome falſe ones,) *we have heard God is with you.* And as Chriſt when lifted up and riſen, ſo Saints draw Hypocrites to them.

Reaſ. 3.

Becauſe the Goſpel brings the greateſt and ſweeteſt conſolations with it. Hence a man under the terrour of the Law, and ſence of curſe for his ſin, will make his laſt refuge hither, and hide himſelf under the wing of the Goſpel, not ſo much out of love to Chriſt, or Goſpel, but becauſe they ſerve his turn, and give him eaſe. Like men ſcorched with heat, and almoſt ready to die, the ſhadow of a Tree is now very comfortable, and therefore there they ſit; ſo theſe: Or as men with ſcalded

arms,

arms, they put them into water, which gives them ease, no cure; but because it gives them ease, there they keep them, so here: Men have been scalded with wrath, Oh now Gospel is very sweet, and so are eased by it, never cured by it. Therefore here you shall find them disclaim all Works, and cry up Grace only; where the purest Churches are, there are usually great awakenings, there God is very near men, and made most manifest to mens consciences, and there are most soul-plagues, contempt of the Spirit of Grace, and hence most dreadful torments of conscience, and fearful lookings for of Judgement. Now hence it comes to passe when Christ is offered, and general notice given to mens minds, that yet there is hope and mercy for great sinners, this fills them with joy and peace, as *Johns* hearers, *John* 5.35. and hence they beleeve as the stony ground that had some plowing, and hence received the Word with joy and believed, *Psalm* 66.3. It's a Prophecy of the Kingdom of Christ, Antichrist he tormented the consciences of men, *Rev.* 9. Men have no peace within or without. *Luther* is raised up, and preacheth the Doctrine of Free Grace, which a world of men looking to their ease, others in truth receive it; for some time before his death he cries to God that he may not live to see the ruines that were coming on *Germany* for their contempt. The Law is the Ministry of Death, the Gospel propounds great priviledges, with much more sweetnesse to sinners, and hence hither men fly.

4. Because the Gospel yields the fairest Colours for a mans sloath, and strongest props for that. Hence you shall see them walking in this garden. For the last sin God conquers in a man is his sloath. When the swine have no swill to eat, yet you shall find them in the mire of sloath; this *slaies the foolish.* Hence the best Hypocrite will plead the Gospel, its troublesom to the flesh, to bear a daily sense of the sins and wants of the soul. Hence you shall have *Capernaum* receive Christ, and wonder at his Doctrine; and yet Christ upbraids them, *they repented not,* *Mat.* 11.20. Its troublesom, nay impossible for a man to break his chaines and get his soul loosed from his lusts, and free for the Lord. The Gospel shews all fulness in Christ, & that he must do all, a sloathful false heart therefore closeth with Christ as the end, but neglects him in the means. Why? Christ must do all, say they, and hence if Christ do drop upon their heartes, well and good, if not, 'tis Christs fault, he is a hard Master that gathers where he did not sow, and hence wrap it up. A mans false heart is weary of the yoke of Christ, and hence would fain be eased of it. Now the Gospel promiseth liberty from the bondage and curse of the Law, and a sloathful heart can find out reasons to free himself from the Rule of it, as part of Christian liberty, *this is our Liberty in Christ Jesu,* 2 *Pet.* 2.19. And they rejoyce exceedingly that the Law is dead, as they did, *Rev.* 11.10. for the death of the witnesses, because they tormented them: I say again, they rejoyce not because the Lord makes them like himself, and because of his Image restored by the Gospel, and because they feel the power of it, but because they are free from the power of it. Its an old deceit, yet subtil, to rejoyce, and love, and blesse Christ, because he will pardon sin, though I lie and live in them. Or if they do not free themselves from it, the Gospel shews the Law within closing with the Law without, to be an evidence the Lord will not impute it, and that 'tis not therefore they, but sin in them. Hence a sloathful heart will continue in his sloath, and to ease himself of trouble for sin and obedience too, say, 'tis not he, but sin. And hence *Arminius* makes a strange interpretation of *Rom.* 7. Because he saw *German* Professours plead that for themselves. The *Israelites* entred not into *Canaan,* unbelief caused it: And why did that shut them out? Oh there were walled Towns and difficulties, and this was the last shock, and hence they fell off; so 'tis in Hypocrites now. The safest place to lie asleep is in Christs Lap.

5. From the mighty cunning of Satan, the strength of whose Kingdom is made and continued by peace, *Luke* 11.41. Hence *he will turn himself into an Angel*

Reas. 4.

Reas. 5.

of

of light, and suffer men to go to Christ and Gospel, to avoid the search, that they may be Christs in appearance, and his indeed, 2 *Cor.*4.4. He hath a mighty power over men to blind them : For there be three things which trouble men usually, and make them question their estates, and the Gospel quiets and absolves them from all.

1. Conscience, that cries dolefully sometimes, these sins shall have these woes. Yes, unlesse I believe; but I believe, and trust to Christ, and flee to Gods Mercy.

2. Ministry, that cries and searcheth into the deepest windings of mens hearts, that men cannot but see that Christ hath eyes of flaming fire to see through them. Now hence men avoid the stroke and power of all Ministry, thus it is with me, thus it will be with me, but I believe and trust to Christ. And hence men bear back like Brazen Walls all Blowes.

3. Gods judgment-seat. What though men see you not, yet God seeth. Why, they have sinned they confesse, but Christ hath suffered, they have sinned, but they trust, &c. Micah 3,11. *Is not the Lord among us ?* Look as it was with *Joab, he runs to the Horns of the Altar,* yet there he perisheth, there he would die, there was the last refuge from search and death, so here.

SECT. III.

HEnce do not think your estates good, because you look only for justification by Christ, and look only to Gods free Grace, and count of Grace in Christ. Its a common errour for men to think, being they be of this opinion, only to look for Grace in Christ, to think that therefore their estates are safe, and they are justified by Christ. Why there may be such a power of Word and Spirit to conquer their judgments as those Papists that have been pleading against it, have been overcome by it. Thou maist receive the Notions of it in thy Head, but the power of it never into thy Heart.

Obj. 1. But my heart hath been affected with this, to see when my sins deserve death; yet there is mercy for the vilest in Christ.

Answ. Thou maist tast and joy, and yet fall off at last.

*Obj.*2. But I have Fellowship with the Lord Jesus.

Answ. Thou maist eat and drink in his presence, and yet be bid *Depart, I know you not, a worker of iniquity.*

*Obj.*3. But I have *escaped the pollution of the world,* 2 *Pet.*2.20. And that through this knowledge of Christ, his love hath much moved me to part with my sins.

Answ. It may be so, and it may wash thee from all external pollutions, and yet thy swinish nature remain still hidden from thee, but seen of an all-seeing God.

*Obj.*4. But I look for Christ, and wait for him and desire him, and all that are wise think well of me.

Answ. You may do all this, and yet you may be found foolish for all this. Evangelical work which is accompanied with Salvation in some, it may be Hypocritical in thee: And therefore take heed you do not take shews for substance. For look as in the Gospel Gods utmost perfection of wisdom and love appears, so the most hidden and admirable delusions of Satan are Evangelical. There his power is employed to undermine, and so to keep his head. Oh that we could but imagine and set before our eyes the amazing condition of such a man ! whose plagues shall be made wonderfull, that hath been troubled with sin a long time, at last looks to Christ, and there rests, and so hears all Sermons, and there still sleeps, and considers often that his waies are evil, but never suspects his Faith to be evil, then he comes to die, and then looks for Christ ; at last the week or snuff

dies,

dies, and Sun sets, and darknesse approacheth, and then suddenly slips into Hell, where he sees Christ and Saints afar off : And what hath deceived them ? Oh their Faith hath deceived them, to see Christ shaking them off as dust : Oh they wish, Oh that I had known or feared this before ! and will you not fear now ? as for you prophane ones that can scoff, and drink, and break Sabbaths, and live idly, your judgement is writ upon your foreheads : but Oh take heed you that have escaped these pollutions, lest you deceive your selves here. To shew you that deceit particularly, it's not my time yet ; but go alone and think sadly of it, I may look for justification by Christ, and wait for Christ, and yet perish. Oh let me be sure I get such a Faith as will not deceive me here : Should not a man you will say trust to Christ ? yes when you can in truth ; but thy Trust may be but Presumption.

II. Take not up therefore every Opinion and Doctrine from men, or Angel *Use 2.* that bears a fair shew of advancing Christ, for they may be but the fruits of Evangelical Hypocrisie and deceit, that being deceived themselves, may deceive others too, *Mat.* 7. 15. *Beware of them that come in Sheeps clothing, in the innocency, purity, and meeknesse of Christ and his people, but inwardly are Wolves, proud, cruel, sensorious, speaking evil of what they know not; by their fruits you shall know them.* Do not think Beloved that Satan will not seek to send delusions among us, and do you think these delusions will come out of the Popish pack, whose inventions smel above ground here ? No, he must come, and will come with more Evangelical fine-spun devices. It's a rule observed among Jesuites at this day, If they would conquer Religion by subtilty, never oppose Religion with a crosse Religion, but set it against it self ; so oppose the Gospel by the Gospel : and look as Churches pleading for Works had new invented devised Works ; so when Faith is preached, men will have their new inventions of Faith ; I speak not this against the Doctrine of Faith where 'tis preached, but am glad of it, nor that I would have men content themselves with every form of Faith ; for I beleeve that most mens Faith needs confirming or trying, but I speak to prevent danger o ther hand. For it was that which Christ did fore-tell, *Mat.* 24. 24. *Many false christs should arise,* i. e. such as should misapply Christ, that had a spirit for Christ, which was a spirit against Christ, and would *deceive if it were possible the very Elect* ; for coming with Christs Spirit, they dare not oppose them, lest they oppose the Spirit of Christ ; the only remedy is to hold to Christs Word, and not to depart one hairs bredth from it, *Rev.* 3. 10. and to a Word well understood, and then dispute no more. Satan comes to *Eve,* and bids her eat, no, God forbid, yet eat to be like gods ; He dazeled her eyes with that which was not : now she fell. Take the truth from what the Word saith, and depart not from it.

III. Here see the dreadful estate of all them that be found false-hearted in the *Use 3.* purest Churches, and that in these three respects.

First, That they should so horribly forsake and blaspheme the Name of God, to make the glorious Gospel of God, and all the sweet Doctrines of Grace a cover for their hypocrisie and sin, as indeed it is, for were it not for this, they might be found out in their sins, but now they are beyond the discovery of all men, or means.

Secondly, That they should be so lamentably forsaken of God, as to be left,

1. To the most subtil and spiritual Hypocrisie in the world, which being most crosse to God, shall receive most fierce and searching wrath. For as, Divines say of Christ, he was forsaken in Soul, because man had sinned with his Soul : so Gods wrath will search deep in their hearts, whose hearts have guilefully departed from the Lord.

2. That he should lead them so far, and yet in the main forsake them ; Oh this is heavy wrath, for a man to be lead in the day-light of the Gospel, almost to the end of his journey, and at last the Sun sets, and he left to wilder.

Thirdly, In

Thirdly, In regard of the cries of the very Gospel it self against them. Oh that the precious Gospel of God coming with so much Peace, Love, Grace, mercy, should win them to be Hypocrites, but never to be Friends. Beloved as there is vengeance of the Law, and of the Temple, so there is vengeance of the Gospel when the soul shall be drawn before the Tribunal of Christ, and shall stand there quaking, all sins set in order before you, and your mouth shall be stopt. What say you then for your life? Oh Grace and mercy Lord, Oh now shall the Gospel come forth and say, all this I did, I spake, I strove, I comforted, I terrified, and yet he hath opposed the Lord, and me, he hath made a cover for all these evils, and therefore Lord let him never be comforted more, *John* 3.19. Oh Christ hath heavy things against these Times, that take light of the Gospel to see to commit their sin by! And therefore lament your present estates you that know your selves naught, never yet drawn to Christ, never yet humbled at the feet of Christ, and look up to the Lord what-ever misery he inflicts, not to suffer thee to be deceived here; not only to have such a Faith as may catch hold on Christ, but he on thee, and come unto the light to manifest the hidden enmity there. Never was yet man deceived, but he that was willing to be deceived, that would not use the means, and search.

SECT. IV.

Use 4.

ALL you therefore that live under the light of the Gospel, consider if it doth not nearly concern you to search and try your selves whether you, or some of you may not be Evangelical Hypocrites; the time is coming that you shall stand before the Tribunal of God, wherein the hidden things of darknesse shall be brought forth to light, and it will be too late to know your selves then: Oh therefore search now. No mans misery will be so great as this, if your heart be found false. I shall speak in a manner but generally now.

Sign 1.

1. Those that do believe, and yet fail in respect of the efficient cause of Faith, it never had the right maker, never came out of the right shop, nor mint, it was never a Faith of Gods making, but a faith of your own making, so that it's a base bastard Faith, that though it be born in the House, it shall never possesse the inheritance, because it was never begotten of the right Father, the Lord never wrought it, but themselves, for many a man is convinced by the Law, and spirit of bondage that he must die, and that he is a most grievous sinner, and that when he hath done all he is unprofitable, but yet he trusts to Christ, and Gods mercy, and so believes, he finds no great difficulty in this, nor no great need of the Almighty power of the Lord to work this, and all men living shall never make him think but that he doth heartily and truly beleeve: but ask him, have you no doubt of your estate? and of Christs not taking hold of you when you take hold of him? Yes, but seeing he hath been troubled about his estate, and repented of his sin (in his fashion) and reformed himself and Family, and loves the best things, he believes without question, and so misapplies promises to himself, never feeling a need of the revelation and donation of Jesus to him by the Father; and thus the Lord finds this man a Christ, and this man finds the Lord a Faith, and the Lord Jesus redeems this man by price, and this man redeems himself by power, and so the Father shall have some Glory for providing a Saviour, Christ shall have some Glory for paying a price, and the Spirit of Christ which only can draw to Christ, shall lose his Glory, and so this man may take it to himself. And is this good think you? *Col.* 2. 12. *Risen with Christ through Faith of the operation of God*, 1 *Pet.* 1. 3. *The same power that raised Christ from the dead, must raise you to a lively hope.* Mat. 22. 1, 2, 3. One man came from his hedges and High-wayes to the Feast of the Promise, and Ordinances of the Gospel, till the Lord saw him without Christ; but *John* 6. 64, 65. *Unlesse the Father reveals Christs face, the Father perswades thee of*

Christs

Chrifts love, *you can never come to Chrift*, men know not thy Hypocrifie, thou doſt not, but Jeſus doth, and what good will thy Faith do thee then? It was a fweet fpeech of Chriſt, *Thy Faith hath faved thee.* Oh heavy when it ſhall be faid, thy Faith hath damned thee, that which I thought to be the way of life, is the way of death; truly ſo it will if you do not fetch it out of Heaven.

II. Thoſe that do believe, but they fail in the object, *i.e.* they cloſe with Chriſt, but they know not who he is: that as the Woman of *Samaria* that had ſome lookings to the *Meſſiah*, ſhe did worſhip whom ſhe knew not: ſo men beleeve in one whom they know not, only have heard the fame of. For there are two things in the Goſpel. 1. The outward words and letters. 2. The things contained in thoſe words: Hence there is a double knowledg of Chriſt.

1. A fantaſy knowledg, as a man that hears of any thing abſent; preſently fancies the thing in his head.

2. There is an intuitive knowledge whereby the ſoul doth not only ſee words and fancies, but beholds the things themſelves: Hence it comes to paſſe that many a man hearing the Fame, and receiving the fancy of Chriſt, beleeves in him, but not feeing him indeed as he is, therein he beleeves in one whom he knows not: and hence the Lord Jeſus may be a hid thing to many a man, and the Goſpel a ſealed Book, though he lives and remains in the very light of the Sun, and that all his daies: Hence Chriſt laments *Jeruſalem, Oh that thou hadſt known, but now hid, hid*; and yet Chriſt Preacht. Yes, *Deut.* 29. 4. *You have heard and ſeen, and yet the Lord hath not given a heart to ſee to this day*; So 'tis with many a ſoul, you have heard with your ears the great things of the Kingdom of God, yet the Lord hath not given you eyes to ſee: you have ſeen deliverances on Sea, yet the Lord hath not given you hearts to underſtand: and if ſo, all your Faith is naught, and profeſſion and affection vile, and eſtates miſerable, 2 *Cor.* 3. 18. *All we with open face*, &c.

But many ſee it not ſo.

I confeſſe ſome may ſee more darkly, and be mourning under it, yet he that doth not in part, he to whom it is hid, 2 *Cor.* 4. 3, 4. is one of them that be loſt, whoſe *eyes Satan hath blinded*, *John* 6. 45. *He that hath heard and learn'd of the Father* Many hear, but never learn of the Father; hence never come truly unto Chriſt; 'tis in this caſe as 'tis with a Traytor, he comes to the King for his life, and prayes for his Sons ſake; the King ſends for him, and ſaith, here is one that beggs for your ſake, do you know him? For my ſake! I wonder on what acquaintance, he is a ſtranger to me, and therefore I regard him not. So here.

III. Thoſe that have ſome kind of ſight of the Object, and ſee Chriſt, but there is a wound in the ſubject, becauſe their Faith ariſeth and ſprings out of an ill ſoyl, it's in ſuch a party that never was yet throughly rent from his ſin, and here is the great wound of the moſt cunning Hypocrites living: for there are two things in him,

1. A carnal heart, which cannot be ſatisfied with a ſpiritual good with Chriſt; hence he muſt have his Luſt.

2. A convinced conſcience, which cannot be quieted without Chriſt and mercy; hence men cloſe with Chriſt, and their Luſts too. Look as it was with the ſtony ground, and thorny ſoyl, they beleeved, but had a ſtone at bottom, *but roots of bitterneſs*, &c. Theſe men can ſometime plead acquaintance with Chriſt, *Luke* 13. 26, 27. yet *workers of iniquity*, 2 *Pet.* 2. 19, 20. Some had eſcaped the pollution of the world, that you may do, but a ſwiniſh nature laſts, that they never felt, or grew not in the feeling of it, and looſening from it: as with Apricock-trees rooted in the earth, but leaning on the wall; ſo they on Chriſt. Oh conſider of this, let a man be caſt down as low as Hell by ſorrow, and lye under your chains, quaking in apprehenſion of terrour to come, let a man then be raiſed up

to

Sign 2.

Object.
Anſw.

Sign 3.

to Heaven in joy, not able to live; let a man reform and shine like an earthly Angel, yet if not rent from Lust, that either you did never see it, or if so, you have not followed the Lord to remove it, but proud, dogged, worldly, sluggish still, false in your dealings, cunning in your tradings, Devils in your Families, Images in your Churches: you are objects of pitty now, and shall be of terror at the great day, for where sin remains in power, it will bring Faith, and Christ, and joy into bondage and service of it self.

Sign 4. IV. Those that beleeve, yet fail of saving Faith in regard of the very act of beleeving and closing with Christ, *viz.* they close with Christ, but 'tis without a high esteem of him, or love to him, they have some, but right Grace consists in a kind of summity, or excellency, else 'tis not right, 1 *Pet.* 2. 5. To you that beleeve he is precious, and hence it comes to passe,

1. That some never come to find or enjoy Christ, because they will not come off to the price of him, to sell themselves out of all for him.

2. Some sell him away again in time of Temptation, like *Esau* that sold his Birth-right, and never make any thing of it; because the Bond is not strong enough down, they fall from him.

3. Hence comes all a mans uneven carriage.

4. Hence comes sometimes the unpardonable sin, *Heb.* 10. 29. Many a man laies claim to Christ and his Blood, and righteousnesse, that never knew the worth of it; and this is Christs complaint me thinks in Heaven, (and of Saints on earth) *He comes unto his own, and his own esteem him not*, his own love him not, his own receive him not: him that is the glory of Heaven, the beauty of the Father, the delight of Saints, the wonderment of Angels, he I say is not esteemed by many a man, that in his judgement esteems him, and in his heart doth despise him. There are two parts of this esteem. 1. To esteem him only, *John* 5. 44. 2. Him ever and alway, *Psalm* 73. 26. *Thou art my portion for ever*, Many say they esteem Christ, but to be ever loving him, ever looking on him, this is not their frame. Oh think of this, fail here of your valuing of him, and you fail every where.

Sign 5. V. Those that beleeve, but they fail in their end; and these may for a while in a hot fit prize Water, prize Christ and mercy above all things in the world, but their end is naught: so that men here may ask and never have, because of their Lusts: As a man that lies on his death-bed, or in a Sea-storm in fear of Hell, he may now prize and take hold on Christ to save him. A man lies upon the Bed of horror of heart, he may prize Christ to comfort him, and getting a conceit of it, be wrapt up almost in an extacy of joy, that a man would think he was sealed with the Spirit of Christ, and yet his end being naught, Christ only to comfort him, misseth of Christ in conclusion; for when a man beleeves indeed, he receives Christ for the end the Father sent him, *viz.* to be King and Soveraign of the whole man as well as Saviour. *Psalm* 24. 7. *Open your gates that the King of Glory, &c.* Rom. 8. 38. *I am perswaded nothing shall separate us from the love of Christ Jesus our Lord*; our Lord as well as Jesus. Indeed *John* 6. 15. some did receive Christ to be King, but it was that he might be their cook, he provided loaves for them; so here. *Psalm* 66. 2, 3. *Because of thy power thine enemies shall flatteringly submit*: 'tis but flattery, not Faith; look to it therefore.

Sign 6. VI. Those that beleeve, but fail in regard of the use of the Gospel, and of the Lord Jesus, and these we read of, *Jude* 3. *viz.* of some men that did turn *Grace into wantonnesse*, for therein appears the exceeding evill of a mans heart, that not only the Law, but also the glorious Gospel of the Lord Jesus works in him all manner of unrighteousnesse; and 'tis too common for men at the first work of conversion, oh then to cry for Grace, and Christ, and afterward grow licencious, live and lye in the breach of the Law, and take their warrant for their course from the Gospel; I shall not name all the wayes that men do so, but I will only speak that which

which conscience and compassion moves me to ; not to begin ; but if possible to still division, and what I shall speak shall be by way of prevention:

1. Take heed of making Graces in a christian the weaknesses of a christian, for this is to make darknesse light, and Grace wantonnesse indeed: Is it not? Take heed then of thinking or saying counterfeit or false Sanctification consists in feeling something in a mans self, as love to, delight in the Lord and his wayes: True Sanctification, in seeing nothing, no love, no delight: why the Apostle *Paul* knew that in him, i.e. in his flesh dwels no good thing, but he calls it flesh there, and groans under it, yet he felt a Law within closing with the Law without, and blessed the Lord for it, and that was himself. Do you think the Holy Ghost comes on a man as on *Balaam*, by immediate acting, and then leaves him, and then he hath nothing : Yes Beloved, know you not Christ is in you (2 Cor. 13. 5.) as well as out of you ; in you, comforting, dwelling, sanctifying, preparing the heart for himself. Indeed to be puft up with Grace, or rest in it is a sin, yet that Grace is not that sin.

2. Take heed of making weaknesses Graces or Duties : as

First, To make poverty of spirit, the sight of nothing in a mans self ; why, he that is poor hath Heaven for his, and so Christ and Promises his, and hath Faith his, at least some seeds. Now to see nothing now, is to see an untruth, and to tell a flat lie to God, and Men, and Scripture too. Indeed a man that is poor doth usually see nothing, but that is his weaknesse, not any Grace.

Secondly, To say there is no difference between Graces of Hypocrites and Saints. Why so? Because I cannot see any. Is this your weaknesse or your wisdom? you can see none, and will you make your weaknesse your Religion?

Thirdly, That a man must not evidence his Justification by his Sanctification, I speak of that which accompanies Salvation. Why so? Because then there will be comfort to day, and sorrow to morrow, grant it, but then consider, 1. That is either a mans weaknesse and ignorance that he doth not see it, or 2. his wickednesse and carelesnesse that hath stained that work : And will you make this a Duty, a Grace? Oh but many have been deceived here ; grant it, and will you make your wretched basenesse of heart the foundation of this conceit?

Fourthly, That a man must see no saving work, nor take comfort from any promise until he is sealed: No, why so? Because many tall christians have deceived themselves so, and deluded themselves there, and been kept off from Christ, and truly I believe it in part. But what of that? Shall mens weaknesse be my Religion or work? No Beloved, for a man beleeves before he is sealed, *Ephes.* 1. 13. And hence Christ is his, and now for him to deny Christ to be his own, 'tis to make Christ a lyar, 1 *John* 5. 10, 12, 13. not that I would have christians content themselves here (it's a sign you never knew what Christ meant if so you do) till he shall send a more full gale of his Spirit.

3. If you do account them weaknesses, yet take heed your closing with Christ do not cause you to make a light matter of sin, either not to take notice of sins at all, only look to Christ, ('tis not I but sin, as being the act of the outward man: one calls this to unknow a mans self) or not to be deeply sensible of them, and so use Christ as your shoe-clout to wipe them off, Oh this is dangerous ; the Spirit of joy never quencheth the Spirit of Sorrow. *Capernaum* entertained Christ, and yet perished, Oh she repented not! What must we repent after we be in Christ? Yes, *Jer.* 30. 19. *After I was turned I repented*: It argues a bold conscience, when men as they look to no good in themselves, so to no sin in themselves, but wholly to Christ.

4. Take heed of those Doctrines which in shew lift up Grace, but indeed pull it down, or any part of it, as

First, to think that the letter of the whole Scripture holds out no more than a Covenant of Works, a most prodigious Speech, though coloured with advancing a

S   Spiri-

Spiritual Covenant of Grace, and no Word but Christ.

Secondly, Under a shew of advancing Gods Grace in doing all, to say the Ordinances are not means, but only occasions of conversion.

Thirdly, under a shew of giving all to Grace, to abolish that plain truth, as to say we are not justified by Faith, which though it be true, not really, *i. e.* not simply, by Faith in it self considered as a work, yet to say [not relatively, as the Lord is apprehended by it] it is false. If we cast off the power of the truth, yet let us not cast off the form of it: keep the form of wholsome words as well as truth.

Fourthly, Take heed of maintaining that a man until sealed is not to be perswaded to beleeve, under a shew of letting the Spirit of Grace do all. And Brethren, doth not the Spirit of Grace accompany the word of Grace; are not Evangelical commands part of that Word? is there not a power going along with them? what is this but to take from Gods Book, and he that so doth, God will blot him out of the Book of Life, *Rev.* 22. 19.

Fifthly, That a Christian is to gather no assurance from particular conditional Promises under colour of receiving all from Christ and Grace. True, them that have nothing to do with them, ought not; but for those that have to do with them as their Inheritance, not to apply and make use of them for their comfort, 'tis to trample under-foot Christs blood that hath purchased them for that end, and 'tis to rase out in our practise the greatest part almost of the Covenant of Grace.

Sixthly, That the Law ought not to be our rule of life under a shew of being freed from it by Christ, as though Christ came to set Hell-gates open for men to do what they please. Shall I say any more? I am weary with speaking, I desire rather to go aside and mourn, and to think there is somewhat amisse why the Lord lets these out. You that are sincere, search and keep close with Christ, and fetch more life from him, and though accounted under a covenant of Works with men, yet rejoyce, you know it is better with you in his sight. And you that are weak, beware and take heed, and do not consider what I, but the Holy Ghost hath cleared this day: and as for all them that do turn Grace into Lasciviousnesse, not intentionally, but practically, not in all things, but some things: consider this Scripture, *Jude* 4. Men *ordained to this condemnation*; they thrive and have no hurt, and they joy, Oh but they have condemnation enough upon them. Do but consider *ver.* 12, 13. *Twice dead*, dead in *Adam*, then quickened by Christ with common Gifts and Graces, then dye and turn Grace into wantonnesse, for whom is reserved the very blacknesse of darknesse for ever. They bring in painted prophanenesse.

Use 5.   Oh take heed then, lest you fall short of Christ by unbelief, *Heb.* 4. 1. Christ must do all; Oh but take heed, use meanes, and then put the work into his hands to make Faith right, *Heb.* 12. 1, 2. *Looking to Jesus the Author and finisher.* Suppose Christ was here on earth, and thou shouldst beg it, would he deny thee? Oh no, begg hard therefore now.

CHAP.

CHAP. XIV.

Shewing that there is a vast difference betwixt a sincere Christian, and the closest Hypocrite.

SECT. I.

THat there is a vast and great internal difference between those that are sincere indeed, and the closest Hypocrites. Or, There are certain qualifications within, and operations of God upon the Souls of the faithful, which make a very great difference between them, and the closest Hypocrites.

Doct. 3.

For the Lord Jesus here sees the difference, and shews the difference, though but generally I confesse in this Verse; some were *wise*, others were *foolish*; wisdom and folly are different qualities, and though these keep their residence chiefly in the mind, yet the Lord never did infuse any true wisdom into the mind, but there was a great change of the heart, nor never was any man left unto his own folly, but it did not only argue an evil heart, but did ever arise from thence, *Ephes. 4. 18.* so that Christ not only sees, but discovers to the Churches a vast difference for them to take notice of: I confesse the difference was not only in regard of open prophanenesse, or common conversation in living like men of the world, yet a difference here there is. For the opening of this Point, I shall open these Particulars.

1. That the Lord doth make this inward difference.
2. That 'tis so great that the faithful do see it.
3. That 'tis so great that others cannot receive it when 'tis offered.
4. That 'tis so great that they cannot understand it.
5. The reasons why the Lord makes this internal difference.

I. That the Lord doth make it: only some Scriptures now, *Eph. 5. 8. You were darknesse, now are light.* *Ephes. 2. 1. You were dead, now are alive.* It's true there is a life Hypocrites have, which puts much difference between them and others, but if that doth, what doth the life of Christ in a man, arising from the death of every sin? *Acts 26. 18.* The Lord turns not only from *darknesse to light*, but *from the power of Satan to God*, together with which ariseth remission of sins. What is this then but a greater change than from Hell to Heaven? Is it not worse than Hell to be under his, not only Temptations, but power? and is it not better to be with God, than be in Heaven?

II. 'Tis so great that the faithful do see it. I confesse at first work it's like a confused Chaos, they know not what to make of it, but afterwards they can and do, *1 John 5. 18, 19.* We know we are *born of God, free from the dominion of sin*, of which he speaks, and that the whole world lies in wickednesse. Before a man is born again, he sees no difference between him and other men, but now he doth; and hence 'tis frequent in Scripture for Saints to expresse their experience of their double estate, *Tit. 3. 2, 3.* and they are commanded to try themselves, and may not only see Christ out of them, but Christ in them, except they be Reprobates, *2 Cor. 13. 5.* and hence commanded to give thanks for this, *Col. 1. 12, 13.* which commands being Evangelical, have a power to all the Elect.

S 2   III. 'Tis

III. 'Tis so great that others cannot receive it when 'tis offered, they are so far from having it in them, or counterfeiting, or making this inward work, that they cannot receive it, no not when the Spirit it self comes to work it, *John* 14. 17. *The Spirit of truth which the world cannot receive*, it doth receive Prophetical Gifts, and common Graces ; but there is a higher and more Divine work which they cannot receive, *Rom.* 8. 7. *'Tis not subject, nor can be subject to the Law of God*, where the holinesse of God appears.

IV. 'Tis so great that they cannot understand it what it is spiritually, only in fancy, 1 *Cor.* 2. 14. *neither can he know them*, and hence men lie groping all their life for Grace, and ask and have not, because they know not the thing they would have, *John* 4. 10. *If thou knewest thou wouldst ask, and he would give.* A Beast cannot conceive what a life a man leads.

V. Now follow the Reasons why the Lord doth make this internal difference, or shewing that there is this difference.

SECT. II.

Reas. 1.

IN regard of the infinite love of the Father which he bears to the meanest Beleever above the most glorious Hypocrite that ever lived. It's an everlasting love, and it's like that love he bears towards his own Son, *John* 17. 26. Now if the Lords love be not common to both, neither is the work, or fruits of his love common in both, but a great difference there must be ; for as 'tis with men, so 'tis with the Lord. There are three expressions of love. 1. Their looks. 2. Their Promises of Love. 3. Their works of love : so the Lord doth,

1. Create in his people glorious apprehensions of his blessed face appearing in the glasse of the Gospel, *Rev.* 22. 4.

2. The Lord makes many Promises of love unto his people, which go to the very heart to chear them, *Hos.* 2. 14.

3. The Lord confines not his love to looks and words, though it's wonderful to have the least of them, but you may read his love in his works of love. Now those works peculiar to them, are first and chiefly the donation of Christ, *for* a man in redemption, *to* a man in vocation : and then the peculiar fruits of this love exprest in peculiar operations upon the Soul, and in the Soul, which Gods truth in the New Covenant promiseth, and Gods faithfulnesse executeth, *Jer.* 31. 33. & 32. 40. to take away the *stony heart*, to write *Laws in the heart*, to *put fear into the heart* ; these are the peculiar effects of this New Covenant, and they are operations in a man, which only the Elect feel and wonder at Grace for, *Ephes.* 2. 4, 5. *According to his great love hath he quickened us together with him* : there is a kind of Resurrection of a mans soul when 'tis brought home to Christ. And look as the bodies of the Saints shall be different at last day, so when God raiseth their souls from the Dead here, there is a difference now.

Reas. 2.

2. In regard of the Death and Blood of the Lord Jesus, which was shed not only that he might be a *God* unto them, but that they might be a *peculiar people* unto him, *Tit.* 2. 14. *He gave himself for his people*, not only to justifie his people, but also to cleanse his Church, *Ephes.* 5. 26, 27. for this hath been Gods great plot : first to perfect his people in their Head ; and then lest there should be a golden head, and feet and hands of iron and clay, and because the Church is not found lovely, therefore the Lord makes it lovely by little & little here, until it *appear without spot or wrinkle* at the last day. Do you think Brethren that Christs Blood was shed to work no more in his people than in Hypocrites ? was it only shed to take away guilt of sin from Gods sight, and then to let a man wallow in the sins of his own heart ? 'Tis true there is a work of Sanctification which Hypocrites have, which Christs Blood purchaseth, for I beleeve all common mercy and patience

comes

comes by Chrifts Blood, and fo all common Gifts and Graces ; but yet Beloved there is a vaft difference ; their wills were never changed though their minds were much enlightened ; hence they finn'd wilfully. The Lord never was dear to them, hence fecret defpight grew up, that at laft they committed the impardonable fin, *Hof.* 10, 26, 29.

Reaf. 3.

3. Becaufe thofe Graces or Qualifications, together with the Operations of them which are in the faithful, are the fame with Chrifts, the fame in kind and nature, *Joh.* 1.16. *From his fulneffe we have received Grace for Grace* ; hence we are faid to *bear his Image,* and becaufe it's but little at firft, hence *from Glory to Glory,* 2 *Cor.* 3.18. Now the Lord Jefus had not only the Spirit which he had without meafure, but alfo he had many Divine qualities, habits, or Graces, which it is blafphemy to think that they were hypocritical or common, which the faithful receive from his fulneffe, and wherein they are made in their meafure like unto him : fo the Saints have not only the Spirit, but alfo thofe peculiar operations of it wrought in them by the Spirit, whereby they come to be made like unto the Lord Jefus : Hence as there was an infinite diftance between the Lord Jefus, and the beft Hypocrite, fo the likeneffe that they have of the Lord Jefus, makes a difference now. And look as there is a difference between a Plant and a Beaft, a Beaft and a Man, fo there is a glorious life which Saints have begun here in this life, which none have but themfelves, 1 *Pet.* 5. 10. They have the *Firft Fruits, &c.* the which is meat and drink which no man knows of that lies in his hypocrifie and fins.

Reaf. 4.

4. If there fhould be no difference, then thefe evils would follow : 1. This laies a foundation of contempt of Grace, and of the Beauty of Holineffe in the hearts and lives of Gods people : for look as 'tis in the work of the Son in Redemption, if Chrift fhould have dyed as much for *Judas* as for *Peter,* and fufpended the act of Faith to apply this on the Free will of either, then *Judas* had as much caufe to thank Chrift for his kindneffe as *Peter* : and *Peter* had no more caufe of bleffing Chrift for his love in redeeming him, than *Judas,* and what cold praifes will he then give him : So if the Spirit of Chrift fhould fanctifie or call a Saint no more than an Hypocrite, then the one hath no more caufe to be thankful for the work of the Spirit than the other : and when a man comes to look upon the wor of the Spirit, and the Graces of it, there is cold water caft upon thofe ; this is no more than what a Hypocrite hath. Chrift hath not only redeemed by price, but alfo by power, from the power of Satan, Sin, Darkneffe, Delufion, and not to be thankful for this, is not to be thankful for the Redemption of Chrift : Thou fhalt never have it then that doft defpife the Spirit of Grace, whereby thou art but commonly fanctified.

2. Becaufe this abolifheth the ufe of all conditional Promifes made in the word : for you know they are made to fome qualification or work of the Spirit in a man, fome to Mourning, Poverty, Faith, Hunger, Loftneffe, &c. now if there fhould be no difference between feeming works in Hypocrites and thefe, then 1. the truth of the Promifes is deftroyed, for the Lord faith, *They that hunger fhall be fatisfied.* I'le anfwer, Hypocrites may hunger, and yet not be fatisfied. 2. The ufe of thefe Promifes fhould be loft, for why fhould a man then caft his Soul upon Gods faithfulneffe in the Promife, when 'tis but common love to him and Hypocrites : If it be replyed the one hath Chrift, the other not. I anfwer, 'tis very true, but then I ask, Who is he a Chrift to ? it muft needs be to a particular People defcribed in the Word by their peculiar qualities, flowing from their forms and fubjects by which they are known ; and now confider *Rev.* 22.19. *Is God a God of the dead ? and not of the living only ?*

3. Becaufe this makes the moft holy men that ever lived deceivers of themfelves and others ; only look upon *John* Chrifts beloved Difciple, and bofome-companion, he had received the anointing to know him that is true, *and he knew he knew him,* 1 *John* 2. 3. But how did he know that ? he might be deceived (as

'tis strange to see what a melancholly fancy will do, and the effects of it ; as honest men are reputed to have weak brains, and never saw the depths of the secrets of God.) What's his last proof? *because we keep his Commandments, i. e.* we have them writ in our hearts, and keep them, though we cannot fulfil them, it makes us every way more holy: Christ doth not keep them only, but we through his Grace keep them ; thus he proves it by a work in him. Now thus I reply, if all works in the souls of Saints be common to Hypocrites, then *John* went upon false grounds, deceived himself, and all that heard him, and all the Churches that ever were to this day.

Use 1.
Of Confut.

TO the Papists, who in their writings seek to shame the Churches of Christ, saying that they deny all *Inherent Righteousnesse* or *Graces*, making a man just by the righteousnesse of Christ, and in the mean while to remain like a Carkase or Ghost, or a painted Sepulchre full of rottennesse within. Three or four of these Archers that have shot these arrows I have met with, whereby they wound the heart of Profession, and keep the people in a professed enmity and opposition against the waies of Gods Grace: Now we do not only deny this, but we professe that the Lord doth not only out of the riches of his Grace accept us in Christ, but out of the same love sends down the Spirit of Grace, not only to make us civil and moral, or hypocritical, but that the Lord works thereby such a change as is not to be found in the most refined Hypocrites breathing. And we professe though our Justification doth not consist in this, yet who-ever hath not this is not justified (what-ever he may imagine) in the sight of God. And the Lord grant the Churches of the Lord Jesus may never open the mouths of those Blasphemers of his Name, in denying all righteousnesse in our selves at all ; Deny it to justifie, deny it not altogether.

Use 2.
Of Confut.

Of an old *Arminian* error ; for they hold and maintain an *Inherent Righteousnesse*, but that there is no difference between the Graces of Beleevers and Hypocrites, only in their continuance, and that is by chance too, and doubtful, *viz.* if they hold on, and for this purpose cite many Scriptures, three especially, that of *Ezek.* 18. 24. *If the righteous man forsake, &c.* which is spoken of rotten Pharisaical Hypocrites falling far short of what the Saints have. And the Parable of the Seed, *Mat.* 13. *They all sprang up:* where 'tis manifest the soyl was naught out of which they that fell away did grow. And *Heb.* 10. 29. *Blood wherewith they were sanctified*, which is meant of such as had some inward enlightning, and lasting, and external profession really, not in appearance only in them, yet not any saving and effectual work, but thus by making Grace common they make it vile, and under a colour of making all men watchful, they destroy all Faith in Gods faithfulnesse and Promise, especially until a man come to die. Divines have many strong arguments against them, and shew however there may be decaies, and relapses, and winter-seasons of the Saints, yet ever there remains in them the *Seed of God,* 1 *John* 3. 9. *John* 4. 14.

The main ground of this their conceit hath been double.

1. False observation, in beholding many fall off that were not Stars, but Snuffs, glorious Professors for a time ; and lest they should be mad without reason herein, they search the Scriptures, and in four thousand years find but four or five that fell away, *David, Solomon, Hymeneus, Alexander,* and *Demas,* none of which if examined will serve their turn.

2. A great mistake of the work of Grace, together with their own experience, for they conceiving Grace to be but a mean thing, and not understanding it, because they never felt it in themselves ; hence make no difference between one man and

and another, and hence maintain apostacy from Grace. I hope I need not stir you up to abhor this conceit, considering what hath been said. I grant indeed a man may fall away from Grace, considering Grace without Christ to keep it. But yet 'tis in it self such a living Fountain, as in it self doth not perish, though it may; and in respect of Christ, it cannot.

Obj. Did not *Adam* fall from all his Grace?

Answ. Yes, because he had neither the Covenant of Grace, nor the Spirit of Grace, nor power of Grace to support and keep him; but its Gods covenant now to write his Law, to put his fear in the heart, never to depart, and to give the Spirit of Christ, who is now risen from the dead. *Because I live, you shall live also,* John 14.19. And *power to keep us,* 1 Pet. 1. 5. So that though 'tis Christ that keeps a man from falling, yet the truth is, he that doth fall from Grace, as though it was a common fading thing, or doth fall from Christ, he never had Christ at all, John 4.14. *The water that I shall give, shall be a Spring of living water,* not of dead Graces, yet quickned by the Spirit, and helped continually. And its kept till life of Glory comes, where 'tis swallowed up in the Ocean of perfection.

Hence we see the difference between the Graces of Hypocrites and Saints doth not only lie in the efficient cause, *viz.* the Spirit of Christ barely considered in it self, for then there should be no difference at all, for there are not two Spirits, and the same Spirit that works in the Faithful, the same Spirit is in the unfaithful, to work many strange works in them, 1 Cor. 12.3, 4. Neither doth supernatural power of the Spirit distinguish (I mean that which is above the strength of nature, not that which is above the use of nature, for nature crooks all Gods works to it self) for the gifts of Prophecy and common joy are above the strength of meer nature, but the difference lies in the work it self. As 'tis in creation, the least spear of grasse hath the same power to make it, that made Heaven and Angels. Is there no difference then? Yes, it lies in the very work or effect of that power. And as 'tis in a Cedar and a Fly, there is more excellency in the former in some respects, but the latter hath another life, which the other hath not: So the meanest Believer is better than the most glorious Hypocrite. And look as it was with *Saul,* when he was anointed King, there was a new Spirit came upon him, the Spirit of a King, which common Subjects had not; so when God makes us Kings and Priests unto Christ, there comes another Spirit upon us, which common men have not. I know there is the Spirit it self in the Saints, as 'tis not in other men; But how is it there? I know 'tis there by Faith, but not only by this, but by certain peculiar effects which are not in other men. As 'tis with the soul, 'tis in the body, hence works a life which is not in any brute creature, so 'tis here. And hence 'tis said, *The world cannot receive it,* John 14.17. Mal. 3.2, 3. *Who is able to bear his coming, because he comes to purifie,* &c. Yet still the Spirit barely considered in it self, puts no difference, unlesse it be in respect of the work it self. Oh therefore look to it, do not say, I have now the Spirit and Christ. But what doth Christ work there? John 15.1, 2. There are but two sorts of Branches there, fruitlesse, and fruitful; the difference is in the very fruits of them, &c.

Oh then terrour to them that content themselves with common works, and so think their estates good. You have been terrified, confessed, and repented, *Judas* did so. You have reformed many things, and take delight to draw nigh to God in Ordinances, those Hypocrites did so, in *Isa.* 58. You have seen nothing in your selves, the Devils do so. You have had great ravishments, and seen the Glory of Heaven, of Saints, *Balaam* did so. You have beheld and seen the Lord Jesus, as if present on earth; Many saw him, heard him, and were lifted up to Heaven by him, and shall see him at last in Glory indeed. Oh but my desires are good! Many shall seek, and not enter. Oh therefore consider of

your

Use 3.

Use 4.

your eftate, and tremble, and fet before thee all the mercy the Lord embraceth his people with! and fay, Oh that mercy for me! and follow him till he hath done it.

SECT. IV.

HEnce it may appear that the true Believer may know the bleffedneffe of his eftate, by the peculiarneffe of a work within him. For if indeed there fhould be no difference between thofe Graces that be in Hypocrites and in Saints, if no difference between Love, and Faith, and defire in one, and that which is in another, then none could know the bleffedneffe of their eftates by any work; but feeing that the Lord hath made a vaft and a known difference, fo that God knows it, and themfelves know it, as hath been proved, and all the world might know it, but that they want eyes to fee mens hearts, and they fhall know it at the laft day to their eternal anguifh, *when the hidden things of darkneffe*, and *the fecrets of all hearts fhall be opened*, then it muft needs follow from the knowledge of fuch a work, a man may conclude his bleffed and fafe eftate. By work, I mean, no Popifh good work, nor confider a work without a peculiar word of promife made thereunto. If we fhould ask a woman married to another Husband, how fhe knows fuch a one is her husband, fhe would manifeft it by thofe peculiar acts or works or manifeftations of a husband to her. She hath known he hath forfaken great offers, and come to her: Her heart that was moft oppofite, was at laft overcome to forfake all, then they entred into a peculiar bond of covenant, fo that they cannot part, and though they do depart, yet they ftay not long. So here: If you fhould have asked the *Ifraelites*, how they did know they fhould be faved from the deftroying Angel? Why the Lord hath promifed to fave us. You that do what? That *fprinkle the door-pofts with the Blood*. So the deftroying Angel of Gods prefence fhall deftroy millions of people, and that in the night-time, when they leaft fufpect it. Notwithftanding all deliverances, miracles, plagues and repentances, Shall you be preferved? Yes, the Lord hath promifed it, and reveal'd it. To whom? To them that have their door-pofts fprinkled with Chrift's Blood, apprehended by the work of Faith, *Rom.*3.24,25. *Heb.*10.22. If one fhould have asked the Lord Jefus himfelf, whom he loveth? he would *John* to anfwer, *his fheep*, for *for them he layes down his life*; be they feeble or ftrong. If one fhould ask further, who are his fheep? he would defcribe them by feveral properties, as he hath done, *John* 10. Such as *know me*, as *hear me* only, as *follow me*. So if you ask a believer that queftion, How do you know you are loved? Is it good to anfwer with Chrift, I am his fheep, for whom he hath laid down his life, when I was loft and went aftray. But how do you know that? Is he now to anfwer like Chrift, by thefe properties wrought in me, or no? If you fay, No, becaufe all thefe an hypocrite may have, then the Lord Jefus hath done very weakly in defcribing his own fheep, by fuch properties to be his, which difcover them no more than fo: Its true an hypocrite hath fomthing like all thefe, but not thefe indeed. If you fay, yes, then a man may know his bleffed eftate by thefe. The promife is, *Prov.*8.17. *I love them that love me.* But how do you know you love the Lord? There is the queftion, If Satan and blind carnal reafon ask this queftion, you will be filled with accufations, and never fatisfie them; for he that accufed *Job* to Gods face, will much more to their own faces, accufe Saints of hypocrifie. If uncharitable men that never had the love of Chrift abiding in their hearts, you will never fatisfie them; but if the Lord ask the queftion in his Word, hold there, and the work is fo clear, that though there hath been much decay, yet after recovery, the foul dares eye the Sun, and fay, *Lord, thou knoweft all things, thou knoweft that I love thee*, *John* 21.17. Hence by this work you may come to know your fafe eftate.   I. A

1. A man may know his blessed estate in respect of time past, by a work, *i. e.* with a word or promise made to it, and the Spirit revealing of it, *viz.* the everlasting thoughts and election of God toward him, Rom.8.28. *Them that love God, who are called according to his purpose,* notwithstanding all their miseries and sins; yet *love him,* and *so called according to his purpose,* for so the Apostle raiseth up his thoughts. I know the world is full of want of love, and think it easie so to do, and like the Devil, are very kind to the Lord, as they think, while the Lord pleaseth them; who yet when the time of patience is out, shall be eternal blasphemers of him. But there is such love whereby Saints may raise up their hearts thus to see Gods love, 1 Thes.1.4,5. *Knowing your Election of God.* How so? Immediatly? Some Divines think Angels see it not so, and that its peculiar to God so to do: But mediatly, for our word came in power and, in much assurance to make you enlarged for God, to turn you from Idols unto God, and to wait for Christ in Heaven, seeing him here, but as in a Glasse. And by the same Spirit *Paul* saw it, by the same Spirit they might much more see it, and so the Elect may see it. And if experience may be added to the Truth; How many of Gods people dayly, knowing their work of vocation and glory, ascend from these lower stairs of the Lords Ladder, to the highest of Election, and there are swallowed up with eternal wonderment, filling their hearts with that joy and peace, that the weak Tabernacle of flesh and blood cannot bear the weight of that Glory long; That by works see the promise, and by the promise of love behold eternal thoughts of love: And hence promises are said to be given to Saints, *before the world began:* Because promises to them that thirst, mourn, believe, *&c.* are not bare words, but eternal counsels, in which you see Gods purpose.

2. In respect of time present, by it we know our present union to the Lord Jesus, 1 John 2.4. *He that saith I know him, and keeps not his Commandements, is a Liar.* Yes, that is true negatively, but may a man, ought a man to see or know his union positively by this? *Answ.*5. Many said, they did know and love the Lord, but *he that keeps his words,* Oh they are sweet! Its Heaven to cleave to him in every command, its death to depart from any command. *Hereby know we that we are in him.* If it were possible to ask of Angels how they know they are not devils? they would answer, the Lords will is ours: So here. How do you know you have not the nature of Devils, and so in state of Devils bound there till the judgment of the great day? Because God hath *changed our vile* natures, and made our wills *like unto his glorious* will, *&c.* So for forgiveness, Luke 7.47. *Much is forgiven her,* &c.

3. In respect of the state of Glory for time to come. We may know our blessed estate by a work, 1 Cor.2.9. *Eye hath not seen what the Lord hath prepared for them that love him,* Psal.31.19. *Oh how great is thy goodnesse laid up for them that fear thee* 2 Cor.5.2. If *cloathed with Christ,* whole Christ, *v.*5,6. He hath fitted us for this, and *given the earnest of the Spirit,* which, Rom.8.23. are *first-fruits of Glory,* therefore we are confident.

Obj. But if you look to your selves, you will have peace to day and sorrow to morrow.

Nay, *we are alwaies confident,* and yet *Paul* did not now go on in a Covenant of works. Now whether a man first comes to know his estate by a work, word, and spirit, so that there are three things to evidence our happy estate, or whether by two things only, *viz.* a general word and spirit, I intend not to dispute, because it makes nothing against the truth in hand: Only this I say, its very dangerous to *limit the Holy One of Israel,* especially in his freedom of working, to breath light, and life, and divine consolation, when and by what means and promise, and in what measure he will. Christ when he was here on earth, would say somtimes, *thy sins are forgiven,* Mat.9.2. Somtimes *be it unto thee as thou believest,*

Mat.9.28,29. Nay, *be it unto thee as thou wilt*, Mat.15.28. If in these inferiour things, much more in greater. Christ is now gone, and we have no immediate speech with him, but in his Word, and he is free to speak to his people according as he pleaseth, and when they need. And therefore let me entreat Brethren to be wary in their speeches in dashing all promises in pieces. What Christian heart can see Gods Truth mangled, without being angry and mourning for the hardnesse of mens hearts? The Lord hath spoken peace to some mens hearts thus, he that is lost shall be found, *He that believes in me shall never hunger, and he that comes to me shall never thirst*; and seeing this, they conclude, the Lords Spirit helping them (for somtime they cannot do it) peace. For the *Major* is the Word, the *Minor* Experience, and the Conclusion the Lords Spirits work quickning your spirits to it. Now say some, how do you know this? Thus you may be mistaken, for many have been deceived thus. Grant that, And shall a child not take bread when 'tis given him, though dogs snatch at it? What should one do then? Bring their work to the light, to the triall of the Word, which you know doth but two things.

    1. Shews what God is. And

    2. What man is, and so discovers and describes all hypocrisie of men, and all grace of men, now if it will not bear the trial of the Word, convince them they have gone on in a covenant of works indeed: But if it will, hold there, take heed then of false witnesse against the Truth of God; so that do not condemn the work of Christ in any man, where 'tis of the right stamp, and hath Christs Image upon it, and so pluck men from their claim to Christs love revealed in his promise. But learn to difference it once, and then I am perswaded the sad differences that begin to appear, would soon be ended among all them that *love the Truth in Christ Jesus*, 2 Pet.1.4. *Whereby are given to us* that have precious Faith, *exceeding great and precious promises*, The Lord gives little to his people, Oh but he gives them rich promises! Bonds, and Bills, and writings to shew for rich Grace, and riches of Glory, and riches of peace. Oh but these promises Hypocrites may have! they may be lost, and hunger and thirst, and believe. What as those do that have their interest in these promises? Why are they called *precious Promises? Precious promises* are not common things. *Precious promises* are not the portion of a base world. Precious things God never gives to dogs, and believe me, you may come to know the price of them in the times of your horrour on death-bed, that account them common now. Oh but many rest on promises without Christ! That's all one, the faithful by them come to partake of the Divine Nature, of Christ, of his Spirit, of Divine Consolations, Peace, Grace, and this is not building on a work, or resting on a bare promise, when it carries you to Christ and the everlasting embracings of him. Its no matter what promise gives peace, so long as it lands us in Christ. And therefore a man may know his blessed estate by a work, only let me put in three Cautions.

    1. Take heed you do not in your judgment or in your practise go about to move the Lord to love you by your work, though it be of his making. For all works are fruits, no causes of the Lords love, for this is Popery indeed, and 'tis Hypocrisie, Isa.58.3,4. *Why have we fasted, and prayed, and delighted to draw near unto God?* &c. but look upon the work and promise, and be the more vile in thine own eyes, that the Lord should promise, or do any thing for thee. So that when you feel any saving work, go not to God with expectation of any good in the name of that work, but in the name of that free Grace and Faithfulnesse of God, which hath moved him to make such precious promises to such as those are that have it. *Hast not said Solomon shall reign?* 1 Kings 1.13. So here.

    2. Take heed you do not sit down contented with the work, and quiet your selves with that, never looking to behold his face that gave it, that wrought it. The *poor blind man*, *John 9.* had a mighty cure upon him, and some seed of

Faith,

Faith; the Lord wrought the work, but hid himself: He wondred at the great change, was affected with his love, at last the Lord Jesus comes himself, *Dost thou believe?* faith he, *Lord who is he? I am he;* then he worshipped him, *v.*36,37, 38. So 'tis with the Lord in his way of working Grace: Oh therefore long to see him here in his glasse, and in Glory, in his face fully! Truly there is no work of Christ that's right, but it carries the soul to long for more of it, and to be with him that hath done it. Many Christians when they have the work, run away with it as a good sign, and look to the promise, Oh but long not, look not to behold the Lord! *Do ye thus requite the Lord, Oh ye foolish people and unwise?* Were it not enough that your sins make? but will you make works & promises also a partition wall between the Lord and your souls. I professe the Lord will fire such work about your eares, and drie up all your pits, that you may long for to drink out of the Well of life it self. And 'tis a black mark of Unbelief that shall keep thee from rest, *Heb.*4.3,10,11. Oh but when you long to see him, *Oh when shall I appear before God! Psal.*63.2,3,4. Then the Lord will fill thee. As Leaden Rings with a Pearle, so Promises and Christ put together (not divided) are exceeding precious.

3. Do not look to see the work or promise yours, nor receive any consolation from either, unlesse the Lord appear in both, John 10.16. *They shall hear my voice;* for so most men bring home Humane, not Divine consolation from a work. But Oh fetch it you from Heaven! as in *Peters* redemption, *Acts* 12. You reason, and others tell you, and yet you are full of fears and doubts; and thou criest, Lord perswade me, Lord perswade me, yea, hold you here, now you are where you ought for to be. Do you think Christ is filled with Grace and Life for you, and not with Consolation for you too? Only use means, and so look up to him.

SECT. V.

Use 6

OH therefore content not your selves with any hopes your estate is right, until you find this difference, for the Lord speaks peace only to his people, and his people are differenced from all others. Hence how can you say peace is yours, till this be cleared up unto you?

I shall speak to two sorts of people.

1. Those that content themselves with any thing that may stop and quiet Conscience, any slight work, any poor desires, any hedge-Faith, any moral performances, any groundlesse conjectures will serve their turn. And being full, they can hear all Sermons, no wind will shake them, no searching, threatning Truths concern them; they are so good, that they think the Lord means not them. Well, I say no more to you but this, know it that the time is coming that the Lord Jesus wil try you, and examine you to the very Bran; and will descry all thy paint, and open all thy lusts and thoughts, and thy nakednesse, and shame, and confusion shall be seen of all the world.

II. Those that content themselves with the revelation of the Lords love, without the sight of any work, or not looking to it. I desire the Lord to reveal himself abundantly more and more, to all that have the Lord savingly revealed unto them. For this is the misery, Christ is a hidden thing, and so is his love: Yet consider,

1. God reveals not his love to any Hypocrite, but to his people, that have a work far beyond them.

2. That the testimony of the Spirit doth not make a man a Christian, but only evidenceth it. As 'tis the nature of a witnesse, not to make a thing to be true, but to clear and evidence it. And therefore whether the Spirit in the first or second

cond

cond place clears Gods love, I dispute not, because 'tis doubtful ; yet be sure you find out the difference, *viz.* some work in you, that no Hypocrite under Heaven hath : Else what peace can you have ?

1. Hereby you come to prevent the strongest delusion that Satan hath to keep men in bondage to himself, *viz.* to give men great peace, and sometimes great ravishment, while they are in their sins, that so he may harden them there still, *Luke* 11.21. Now by taking this course, and going to Christ to untie the knots of Satan, you do now undermine the main plot of Satan, you break his head, having recourse to Christ to do this. His policy is, Let your heart alone, let Christ alone with that. But now you may be sure all your consolation is of the right make.

2. Otherwise you quench the Spirit, and resist the testimony of the Spirit, at least one great part of it. For the Spirit when it doth come to witnesse Gods love, it answers all the doubts and objections of the soul that it had before. Now the great doubt of Gods people is not only, Am I elected, am I justified and accepted? But am I called, am I sanctified, are not my desires, my Faith, my love counterfeit? which I may have, and yet go to Hell ? Now the Spirit when it comes, clears up all doubts, not fully, but gradually, for 'tis the most clearing witnesse, and therefore, John 14.18,19,20. *At that day you shall know that I am in you, and you in me, and I in the Father.* The Spirit doth not only say Christ is out of you, in Heaven, preparing and interceding, but in you, sanctifying, preparing thee for Glory, that art a vessel of Glory ; *and you in me* by Faith, by Love, desire, &c. Now when a man shall say, I look to no work, but only for the Spirit to reveal the Lords Love ; in seeming to desire the Spirit, he doth resist the Spirit of God.

3. Otherwise you shall be deprived of all that abundant consolation which the Word holds out before you. For suppose you say, I look not to the work of God in me, to receive any consolation from that, or any promise made to that. I look only to the revelation of the Spirit.

*Ans.*1. There is never a promise but the Comforter is in it, and they are given for that end, to give strong consolation, now if you look to no work, nor no conditional promise, nor to find the condition in you (which yet Christ must and doth work) Lord! what abundance of sweet peace do you lose? *Rev.*7.17. The Lamb leads them to the *living Fountain of waters, and God wipes away all tears* : And for ought I know you shall die for thirst that refuse to do it. Oh slow of heart to believe all that the Scriptures have writ ! all that God hath spoken ! Ought you not thus to be comforted ?

But 2. If you look to a Spirit without a work, whilest you do seek consolation from the Spirit, you cannot avoid the condemnation of the Word. You say the Spirit hath spoken peace to you. But do you love Christ? I look not to that, but to the Spirit. Why the Word saith, *He that loves not him, let him be Anathema.* So, Is the League between your sins and your souls broken ? *Ans.* I look not to that. Why John saith, *He that committeth sin is of the Devil,* 1 John 3.8,9. Are you new creatures ? I look not to that. Why the Word saith, *Unlesse you be born again, you cannot enter into the Kingdom of God.* And the Lord knows, but on your death-beds, thus Satan may assault you, and then will the Lord say, nay, look to your self. The Word shall be *Belshazzars* terrour. Consider, *Psal.*32.1,2.

4. Look to it, else you shall be deprived of further manifestation and communion with the Lord Jesus. The Lord reveals not all of himself at once, the day dawns before the Sun riseth, and there is a further manifestation of the Lord in this life to his people, not for, but when they indeed maintain such works before him, John 14.21. *I will manifest my self unto him.* How ? Oh saith Christ, *He come and sup with him.* Never think the Lord will dishonour himself so far as to come into a filthy heart. Sin doth and will grieve Gods Spirit, that he will only
accuse

accuse, nor speak peace to you, till all is mended.

5. Else you may fall everlastingly away, as those, *Heb.10.29* They had *received the knowledge of the Truth, and were sanctified,* but their wills and hearts never changed. Oh take heed there be not left *only a fearful looking for of vengeance!* You stand on the brim of destruction every moment, that do it not. For 'tis plain hypocrisie, not to bring works to the light; 'tis not ceasing to go on in a covenant of works, *John 3.20.* And if the Lord do'h love you, and you will not take the counsel of the Word, the fire of the Lord shall try you. And when that comes, and Conscience shall ask, wherefore comes all this great evil up on me? when your miseries shall be great, Oh it shall be said, this was because I loved not the Lord, I forsook the Lord, &c.Oh therefore look to the Lord now to cleanse you! *Zac.13.9.*

'T s true, there is a difference, but is it possible to know it, seeing that a false *Obje?.* heart may go so far? especially to know it in it self?

'Tis true, 'tis difficult for men, Ministers, or Angels to reveal it, yet 'tis easie *Answ.* for the Lord Jesus to reveal it, and this he doth do. This light discovers hidden things as they are, his *Spirit leads into all Truth.* And this is a peculiar priviledge and honour, as for God to know, so they partaking of the Divine Nature, for them to know their own hearts, *Jer.17.9,10.* And although it be an easie thing for hypocrites, that never knew what Grace meant, to be mistaken, yet after the Lord hath made it known to the elect, 'tis no easie matter to deceive them. As 'tis with Apothecaries, that know when they meet with counterfeit drugs; or Jewellers, that know the difference between Bristow-Stones and Pearls. As the blind man saith, whereas I was blind, now I see, so I was dead, now behold I live. *Old things are passed away, all things are become new.* 1 Pet.2.9. They are *called out of darknesse into marvellous light.* If they could not know a difference, why would the Lord command them to add one Grace to another, and *grow in Grace?* May they not well reply? Alas Lord I know not Trash from Treasure! I know nothing thou hast commanded me to do, but hypocrites may have and do. I say therefore the work may be seen in it self, and that by a threefold light.

I. The light of the Word, which is a Divine Revelation of or concerning God and man, and of man, not only as fallen in *Adam* (which discovers all his sins, their nature, their end, &c.) but as risen again and recovered in Christ, the birth, being, breeding of the new creature. It discovers all hypocrisie of the heart, so that they shall be forced to say the Lord hath found me out, and Saints shall say the Lord hath done me good. As if the question be, Whom doth the Lord Jesus love? You need not go to Heaven for it, *the Word is nigh thee.* Those that love Christ: Who are those? *Those that keep his Commandements,* &c. So that the Word is a light to discover Truth from falshood, the work of Grace from the work of hypocrisie; and by this light Saints may and do know what the work is. And it argues dreadful unbelief and Hypocrisie not to do thus, *John 3. 19, 20, 21.* And this all the Saints are commanded to do, 2 Pet.1.19. *We (sealed with the Spirit) have a sure word of prophesie,* &c. *Which is a light in a dark place;* both to reveal Gods heart and our hearts unto us; hence *it makes us wise to salvation.*

II. The Light of the Spirit going with the Word, reveals the work; without which the work cannot be seen, no more than a Book written in the fairest hand or print, can be seen without light to see it by: And hence Gods people cannot presently read what the Lord hath written, &c. 1 *John 3.24.* That look as 'tis with Scriptures, Papists say they are obscure, and how do we know them? We answer, there are Divine Characters of Majesty and Glory stampt upon them, whereby we by the same Spirit that writ them, see them, and are perswaded of them; so here. Or as tis in the work of Creation: How can any see God in it? We say, in the very workmanship appears his Power and Eternity, Wisdom, Goodnesse, &c. Now although Atheists cannot see these, yet others do and can.

So in the workmanship of the Elect, 'tis so. Its the Glasse of Gods peculiar mercy and love; now they that never had it, know it no, but the Saints do, by the Spirit especially. Thus far we grant the Spirits Testimony, that it must reveal it.

III. The Light of experience and sense: For Saints have an experimentall knowledge of the work of Grace, by vertue of which they come to know it as certainly (as we dispute against the Papists) as by feeling heat, we know fire is hot, by tasting honey, we know 'tis sweet. Now this is diversly apparent to experience.

1. By meditation of the work, in comparing it with the Rule, for no dead creature can perform one spiritual living act of life, no not a good thought, though they may think of good things. Now the Lord hath given to his people a most exact Rule of life, hence by meditation they may see how far it agrees or disagrees with the Rule, and judge of a living act by it; and so of the God and Lord of life to be there. Hence *try your selves, know you not Christ is in you, &c,* And hence I never knew yet a thinking Christian deceived, and hence I fear all that make not this their trade, will be to seek, and so to begin again: Oh the Lord teacheth his people hidden mysteries by this.

2. By the operation and working of it, for Grace may be in the heart, and yet lying asleep, and raked up under the ashes, not seen, not felt, but in the operation of it, it may, which is peculiar as the form is. For how do we know we love or delight in any creature? By the operation of love and delight. How did Christ manifest to the Pharisees that they were *of their Father the Devil?* Why *his lusts they would do.* So how can any tell he knows the Lord, or loves the Lord, or beleeves in the Lord? The operation discovers it, *James 2.22.* And hence, Gal. 5.6. *Faith which works by Love.* And though hypocrites act like them, yet there is a peculiar vertue in the one that is not in the other.

3. By their temptations and trials, Deut. 8.2. *The Lord hath led thee forty years to prove thee and shew thee what was in thy heart.* Rom. 5.4,5. *Tribulation breeds experience, and that hope* or expectation of that which shall never make us ashamed. Ile name no more. But look as we said to them that cried out against Prayer without a Book, we answer, Hath a man dwelt in his own heart so many years, and not known his wants, to make him pray? nor the Lords work of mercy, to make him blesse, so here.

Object. 2.
Answ.

2. But if a man looks to his work, this will interrupt and break his peace.

1. It may and doth break and interrupt a false peace; as many say, yet they trust in the Lords mercy, Oh 'tis a presumptuous peace.

2. Neglect of this yields most unpeaceablenesse, even in them that are sincere. You have peace, and then break out into pride and passion again; then question all. The Spirit will sigh, not sing in that bosom, *Psal. 32.1,2,3. Judg. 16.20.* Neither can you avoid the condemnation of the Word, though you maintain consolation from the Spirit, nor suspition of hypocrisie.

3. This is the way to peace, *2 Pet. 1,7,8,9. Mat. 11.29,30.* Christs *yoke is easie* and yields peace, in life and after life too, Rev. 14.13. *Their works follow them.* So that hereby comes double peace and rest.

1. From horrour.

2. From sin, which is wonderful great.

Object. 3.
Answ.

3. But I look to Christ, I look to no work. If I have him, I have all.

True, First look to have him, to be comprehended by him, that so you may comprehend him. But because you look for all in him, will you look for nothing from him? Will you have Christ sit in Heaven, and not look that he subdue your lusts by the work of his Grace, and so sway in your hearts? You despise his Kingdom then. Do you seek for pardon in the Blood of Christ, and never look for the vertue and end of that Blood to wash you, & make you without spot, &c? You

despise

despise his Priesthood and Blood then.   Do you look for Christ to do work for you, and you not to do Christs work, and bring forth fruit to him? You despise his Honour then, *John* 15.8. If I were to discover a Hypocrite, or a false heart, this I would say, It is he that shall set up Christ, but loath his work. To have Christ, is sweet, as *Capernaum*, to follow Christ, is heavy, *John* 14.21,23.

4. But if I have the witnesse of the Spirit, what need I have any other diffe- *Object. 4.* rence.

1. The witnesse of the Spirit makes not the first difference. For first a man *Answ.* is a Believer and in Christ, and justified, called, sanctified, before the Spirit doth witnesse it ; else the Spirit should witnesse to an untruth and a lie. For un-believers are under wrath.

2. If the Spirit doth not witnesse this peculiar work to be in you, and clear it to you, tell me how you can escape the anguish of Conscience and the terrours of Hell in your hearts, unlesse Conscience be seared and blinded ? When the Lord shall set Conscience to ask and say, I chuse none but whom I call, I call none but whom I justifie, I justifie none but whom I sanctifie, and that not with a common, but a peculiar work; Is it so with you? If it be dark or doubtful, can you but think all your joyes have been dreams, and your witnesse delusions ? Therefore look unto this.

5. But if I should do this, I should look to find some cleannesse in *Object. 5.* my self, whereas I am to see nothing but ungodlinesse: Goats are clean crea- tures.

1. When you stand before Christs judgment-seat to receive pardon, you are *Answ.* here to look upon all as unclean, and your selves ungodly.

2. When you come to look upon your Sanctification, you are to see it as 'tis, mixt with sin and corruption, and so cause of being abased as low as Hell for what is done ; yet that cleannesse and truth there is, you must see too, *Rom.*7. He felt a *Law warring against the Law of his mind*, yet he felt another Law too which he made an evidence of his being in Christ, *Rom.*8.1.   Giving all the Glo-ry of it to Christ. *Not I but Christ*. And yet *Paul* was no Goat, Its one thing to see Grace in my self, another thing to look upon it as mine, to clear me withall. You are to see the Lords work and not appropriate it to your self. And this let me say, if there be no more than ungodlinesse in thee, and thou seest no more, thou shalt never see God in Heaven, *Heb.*12.14. Nor didst never see him yet, 1 *John* 3.6,8. Oh therefore look to a work *!*

1. If you do not , you have no peace. For the Lords sake do it before fire try you, or you stand scorching before the Tribunal of God.

2. The sweet of it will be great, as there is nothing more bitter than Christ de-parting with his holy presence; so nothing so sweet as Christs cleaving to thee in his holy presence. And truly sin was never bitter to that soul to which the work of the Lord Jesus was not sweet, though its accounted by some almost Popery to speak so. To this all promises are made, 1 Tim.4.8. *Godlinesse hath them.* 'Tis true, they are made to Christ, *i.e.* to Christ mystical, 1 *Cor.*12.12. Yet to the head as the foundation and conveyer of all to the elect, *Eph.* 1.23.   2 *Pet.*1.3,4. If you despise work, you despise Promises, and so despise Christ, and the Lord knowes what use you may have of them before you die.

SECT.

SECT. VI.

TO the people of God, in whom the Lord hath made this great change, and made a difference between you and all the world. Take heed of denying your work, and this real apparent expression of the Lords love. How many doubting drooping Spirits are there, that though others may see, and though themselves have felt the sensible expression of the Lords love, yet oft come to this conclusion, or fear that the Lord did never yet good unto me? And dispute against it, and think that this an hypocrite may have, *Isa.*49.14. There are two waies whereby Grace is despised.

1. By making common Grace special.
2. By making special Grace common. The Elect are apt to do so before they are called, as *Paul* thought his innocent Godlinesse gain; they are apt to do the latter when once in Christ. All this we may have, and yet to Hell. Oh take heed of despising this kindnesse which the Lord Jesus hath not shewn to the greatest Potentates of the world.

Yea, if I did but know it; but I am put to such fears and doubts about it, that I know not what to make on't.

1. Do not think that thou art under the power of thy sin, when thou art at war with thy sin and it with thee. For the Lord many times clears up his love to the soul, and 'tis better than life to him, but then winds arise, and storms come, and sin and Satan assaults, and now he cries out, he perisheth, and that he was never redeemed by Christ, nor never saw Chrifts love. Should his soul be thus ensnared, thus assaulted, and no strength against it, and therefore being under the power of it, hence he never had pardon; they cannot overcome their corruptions, though they strive against them, hence think they are under the power of them, and then say, where is Chrifts Spirit? *&c. Answ.* When *Rebekah* had Twins, so that she was troubled, she went to the Lord, who told her, *the elder shall serve the younger:* So there is Flesh and Spirit in Saints, *and these two are contrary, so that you cannot do the things you would*; and sometimes cannot will, yet somthing opposeth this. Well, know it, that the elder and stronger shall serve the younger, it shall be Lord. A man that is at war with another, hath received power against him, but victory is not gotten presently, so 'tis here: *Judgment shall come to victory.* Though thou art bruised and canst not raise up thy self; now there is no fear of breaking, if God will not do that, none shall do it, and therefore thou shalt get victory. Only know for the present thou hast power. Thou goest to all Ordinances, and when no help there, raisest the power of Heaven. Oh Lord awake! *Awake Oh Arm of the Lord! Isa.*51.9.

2. Do not think that the being of Grace is lost, when 'tis hid, by the cessation of it for a time from act. For 'tis hard to know whether Grace be there, when acts are not seen or felt; now sometimes 'tis so: The heart growes carelesse and negligent, ceaseth from acting, quencheth the flame of the Spirit. Hence come fears, was there ever Grace here? The Sluggards Garden grows full of Nettles, and he saith, was there ever good seed sown here? *Answ.* Consider 'tis in this case, as 'tis in sin. Though the act of sin ceaseth, yet there is a bent of heart still toward it; and a carnal heart will return to his old Byas and bent again: So though the act of Grace ceaseth, yet there is an inner man, a gracious bent and frame put upon the will, that though for a time it ceaseth acting, yet it will return to its old bent again, to its own nature, which is called *the seed of God,* 1 *John* 3.9. From which a man can never fall. For in sleep there is cessation from acts, yet the frame remains still. In the old Law, if any unclean thing fell on a Pitcher, it was accounted unclean, but if in a Spring, not, because it would work it out again; so here: There is a Spring of Grace, which may be muddied and stopt up,

yet

yet it will work it felf clear again. And this Gods people fhall find; there is fomthing in them that fprings up to everlafting life all their daies.

3. Do not judge only of the truth and meafure of Grace by what thou haft in thy hand of feeling; but by what thou haft in thy hand of Faith in the promife. God hath ever delighted to keep his people fhort of what they would have, and to give them but little, infomuch that they often queftion the truth of Grace, feeling fo little meafure of it. Yet they look to the riches of Gods Grace, to the freeneffe and riches of the Lords promife, and hang there, and pleafe that, and fuck that breaft. *Anfw.* Oh now confider thou art empty, but remember the Lord Jefus is full, and the promife is free and full. Oh the riches of it, to give abundantly, and to work Truth in thee! Hence 'tis there in the promife, and thy Faith hangs on the promife for it: Why, tis thine by Faith then. The nature of Faith is to carry the foul empty to a promife and the Lords Grace, and Chrift there, fo that it knows not whither elfe to go but for bread here. Now Faith doing thus, it makes the promife and all of it thine, *2 Pet.1.1,4. Abraham* had his child firft in the promife, when he felt a dry body, and faw a barren womb. And know it, its infinite mercy to be kept up in the promife, and thou giveft the Lord infinite Glory by embracing of it now, and thou maift triumph here. *Haft not faid, Lord, that Solomon fhall reign,* and fin fhall not? It fhall not. Oh rejoyce on Heavens and Earth at this, for the Lord hath vifited me! God took from *Paul* his revelations, and fent diftempers, that Grace might be manifefted in the promife.

4. Do not think that the Lords heart is not towards thee, while he hides his face from thee. For there may be frowns in a Fathers face, and yet love in his heart: The Lord purpofely hides himfelf from his people fomtimes, efpecially when they begin to grow weary of him, or proud, but yet his heart is towards them ftill. Now they think not fo, when in utter darkneffe, then they think there is no love. The woman of *Canaan* befought Chrift oft, yet he heard not, yet his heart was towards her. How did that appear? Her heart and Faith was ftill toward him, fhe would not leave him though fhe fhould have but crumbs. *Ifa.*45.15.& 8.17. And the Lord doth purpofely hide his face in love, that his peoples hearts may be towards him, *Hof.*5.15. & 6.1.

5. Do not judge of the Lords love and heart toward you in thefe fad times by prefent feelings, but by the iffue of them. For fuch is the Lords cariage towards his people fomtimes, that God feems wholly to croffe them, and appears in all their wales with a drawn fword againft them. He doth not only leave them to their enemies, as he did *Samfon,* but to their fins, and to Satan to buffet them, that there is nothing but clouds of wrath and no Star appearing. Now look to the iffue, and *mark the upright man, his end is peace*; and confider this, Chrifts Kingdom is hid, and he brings contraries out of contraries, he makes darkneffe light; Hell Heaven, guilt pardon, weakneffe ftrength, and calls things that are not, as though they were. Then think within thy felf, Ile conclude nothing againft my felf, but ftay and wait what the iffue will be, which is ever glorious, *James* 1.2, 3,4. 1 *Pet.*1.5,6,7. Confider hath not the Lord done thee much good already? Oh confider what is then behind!

6. Never enter into difpute with Satan, or thine own felf, about thy eftate, but by taking and making Scripture and Word to be the Judge of the controverfie. Fears come in, you fhall never have mercy, never have power; Who told you fo? Doth the Word fay that? The Lord never gave himfelf to me, I fear it! Doth the Word fay fo? Never was any as I; Doth the Word fay fo? Or doth not the Word fay, God delights to pick out the vileft; to fend the Phyfitian to them that be fick. I cannot fee nor conceive any mercy; Doth the Word fay fo? Are not the Lords thoughts above thine? I have not that peace that others have, therefore the Lord intends none toward me; Doth the Word fay fo? Oh but o-

thers

thers if they knew me, would loath me! Doth the Word say so? When as it saith, *Doubtlesse then thou art our Father*, *Isa.63.16.* And bring before this Judge both sides, not only what sin can say, or may do against thee, but what the Word of the Lord Jesus can say for thee, *Jer.31.18,20.* *Ephraim* cries out of stubbornesse: Oh *but is not Ephraim my only Son?* Hear *Ephraim* lamenting too. And hear nothing against a Word. Look on *Paul* warring against Christ, and yet the Law of Christ in him also, *Luke 24.25.*

7. In times of greatest and smallest fears, remember to be humble and vile in thine own eyes, worthy never to be beloved. And let the Lord have his Will of thee, and this will give you peace. God denies mercy to that man that will be Lord of it: To be sure, evidence mercy then he will not; and when he doth manifest it, 'tis then when poorest and vilest, and the heart is meek and humble, *Isa.57.15,16. Mat.11.29.* Oh the Lord opens his heart and love, when once his Will is dear. The Lord casts by his rod and frowns now, and creates peace. Thus you may come to see the work, or the Lords Grace in you.

Use 8.

To Ministers, to take heed of making precious things common, by giving in false Signs and Evidences of love, but look up to the Lord for a special Spirit here.

Use 9.
Of Consolat.

To Gods poor people, and thankfulnesse. Oh that he *hath called thee from darknesse into marvellous light, into the Kingdom of his dear Son!* Oh that when so many come near to mercy, and fall short of it; yet me to be let in! *Caleb* and *Joshua* to be let into *Canaan*, when the rest so near, and all perished! Blesse the Lord for all Afflictions, Fears, Temptations, Enemies, Evils, Hidings of his Face, hereby he hath but tried thee and purged away thy drosse; and be comforted against all reproaches of Hypocrisie and Apostacy, and a proud world that casts filth in the face of Holinesse. *Now we are Sons of God, it appears not what we shall be, but we shall be like him in Glory,* in Grace, in Honour, in his Kingdom, *for we shall see him as he is.* And as for you that live, and lie, and bed it with your ease, lusts, sloath, and God sends you means, but the Bellows are burnt, the Lead is melted, and your Drosse not consumed, *Reprobate Silver shall men call you, and God shall destroy all your confidence.* But you that are the Lords, Oh that you could see what the Lord hath done! he hath put Heaven into thy soul, and his work which is more Glorious than the Creation of Heaven and Earth.

CHAP. XV.

Shewing that the Hypocrisie of the Heart proceeds from a want of a Saving Illumination in the Understanding.

SECT. I.

Observ. 4.

THE *Spring or one great cause and original of Evangelical Truth and Hypocrisie is the mind of man.*

For here there was an apparent difference between the Virgins in their practise and in their wills, as hath been shewn; yet the Lord expresseth it in general thus, that some of them were *wise* (which is one part of the perfection of the understanding) and some of them were *foolish* (which is the great

great defect of light in the mind or understanding) because the truth of the one and the falshood of the other, manifested what their hearts were, in their heads and minds; and the Truth in the one, and Hypocrisie in the other did arise and was maintained by wisdom in some of their minds, and by folly in the mind of some others. Folly or want of Divine Light made the one unready for Christ, wisdom or having of Divine Light, made the other prepared for him : Not that it doth exclude the evil or change of the will and affections, but because they manifest themselves, and are maintained in the mind. Hence I say, one great reason or Original of both lies in the mind, Mat.6.22,23. *If thy eye be single, thy whole body is light,* &c. The eye or mind of a man sits like the Coachman, and guides the headstrong Affections; if now this be blind, there will befalls and deviations into crooked waies, John 3.19,20. *Light is come.* Now what is the *condemnation?* *Men love darknesse, i.e.* will be blind, and having sore minds and hearts, will not look up to the Sun. They see not, nor receive not the Truth in love, and hence condemned, and *è contra.* Hence Deut.29.1,2,3,4. *Moses* sets down the causes of all their evils : *The Lord hath not given you eyes to see to this day.* They did see and hear by natural and acquired knowledge, but not by a Divine, created, infused knowledge, all that God had wrought and done for them. Hence when the Lord intends to send down the *Jews* under unbelief, Isa.6.10. The Lord then said, *shut their eyes lest they see and so be converted.* The heart makes the eyes blind, and the mind makes the heart fat. A man that is at enmity with God, the Lord sets him against himself. Hence men are left of God to their own lusts, Luke 19.42,44. *Oh that thou hadst known!* and *they knew not the day of visitation.* Hence Deut.32.29. *Oh that this people had been wise to consider their latter end!* You know 'tis in the *Proverbs of Solomon* the frequent title of those that are sincere and falshearted, the one is called *wise,* and the other *foolish:* Insomuch that some Divines have made a necessity of a change and turning about of the will, when there is fulnesse and clearnesse of light in the mind. Else they say a man might be *sapiens* and yet *impius* too, which cannot be. But I dispute not about that; there be many bruit creatures that imitate the knowledge of man, yet there is no mind of man or reasonable soul in them; so hypocrites may have excellent abilities of reason, and yet fall short of that new mind, the eye and director of the whole man, that Saints have. Its ever dark night with them the Sun of Glory never did yet rise upon them.

SECT. II.

1. BEcause all Divine Light of Glory is ever powerful through Christ to change the heart. Hence if hypocrites had it, their hearts would be sincere, which is not so, and hence they ever want it, whatever light else they have; and hence those that have it must be sincere, John 8.32. *You shall know the truth and it shall make you free, i.e.* from your bondage of fears and sins, hence *David* prayes for light, Psal.119.33,34. And then he shall be set at liberty. As Iron is drawn to the Loadstone by a secret hidden vertue, so there is a secret vertue of Divine Light that drawes the most Iron heart, nay changeth it, John 17.17. *Sanctifie them through thy Truth,* &c. For this is the difference between mans and Gods teaching: And hence when the Gospel comes in power, it comes in demonstration; whereby the heart is mightily overpowred, that it cannot but fall down before God, whose voice and truth it hears. And hence the young man saw some worth in Christ, but not enough, and hence he forsook Christ. Truth is not stones, but bread to them that see it indeed.

2. Because the mind is the first inlet of all sin and all Grace, and hence all hypocrisie springs from thence. Hence when Satan laid his Train to blow up all the world

Reas.1.

Reas.2.

V 2

world by fin, he firft enters into difpute and parly with *Eve*, and as the Apoſtle ſpeaks, deceived her, 1 Tim.2.14. *The woman was firſt deceived.* And hence when Satan came with his laſt and ſtrongeſt temptation, to draw away the heart of Chriſt to him, he attempted it by a ſudden preſenting to his mind the Glory of all the world, hoping hereby to get in. Nay in the unpardonable ſin there is *ſumma cæcitas*, to call evil good, and good evil. And hence the Phariſees that did commit it, were called blind; and when ſin is entred, it ſtrengthens it ſelf by the mind, Heb.3.13. *Leaſt any of you be hardned through the deceitfulneſſe of ſin.* As 'tis with Cities, they might be eaſily taken, but for the Forts that are built about them, and the Souldiers that are in them: So men ſet up their hearts and minds above, and againſt the Lord Jeſus. The power of ſin lies in the power of darkneſs, as the power of a weak State in the wiſdom of its Council. And hence when the Spirit comes, all the work of it is expreſſed by conviction *of ſin, righteouſneſſe and judgment*, becauſe convince one effectually, and you convert him. And hence when the Lord comes with life, he comes in by light, Eph. 5.14. *Chriſt ſhall give thee light.* And hence when the Goſpel comes to take away all darkneſſe and ſin, 'tis ſaid Satans chief policy lies in this, to blind mens eyes, 2 Cor.4.4. Either by obſcuring the Light, or by kindling a falſe Light in their minds, that they ſhall think they ſee, when their darkneſs remains; not but that there is filth enough in the will, but Satan knows that Chriſt ſhines into the heart by the mind; and hence he blinds men, and then he knows he ſhall damn men. Beloved, if men had the Spirit, it would *lead them into all Truth, now this the world cannot receive*, becauſe John 14.17. *It knowes him not.* This is that which opens and ſhuts to all life and ſin; not that bare light can change the will, but the Lord doth it by the power of his Truth and Light: And as 'tis with water coming through ſome Mines, there is a healing vertue in it, ſo Light coming from everlaſting love, it heals men of their evils.

SECT. III.

Uſe 2.

Hence ſee the danger of two ſorts of men eſpecially.
1. Of thoſe that flie from the Light, which is done ſundry waies. He mention onely one, that is uſed by a falſe heart. A man is troubled in mind concerning his eſtate, fears death and Hell, and ſo few ſhall be ſaved, how can I be one, *&c.* How comes he to fear? The Lord hath by his Spirit in the Word diſcovered and found out his ſin, the thief is taken and apprehended, and condemned, he hears ſtill, but yet can find no peace, Why? Becauſe he lives in thoſe ſins that he is convinced of. Hence the Word raiſeth damps and heart-qualms, that he hath no peace, but is ever pulled from his own bottom and hypocriſie, and the Word diſcovers more ſins, and hence hath no peace: The Word will not give nor offer Chriſt and a baſe luſt together, nor will not ſuffer any to have them both in peace. Hereupon the ſoul finding no reſt nor peace (which the falſe heart ſeeks for chiefly) flies from the Light, eſpecially if it hath found out a ſhorter cut to its peace, by any device or golden deluſions of men. And now they will hear there no more, and now the Publiſhers of Gods Truth are tyrannical tormenters of the Conſciences of them that be weak, falſe Prophets, that lead them out of the way of peace. And becauſe of this, they think they were led out of the way of truth, becauſe out of the way of peace. Or if they do come, they can ſit with diſdain and contempt of men (alas they ſpeak according to their light) and of all the truths of God, which ſhall one day be preacht over again in flames of fire to their eternal horrour, Rev.6.2. Its ſaid, *Chriſt rides on a white Horſe, conquering and to conquer.* Men have unruly hearts and ſtrong hearts, and they will not die, nor yield preſently. And hence when one ſin is caſt away,

another

another steps into the room of it; and when that is gone, another supplies the place of it, and commonly the strongest sin and temptation is the last. Now hence Christ goes on, rides on in the Chariot of the Word, conquering and to conquer still. Those that do yeild, he saves, those that will not, he slaies. Now these poor Creatures have had Christs arrows in them, and are wounded for some sin, but the Lord discovers more still; hence at last they flie away with the arrowes in their hearts for ease. Oh poor creatures know it, the Lord Jesus will find you out! You will not be conquered by him, you shall never be saved by him. You have light, you shall have delusions, endlesse unknown hypocrisie and darknesse to be your portion. There is never a plain heart but he accounts that wound and trouble greatest mercy, and blesseth the Lord, that he will not give him his sins and peace with them too.

2. Those that flie not from the light of the Truth, but give it the hearing, but yet let it slip; either not minding it then, or not pondering it afterward; that before they come, thirst not for more light, look not up for it, nor are mourning when the Lord hides it from their eyes. Some there be that be such all-sufficient men, so good they need be no better, so wise that they need know no more; some insufficient indeed to know, and hence *ever learning*, hearing, *but never coming to the knowledge of the Truth.* If Light breaks not in, they can lie in darknesse still, and not mourn; and think no more of it than a tale that is told, or news that is brought. Oh look to your standing, for you are in the high rode to hypocrisie, and its impossible you should be kept from it that lie so, John 12.35. *Walk while you have the light, lest darknesse come upon you.* Satan knew if light came in, Christ would come in: And therefore know it, all that time thou hast heard and heard, but not with Divine Light, hast got only somwhat to prate on now, to be of another opinion now from what thou wast: Oh now Satan hath been let loose, by the dreadful vengeance of Almighty God, to blind thee, that so thou mightst die in thy hypocrisie and sin. Oh poor Captives, mourn under this; and behold your danger for time to come.

Hence see the reason why many that have had mighty strong Affections at first *Use 2.* conversion, afterwards become dry, and wither, and consume, and pine, and die away, and now their hypocrisie is manifest, if not to all the world by open prophanenesse, yet to the discerningeye of living Christians, by a formal, barren, unsavoury, unfruitful heart and course, because they never had light nor conviction enough as yet. You shall have some ignorant creatures awakened by some thundring Ministry, weep and mourn for sin, and after vanish into smoak, being never convinced of sin. Land-floods of sorrow without a Spring of light, are dried up, and make the heart more fruitful in sin afterward. Many go under fears of wrath, and never get peace, because never convinced of wrath. Many are affected with Christ, and with joy of the Gospel, as the stony ground, but they wanting depth of earth, of conviction, die away again; and hence all the world can never stop a Christian in his shining Profession, no more than they can the Sun in his course, as *Paul*, 2 Cor. 5.11. *We knowing the terrour of the Lord perswade men.* And hence *Moses*, *Heb.* 11.27. feared no frowns of *Pharaoh*, cared for no honours from *Pharaoh*, he saw the God that was invisible, and hence Christ praies for his Disciples, to be kept from evil. *The world hath not known me, but these have known me, John* 17. When men are condemned to die, they take on because now they see death, but here in time of health they see it not. If men wrong a child, their heart smites them and grieves, but the Lord is abased dishonoured, and men are not affected, because they want light, and see it not: If men be to match with a Prince, or stand before him, 'tis counted blessednesse; but before Christ, 'tis a burden, because men know it not. 'Tis strange to see some people carried with mighty affection against sin and Hell, and after Christ. And what is Hell you fear? A dreadful place. What is Christ? They scarce know so much as Devils do,

but

but that is all: Oh trust them not! Many have, and these will fall away, to some Lust, or Opinion, or Pride, or World; and the reason is, they never had light enough, John 5.35. *John was a burning and shining light, and they did joy in him for a season,* yet as glorious as it was, they saw not Christ by it, especially not with Divine Light. Its rare to see Christians full both of light and affection. And therefore consider of this, many a man hath been well brought up, and is of a sweet, loving Nature, mild, and gentle, and harmlesse, likes and loves the best things, and his meaning, and mind and heart is good, and hath more in heart than in shew, and so hopes all shall go well with him. I say, there (may lie greatest hypocrisie under greatest affections; especially if they want light. You shall be hardned in your hypocrisie by them. I never liked violent affections and pangs, but only such as were dropt in by light; because those come from an external Principle, and last not, but these do. Men are not affrighted by the light of the Sun, though clearer than the Lightning.

Hence take heed of contenting your selves with every kind of knowledge: Do not worship every Image in your own Heads; especially you that fall short of Truth or the knowledge of it; for when you have some, there may be yet that wanting which may make you sincere. There are many men of great knowledge, able to teach themselves and others too, and yet their hearts are unsound. How comes this to passe? Is it because they have so much light? No, but because they want much; and therefore content not your selves with every knowledge. There is some knowledge which men have by the light of nature (which leaves them without excuse) from the Book of Creation, some by power of education, some by the light of the Law, whereby men may know their sin and evils, some by the Letter of the Gospel, and so men may know much, and speak well, and so *in seeing see not*; some by the Spirit, and may see much, so as to prophesie in Christs Name, and yet be bid *depart, Mat.7.* Now there is a Light of Glory, whereby the Elect see things in another manner; to tell you how, they cannot, its the beginning of light in Heaven, and the same Spirit that fils Christ, filling their minds, that they know by this anointing all things; which if ever you have, you must become Babes and Fools in your own eyes. God will never write his Law in your minds, till all the Scriblings of it are blotted out. Account all your knowledge losse for the gaining of this. 'Tis sad to see many a man pleasing himself in his own dreaming delusions, yet the poor creature in seeing sees nor, which is Gods heavy curse upon men under greatest means, and which laies all wast and desolate, Isa.6. *How long? Until all be wast,* v.11.

Use 4.
Hence see the right way of living a life of Truth, of being *an Israelite in whom is no guile.* Keep light in your minds, and you will keep Truth alive in your hearts and lives. Many a sincere heart may have Hypocrisie and much unsoundnesse in him, though he be no Hypocrite. But how comes it so to be? and whence so little Truth? and hence so many fears and doubts about their estates continually? Oh! men lose that Glorious Light that somtime they have. For when you have it in an Ordinance, Oh how sweet is the Lord and all his waies to you! Afterward you have lost your hearts, truly 'tis because you have lost your light.

Two waies Hypocrisie vents it self, which Gods people oppose.

1. In secret withdrawing of the heart to sin. Oh now get light! for sin never draws away, but by appearance of some good at least, *pro hic & nunc. Jam.1.* 14. Now put off the covering, keep the mind from being deceived, you will keep the heart from being hardned, deaded and withdrawn from God.

2. In performing duties, but not for Christ as their utmost end; now the heart is bent this way, yet it failes, because light is gone, to see and behold the Glory and blessednesse of this. Men that have honour or gain in their eye, are carried violently after it. Men that are bound for a voyage will go through, their

their eye leads them. *Stephen* speaks till the stones were about his ears, *I see Jesus* saith he, *at the right hand of God.* 2 Cor.15.58. *Be abundant in the Lords work, knowing that your labour is not in vain.* Hence *David* Psal.119. begs for knowledge of this and that, and then he will do it. Oh therefore keep it in your minds as precious, Prov.2.10. *If knowledge be pleasant,* &c. And pray to God to keep it for you. Light is in the Sun, and not ceased to this day: so if the Lord would put in this Light, and be the perpetual Fountain thereof to you, it would abide, &c. *Thy Word I have hid in my heart,* &c. Psal.119.

SECT. IV.

HEnce learn the cure of hypocrisie, *viz.* Remove the cause, which is folly; and if you would be sincere, Oh prize, and beg for more light, and love it, and you shall then after you have digged for it, find it. Would it not be sad to be led blindfold like them till they were in the midst of *Samaria,* so till in the midst of Hell? Would it not be sad to be like *Sodomites,* groping for the door? Especially you that are come over to this Countrey for more of the Knowledge o Christ. Oh then Beloved, take heed you bury not your minds in the earth, lose not your thoughts in the dung. And you must stand one day before God, when the Book of the secrets of your hearts shall be opened, when if found too light, then would it not be a doleful parting to lose the Lord Jesus after such light and affections, for want of a little more Light? Oh look to your selves now!

Use 5.

1. Stick close to the guidance of the Scriptures, and love them. *Moses* saith, *Then other Nations shall say, what people so wise?* Deut.4.6. And these make *the men of God* (2 Tim.3.15.) full of Gods Spirit, *wise unto salvation,* and for neglect of this, the Lord gave, and doth *give men up to strong delusions, that they believe lies,* viz. *because they loved not the Truth.* Never a Truth but is unsealed by Blood, and revealed to be the infinite wisdom of the Father, and love to poor lost men, where God opens all his heart; if men will despise these, 'tis pity but they should be blinded. Do not scoffe at those that know the Lord here, they are Scripture-learned men, if not, never Spirit-learned. Take this for your Counseller, in all your doubts and fears it will reach you. A man gets an opinion, or falls in love with a sinful corruption, both deceive him. Why so? Is there no word against it? Oh yes, but they will not hear it, but make God and Scripture bow down to them, they will not be led by it. Oh intreat the Lord to keep thee from that.

Means 1.

2. Be abundant in meditation dayly, Psal.119.99. 'Tis an hundred to one else if not miserably deluded. And as the Spirit convinceth first of sin, righteousnesse and judgment, so let your thoughts be. This makes a man see far, and see much.

Means 2.

3. Practise what you know, and tast the sweetnesse of it there, Psal.119.100. And then the heart will grow savingly full of Divine Light. Nothing makes men foolish but this. *Oh tast and see!* Oh if men knew the sweet of this way of Truth, they would ever walk in it, and bring others to submit to it! *Shall I hide from Abram, that will teach his Family?* Gen.18.17,19.

Means 3.

4. Cast up your eyes to Christ glorified, being full of the Spirit for thee, and beg of him, as if he were with thee to send it down. As *Solomon* asked this. See, *John* 7.39.

Means 4.

Oh learn to be exceeding thankful for any saving light the Lord hath kindled in you, if ever it hath been powerful to discover and remove the hidden hypocrisie of thy heart, that now the Lord hath made thee plain and serious for him, that its death not to live, Heaven for to live unto him. Oh then blesse the Lord for that means that did it for thee, that mightst have perished in thy own delusions and dreams.

Use 6.

dreams. Time was when thou waſt deceived, now the Lord hath made thy eyes brighter than the Sun, to ſee ſuch things as are hid from great ones in the world. Oh though it be but a little, yet if real and ſaving light, bleſſe him. A man that hath been in midſt of Sands, and without a Pilot, afterwards looks back, and ſaith, there I might have ſplit. Oh this is wonderful to him! Oh Chriſt did thus! *I thank thee thou haſt hid*, &c. *Mat.*11.25. The Lord hath hid them from heads and hearts of many wiſe and prudent, and ever they ſhall be hid, and *è contra*, revealed them to thee, a babe, a weak one, a poor ignorant one, Mat.16.17. *Fleſh and blood hath not revealed it*, ſo as to build here on this righteouſneſſe, to fetch all light and life from Chriſt, and cleave alone to him. Oh remember you are called *out of darkneſſe into marvellous light to ſhew forth his vertues?* What canſt deſire more than eternal life? And this is it, 1 *John* 5.20. *John* 17.30.

CHAP. XVI.

That Hypocrites diſcover themſelves in an un-effeǔual uſe of the Means of Grace.

Secondly, *The difference between the wiſe and fooliſh Virgins is ſet down more particularly*, v.3,4.

SECT. I.

THIS particular difference is declared by the different practiſe of the fooliſh and wiſe Virgins each from other.

1. That the Fooliſh though they had ſo much wiſdom (like the wiſe) as to take *Lamps*, yet ſo much folly was bound up in their hearts, as that *they took no Oyl in their Veſſels for their Lamps.*

2. That the wiſe did not only light their Lamps, but they did alſo fill their Veſſels with Oyl, that either their Lamp might never go out, or if it did, it might be ſoon kindled again. More plainl, The Fooliſh contented themſelves with the name and blaze of outward Profeſſion, kindled from ſome inward, yet lighter and more ſuperficiall ſtrokes of Gods Spirit, neglecting the great work within: But the wiſe did not only carry their Lamps of outward Profeſſion, but they filled their Veſſels, and got an inward Principle of the Spirit of the Lord Jeſus to maintain their profeſſion before man, and their uprightneſſe before the Lord. So that me-thinks here is a double difference, the firſt is implied, the ſecond plainly ex-preſt.

1. That which is implied is this, that the Fooliſh made choice of a good end, *viz.* to meet Chriſt, but it was with an ineffectual uſe of means to that end; their Lamps were to light and lead them to Chriſt. Theſe Lights might blaze for a time, but they would conſume without Oyl. They neglect that, the wiſe were better inſtructed than ſo.

2. The Fooliſh glory in an outward Profeſſion, as alſo in ſome ſuperficial affection, without an inward Principle of the gracious preſence of the eternal a-nointing and Spirit in them; but the wiſe have it, and are carried to Glory by it. And more at this time of the Lamps and Veſſels I ſhall not ſpeak.

Doǔ. 1.

1. *That the cloſeſt Hypocrites of Virgin-Churches diſcover themſelves (at leaſt be-fore the Lord) in an ineffectual uſe of thoſe means that do conduce towards their deſired and expected end.*   The

The Bridegroom is here looked for, the presence of Christ Jesus is longed for, he comes in the night, they must meet him in the night. Now means they use, Lamps they take, and so much Oyl as kindles their Lamps; but Oyl they take not in their Vessels, the only means to preserve their Lamps from going out, that so they may meet the Lord and not be shut out from the Lord, as at last these carelesse Virgins were. Search the Churches for the present, search the Records of Ages past, many have desired the Lord and looked for the Lord, and yet have lost the Lord their end: Why so? They never had hearts effectually to use and improve the means to that end, either outward or inward. Look upon men out of the Church, they perish because they have no remedy, they have no Lamps to light, they have no Bread to eat, no Means to help. But why do those within the Church perish? Is it because there is no remedy? No, but because they do not use the remedy. Is it because they want Means? No, but because they do not effectually improve means. Here they fall short, herein they discover themselves. Look but upon this next Parable of the Talents, v. 25. One of them was cast off, and cast out. Why? Because he had no Talents? No, But because he had no mind nor lift to use his Talent, he did not make his gain out of it to attain his end. All Ordinances of God, and all that time we have under them are Talents. Now wherein do Hypocrites fail? There is a secret gain of Ordinances which Hypocrites regard not, and hence the best hypocrite lives in debt, and dies a Beggar. For Prov. 16.17. *Wherefore is there a price in the hand of a fool, but no heart to use it?* Precious Liberties, Ordinances, that many have desired to see, and have not seen them. Why doth the Lord betrust him with such that useth them not? Oh he hath them, but here is his wound, he hath no heart to use them! Look throughout all the Word, Why have many set a great price on Christ, and yet have lost him? Because like higling Chapmen, they have had a desire to the Commodity, but they have been loath to be at the cost to use the means for it. The Gospel brings Christ and Immortality to light, and this Serpent is lifted up, this Lamb slain before mens eyes, and this Bread put to mens lips and mouths. Why are not all possessed of him, blessed in him? The Lord saith, come, and *the Spirit saith, come, and the Bride saith, come*; Why the reason is, men will not use the means for him, Isa. 55.2.3,4. Men will lay out their money, though it be for *that which is not Bread*. Jer. 2.5,6,7,8. *I brought them through Pits into a pleasant Land, to eat the goodnesse thereof.* And doubtlesse he brought not a herd of swine into *Canaan*, only to enjoy the outward blessings and swill of *Canaan*, but to enjoy the good of his Temple, Ordinances, &c. But where was their wound? *Neither Priests nor People said, where is the Lord?* i.e. Where is the Lord in these waies, that we may come at last to the full enjoyment of him by these? This they neglected. Methinks 'tis with the best hypocrites as 'tis with divers old Merchants, they prize and desire the gain of Merchandise, but to be at the trouble to prepare the Ship, to put themselves upon the hazards and dangers of the Ship, to go and fetch the Treasure that they prize, this they will never do. So many prize and desire earnestly the Treasures of Heaven, here is their end, but to be at the trouble of a Heaven-Voyage to fetch this Treasure, to *passe through the Valley of Baca*, Tears, Temptations, the Powers of Darknesse, the Breaches, Oppositions, and Contradictions of a sinful, unbelieving heart, good and evil report, to passe from one depth and wave to another, this the best hypocrite failes in, and hence loseth all at last. And this I conceive to be one of the great differences between the strong desires and esteems of Hypocrites and Saints.

X   SECT.

SECT. II.

I. IN regard of God, becaufe this neglect is one of the great means by which he doth execute his eternal rejection of men, and hence here they ever do fail.

For 1. The Lord hath chofen fome to life, the end.

2. He chufeth certain means to lead to this end.

3. He purpofeth to carry all his Elect by thefe means to that end; themfelves cannot; hence the Lord doth. And hence arifeth the great peace and fupport of the Saints, when they look upon the everlafting mountains of hindrances and impoffibilities in their way, the Lord hath undertaken to carry them through them, *John* 17.15. That when heart and ftrength failes, he will be heart and ftrength, and guide by his counfel, and bring to his Glory. And hence as all the Elect are to be certainly carried through all means to their end, and this is proper to them, fo hence the beft Hypocrite being never appointed certainly to come to this end, ever failes in the ufe of means; there he is and fhall be forfaken of God, and forfake God. Hence *John* 6. When many ufed the means, and followed Chrift for a time, that they might have life, at laft they forfook Chrift and means to have him. Why? *v*. 65. Becaufe *none can come to me, except it were given him of the Father*. Hence look as certainly as the Decree of Reprobation fhall ftand, he having not appointed them to the end; fo he never carries them through all means to that end, and therefore here they do ever fail. As 'tis in a Family, thofe that the Lord of the Family intends to give his eftate unto, he keeps a ftrict eye upon them, keeps them under the Government of the Family; as for others, let them go where they will, and do what they will; fo here, all that fhall enjoy God, are put under the Kingdom of the Son. Hence he is faid to give it up: To others he will fay, you love Liberty, take it then.

II. Becaufe the Lord and Fellowfhip with him, is never indeed their laft & utmoft end, or their only end, but they have fome other end of their own; & hence they are never carried ftrongly through all means to that end. For this is the nature of a mans laft and utmoft end, it carries a man without any ftop toward it, and that with delight. As a man that hath ho our and preferment, and great hopes in his eye, that is reaching to the top of his afpiring thoughts, he will ride, and run, and flatter, and fin, *&c.* A man that hath riches in his eye, he will *rife early, and go to bed late, eat the bread of carefulneffe*, and he never hath enough. A man that is fick, and hath health in his eye, takes his Phyfick, obferves his feafons, wafts his eftate, for this is his end. Hence a Hypocrite never making Chrift his laft end, but being ever *a double-minded man, James* 1. And having his own ends, and lufts, and felf to attend upon, hence the Byas draws him from following Chrift effectually, but he muft follow his own ends, and hence ever neglects the means that lead him thereunto, *Mat.* 6.24. Look as 'tis with men that have two Trades, or two Shops, one is as much as ever they can follow or tend, they are forced at laft to put off one, and they muft neglect the one: So here.

III. In regard of that Spirit of floath and flumber, which the Lord ever leaves the beft Hypocrite unto; which is the deareft luft and laft enemy that the Lord deftroyes in all his, but never deftroies in thefe. Which fo might'ly oppreffeth all their fenfes, that they cannot ufe effectually all means to accomplifh their ends. And hence a man defires the end, but hath it not, *Prov.* 13.4. The Lord propofeth the moft Glorious end to his people, but its through many difficulties that we muft come to it. Now there being the Spirit of floath within, and thefe difficulties without, a Hypocrite fits down and refts under the fhadow of this growing, fpreading fin; and faith 'tis hard, and becaufe he cannot do fo, he hopes 'tis but an infirmity, and God will accept of his desires, and here perisheth, Mat. 7.14. *For straight is the gate that leads unto life, hence few there be that find it.* Look as it was with the *Israelites*, *Canaan* they were bound for, they came at last to it, but when their Spies had told them of the difficulties, they sank, only *Caleb* and *Joshua* of that mighty Host that had upright hearts here. Heavy things must descend, though cast up ; for their place is downward. Light things, cast them downward, yet they must up again, for their place is upward ; So 'tis here : A sluggish heart may be lift up by means, but they cannot hold it, their place is downward, here is their rest ; so Saints, *è contra*, like fire will consume all difficulties, their rest is upward.

SECT. III.

Use 1.

HEnce we see one ground of many complaints that are in the mouths of many Professors of the waies of God, that never find the sweet which is the end of their Christian course, that are ever complaining of wants, but never feel supplies, ever learning, never knowing, ever hoping, never having, ever confessing of their sins, never triumphing over their sin, ever wishing that they had the Lord, but never possessing the Lord. And hence have minds full of fears, and mouths full of complaints, and hence finding no sweet in their course, could be content but for shame, to throw by their Profession. Why ? Where is the cause of this ? Is Heaven so barren and beggarly, that there are no Jewels to be had there ? Are the fields of Gods Ordinances so empty, that there is no Treasure to be found there ? Oh yes ! there 'tis, but Christians are idle, there is the Treasure, but they cannot beg, much lesse dig for it, *Prov*.2.3,4,5,6. If there be a treasure in the ground, and a man can find nothing, and so is ever complaining, the fault is in the man, he doth not dig long enough, nor deep enough ; so 'tis here : There is never an Ordinance, but the Lord is in it ; *he never said to the House of Jacob seek his face in vain*. Men pray, and if a few sighs will fetch in relief, well and good, if not, they cast that Shovel by, *dig I cannot* ; they spend some time in laying sin to heart, but if I cannot presently feel the bitternesse of it, I cannot help it, *dig I cannot*. A man can be content to hear the Word, and to listen after it, but to stir up the soul to lay hold on the Lord, that their sleep forbids, Prov.13.4. *The soul of the diligent shall be made fat*. Why do you famish under means ? Is it because the Lord is unwilling or unable to relieve ? No, *John* 6.27. You *labour for that bread that perisheth*. Labour not for it, but for the other, and the Son of man will give it you, for he is sealed for that very end. You complain your hearts are alwaies out of frame. Tell me, do you keep them with all diligence ? *Prov*.4.23. With all your Guard about it ? You complain you never get assurance. Do you use all diligence to make it sure ? You complain you seek and find not. Do you seek him diligently ? *Heb*.11.6. Oh this is the cause ! *The Lord hath given you the Spirit of slumber*. Oh lay not the fault on the Lord, but on thine own carelesse heart, and lament over it, and say, this hath been the cause of all my complaints and woe. Oh I remember what the Lord by *Jeremy* speaks ! *Go into the strong Holds, for the Lord hath poured upon us the Spirit of deep sleep, and given us the waters of Gall to drink*. I confesse the Lords choicest servants have their complaints, their sighs and groans unutterable, they have their fears, temptations and tears : Who more abundantly ? Yet Beloved, methinks, 'tis with them as 'tis with Passengers and Travellers towards their home, that they see it Twenty Miles off sometime, when they be on the Top of an Hill, after they have gone a little farther, they come into a Valley, and then they complain they have lost the sight of it, and cannot see it again scarce till they be upon it ; yet they sit not down in their Valley, but are going towards it. *They go from strength to strength*,

though

though they come tired thither ; as Psal.84.7,8. *They passe from strength to strength till they come to see God in Sion.* They rest not in their complaints, but get on ; and the star before them, the Means that lead them to that end, make them (as Mat.2.10.) *rejoyce with exceeding great joy.* I confesse they may for a time give way to their sloath, and sit in their vallies, and turn day into night, and sleep out almost the season of means ; yet you shall ever find this, if ordinary means a-waken them not, terrible Flashings and Lightnings of wrath do ; and in their afflictions and terrours and wounds of Conscience, Hos.5.15. *they shall seek the Lord early.* Ponder therefore of this cause, and in a time of sorrow they shall complain for somthing, *viz.* for their sloath. This may be the greatest sin of some, they live in no sin, but complaint, thy complaints may be fruits of sloath in not using means, and this may be thy great sin.

Use 2. Hence learn 'tis not having of Means in this place, nor coming hither for Means, that will do you any good or evidence your safe and good estate, but an effectual use and improvement of them ; not only the use of outward, but inward means too. Men that have never so great a stock may die Beggars, by not im-proving it, *Deut.*29.3,4.

1. Many seeing and beholding that Sun which is set with them, to be risen here in these Western Parts, partly out of fear of persecution, partly by Friends per-swasion and company, partly to enjoy Gods Ordinances, have taken their flight hither.

But 2. Being come, wish Oh that our eyes had never seen it ? partly through plenty of means, despise and loath them, partly through multitude of coveting or vexing cares have no hearts to, or time to use them.

And yet 3. Are comforted in this, that they have them, though they see no God in them, tast little sweetnesse, receive little power from them, and hope to go to Heaven at next remove, that have come so far for these, &c. I would to God it were so. But oh consider,

1. If you improve them not, your coming hither is but the discovery of thy hy-pocrisie to men and Angels, for this is the stage wherein the most fine-spun hypo-crisie and real sincerity shall act its part.

2. Nay thou art so far from being blessed in having them thus, that Gods fier-cest plagues shall here approach thy dwelling. The Arke among the *Philistims* made the Lord plague the *Philistims.*

3. Nay this shall lay all desolate one day. They cried *the Temple of the Lord,* Jer.7. *Go to Shiloh.* So I say, Go to the *Palatinate,* Go to *Germany, France,* go to the places whence you came, and *see what the Lord hath done.*

4. This shall be as to Saints greatest joy, when they shall look back, and see all the difficulties they have passed over, that here and there hearts and help failed, and there I lingred, but the Lord was merciful, and pulled me out, and they shall wonder at that Faithfulnesse and Grace ; so here : This will be terrour and anguish, that I came so far, and had means, and took some pains, and was almost perswaded one time, almost confuted another, almost conquered and had yielded up all at another, but oh my Lump fell down to the dust again, and my soul forsook the pursuing of the Lord again ? and this shall be the portion of Hypocrites. You may neglect and wrap up your Talents, but the Lord hath a time to call you to an account what gain you make. Look therefore to it, it may be some of you have need to improve means, you despise them in one place, and hither you come for them, and poor hearts, eyes dim, hearts hard, Consci-ences asleep, ears deaf, breath gone, life lost, God departed, and nothing left but a dead Carcase. It may be some are sincere, and the work of Gods Spirit is set back, your Lamps are out, your watchful minds and tender hearts and earnest pursuit after the Lord is gone. Oh then consider what little cause you have to boast in means ! Men that have no part in ships, look for no gain ; but if you
have

have any part in the Blessing of Ordinances, rest not without it.

Hence see what need you have of a mighty and unresistable power of the Lords Grace and Spirit, to carry you an end in your Christian course, if ever you come to life. For if Hypocrisie discovers it self in an ineffectual use of means, then you will find all the powers of darknesse resisting and seeking to surprize you here. That as 'tis with Thieves, you shall not see nor find them lying in the City, 'tis in vain there to offer any violence, but in the way; So Satan cannot step unto the Gates of Heaven to keep you from thence, and hence all his power and policy lies in the way of means, to keep you from thence. And hence look upon the best man, how many hindrances to Prayer sometime, though he hath tasted the sweet of it, he had rather die than pray. How soon are the thoughts turned from God, when we come to draw nigh to God, how unable to wake one hour? That if it were not the invincible strength of a God that did support them, 1 Pet. 1.5. they could never go on. Tell me you poor Creatures that never were effectually carried to your end by means, Do you not oft find checks for sin, desires against it, Christ and mercy weeping at your knees, melting over you, and your hearts almost perswaded? Do you not find a want of Christ, and Grace, and Spirit, and Promises, and you hope it will be better? Do you not find some movings towards the Lord, but yet withal do you not find a dead, sloathful heart slayes you again? The veriest reprobate in the world may have as good an assurance of heaven as thou, there may be better in Hell than thee. And who can mend this? long, long it hath been thus. Oh then feel a need of the Lords irresistable power! Thou indeed hast an end, but say, Lord thou must carry me like a lost sheep on thy shoulders to that end! *Seek the Lord and his strength, seek his face evermore*, in all means, at all times, but seek his strength then, Col. 1.29. *I labour thus, striving according to his working, which works in me mightily:* and so I strive. Oh see need of this! Many of you make work with your own hearts, and strive, and endeavour, and yet cannot stir. Oh look then for this mighty working, and feel a need of it!

SECT. IV.

Hence judge what your estates are this day before the Lord. I know and believe that you prize, pray for, long for the end, and if ever the Lord saves and pardons you, you shall have cause to blesse him. You may do as hath been said, but never find a heart given you by the invincible wrestlings of a God to use and improve all means to that end; and thus your practise in the habitual neglect of means is a clear and manifest witnesse, like the day against you, that you do not desire sincerely the end (as you think) in having so little respect to the means that conduce thereunto. Did you ever see that man that did indeed desire life, but he would use all means, wits, and friends, nay cut off his Limbs to preserve it? But however, put that name upon it, say you do desire and prize the end, yet if the Lord leaves you, or you forsake the Lord in a neglect of means, that lead thereto, and that effectually; what you may be, and what the Lord may do, I know not, but to this day your estate is no better than a painted salvation and pictured hypocrisie before the Lord. That stone at which the closest hypocrites have stumbled, that rock on which the best hypocrite hath been broken, thou art fallen upon, that enemy of sloath, which hath carried Kings (men that have worn the Crown of Profession in the world) miserable Captives, (notwithstanding their lamentable cries, Lord save us!) to hell, the same enemy hath already bound thee up in Chaines, and what will become of thee, 'tis only known in his Breast, that by the voice of his Trump can awaken the dead, and break the bonds of sloath and death it self. But you will say, there are no Virgins among us that neglect to take their oyle, that so far forget themselves as to neglect the means, that are come so many thousand miles for means; there is not a day but some line is drawn, not a Sermon, Sabbath but some good got, or else they think themselves half undone, not a prayer but one step nearer to glory: The day is not long enough, and therefore the nights are spent in wrestling with the Angel; nay, in prevailing with God for themselves and Churches, and blessing on both; Sabbaths are the day-breaks of heaven, the fellowship of Saints better then to stand before Kings, the fellowship of Christ in heaven so sweet, that in seeking of him men forget themselves, nay to eat their bread; that if the Lord should have let out the vineyard of Ordinances to any Husbandmen in the world, who could or would have taken more pains to dig it, to dress it, then we doe. Beloved, those enlargements that are in any after the Lord, the Lord cherish and increase them, but I fear we may go five times about the tree before we see such loaden boughs. I am much mistaken if the best may not be discovered here, the fairest flowers in the field must wither, they cannot last, and the best affections that are but temporary, that have acted men mightily for a time in the use of means, must perish in the neglect of means at last. I shall not therefore meddle with profane or carnal Gospellers, so much as with close deceivers of their own souls; and look as 'tis in all sores, you may know where the sore is by the lappings, so you may know a sluggard that neglects means by his shifts: For if you observe, no sin hath so many shifts and excuses for it as this; *Saul* when he had not gone through stich with the Lords work in slaying the *Amalekites*, what adoe had *Samuel* to convince him? He tells a lye, lays the blame on the people, propounds the good end and affection he had; So here: Thus it is with many, as *Viz.*

4. Those that live in a secret neglect of means, and yet hope to come to their end, because of their desires; we shall finde the Scripture gives us two sorts of desires. 1. Of the righteous. 2. Of the sluggard. 1. *The desires of the righteous*, Prov. 10. 24. *shall be granted*, being breathings of Gods eternal Spirit, not a sigh or groan unanswered. 2. Of the sluggard, *Prov.* 21. 15. *The desire of the slothful kills him, for his hands refuse to labour*: the desires of the righteous are ever spurs to quicken them up in the use of means mightily, the desires of the sluggard bridle him up, they binde his hands, and fetter his feet, that he cannot but neglect means: Some desires there be that arise from the need of a good, and here will not only be desires, but all means used, as in point of famine; some only from want of a good, and here a man usually contents himself with bare desires, never hath a heart to use the means mightily for that end. Many a one is convinced his state is miserable, and fears it, and *Balaam*-like, sees the blessedness of the people of God, and knows he wants pardon, and life, and peace, and promises, and Christ, and desires it; oh that I might die their death, oh that I might live and drink that water, that I might thirst no more, oh that my sins were pardoned, oh that my heart was humbled. But what if the Lord grant them no peace nor pardon? Do they make earnest enquiry after the Lord Christ with restless pursuits and groans because they need it, is it worth that? Oh no, but yet they hope God will be so merciful as to accept their desires, and so they rest, and live and die in that rest, oh poor creatures your desires kill you; as a man is undone with slothful servants that cannot earn their own, much less get their masters bread. And many in Hell, say I had thought my desires would have carried me to glory, but now I see they have been slothful, and here I must perish and famish for ever; had I known of this, I would rather have wept out my eyes, and filled the world with my sorrowful complaints, my meditations of the Lord should have been at midnight; I would have deceived my eyes of sleep at night, and deprived my self of bread at day, and lost my limbs, had I but known that by contenting my self with these desires, I should have lost my life. Here many Christians are falsly bottomed, they are troubled about their

estate,

eſtate, come to ſome or other and profeſſe their deſires are after Chriſt and grace, &c. And then conforme (as in ſinking firſt a man ſnatcheth at any Flag or Twig) with theſe deſires, before they have followed the Lord in the uſe of all means to get the thing they deſire. And here is the firſt beginning of the Lords forſaking of them, and theirs of the Lord, and he is left alone only with his deſires, that if any duty be neglected, deſires comfort him; if grace reſiſted, deſires quiet him; if ſin keeping him captive, deſires fill him; *Luke* 13. 24. And ſo like a Bird that lies in the neſt, but its wings never grow, there it periſheth. I know Saints may comfort themſelves with deſires before the things be given, becauſe promiſed, but you ſhall ſee an endleſſe reach in them in the uſe of all means, *Phil.* 3. 13. Others think their neglect of means to be but an infirmity, & that their deſires will ſerve, & hence abuſe that Scripture, *Rom.* 7.

2. They that neglect the means and yet hope to come to their end, becauſe of worldly clogs and incumbrances here; for this is the very ſpirit of many a man. If God keeps the houſe from being burnt, and family from being ſick, it may be family prayer is neglected, if not that, yet ſecret is omitted; if not that, yet meditation; a man can get no heed nor heart, nor time for it, if any good is got, its loſt again; Sabbaths ſpent, and no good gained; a man knows his ſoul lies waſte and common without any fence or watch, and that he would not let his fields lie as he doth his heart, overgrown with cares and luſts and vain thoughts. Now many a man though he doth diſlike this, yet lives in this. Why? Is this your home, are theſe things your portion? No, but yet thinks he may with a ſafe Conſcience continue thus, and God forgive him too; why the family is great, children encreaſe upon me, (and they are ſo buſie and long a dreſſing on the Lords day, that Sermon is out before they come) and we are not called to book it all day as Miniſters can, and worldly employments are ſo many, and the beſt are entangled here; and they think this is an excuſe, *Luke* 14. 18, 19. Nay many a one convinced of this, yet lives in this againſt the light of conviction, hoping that one day the ſtream of worldly occaſions will be run by. I confeſſe, as the Lord hath given us his Ordinances to ſeek him in, ſo he hath appointed our callings to walk with him in: *Adam* in Paradiſe muſt not be idle, but look to the garden; and in this land thoſe that will be good husbands for God (leaſt they diſcredit their profeſſion by bringing themſelves to a piece of bread) muſt be good husbands for themſelves: But here is that which ſtings, when to worldly employments, men are ſervants, not Lords of them, when men do not make their occaſions bow down to them, and ſerve them, that they may ſerve and ſeek a God, but they bow down their knees, nay baſely their backs, under the feet of any mean imployment, and that muſt be followed with neglect of God. Do not ſay who is not entangled here? I tell you if Chriſts prayer can prevail ſome are not, *John* 17. 15. *I pray not that thou wouldeſt take them out of the world, but keep them from the evil:* If blood can prevail it doth, *Gal.* 1. 4. Oh look to this! it may be ſome of you do not only neglect the Lord in means, but when the Lord comes to you in means and quickens your hearts and kindles many reſolutions in you; you neglect the Lord, all dyes again, oh it is the world! know your eſtates by this.

3. Thoſe that depart from God in the neglect of means, becauſe they finde no good, and do not feel themſelves a whit the better for them; they neglect this trade, becauſe they finde it a gainleſs trade: For this God executes his eternall rejection upon many a ſoul: As it was with *Saul*, it was one of the laſt Vials God poured out upon him, 1 *Sam.* 28. 5, 6, 15. ſaith he, *I am ſore diſtreſſed, and the Lord anſwers me not by Urim nor by Thummim, and therefore am I come to thee;* let a Devil comfort me if God will not: So many a ſoul having committed ſome ſin that lies glowing on the Conſcience, is ſore troubled, and firſt it goes to the Lord, and the Lord anſwers not, there is ſilence in heaven, and

in all means, but the noise of fears within; now at last the soul doth not forsake the Lord for Satan plainly, but what means can comfort them that they seek for, and in time a man is weary of waiting at Gods gate, and hence a form of duties, and prayers, and custome of devotion is kept to quiet the conscience; but they are not restless for the gain of them, for the Lord in them: they think 'tis in vain, to no profit, as those in *Mal.* 3. 14. to walk mournfully. *Jonah* was cast out of Gods sight, yet through *the belly of a Whale he would look toward the Temple.* So 'tis with the people of God, though they sometimes conclude thus, and think not to seek any more, yet their hearts have tasted the good, and their faith beleeves there is that hid in the Lord in his Temple, that it never saw yet, hence they look still. What made the man *Mat.* 25. hide his talent in the earth? I thought thou wast an hard Master, and lookedst for so much gain, and I could not get it, and hence he hid his Talent. Hence men keep the means, without use of the means, and some that have for a time been used to do so, keep it as their custome without making any such work of it, as to gain the end of the means.

4. Those that do neglect the Lord in means by an effectual pursuit of them, because of some sips and taste of some good in them; and some thinks 'tis in this case as 'tis in some Countries where if a man comes to their house in the afternoon, and both have a minde to part, yet loth to part without shewing some kindness, and the other without tasting of it, they lay their voiding napkin, and finding that refreshing there, they are content to lose their supper. So 'tis here, a man comes weary to the Lords House, to his Ordinances, the Lord will not let him go without some expression of kindness, nor they depart willingly from the Lord without it, and hence the Lord gives them light out of darkness, joy out of sorrow, peace out of trouble, a taste of his sweetness, after tasts of sins bitterness, and then they take their leave; as they *Hebr.* 6. 2, 3, 4, 5. And here the Lord leaves many a poor creature, *Deut.* 29. 2, 3, 4. they did see something, and tast something, and there they rested; Oh but the Lord gave them not eyes to see, &c. For no Hypocrite living is fully emptied of his lusts, but hath somewhat to fill him; but some emptiness he may have, hence may have some desires after the Lord, and hence it is not the fulness of God onely that satisfies him, but some tasts of Gods kindness, and small things do and must fill him; his lusts fill him in part, and something of God is wanting, and that some little matter doth make up. Hence when this is done, means is neglected fearfully, a mans heart is hardned and ignorant, a little light and sorrow stays him, as the stony ground though there be a stone at bottom; a man is full of doubts, and a little hope which frees him from fears quiets him, hence he never conquers unbelief: A man hath lived a loose course, a little resolution of heart stays him, though the heart will depart again, as those *Deut.* 5. 27, 29. the Lord hath but little of their hearts, and the Lord shews them but little of his: And hence this is usual to see a false heart most diligent in seeking the Lord when he hath been worst, and most careless when 'tis best. Hence many at first conversion sought the Lord earnestly, afterward affections and endeavours die, that now they are as good as the Word can make them: Hence the Lord when in mercy he deals with men, keeps them long fasting till the time of extremity comes, and then he poures waters on the thirsty. Hence better for those never to have known, 2 *Pet.* 2. 21. and an hypocrites last end is to satisfie himself, hence he hath enough; a Saints is to satisfie Christ, hence he never hath enough.

5. Those that do neglect the Lord under this colour of receiving Christ, they can do nothing themselves, and Christ must do all; and hence neglect the Lord secretly, and sometimes quarrel with the Ministry privately, when pressed to a duty or to beleeve. Alas what can a man do, when all the Ministers in the world

world have preached their hearts out, at last they must bring us to Christ ; what
else should the Apostle mean, *Rom. 4. 5. Not to him that worketh, but beleeveth
is faith accounted for righteousness. I must not live, I must let Christ live,* &c.
And hence say they the cause of perishing is not mens wills, but Gods, he elects
not, he gives no heart; such hypocrites the Lord prophesies of, *Mat. 7. 21. Many
that say to me Lord, Lord,* i. that advance the Lord Jesus, and live in neglect of
all duties, and bring the Lord of glory not from his Throne in Heaven to Hell,
but which is worse, debase him from his glory to sin; to be the cover of sin, and
protector of it. Beloved, I know no surer sign of a vessel that God intends to
break in peeces then this, to live in this neglect, *2 Tim. 2. 20.* Nay 'tis an e-
vidence there is no hope, no living hope, *1 John 3. 3. He that hath this hope,
purgeth himself as Christ is pure.* Many it seems boasted of hope in Christ, so
do Saints, but he gives this Note, He purgeth himself, he will not sluggishly put
all on Christ. Tis true, 'tis the mighty working of Christ that must conquer
thy lusts, but must this put you to neglect striving, *Col. 1. 29. I strive according
to the working.* And for mine own part, though Ile not dispute the point at large,
I beleeve, there is a constant assistance of the mighty power of the Lord Jesus
in the souls of all the Saints, *1 Pet. 1. 5.* And hence *1 John 4. Greater is he
that is in you, then in the world.* The Saints as they receive the Lord Jesus to
rule them, that he alone may be Lord and King not only in heaven, but in their
hearts; So a false heart receives Christ lastly for to ease him : Sometime for to
ease him of the burden of Conscience ; sometime to ease him of the Lords work,
the burthen of his will; and hence some at last have complained, though hardly
convinced of it, that they could be contented the Lord should act them ; but
their end was, that hereby they might be rid of their burden, and so eased by
him. I have heard a Question should be askt, What is the difference between
the workings of Gods Spirit and the Saints ? And that the Answer was, 1. The
one is by graces, the other immediatly. 2. The Spirits is, when a man labours
least : quite cross to the stream of truth : Take heed how you understand these
points aright, the depth of the most hellish villany in the world lies un er them.
Wo to thee that canst paint such a Christ in thy head, and receive such a Christ
into thy heart as must be a pander to your sloth ; the Lord will revenge this
wrong done to his glory with greater sorrows then ever any felt : To make
Christ not only meat and drink to feed, but cloaths to cover your sloth. Why
what can we doe? what can we doe? Why as the first *Adam* conveies not
only guilt but power : So the second conveys both righteousness and strength ;
as Christ is now triumphing by his eternal Spirit, and his life is heavenly ; so
if you be in Christ, there is a Spirit of Christ, whereby a never dying life is begot, that can and doth conquer ; though it be but a spark, Christ maintaining it,
it shall come to victory. You are forsaken of Christ if you want this, or else
take heed this colour make you not forsake him.

6. Those that neglect the means, and yet look for the end in hope of future time, and so neglect the present season. Thus 'tis with many a one ; the
day of life and health, and day of Ordinances continues ; and hence the sluggard cryes, *Prov. 24. 33. Yet a little more slumber,* i. Ile have but a little while
longer, &c. Hence when Conscience checks, Ministers warn, the Lord wooes,
the Spirit cries ; a man puts off all with this, I hope it will be better : And
hence it falls out with them as with those *Matth.* 24. *The Lord comes in a
time they look not for him* ; and of this many on their deathbeds have cryed
out. Think of this you convicted persons that know its miserable with you,
before God stop your breath ; you have nothing to plead for your neglect, but
hope of time. Know it, Gods present seasons are golden, one moment worth
eternity ; and now is the time, if you neglect his season, he will not regard yours.
God is never found in your time, but in his time. Oh lay these things to heart !

Y

especially you that are grown weary of means, that faint in your way; God is not yet weary of continuing means, art thou weary of gaining by means? Oh consider this you that have had many hopes, desires purposes, but all blasted, your time and means neglected: Think on this you that have had marvellous affections, but your spirits are gone; Nothing can make you mend your pace, not all Ministry and Word, but you are clog'd with means. Remember that *Isai.* 65. 8, 9, 10, 11, 12, 13, 14. *For my people that have sought me,* &c.

SECT. V.

TO all those that do effectually seek the Lord in the use of means. And for discovery thereof, Consider:

1. If ever the Lord gave you a heart effectually to seek him in means, you will finde mighty opposition, temptations springing up one after another, &c. from within, from without, and the oppositions will make you seek him the more. Hence *Rom.* 13. 11, 12. he bids us *put off the works of darkness, and put on the armour of light.* When a man desires and lies in his sloth, he meets with little opposition or trouble of his own heart; but here 'tis otherwise, therefore put on armour. And I say the soul is made hereby to seek the Lord the more, as the blinde man, *Mark* 10. 48. *Redeem the time, because the days are evill.* As 'tis with Mariners, they will not only use fair, but side, and almost contrary winds to come neer the shore they are bound for; let the Lord give any grace, oh more of that mercy, as *Moses,* Deut. 3. 24. Let the Lord deny, yet the soul cries the more; let agonies come, Christ prays the more; let the will oppose, he will yeeld himself to the Lord to cross his own will, and deny himself; peace makes him love, and affliction makes him seek the Lord early. Hence because thou art troubled at the feeling of a slothful heart, that will make you seek for more help.

2. You will seek him with your whole heart, so that 'tis the Lord only that the heart is bound for, *Psal.* 119. 2. *Phil.* 3. 12. The feeling of the Lords power and eternal life, and that not only while means last, but when in want of, and banisht from means: As *David* forgets his Crown and Kingdom, and saith, *Psal.* 27. 4. *One thing I have desired.* Hence *Hezekiah* had a promise of life, and going to Gods House when recovered, It was not life he minded so much as this, *What is the sign that I shall go to the House of the Lord?* Hence Saints though they neglect sometimes, yet as a Ship driven back by neglecting winds, or as a Tradesman he is altogether for his gain, yet proves an ill husband sometimes, but when he hath felt his losses he falls to his trade again: So here, like Merchants seeking pearls, &c. *Matth.* 13. 45. Let this comfort you, though you finde nothing, yet Saints are a generation of Seekers, finding time is not come, yet certainly you shall come to your end at last. You have no lappings for the sores of your sloth, but opening them before the Lord, the Lord will heal and help in time.

But I feel no good, hence I am afraid I seek not aright.

Gal. 6. 9. *You shall reap in due time,* and Hebr. 11. 13. All things were cross to the promise yet *Abraham* holds on still.

But I finde my spirit faint, and grow litless and weary.

When heart and strength fail, yet God doth not. God will desert that you may know where your strength, and heart, and help lies.

But 'tis so great, I know no difference between mine and others neglect.

That is sad, yet as 'tis in all sins, falls into them do but undermine them the more. *Peter* denies Christ, as well as sleeps, yet he is the first that preacheth

eth him. When a mans meat is so far from doing good, as that it doth him hurt, he is dying; so that sin is dying, that so h is dying, when food given to it doth kill it. *David* is ready to give up all, yet saith, *Its good for me to draw neer to God,* and there the heart will repose it self again.

Use 6.
Of Exhort.

OH be not slothful then, neglect no means, but use all means, get oyl in your vessels that you may get your desired end. Mariners that are bound for a voyage, when set out, will not be at rest till they are landed where they would be. It was one of the Churches sorrowful complaints, *Isai.* 64. 7. *None that stirs up himself,* &c.

Object.

But I finde many hindrances without me, many sins within me, I have sometime neither strength (nay which is worse) nor yet heart to seek the Lord, though my wants are many, though my days decline; how shall I doe?

Answ.

1. Finde out that which clogs thy heart from seeking effectually, and causeth that neglect, and that makes the Lord neglect thee in thy ineffectual seeking; else thou mayest seek and never finde; and that is some lust, something that easeth the heart which is not God. When the soul hath not bread, it will with the Prodigal then resolve for home; men could not live as they do, so many days without God, unless they did feed on somewhat else beside the Lord. Hence its usual for men in means, to use means for a good, and out of means to resist that good, *Isa.* 58. 1, 2. *Zac.* 7. 6. Men that would have their load drawn, must first take their wild Horses out of it: So do with these lusts. If therefore not for your own, yet for the Lords sake, who else will not be accounted worth the seeking, finde out whatever contents you; necessity hath no Holidays, oh you must have him!

2. Use means, but trust not to them, nor to any strength received to carry you along in this work: you will else neglect and fall from the Lord, and the Lord from you. Its said of *Asa,* 2 *Chro.* 16, 12, 13. *Asa was diseased in his feet in his old age, yet he sought not to the Lord, but Physitians:* So 'tis with many a diseased Christian, they seek not to the Lord, to cure their feet, but means, or themselves, hence he decays and dies. You have the stream of all temptations against you, 'tis not your own Oars, but the Lords winde that must carry you against it; look therefore to an almighty power in means to help you, plead Gods Covenant to put his fear into your hearts, that you may not depart from him, as he will not forsake you, 1 *Cor.* 15. 10. *Paul received not grace in vain, but laboured abundantly; yet not I, but grace.* There is little fear of drowning so long as we keep head above water, so long as we cleave to the Lord Jesus.

3. Love the presence of the Lord and his company. If there be any love between you, you will then finde time, and nothing shall keep you from him, *Jer.* 2. 1, 2, 3. *I remember the love of thine espousals, when thou followedst me in a wildernels thorow pits and deserts.* Remember he hath been in heaven praying for thee, when thou hast been provoking of him, he hath been blessing thee, when thou hast been abusing him, it may be he hath let out his heart blood to make room for thee in his heart, it may be he intends through all eternity to express his dearest love to thee, and is he not worth your love? Love him, and you will be with him, love will be stronger then death, it will break all these bonds.

4. Set before you the greatness of the good you are to use all means to gain; why do men hunt after flesh-pots? The world is esteemed great, 'tis near us, and so for honour: Now Christ and eternity are afar off, and hence they seem little, and hence to seek them is not made a business of greatest weight and im-

portance, 2 *Cor.* 4. 16, 18. *We faint not while we look to things that are eternal*, *Acts* 24. 15, 16. There is not the vilest Reprobate, but when he shall see the glory that shall be revealed, shall stamp and tear his hair and say; Oh, if I had known this! I hope I should never have dreamed out my time so as I have done! We look on the Picture of Goodness in the volume of the Creatures, which satisfie not; Oh never cease looking upward, till you see what you seek for in the greatness of it. Suppose a man should sleep all his life-time, and be in a dream, and in it have all the delights and glory of the world presented before him, at last the ground opens its mouth and swallows him up, and then he is a-wakened, Lord how will he cry? Truly Christ and grace and fellowship with God are not thought of, sought for, are small things with men, but the World is great, and this is your delight; truly 'tis but your dream: What will your souls be when death opens its mouth? what a sad thing is it to see men spin Cop-webs that must be swept down.

Motives.

I. To those that never sought the Lord effectually to this day, not to neg-lect him now; those that are like children born before their time, that have had some sorrow after the Lord, but comforted before it was deep enough; have some desires, but eased with other things before they were satisfied with Christ himself; that have run for a spurt, but are grown weary before they come half way home, and so sit down in the way; like Clocks set slow in the first hour of the day, run slow all the day after: So these set back and think they are set right too, run slow all their life after. That as he said of a covetous man, he had a strong desire for heaven if any would bear his charges thither: So these. And to you I speak, not that never sought, but that have been seeking; yet effectually to use all means, this you never did.

1. Consider how far men have gone? What means they have used? yet have never found to this day, *Luke* 13. 24. *Strive*, saith Christ. This I speak because men think they may neglect their seasons of earnest pursuit after grace, men may sit still, and put all care from themselves to God, and live in their sloth. Oh no, Consider so many snares, so many by paths, so many deceits within, so many fins and lusts to subdue, all time and means is little enough: Take heed of spending prodigally, and think Christs grace will bear you out. Oh! look upon the cries at death-bed, to see some men that have been like famishing men that have wanted bread, and then have cryed bread, bread, but could not eat it. Oh saith *Paul, I beat down my body, lest in preaching to others my self become a cast away.*

2. Consider how others have broken down the greatest difficulties, and are now in glory, as *Rev.* 12. 11. *They loved not their lives to the death.* They have not only spent their time, lost their name, their comforts, but their blood, that have passed through waters, fires, bonds, imprisonments, and with *Paul* have not *accounted their lives dear, that they might finish their work. David* was full of God one would think sometimes he had enough, yet when he awakes, he is with God at midnight, *his thoughts and reins instruct him; the Law was his meditation day and night.* You shall see him in the Temple blessing God, on the Throne advancing the Lord, on the dunghill, in banishment longing after him, when he sate among Princes meditating; and was there here too much cost, might any of this oint-ment have been spared? Consider Christ himself, *Heb.* 12. 1,2,3. cast off sloth, *Looking to Jesus, who for the joy, despised the shame, endured the Cross,* and that not for himself, it may be for thee, that thou mightst not, now he is at the right hand of God: So are the Saints in Heaven, and now rejoycing that ever they sought him, that they spent so much time on him.

3. Consider, There is a time of neglect of Christ, which when past, you shall never finde him again, *John* 7. 3,4. *Ye shall seek me, but never finde me.* You have had

had many Diamond-days and seasons, and God gives you a space to repent, and saith, *My Spirit shall not alway strive*, it may be some are but within that space, that the Lord is at the last cast with you.

4. Consider whatever your condition be, shake off your sloth, and set upon the means, the Lord will be found; do it in good earnest: This will be good news to you that think he will never, but be thy heart like steel, and hard, the Lord will break it, *Hebr.* 11. 6. *he will be found of them that seek him diligently*: And the greater things thou seekest for, the more like to get them; as one of the Fathers thinks that to pray with repetitions, is to pray for small things. *Open thy mouth wide Ile fill it*, and it may be presently in a moment, when thou thinkest least of it, it may be at that time when thou findest most unwillingness and difficulty to seek, seek then and the Lord will be found. Oh this damps many a man in the use of means, he thinks the Lord will never help, and hence is tormented with this thought, and sits down and rests: If you would keep a Labourer from work, or a Traveller from walking, put thorns in their feet; now the work is neglected, there is pricking stuffe, he cannot follow on his businefs now? So 'tis here, *Prov.* 15. 19. Take heed therefore of sitting down with such thoughts as these; its strange thou shouldst be killed for every cut, and because wounded for sin, to fall off from the Lord by unbelief too.

II. Motives to you that have followed the Lord, but now have begun to neglect him: For what cause I know not, but I am sure the Lord hath given you none: Yet a spirit of slumber and sloath is upon you, that you are not the men you were. It may be some for want of place, want of time, many occasions, many sorrowes and temptations in this wildernesse; and hence no means sweet, no bed easie, your bones are broken. It may be a little time of neglect hath emboldned you to a custome: It may be loose examples, the spirits of others flat, and thine is so too, whom God sent into Church-Fellowship to quicken them: It may be an ill Husband is an hindrance, a bad wife, as *Jobs* wife, or whatever 'tis, Oh that God would speak this day to you!

1. Consider thou art nearer to thy salvation than when thou didst first believe; and then you thought no time, no pains too much, but all too little, *Rom.* 13. 11, 12. Mariners near the Shore, look out for Rocks, Lord that I may not split now. Truly as it was with Christ, the longer he did live, the more sorrows, so with you. God hath carried you near salvation, Oh now being neerer, there are worse rocks, look about you now. Satans last temptations are strongest. Oh give not in now! It may be not many daies nor weeks hence thou shalt come to thy journeys end: Awaken then out of sleep.

2. Consider how glad the Lord is of thy company, he hath been so, and will be so again; thou canst not come in too late, 1 *Sam.* 12. 21. as poor and vile as thou art, *Prov.* 8. *His delight is with the Sons of men.* Witnesse mercies, witnesse afflictions. Oh then seek him! Witnesse desertions, then seek him; witnesse his sweet entertainment of thee, many a time when he hath given thee meat that the world knows not of; witnesse so many hindrances which Satan laies in, who knowes how crosse 'tis to Christ, *Jer.* 2. 1, 2, 3. *I remember the love of thine espousals, when thou didst follow me*; especially when with most difficulty, when little strength within, when little hope without, yet Ile not give over. He never forgets this. The Lord hath never such sad daies as when thou turnest thy back on him, and thou never so good, as when thou seekest him.

3. Consider thy gaines, there shall not be the least endeavour, desire, pursuit after the Lord, not the least Word, Prayer, Thought, time spent, but an abundant recompense is in Christs hands; 1 *Cor.* 15. 58. *Ever abounding, knowing that it shall not be in vain.* A man that rowes against the stream, a little neglect of rowing carries him down again. But oh *be ever abounding in the Lords work, for your labour is not in vain in the Lord.*

4. Consider if after admonition again and again, yet you nourish sloth, there is some heavy stroke neer thee. Believe it, he will not alway bear with thy neglect. As nothing joyes him more than your company, so nothing cuts him more than your neglect: But though he save you from eternal misery, yet sometimes your greatest comfort is lost by this means; *Mat.*26,38,40,44,45. First he stirs them up once and again, then leaves them, and comes again, and saith nothing, but the third time, *sleep on, the Son of man is betrayed.* So your comfort, and Christ and his presence are betraied. Some have had their husbands, wives, children estates gone, but which is worst of all, the Lord betraied, the comfort of their hearts gone, and hence horrours and fears surprize them.

III. Motives to us especially in this Countrey.

1. God hath put the price and wealth of the world, better than all Gold and Silver into our hands, who are most unthankful, most unworthy; and will you come so far for means, and here neglect them? Will you thus neglect the Lord? Like men in Consumptions, they long for any thing, and when it comes, they cannot touch it. If it were night, you might fall to sleep, but the day approacheth. Shall God plant his Vineyard, but you never come to eat the fruit of it?

2. Your Temptations are greater here to neglect the Lord. Others are tried with the scorching Sun, there is no sleeping there. God tries us with the shadow, sets us under the Vines of Ordinances; others are in storms, we in calms. *When thou eatest and art full,* saith *Moses, Deut.*8.10,11. Oh *forget not the Lord!* You lose in your estates, and now you are hungry after the same again. Satan when Christ was hungry, assaults him. 'Tis a thousand to one if he makes you not fair offers, and overcomes. Things that cost us much, we prize, and keep, and improve, if of any use. When we go Twenty mile to a Sacrament, Oh then its precious! While under the bondage of oppressors, oh liberty of Conscience, and Ordinances are precious? But when at liberty, we have liberty to have them, hence take liberty to neglect them.

3. Our enemies will be upon us. Who sees not (that observes the Lords dealing) that some sorrows are toward, unlesse the Lord awaken; some sudden blasting blow. If any wind be stirring, men on the tops of the mountains will feel it. The Lord hath set his mountain above all others, and its folly to think to flee from the Crosse, unlesse we flee from Christ. 'Tis part of the portion he doth owe us here, if he loves us. Yet seek the Lord, neglect no seasons to gain him, and you shall he hid, *Zeph.*2.2. Nay when worst times come, 2 *Chron.*15. 3,4,5. when there is no peace, they that seek him shall find him.

I do fear there is at this day as deep mischief plotting against *New-England* as ever the Sun saw. Enemies will first deal subtilly before cruelly, but subtilly that they may deal cruelly. When *Pharaoh* deals wisely, he means to kill. Yet the Lord shall be with us, as of late hath he not been seen in the midst of us for a refuge? Whatever any think, I believe never did the Lord stir up such prayers, Faith, &c. amongst us.

1. Oh therefore seek the Lord still in private. If you find no good, find out the sin. Is not meditation neglected? Communion of Saints not improved? Do not say, we can do nothing, and why are we prest to it? If you cannot, yet 'tis your duty, and you must be prest; and perish you shall if you seek not; or if you be called, there is some spirit of the Lord in you that is mighty.

2. Being come hither for publick helps, and means, and all Ordinances; Oh do not betray your Liberties! but lose your Bloud before you lose them, and the Lord in them. Bear the Arke still on your shoulders, that the Lord may dwell with you. Hence,

1. If you would have the Walls of Magistracy be broken down (the means to preserve the Church and means among you) If they make Laws, deride them; if they execute Laws, appeal from them.　　　　　　2. Would

2. Would you have confusion the mother of discord among the people ? let every man then once one day in the year turn Magistrate, and out-face Authority, and profess tis his liberty.   Would you have rapines, thefts, injustice abound ? let no man know his own, by removing the Land-mark, and destroying Propsieties.

3. Would you have Gods Ordinances in the purity of them removed ? keep out the load of Superstition, but yet for peace sake, suffer a few seeds to be sown amongst you.

4. Would you have all the Messengers of the Gospel at first reviled, at last massacred ? Profess they are no better than Scribes and Pharisees, persecuting Egyptians, enemies to the Lord Jesus, and the more devout the worse; as those that stirred up storms in *Germany* said, Christ had four great enemies : The Pope, Anabaptists, *Martin Luther*, but especially *John Calvin*.

5. Would you ruine the Gospel ? set not Popery against it, but Gospel against Gospel, Promises against Promises, Christ against Christ, Spirit against Spirit , grace against grace, and then he is twice beaten, that falls by his own weapons.

6. Would you have oppressors set over you, to remove ordinances, to encrease your burdens ? Maintain this Principle then that they will not assault us first by craft and subtilty, but openly and violently.

7. Would you have this State in time to degenerate into Tyranny ? Take no care then for making Laws.   When they are made, would you have all Authority turned to a meer vanity ? Be gentle and open the door to all comers that may cut our throats in time ; and if being come they do offend , threaten them and fine them, but use no Sword against them.   You Fathers of the Country be not offended, this I speak not to disparage any, the practise speaks otherwise ; I onely forewarn : I hope the Lord hath prepared better days and mercies for us, I am sure he will, if what means we have we preserve, and what we preserve, we through grace shall improve.

CHAP. XVII.

That the hearts and souls of Believers are made as Vessels, onely for the reception of Christ his Spirit, and the graces thereof.

SECT. I.

2. THe Inward Principle, wherein lies the second Difference which is plainly expressed.

We are now to inquire further concerning these Vessels and the Oyl in them.   Vessels were the place onely of receiving and preserving the oyl for the continual burning and shining of the Lamps : So that though in some Scriptures, by Lamp is understood both the Vessel and the Lamp by a Figure, yet in distinct Phrase of Speech, that is properly the Lamp which burns and gives light, and that which contains the oyl to nourish this is the Vessel : So that the Vessels were not separate things from the Lamp, as though the Lamp was in one hand, and a Vessel in the other ; this was neither the custome, nor comliness of that age to cumber themselves thus ; but the Lamp (as 'tis in ours) was that part which was kindled and lighted , the Vessel that

which

which kept the oil to serve this end: And hence the folly of five of them appeared, that they would carry burning Lamps with empty Vessels; just as if a man should draw the wick through the oyl that it may burn for a time, and provide no oyle in the Vessel to maintain the Lamp; however all comes to one (if they be separate) in respect of that that I aim at.

Thus Literally we see what the Lamp, Vessel, and Oyl is : Now what is Spiritually meant thereby.

1. For the Oyl : What is that? I intend not here to shew the fond and various apprehensions of Popish Writers, who understand by oyle, alms, good works, a good intention, &c. But by Oyl is meant the Spirit of Christ, and the graces of it, peculiar to all the Elect ; and thus in Scripture phrase, 1 *John* 2. 27. the Spirit is called *the anointing* ; and the graces of the Spirit, *Cant*. 1. 3. *The smell of Christs ointments* : Harlots love him for the gifts he sends, but Virgins for the grace he hath. That oyle which ran first on our *Aarons* head, and runs down to his skirts is here meant. Now as Christ himself had not the Spirit without graces, nor these without the Spirit, but both: So both these being in him as in the Fountain, they are in us as in the Vessel.

2. Christ being the Fountain of all grace, and having the Spirit without measure, and therefore hath enough to spare ; he cannot be meant by these Vessels which had but their measure, and such a measure as that they had none to spare for the other. Therefore by Vessels are meant principally the precious souls of the faithful, into which this golden Oyle was put, and therefore, 2 *Cor*. 4. 7. *We have this treasure in earthen vessels.* And *Rom*. 9. 23. *They are vessels of glory, prepared unto glory*, and so frequently ; so that herein the foolish fall short, for the foolish boasted of Christ out of them, but where was the Spirit and vertue of Christ in them ? And this is conceived to be the reason why the main difference is not made, by the want of the external principle, *Viz.* Christ, but by want of the internal principle and work ; this they had not. 1. They had so much oyle, *i. e.* lighter strokes of the Spirit, as kindled a profession but they had not enough. 2. They had so much oyle and light as continued their profession for a while, but it continued not long :

Here therefore observe these four things :

Obs. 1. *That the precious souls of the faithful are Vessels made only or chiefly to receive and preserve the presence of the Spirit and grace of Christ.*

Obs. 2. *That within these Vessels there is an inward principle of Grace and Life.*

Obs. 3. *That there is a certain measure, degree, plenitude or fulness of the Spirit of Grace in the hearts of the Faithful, which the unsound, though most glorious Professors of the Gospel fall short of.*

Obs. 4. *That the graces of the Saints wherewith their hearts by the Spirit are filled, are constant, and of an everlasting, and eternal nature.*

These three last answer three Questions, If any ask the difference between the Virgins ; the foolish want, and the wise have an inward principle of the Spirit of life. If it be said, Hypocrites have an inward work, yet this inward Principle is such a fulness of Spirit which they ever fall short of, and this will make them known for the present. If again it be said, That many flourish gloriously for a time ; yet its of an everlasting nature : And this will manifest them one from another in time to come.

The First Point therefore Ile only touch on now.

SECT.

SECT. II.

THat the precious souls and hearts of all the faithful are vessels made chiefly and onely to receive and preserve the Spirit and Grace of Christ, Or the gracious presence of the Spirit of Christ : That as it is with the souls of the wicked, they are made onely to hold Satan, sin and wrath, and so fitted for destruction; so the souls of the Saints are made and fitted onely to receive and nourish the Spirit, grace, and love of Christ. That as 'tis with Princes, the best rooms are reserved onely for them; their Attendants may come in and out to serve them, but its their room, their lodging: So here, the hearts of the faithful, and the best rooms, best affections of it, are onely to entertain the Lord, and his grace and Spirit; yet other things may come in and out as Attendants to him, to serve him, but the rooms themselves are onely for his proper use, 2 *Tim.* 2. 20, 21. The Church is Gods House; now there are many Vessels (many souls) some baser of wood, and earth, some of honour; what are these? *Answ.* If a man purge himself from these; for no man is born with a next disposition to receive grace, as a Vessel full of puddle water that must first be cast out: Now when this is done, he is a Vessel meet for his Masters use, prepared, &c. The best Vessels abide in the house, not for their own or servants use, but for the Masters use onely. And though the Spirit may withdraw for some time, and they be unable to do any good work, yet they are prepared for the Spirit, and so for every good work, and here is all the use of the vessel of honour. Hypocrites are vessels of Pompe, and State, and Ornament: Oh the brave Church of *Sardis* ! the profound judgments, deep heads, eminent Christians, but not Vessels of honour, because not Vessels of use onely for their Master, onely to receive the eternal anointing of the Spirit of the Lord Jesus. If you would know the certainty of this more fully, 1. Go and ask themselves; Is it so or no? If they be of age, and know themselves they will say, I am the Lords onely, *Isa.* 44. 4, 5. *When they spring up as willows by the water-courses: One shall say, I am the Lords.* As that eminent Light said, when dying, Oh Lord, I will be thine: Ask the world whose they are? and to what use and purpose they serve? they will answer, they are none of ours; and therefore *John* 15. 19. *The World hates them.* Ask the Lord himself, he will profess though many wants and weaknesses in them, nay, though sometimes they are weary and neglect him, fall and foul themselves, yet *Isai.* 43. 21. *This people have I formed for my self:* Vessels formed and fitted of God onely for his glory.

1. Because all the creatures in the world are theirs, and servants to them, and therefore they are for the Lord onely, 1 *Cor.* 3. 21, 22, 23. If the more we took care for, and set our hearts upon the creature, if the more we were conversant with it, the more we should have, and the better we should live; Or if they should not serve us, unless we did first bow down our knees to worship them, and our backs to bear them; Then seeing the world lives by catching, we might then dis-robe and dis-throne our souls, and care more for these things, and less for the Lord; love these things more, and the Lord lesse; but the Lord Jesus having taken all care for his people, and bearing more love to them, and having more care of them than themselves, and therefore having given all creatures in the heavens, sea and dry land to serve them, they ought to be, and are onely for him, *Hos.* 2. 21, 23. When a man is the seed of God, and born for him, Now all creatures serve him; hence 1 *Tim.* 6. 17, 18. Tis a prevailing Motive with all the Saints, we have a living God that gives us all things; all creatures being dead, and not able of themselves to help us, therefore trust not on these things, but him onely, be not high minded in these things; but magnifie him onely. We know how angry God was with *Belshazzar* for profaning the

Z   Vessels

Doct. 1.

Reas. 1

Veffels of the Lords Houfe in making them quaffing bowls, and turning them to common ufe. When a man is brought to that mifery that he hath none, nor knows of none to be a friend to take care or thought for him, none that loves him, then he fhifts for himfelf and becomes a fervant. But thofe that know, as women that they have rich husbands to live on, they take care 1 *Cor.* 7. 34. how to pleafe them : So here. Whats the reafon that men are mad for this world? Becaufe they poor creatures have no friend, know no friend ; but Saints have him, and know him, *John* 17. 2. The Saints are given to Chrift, Chrift to them, and all the world put into Chrifts hands for us, (for the creatures are not given to us immediatly to our own difeofe, and hence we have not much of this world) to what end? That fo he might give eternal life begun here. This is the only gift, and laft, and beft, and worthy of himfelf, and this only we receive.

Reaf. 2.

2. In regard of that bleffed Liberty all the faithful are brought into, for what is a Chriftians Liberty? Is it to ferve men? No, 1 *Cor.* 7. 23. Therefore ferve not your felves : Is it then to ferve your own lufts? No, *Rom.* 6. 22. *You are made free from fin, and fervants unto God.* Is it then to ferve any Creature out of your felves? No, *Gal.* 1. 4. The world is yours already, 1 *Cor.* 3. 21, 22. given to you, bought for you, fpend not therefore one groat more to purchafe it, but keep thofe affections and hearts for the Lord ; much lefs imprifon not, and imbondage not your felves for it. A Chriftians liberty which God crowns him with above all the Princes of the world, is to be onely for the Lord, which liberty all creatures groan to be in, *Rom.* 8. 21, 22. To be for God and a luft, for Chrift and this world, its a fhameful bondage, and moft lamentable, and you are not at liberty yet, if not onely for the Lord. When the children of Kings and Peers, of Princes fhall be made to come at the call of their Grooms and Kitchin-boys, if ever they ftood before the face of Princes, they will count this a heavy thraldome and bondage : So if ever you ftood before the God of the whole earth, you will account it an heavy bondage, to have an heart fometime for, and fometime not for the Lord. Is not this liberty? No, but to have a heart only determined to the Lord ; as 'tis in Angels, and in the man Chrift Jefus. Verily look as the Lord leaves his people for a time to their liberty in fin, fo that their hearts are determined onely to fin, that they are fit onely to receive the fuggeftions and pleafures of it, but fit to quench the Lords Spirit : So the Lord Jefus making himfelf and grace more fweet than their lufts, their hearts are determined onely for him, their Veffels are onely for his Oyle, *Rom.* 6. 19. The liberty of will that *Arminians* plead for is nothing but the hypocrifie of a falfe heart, whofe heart being roucht partly with God, and partly with the creature ; hence is alway falling from one to the other, *Jam.* 1. *Double minded men* ; but the Saints are determined unto one, and hence made perfect in one.

Reaf. 3.

3. In regard of the fulnefs and all-fufficiency of the Spirit of Grace which their hearts are made fit veffels to receive, and do receive ; they finding enough there, God referves them, and they referve themfelves onely for the receiving of this, *Joh.* 6. 68. *Will you depart? Lord, to whom fhould we go? Thou haft the words of life* ; and fo the Spirit of life, that have quickned our hearts when dead, that do put frefh life to us when dying, that comfort our hearts when forrowing. Here is the life glory, the life of Chrift, the life of God ; other things do but dead our hearts, thou haft words of life, *John* 4. 14. *The Water that I give fhall,* 1. Be that which fhall quench all his thirft to other things ; fo that though a man wants them, yet his ftomack is gone, which the damned fhall find otherwife. 2. A Well of Water in him, ever near him ; men have their accommodations far off, but this is in him. Your hearts within are troubled, perplexed, and behold this is in you. 3. Springing up, continually increafing, for to have a good thing, and not to be fatisfied in our defires with it, what is it but a mifery? Hence it fprings up unto everlafting life, which is the Fourth, *Viz.* The Continuance of it, this will be

be here till my mortality is swallowed up of life. Like a leaking ship that takes in water by little and little, till at last it is swallowed up in the sea.

SECT. III.

HEnce we may see the reason why the Lord doth not abundantly reveal and communicate himself to the souls of many men. What is the matter? Is it because they find no want of his spirit, and life, and grace, and peace, and glory? Yes they doe, and hence expresse their wants to men, and complain of their wants to God. Is it for this, that Christ hath not wherewithal? Yes, he hath received the Spirit without measure, *John* 3. 34. and fountaines alway run, though men seldom drink. What then? Is it because they bring not their hearts, hold not their vessels under the Lords horn of oyl? Yes that they do, but their vessels are naught, they are not only for him; they feel their want of grace and Christ, but not only or chiefly of this. Special Grace shall never be poured into a common vessel, a common heart, that lies in common for God, and lust, and world too. The honour, peace, life, gain, of a God, are sweet and precious. *Lord ever give me that water to drink.* But you have five husbands, and seek not this only: Hence, if the Lord denies you, you can be content, because you have something else to fill your vessels; if the Lord gives, you undervalue it and grow worse: and the very rising of that common grace you have, is the beginning of your apostacy, and setting off from God. And hence, no wonder why you pray but never have, *Jam.* 1. 6, 7. you want, and crave, but never find; your vessel is naught, though the Lord is good. 'Tis a black mark that thou art in bondage to the creature, and didst never know what the liberty, even the glorious liberty of a son means. And 'tis a most grievous bondage to be half unloosed and yet to be in bonds. And I assure you, if you knew the gift of God, if ever you tasted how sweet the Lord is; this is the only thing your souls will cry for: That when you come to ask, and the Lord saith, what would you have? Oh the spirit of life! Oh the anointing of my blessed head! And what else? It only; this is it only my vessel is made to hold, I am not made for my lust, nor sins, nor world: I would I had a bigger vessel, a larger heart to receive thy Grace only. I confess, a gracious heart may for a time be carried too violently after other things; and yet seek the Lord too, as *Solomon, Eccl.* 2. But after it knows Christ better, it's more reserved now for him, as *Gen.* 39. 3, 4, 5, 6. *Josephs* master for a time kept things in his own hand, but when he saw the Lord was with *Joseph*, and that he was prosperous, and blessed, then he made him overseer, and he knew not 'tis said, what he had, save only the bread that he did eat: So it is in our *Joseph*. As the poor woman that knew the Messiah, she leaves her vessel, her water-pot with him, and now would have all the City to come and see and believe in him, and depend on him only, trust to him only. *&c.* Dost therefore seek, and find not? Hast bin long waiting, and feelest not? And thou wondrest at it! Others comforted, and I not! Search if this be not the cause; it may be thy heart is not set only for this, but on thy back, belly, lots, ease, what shall I eat, drink? *&c.* As some women, because God doth not feed so liberally their sweet tooth, their licorish longings; build them seiled houses, measure their present condition according to their sinful humour; nothing can please them: neither husband, servants, Ministers, nor Gods Ordinances. Is this a vessel for the Lord and his Grace only? You must, you will have a longer coat than you can well wear; Hold here. Never think to have one prayer answered: If this night thy day of misery should come, cry thou mayst, but no God to hear thee or help thee. Oh a little oyl, now a little grace, now a little mercy, Lord now, Oh no, you have no vessel to hold it. But oh bless the Lord you know it. Others it may be are not so full of these sores of impatiency: but you pray for God, and Grace, and have it not. Why so? These are not the things that you are only set for. Why? Because you are content without them. I am not, you will say; But you are; for you doe not lament daily after the Lord for these things only :that which only satisfies, that thy heart is not at rest till it find : I hope I may have help for all this : No saith *James*, think not so. Oh therefore bless the Lord. You know what hurts you; Saints have hurts thus : but they purge themselves, and hence are blessed vessels still. When *Moses* was begging for *Israel, mine Angel*, saith God, *shall goe with you*, I will not. No, thou only, *else let us die here, Exod.* 33. This prayer wins the field & wears the garland. The evils of the Churches are many, an hour of temptation is coming on; scandals are like to be great; the subtilties of enemies many. Now we pray, and yet these have come, and we fear they will come. Oh beloved, go to the Lord, and plead with him only for this; and when thou canst procure nothing for thy self, yet let it fare well with *Sion* : and this only I must have. *Psal.* 27. 4. *One thing have I desired.* You shall have it then, else not.

Use 2.　　See the great sin of those that lose their life, preserve not the Spirit when he comes to them in Ordinances; you are vessels onely made for the Lord, and will you lose that which He drops in? There is no others can receive him, *John* 14. 17. and when He comes to you, do you thus requite Him? *&c.*

CHAP. XVIII.

That the Holy Spirit is in beleivers as the Principle of their Spiritual Life and Holinesse.

SECT. I.

Doct. 2.　　**T**Hat *within these Vessels, is an inward Principle of Life and Grace.* Or, *The burning shining profession of all the faithful, it proceedeth from an inward Principle of the Spirit of Grace, by the means of which, their Lamp burns, and their Profession shines.*

For this I understand by oyl in the vessel, the Spirit of Jesus, not out of us, but received in us; not coming only upon us, for so he may on foolish virgins, by *Balaamitish* ravishments, and hypocritical pangs, and land-flood affections ; but abiding in us, and that not as it doth in hypocrites, but as it is in Christ Jesus, without measure, both Spirit and Graces, so it abides in us in measure: in Him as the fountain, in us as the vessels, from whose fulness, we receive the same. So that by oyl is not meant the external Principle of all Life, the Lord Jesus having Spirit and Grace enough, but keeping our hearts empty of it : but the Lord Jesus in us, who is not in us, but by his Spirit, even the Spirit of Life, from whence all our actions spring, and from which oyl our lamp burns. This therefore I say, the Profession of the faithful, springs not from outward motives, or principles of motion, as the actions of hypocrites ; sometimes sudden praise, sometimes gain, sometimes fears, sometimes fleshly hopes, sometimes sudden conceipt and fancy, sometimes irruption and rushings of the Spirit upon them; but there is a spring within, there is a life within ; there is oyle in the Vessel to fill the lamp ; and so hence it burns.

burns. *Eph.* 2. 1. *You hath he quickned, who were dead in sins,* i.e. you were held as fast under the power of your sins, as a dead man is under the bonds of death: but now in the room of that death, there is the Spirit of life, and the life of the Spirit. Now life is an inward principle of motion, of any thing in its own place; as the sun, and trees, and grasse, and cattel. You may take a stone, or, milstone, or wheel, and move it, yet they have no life, because this is not from an inward Principle so: hypocrites may be acted, and moved by the great power of the Spirit in an Ordinance, yet not living but dead stil. *John* 4. 14. the water (which is the Spirit *) is a spring of living water in him.* Cisterns may have water in them, but no spring that is running winter and summer. 1 *John* 3. 9. This is called the seed remaining in him: which is that new creation, new birth, which the verse it self expounds, so that he cannot sin; it is against his nature, now he cannot be a sinmaker. *Balaam* could not curse the people of God; and many cannot do as others do. Why, is it, because they are born of God? No, but from some other respects: and hence, *Mat.* 13. 21. the stony ground fell away, because they had not the root within. This is called the inner man; the good treasure of the heart, opposite to the evil treasure of the heart of a wicked man. Now, as an evil man acts not only from Satan, the evil spirit; but the inward power of lust; so the Saints, *Mat.* 12. 35. And here I intend not to shew what this inward Principle is particularly, for that I reserve to the two last points. Yet, least any should stumble, let me speak to two sorts.

1. Know some of you, that there is not only external actings of the Spirit from whence we act, but a new nature in the Saints.

2. Let others know, 1. That as before the Lord cals we are dead, so after we are alive this inward principle is not perfect here: Hence actions sometimes cease, and when they do not, yet are corrupted, as *lasa principia* act, but ever erre in their act, hence have need of pardon from and acceptance in the Lord Jesus. 2. That this is not in us as in *Adam*, who did not need to borrow life of another, but it stands in daily need of the Lord Jesus, and hence this inward principle acts, but 'tis by faith, the operations of which are the wagons to victual the camp continually, especially in time of need, and which is part of this inward principle; and hence 1 *Pet.* 1. 5. *You are kept by power and faith,* i. your souls, graces, lives are kept by the Spirit, but through faith in us *to salvation.*

Let me therefore prove these three things to you for opening of this point.

1. That the Spirit of the Lord Jesus is in the souls of the faithfull.

2. That there is a principle of created graces, or the life of the Spirit in them.

3. That from this principle of the Spirit dispensing himself by his graces, our lamp burns, our acts of profession spring and shine forth.

First, That the Spirit of Jesus is in the soules of the faithfull, 1 *John* 2. 27. *The anointing teacheth you all things.* Rom. 8. 11. *The Spirit that raised up Jesus from the dead dwels in us.* The manner of his being in us I intend not to meddle with, unlesse I saw more cause: I do beleeve the manner of his abiding in us, and his nearnesse to all the Saints, when seen of us, may astonish our own spirits, and shall one day confound all the world; Only know, as the Martyr said, *He is come, he is come.* The spirit of the world and Satan is cast out, 1 *Cor.* 2. 12. and in room of them enters the Spirit of God.

Secondly, That the Spirit so is in the faithfull, as that there is a principle of created graces in them, or an inward principle of life and grace. Not that these alone make this inward principle, but the Spirit in us working of them, working by them. And truly 'tis a sad thing if the proving of such a principle shall be an attributing too much to grace in us.

1. Therefore to deny this is to deny Christ to be our sanctification: For beside the passive obedience of Christ, we are justified by his active obedience also,

i. e. his inward conformity to the Law, and his external obedience to the Law. So that graces as they are in Christ become our justification; and hence he is said to be *our righteousnesse.* No man can stand before God but by perfect holinesse, but by doing whatever the Law requires, and continuing so to do; this is not in us, this is in Christ: This as 'tis in Christ is properly our righteousnesse or justification. Now what is our sanctification? if not graces in Christ, then graces received from Christ Jesus, which is this inward principle now I speak of; and therefore to deny this is no lesse than to say Christ is not our sanctification: But saith *Paul, The Lord sanctifie you in soul and body and spirit;* 1 Thess. 5. 23. And if it were so, a man may have a heart unsanctified and Christ too.

2. If there should not be those graces, then a Christian was not bound to adde one grace to another, but then the Apostles precept should be broken, 2 *Pet.*1. 7, 8. and so a Christian could not grow in grace, for graces are perfect in Christ; and the Spirit doth not grow in grace, and the immediate operations of the Spirit increasing in us, are not properly graces, no more than the act of seeing is the eye, no more then giving goods to be burned is love.

3. Then we are not to pray for graces, if there be no such things to be found in the hearts of Saints, but *Psal.*51.10. *David* praies, *Create in me a clean heart;* now if it be a thing created in me, 'tis not the Spirit only in me, for that cannot be created. I doubt not but *David* had a clean heart, but he fell in part; and therefore look as there needs a creating power to make, so there is a creating power to restore us again to what is lost.

4. Then the Saints have none of their sins mortified; for 'tis as with the eye, being made to see; if sight goes out, darknes comes in, and if that be subdued, sight is renewed: So the Soul being made only for God, and to bear his image; blot out that darknes and sin comes in: cast out sin, the Lord and his Image and Graces come in. If therefore there be no Graces in the Saints, then no sin mortified: truly if so, then the end of Christs coming, and dying is quite abolished, 1 *John* 3. 8. & *Rom.* 6. 2, 3.

5. Then the Lord should be false in his Covenant, and break Oath, and be forsworn: for, *Jer.* 31. 32. *I'le write my Law in their hearts* . *Luke* 1. 73, 74. So that if you will not believe man, yet believe God: and if you will not believe his Word, yet his Oath. Oh, but many good Christians find no such thing. But is it so, as they find it indeed? Either then they are no Christians, or else the Lord is forsworn.

Thirdly, That by the inward principle of Spirit, and Graces, our lamp burns, and shines, our actions issue. The Spirit enables a man to know, & hence the act flows, he doth know the Lord. The Spirit enables inwardly so to love the Lord, and hence it doth love him. That as Christ saith, *a good tree brings forth good fruit,* from an inward sap received from the root, and by abiding on the root; So here.

1. Those that are renewed to *Adams* image in their measure, have according to that measure, power to act; or in those Graces there is power to act, for he had power so to do. Every creature in the world had a Law of Nature to carry them to their end; and so were carried to it. But *Adam* had a Law of Divinity, whereby he being a cause by Counsel, was enabled by God to carry himself toward his end. Now we are renewed to that image in part, Eph. 4. 24. I know there is difference between *Adams* power to act, which had no Faith, ours that hath. And do not think that this doth advance nature, & the power of man, no more than the execution of the Promise of the Covenant of Grace, doth destroy Grace and advance nature. For the writing again the Law in our hearts, is that which this Covenant promiseth; nay, this doth honour the riches of Grace: that a man being under the power of sin, and cannot get deliverance, the Lord should now give an humble conquering Spirit: never a precious heart but will be thankful for it.   2. Because

2. Becaufe the Graces in us, are received from the Lord Jefus his fulnefs, *John* 1. 16. Now the Graces in Chrift are not dead, but living, are not weak, but powerful; the Spirit of Grace 'tis now triumphing in him, 'tis fo in us only: 'tis in him in the higheft degree, in us in a lower. And therein confifts our like-nefs to Chrift, 2 *Cor.* 3. 18. And to deny this, is to deface the Image of the Lord Jefus; and this is part of the Beauty and Glory of Chrift: hence to deny this, is to obfcure the glory of the Lord Jefus. Without Chrift a Chriftian can do nothing: but how doth Chrift do all, by the Spirit without Graces? (I fpeak not of Con-verfion where 'tis without Graces as caufes) No truly, as he acts, fo we act in part. Unlefs any will fay, we have not received grace for grace; or are in no meafure like the image of Chrift.

3. If the firft *Adam* hath conveyed to all his members a power of corruption, then the fecond *Adam* alfo a power of Godlinefs, contrary to that, 2. *Tim.*3. 5. yet in meafure ftill, fo as the Apoftle faith, *we can do nothing againft the Truth, but for the Truth.* 2 Cor. 13.8.

But what meafure of power is it? *Queft.*

Anfw. I know no man that can from any ground limit the meafure of it. For it may be in fome men in greater power, in fome men in lefs, in the fame man at one time in a greater meafure, at another time lefs. If one afk of trees, what meafure of fruit they can bring forth; we cannot tell, becaufe fometime more, fometime lefs: and the fame tree more one year than another, and more at one time of the year then another; for they have their winter feafon. Only this, whereas be-fore converfion he is ftark dead to act, now he is alive and is not dead. And if a man fhould after converfion be but in the next difpofition to receive Grace, then how could one Chriftian be more grown and ftronger in Grace in his inner man than another? I know not any to queftion this, only I fpeak it to cut off their carnal hopes, that think Chrift is theirs, when they have nothing, can do nothing, and fleightly fay he muft do all; I cannot, I tell you the Saints can, they cannot but love the Lord, and choofe the Lord. *&c.*

But muft not a Chriftian deny himfelf, and alway go to Chrift for power to do, and fo be humble, and empty? *Object.* 1.

Anfw. 1. You muft, becaufe this is the meanes to live to Chrift; but this doth not argue you have no power at all. A man muft pray for his *daily bread*, much more for *daily grace*; but doth this argue a man hath no bread in his houfe? No, this is the means to have it continued and bleft. Eafily can the Lord take away bread, or the ftaff of bread. Graces extinguifh not Faith, but help it.

2. A Chriftian can do no duty perfectly, hence muft repair to Chrift to help him to do every duty better; hence though he muft ufe that power he hath, and do what he can, yet he muft not content himfelf with what he hath, but feek for more, and what a fweet life is this? What honour would here come in? God lets in a new light into my minde, now I may and muft fee his truth, I faw it yefterday, but I may and muft go to Chrift to do it better; I muft not quench the Spirit of prayer, but carry the key with me, and next day pray better. And thus the foul is thankful for what it hath, and emptying it felf notwithftanding that, and daily then receiving from Chrift. And I beleeve many Chriftians fail here: As in the body, meat feeds and ftrengthens life, fo I cannot live without Chrift.

But doth not this make a man truft to graces? *Object.* 2.

Anfw. To act from them is not to truft to them, no more then for a diligent hand to truft to his diligence, when he acts diligently that fo he may be rich.

But doth not this difhonour grace to do all by the power of it? *Object.* 3.

Anfw. Then the Saints in heaven that are made perfectly like Chrift, and that love the Lord perfectly, fhould not honour grace by this means, when as this is it that makes them honour it moft of all. As *David*, Lord what am I, and

and my people, that we should offer willingly : So here.

SECT. II.

SEE hence what cause of thankfulness to all the people of God, that the Lord should make their souls the Vessels (which he might easily and justly have dashed in peeces) to receive and preserve this eternal anointing ; I do beleeve there is no man that knows the bitterness of sin, the plague of his own heart, but when he sees Christ is his, yet it makes him mourn that there should be so little suitableness between the Lord and him, so little likeness between his life and Christs ; what thorgh the Lord love me, and yet my heart weary of him ? what though the Lord bless me, and my heart abuse him ? and hence this makes it thankful, *Rom.* 7. 24, 25. This is so far from dishonouring grace, as that the Apostle makes this the matter of admiration of Gods grace, *Eph.* 2.3, 4. *God who is rich in mercy, when dead in sins hath quickned us* : Not only quickned our head, for hence is cause of eternal praise, but us ; and hence he hath set us up *in heavenly places in him* : This is the state of all men, they cannot do one spiritual act ; now that the Lord should help when all creatures left us, is wonderful, but that it should be with such a life, even the life of Christ Jesus himself, for the same Spirit that raised him from the dead dwells in us, and the same Spirit that is now in glory with him, is in us, 1 *Pet.* 5. 1. This is mercy indeed ; that he should not only die for us, and live in heaven for us, but that he should love so dearly as to come and live in us, that when our sins had slain him, he should not onely come and dwell in our houses, nor onely lay his head in our bosome, but live in our hearts, where he finds such poor welcome, and ill entertainment at our hands, I tell you this is wonderful, to make his habitation in us, that before we go to live with him, he should live in us : Let them that never knew what this meant refuse to be thankful, but if you find it so, forget not this love, *John* 14. 17. *He send the Spirit whom the World cannot receive, because it knows him not.* The Lord sends the Spirit in common graces, and the World doth receive that also in prophetical and miraculous gifts, and it doth receive that ; but this Spirit which God pours on the thirsty, this Spirit with which God fills the empty, they cannot receive this. Oh that you should have it, when as they know it not.

1. Hence therefore take heed of not owning the Spirit in this his presence. Do you thus require the Lord, oh unthankful world ! not so much as to own the presence of such a friend, neither in your selves, nor yet in others. How like the world is it to think that there is no such thing ?

2. Take heed therefore of not esteeming highly of it. If ever God broke thy heart, thou wilt esteem this life, this principle as the greatest piece of love ; and say, Lord I shall account this as the greatest part of love in the world, *Psal.* 119. 68. *Thou art good, oh teach me thy Statutes:* Now to undervalue this, and to account it common, and hence as no sign of love, 'tis a part of unthankfulness.

3. Take heed of imprisoning the Spirit of grace, common truth, *Rom.* 1. 18. It was fearful to imprison and silence that, much more this. It was the complaint of the Church in those days, *None stirs up himself*, Isai. 64. 7. What strength the Lord gives, let me use ; what I want, the Lord hath enough to help me withal ; put it to exercise, or else affliction will.

4. Take heed of enfeebling this Principle, weakning of it : The Church of *Sardis* things were ready to die in it, you should strengthen this inner man, not weaken it, either by not feeding it with Christ, or wounding it with known sins against Christ. Therefore let all the Churches know this, and take heed that

you

you do not refuse to own this : where elfe will you make the difference between men, that either Churches may difcern them, or you may difcern, and fo have peace your felves.

Hence fee the reafon of that inward hypocrifie that is in many mens hearts, fo that the beft profeffion of many a man is but a *Scheme*, an Image, a very craft, a very artificial form ; all the duties are fair without, but faplefs, livelefs, within : Here is the reafon they have no inward principle of life, or if they do go to Chrift, they have no fuch principle within them, to carry them to him, fo as to receive life from him ; and hence confefs fin without forrow or fhame, petition without thirfling, live without love, do without life, becaufe there is no fpring, but a dry heart within ; and hence they muft do duty , but they muft make dead work of it, and hence all is but an appearance, and at beft but a would be : This is in a great meafure in Saints when the Spirit within is quenched, but it is in full age and ftrength in hypocritical hearts, *Jer.4.14.* when the profeffion of *Judah* was great, and the Prophets had fcarce any thing to fay againft them for outfide, *Oh Jerufalem, wafh thy heart from wickednefs*, there thy wo lies, it enters to the very heart ; fo Chrift, *How can he that is evil, bring forth good fruit.* And this is that which may make men mourn, if I forfake all profeffion, I fhame my felf before men, if not, I muft blafpheme the Lords Name, and play the Hypocrite before the Lord, *Matth.* 12.33, 34, 35.

SECT. III.

TO take heed of denying the grace of God, or this inward principle, in whole, or in part, for this inward principle, being the life of Chrift in us, to deny this is to deny Chrift, and to take away his life ; and fuch the Lord will deny before his Angels another day : When they fhall fay, *Have we not eat and drank in thy prefence, he fhall anfwer, I never knew you :* I fhall therefore here direct my fpeech to four forts.

Firft, To thofe that deny created graces in the Saints peculiar unto them only, its faid there are none fuch in the Country, if there are not, it may be there have been, and it may be will be, and therfore ile fpeak: For I beleeve 'tis a delufion digged and hatcht out of the ftem of the lowest fink in Hell : And therefore that all may take heed of the evill of it, I will firft fhew the evill of it, then the caufes that do beget it.

I. The evils of this delufion are thefe.

1. It fettles and faftens a man under the power of all his fin, and yet with a quiet Confcience, and yet to keep his Chrift too. It tranfcends my capacity from whatever I have read, or have heard, or have felt, or can imagine how the power of fin can be taken away, but where the Spirit infufeth the contrary grace ; an empty houfe fwept and garnifhed with common gifts, is but a fitting houfe for Satan to return into : Say therefore a man may have no fuch graces, and yet have Chrift, and them in Chrift, you ftake this man down under his fin, and make this member of Satan, a member of Chrift Jefus. And upon this ground all Churches in the Land may be forced in Confcience to take in all prophane members, if they plead Chrift, and their allnefs in him.

2. This blurs all the glory of a Chriftian, or at leaft the greateft part of it : For what is the glory of a Saint ? 'Tis to be like Jefus Chrift the Lord of glory, to bear his Image before God and men : As to fee a man with a Swines face would be the fhame of a man ; to fee a Chriftian with Satans Image, is the fhame of a Chriftian ; but to be like our Head, this is our glory, though it be in fufferings, 2 *Cor.* 3. 18. heavenly, humble, compaffionate, holy, as he was ; and hence when God hath a mind to make Churches or Chriftians bafe in the eyes of the

A a   world

world, he will withdraw here, and when he intends to draw the world after him, he will glorifie it with his glory, *Isai.* 60. 6, 7.

3. It cuts off a Christian from all hope of glory, how many be there that scramble and catch at Christ, and every one faith he is mine, The proud man faith, he is mine, and hopes now verily to be saved, but that hope is vain ; they have Christ out of them, but where is Christ in them ? The life of Christ, and the Spirit of Christ ? *Col.* 1. 27. *Christ in you, the hope of glory.*

4. Give me but one place in all the Book of God, where blessedness is bestowed upon, or conveyed unto any, or promised but to such as have these graces. *Blessed is he that feareth the Lord, and greatly delighteth, &c.*Psal.112.1,2. If there be no such thing, let any man expect it if he can.

II. The Causes.

1. A magnifying Christ, and making him our Sanctification, when as you heard the last day, this is to deny him to be our Sanctification : He becomes our righteousness by imputation of his holiness, and our Sanctification by infusing of it. Nay, hence a man deprives himself, of all good in the Lord Jesus, when a man denies all grace in himself, and then flies for Sanctuary unto Jesus Christ, 1 *Iohn* 1. 6, 7. *If we say we have fellowship with him, and walk in darkness, we lie,* &c. And hence it seems they denied men to have sin, *vers.* 8. boasting of fellowship with Christ, *vers.* 6.

2. Because there are (say men) onely immediate actings of the Spirit. If this be so, then there is seeing in a Christian without an eye, and hearing without an ear, and knowing Christ without an understanding, and loving without love, and living without life, and feeding and eating without a mouth ; and then when these actings are over, a Christian is like another man, there is no Law remains written on his heart, and so Christ should enter into his Saints, like Satan into the Serpent, who only acts the Serpent, and when that is done, he remains a Serpent again. Know it, the Lord Jesus his greatest work is not onely to change the acts, but to change the frame of the heart, not only to put new actions, but a new nature into men.

3. Because men know not the Spirit, never felt the presence, nor power, nor comfort of it themselves ; and hence men do as some Countries, because themselves are black, they paint the Devil white. *Iohn* 14. 17. *The World cannot receive, because it knows him not.* Give me any Christian living that ever found the sweetness of it, but his longings were to have more of that grace, to *forget things behinde, and reach to things before, even to the resurrection of the dead,* whom I believe none will say want all habits of grace : I look upon the Opinion as coming with a curse from God : A man hath been a dry Professor long, Conscience faith, There is no grace in the heart, and hence is troubled ; True, faith he, there is none in Saints, it is in Christ, and there he catcheth and deceives himself.

Secondly, Those that do acknowledge them, but any power or activity in them they deny ; they say there is oyl indeed in the Vessel, but it helps not, 'tis no means to make the Lamp to burn or shine ; there is the life of Christ, but it is a dead life, they call them the graces of Christ, but they are but fruitless graces. I confess it, if you consider them without the Spirit of Christ, they are no true graces, much less active or living ones ; but consider them thus, they have a power, as take the least grain of corn, there is a growing power in it, & fructifying too in it by dying first, though it actually doth not fructifie presently, and though there must be rain, and Sun must shine also, and a providence accompanying of it , so it is in the graces of Saints : And hence its called a *Law of the mind,* there is a power of a Law, as of sin; and hence as Christ grew in wisdome and stature, so all the members of Christ are like unto him.

I. The evill of this.

1. This abates of the excellency of grace, as from a Jewel to take away the
operative

operative vertue of it. For it's not like Carifts now, which is ftrong through God, not weak; which is living, not dead. This is not like the glorious Graces of Saints triumphing. This makes the Graces of Saints of lefs excellency then common Graces: common Grace will make a man ride over many a fin, and run exceeding faft, though he fall at laft. A man that hath bin angry, it will make him very quiet and ftill, and is there no more power in this?

2. This will make a man content himfelf with a bare form, with a falfe confidence if this be true. For take a man that hath bin long feeking to get ftrength againft a vile heart, and he finds none; there is no power of heavenlinefs, he is earthy; no meeknefs, he is proud; I would fay to him, do you ever think to get any power of meeknefs, love, faith, &c. You fhall never do it, never have it here; all your ftrength is immediatly from Chrift, look for it there; in confcience a man muft ceafe there. And 'tis certain all our ftrength is in, and from the Lord; but 'tis difpenfed mediatly, *Eph.* 3. 16. Paul prays *he may be ftrengthned with might in the inner man.* Or thus, a man may not pray for ftrength of Grace, which *Paul* refufed not.

3. Then the Saints if they be asked whether they believe, or can love the Lord Jefus; their anfwer muft be, no I have no power to love, nor beleeve, and then *Peter* did ill to anfwer fo, *Lord thou knoweft that I love thee.* Then *Paul* to fay, *We can do nothing but for the Truth.* Then that Martyr that to then that faid, *the Lord ftrengthen you:* yes faith he, the Lord doth. I know if the Lord withdraw his Spirit, we are gone, as *Adam*; but is there not the immutable affiftance of it? Is there not the Promife, *I will never leave thee,* though fometimes weaker, fometimes ftronger?

4. This will make a Chriftian hide and not improve his Talents; he hath Grace, but no power to put it forth. Then fuppofe God gives power to fee Truth one day, I muft not fee it with this eye the next; but look up to Chrift, and fay, I cannot fee at all.

II. Caufes of this.

1. In oppofing the outward principle of life, or firft principle, and this fecond, I muft live on Chrift; hence I muft not, I have no power to act my felf in any meafure, becaufe all my ftrength is in him. When if this were true, a man might argue, becaufe all Grace is originally in Chrift, hence no Grace in me, becaufe all Glory is in Chrift originally; hence no Glory fhall be conveyed to me. No, this Scripture reconcile thefe: *Becaufe I live, therefore you fhall live alfo,* John 14. 19. Becaufe Chrift is ftrong, hence he will make us ftrong in the inner man, and not in the Spirit only: becaufe Chrift is glorious; hence we are predeftinated *to be made like unto him.* Becaufe all fap lies in the root, to fay therefore there is no fap or power in the branch to fructifie; this is falfe.

2. The hypocritical activity of falfe Profeffors, who having no fpring to feed their wells, no Chrift, nor bucket to draw fron him; hence are their own men, and fee up for themfelves, till they turn bankrupts. And now becaufe a Pharifee is fo active as to go through fea and land to make a Profelyte; therefore *Paul* hath no activity of Grace of Chrift in him to go from land to fea to make Chriftians.

3. Sloth, A man fets upon a duty, and now becaufe he cannot do it eafily, nor quickly, he cannot do it at all. A man would have Grace active without means; and God will not help in that way: and hence many Chriftians cannot cleave to Chrift by love, or defire; no, fo long as they pore upon their wants, no encouragement, but turn the mind, and confider well of the love and glory of Chrift, then with *Paul,* 2 Cor. 5. 14. *Chrifts love conftrains.*

4. Judging that to be the power of Grace at all times, which is at fometimes; A man hath given fpecial occafion for the Lord to leave him; as the Camp in *Jofhuahs* time, *Jofh.* 7. and he thinks there is no more power at any time in any man. For then a man fees all the world cannot help, when if *Achan* were

removed, the Spirit of the Lord would return again.

5. That hereby a man may have his sins without trouble, for a man hath bin troubled, and cannot get power, now he hears there is no such power to be expected, he looks to Christ, and if power come, well, if not, saith he, 'tis not my fault.

III. Those that deny the evidence of it, the evil of which apprehension, I conceive to be no less then taking away that which is the chief, if not only difference between hypocrites and Saints in virgin Churches, for so 'tis made here. A man saith I have Christ, and so have not they : I ask, where is the Spirit ? You have the Deed, where is the Seal ? You have the Testator, where is the Executor, the Spirit in you ? Yes, I have it, it hath witnessed Christ is mine. *Answ.* It hath witnessed, but what hath it wrorght ? Where is the power of his death, killing thy lusts ; Where is the life of the Spirit of Jesus in you ? Where is the Oyle in your vessel ? Truly I look for the Bridegroom, but I regard not that, neither are others to regard it in way of evidence. Then I say the chief evidence is destroyed in the Churches. I have known many that have had assurance; yet never saw them prove right, till it witnessed this was here. What should be the causes of this and that men should make blusters in the Churches, because of this, as though it was building on works ? In several men they are several.

1. An aptness in mens hearts to outrun the Truth, and to fall from one extream to another. Many men there be that fall short of Christ, and the Grace of God in and from him : and from their loose prophane life, fall to duties, and imitate Gods people, and then when they have got credit with good people, they judge well of them : and having made their peace hereby, with conscience, and not with God the Judge; never look after the saving knowledge of, and fellowship with, and life from the Lord Jesus. Now, because men rest on this, these duties are no evidence ; hence none are at all. The *Corinthians* first mourned not for the incestuous person; and when cast out, wanred pity towards him. *Calvin* preached against Holidaies, hence intrench'd upon the Lords day. Some of the separation see many Churches where they have come corrupt, hence make them all no Churches. A man is apt to think, because I have rested on my self, and found those signes which now are not found, hence all others do so too. And I beleeve divers Books have occasioned it, which give signes that will not hold without a fuller explication of them.

2. The apostacy of eminent Professors, who have bin deceived in their evidencing thus : And truly it would make one think the honesty of the World is but a fashion, and no evidence of any good estate ; hence men say you have joy, so had the stony ground; you are blamelefs and strict, so was *Paul* a Pharisee; and Satan hereby shakes many a soul : hence the Apostle comes in, *Heb.* 6. 9. and speaks of better things, and things that accompany Salvation, and these should you follow. *Hymeneus* and *Philetus* fell both, 2 *Tim.* 2. 18, 19, 20, 21. Yet purge your selves, and you shall be vessels of honour for the Masters use.

3. Corrupt experience, it may be a man walks so loosly without fear, or life, or love, that the Lord leaves him, and he can see no clear through-work, sometimes hath pangs, and then hopes, sometime dead, then doubts ; hence being vext here, and finding no peace ; if he find it any other way than this, there he rests. As 'tis observed with man, cloaths hide their shame : but when dead, their face is also covered, all their glory being then gone: so some Glory of God appeares here, but when Christians are dead, they cover this, I'le look no more to it, all the glory of it is now gone, and here lies a deceit to love Christ for freeing me from this way of evidencing.

4. A heart that never felt the bitternefs and bondage of sin as the greatest evil. Take a man full of fears of wrath; oh now assurance is his chiefest good, and he will account it so; but if ever God did load the Soul with sin, *è contra*, you will account

of deliverance from this highly, nay a promise he will do it is sweet: but to be feeling those sinews of sin crack; oh its the joy of Heaven that now fils that heart! The greatest evil in Gods eyes is sin; the greatest good we have is redemption from it by a mighty hand : now not so much as to account of this highly, this is hard. Thus I have left these things to be thought of, I cannot avoid it, it lies in my text; and the rather, because of that Scripture abused, *If any say, loe here is Christ, or there, believe it not.* i. e. by signes : or in a wildernesse, *i. e.* in a sorrowful estate, or in the privy chambers in frames of heart, believe it not neither. Take heed you do not wrest Scriptures thus; I'ts said, *Esau hated Jacob for the blessing*, Gen. 27. 41. This Spirit of Grace is the blessing which Saints account as the evidence of the dearest love ; to separate from Churches, from Messengers of God , for this will yield you sorrow enough one day. I tell you, you shall not be found *fighters against men, but against God*, and the Spirit of his Grace, and the Life of him who lives in Heaven for us. Take heed you forget not oyl in your Vessels.

IV. Those that acknowledge in their judgements all these things, but deny it in their lives, regard **not** the having this principle of Life, and have peace in this, from a double ground.

1. By a fruitless Faith which hangs on Christ ; but never receives nor brings in this principle, as those, *John* 2. 24, 25. and hence though they receive none, yet they hang on him. And so their Faith like a bucket without a bottom, draws up nothing.

2. *A form of godliness* before men. If a man should neither speak well, nor pray, *&c.* He would have no love, no respect, no receiving into Church: but he cannot do it with life, and hence a form contents him, and there rests. So that now if Conscience troubles, and says, those duties are done with no life of Christ, and Spirit; he answers, yet I goe to Christ : If this be all, why do you not cast off your form ? Oh then I should have no love from men : oh this life of Christ is not prized, till with these Virgins they feel the want of it, and 'tis too late, know this will be your woe at last. Look upon thy dead Soul, all thy glory is gone, and wait upon the Word that the Lord may make thee live. Could you know this Well of water and ask he would give it you. Oh beg for it then as for your life. Only first seek it in Christ, and so from Christ.

SECT. IIII.

WE live in a Country which hath goodly trappings, rich hangings, glorious Profession, burning Lamps : and hence many think themselves rich, when indeed poor ; many look to meet the Bridegroom, when indeed they shall be shut out from the fellowship of the Bridegroom. How shall I know that ? That all my sorrows, prayers, reformation, profession, is but a point, an appearance, a fashion, a Church-craft, which will stand me in no stead when the Lord shall appear, who shall judge the secrets of all hearts, by the Word you hear this day. Try it therefore by this Rule, doth it come from a principle of life or no? Your Lamp burns, but look what is in your vessel that feeds this flame. That as our Divines speak, how the Disciples could do greater works than Christ, and others wrought Miracles besides Christ : how then do they prove that he is Christ ? 'Tis answered, in all his miraculous works we are to consider not only *quid fecit*, *i. e.* what he did, but *qua virtute fecit*, from what power he did it. The Apostles and others wrought Miracles, but it was *alienâ virtute* : Christ did them, but it was *propriâ virtute*. So many an unsound heart he may do greater works then Saints, and his lamp burn brighter. Therefore in this case we are not to look so much to what is done, as from what power and principle it is done : for therein the best hypocrite ever failes. We shall ever observe in some beasts there are *umbra va-*

Use 4. Of Tryal.

riones

tionis, yet there is no rational soul, nor any wise man will beleeve that their acts proceed from such a Principle : So there are shadows of the power of grace in a carnal heart, and yet no Judicious Christian will say they come from an inward soul, or principle of life. Consider therefore whether there is this principle or no ; you see there is profession, you have a name to live in the judgement of all the Church, but search your hearts, and see from what principle it proceeds, for if this be wanting, all is naught : As he that had Beer given him, when Milk and Wine, and Sugar was put into it to mend it, said, The Wine is good, and the Milk is good, but the Beer is naught : So Profession, affection is good , but the heart, the man is naught, *Jer.* 2. 22. *Though thou wash thee with Nitre , thy sin is marked before the Lord.* And that the Trial may be full and fair, I shall shew Negatively, the several sorts of men that act not from an inward Principle, yet carry it out as though the bitterness of death was past, and the Bridegroom theirs.

1. When a mans Principle is nothing but the power of created nature expressing it self, and setting the best face forward, in the gilded rottenness of some moral performances, wherein a man saith, he doth what he can ; for there is this principle in most men, a desire to be saved, nature saith so, and according to the intention of this desire, so accordingly will men do more or less ; and hereupon sooth up themselves, when they see they cannot do as others do , or as the Lord commands ; I do as well as I can. Nay, when condemned by the Word which meets them, I do as well as I can, I beleeve, I repent, I pray, I remember the Word, I do as well as I can, and so they hope God accepts of that ; and though I beleeve no man but may be hired to do more than he doth, yet nature may do much ; hence I heard an Arminian once say, If faith will not work it, then set reason a work, and we know how men have been Kings and Lords over their own passions by improving reason, and from some experience of the power of nature, men have come to write large Volumes in defence of it ; and its known the *Arminians* though they ascribe somewhat to grace, and in words all to grace, yet indeed they lay the main stress of the work upon a mans own will, and the royalty and soveraignty of the liberty of that : But to leave them and come to our selves, Is it not a common thing for men *to make lies their refuge*, and to say , I was in a woful condition once, and never looked after God, but now I blesse the Lord 'tis otherwise with me. How? Now I beleeve, repent, *&c.* And so I confess all I do is full of weaknesses, yet I do what I can ; and thus they are like to men that have old garments new dressed, they have made them as good as they can; and like the young man, *Luke* 18. 21. *All these things have I done from my youth, yet one thing was wanting*, which was to *forsake all*, and so himself, that the Disciples said, *Who then can be saved: With man 'tis impossible, but with God all things are possible.*

You say you do as much as you can; I say do so, but 'tis impossible with man, from any strength of man, and you have no more yet, *John* 1. 13. *Born again, not of the will of man, but of God.* There is in some men a birth, like to the new birth, which is of the will and power of man, but oh this is not this inward principle which the Almighty power of God creates ; and therefore know it, if you get no other oyle in your Lamps, you shall never meet the Bridegroom.

2. When a mans principle is the power of holy example, whereby many a one is drawn to do more than otherwise he would. Many men think for a while as that man spake; Men talk of being worth thousands, I would fain see the men. Ministers preach and others speak well, we must do this & that, but I would fain see the men that do it. Now it sometime falls out that the Lord sets before mens eyes some pattern-Christians, hereupon they think thus; here are two contrary ways, they cannot both lead to heaven, their way is better than mine, and doubtless leads to life, mine doth not, and therefore let me live like them. And hence there shall not be any Fast, but they will be at it; not a Sermon near, but they will go wet and dry to

hear

hear it ; nor any duty in Family, but they will imitate it, and hence read and learn, that they may be like them. No Christians in the Country hated, but they will love them, nor Ceremonies cast off, but they will abhor them ; and hence they reflect upon their patterns, and think their estate safe, because they are as good as a Christians outside : And hence like some dead Cattel, there is nothing good but their skin ; so there is nothing good in these, but their imitating outside. Thus it was with *Joash* while *Jehojada* lived, 2 *Chron.* 24. Hence he fell like Ivy with the Oak, when God cut him down : Thus it was with these five foolish Virgins, a man may follow good examples, but not rest in bare imitation of them : And hence a blessed man is described, *Psal.* 1. Negatively, from not imitating the wicked, not from imitating the good ; because good men may be in many things ill examples, and it ever proves so in these men that have no more then this Principle ; hence if they be loose in their tongues, or on the Sabbath, their plea is, they are like unto them. And hence come all your acquired excellencies ; a man is an imitating creature, led by example, and a carnal man out of the heart of hypocrisie in himself, will imitate the divine nature which is in another; and hence men not only take up such practises, but such opinions only, because such and such are of that mind : And hence men change practises and opinions as Examples do change ; in *Joshua's* time great Reformation, he no sooner dead, but all fell off again : then they were for purity of Ordinances and Gods Worship, now they serve *Baalim* : Oh consider, here is an outward, but no inward principle !

3. Those whose principle is nothing but external applause and praise of men, and this will carry a man beyond all the best Examples : Nay, sometime to be singular, and a man alone ; a Pharisees Trumpet shall be heard to the Townesend, while simplicity walks thorow the Town unseen Hence a man will sometimes covertly commend himself, and my self ever comes in, and tells you a long Storie of Conversion, and an hundred to one, if some lie or other slip not out with it. Why, the secret meaning is, I pray admire me, hence complain of wants and weaknesses ; pray think what a broken-hearted Christian I am ; and hence if comforted they complain, if not, they will comfort themselves ; hence many lift up eyes and hands, and fetch deep sighs in prayer, remember and note Sermons, look now what a gift I have : Hence if you come to their companie, they will have so many good words as may make you think well of them, and then the Market is almost done with them : Hence men forsake their friends, and trample underfoot the scorns of the world, they have credit elsewhere : To maintain their interest in the love of godly men they will suffer much : Hence men in the Ministry pray for grace to beautifie and perfect their parts, that so they may preach and convert and have credit : Hence men meditate new Light, and profess deep things that few know, that men may worship the rising Sun : Hence the Lord is neglected secretly, yet honoured openly, because there is no winde in their chambers to blow their Sails, and therefore there they stand still : Hence many men keep their profession, when they lose their affection, they have by the one a name to live, and that is enough, though their hearts be dead : And hence so long as you love or commend them, so long they love you, but if not, they will forsake you ; they were warm onely by anothers fire ; and hence having no principle of life within, soon grow dead : This is the water that turns a Pharisees Mill, and the Lord passeth a heavy doom, *You have your reward.* I have wondred that the opinion of men, nay, dream of mens thoughts should act men ; onely 'tis a curse of God, that when men despise his honour the greatest good, they shall be fed with the basest good.

4. Those whose Principle is nothing else but their own gain of outward blessings. Many there be that make not their honour, so much as their bellies their gods, and thy rule them, *Phil.* 3. 19. hence the Shop-keeper will give good words

when

when he sells his commodity, he should lose much of his custome else ; and hence
the Minister preacheth contionably that his guine may come in, 1. *Thes.* 2. 4, 5.
Hence people would be as good as the best, they cannot get a lot in all the Country else. Hence a man is sometime content to forsake all for Christ, that he may
make a booty of Christ, as *Judas* did. Hence when Christ feeds them with
Loaves, then the people will make him a King, *John 6.* though afterward they cry
Crucifie him. So men deal with Christ as the Souldiers did, that caught him,
that they might strip him of his garments. And hence many men if they see sorrows and wants attending them, if they attend on Christ, forsake him. Look
upon our own Land, many so long as they could enjoy Christ with fair weather,
cry out of Ceremonies, and pro-haning of Sabbath : yet this not being to be had,
creep to them, and read the Book for prophaning thereof. Many shadows
have been seen since our Sun hath risen here , and this way they looked : but
viewing other mens wants , and fearing their own losses, and conceiving they
may meet with *Massah* in this Wildernesse, refuse to follow. And least this
should seem to be the cause, cry out we are Separatists, or strongly possess themselves against all relations, there is no living at all here.

Look but at home, how many Dove: (that prove but Ravens, and live on the prey)
come hither to our windows , and have followed Christ to this Worlds end ; when
he fed them with loaves, they made him their King but now he hath taken away
what once they desired ; because there is better Bread to be laboured for ; now
they forsake him, and live on the spoyl. This is no inward Principle. And hence
when mens Expences for Christ, exceed their Receipts from Christ, they cease
spending, and fall in the high way to begging at the door of the World.

5. Those whose Principle is nothing else but the strength of natural Conscience,
which will set men a doing, when they have neither praise from men, nor gain
from Christ for their labour. For the Lord deals with some men, as the *Romans*
did with some of their Prisoners ; they would chain a Prisoner and his keeper together, and let them go up and down : so God chains many a poor Prisoner of
hell and his conscience together, and lets them go together. And hence many a
man keeps pace with his conscience, and cannot give it the slip for all the world
heaped up with gold, as *Balaam* said.

Now there are two things in a natural conscience, *Rom.* 2. 15.

1. To accuse, Hence a man dares not omit prayer, dares not commit a sin
he hath a mind to; conscience would then roar. Hence many keep constantly
set duties in private, and tremble at small sins : not because they take any delight
in the one, or are weary of the other ; but because they are ever under the eye of
this Judge.

2. To Excuse, and to give much sweetnesse when a man follows the dictates
thereof, hence a man though carnal, will die for his Religion, and that with some
cheerfulness , because conscience chears within, and sings him asleep in trouble.
And hence a man will cry out of all the glorious hypocrisies of men, because to
walk according to Conscience is sweeter to him. And hence a man comforts
himself , tis my Conscience, *Mark* 12. 33. To love God *is better than burnt
Offerings.* Hence a man will profit exceedingly in what he holds, *Gal.* 1. 14.
because zealous for it for Conscience: and yet this is but a Principle of Nature,
not an inward Principle of life, whose property is to seek the subversion of corrupt Nature , as natural Conscience seeks the garnishings of it and the actions
thereof.

6. Those whose Principle is the fear of death, and hell; raised not so much by
the power of Conscience, as by the power of the Word. And hence come complaints about a mans Estate ; that a man can have no rest by all duties that he
hath done, or doth. Hence following of the means, running to the best Ministry, mourning, and lamenting, and confessing sin, *Mat.* 3. 7. *Oh generation of vipers*

pers &c. And hence prizing of favour and Comfort, Pfal. 78. 34, 35. Hence many do take this for their Conversion, and say, I heard such a Minister at such a time, and then I cryed out I was damned, and thought I saw the Devil, yea, and to Hell you may for all this, if no other Principle. Indeed, there is this fear in the elect, but drives them to the Ark, as *Noah* : But those, when their fear is over, they fall to fight against the Lord.

7. Those whose Principle is nothing else but the immediate actings of the Spirit of God upon them. For sometime the Spirit of God comes upon men, as Light shines on the mud wall, yet dwels not there as in the Sun. And hence many speak, pray, prophecy admirably, as *Balaam*, Numb. 24. 3, 4. Many men like Carriers bring others goods, that are not possessors of them. Now these are 1. External enlargements, and hence a man doth many things which he hath no inward power to perform, the Spirit is there assisting ; hence he cannot do so at another time, but 'tis the Spirit only assisting. And hence a man may have abundance of knowledge, and he not affected with it ; he may live, and pray with applause of men; others wish they were like him, yet live without love, & speak without feeling, and do without life, hence men leave themselves here. 2. Internal pangs, the Spirit of God begets some inward grief, especially when outward evils press, then inward flashes and desires, but they are soon done. There is no Spring, no Principle within. What the difference is between Saints uneveness, and this unconstancy, you shall hear hereafter : yet these are wrestlings of Spirit not yet conquering, and hence it possesseth not the Soul.

8. When mens Principle is nothing else but common gifts, which are inward, and abiding long in the Soul. That a man now thinks he hath Grace, and sure signes of the Lords love, and here is fastned : when there be two things wherein it appears here is no inward Principle. 1 These gifts ever puff up, and make a man something in his own eyes, as the *Corinthian* knowledge did. And many a private man thinks himself fit to be a Minister, many a Minister better than all the Parish besides ; when *Paul* was the least of all the Saints. And hence commonly they degenerate to pride & form. 2. These keep men strangers to Christ, & the life of Faith; they have these affections, yet ignorant of Christ, take these as signes of his love, & live without him. And this is indeed the inner Principle which all the wicked in the world want; there is in true Grace an infinite circle: a man by thirsting receives, & receiving thirsts for more. But hence the Spirit is not poured out abundantly on Churches, because men shut it out by shutting in, and contenting themselves with their common graces and gifts, Mat. 7. 29. Examine if it be thus. If so,

1. You cannot come to the Lord, John, 5. 44. *how can ye beleeve ?*

2. Nor to receive any thing from the Lord if you do, Jam. 4. 3. *When you ask to spend it on your lusts*, when that carries you.

3. This puls down the Kingdome of the Lord Jesus, when other things rule us, and not himself alone.

4. Satan will have this against you, as against *Job, You serve not the Lord for nought.* To what purpose are *your new Moons*, Church-reformations, if it be thus ? Now, because it hath been replyed to what was formerly said, that Christ was the vessel, not our Souls. I shall therefore confirm the latter to be the truth, by these reasons.

1. Mystical places of Scripture are to be interpreted by plain. Now though Christ may be the Antitype of these Vessels of the Temple, yet he is not plainly said to be a Vessel ; but Souls are called so, Rom. 9. 23. 2 Cor. 4. 7. Acts 9. 15. *Paul is a chosen Vessel.* 1 Thes. 4. 4. *we are to possess our Vessels in holiness.* 2 Tim. 2. 20. *Vessels of honour.*

2. The Spirit is not in Christ as in a Vessel, but as in a fountain ; hence *Joh.* 3. 34. *Christ hath received the Spirit without measure.*

3. The foolish Virgins had Vessels ; because its sayd, *they took their Lamps, but no Oyle with them.* Their folly was not in not providing Vessels. Hence the foolish

Bb

lish Virgins did not afterward beg their Veſſels, but their Oyle.

4. The wiſdome of the Wiſe did appear, in that they did provide Oyle for their Veſſels. If therefore the Veſſel be Chriſt, therein lyes the wiſdom of the Wiſe, that they got the Spirit for to put into Chriſt, and the folly of the fooliſh, they got not the Spirit to put into him. Or the one go: Chriſt Jeſus full of the Spirit; the other, Chriſt Jeſus void of it. When whoever hath Chriſt, muſt have in him the fulneſs of the Spirit alſo.

5. The other interpretation croſſeth the main ſcope of this part of the parable, which is to ſhew the difference between the Virgins; all profeſſed Chriſt, went to meet the Bridegroom; but here was the difference, they never looked for to get the Spirit in them: and this is moſt ſuitable to men raiſed out of the dregs of Popery, where Works being aboliſhed, Chriſt is owned, and therein do well, but herein fail.

Thus you have heard the uſe of Tryall negatively. What this inward Principle is affirmatively, you have generally heard; and ſhall more particularly in the other two Doctrines. Only this I will add; it conſiſts of two parts.

1. Our life in Chriſt by Faith.

2. Chriſts life in us by his Spirit. Faith empties the Soul, and looks upon it as dead, and ſees its life laid up in Chriſt; and hence forſakes it ſelf, and embraceth the Lord of Glory. Secondly, the Spirit comes and poſſeſſeth a forſaken empty Houſe, and there lives and dwels. Both theſe the Apoſtle mentions, *Gal.* 2. 20. *Eph.* 3. 17. *Joh.* 15. 4. As two married together, their Souls live not where they are, but in each other; The one cares not how to pleaſe her ſelf, but her husband; and *è contra*. So that leaſt any weak Soul ſhould be diſcouraged, that thinks there is no Principle of Life, becauſe ſuch a blind, empty dead heart, wandring from God, &c. Nay, when the Lord quickens it, Oh its loſt again! Nay, when quickned, oh then when it comes to, it is feeble! I tell you it muſt be ſo. This makes you lay up your life in him: this death is your life. And leaſt any falſe heart ſhould be here deceived, that ſaith he hath Chriſt; *If you have not the Spirit of Chriſt, you are none of his*. The Saints [have] this ſometime, their Temple is filled with Glory; and for their general courſe, they are Admirers of the Lord Jeſus; and account his Life, to be Life, and all their life beſide to be a continual death. There is not any Grace but they ſay, oh that I had it!

SECT. V.

Uſe 5.
Of Exhort.

TO every man, as ever you look to be with Chriſt Jeſus another day, get this oyle in your Veſſels. The Lord doth in this Parable ſet before your eyes the eſtate of the pureſt Virgin-Churches and Profeſſors in the world, and it is his infinite love to tell us before-hand, before the time be paſt; to tell us, that many of theſe ſhall be ſhut out from the preſence of the Lord Jeſus, whom themſelves and others think ſhall not; and yet this love would be but little, unleſs the Lord had made known the cauſe or defect in not getting oyle to their Veſſels. Oh conſider therefore, here you are like to fail; you that have Lamps before the cry and Bridegroom comes, acknowledge Chriſts love, and be overcome by it to get oyle into your Veſſels; when *Rahab* knew that the Lord would deſtroy all *Jericho*, now ſhe lays about her to preſerve her life. What's the means? To tie the Scarlet thread at the window: Oh ſhe would be ſure to get and keep that there. You know the Lord Jeſus will come and diſcover the unſound profeſſion, and deſtroy the glory of the World, and Churches too: It may be you have had ſome fears, what if he ſhould cut me off, and caſt me out as poſſibly be may? and I may as well as eminent Profeſſors. I tell you, none ever

periſhed

perished but becauſe of this. How juſt had *Rahabs* judgment been, if ſhe had refuſed to get her ſcarlet thread there, and yours if now you get not your Oyle in your Veſſel? How many are there that have lived fairly and died quietly, and when they are dead and knock, the door is ſhut': That then wring their hands, Oh had I but known of this! I would have ſpent my care and ſtrength, and tears, and thoughts how to have filled my Veſſel, but I knew it not.' This time will ſhortly come, and if you know it now, and do not ſet upon it, what a cut will this be? As therefore the Apoſtle exhorts, *Heb.* 4. 1. *Having a promiſe of entring into reſt, fear leſt you fall ſhort of it.* I ſay ſo much more here, knowing how only you ſhall enter into Chriſts reſt, fear leaſt you fall ſhort of this; I hope I ſhall not, I thank God my courſe is blameleſs, ſpotleſs, I have forſaken the ſins of places, and pollutions of Ordinances; ſo theſe were Virgins alſo. Oh but my Lamp burns as bright as any mans I know: So did the fooliſh Virgins, oh but they all think well of me, ſo were theſe thought of, till the Lord ſaid, *I know you not.* Oh but I look to Chriſt, to meet with him, and ſalvation from him; So did theſe, and yet were ſhut out from Chriſt. If the Lord ſhould have ſaid it was becauſe they had not wealth enough, nor world enough, every man would not have been wanting here, but would have ſtriven to have got enough of that, though it were not to be had; but there is enough in Chriſt to inrich you, who hath the Spirit without meaſure to do it: The Spirit may breath now.

Labour to feel and mourn under thy whole corrupt principles, that have acted *Means* 1. thee hitherto: For many men are ſenſible ſometimes of ſome particular acts, and jarrings of their hearts and life with the rule; and then they ſeek forgiveneſs of, and grace againſt them, and then they hope all is well, then they do many things, and hear *John* gladly, and in plainneſs and integrity of their hearts think that all is well. But ſtill they fall ſhort of a Principle of life, becauſe they never felt a whole corrupt Principle, and how in every thing it croſſeth God, not only in the corrupt, but moſt glorious actions. For all men living naturally turn from being open, to ſecret enemies; and from being ſecret, to be ſubtil enemies, and to undermine the Lord in all they do. Now many ſee it but not the evil of it, nor mourn under it. Hence the Lord never ſends another Spirit, becauſe they have not the Spirit of heavineſs for want of it. But when a man ſees that in every thing he is carried and acted by a principle of bitterneſs againſt the Lord, and lives without the Spirit of the Lord to act him; the Lord is not far from that ſoul when he feels this, and mourns before the Lord, becauſe of this, and the want of that, 1 *Kings* 8. 38. So Chriſt ſaid, *Becauſe I ſaid I go away, ſorrow hath filled your hearts,* John 16. 6, 7. This is the very reaſon why Saints have the Comforter, his abſence fills their hearts with ſorrow; becauſe when he is gone, oh the ſtraitneſs, vileneſs of a corrupt heart! you ſay it may be. If this be not a right Principle, what is? *Anſw.* To undermine all falſe works; oh therefore, feel this plague! If ever God works this grace, feel you muſt the want of it, and if you do mourn then you are under it: And oh mourn, 1. By conſidering the evil of it, you can mourn after a dead father, and ſhall you not over a dead heart. 2. To think there ſhould be ſo much Spirit in Chriſt, and not a drop for me. Is he ſo angry with me? See therefore I pray you that you are led by ill principles, or falſe principles. I pray, but ſelf-love ſets me a work; I profeſs, but praiſe of men acts me; I obſerve duties in ſecret, but natural Conſcience only carries me. No ſurer ſign of ruine then for the Lord to hide theſe things from you; nor of love then when he ſhews this, and gives you not only ſenſe of ſome one act, but a ſpirit of heavineſs under this. This empties the Veſſel, and ſo makes us Veſſels of honour; do not therefore ſet thy ſelf ſo much to do, as to ſee where thy evil principle is, in all thou doeſt.

Repair now to the fountain of life, for a principle of life from him, and fetch *Means* 2. it from him.

What is that ? and how ſhall I fetch it from him ?

1. Tis not a mans own ſtriving, a man may imitate nature, but cannot make nature : All the world cannot make one poor flie. And as 'tis *artis celare artem*, ſo when he hath done he may deceive himſelf and others, but nothing elſe. *Born not of the will of man* : A man is in great diſtreſs of Conſcience for ſin paſt, fear of death for time to come, and now he comes juſt as far as a Devil ; then prays Lord ſave me, and now comes as far as nature can carry him, and therefore is eaſed, and now he hath Satans black ſeal upon him, and ſelf-flattery hath carried him on. The fountain of life is not here.

2. 'Tis not the Law, it convinceth one, and he complains, it condemns another, and he cries out, it irritates another, and he falls to do what he can ; but the Law cannot give life, *Gal.* 3. 21.

3. 'Tis not bare Ordinances, which are of themſelves but husks and ſhels, and empty pipes ; witneſs the cries of many a man Sabbath after Sabbath, no life, and that for a long time : Nay, he grows worſe.

4. 'Tis not God ſimply conſidered, He is indeed the fountain of life, but ſin hath ſealed that fountain ; hence many a one goes to him, and departs from him with frowns.

5. Where is life then ? In Chriſt : I know he is Lord and Prince of Life. Yet conſider, as God-man no life is in him for you, as to be communicated to you. Where then ? 'Tis in the blood and death of the Lord of life : You are ready to undervalue this life. Oh conſider, what it muſt coſt the Son of God ? and where it muſt lie, *Hebr.* 9. 14. *If Buls and Goats blood waſhed the fleſh, much more this blood, &c.* Many a man feels a blind dead heart, and all duties dead : And hence uſeth many perſwaſions to himſelf, yet they continue ſo ſtill, becauſe he never looks to this blood. There is this excellency in Chriſts blood, not only to cleanſe from guilt, and power of ſin, but from dead works, and none elſe can. Now therefore repair hither for it ; know what your lives will and muſt coſt. Now how ſhall this be done ?

Anſw. 1. Prize this blood, and ſatisfie thy Soul with it, chooſe it, and reſt in it, in the Lord himſelf as ſufficient, *Joh.* 6. 53. *Except you eat and drink, &c.* many account it a common thing ; you receive it not then, but trample it under their feet, many eſteem of it, but they feed not themſelves with it, nor quiet their hearts with life there firſt : and hence it falls out thus,

2. Keep this Rule, content not thy ſelf with that meaſure which thou haſt from Chriſt, but be thankful for it, and falling ſhort, call ever for more ; but ſatiate thy ſelf with that which is in Chriſt.

If thou canſt not do this, and it is beyond thy ſtrength, then conſider Chriſt hath words of life, *John* 6. Oh beg for that, and for thoſe words ! *Hear what the Lord will ſay, Pſal.* 51. 8. You cannot ſee nor come to Chriſt : Then *hear, and your ſouls ſhall live.* Who knows what the Lord may do. 'Tis not poſſible for man to do it, but the Lord Jeſus may and can.

Oh then you that have this Principle, Let all your actions iſſue and ſpring from hence ! As *Paul* exhorted *Timothy*, *Stir up that gift that is in thee. Up Deborah, up. Awake Harp and Lute,* ſaith *David.* Do not ſay, I can do nothing, and ſo the Lord muſt do all. Do not ſay, I have a dead heart, and can do nothing, but ſtir it up. It was the Lords complaint, Iſa. 64. 7. *None took hold of the Lord nor ſtirred up himſelf* to that end. It may be ſome of you have ſome ſtrength. Oh put it forth ? I know all ſtrength is from Chriſt, but there is a pertinant ſtrength in you. You are not dead to act, you wrong the Lord and his Grace if you think ſo. As 'tis a heavy ſin to ſhut up and impriſon natural truth, *Rom.* 1. 18. So much more the power of Grace. Others have loſt it, oh recover it ! And hence *Paul* praies for this earneſtly, Eph. 3. 15. *The Lord ſtrengthen you with might in the*

inner

inner man. And therefore put this forth to act, and be sure you act only from this Spirit of Grace.

How shall I do this ?

1. Set the Lord Jesus in all his Glory before you. There is that excellency of the knowledge of Christs Person, that it makes us be and live like him, and according to the propinquity of our souls and eyes to Christ, so we are like him. As 'tis with the Sun, when it is gone from the earth, there are not so much as leaves on the Trees, yet when it returns, the Trees bring forth fruit. Or as 'tis in Heaven, 1 *John* 3.2. so in this life, when we see him in a Glasse, 1 *Cor.* 3.18. That look as 'tis with an ambitious man, when he is in the presence of men he will manifest all his excellency, nothing shall be done to gain discredit. So if the Lord and his life be your excellency, when you see Christ, you will approve your selves to him. See him therefore beholding and accepting ; and that Grace you would put forth, see it in him : 'tis strange to see what a stream of spirit comes somtimes this way.

2. Keep the remembrance of the exceeding greatnesse of his love fresh in your minds, in that *he hath quickned you, Eph.* 2.4,5. and that this life was by his death. All the Flowers of the field cast their favour but for a time, and then away with them ; but Christs love and Christs death do usually alwaies breath a favour of life to a sincere heart that ever knew what the sting of death meant, 2 *Cor.* 5.14,15. Christs love constrains, because he dies that we should live. But how ? Because we thus judged. God hath made man an Agent by counsel. Now some Christians go to the Lord to help them, but set not prayer of Faith a-work, and hence have no water of life : Some do, but use not other means to set the understanding (the mind of Faith) on work, to quicken it up to act, and so would have life brought in, but not by the right door : An empty Vessel will not be full of this water till now, that the mouth of the understanding is open. Now many things are to be considered to act every Grace, as Gods Command and Promise, *&c.* But this is that which in the general quickens, oh Christs love which constrains the Soul to live to him ! According as a man thus receives from Christ, so he returns to him. As 'tis observed, one sign that when a people visit not their Minister, they receive no good ; so here : That is sign of a decaying Christian, for usually they that get good by Christ, cannot by their good will stay a-way from Christ. So then the soul will return in all fruitful obedience to the Lord, when he receives the sweet of the Love of the Lord. The Lord doth me good methinks, and hence he follows the Lord. Satan hence prevails with the heart, because of his external objects, and a party within ; so here Christ prevails, because there is a party within, when external Objects are propounded. Let a man have life, if he have no food he will never live. If bread be before him, and he feed not on it, and that abundantly, he will never have strength, so this love of Christ in us, is life in us, and food for us.

3. Famish the contrary principle, the strength whereof is by sucking in the sweet, and receiving in carnal content from the creature, *Rom.* 13.14. *Put on the Lord Jesus,* his Spirit, his Righteousnesse, his Life, his Graces, *Make no provision for the Flesh.* Many Christians look up to Christ in all means, but can do nothing, because they have some delight either in lawful or unlawful things, that lies between him and Christ. Hence that grows strong, the other feeble.

4. Die to all self-confidence in Grace received, or self-contentment with any measure of it ; for thereby you stop the Spirit : For we of our selves cannot think a good thought. Therefore be strong in Christ, and hence *Eph.* 6.10,11,12. A man is apt to fall to a double extream, to be strong in the Lord without putting on Graces ; and to trust to them without being strong in him. Corn must die before it lives, so must you : and rest not content with the measure received, but look

for more, and hence be thankful, and say, 'tis not I but Christ; yet look for more.

5. If no means come to give strength, consider sadly if you have not broken covenant with God, as in *Samsons* case, God was in covenant with him, but he had broken it on his part, hence his strength was gone. I know no place that breeds men of larger Covenants than this place, by Sea and Land, personall, and especially Church-Covenants. Now thy strength is gone. Dost not live in breach of Covenant? Not only it is broken, but you live in it. You covenant to cleave to the Lord, or if you depart, to return soon again, but you lie in your falls. Nay your Covenant and returning heals your horrour only, not your sin. You covenant to love Brethren dearly, but a little offence one gives; or hopes of a bigger Lot, will tempt thy heart to leave them to their own shifts. You covenant to submit to Officers in the Lord, but some take liberty to speak what they will, and others do what they list. To watch over your brethren to put life in them, but you grow a stranger, and it may be see them not once in a quarter, unlesse at Church: But can it be said they are any better for thee? Oh your sins are double, and hence your plagues of heart are worse now, more hard to be wrought upon, and hence sin and Satan lead you, *Psal.*78.57,60,61. Oh consider this sin, the strength of God is taken as Captain of the Camp, that when you cry, Lord help, there 'tis. But alas 'tis gone from you, and 'tis in Satans hand, not only your strength, but Gods strength, and the soul is taken captive. Oh therefore mourn for this, lest you mourn at last.

CHAP. XIX.

Sheweth that there is such a fulnesse or mea-
sure of Grace in the hearts of Believers,
which the most Refined Hypocrites never
arise unto.

SECT. I.

THat there is a certain plenitude, fulnesse, or full measure of the Spirit of Grace in the hearts of the Faithful, which the most Glorious, yet unsound Professors of Virgin-Churches want, and have not in their Vessels, but fall short of.

Just as these Foolish Virgins, they had their Lamps, a burning and shining Profession. And had they no more? Yes surely, for their Lamp how could it burn, but by means of some Oyl? They had their wiek toucht and dipt in Oyl, some lighter stroaks and superficial impressions of the Spirit. They had not their Vessels filled with Oyl, they had not this degree and full measure of the Spirit. This they fell short of, and herein appeared the difference. There are certain inward touches, an inward lighter Dye of Gods Spirit, which serves to beget a most eminent Profession before men, but never to make the Soul sincere indeed before the eyes of God. That look as some Naturalists make three or four kinds of life, differing only as higher or lower degrees of life, though not of the same life; as Plants have a Vegetative life only to grow, but no sensitive to see; because

cause their forms are more drowned in their matter; sensitive in beasts, yet not rational; rational in men, but not Angelical, &c. So here; a greater degree of the Spirits working, makes a difference in kind between Christian and Christian. 'Tis the Spirit that makes a man live a civil moral life, 'tis the same Spirit by a greater stroke, makes a man live the life of God, *Eph.4.18.* Yet here are two kinds of lives as far different as sensitive and vegetative; and though the rational hath both, yet 'tis neither of both. So though a Saint lives the life of reason and morality, yet there is another life he hath, which doth differ from these of a higher degree, and of another kind. I do not say therefore that a sincere soul only hath a greater degree of the same Grace, but that he is distinguished by a greater degree of Grace and working of the Spirit of Grace from an unsound heart. As a man may love another, but not with a conjugal love, here is now a degree of love, but not of the same love, for 'tis not a whit conjugal; it might then be sinful in some men, so 'tis here. A man that hath filled his stomach with meat may have some desire after it, but not an hungry desire, nor in that degree; hence not hungry at all. So *the sluggard desires and hath not,* a carnal heart desires, and another desires the Lord Jesus; a carnal sluggish heart desires and hath not, but another hungers and is filled; he hath not any degree of the same hunger. 'Tis therefore granted there are desires, and joyes, and light, and growth in false hearts, but there is not that fulnesse of joy, that fulnesse of light, that fulnesse of the Spirit which is in the Faithful, and here they ever fall short. Yet note,

1. There is not a perfect measure; nor the fulnesse that shall be when our souls shall be gathered to them that are made perfect.

2. Nor yet that there is that fulnesse the Saints aim at; for 'tis the resurrection they aim at, *Phil.3.12,13,14.*

3. Nor yet a glutting fulnesse, that men have Manna enough, and say, the main work is wrought, and that is enough: Not such a fulnes as satisfies their appetite from longing for more. But which satisfies and quiets their Conscience in regard of the uprightnesse of their souls before the Lord.

SECT. II.

BUT for the more full and clear explication of this point, I shall shew you these three things.

1. That Hypocrites may have some inward touches of Gods Spirit.

2. That the very reason of their falsenesse is because they have no more than such touches or stroaks.

3. That there is a fulnesse the Saints come to, which others want.

To be shewed { 1. Positively.
{ 2. Negatively.

I. That Hypocrites may have not only outward shews, but some inward lighter stroaks of Gods Spirit. As

1. Of the Spirit restraining and confining, nay benumming of corruption, as *Paul* was blameless, nay he had no mind nor will to many sins, nay did not think he had any living contempt and enmity of God in his heart. Hence *Rom.7.9.* 'tis said, *When the Command came sin revived.* Was it not living before? Yes, but it was asleep, it was benummed, like cold Snakes, but not killed.

2. Of the Spirit preventing and exciting unto many, nay, to any duty of the Law in general, and that sometime by fears of misery and terrours of the Law, *Deut.5.23.* And sometime by love and mercy, morally affecting the heart, *Exod.19.4,5,6. You have heard what the Lord hath done, Will you now enter into*

Covenant?

Covenant? Yes, yet what is said of them? Psal.78.37. *They were false in Gods Covenant.*

3. There may be some operative and quickning Grace of the Gospel, Heb.6.4. *They were enlightened,* &c.

4. There may be some edifying and cooperating glits of Law and Gospel, whereby a man may not only be useful and helpful to some, but to the Church of God, as those that did prophecy in Chritts Name. And these may be so inward, that they think themselves clean and sincere; as *Abimelech.*

II. That the reason of their unsoundness is because they have no more than lighter stroaks of Gods Spirit.

As I might shew in all these, *Paul* is blamelesse, yet far enough from having sin mortified by Christ, and hence professeth, *We did serve divers Lusts,* Tit.3.3. The *Israelites* cry out, they *will do what God will have them :* Yet *Oh that there were such an heart!* Deut.5.29. They in Heb.6. *were enlightened and tasted,* yet fell. He therefore adds, *We are perswaded* (v.9.) *better things of you.* They did *prophesie in Chrifts Name,* Mat.7. Yet *depart from me you workers of iniquity.* But see it more particularly, Mark 12.33. Saith the Scribe to him, *To love the Lord,* oh *'tis better than all burnt Offerings.* Some *Jews* did rest there, but neglected the inward work; but this man, the inward work was prized in his judgment, he had both profession and some affection: And was he now entred into the Kingdome of God? No. Here was his wound, he fell short of it some degrees. Hence its said, *thou art not far from the Kingdom of God.* So the *Israelites*, Why did not they enter? Was not the Land good? Oh yes! That report the worst of the Spies brought: But their hearts were not taken with the goodness of it, as *Calebs* and *Joshuahs* were. And hence they were shut out, *Numb.*13.27. & 14.7,8,24. So it is here. So an unsound heart may be enlightened, as 'tis there, Heb.6.4,5. But there is a marvellous light which they never have, they have not such a degree, 1 Pet.2.9. And hence, Deut.29.2,3,4. *The Lord hath not given you eyes to see to this day.* Did the Lord give them no eyes to see, no hearts to be affected with what they did see? Why came they then out of *Egypt?* Why did they sing when they saw *Pharaoh* drowned? Why they had not such eyes and such hearts as *Moses* had, not unto that day.

So for turning to the Lord. Do not many unsound hearts turn over a new leaf? Do they not, not only outwardly, but inwardly too? Where is the flaw then? In the degree, Jer.3.10. *Judah hath not turned with her whole heart, but treacherously.* So there may be some growth and life in false unsound hearts, that may after fall away: But where is the wound? Look in the Parable of the Seed; Some grew not at all; some did grow, but not having depth of earth, fell again: Others fell not in persecution, but there were the roots of Thorns that choakt the Seed; the good grounds feed came to ripenesse and fulness of fruit, though some in a greater degree than others; yet none at all (no ripe fruit) in the rest. Hence the Lord is said to *weigh the heart,* Prov.16.2. Men think they are humbled, and do believe, but God finds them too light, as *Belshazzar was weighed and found too light.* And thus it will be seen at the last day, when Christ Jesus shall appear, that all the most glorious Profession of many a man is therefore rejected, because found too light.

III. That there is a fulnesse which the Saints have, and which others fall short of. Which I shall shew,

I. Positively and affirmatively from what hath been said, Prov.12.26. *The righteous is more excellent.* John 14.17. *Whom the world cannot receive, because it knows him not.* There is that Spirit in Saints which no unregenerate man knows, hence desires not. Because he dwells in you, he doth not only send some gifts, or work somwhat there, but he dwells there, he fils the heart. Hence the end of Chrifts death is, *to purchase to himself a peculiar people,* Tit.2.14. Of such a

spirit,

spirit, such holiness that only themselves know. So 'tis that which all the Prophets press to, to a higher pitch ; and hence that charge of *Josh.*22.5. And 'tis a peculiar fruit of Election, *Eph.*1.4. 1. *To be holy.* 2. *Before him.* 3. *In love.*

II. Negatively. If there should not be such a distinguishing fulness,

1. Then the whole Ministry of Christ is in vain ; and so destroyed, for what is the end of that, that God raiseth up any Ministers in the Church, but this, *Acts* 26.18. *To turn men from darknesse to light.* If this light was only that in *Heb.*6.4. then the end of the Ministry was to work hypocrisie. *And from the power of Satan to God,* there the Lord leaves them not, but *that they may receive remission of sins,* &c.

2. If there should not be this fulness, most of the Promises should be destroyed, and Gods Faithfulness fail, and the Saints be deceived. For Promises are made to them that mourn, to them that hunger, to them that believe, &c. Now many Hypocrites mourn, and desire, and the stony ground believed. Then it seems the promise is not true. Yes, and therefore there must be another kind of mourning, another and higher degree of the Spirit of Faith, &c. *i.e.* not of the same Faith, but of another kind of Faith.

3. If not, then all Christian endeavour after a higher measure of Grace should be destroyed. For if any man only hath Christ in his eye, that he may have him, I say that is sweet ; but I say you shall never have him, unless you receive him. Oh but many receive him! as *John* 2.23. yet Christ *committed not himself to them, for he saw what they were.* Now therefore if you regard not the measure, *i.e.* such a kind of receiving of him, you will never seek for it, pray for it, nor learn to know it. And hence 'tis said, Prov. 15.24. *The way of life is above to the righteous,* If it were not above, of that height, he would never come over difficulties to it.

4. If not, there is no true hope that any man can have : But 'tis utterly destroyed, 1 John 3.3. *He that hath this hope purgeth himself.* I am as good as such a one : But, *as Christ is pure.* That is his Copy and his Pattern.

5. The very people of God are destroyed from having a being in the world, if this measure makes not the difference. If it be replied, the Lord Jesus makes the difference, 'Tis very true, those that are in Covenant, they have God to be their God, that makes one difference ; but if there be not some peculiar workmanship of the Spirit in them, then though they have God their God, yet the second part of the Covenant is destroyed, *i.e.* They are not the Lords peculiar people that have more than common wash-work. For we are not only the Lords people by choyce and purchase, but by new Creation also, *Isa.*64.7,8,9.

SECT. III.

HEnce we see the sight of no Grace is no part of a Christians Grace and Holiness. The five Foolish Virgins were not shut out because they did not see they had no Oyl, but because when they did see it, (as the Lord will make you see it first or last) they did not get such a measure and quantity of it as might fill their Vessel. You may go down to Hell with complaints I have nothing, unlesse the eternal Spirit work something at last in you.

Hence take heed of quenching and limiting the Spirit of God, when it's working upon and breathing in your hearts at any time, in any means. Because you may then fall short of this measure of it, and so be shut out at last. Look as it was with the *Israelites,* 'tis said of them, that *they could not drive out the Canaanites,* i.e. they would not by reason of their sloath ; and hence they were pricks, nay snares to them. So the Lord begins to work strangely upon some men, but they

they are presently humble enough, and have comfort enough, and Grace enough, and cannot be better, and hence God makes their sins snares and thorns to their sorrow and ruine afterward. Nay Beloved, many a one will quench the Spirit. Oh take heed of it! Thus,

1. The Spirit not only convinceth, but humbles his heart, and shakes his spirit with fears of sin. Now what should he do? He should welcome it, and say, oh blessed Spirit, dost begin to cast me down to the dust for my sin, before I am cast to Hell for my sin? What wilt have me to do? Oh humble me more. Give me not only an act of heaviness, but a spirit of heaviness? As she said of affliction, *I pray God this Plaister may never cease cleaving, till healed.* Now what do many men? Why either game it, or work it, or sleep it away. The young man will not so soon lose all his mirth: The man that hath thought his estate good so long, will not believe 'tis so with him now. Or as *Solomon* speaks of Gods hand, he gro vs weary of his chastisement, and so casts it off, and catcheth hold on Christ and comfort, and there staies, before the Spirit hath done it.

2. If they dare not shake it off thus till the Spirit easeth, then they satisfie themselves with some hopes the Lord gives, and some tast of his sweetness, before they are satisfied with it, as those did, *Heb.*6.4,5. And hence Psal.90.14. *Oh satisfie us with thy mercy, so shall we be glad all the daies of our lives!* So satisfied, as to live upon it alone. As many say, they could be contented it should be so, but they do not live upon it. As if you should ask a man, could you be content to be made King, and come from Beggery? Yes; but he is left there, 'tis not so; and hence lives a Beggar still. Men cannot live without their lusts. Yet saith Christ, *My flesh is meat indeed; and drink indeed,* i.e. This gives real consolation, satisfaction indeed. And here many a Christian sinks, and goes up and down short of saving good.

3. Hence many walk in some desires which the Spirit hath wrought, but to break through all difficulties, and follow the Lord indeed, and come to that they know they must indeed, this they will not do, but depart from Christ sorrowful, and hope the Lord will accept of them; and hence the Lord complains, *Mal.*1.8. of this generation that had desires in their flocks, but lame ones. *Will thy King accept this?* And so all their work is overly and superficial by stinting the Spirit. Thus far you shall go but no farther. Oh Beloved, this is the frame of a sincere heart, the Lord empties him, but he is never content till the Lord fills; and when he finds it, he sits not down content that the work is done, but as his want made him beg before, so his tast makes him long more now, as *Moses,* to see more of the Lords Glory: As *Paul,* Phil.3.12,13. Oh therefore when the Spirit comes, intreat it to go on and finish. And hence *David* begs, *Psal.*119. 132. *Oh the mercy that thou usest to shew to them that love thy Name!* Why so? Oh *David* saw mercy to others, that sets God awork to do somwhat for them, work somwhat in them, but 'tis not such mercy. Oh beg for that mercy that humbled others, quickned others, that are now in Glory; that, or no mercy Lord!

Quest.
Answ. *How shall I know whether the work is overly?*

1. If sudden and violent, 'tis usually overly. A Picture long a drawing is exact, another soon done is lightly done. A man hath Leopard-spots, which in our garments cannot be washed out easily. Gods through-work is soaking and searching. Hence violent sudden sorrows and joyes and reformation which all were in the stony ground, proved unsound, *Mat.*13.5.

2. God hath thy time of trying thee, *Mar.*13. The seed was sown. Which now is good ground? Where is there fruit to be seen and ripeness of Grace? Look upon persecution, if that doth not drive thee from Christ. If that doth not, see if the world doth not, which by a certain deceit and cozenage will befool you. I am perswaded, as *Calvin* is, that all the several trials of men are to shew them to themselves and the world, that they be but counterfeits, and to make Saints

known

known to themselves the better. As *Saul*, he hath a temptation only of a command, when he had nothing to cause him to stoop but it, yet he fell there. So 'tis with many others that God doth much for, he tries them, Rom.5.5. *Tribulation works trial, and that hope.* Prov.17.3. If you would know whether it will hold weight, the trial will tell you. Look you there, and in special, if it drives to Prayer, fear not.

CHAP. XX.

Wherein is given a more Large and Full account of that Fulnesse of Grace that is in Believers, as to the Several Parts thereof, and how the most Glorious Hypocrites come short in all.

SECT. I.

MAke therefore a narrow search whether you have this Fulnefs of the Spi- *Ufe 3.* rit or no.

What is this Fulneffe ? Queft

When the Spirit comes in the room of those things which a man is full *Anfw.* of now. For fulnefs or filling implies emptinefs, and the removal of that.

Now there are six things every man is full of.

| 1. Sin | 3. Unbelief. | 5. Self. |
| 2. Darknefs. | 4. Satan. | 6. World. |

So there is answerably in every Saint,

1. A Fulnefs of humiliation for fin.

2. A Fulnefs of illumination and revelation, in the room of darknefs.

3. A Fulnefs of Faith, in the room of unbelief.

4. A Fulnefs of the Spirit it felf, in the room of Satan.

5. A Fulnefs of Sanctification in acting for God as their laft end, in the room of felf-feeking.

6. A Fulnefs of Glory and Confolation, inftead of the world.

I. Fulnefs of humiliation under fin, oppofite to fulnefs of fin.

For every hypocritical heart hath commonly fome humiliation and cafting down, which is the firft Principle of all his Profeffion, and hence can tell you of his miferable eftate that once he lived in, and for which he was troubled, but it was never deep enough. For as there was before his terrifying, a full power, a fulnefs of the dominion of fin, his humiliation for fin, never reached, never came to that fulnefs or meafure, fo as to deliver the foul from that. For I do not account that true humiliation whereby a mans heart is rent, troubled and tormented with fin, but whereby 'tis rent from fin; not from the being, but from the power, not from the bondage of fome, but yet from the power of all. For if rending with fin fhould be humiliation, then the Devils fhould be more humbled then any. Then alfo a man may have too much of humiliation, and of Gods Spirit. If rending from the being of all fin fhould be humiliation, then no man living should be sincerely humbled ; unless we dream of an estate of perfection before it comes, and of the day of triumph in the time of warfare. If rending from the bondage of some sins should be humiliation, then a man might be truly humbled for sin, and yet under the power of it. And therefore look as in every one the Lord humbles, there was once a fulness of the reign and power of sin in the full strength of it ; so that full measure of Humiliation which the Lord works in his, it ever comes to that height, as to break that power down, *Ehud*-like, it not only wounds the flesh, but leaves the dagger in the heart of this Tyrant ; *2 Cor.* 10. 5. *The weapons of our warfare are mighty to cast down every thing that exalts it self.*

If I should leave this Point thus, I should but leave you as doubtful as you came, and so in the dark ; therefore for the better clearing of this Point, let me explain five things to you : The Scope of which is to shew you, what I mean by sin, and the power of it, and that Humiliation that removes it.

I. That besides the outward acts of sin, and inward lusts and breathings of sin, and the spiritual plagues with which God strikes men for sin, as blindness, hardness of heart, there is in every man living another sin, commonly called the sin of nature : (as in the Serpents, besides the spitting of poyson, their nature is poisonous) which sin is generally beleeved and confessed, but felt by few. This is called in Scripture by the name of *Flesh*, Joh. 3. 3. *The Law of the members, The old man.* For as in men, there are actions, breathings, and the man himself ; So here : Which sin of nature is the deordination of the whole man, or a corrupt bent and set of the whole man against God: And it expresseth it self in two particulars ; 1. In a constant departing from God in every action, Civil and Moral : Like a man set out of his way, every step he goes is out ; or like a Clock out of frame, every stroke is false, *Psal.* 58. 3. *The wicked go astray from the very wombe.* 2. In a fierce, invincible, resisting and contradicting of God, when he hath overtaken the soul to draw it home, and turn it back, *Rom.* 8. 7. We account it a doleful thing for Christ to bid the soul depart at the last day, that wo is past upon all the sons of men by this sin now ; only with this difference, 1. They are forced to depart then, men willingly depart now, and hasten away in every thing from God as fast as they can. 2. They depart into fire, these to broken Cisterns of creatures. I do 3. Believe they would not resist the Lord, if he should come to save them from their separation then from him, this makes nature resist him now.

II. That this sin of nature is most properly only the reigning sin. The text is evident for it, *Rom.* 6. 12. *Let not sin reign, to obey it in the lusts thereof.* There is 1. Obedience, *i. e.* the outward acts. 2. Lusts, the inward breathings. 3. Sin it self where those lusts are seated. It hath been a Question, What a mans raigning matter sin is, and many discoveries have been made of particular sins, as that which riseth and awakeneth first in the morning with us, that which rides and labours a man upon the Sabbath day, when the Lord or sin must ride in triumph : yet that is the misery of a carnal heart, that when he gives his beasts rest, yet such is sins tyranny, he being sins beast, that he shall then have no rest. Now if their meaning be, that some particular sin may be a raigning sin, or a mans personal reigning sin ; then 'tis true, *Judas* loves his bag best, and *Achitophel* and *Haman* his honour most, and *Herod* his whore most. But if they mean a mans natural reigning sin ; the reigning sin then, 'tis not any particular sin so much as this : For no sin is able to reign over any man but by commission and power from this. As the Weeds can never grow tall, but by vertue of their soil where they grow, *Mat.* 15. 19. All the boughs flourish by vertue of the root whence they grow. And hence we shall see, let Satan sow his seeds of pride or lust or passion in a man whose nature is changed, its impossible they should come to any perfection there, but they will die away within a time, because the heart of the

soil

tou is gone, and power or unremoved; and hence also it comes to pass, that a mans master sin may be changed: Those sins that are his master-sins in his youth, are not in his old age, those that are at one time, in one place, are not in another. Now there could never be such change of Governours and Vice-roys, unless there were some great King, that sets up one, and pulls down another, *satis pro imperio*; This is therefore the raigning sin, which hath taken possession of every part, which hath its hand in every act, which pulls down one sin and sets up another under it, which gives strength to every sin that hath any, which fights it out till the last: This is, I say the reigning sin; hence think not that then the reigning sin is down, when your personal sins are destroyed, though it be with a most sudden and fearful destruction.

III. That when the Spirit of God humbles the soul indeed, he strikes the head, and wounds the heart of this sin; he doth not only cut off some limbs of it, nor only binde it, but slay it of its life and power. That as 'tis with some men, they may have many pains, gripes, diseases, yet live and recover again, but the pangs are not so strong as to separate soul and body, for then the man is gone: So a carnal heart he may be troubled, and have many gripes of Conscience, and apply the promise, *Come to me you that be weary*, and so he may finde rest, and as he recovers his peace, his sin recovers its strength; but when the pangs are so strong as to separate body and soul, sin of nature which hath lived there; now the man dies, now the soul falls down indeed. Now this effectual humiliation carries the soul unto Christ, and hence *Acts 26.18. turned from the power of Satan to God*, Col. 1.13. *He hath delivered us from the power of darkness.* And hence Gal. 5.24. *They that be in Christ have crucified the flesh, as well as the affections and lusts*: For if the Lord should only humble a man for the sins of a wicked life, and some wants in the heart, the Lord should only bruise Satans heel, but never strike his head; the Lord should slay the *Amalekites*, but spare the *Agag*; 'tis true, the Lord usually at first conversion sets one sin upon the soul that brings to minde many other, and the Lord humbles for them, and here the soul is apt to rest as many do, but when the Lord comes indeed to work, he cuts thus deep as now I speak. 1 *Cor.* 15. 'Tis said, *The Lord must reign till all his enemies are put under his feet.* Look therefore as this sin is the greatest enemy Christ hath, so if he reigns in heaven, he will be sure above all other sins, to strike the head of this, and disthrone this; and we shall find that there may be deep terrors upon the false hearted Virgins, but they only assault the soul; So on Saints, but Christ then strikes at the sin and saves the soul, *Isai.*57.16, 17. And this I add, there may be a great power of Christ put forth to humble the soul, but mens hearts resist this; and even *Pharaoh* was humbled, but its never saving, unless it strike the very power and throne of sin, and so this sin; and now the soul is humbled indeed.

IV. That no unregenerate man ever had such a measure of humiliation, as ascended to, and ended in this, though he may have all that Humiliation which is precedent unto this. As,

1. The Lord may arm first some few, and then many of the sins of their lives upon them, so as they may feel the most intollerable burthen of them; not only to stand convinced they are most grievous sinners, but to shed many tears; nay, to be sore troubled and distressed, oh the heavy wrath that lies upon my soul! Thus *Saul*, 1 *Sam.* 28. 15. And hence many make heavy complaints, oh the Lord hears me not! *Send for Moses*, saith *Pharaoh*. *My sin is greater than I can bear*, saith *Cain*. Nay, not only so, but they may feel more terrors than many of the Saints, as the damned now; for the Lord lays this burthen upon his peoples backs in measure, but the Lord empties out the whole sack upon them, and the ground of this is but the sting of sin, or the gnawings of particular sins in the Conscience, not the burthen of the sin of nature as yet.

2. You

2. You will say, thefe fell from God, never looked to Chrift, nor left their fin ; but I have done fo. I have feen the mercy of God in the Gofpel, the Lord Jefus hath been revealed there, and I have feen fin, I muft part with my fin, if ever I have him, and fo I have. And this you may have, you may fee an excellency in Chrift, and be fo affected with hope of his mercy, and melt at the thoughts of his Love, as to caft off all outward evils that thou haft, or the world lives in, 2 Pet. 2.20. So that thou maift efcape thefe, by coming to him to remove them, and by feeing that elfe thou fhalt have none of him ; and hence hated thou maift be of the world. The reafon is, Chrift hath only wafhed thy skin, but never changed thy nature as yet, fo that you may thank God my Confcience is clear.

3. You may have not only outward acts, but for a time inward lufts quenched, that a man hath no mind nor heart to any finful way, nor to the deareft fins he hath lived in, whilft horrour lies upon him. As in *Judas*, when God did heat his Confcience, his luft, after his Bag was gone, he had more mind to an halter ; And hence flings away his pieces of filver, and innocent blood lies heavy. Oh the mercy of a Chrift that I have fleighted ! He thought he might have had his money and Chrift efcaped with his life, and his fin pardoned afterward. And hence its faid, Mat. 27.3. *When he faw he was condemned, he repented,* and as a man not worthy to live in his own thoughts, *he goes and hangs himfelf.* 'Tis with the foul as with water, all the cold may be gone, but the native Principle of cold remains ftill. You may remove the burning of lufts, not the blacknefs of nature, from a carnal heart, and the ground holds, nature is not changed. This I fay an unregenerate man may have, but yet never find this change of nature, where the power of fin lies : change of Confcience from fecurity to terrour, change of life from prophanenefs, and civility, and fafhions of the world, to efcape pollutions thereof ; change of lufts, nay quenching them for a time ; but the nature is never changed in the beft Hypocrite that ever was. As 2 Pet. 2.19,20. *They were wafhed,* but never from their fwinifh nature ; And here they ever fail, Prov. 30.12. *There is a generation clean in their own eyes, yet not wafhed from their filthineffe.* 2 Tim. 2.18,19,20,21. *Alexander* fell, and *Hymeneus* ; they talked of the glorious eftate of Saints, and that here was all the refurrection that is to be expected ; and it feems it was fuch a fall of fuch perfons that many ftumbled, and faid, How fhall we know who are the Lords ? Doubtlefs we may fall. No, *the foundation remains fure, and the Lord knows who are his.* They were none of his all that time, *and let all that profeffe Chrift depart from iniquity,* for *he that purgeth himfelf fhall be a Veffel of honour.* And therefore read through all the Scripture, conftantly never any Hypocrites but they had this brand, Mat. 7.23. *You workers of iniquity.* *Herod* and *Judas* had their haunts, *&c.* And *Rom.* 1, & 2. The Apoftle fhews that all were under fin. He may in every thing elfe be humbled, for all the humiliation befides this ftrengthens fin in its Kingdom, and binds a man fafter under the dominion of it. And hence fuch men are more hard to be convinced than men that were never caft down at all.

But this he never finds, for if he fhould, then,

1. A gracelefs heart might partake of the greateft Benefit of the Covenant of Grace, and love of God. For Rom. 11.26. *This is my Covenant, to take away their fin.* For to fubdue fin is greater love than to conquer Devils, death, and Hell, *Ifa.* 11.6. 'Tis turning Lions into Lambs.

2. Then an unregenerate man may partake of the laft end of all the fufferings and forrows of Chrift, which is *to fave his people from their fin.* And hence, John 1.29. *Behold the Lamb of God which taketh away the fins of the world.* 1 John 3.5,8. *Chrift came to deftroy the works of the Devil.* This therefore he ever falls fhort of. He that hath found this eafe, and accounts this work common, never had it yet.

Queft. *How may a Chriftian know when the Lord hath changed his nature, and taken down the power of his fin ?*   *Anfw.*

Answ. It might suffice to evidence this against all gain-sayers, that thus 'tis, and so to know it by the Spirits witness, which shews us the things freely given of God, who to save the Lord a trying another day, tries us now, and makes known these hidden works. Especially seeing some Divines think, that as the first *Adam* conveyed this sin of Nature, I not knowing; so the second *Adam* doth also remove this by an immediate stroak, I conceive 'tis so also, but not only by it. And therefore take two Evidences now.

1. Where-ever this is done, that soul doth not only see this sin, for so an unregenerate *Paul* did, *Rom.7.9.* Where *sin revived,* &c. And the Word is a *divider of joynts and Marrow.* Nor do they only feel this as an evil, and so be much troubled with it, but when the Lord makes the dejected soul feel it as its greatest evil, so long as it remains in its being; (as it will) worse than death, than hell, than all afflictions, and miseries. 'Tis not a particular sin, but this that he feels thus. You will say, this is a high pitch. I say, consider if any man was ever humbled under sin, but he that felt sin as it is. For if I feel it not as 'tis, I am deceived. Now 'tis the greatest evil; To depart from a living God is worse than for soul and body and all creatures to depart from me. To make God miserable is worse than for all creatures ever to be made so, and sin in its tendencie doth so, being a cross to his Will, *Isa.1.24.* Hence he that feels it indeed, feels it so; the beginning of which is a sorrow and mourning after God, that it might be so, *Isa.63.17. Why hast hardned our hearts from thy fear?* But thus 'tis indeed, *Rom.7.24.* And when 'tis thus, it will hold thus till death, while the cause remains; nay the more life and love, the more tender it grows; setting aside some careless fits. And hence its greatest joy is to think of the time it shall be for ever holy. And hence accounts no such mercy as to be set at liberty to live to God indeed. A graceless heart sees and fears it, and cries out of himself for it; but stay a while, and he loseth his tenderness, either because he cannot part with it, or because of Christ, he looks now to him, or because he hath now some sprinkling of the Spirit, nature is eased thereby, and he is quieted; and hence never any carnal heart, but some root of bitterness did grow up at last in this Soyl. Hence Ordinances profit not, because feeling is lost. But the soul thus feeling it, beholding the Holiness of God and Love of Christ, and its constant withdrawings, resistings, oh it cuts deep!

2. Then the nature is changed, when the Conscience being still and quiet, and the soul assured of the Lords love, yet nothing gives the heart quiet till 'tis contiguous to God in Christ to enjoy him, in his Holiness, and in the love and delight of his whole will. For this is a certain Rule, If the nature be not changed, if Conscience be but once quieted with the sence of Gods love, and affected with it, and hath not God indeed, nor his work to quiet it, it will fall to lusting after Creatures and live upon them, and feed the heart there. For as 'tis impossible for a man to live, or to be without provision, so the world being provision for the flesh, meat, drink, sleep, and these lawful things, there it doth and will lie quiet without God. But now where the nature is changed, and there is another nature, there is something else provided for it to live on, and that is the Lord and his Will. As Christ said, *'tis my meat and drink to do his Will.* And *Rom.7.22. I delight in the Law of God in the inner man.* There was somwhat that loathed it, but there was somwhat else delighted in it, and there lies its life, and though the heart would rest and give over somtimes, yet 'tis a Law of the mind that the soul hath, he can have no rest, *Rom.8.5.* And therefore take a child of God, let him have meat, drink, sleep, blessing in his Calling, preach, pray, and have honour, yet he will constantly come home to the Lord mourning. What doth all this do me good? When I rise up, lie down, eat, drink and pray, and do all without him? An unmixed heart all this while. The world stands between him and the Lord all this while, but this doth not. Many a sincere heart hath heavy complaints;

plaints, and many doubts, becaufe 'tis not thus ; this rather is an evidence of
peace, than Gods war againſt it. Its an old Rule, he that can live in Heaven,
ſhall ; and there is nothing but a God to ſuck in, and breath out, and live unto.
Is this thy Element now ?

Oh conſider and examine your ſelves here you poor Saints, that you may be
comforted. Others of you, if now you do not, the Lord Jeſus will another day,
and bring theſe ſecret things of darkneſs to light. If thou findeſt this was never
yet done, know it, all thy tears, and fears, and prayers have been in vain ; and
under the power of ſin and Satan thou ſtill art, through the fierce wrath of God a-
gainſt thee: And there I leave thee till the Lord find thee out.

SECT. II.

II. A Fulneſs of Illumination in the room of darkneſs.

BUT let it be firſt noted that I ſpeak not here of Revelations of future E-
vents. When Virgin-Churches ſhall fall a dreaming, 'tis a ſign he fall a
ſleeping. Nor of revelation of new Doctrines, nor yet of the Love of Chriſt and
aſſurance thereof ; but of the Perſon of Chriſt, a work common to all the Elect,
and not peculiar to ſome, for Chriſt may not appear in his promiſe of love for a
time to a ſincere heart, yet this is then wrought. I ſhall therefore expreſs my
thoughts herein in four Concluſions.

Conclu.1.
1. That all unregenerate men are under the power of darkneſs, of ignorance,
Eph.5.8. *You were darkneſſe* in the abſtract, *Eph.4.18.* So that *they cannot
underſtand the things of the Spirit of God,* 1 Cor.2.14. Eſpecially the Lord Jeſus,
for the knowledge of him is above nature, not only corrupted but pure nature.
Nay though the Lord gives the beſt and cleareſt means of revealing himſelf, yet
they cannot ſee, John 1.5. *Light ſhined in darkneſſe, and it comprehended him not,*
no more than he whoſe viſive faculty is loſt, when the Sun ſhines round about
him. Nay, that light which is in them is darkneſs, *Mat.6.23.* And then how
great is that darkneſs? For many men might have known Chriſt, but that they
thought they did know him before, and ſo are delivered up in theſe chains of
darkneſs to the Prince of darkneſs, but are like wilderneſs-ſhrubs, ſhall never
ſee when good comes. Miniſters (as Chriſt did) may mourn over them, but
can never help them until the Lord pull off their ſcales. For they pleaſe themſelves in darkneſs, and love it more than light, and are not as *Paul,* praying and
mourning under the Scales that are upon their eyes.

Conclu.2.
2. That there is a ſtate of light to which God calls his people only ; or rather,
that there is a ſpirit of Light, Illumination or Revelation let into the mind,
which is Peculiar to the Beloved of Chriſt, 1 Pet.2.9. As of other things, ſo eſpecially of the Lord Jeſus, 2 Cor.4.4,5,6. And 'tis ſo Glorious a work that
Chriſt himſelf admires the Father, and ſtands in a raviſhment at it, Mat.11.25.
To Babes, uncapable of all others of knowledge ; yet to them doth the Lord reveal ſome things that the wiſeſt in the world never knew. I do believe that the
greateſt Scholar that ever lived, never had one ſuch thought or apprehenſion of
the Lord and the things of the Lord, as the Saints have. And hence Chriſt pro-
feſſeth, oh *bleſſed are your eyes that they ſee* ; and themſelves bleſs him, and fall a
wondring many times, *Lord why doſt manifeſt thy ſelf to us, and not to the world* ?
And therefore 'tis an injury to the Grace of God, to make precious things common, and all the work of the Spirit on the underſtanding to be common to Reprobates, and to ſay, the difference lies only in the work of the Spirit upon the
will, John 6.45. *He that hath heard and learned of the Father, comes to me.* If
the Learning of the Father be common to a Reprobate, then either they may
come

Conclus. 3.

come to Chrisl, which is there denied, or Chrisls promise is false, for then a carnal heart may hear and learn of the Father, and never come to Chrisl.

That notwithslanding 'tis thus with them, yet foolish Virgins may have some light in their Lamp, some sight and knowledge of Jesus Chrisl. It is said we live in dayes of light, and so indeed we do, but as the Lord said to them that had seen his Miracles, *yet the Lord had not given them eyes to see to this day*; they were inlightned, yet fell, *Hebr.* 6. 4. I shall therefore speak not of the revelation of all the Word, but of Chrisl the end of it, and the knowledge of whom comprehends all the rest.

1. There is a knowledge of Chrisl in many a man which is begot by common fame, and humane private inslruction, which men hearing from credible men, conceive of and believe; As that Chrisl is the Saviour of the World, is come, is dead, is risen, is at Gods right hand, that in him Gods jusltice and mercy is reconciled, that there is mercy with him for the greatelt of all sinners, *&c.* And according as men are more or less inslructed; so do men conceive and beleeve. But now this knowledge is but traditional, and begot by common fame and humane report, like *Herods*, that heard many things of Chrisl, and yet indeed despised him. The Lord I know doth make use of this to cause the soul to come to further sight of him, as in the Queen of *Sheba*, but its far enough off from giving any saving knowledge of the Lord Jesus; and hence *John* 1. 46. when they had been with Chrisl, they do not wish them to resl in the report, but *Come and see*; so you hear of these things, but come and see these things. You have learned them from man come unto the Lord that he may teach them; and hence we shall see many of the people of God that have been put to a Quesltion of all things that ever they learned, and learnt them over again; as, Whether there be a Chrisl or no, *&c.* And they never saw these things indeed, until the Lord taught them a second time; hence therefore those that have been thus trained up, and have been troubled and comforted by some conceived promises of Chrisl, but never saw any more of his person, then what you have learned before; *Your eyes are closed up to this day.*

2. If any man should see and behold Chrisl really, immediatly, this is not the saving knowledge of him. I know the Saints do know Chrisl as if immediatly pres[e]nt, they are not slrangers by their dislance, if others have seen him more immediatly I will not dispute it, but if they have seen the Lord Jesus as immediatly as if here on earth, yet *Capernaums* saw him so; nay, some of them were Disciples for a time, and followed him, *John* 6. and yet the Lord was hid from their eyes; nay all the world shall see him in his glory which shall amaze them, and yet this is far short of the saving knowledge of him, which the Lord doth communicate to the Elecl. So that though you see the Lord so really as that you become familiar with him, yet *Luke* 13. 26. *Lord have we not eat and drunk*, *&c.* And so perish.

3. A man may see the Lord in his wonderful works, and glorious kingdome and government, and yet not know him savingly, wondrous deliverances, preservations of himself, and of Gods people, dreadful desltruction of enemies, such as they cannot but say, *This is the finger of the Lord*, and yet know not, *Deut.* 29. 1, 2, 3, 4. And hence *John* 15. 24. and hence men think such things are done, and shall I ever be vile again, yet they become as bad as ever.

4. He may see the Lord Jesus yet more clearly by the letter of the Scripture, which though it brings to the saving knowledge of Chrisl, yet to see the Lord Jesus no otherwise then by the slrength of fancy and underslanding, from thence is no saving knowledge of Jesus Chrisl; and hence *Rom.* 16. 26. the Mysltery of the Gospel was hid from the Jews, but now 'tis revealed to all Nations; literally, to all where it comes, savingly to some few. For between the saving knowledge of Chrisl in the Gospel, and palpable ignorance of him in the Gospel, there is this middle knowledge which is literal, whereby a man doth see, *yet in seeing, sees not,*

not, Ifai. *6. 9.* which is the State of a Church which hath been long trained up under good means: And hence we fhall fee many men of great learning have been able to write Volumes of the Myftery of Chrift, and yet in *feeing never faw.*

5. There may be in a falfe heart a ftrange knowledge of Chrift without Scriptures, which may ravifh a mans deluded heart ftrangely, which is ufually the firft Temptation of the Virgin-Churches, that are of much knowledge, and little love, *2 Cor. 11. 2, 3, 4.* Wherein Satan doth not feek to pull away men to forfake the Gofpel, but from the fimplicity of the Gofpel, *Repent, and beleeve, and be faved.* For faith he, *Satan is transformed into an Angel of light* : And hence we have heard that fome have heard voices, fome have feen the very blood of Chrift dropping on them, and his wounds in his fide, fome have feen a great light fhining in the Chamber, fome wonderfully affected with their dreams, fome in great diftrefs have had inward witnefs, *Thy fins are forgiven* ; and hence fuch liberty and joy that they are ready to leap up and down the Chamber: O adulterous generation! This is natural and ufual with men, they would fain fee Jefus, and have him prefent to give them peace ; and hence Papifts have his Image ; and hence Chrift gives the Sacrament to fhew himfelf as familiarly as can be. Hence *Thomas would not beleeve, unlefs he might put his finger in his fide,* and the Lord tendred him, yet pronounced *them blefed, that have not feen, and yet beleeved,* Joh. 20. 29. So I fay *è contra,* Wo to them that have no other manifefted Chrift, but fuch a one. Little do you think what wrong you do to Chrift, for you do as much as in you lies Eclipfe all his glory at the laft day, as the wicked by their fins Eclipfe his glory at this day. *2 Thef. 1. 10. He fhall be admired in all that beleeve.* Why? Becaufe our Teftimony was beleeved ; That Faith which clofeth with, and fees Chrift in a Teftimony, is that whereby Jefus fhall be admired at the worlds end.

Concl. 4. That the faving knowledge of Jefus Chrift is this, Whereby the foul being fenfible of his Ignorance of Jefus, beholds fuch a glory in Chrifts perfon, as that he efteems him in all his glory, as his prefent, greateft, and only good. I will take this in pieces.

1. I fay that foul which hath truly and favingly feen the Lord Jefus, hath been made fenfible of his ignorance of him ; I fee him not, I have heard of him, and read of him, and taken his Name into my mouth, and profeffed him ; and I beleeve others fee him, and bleffed are their eyes, but I fee him not, *John 9. 26, 37, 39. For judgement am I come into this world,* and look as all the increafe of the knowledge of Chrift comes in by this door, fo the beginning of it , and therefore thofe that have been caft down and heard of Chrift a Saviour, but never felt their ignorance of him before they have apprehended him, their light is darknefs, and their knowledge full of delufion and idolatrous.

2. It beholds a glory in Chrifts perfon, for before the Lord reveals his Son to any, look what he was to the Jews he is to every man, *Ifai. 53. 2, 3. He is rejected and defpifed of men,* nothing fo mean as Chrift, every vanity preferred above him, and men can do no other, becaufe they fee not his glory and beauty, *1 Cor. 2. 8. If they had known, &c.* Therefore the Lord reveals his hidden glory to them, fuch as never entred into their hearts before, or into the minds of other men , which though others may talk of, yet they cannot fee it in that manner as they do ; it is called therefore *marvellous light* which he doth reveal, when the foul hath been viewing its own fhame and filth, when all the grafs and glory is withered, *Ifai. 40. 6.* then the glory of Chrift is revealed ; One every way fo fit and fuitable to them, according to all their wants and woes , by fome Sermon or other, which when the foul doth fee, it ufually fills the head, and heart, and eyes with tears. Oh that I have defpifed him fo glorious! *Acts 2. 36, 37. 2 Cor. 4. 5, 6.* If the foul fhould not feel its ignorance of him, it would never efteem the

fight of him, but now it doth thus, and now that Glory is revealed, *John* 1.14 *We beheld his Glory as the Glory of the only begotten Son.* In every Truth there is Glory which men fee not, and this is called in Scripture, *the finding of the Pearle* Mat.13.45.

III. He fo beholds him in his Glory as that he now esteems of him in all his Glory. For a *Balaam* may fee the Glory of the Tents of *Ifrael*, and *the Star of Jacob*, but they esteem not of him in all his Glory. The damned in Hell fee a Glory in Christ, elfe they would never grieve for the lofs of him, but 'tis only in regard of fomthing in Christ, delivering Saints from forrows they feel. Nay many Reprobates under a lively Ministry, fhall fee fome Glory in Christ and in Saints, to think them the happy men, yet not esteem of him in all his Glory; but 'tis otherwife here. The Lord arifeth as the Sun upon the earth, which makes all things that have any Glory to appear therein, and it puts a Glory on every thing, that was hid before. So Christ puts a Glory on every thing of himself: So that,

1. The foul fees a Glory in the Grace of Christ, *John* 1.14. For the Glory of Chrifts Perfon is not feen without these excellencies, *Luke* 1.46. *My foul magnifies the Lord.*

2. A Glory in the Holinefs of Christ, *Ifa.6.3.* Especially to confider it's in him to make me holy, *2 Cor.3.18.*

3. A Glory in his Covenant and Promifes, *Pfal.45.1,2.* Oh that all thofe Promifes might be made good to me! This is all my defire, *2 Sam.23.5.*

4. A Glory in the Government and Commands and Will of Christ. Oh if once I could in every thing give content to his heart! *Pfal.19.10.* That the foul had rather lofe all than crofs his will in a fmall thing, feeing a Glory in the leaft Truth, in cafting off a Ceremony, &c. *Zach.6.13.*

5. A Glory in all the Ordinances of Christ. *Oh how amiable are thy Tabernacles oh God!* Oh the Fellowfhip of Saints! Oh the peace on Sabbath!

6. A Glory in all his cariage. Let him blefs me with outward estate, though but a little. This is the allowance that Christ in Glory provides for me. Let him threaten me, *good is the Word of the Lord.* Let him defert me, his anger is love: Oh that is Glorious! Let him take all from me, reproach me, *Mofes esteems Chrifts reproach greater riches than Egypt,* which is our estate here. It fees a Glory in all Chrifts waies, and quiets it felf here, *it is the Lord,* as *Eli* faid. Thus Saints fee and esteem of Christ in all his Glory, and we fhall find a falfe heart ever falls fhort here, a fincere heart never, but commonly is fo taken up with it, that if you ask, fuppofe you fhould have all Grace, Holinefs, Promifes of Christ, &c. Would not this be mercy? Yes, enough: I fhould then boaft in him, and blefs him for ever. And hence Christ is called, *Luke* 2. 33. *the Glory of Ifrael,* becaufe they fo esteem him. And *Ifa.28.5. In that day the Lord fhall be a Diadem of Glory.* Others may in horrour prize Christ above the world, but 'tis only to eafe them.

IV. I add, he esteems him thus,

1. As his prefent good; fo that if the Lord doth withdraw or deny himfelf now unto him, nothing in this world can for the prefent quiet him, *Jer.50.4,5.* Hence thofe in their judgments acknowledge Christ the greateft good, and when they are dying, and fee he will be fo at laft day, yet now for the prefent a little more liberty in fin, floath, luft, honour, gain, Lots, large accomodations are better. You never faw him. Oh vile world! the Lord will one day condemn thee out of thine own mouth; thy own will was more dear to thee than his; this worlds eafe better than his peace, &c. When you lie on your Death-beds, you esteem him then. Why? Becaufe he ferves your turn then: Hence before you did not.

2. As the greateft good, *Deut.33.26.* *Jer.10.7.* Hence thofe that fee fome

good in Christ and desire him, and offer fair for him, but prize him not as the greatest good: And hence with the young man, though content to part with somwhat, not with all, they will cast their rags down at Christs feet, and intreat him to take away their sins ; but will not cast their Crowns down, the dearest things they have: And hence the thorny-ground-Professors ever fall away. The good things of this world which they forsook in time of persecution, were dearer than Christ, and hence they fall away. 'Tis a dishonour to a King to be valued as other men are, *Zach.*11,12,13.

3. As the only good, *Isa.*24.23. *The Sun shall be confounded*, &c. And though other things may steal into their hearts for a time, yet they recover themselves ; this is the *one thing*, *Psal.*27.4. that they beg in this life. And hence do fall short.

1. Those that esteem Christ as men do Merchandise ; they would fain have it, but are loath to fetch it. Men may esteem Christ, as they think, the only good ; but here in their falseness appears, that they neglect means to it, because they have some good else to quiet them. And here is condemned all lazy Profession.

2. Those that would have Christ, and esteem him highly, and use means for him diligently, but they must have Christ, and world, and lust, and ease too : Christ to quiet their Consciences, and the world their hearts ; Christ to rest on, when their duties fail them, and world to rest in, when the Consolations of Christ are denied unto them. *The Land is good, go up and possesse it.*

Object.
Answ.

1. But do the Saints come to this pitch ?

2 *Cor.*4.3. *If our Gospel be hid, 'tis hid to them that be lost.* Who are those from whom Christ is hid ? When is he hid ? When his Glory is hid. I know Saints may feel a want of, and mourn for it, but it will appear if they are the Lords, at some time. Nay this they will find, some and much contempt remaining which they oppose, yet this is here, and at parting times it is seen.

Object.
Answ.

2. But Saints cannot know this.

Yes (as well as they can know their contempt) by means of Gods Spirit, he that is carried from one contrary to another shall know it.

Object.
Answ.

3. But Hypocrites may attain to this.

1. Then the Gospel may be revealed to an hypocrite and to them that are lost.

2. Then they may believe ; for to them only the Lord is precious, 1 *Pet.*2.7. Then a thing is precious, when we value it according to the worth of it. Now the Lord is the greatest and only good, and then when we esteem him so ; this is the work of Believers only.

3. Then Christ may be a carnal mans Treasure. For that is our treasure which we esteem most.

4. Then a carnal heart may honour Christ with one of the highest degrees of honour, which consists in this high esteem, *Luke* 1.46. *My soul magnifies the Lord.*

5. Observe we, that never any lost Christ but because they undervalued him. Forsake all, and take the Pearle. That it shall lie upon you one day, oh if Christ had had that esteem which lust and world hath had, I had had him now ! Examine, if it be thus, if you thus see and prize the Lord Jesus. Oh be thankful that ever the Lord sent that Messenger to reveal Christ ! If not, oh go and mourn ! *Paul* did so three daies, *Acts* 9. when *he saw nothing.* Oh Christ hath been long hid from thee. Oh few have this ; but lay about for it, for else that in *Mat.*23.39. shall be your portion.

SECT.

SECT. III.

III. Fulness of Faith, in the room of Unbelief.

FOR 'tis not unknown how strongly this sin keeps every mans Palace, and that not *Moses*, but the Lord Jesus is the stumbling stone even of the *Jews*, the peculiar people of God. When men are at their last cast, that the Lord intends to wait to pity no more, at last the Son comes, and an unbelieving heart casts the Ballance and refuseth him. After that the Lord hath tried men by miraculous preservations, deliverances from *Pharaohs*, provision at *Massah*, then *Canaan* comes to be entred, and men cannot enter because of unbelief. This sin stands in open view, and keeps the breach, when all other sins in appearance are beaten out of the field. Now there is a Spirit of Faith, which comes in the room of this unbelief, dispossesseth the soul of the power of it; for there may be some lighter stroaks of the Spirit, which are lighter Skirmishes with it, but yet it wins the field again; as in the stony ground, that believed, but unbelief got head again in time of persecution and temptation, and then they fell away.

Quest. 1.
Answ.

What is this Faith, or that fulnesse or full measure of it?

I shall not speak here of Historical or Miraculous Faith: The first of which is in the Devils, the second in some men only, that may perish afterward. Nor yet of that Faith which we call, of Assurance, we shall not come yet to that. But of that which we call justifying Faith, and that which doth first unite to Christ, and justifie. Now this Faith is the coming of the soul to Christ. This is the general. For *Adam* had his life in himself, but now 'tis lost in us, but laid up in Christ, *Col. 3. 3.* Now hence they that would have this life, must go out of themselves to the Lord for it. Now the motion of the soul between these two extreams of emptiness and death here, to life and fulness there, what is it but Faith? Which *Adam* had not, nor could have in that estate; and therefore none of the Sons of *Adam* naturally can share in it.

And that this is Faith it appears,

1. From *John* 6. 35. *I am the Bread of life, he that comes to me shall never hunger, and he that believes in me shall never thirst.*

2. Because unbelief is the departing of the soul from the God of life, *Heb.* 3. 12. Not from a holy Law, but *from a living God.*

3. Faith is the proper effect of Vocation; or rather the chief part thereof. Now look as ineffectual vocation is when the Lord calls, but the soul never comes; so effectual vocation is whereby the Lord calls, and the soul answers, and so comes. So that to sit still and see nothing, and do nothing, is not Faith, but sloath. No, Christ cannot be in that soul that is yet in himself. Therefore Faith is not a passive possibility of the soul to receive Christ, though that may prepare for him, but the going out of a mans self unto Christ.

Quest. 2.
Answ.

But may not a man come to Christ, that never shall have mercy from Christ?

Yes, there may be many lighter stroaks, as in temporary Believers. The world is at this day full of Faith: Every man thinks and saith he believes, though his Faith be weak. 'Tis mens Buckler against all means, they know these sins, but as long as they believe all is well. And 'tis their comfort in all their troubles, though the Lord kills, yet they will believe. And I say, some men have departed indeed from the Lord: The Gospel hath been preached, and they have made out of themselves to Christ, but missed of him. There is a Bramble-Faith that catcheth and scratcheth Christ, kisseth and betraies him. That coming to Christ therefore which none else have the full measure of, it appears in these particulars.

'Tis that work of the Spirit whereby a sinner sensible of his extream nakedness, emptiness and wants, being called of God, his whole soul comes out of himself to Christ, for himself. I speak not of assurance, for if that were Faith, all Reprobates then were bound to believe an untruth, *Viz.* That God the Father loves, and Christ hath died for them.

1. 'Tis a work of Gods Spirit, and hence 'tis called the Spirit of Faith, not only because wrought by it ; but because the Spirit is in an admirable manner fastned to it, and clasped to the soul, and the soul to Christ by it.

2. The Subject in which 'tis wrought : A sinner sensible of his extream wants; for Faith springs out of the destruction of our own excellency, and ruines of it ; like Christ that did *arise a root out of a dry ground*, for the Lords great plot is to advance Christ and his rich grace. Now look as 'tis obscured by bringing any thing of our own to it, so 'tis advanced by fetching all from it ; this can never be till the soul is sensible of his nakedness, emptiness and wants ; let Christ be never so sweet, a full soul will loath him ; and I say extream want. The Prodigal never comes home, till he dies for hunger : For such is the sencelesness of men, and dislike of Christ, that extremities only drive them hither, as *Judges* 5. 6. When the *Midianites* came, they ran like beasts to their den, and untill bread was taken from them, they cry not unto the Lord, but then they do : So men have neither hearts, or if so, no heads to come to Christ till now ; and usually the Lord makes this the ground of the souls first motion towards Christ. I die here, and because of my wants I therefore come. *Pardon sin, because great*, Psal. 25. 11. *Be merciful, because 'tis a stiffenecked people*, Exod. 34. 9. That so when the Lord pardons the soul may have nothing to boast off but misery, and now 'tis hard to beleeve. But this is not all.

3. It must be called of God, for else the soul though never so sensible of misery, could not, would not, durst not come ; but it would either sink under its burden, or plead against all means : it shall presume, as *Judas* that had no look of Christ (as *Peter* had) hangs himself : And hence *Jer.* 3. 23. *Come unto me, Their heart answered, We come.* For this is usually the Objection of the soul when it sees the riches of mercy, What have I to do with it, that am so vile, and have fallen so oft, and rejected the Lord, and am like to do so; I shall sin the more by this means. No, the command of the Gospel comes, oh come, notwithstanding all this, nay because of this, for I will heal you of them. Now this call hath two things in it. 1. 'Tis particular, for general invitations to beleeve and come in, are made particular to the Elect, who else would not come in : And hence *Isai.* 43. 1. *I have called thee by name.* For we shall finde that the hearts of men when they see a promise cannot think it concerns them ; all that hunger shall be satisfied, but shall I ? And hence shew them 'tis as particular as the Law, they cannot think it is to them ; and hence they say sometime the word *All*, is not put in. Now that is the mighty power of unbelief, a word spoken to all is regarded by none, till the Lord make it particular ; and hence *Isai.* 2. Christ is said to judge the Nations, now when Judges ride their Circuits , they do not make Laws, but only apply Laws. One man is brought before them to be condemned, he hopes better, but he is so; now he trembles : Another to be acquitted , he fears, being falsly accused, he is freed; and now he rejoyceth. 2. 'Tis a living call, or powerful call, *John* 5. 25. And hence a man may live under the calls of the Minister long, and never come, because 'tis not made living from the Lord of life ; and hence not irresistable.

4. Upon this call the whole soul comes out of it self to Christ ; for if a man could climbe the clouds, and unlock the doors of heaven, and come *Elias* like in his body to Christ, he might miss of Christ, as well as those that came and followed Christ for a time with their bodies while he lived on the earth ; a man may come to Christ with half his soul or heart, there may be some hope, and some desires,

some

some love, and some cleaving to him, and choice of him really, inwardly, and yet not savingly, because the whole soul is not here come, but half of it, *James* 1.7,8. Now the whole soul then comes, when all the affections and will take their flight to the Lord, and fasten there. When all the affections are gathered from all other things and changed, and so they come to, and embrace the Lord; so that hope waits only here, when will the Lord pitty me? Desires that were set on a thousand things before, all long after him, love only tasteth him; the Lord letting in some sight of the freeness of mercy, hope looks out hither; the Lord shewing the want, but the way to it, desire breaks down stone-walls, and all means, and the difficulty of them, to have him: The Lord letting the soul tast the sweetness of Jesus and his grace, the soul joys, and love imbraceth, and the will softers; a carnal heart desires, loves, joyes in other things, and the Lord also, and so hath a false heart. But the whole heart comes hither, and when 'tis here, thinks one heart too little, nay one life, one soul, and when any part of the affections are left any where else, then the soul mourns, hates that bondage, is ashamed of it, &c. So that the stream of the whole soul runs now hither, *Psal.* 119.2. *Jer.* 3.10. *Psal.* 45.10. So 'tis with the soul, as with them when they were to come out of *Egypt*, they would not leave child, nor hoof behinde, lest there should be any occasion of return; it is with the soul departed from the body, it only minds the Lord, it hath taken leave of all; so by Faith the whole soul leaves all, and comes to the Lord; otherwise the soul is not come to Christ, but reacheth after Christ; like men that waded after the Ark, but perished in the waters: Their arms are not long enough, their desires and love are not long enough to reach Christ, the bent and stream of the soul is set and runs here. 'Tis with the soul, as 'tis with two Rivers, both run with all their strength to the Sea, but the great River is bigger, and runs faster, yet the others stream is wholly carried thither. So some men may be more full of Faith then others, yet both run to the Sea, and as Rivers, they run in their Circles, this way and that way, and are sometimes damned up, yet end there: So the souls of all Saints run to this and the other creature, yet they end in the Lord at last. As *Peter* and *John* that ran to the Sepulchre, though one out-ran the other, yet they came both to the Lord at last; when both of them had for a time forsook him, though all the world draw the soul back, it cannot live without the Lord; nay, though the Lord beat away the soul from him, yet it follows after him.

5. 'Tis to the Lord for himself, for *John* 6. some came to Christ for loaves, and could have been glad if Christ had been King for it, but did not care for himself: And hence *verf.* 27. he points and turns them to himself; some came to him for higher ends, therefore were his Disciples, that is, for life from him. But when he told them, *There is no life, unless you have the Son, And eat and drink his flesh and blood, or else you die*, it was a hard saying, they could not understand nor see what that meant; and hence forsook him, but when they come and receive him himself; now life is indeed theirs.

So that its Christs person that this Faith first pitcheth on, as 'tis in Marriage, and those that come for this, were never sent away. Now the soul is truly come to him for himself: 1. When himself gives rest to the soul in the want of all things, *Hebr.* 4.3. If friends, protection, strength, life, glory be wanting, yet having him, in him I have all these; when all is sold away, not the treasure only, but the Field contents him: For it looks on this, as better then heaven, then glory, it comforts the soul that the Lord himself should be mine. 2. The soul that taketh him, 'tis not only to make boast of him, as *Capernaum* had him, nor to cover sloth, and sin, and delusion by him: I have Christ, and I have no more to care for, &c. but to live on him, *John* 6.57. *He that eateth me, shall live by me.* Phil. 3. 9, 10. A man takes not Christ as Medicine to ease him; nor as stately, hangings to adorn him; but as bread to receive life from him. For many receive Christ, rest they do upon him, and rest they say in him, but they do not suck any good from

from him, nay before they had my Chrift, or affurance of him they were better than now. You have nothing to do with the Lord Jefus, you are out of your place. As in *Jothams* parable, the Olive and Vine would not be pulled out of their places, to be fet on the tops of other trees, as Kings; left they lofe their fatnefs and fweetnefs: So fince you have clofed with Chrift, you have loft your fatnefs and fweetnefs that once you had, you are now out of your place, go to your horrors and forrows again, till the Lord fo give himfelf to you as that you may receive life from him.

Queft. 3.

But muft all come thus to Chrift with their whole foul, will not part of the price ferve?

Anfw.

No, the whole foul muft come, and cannot but come.

1. In regard of the Jealoufie of God; who is like a jealous Husband, can bear with many weakneffes, but will have the whole heart; and they that do not, fhall be deftroyed for fpiritual Whoredom, *Pfal.*73.27. He fhould difhonour Chrift elfe, to fell him fo cheap.

2. In regard of the excellency of Chrift: The Lord draws the foul by the revelation of him, *Rom.*1.16,17. *Ifa.*55.3,4. Now look as men in this world, when they fee a feeming good, their whole foul is over-powered to be drawn after it. So here, when fuch an Object is feen, efpecially the Soul having been at his Sepulcher weeping, as Iron never ftirs till the Loadftone comes, and then it makes to that only, not to things toucht with it: For *as we love him becaufe he loved us firft*, fo Chrift loving the foul with all his heart, and his whole heart fet upon him, the whole foul is *è contra* fet on Chrift.

3. In regard elfe a man can receive nothing from the Lord, *Jer.*29.12,13. As 'tis with Conduit-Pipes, let them be laid, but not reach the Conduit head, no water can come to that Family; fo here: And this is the reafon why men live, and pray, and receive nothing, their hearts reach not hither: Mens hearts reach but half way to Chrift: Tell me elfe, did you ever not receive?

4. Becaufe elfe 'tis indeed no coming to him, but a leaning on him or toward him. So as 'tis with trees, if not cut off quite, or not pulled up quite by the roots, they cannot be fet in another Orchard, if the tree be left with never fo little twigs in the ground, fo here: Nay the Lord accounts this worfe than if a man had not come at all, *Jer.*3.10. The Lord abhors a double heart, that *Judas*-like forfakes all for the Lord, but then loves the Lord and the Bag too. You are not the Lords. As it was with that man that quarrelled about the tree, it leaned over the Pales, but the root being found to be there, his it was: So though he lean on Chrift, he is none of his.

*Queft.*4. *Anfw.*

But do all Saints come to this meafure?

Ponder thefe grounds elfe.

Object. But are not our hearts partly carnal, and fo clofe with the Creature?

Anfw. True, but yet,

1. So far as 'tis carnal 'tis lamented heavily; fo that they grow not there, but are dying, withering dayly, *Jer.*31.18,19. When a mans affections grow out of the world, and there is no fear nor forrow, in this refpect now, no Chrift is there.

2. The Bent and Byas of the Soul carries the whole Soul hither. For I would not judge of this fo much by fudden pangs, as by an inward bent; for the whole Soul in affectionate expreffions and actions may be carried unto Chrift, but being without this bent and change of affections, it's unfound. As in *Gideon*, they would on a hurry make him King: He would not: He knew it was a fudden pang which would die. And the reafon is, the true turn of the whole Soul is not by turning old affections upon another Object, but changing them firft by this bent, and fo turning them. For a carnal heart may have the firft, as the fame eye

may

may see the Sun and a Dunghill, and the eye not changed; So here. Now when the whole Soul is set here, it is never at rest till here.

But may not Hypocrites come to this?

1. Then they may be blessed, *Psal.*119.2.

2. Then they shall never be cast off from Christ, *John* 6.37.

3. Then they may partake of that which the Lord only looks for. For why is the Lord angry? The heart is gone from him. Why is the Ministry ordained, but to win the whole heart to him? *John* 3.19,20,21. Oh therefore consider whether it hath been thus with you or no? If not, wo to you? Oh be very careful here? 'Tis a thousand to one if some part of your heart be not fixt elsewhere. If Christ were at Judgment, and should say, *Come ye Blessed*: How glad would ye be? Oh he saith now, Come and take my self!

SECT. IV.

IV. Fulness of the Spirit it self, in the room of Satan.

I Shall not speak here either concerning that fulness of the Spirit in extraordinary gifts, spoken of frequently in the *Acts*; nor yet of that Fulness of the Spirit which some Christians that the Lord sets apart to do and suffer more for him, shall receive more than others. For *John* 14.17. the Disciples had the Spirit, and yet Christ promiseth to send them the Spirit. And *Stephen* was a man *full of Faith and the Holy Ghost*, *Acts* 6.8. And *Barnabas Acts* 11.14. *was a good man full of Faith and the Holy Ghost*. But I shall speak of that Spirit which is in every Believer, without which we are not Christs, *Rom.*8.9. And this is that Spirit which is opposite to the evil Spirit, the Prince of darkness, which possesseth with craft and power all the souls of the sons of men, who doth not only encamp about men, 1 *Pet.*5.7,8. Nor only *work within them*, *Eph.*1.2,3. but he inhabiteth and dwelleth in men. He doth not only take men captive, 2 *Tim.*2.26. but he dwells in and possesseth the souls of his Captives, *Luke* 11.21. And though he doth depart for a time, yet, *v.*26. *They return and dwell there.* Now in the room of this, comes Gods Spirit, who *v.*22. is said to be stronger than Satan, which cannot be meant but of Christs Spirit: That as 'tis with a man whose heart is turned from the Lord, he is not left only to be carried by the power of his sin, but by the power of Satan also. So when the whole soul is turned unto him, the Lord leaves not the soul to be carried along by the power of his own Grace or Faith, but the Spirit it self fills and acts that soul. And as the soul was carried by the mighty power of Satan before, 'tis now carried by the Almighty power of the Spirit it self, Hence 1 *Pet.*1.5. *Kept by the mighty power of God through Faith.* And hence *Acts* 26.18. *Turned from the power of Satan*, not to duties, but *to God* himself, *i. e.* the Spirit of God, and so to close with him.

What is this Spirit which the Saints have?

I shall express my self in these three Conclusions.

1. That if *Adam* had stood, he and all his posterity should have had that power and presence, and constant assistance of the Spirit of God, as that they should never have fallen, nor have been able to fall in respect of the assistance of the Spirit: He should have been green all the year long, his Blossom should not have been blasted, his fruit should never have withered. And the ground is the Rule of Justice; for if he falling, all his posterity are forsaken of God, and under the reign of sin, and death and Satan, *Rom.*5.18,21. Then he standing, all his posterity should have had the everlasting presence of God, and should have bin under the reign of the Spirit of Grace & life. Thus also the Covenant ran, *do and live.*

2. That

Conclu.2.

2. That the Lord Jesus the second *Adam* standing and rising in the room of all his people, hence he doth convey and propagate to all his posterity the immutable and constant assistance and presence of his Spirit, whereby being once begotten of him, & called to him, they never afterward depart from him. And though weak in themselves, yet assisted by this Spirit, do not, cannot depart wickedly again. The Lord Jesus having stood, they cannot fall, because by vertue of his standing they have this presence of the Holy Ghost, *John* 14.19. *Because I live, you shall live also*. John 6.57. *As the living Father sent me, and I live by him, &c.* Christ standing next to the Father, lives by him; we standing next to Christ, live as infallibly by him. And I say the ground is Christs standing. For though there be many reasons why the Saints can never fall from Christ, as the Spirit of Grace, Covenant of Grace, Intercession of Christ, yet the main ground is Christs standing without the least fall from the fulfilling of the first Covenant, which we having the first moment of believing kept in Christ, hence the Spirit is given, and the Covenant of Grace, of strength. And hence *Rom.*5.21. & *v.*17, 18. And hence the Spirit is said to dwell in Believers, *Rom.*8.11. And we are the Temples of the Spirit, whether he dwell in them in his person personally, the well is here deep, but he dwells in them so as he never ceaseth assisting of them, so that they cannot depart from the Lord again; hence *Isa.*59.21. *My Spirit shall not depart from thy Seed*. *John* 14. 'Tis called *the Spirit that abides for ever*. It knits the soul to the Lord, and keeps it so for ever: Never suffers that love-knot to be untied again. When the soul is weak, the Spirit helps him, when careless of it self, the Spirit keeps him, though the soul offers to run from the Lord, yet this Spirit follows him; though he grieves the Spirit, yet this Spirit still keeps his own house, will not depart from him; and so not suffer the soul to depart from the Lord. And this is the reason why the Saints never fall from the Lord, though they have weak Grace, poor beginnings, many sins, and *Adam* stood not, though with the perfect Image of God upon him, because he had not this Spirit yet given; though he had the Spirit of God, yet not this Spirit, which some call the Spirit of Adoption given to him, because he had not fulfilled the first Covenant, which we in Christ have, which is not only the ground of our never falling, but of assurance we shall never fall. For what breaks a mans peace after Faith? Apparition of sin in the Conscience: What makes that terrible? The Law. Now when I see in Christ, I have kept all things in the Law, not only the cry and accusations of the Law and sin are stilled, but also there ariseth a holy boldness and confidence and joy, even before the face of an angry God, *Eph.* 3.12. And as soul and body are ever knit, so here, &c.

Concl. 3.

3. This Spirit thus assisting, no unregenerate man ever hath. I speak not now of keeping the soul from falling from Grace, but from Christ.

1. Because the Spirit of Satan fills them, he is the strong man that keeps the Palace, under whose Kingdom and power they are; and therefore this Spirit which destroyes the Kingdom of Satan is not in them.

2. Because this was a Prerogative that *Adam* had not, though he had great Gifts and Glory otherwise: So this is not the Gift which is given unto them.

3. Because this ariseth, and therefore is given because Christ stood, and therefore those he never stood for, rose for, suffered for, never have it.

4. Therefore we shall see in experience, take the best Professors living, though they may come, as they and others judged, to the Lord, and follow the Lord, yet they will in time depart, sometime outwardly, *John* 6.64. *There be some of you that believe not*. See them, *v.*66. And why did they depart? *It was not given them of the Father*. The Spirit never was given effectually to draw them, nor yet to keep them.

It not outwardly, at least inwardly ; and hence Hypocrites though they have marvellous affections unto Christ, and so have spoke of him and commended him, and seemed to be carried above all creatures and duties toward him, yet himself and his mercy, and his blood, becomes a common thing to them, and his knowledge and promises common : and hence they slight and loath him, and mourn not for it, and so are so far from being kept close unto Christ, as that they are nearer the unpardonable sin then him. But all they have is like *Jonahs* gourd, which suddenly riseth, but there is a Worm at the root, that pulls it down again : And so their love dies to Ministers that Christ sent ; and to his Truth and Ordinances.

But if the Spirit doth thus, Who then shall be saved? for who is there that departs not ? *Quest.*

When I say the Spirit doth so assist the faithful, as that they never depart : The meaning is not, as though the soul should now never fall into any more sin or unbelief, for what do the Saints more complain of then their backslidings, *Isa.* 63. 17. *Heb.* 12.1. Saints hearts are no sooner raised up, but their weights grow heavy and press them down ; no sooner do they walk in the way, but they begin to fall off : But when I say so, I say three things. 1. Their whole heart never departs. 2. They do not depart for ever. 3. Though they do depart from the Lord, yet the Spirit doth not depart from them; as it is in common reason, the same thing may go either in a straight or crooked line to the same point. As a River may run in a straight or crooked line to the Sea. So the Saints, their springs (their hearts) being set a running after the Lord, though they do not follow him in a straightline, so as never to depart to the right hand or left ; yet they are so kept by the Spirit that they are continually making after him, cleaving to him ; though with many crooked windings of their hearts, this way and that way from the Lord. And therefore as it is in a wheel, it stands bent for such an end, yet runs at one side, but is turned by the skill of him that guides it into the way again, and so let it run the man is with it : So 'tis here. And because somthing is like this in Hypocrites, I shall endeavour to cut the thread. *Answ.*

I. Their whole hearts never do nor can depart from the Lord, all their sins and departings are against their new nature, which the Lord hath given them. Its against the grain, which as it aggravates their sin, so it shews the difference between their sins and the sins of other men ; they may be drawn aside, but its against their wills, or if so, yet against the bent of their hearts, which is set toward the Lord, and Sion-ward ; they may be carried captive against their wills, as *Paul* complained he was, and made his moan to heaven of it ; or if with their wills, yet it is against the active bent of their wills, which inclines them another way, 1 *John* 3. 9. *They cannot sin, because the seed remains in them* ; so that they cannot sin with their whole hearts ; nor depart from Christ with their whole hearts : As it is with a Woman, though her Husband hath her whole heart, yet there is much weakness and sin mixt with this love; So that whatever unkindness she shews, it is not with her whole heart, but against it, and hence she is not cast off : So much more here. Or as it is with the unregenerate man possessed by Satan, though he may forsake many sinful courses, take up many duties, despise the World, yet it is not with his whole heart : And hence he is pulled back like a Bird by the leg, Satan having an end of his heart, and he that is unholy and unclean will be so still. So *è contra* : As 'tis with a stone, cast it up its against the bent of it, because the nature of it is to rest in the Center, and hence it comes down again. It is not by internal bent, but by external *vis* or force : So sin and Satan being cast out, though they work in the soul, yet they are external Agents, (it is not I, but sin) and hence it is against the bent. The whole soul therefore never departs from the Lord Jesus, but the Spirit keeps it there. As 'tis in the body of a man, he grows sick and inclines toward a dissolution or consumption, and operations are hindred, and little delight in any thing, yet the soul and body are not yet parted wholly hereupon, for even then they are kept close. So though the heart may depart and incline towards consumption and death, and little can the soul do but lie still and grieve, yet the union between the Spirit and the soul once made, is never broken. For as the whole soul departed and made dif-union, so the whole soul returning makes the union. And hence if ever after the whole soul should depart, the union should be broken; and hence look on a Christian when he is himself, he cannot stir, nor depart; partly by a spirit of fear, *Jer.* 32. 40. Like a man in a Ship, he cannot cast himself into Sea, it makes him tremble to think, what if I should fall in, and hence keeps close in the Ship, what-ever storms come, what-ever calms come, for he sees death before him. Oh the loss of Christ and his fellowship hereafter, nay here, is dreadful to him: Partly by a Spirit of love, it constrains us, that when the heart sometime cares not for Christ, yet the Spirit of love springs up: Shall I now leave him that pitied me, That brought me a Pardon, when my neck was on the block, &c.

11. When he doth depart by reason of some evil in his heart, yet 'tis not ever, but he must return sooner or later to him again, it was best with him then. For look as 'tis with Satan, How doth he carry the heart from God? You shall see it in *Judas*, John 13. He stands at the door and knocks by a sinful thought liked of, *verf.* 2. Then he enters the house by causing the will to resolve of it. He doth not carry men like those Herds of Swine against their wills, but prevails with the Will to resolve thus, *verf.* 27. Hereupon Satan having a Commission carries him out, and he must needs go whom the Devil drives; so 'tis here, the Spirit in recalling the soul will have him come back. 1. Puts in secret sweet living thoughts again, and makes the soul consider and remember from whom 'tis fallen, or who the Lord is. 2. Then causeth the will to resolve of a return, and then he must go whom the Spirit draws, *Pfal.* 63. 6. *David remembers the Lord on his bed*, though now driven from all Ordinances: Hence *verf.* 7. *Under thy shadow I will rejoyce*: Hence *verf.* 8. *My soul followeth hard after thee*, or, *cleaves to thee.* But *David* was weak and feeble, how came he to do this? *Thy hand* verf. 8. *upholdeth me.* Look as it was with *Sampson*, when his locks were cut, he was like other men, and was made to grinde, but they grew again, and then he was like himself again: So when the affections and hearts to Christ are cut, they are like other men for a time; but they are continually coming and growing again, and then they are like themselves again. And I say they must return, for when the Spirit carries a man indeed, there is a necessity put upon him, *Acts* 4. 20. *We cannot but speak the things we have heard*; and 2 *Cor.* 13. 8. *We can do nothing against, but for the truth.* For here we shall see the broad difference between a convicted Hypocrite that knows all is amiss with him and the Saints: He sees his falls from the Lord, and is afraid in his Conscience of Misery if he doth not return, and desires and endeavours for to do it; but what if it be hard? and it seem impossible to be better? Now he falls down and thinks this is an infirmity which God will pardon, and so Satan conquers him; I say again, not temptation, but Satan conquers him: For then a man is conquered, when faith is conquered, 1 *Iohn* 5. 4. then Faith is conquered, when returning to Christ with the whole heart is conquered; the whole heart returns not until a mans will resolves by being prest with a necessity of a return and staying there. Now therefore the Spirit of God puts the soul upon a necessity of returning to the Lord, that when the heart saith, It cannot be that ever your heart should be better, or the Lord help; it must be saith the soul again, and it is so, I am not able to bear this evil, for mercy must help, and Spirit must draw, and hence the soul must come, *Pfal.* 42. 7, 8. The soul thinks mercy can and is willing, but will it? Why the Lord commands it, when one wave calls in for another, mercy must step in, and hence *my prayer is to thee.* Now this necessity of return to the Lord

appears

appears chiefly in breaking down all oppositions against its return; which are four.

1. Somtime snares of the world and other things beside. The Lord easeth them, the Lord sends no crosses, gives them their hearts desire, under which Vines they rest, yet if the Lord takes not all from them, he puts such a cloyedness in them, that the soul cannot but return to the Lord again, it cannot live on such course bread, things that satisfie not, it had better once, *Eccles.* 2. 3, 4,11.

2. Fears and discouragements of spirit, for when delivered from snares, then fears come, and discouragements, either by reason of outward losses or the Lords anger: So that the soul fears it never had, never shall have any mercy, that hath thus abused it; and it hath thought God himself to say so, and his behaviour in not hearing and helping in so long a time, to witness so: Yet it will return, though the Lord never save it; it will not sin: *Jonah* yet looks again to the Temple, when he could not come to it, yet he would look to it. The soul will turn up its eyes and mourn; Oh that I have so abused the Lord and mercy! that Love it self should be angry and frown! *Psal.* 77. The Psalmist *refused to be comforted,* v.2. Nay, v.3. Though *he remembred God,* and all his love past, yet *troubled,* this brought greater trouble, yet v.10. *I'le remember the years of the right hand of the most High. Saul* did not thus.

3. Thoughts of impossibility and unlikelihood to get peace or pardon, or victory over sin now. For somtime the Saints think, the Lord loves me, and yet lets these evils lie here, but I can get no help now, especially if after many prayers. I know help against all sins they cannot get, and hence are humbled, but against them sins that help can be got, wherein the Lord hath done it for others, and which make the Lord estrange himself it must be had (for this temptation to a Saint is an Hypocrites overthrow.) *Psal.* 18.21,22,23. If earth cannot help, cannot Heaven? What, not the Spirit, Word, Bloud, Mercy, of a tender-hearted Redeemer? What though not now? yet I will not give him over.

4. When Gods Providence seems to cross his Promise, yet they will cleave to him or return to him. For many times Saints have their estates in the Bonds of Gods Promises, and hence they wait for accomplishment of them; but the Lord carries it quite cross to his promise to their seeming. He promiseth to make alive, to comfort, to sanctifie, to be with me; and he kills, sads, lets out sin, never such a heart, and forsakes me. Oh now Faith shakes! yet they will not away, *Heb.* 11.15,16. The Lord calls them to forsake their Countrey; *Abraham* is a stranger there, and that among Cut-throat *Canaanites,* and dwells in Tabernacles, and four hundred years after, his posterity being afflicted should have it; yet he would not return, though they might, God had said here, *I'le blesse thee,* so here. The murmuring *Israelites* fell short of this.

III. Whenever the soul doth depart, yet the Spirit of God is ever in it and with it, *Psal.* 73.2. The Psalmist *almost fell.* Why did he not? *Thou art ever with me,* thy hand v.23. *hath upheld me.* So that as the Spirit keeps the soul to Christ, so it keeps Christ in the soul at all times. And hence Saints in the closure of all their dealings with God, and he with them, they have seen his love, working good in all; that now the Soul can say, lo *the Lord was here, and I knew it not,* *Isa.* 25.9,10. That the soul admires somtimes, and hence after all sees the Lord more clearly and fully and sweetly, till at last it sees him in Glory. Thus you see the Spirit that follows Saints is with them, which the world wants. Oh admire at the Lord, if this Spirit be given, that Heaven is come down into thy Hell! That no miseries, no sins can part, but its ever putting thee in thy way again. Hence when

1. They are ready to quite fall off, and give themselves for gone, ready to be

made away by temptation, or to make away themselves, the Lord is with them then, *Psal.*94.18. At the time of parting, love appears.

2. Hence when they are somtime so far gone, as that they mind not their return, or believe not, as in the wildernesse, but are well enough without the Lord, the Lord before they think or desire, prevents them, *Psal.*23.6, *Mercy and Truth followes me.*

3. Hence when they think the Lord is provoked that he cannot save, then he is in the midst of his people, *Jer.*14.11. *Why art thou as a man astonied that cannot save?*

4. Hence at the end of life, all the waies of God have been peace, and all our waies, though sorrowful, though evil, turned for good; as in *Jonas* his departing; and by miseries we are yet humbled; somthing the Lord is doing now for Eternity, *Micah* 7.8. *Though I sit in darknesse, the Lord will be a light unto me.*

5. Hence when the heart and strength fail, and Faith is failing, and the heart feels nothing but pain, yet the Lord then keeps, and this is comfort, *Psal.* 63.26.

Consider therefore your estate, that

1. Do depart with your whole heart from the Lord. Hath not the Lord bowed thy heart toward himself, by mercies, by blows? But when sorrows have been past, and mercies grown common, and truth common, thou hast started back like a broken bow which was bent backward, when stretched forward. And now when God calls to any duty, especially when thy will and ends are crossed, that is a burden, and thou art drawn to that as a Fish to the dry land, It is like a Feaver-fit to thee, and never mournest for this. But when any matter of gain and world is presented, all thoughts, time, strength is too little there, that you smell of the field; or if there be any life or joy, yet *the lean kine eat up the fat kine.* Nay, mournest not under that cursed bent which carries thee from the Lord. Know it, thou art forsaken of the Lord.

2. That in times past had many affections, but now sorrow is gone, and seeking of the Lord gone; and being fallen, feest it not, but thinkest 'tis with thee as with other Christians, hast only the old work past, and some new pangs now and then. Why is it thus? *Jer.*8.4,5. Will you fall and not arise? Wilt let the Lord turn from you, and not return? Doth the *Stork know when winter is near, and not you your season?* Oh look to it! What are you fallen with a perpetual backsliding? Why will you not return, but go away with a perpetual backsliding? Know Satan hath hold of this soul.

3. You people of God, wonder you at this Grace: Let your experience prove it. Is it not so, that a Habitation of Devils should be a House of the Spirit of God, not to sojourn, but dwell there, and though abused, vexed, yet it will not depart.

SECT. V.

V. Sanctification, in the room of self-seeking.

THis work of the Spirit hath had many scratches, and passed under divers censures; that if that question should be asked of it, which once Christ made concerning himself, *Whom say men that I am?* We shall find five several apprehensions of it.

1. Some have made it common, and that this treasure may be digged out of dung-hils, that the Lord casts these Pearls to Swine, that a carnal heart may have all these gifts and graces which the righteous have, and *Adam* had, and perish

at

at last. And hence no evidence from it at all.

2. Some have not made it thus common, but proper to the Elect, and that none are justified but they are sanctified, and *è contra*. But it hath been, and they think 'tis so disguised with the mixture of sin and temptation, and cannot be known, or very hardly. If so, that though the Lord Jesus *come unto his own*, and dwell not only in their Houses, but in their hearts, yet they know him not.

3. Some say it may be known, but not as dwelling in our hearts, but as inherent in Christ, making the inherent Grace of Christ in Christ himself to be our Sanctification; which the Apostle makes to be our righteousness. And so as the Papists abolish Christs righteousness for justification, by making it to consist only in infusion of Grace in us; these abolish Christ to be our Sanctification, by making all our sanctification to consist in inhæsion in Christ out of us.

4. Some say there is a sanctification in us, But wherein doth it consist? Not in any habitual Holiness, or Graces in us, but in the immediate actings of Christ in us, and so the Lord makes his Musick without any strings, and reveals things to us without eyes, and makes us live without any power of life: And so after justification they put a Christian in such an estate of Sanctification as that he is a meer Patient, in next disposition to move if he be moved: Like a weather-Cock, which hath no power at all to move, but as the wind blows it, good or bad.

5. Some grant that there is a sanctification proper to the Faithful, and in the Faithful an habitual Holiness, and consisting in a most blessed, inward, total change. But when they come to the application of this to themselves, they think that if they have some reformation with some inward affection, they think every overly change is presently sanctification, and this must be a good evidence to them. And so like some Herbalists that treat of the Soveraign excellencies of several herbs, but when they come to gather them in the garden, they take their counterfeits in the room of them. The causes of which variety of apprehensions is the rareness of it (and therefore 'tis unknown) and the corrupt experience of men.

I shall therefore lay level these things, by shewing you what that measure of sanctification is which is in us, and which is peculiar to the Elect; and which also may be known by them which have it: And therefore shall not speak of sanctification at large, which is the change of the whole man by the death of Christ, whereby he is separated from sin, and sin mortified in him; and by the life of Christ, whereby he is dedicated unto Christ, and lives his life. But I shall treat of it now so far forth especially as this change may be known by it; and therefore I oppose it to self-seeking.

But why do you oppose Sanctification to Self-seeking? *Quest.*

1. Because this Sanctification, I now speak of it so far forth as it may *Answ.* be seen; now it is seen here chiefly, because it may be said here it is: But Hypocrites have a change, Wherein may it be known to be different from theirs? Why, the change of the heart chiefly appears in the change of the utmost end.

2. Because as the pollution of the whole man, and all his actions civil, moral, and religious, consists chiefly, and appears in this self-seeking, or making our selves our utmost end. This makes the most glorious actions vile, and stains them all. So the sanctification of a man consists chiefly and appears in making the Lord our utmost end of all we do: So that though the actions be never so mean and poor, yet this puts a Glory and lustre on them, and is the Crown of them, even of the *giving of a cup of cold water*, Mat. 6. 22. *If thy eye be single.* Look therefore, as before the Lord justifies the soul, every man living seeks himself as his last end and good; and out of this captivity no power can redeem them.

Dan.

*Dan.*4.30. *Gen.*11.4. So after it, the Lord sanctifies the soul with such a measure of his Grace as makes the Lord his utmost end: And this no other have.

Let me therefore shew you what this Sanctification is morefully, and with all the cheif ingredients in it, that so it may be the better known.

It's the renovation of the whole man, appearing in the change of a mans utmost end. But more particularly,

'Tis that work of the Spirit in the soul, whereby the soul beholding the Glory of Christ, and feeling his love, hereupon closeth with the whole will of Christ, and seeketh to please him, as his happinesse and utmost end.

For look as in self-seeking there are four things.

1. A man beholds himself and some good in himself.
2. Loves himself abundantly.
3. Pleaseth his own will.
4. Doth this as his utmost and last end. So here in this description of Sanctification which I oppose chiefly to self-corruption, are four things.

1. The soul beholds the Lord in all his Glory, seeing of him present with him in all his Glory, and set before him, *Psal.*16.8. For this is one necessary ingredient to his sanctification and seeking the Lord as his utmost end. For why doth a man seek himself? He sees some glory and good in himself, none in the Lord. And hence ye say of some men, whose pride spoyls their parts, they know themselves too well, and hence Saints when they see their own vileness, and see the Lord, they are so far from seeking, as that they loath themselves. Therefore when the Lord reveals himself to the soul in his Glory, this makes them seek him and not themselves, 1 *Cor.*1.30. *Christ is made wisdom, righteousnesse, &c. that all might glory in him.* For this is the Glory of Christ, and the first Principle of seeking the Lord, the soul sees his good laid up in the Lord more than in himself; nay wholly in the Lord, not at all in himself. His wisdom is in him, he cannot but wilder till utterly lost without him. His righteousness is in him, he could never have one sin pardoned by Angels holiness without him. His sanctification is in him, he could not have the least thought nor desire, but the Lord must work it in him. His redemption is in him, there could not be freedom one hour from unknown evils but by him. Hence seeing him such an one, he seeks him. As why do men seek men, especially if great? Why do men desire to stand before Princes, and please them, so that they will not gladly offer them the least distaste? Because they see them before them, beholding of them, apt to be angry, if displeased; and their greatness awes them: So here. Why is not the Lord Jesus pleased? He is not seen in his Glory, nor made really present; and hence *Rev.*5.12,13. When they saw him *on his Throne, they cast down their Crowns and gave him Glory.*

2. The soul also feels his love, and so abundantly loves him again. For how come men to seek themselves in every thing, and they cannot but do it? 'Tis because they love themselves, and that abundantly, necessarily, as fire burns; though they burn so hot in this love that at last they consume themselves. So how do any, can any seek the Lord? We know the Apostle saith, 1 *Cor.*13.5. *Love seeks not her own.* When the Sun hath put out this fire of our self-love, when the sense of the Lords love hath kindled that love to the Lord again, as that it abundantly loves Christ, now it will seek the things of Christ, and not its own things. And as there is abundance of self love, that men are eaten up with it; so there must be much love, which must be abundantly shed in the heart, so as to eat up that; arising from the sense of the Lords love, and that abundantly. For many a man comes to have some good will, and affection, and love to the Lord, but yet never comes to seek the Lord as his last end, and live to him. Why? Because he hath not tasted abundantly of the Lords Mercy, Grace and Love,

Psal.

*Psal.*86.12,13. And hence the incomparable Spirit of *Paul*, *I seek not yours, but you*; Wherein? In being *willing to spend*. But save your self *Paul*: nay, *and to be spent*: With much ado; Nay, *most gladly*. Though you love me not, because I love you: So here, though Christ should not love it, yet he is worthy, he hath done enough, and now the soul will not only do, but rejoice, nay, in sufferings; because his love is not dropt, but shed in our hearts. And hence 'tis a never-failing rule, little love or assurance of it, little seeking the Lord; much assurance, much seeking of him.

3. Hereupon the soul closeth with the whole will of Christ, and pleaseth it, because it pleaseth him. Its with every man, as it was with *Samson*, he would needs have a wife of the *Philistims*, Why so? *Judg.* 14.3. Because *she pleaseth me*. So, why will men seek themselves, save themselves, love themselves, and please their own wills? Because it pleaseth them. Look therefore as the soul when he loved himself, did seek to please only his own will in every thing, and 'tis good because it pleaseth me; so the soul, whose heart is now indeared to Christ, though he cannot perfectly do it (that's in Heaven) yet he seeks to give the whole will of Christ content, because it pleaseth Christ. And this is that that God hath sworn his people shall have, *Luke* 1.74,75. And that Christ hath *delivered us from all our enemies*, (For the great reason why men cleave not to the Lord, and please his whole Will is, because they have many things to care for, and keep, and please, which we account friends, which are the Lords enemies, Satan and world) *to serve him without fear*, i. e. in love, and *in holinesse and righteousnesse*, i. e. his whole Will *all our daies*. And hence *Eph.*5. 8, 9. *They were darknesse, but now are light*, by Faith, now there is sanctity, *Walk as children of the light*. Wherein consists that? *Proving what is acceptable to God*. Hence *Eph.* 6.6. They should *please Christ, doing the Will of God from the heart*. And this is so necessary, that *Gal.*1.10. The Apostle saith, *If I please men*, i. e. their wills, *I am not Christs*. And this is *walking worthy of the Lord, pleasing him in all things*, and this is fruit, the end of the tree and leaves also, and differencing a tree from all other, that be beautiful, but barren, *Col.*1.10.

Quest. *But why do you make this to consist in pleasing the whole will of Christ, and not of God the Creator?*

Answ. 1. Because our sanctification now cannot please God as a Creator, though it may please him that is the Creator in Christ, because only perfect Holiness can please him.

2. Because Christ hath pleased the Father by the Holiness of himself, now this being done, and therefore God having put all things into his hands, having done that for us, we are to give content to him. And herein our sanctification is differing from the Image *Adam* had, who in closing with the will of God, looked upon him as a Creator; ours respects a Redeemer, who hath bought us to himself, and hence we are to respect him in our acts now.

Quest. *But why doth the soul close with the whole will of Christ, i. e. so far as 'tis made known?*

Answ. First, Because the holiness of Christ here chiefly discovers it self, and against this a carnal heart will discover it self. For *Capernaites* may boast in, and give entertainment to the person of Christ, but when they come to repent (which was one part of his will) that they did not, that they would not: *Wo therefore to thee Capernaum*: as many will close with Christ for pardon of sin, and lay their sacks on him, but you must burthen your self with them, or the Lord will never ease you of them. Oh no, and hence they have light sorrow for sin; many will embrace the comforts of Christ, and love of Christ, and this joys them, yet the will of Christ that is wearisome to them, *Rom.* 8. 8. They will pick and chuse.

Secondly, Because this discovers a deep ditch of deceit in the heart, many take up some duties, and why do they do them? Because they please the Lord, and the

Lord commands, and for his fake, when indeed 'tis to pleafe themfelves : for in other things they care not whether they pleafe the Lord or no.

Thirdly, Becaufe this clofing with his whole will only gives the Lord content: As' tis not the ftrings, or ftriking upon one ftring that makes the Mufick, but ftriking on them all according to rule. So here: And hence when they facrificed and obferved new Moons, *Ifai.1.14.Who hath required thefe things at your hands* ? Hence when the people began to put the Lord off with mean performances, any common ftuffe, the Lord takes ftate upon him, and faith he is a King, *Mal.* 1. 14. & 9, 10. *I have no pleafure in you.*

Fourthly, Becaufe this only will give peace; and therefore let any man begin to pick and chufe, and his heart die to the Lords will , if *Jonah* like he will flie from any way of the Lords and continue there, he fhall have ftorms ; and hence 1 *John* 2. 3, 4, 5. *Hereby we know him,* &c.

4. He clofeth with the whole will of the Lord as his happinefs and utmoft end ; as a man made himfelf his laft end before, and defired God and Chrift only to keep his fores from aking, for fo I look upon all men made up of wants ; if the body ake with cold, ftomack with hunger, head for want of fleep, Confcience for fin, all happinefs lies in the eafing hereof, and here lies their blifs.   So now the foul makes the life of the Lord its happinefs to live unto him, *Gal.* 2. 20. He makes it his *meat and drink to do the Lords will* ; for *Jehu* fought the Lord, but his laft end was himfelf, as *John* 16. 2. *A man may kill, and think he doth God good fervice* , but that is not his laft end ; a carnal heart may crofs his own will, but not his own utmoft end, as *Judas* : A man may feek the Lord with delight, and follow the Ordinances, and faft, and pray, but himfelf is his end ftill, *Zac*.7.5,6. *Ifai.* 58. 4, 5. As a man that goes to a City, he will do your bufinefle, but he would not go unlefs he had his own ends to bring about there.   But thofe that are truly fanctified, make the Lord their laft end and happinefs.   It's not only good to do the Lords will (for thus men may feek the Lord) as thinking it good fo to do, but as their blefsednefse, elfe 'tis not their laft end, and fo not fought as their laft end ; and fo 'tis with the foul : As a River running to the Sea, many Springs run into it, but it carries them down all with it ; fo there are many occafions , hindrances, bufinefses, yet it carries them all down with it, even the more violently, the more 'tis hindred, *Pfal.* 119. 126, 127. *Therefore love I them above gold.* And this exprefseth it felf in three things :

1. In admiring at the glory of the Lord, and his will and ways, and accounting them happy men, and blefsed, that thus can do and live.   For fometime the foul is decayed and fallen from this, or fick and weak ; now it accounts them happy, that have health and ftrength to walk abroad, *Pfal.* 1.1, 2.

2. In being never at reft in his minde until now that he comes to this ; for therein a mans making any thing his laft end appears ; as he made his goods his laft end, *Luke* 12. 19. Now therefore *my foul be at reft*, for there is no feeking the Lord but felf-feeking hinders ; Now though it be thus yet, Do I make my felf my laft end ? then my minde would be at reft ; but if fanctified, its not at reft till now : And hence *Paul* when he had run this race, now you fee him leaning upon his pillow, 2 *Tim.* 4. 6, 7. And hence Saints are loth to die and be blefsed in heaven, becaufe they have done fo little work as yet ; little do the Saints for the Lord many times, yet their hearts are upright, for what mourn they for fo much as this, when they have lookt upon it ; oh that the Lord hath been a loofer by them !

3. It carries the foul thorow all difficulties with power and delight, *Prov.* 10. 29. *The way of the Lord is ftrength to the righteous, and joy.* Rom. 7.22. *I do delight in the law of God in the inner man.* Other Nations walk *in the Name of their Gods, we in ours*, Micah 4. 5. As when wealth or honour is a mans utmoft end; with what violence are men carried to it; and hence a man thinks he hath never fuch

good

good days as then when he can do much for the Lord; and hence when any duty is to be done, when fearful to do it, or loth to perform it, when the heart is dead, yet beholding it with a spiritual eye, that this gives *Jehovah* honour, oh this carries the soul headlong even into miseries, *Not my will, but thine be done.* This easeth the heart, even in the belly of Hell, and in times of the deepest desertion.

To this Sanctification all the Saints do come, every one in their measure; and if ever the soul tasted the Lords love, or ever was humbled with the bitterness of sin, the first voice and main care is, *Lord, What wilt thou have me to do?* Nay, though no assurance, and it cannot joy in the Lords love, yet it will in the Lords will; and hence when it hath full assurance, yet finding such a vile heart, if God should give it heaven with such a heart it would be death: And hence when he thinks of going to Hell, yet there (saith he) let me blesse thee.

This Sanctification all unsound hearts do want; much Reformation, much affection, many duties, but their end is not changed, though their lives be, and hearts seem to be.

1. Because they cannot love the Lord, because the Lord doth never shed his love into their hearts.

2. This was the life of Christ, *John* 8. 29. of which life they that are dead in sin never have one act, though they may think they have.

3. This is the end of our Election, which therefore an unsound heart may as soon attain to, as to elect, or to be elected of God, *Eph.* 1. 4. *holy in love.*

This may be easily known, 1. Cannot a man know when he is happy? 2. Cannot *Peter* tell Christ that he loves him? 3. Cannot a man tell whether he be an Hypocrite or no? For he that cannot prove his utmost end is changed, must confess himself an Hypocrite yet, his heart was never changed, whatever assurance or peace he hath had; a thing is never good till it serves its end it was made for.

Oh therefore look that you content not your selves with Reformation, but come to this; else 1. You lose all your obedience, the Lord regards it not, the Lord will take all from you; as Vessels that are made to hold Wine, and they cannot, lay them by, *the Lord hath no pleasure in you*, Mal. 1. 8, 9, 10. 2. If you do, the Lord will accept your meanest and poorest services: Consider,

1. Christ cast by his Robes being privie to his own worth, to become obedient, *Phil.* 2. 6, 8.

2. His infinite Wisdom is in every command, though thy carnal reason like it not.

3. His infinite love for thy good, though thou thinkest 'tis for thy hurt.

4. His glory, though thou gettest no good at all by it.

SECT. VI.

VI. Fulnes of the Spirit of Glory, in the room of the world.

WHom the Lord doth justifie, those he doth glorifie, Rom. 8. 30. *i.e.* with the Glory of another world, which though it be hid for a time from others, and somtimes from themselves, yet they do partake of it now, and it shall be revealed upon them another day, 1 *Pet.* 5. 1. Now though Hypocrites may tast of the Word, nay, of the powers of the world to come, yet they fall short of this measure of Glory. And I say, this fills them in the room of this world.

How are men full of the world? And what is the Spirit of Glory?

Quest.

Answ.
*Conclu.*1.

I shall shew this in three Conclusions.

That the full rest and peace of the soul it's to be found only in the presence of God Almighty, in this Being of Beings. His Perfections are in himself, and hence he keeps a perpetual Sabbath of rest in himself; in this rest only the soul of man can find rest, *Heb.*4.6,10. *Psal.*16.11. He is the journies end of all a mans labours and life and travails. Hence *John* 17.13. When Christs work was ended, now I come not to Heaven, so much as to thee. And hence when *Solomon* had tired out himself in his travails through all the things of this world, to find rest, he returns empty and crying home, and now when he sums up his Glory, *Ecclef.*1.1,2. He stiles himself,

1. A man gathered to the Church, to be as near God as he can.

2. *The Son of David*, to whom the Promises were made.

And then, 5. *King of Jerusalem*, the last and least. He is that house and home of his people, whether in fleeting or setled condition, from one generation to another, *Psal.*90.1. So that the Prophet finding this to be most true, I say, stands aftonished at men; and because men had deaf ears here, and their bellies could not hear, he cries to the Heavens to be aftonished at this, *Jer.*2.12, 13. This wine the Lord puts under his Lock and Key; 'Tis not to be found in earth, in Church-Liberties, you may soon see this Temple not one stone left upon another, nor in Heaven simply, nor in Fellowship of Angels; onely 'tis in the Lord, drawing nigh to the soul in these, and drawing the soul at last near to himself by these.

*Conclu.*2.

That all Reprobates being estranged from God, and God from them, are also strangers to this rest, this life of God, this life of Glory, *Eph.*4.18. and therefore seek for it and suck it out of the Paps of the Creature, and that which is not God. And thus their hearts are full of the world, *Psal.*17.14. *Dust they eat, and upon their bellies they go*, shift for it where they will, they shall never find it in him: And if they do find it any where else in this world, let them fill themselves to the full, for they have their portion, they have their reward. And hence they do (all unregenerate men living) find their rest in somthing out of God; rest to their Consciences in duties, and somthing of God, rest to their hearts in some Creatures, either unlawful or lawful, *Mat.*24.38. And there is never a carnal heart, but give him his imaginary content here, and he would desire to live here as an exile from God, and to be without him, if there were no Hell, no plagues, &c. For here is their treasure, not above; here are thy *good things*: and this is the very reason why a man lives without God, nay when he stands convinced of it, nay when troubled with thoughts of this, and no duties can ease him, because somthing out of God is his bottom to stand upon, and his rest and peace; It may be meat, drink, health, sleep, occasional delights and a quiet life. That as 'tis with Seamen, they can endure winds and weather, and rent Sayls, and torn Masts, because they live upon that Trade; another will not: So 'tis here. Though many troubles of mind, yet they ply that Oar, 'tis their living.

Concl. 3.

That all those whom the Lord intends good unto, those he calls in time out of this world into his eternal Glory of rest and peace, out of this world into another. And as their hearts were filled with another world before, so their hearts are filled with the Glory of this other world now, *John* 17.14,16. 1 *Pet.*5.10. And this rest and peace in God is the Glory of the Saints. That look as 'tis with Reprobates, What is their last and great woe? 2 *Thef.*1.9. 'Tis *separation from the Lord*; So this is the great Glory of the Saints, to enter in to him, as *Moses* did into the Cloud, and so to rest in him. *I go to my God and your God.* Hence the Saints are said to *sell away all for this Treasure*, for this Pearle, for the Lord: And so the Lord is in stead of all, and better to them than all they had before. They can live royally upon him, having but one thing to look to, and

having

having all things in this one thing; and more royally than the Princes of the world can upon their Lusts and earthly Treasures. This is the rest and peace the Saints have, *Heb.*4.3. *They that believe do enter into rest.* God calls them out of the world by some bitterness of it, or by some cloying and surfetting, and making their hearts weary of the sweetness thereof, and then they enter into Glory. The Lord sees nothing can fill their hearts nor stop their cries, but him, and now this Sea of Glory breaks in upon them, and fills their hearts: And this the Lord doth two waies, according as there are two things in that good that fills the heart.

1. Proportion.
2. Propriety.

So there are two Raies of eternal Glory chiefly, whereby the Lord gives full rest and peace, and so Glory to his people.

1. He reveals the good they are to enjoy in another world, in its full proportion, *viz. what is the riches of the inheritance of the Saints,* Eph.1.17,18. For no good satisfies till 'tis known in its greatness, though yet there be degrees of this. For we shall see many Christians have assurance, where is the joy of it? Not affected with it, because he knowes not what it is at that time. At another time his heart is above all the world, because he sees what is that Glory the Saints have, and that he hath it, it swallows him up and confounds him. Why me Lord! And this is the reason why the Saints doubt, whom the Lord hath loosned from their lusts and all things here. What so vile, and all that mine? And this the reason why when doubting, so that there is nothing in this world that doth quiet them, nothing from God that doth ease them, yet their hearts are sweetly eased: Their desires are after him, and their delights in his company, better go to Hell thus than in my sins; and the thoughts of the Lord are sweet, because he hath and doth secretly fill their hearts. Something they have or do see in him, *Isa.*26.8. And hence is the reason of the sorrows of them, when their hearts are worst, now though they have the world, yet are not at rest, because they have and do see somthing of this.

2. He reveals by the Spirit and Light of Glory that this good is theirs, their propriety. The first gives rest to the soul, *viz.* the Spirit of vision incompleatly. This Spirit of Faith whereby the soul knows all this good is mine, this gives it compleatly. Now the New *Jerusalem* is come down from Heaven, and God is among men, 1 *Pet.* 1. 8. For if a Christian sees the greatness of this glory, but not as his, the soul will never cleave to the Lord indeed, nor finde full rest; and hence when the riches of Gods grace is revealed, and the Feast set before them, they do not eat, because they fear they were not bidden. Now both these give full peace and rest to the soul, when the soul hath the Lord *Jehovah* in his arms, and hence he cares not now when death comes: Oh it shall be a welcome day to them! And hence they wish they might sin no more, or cease to be. And hence they wish they could set even the whole world a wondring. Was it ever heard since the world began of such a pattern of mercy? Its true, the Lord indeed keeps his Servants for a time under much darkness and doubts, but it's certain even in the meanest Saint this light is sown for them, and *joy for the upright in heart,* and some work there is for the Lord to do for them, and then he keeps a Sabbath of rest in them.

Quest.
Answ.

But have not many Hypocrites their joyes, their peace, their Glory?

Yes, they have some tasts and likeness to this, but want this indeed; and the difference appears in three Particulars.

1. The peace and joy and assurance of that Glory which eye never saw in the Saints, 'tis from the witness of the Spirit of Glory; not only because that God is their God, but because they are his people. 'Tis I say from the witness of God in his Word, not from themselves, nor from man only that they approve me,

me, not from dreams and Diabolical breathings, but from the Spirit of God, he brings tidings of it, and from such a Spirit (that you may know it) that not only shews you God is your God, and so you rejoyce because of this, for thus 'tis with many a carnal heart, and he hath peace, being in horror, from this, the Lord loves me; but he makes you to rejoyce because you are the Lords people, because he hath changed your heart, now the peace is found, and joy is right; and here I would try the peace of any man, God hath witnessed pardon to thee, but hath he shewen thee thou art his? If so, be thankful. But here is the doubt, for it may be the change is not right. And hence those two are ever joyned together, *Zach.*13.9. *John* 14.20,21,22. Horror lies heavy, hence love is sweet; sin lies heavy, hence this witness, they are changed, they are subdued and shall be so, this is sweet also.

2. The rest and peace the Saints have, 'tis not only from God, but in him. 'Tis with the soul as with a Malefactor imprisoned and condemned, the Jaylor comes and tells him that he hath his pardon here brought him from the King; How shall it be proved whether it be a device of his own Brain or no? Why if it be of the Jaylors own devising, he will never lead him before the face of the King, but from him he shall be carried: But if the Messenger carry him before the King, and sets him down before him, and as it was with *Joseph*, his Prison-garments are put off, and he stands before the King, and glories in his presence, now 'tis right. So many have peace, and Satan sets them at liberty, but carries them from God. But when there is a witness of peace from him, and then you stand before him, now 'tis from Heaven, *Psal.*36.7,8. There is peace from him and peace in him, *Psal.*37.4. *Delight thy self in the Lord, and he shall give thee the desires of thy heart.* When 'tis thus, all you desire is granted.

3. The peace the Saints have both from God, and in God, fills them with everlasting content and peace, *Rom.*15.13. *Isa.*11.9. *Filled with the Knowledge of the Lord as the waters cover the Sea.* The earth is the rest of the waters, and the waters fill all its empty place: So 'tis here, the soul is the rest of the Lord, *Isa.* 11.10. and he fills their empty hearts. A Malefactor may dream he is before the King, when he hath his Fetters on his legs; but his dream feeds him not, but when he awakes, he is hungry. And so 'tis with many a carnal heart that is in a dream for a time, but he meets not with eternal satisfaction, *Psal.*65.4. & *Psal.*90.14. And hence men after they have had their peace, grow more bold to sin, and more impenitent in sin, and more worldly than ever before, because they have not everlasting joy; as those, *Isa.*35.10. *Everlasting joyes shall be upon their head* (whereas a carnal heart hath soon enough of God) not everlasting, without intermission of joy, for they must have their nights and tears, as well as their days and joys; but everlasting, without decay of joy; that though they have their tears, yet God wipes them away; there is nothing else, their joy, their peace, and so their hearts are for ever satisfied here. As Christ, when he knew it was finished, now *he gave up the Ghost*, so when the soul finds he is come, now it dies to the world, and makes its perpetual abode in him. Others will have their Carrion, and their stolen waters, how clean soever they wipe their mouths.

Object. 1.
Answ.

But have not the Saints many sorrowes, reproaches, persecutions?

*Rom.*8.18. *They are not worthy the Glory to be revealed.* 2 *Cor.*4.17. *They work a weight of Glory,* and in these they glory. Oh *the Lords Love is shed in their hearts!* *Rom.*5.3,5.

Object. 2.

But have they not many losses, and wants, and straights? and then where is their joy?

Answ.

A carnal heart he murmures indeed, and sinks, and dies away, but 'tis not so here, *Hab.*3.17,18. A Saint takes it out in him, in the Lord, it makes all the world too narrow for him. Others are burnt and consumed in the fire, but so is not he that hath the Son of God with him.

But he hath many sins and Temptations.   *Object. 3.*

1 Pet.1.5,6,7. *You greatly rejoyce in the Salvation reserved for you, though now your Faith have a precious trial by manifold temptations.*

But are not the hearts of the Saints taken off from the Lord, and taken up with   *Object. 4.*
other things?

No, never as carnal mens are, *Tit.2.12. For Gods Grace that hath appeared*   *Answ.*
to them, teacheth them to deny worldly lusts, as we deny children their asking.
They may greedily carry the soul by fits from the Lord, but he denies them their
fill in any Creature, and calls them all to *come up hither.* He denies them as we
do Beggars entrance, and if they do enter, he denies them lodging, they shall
not have good looks from them. Every vile heart hath either a proud, or
worldly, or covetous heart, and these lusts being urgent and entreating long, he
cannot deny them the best room he has. Oh 'tis the woe of men they cannot
but do thus.

But thus you see this world is cast out, and Glory comes in to all Saints: Oh
this world is the cause of all sin!

1. Why do men neglect duties in secret?
2. Sleep at Meetings?
3. Though so fair abroad, yet passionate at home, and storms there?
4. Whence are wars and wranglings about rates and lots? Oh this world!
5. Whence Apostacy? 'Tis not with you as in former times, worse now
than in persecution; and Sermon-proof now? Oh this world! Whence is
hardness of heart? Oh something of the world easeth you! And whence is it
that men with rich stocks are goodly things, and wondred at; and Holiness and
walking with God, and things of Heaven are nothing? Oh this evil world!
Oh Adulterers and Adulteresses, know you not that you hate the Lord, and the
Lord you? 'Tis the cause of all thy sin, but see withal 'tis the cause of all thy
sorrow, Heaven and the Glory of that would enter, but for it, but that it cannot,
because thou art full of it. Oh poor Creatures, take your Farewel quickly of it,
or the Lord will meet with you for it! Cry to the Lord, oh call me to come up
unto thy self!

Thus you see the Fulness of the Spirit which the Saints have; and therefore
that conceit, that Saints have nothing whereby to discern them, let it for ever
perish and rot.

SECT. VII.

TAke heed you fall not short of the Grace of God, of the promise and Spi-   *Use 4.*
rit of Grace, *Heb.*12.15. Oh get Oyl in your Vessels! When there is   *Of Exhort.*
much counterfeit Gold abroad, every man will have his Scales, and not only
look and rub, but he will weigh every piece he takes: Was there ever more
Counterfeits abroad, or such similitudes of the Truth? Insomuch as some in
their Opinions, think it impossible, others in their practises find it hard and very
difficult to distinguish the one from the other. Oh but there is a vast distance
and difference! As ever you look for Mercy, get this Oyl in your Vessel. As
ever you look for peace, know that you have it in your Vessel. I am perswaded
that there is never a soul that follows the Lord tremblingly and
tenderly, but when he hears of this, sends up his sighs, good Lord let me not
fail here; better never have had thy Name in my Forehead, nor affection in my
heart, than to want Oyl in my Vessel: And I am perswaded he trembles to
think, what if I should perish at the last? And yet how many never have strong
fears of failing here, that have most cause so to do. This Parable is directed to

Virgin-Churches at the last period of the decrepit world; wherein methinks the Lord Jesus speaks unto his people, There is much profession, affection, but oh take heed you perish not for want of oyle in your Vessel. Let all your care be to get that, and fear to want that, wherein the Lord doth answer that fear, and question, and thought of his people: Oh what if I should perish at last? Get oyl in your Vessel then, and if the Lord Jesus had been of that minde that there are no inherent graces in the Saints, or so dim they cannot be known, or if known you are not to respect them as any signs, but to look for a witness of grace upon you, or out of you, without respecting or looking upon grace in you, he would never have recorded this Parable, which to wise Virgins is to prevent those conceipts: Oh therefore how many fall short here, and regard not this!

  1. Some fall short here by trusting to, and omnifying of Christ and grace, regarding not any grace within; they separate those things from one another which God hath joyned, and which a gracious heart joyns one to another: They respect not sanctification, faith or vocation, they look to Christ, and can they honour Christ enough? Hence profess they that regard those things have trusted to their frames of heart, and they scoffe at them that look to be justified by Faith: Tis such a delusion as is likely *to deceive (if possible) the very Elect.* Look as it was with the *Israelites*, 1 *Sam.* 4. They were overthrown in the battel of the *Philistines*; but what's the cause, *Oh send for the Ark where the strength and presence of God was*, but what good did the Ark do them with unhumbled hearts, that looked to that, and trusted to that; but minde not themselves; and hence when *Samuel* bids then *turn from their Idols, and serve the Lord only*; now they do it; so here.

  2. Some only look to the out-side, like those that *built the tombes and painted the Sepulchres of the Prophets:* And hence if they be inwardly zealous for external Order, Ceremony, Ordinances, carriage in garments, speeches, &c. they think the bitterness of death is past, when *Agag*-like they are clad with such soft raiment, and hence if there be transgression here 'tis sad: But what if they walk with unbroken hearts? oh they respect not this! And so their care being taken up in trimming and making the Vessel bright, they neglect to get oyle within.

  3. Some fall short here by thinking this thought, that that grace which is inward is also sincere and unfained: And hence do not judge themselves prophane nor civil, because of their profession, nor yet Hypocrites because they do not make only an outward shew, when as the deepest hypocrisie lies under much inward affection many times: And hence they take every such work upon trust without weighing it, if double guilt, and there is no shew of Copper, put it up, never enquiring where the bounds of truth and hypocrisie part; And hence if they have inward comfort though by a dream, they take it; If upon their sick beds after trouble they have had peace, they take it on trust; if they have any promise of rest and peace, or feel some desires, love to Ordinances, and Gods people; they take hold on promises, and trust themselves without trying, without weighing: Sudden work is superficial.

  4. Some feel a want of these things, and content themselves with desires, and so never come to be indeed what they desire to be; Its true, Saints feel wants and desire supply: But 1. They are never satisfied till 'tis so indeed: *My flesh is meat indeed.* 2. They are humble and vile in their own eyes till the Lord help; but these like *Solomons* sluggard, *desire and have not*; whereas in things of lesser worth they will not do so; They will not only desire, but indeed till the ground; If one neglects to till, though they answer, I desire, and God accepts that, every one will say he is deceived; their hunger is their food; they build the sluggards nest of desire, and there sit: Oh therefore take heed you fall not short here! Take heed your prayers and desires prove not lazie and unfaithful Messengers which you send to your Friends to come and help you, and they go half way and no further

ther, and never fetch them to you indeed. Oh therefore get oyle in your Veſſels, do not only fear the Lord, *but fear him greatly,* 1 *Sam.* 12. 18. Do not only cleave to the Lord, but with the whole heart, and cleave to him onely ; Beg
this of the Lord. Look as poor people when they come to rich men that have full
heaps, do ſay, let me have full meaſure, my family is poor, and charge great :
So here.

Motive 1.

Conſider if once you get this it will never die, it ſhall increaſe exceedingly :
Its a treaſure you cannot part withal, that you ſhall never grow poor with ; but
Luke 8. 18. *From him that hath not, ſhall be taken away that which he ſeemed to have.*
Oh many a one ſaith, I fear I ſhall fall at laſt, and I finde my heart ſo ſoon cool-
ed ; Oh get this, nothing ſhall quench it again ! If you ſay I cannot keep it , I
ſay it ſhall keep you, *Prov.* 2. 10, 11. Not when you have Chriſt and Spirit, and
grace in your head, nor in your Conſcience to give you peace, but in your heart ;
and when nothing is ſweet but that, nothing lies between your heart and that ;
it ſhall now preſerve and keep thee, it ſhall follow thee, fill thee, ſeal thee, live
with thee, go to heaven with thee, &c. Mark this ye feeble ones.

Motive 2.

Oh conſider what a ſad thing it will be to thy heart to miſs of, and loſe the
Lord at laſt ; The ſervants in *Iſaac's* Family did not mourn ſo much as *Eſau*
when the bleſſing was gone. Why ? They never had hope of it, never were
neer it. He was ſo long in the field that the bleſſing was gone before he came,
and he ſold it away for a trifle : So them that never came ſo neer the Lord and
his bleſſing, never will have ſuch ſorrow, eſpecially to think I ſold it away for
a trifle : O thought *Eſau* that I had come a little ſooner, &c. When *Saul* went
to *Gilgal* to ſacrifice, 1 *Sam.* 13. 10. *He ſtaid ſeven days, and then ſacrificed before
the Lord,* but then his doom was paſſed by God : And its ſaid preſently *Samuel*
came, Oh if he had ſtaid a little longer ! So you will one day think, I ſought
and waited but forſook the Lord. Oh had I waited one day more I had been
well. This is the reaſon why the Hypocrites portion is heavieſt in Hell.

Motive 3.

You will ſay, It will be heavy hereafter, but not now ? Yes, now to if you do
conſider the Lord Jeſus is ſo full, and thou not to have one drop of that which is
ſaving, even when you come for it. It was a heavy token of the Lords anger,
1 *Sam.* 14. 17. *when the Lord anſwered not all that day* (when yet he did not ſpeak bitter things againſt them) becauſe he did uſe to do it : It notes the anger of the
Lord Jeſus ; as a man that hath abundance of bread, and yet gives not any, this
argues he is very angry if he continue ſo ; and if ſo, how canſt thou ſleep under it ?

Motive 4.

Conſider , elſe the Lord will try you ; God hath his trying times , and they
were never ſent but to diſcover who were droſs, who were gold, and the main
end of all Gods Tryals is to diſcover this Truth that I now am preſſing upon
you. Some have a thorow work, and now the Tryal diſcovers the Truth, as in
Abraham, Hebr. 11. 17. Some have ſuperficial work, and they fall in Tryal, as
Saul, and it doth diſcover it was but an overly work ; For this is the Queſtion
God makes : Is it through or no ? I, ſaith a carnal heart, Yes, ſaith a gracious heart.
Hence its ſtrange to ſee what men will do when a tryal comes. A man maintains a luſt, he will not ſhew it, nor defend it, he ſhall turn to be of ſome opinion or other , and the corruption of his minde ſhall ſhew the corruption of his
heart : A man loaths the people of God, but he ſaith he loves them ; now this ſhall
be a ſign : Time ſhall come that ſome of them ſhall be matter of offence to
him, and ſhall not honour him, it ſhall try him. A man loaths Ordinances, he
ſaith he doth not, but comes to the worlds end to enjoy them. He ſhall have
plenty of them, and ſome ſad loſſes with them, and then you ſhall ſee he ſur-
fets of them, never quickned by them, to ſhew the work was but overly. A
mans heart is above God, he ſaith he is content to be at the Lords diſpoſe, let
him do any thing with him, this comforts him. He ſhall have a croſs wife, or

G g   ſome-

something that doth not please him, and now his heart quarrels, and thus he shall be tryed, to shew it was but overly work. Men despise the liberties the Lord gives them; they say they prize them. A general Governour shall come with pretences of Religion and Protection, and you shall see this chaffe will take old Birds now. Oh therefore try your selves here, and be sure you fall not short here.

What Means are there to be used ?

1. Look that you make your Vessels clear. It hath been said of old, and I beleeve tis a truth still, 'that the Lord will never send his Spirit to dwell in an unclean heart. Doves build not their habitations on dunghils. Gods Spirit must come as an efficient to take it away, but not as an Inhabitant to dwell in an unclean heart, 2 *Tim.* 2. 19,20,21. *He that purgeth himself*, he doth not say, God must do all, but he under God searcheth and purgeth, he shall *be a vessel of honour*, if from these things, especially from those sins which Apostates are conquered with, of which he there speaks : For there be many sins a man may be purged from, and not be a Vessel of honour. But what are the sins the Apostates perish by, mark them, finde them out, one by pride, another by sloth, another by world, &c. *He shall be a Vessel of honour*. Men see and confess, but make not work of it indeed, the old heart is not better, you consume and languish still, 1 *Cor.* 9. 26, 27. *I beat not the air*, i. e. I lay deadly blows on my enemy, and *I beat down my body, least, &c.* Overly search of sin, hath made overly decay of sin, and hence overly grace and affection. As a man hath not light, nor love, nor esteem enough, because he never felt his wound to the bottome. Oh account it an inestimable mercy when 'tis thus ; oh therefore remember the rule of the Prophet, *Jer.* 4. 3, 4. *Sow not among thorns, &c.* Many mens profession springs up, but withers, never comes to perfection; this ground is not plowed, or if so, not thorowly plowed, but thorns left to choak it. Well saith the Lord, look to your selves lest my *wrath breake out like fire*; why is the Lord so dreadful here ? Oh because men are careless here, I look to Christ, and my desires are good, and I pray in secret, and I am much changed, &c.

2. Look that your Vessel be ever kept empty ; when a man hath no grace, and sees how others can pray and mourn, and how far short he falls of them, its easie now to be empty, as *Saul* when he was no King ; but when the Lord hath given some light and affection, and some comfort, and some Reformation ; now a man grows full here : Saints do for God, and carnal hearts do something too ; but a little fills them, and quiets them, and so damns them. And hence men at the first work upon them are very diligent in the use of means, but after that they be brought to neglect prayer, sleep out Sermons, and to be careless, sapless, liveless, who is the better for them ? Because I say that now they have got something, the main work is wrought, they call not that into Question, and so when God comes to reckon, they are found too light. Oh therefore keep the Vessel empty, never content thy self with any measure. Hath the Lord called thee ? Yes I think so, and beleeve sometimes so, but I am afraid I may at last be found without oyle in my Vessel ; be then every day, as if thou wert but now to begin. And this I say, true grace as it comforts, so it never fills, but puts an edge on the appetite ; more of that grace Lord ! Thus *Paul*, Phil. 3. 13, 14. Thus *David*, *Out of my poverty I have given*, &c. 1 *Chron.* 29. 3, 17, 18.

Its a sure way never to be deceived in lighter strokes of the Spirit to be thankful for any, but to be content with no measure of it, and this cuts the thread of difference between a superficial lighter stroke of the Spirit, and that which is found.

3. Look that your vessel be not broken, nor crackt, that when the Lord pours in, it runs not out again, *Heb.* 2.1, 2. *Prov.* 4. 12,13. Oh here is the wound of many a man, he hath many affections in Word, in Ordinances, and they take

hold

hold on him to convince ; to affect him, but he takes not fast hold on them, he keeps them not as his life, with thankfulness for any little, and with watchfulness. And hence a man is where he was, dry and barren. It's true the Lord will not give that out of an Ordinance which he doth in an Ordinance. But it's one thing to have it lost out of thy hands and the Lords hands too, another thing only to lose it out of thy hand. It's one thing for the Lord to withdraw it, another thing for thee to spend it away by the prevailing power of a lust, viz. either the world without, or contempt of Grace within ; you esteem it not as your life, and hence seek not to keep it, you will lose the Oyl in your Vessels. And I am confident this is one reason why a man lives long under means, and never profits, the Lord sees if he should poure any thing into the heart, it would be lost. He takes fast hold of world or self, and keeps that, and hence all runs out again.

4. Look that you be at the cost to get this Oyl in your Vessel. These Virgins when the door was shut and too late would, but the time was past. For we shall find the reason why mens works are sleight, their buildings, their garments, why, they will not be at the cost ; so mens work of Grace is sleight, because they will not be at the cost. They find a want of Grace, and prize it, and would fain have it, but it shall cost them little : they will not be at the cost of their time. Somtime they can seek the Lord in an Ordinance, but what if he comes not ? They depart from him. Sometimes in pangs, and fits when the Spirit comes, they seek, but to be ever seeking, ever carrying sense of sin, 'tis too much time and trouble, they will not be at the cost. Some affections and hearts they spend, but not their whole hearts: Hence Christ exhorts, oh *strive, because many seek and are never able.* Look therefore as it was with *Jonathan, Saul,* 1 Sam.14.45. said *he should die* : No, the people said, *not so, for he hath wrought with God this day.* Not that a man can get Grace by his own strength, but *Col.*1.29. *I strive according to his mighty working.* Only let me add this, be at cost first to get the Lord Jesus himself ; As *Mat.*13.33. *He sold all and bought the Field* ; and when he had the Field, now he had the Treasure. Oh think no time too much, no lusts too dear, no affections too much for him (and then you have all things with him, and shall receive life from him) and not for a dead, but for a living, risen Christ. Christ bestowed Gifts on *Judas,* on *Saul,* but whom he bestowed himself upon, those never wanted any thing, *Psal.*23.1. But here I might take up a doleful complaint ; Oh that men content themselves with colours and tinctures of Truth and Spirit, *&c.* Some Naturalists observe, that Brass would be Gold, it tends to it, had it but more heat of the Sun to concoct it and to bring it to perfection ; so 'tis with the lighter Stroaks of common Grace.

CHAP. XXI.

That true saving Grace in the Hearts of Believers can never fail.

SECT. I.

THat those *Graces of the Spirit wherewith those Heavenly Vessels, or Souls of the Faithful are filled, are constant and of an eternal Nature.*

For thus the wise Virgins, their Vessels were not only filled, but the Oyl was constantly preserved in them, and continued in their Vessels, until they met the Bridegroom. 'Tis true, their Lamp went out, outward acts of the Spirit of Grace, expressed in the Profession of the Saints may be extinct for a time, yet the Oyl did remain in the Vessel still, which was not so with those which were Foolish, not only their Lamps were out, but their Oyl was spent; so that here is a third Difference between *the Foolish and the Wise Virgins*: That the Spirit of Grace in the one is of a dying, withering nature; in the other, of an eternal and everlasting nature. There is an eternal excellency stampt upon them, *John* 4.14. *The water that I shall give him, shall be in him,* no Pools, but a perpetual *living Spring. Heb.* 6.9. *Some that were enlightned and tasted, fell away, but we are perswaded better things of you.* The Saints have better things, which do not cause, but accompany Salvation. The Lord is so far from suffering it to die, as that he will add to it, *Luke* 8.18. *To him that hath shall be given.* Though it be like Mustard-seed, yet it shall grow; there is a growing vertue in it. But as the Lord speaks of his people, *Isa.* 65.8. *As new wine is in the Cluster, and one saith, destroy it not, for a blessing is in it, so is shall be here.* Nay, though it be not so much as seen, yet the Lord then can see it, and doth then keep it, and will preserve it, *Isa.* 40.29,30,31. Nay, though opposed and resisted by temptation, yet, 1 *Pet.* 1.6,7. 'Tis not consumed, but *tried, that it may be to Glory* another day, notwithstanding manifold temptations. 'Tis one of the greatest Miracles in the world to preserve it, as a Spark of fire in a Sea of water: Nay, though it seems to a mans feeling to be quite quenched and put out, that a man finds no more than a Reprobate, yet the Seed of God then remains, and it will break out again. There is life at the heart and sap at the root, yet the Lord will fetch them again. When the Lord of Glory was crucified, and all the Disciples fled, not one spake for him, none durst confesse him, yet the Lord returns to them, and they again to him.

SECT. II.

HOw comes it to be thus immortal and of an eternal nature?

1. 'Tis not only in regard of the power of Grace received, though it were perfect, for then *Adam* had not fell from it.

2. Not in the freedom of a man from temptations, for then the Angels had not fallen.

3. Nor yet in the power of a mans own watchfulness and care to keep it. For *if the Lord keep not the City, the watchmen wake but in vain.*

4. Nor yet in the power of any means; as many think, if under a powerful Ministry, then they are out of danger. 'Tis not in *Paul*, nor *Apollos*, but in the Lord.

Men

Men may rejoyce in *Johns* Ministry, and be affected with it, but 'tis only for a season. But,

I. In regard of the eternal Election and Purpose of God. Their constancy in the State of Grace depends upon that immutability of his counsel, *Math.* 24. 24. *They shall deceive if possible the Elect* ; but its not possible, they being Elect. Wise men may have their Brains crazed, and *Nebuchadnezzar* like, the use of reason gone, but the Principle of reason continues, and the use of it in time returns again ; and so 'tis in regard of damning delusions, 2 *Tim.* 2. 19. *Hymeneus* and *Philetus* fell ; Hence do not the Elect fall ? No, for that *Foundation remains sure.* 1. The certainty of their continuance in Grace is built upon a Foundation. 2. Not every weak one, but a firm Foundation. 3. Not a Foundation of mans saying, but Gods. 4. Not a wavering and tottering, but standing Foundation, and that sealed with the Knowledge of God, *the Lord knows who are his, i. e.* though some men fall, that one cannot tell by outward expressions and profession who are the Lords, yet *The Lord knows who are his,* and they are sealed by his love and knowledge. And it seems this is the prime cause of the continuance of Angels, 1 *Tim.*5. 21. And Election being free, for his own sake, not for their sakes, the Lord foresaw all their good and evil ; hence they are not cut off.

II. In regard of the Faithfulness and Promise and Covenant of Gods Grace. *Adam* had that Covenant : If he did do, he should live : But he had no absolute Promise he should do, or continue to do ; but the Faithful have ; and hence they stand, not by the strength of Grace, but by the strength of the Covenant of Grace. And hence that which to reason is incredible, to nature impossible, is brought about by Faith ; not by vertue of any power of Faith, but by vertue of the power of a promise. God hath said it, and Faith believes it ; and hence *Abrahams* dead body begets, and *Sarahs* barren womb brings forth *Isaac.* Hence through all the Word, when the Apostle perswades himself of their continuance, he ever puts in Gods Faithfulness, 1 *Cor.* 1. 8, 9. 1.*Thes.* 5. 24. 2 *Thes.* 3. 3. Hence *Jer.* 32. 40. *I will not turn away from them.* Answ. True, if they do not from the Lord. No, but *they shall not turn away from me.* Object. But we see many do fall. Answ. But if he doth, he shall not be broken, but taken up again, *Psal.*37. 24. Yea for a time the Lord may do thus. But will this continue, having sinned against such mercy, and my sin being now greater ? Now the Lord will depart. Answ. 1 *Cor.* 1. 8. *Yea, he will confirm you to the end.* Yes, it may be he will, as he hath done, while I am out of temptation : But I may meet with it before I die. Answ. 1 *Cor.* 10. 13. *He will not suffer you to be tempted above measure,* &c. Yea, if I was such a one as *Abraham* or *David*, that had such hearts, and did the Lord so much honour. Nay, but *Isai.*55. 3. *Even the sure mercies of David.* This is the Faithfulness of God.

III. In regard of the constant abode of the Spirit of the Lord in the hearts of the Saints, whereby they are kept, *John* 10. 28. *None can pull his Sheep out of the Fathers hand.* Look as the first *Adam* sinning, conveys the power of sin and Satan and death, which reigns with unconquerable power over all the Sons of men ; so Christ rising, conveys that Grace and constant presence of the Spirit which reigns to eternal life, and carries the soul through all difficulties, *Deut.* 33. 27. *The eternal God is thy refuge.* Let what evils can come, there is a refuge. Yea so long as I can stand. But what if I fall ? *Underneath are the everlasting arms.* Let a Saint fall never so low, yet Gods everlasting arms are still lower ; where-ever he falls, he falls at last into the Lords arms ; For else it was impossible for any soul to continue, *Isa.*46. 3. 4. *From the womb to the hoar hairs I will carry you.* Saints when they are little, think they shall fall at last, and when strengthened, fear if they live till old age, their hearts and spirits will die ; yet they do not. But how comes this about ? *I will carry you.* And hence 'tis impossible they should ever

die

die or perish, no more than the Lord Jesus, *John* 14.19. So that if Gods purpose is firm, his promise sure, his Spirit able, the Spirit of life and grace in the hearts of the Faithful, shall be kept even to eternity.

SECT. III.

Use.

LET that Opinion that the Graces of Saints are fading and mortal, rot and die, and be had in everlasting detestation of them that know the Lord.

Object.

But we see how many fall off and fall back, and I have found it by experience so.

Answ.

The seed that is cast into the earth, first dies, and then lives and growes; so no sooner doth the Lord fill his Saints, but there is much self-confidence on it, and resting in it, hence it dies, yet it lives and grows again. And hence the Lord keeps his people poor & sensible of their own weakness as long as they live; but if it quite dies and withers, they were never the Lords, nor never had one Dram of Grace, 1 *John* 2.19. If it be taken away, he did but seem to have it. All fleshly excellencies in men, as common gifts be, do wither, *Isa.* 40.6,7. *All Flesh is grass:* But Plants in Gods Orchard never lose their greenness, though Plants and Flowers in the field may, *Psal.* 1.3. *Whose leaf shall not wither.*

Object.
Answ.

But this may make men secure, say the *Arminians.*

1. Nothing puts more life in the Saints. It would sink them else, if it were not thus, as when the Lord told *Joshua, where ever thou settest thy foot, thou shalt prosper, not a man able to stand against thee,* this puts life into him.

2. Though they cannot fall quite away, yet they may fall so as to lose the sweetness of Grace, and presence of God. If a man should eat too much, and ever be sick, though not die after it; or if one should fall and break his bones, though he doth not lose his life ? Is this any gap for any to rejoyce ?

3. Though they cannot wholly drive away nor bear out the breath of the Spirit, yet they may *grieve the Spirit by which they are sealed,* Eph. 4.30. Which is more sad to a holy heart than all evils in the world beside. But therefore let this Conceit die and perish, which is raised up by Satan to disgrace the Image of God and Spirit of Grace in the hearts of the Faithful; for who will make men seek after perishing things, under a colour of making men seek for the Spirit, it is to resist and quench the Spirit of God in them.

SECT. IV.

Use 2.

IT may comfort the hearts of the Faithful exceedingly against fears of Apostacy, when they see great Cedars fall, How shall I stand? And when they hear of some temptation that may be hereafter, then they fear. And when they feel the evil of their own hearts (which the Lord lets them feel to humble them that they may grow lower, and so stand the faster) they say, I shall fall, and when they have found the Lords presence, oh if now I should relapse after this health ! *How shall I know whether I shall stand or no ?*

Quest.
Answ.

'Tis not only discernable by perseverance, but by somwhat begun, though very difficult to be seen. As,

1. Observe Gods several and various dispensations of himself and his Grace toward thee, whether they issue from his everlasting love or no; for if so, then he will everlastingly keep that which he hath given thee. *Quest. How shall I know that ? Answ.* Look as that issues from eternal wrath, that separates the soul from God, or therein 'tis exprest; so that is the expression of eternal love which draws thee to God in Jesus Christ. Observe therefore the Lords carriage,
Doth

Doth it draw thee at laſt to him, nearer to him; and ſo the more he diſpenſeth of himſelf, the nearer thou art brought to him; here is the expreſſion of eternal love, and the Lord will keep thee, *John* 6.37. *All that are given me ſhall come to me.* Let the Lord give his Spirit, though but little, they grow thankful. Oh he is come, whom I thought would never have returned again! Let him deny it, this keeps them humble. Let the Lord diſpenſe himſelf in an Ordinance, they love him; and *one day here, better than a thouſand elſewhere.* Let him not do ſo, they feel the more need of him. Let the Lord free them from temptations, and give them conqueſt, Faith now rejoyceth. Let them fall into many temptations, their Faith growes the more purified than ever. Let the Lord give them outward bleſſings, they grow more vile in their own eyes, *leſſe than the leaſt*, with *Jacob*. Let the Lord deny them, *Hab.*3.18. they rejoyce in the Lord. They get good and are more endeared to the Lord by every carriage of the Lords, at leaſt in the iſſue it is ſo. As 'tis with wicked men, they may for a fit be affected and return to the Lord, but in the iſſue they forget the Lord, ſo 'tis here contrariwiſe. There is not any unregenerate man, but ſomthing or other conſumes him. The wicked ever are like Chaffe driven from God. Gold that is of an everlaſting nature, keep it, beat it, burn it, you cannot conſume, but only purifie it, 'tis not ſo with Chaffe. Let the Lord give him taſts of Grace and joy, it eſtrangeth his ſoul from Chriſt, it doth not bring him near to Chriſt.

2. Obſerve whether thou doſt grow out of, and live upon an everlaſting Covenant or no, *Rom.*11.1. *God hath not caſt off his people, whom he foreknew.* Who are thoſe? *Children of the promiſe*, *Rom.*9.7,8. That are born and bred of the promiſe or whole Covenant of Grace; God hath treaſured up all Grace in Chriſt, laid it up in that ſtore-houſe, Chriſt hath dropt it in his promiſes. Now when the ſoul is rooted in the Covenant, now it ſhall never die nor periſh. As 'tis with ſome trees, ſet them in the ground, they will grow, if they have Sun and rain, but die at laſt! Take another, and ſet it in a Stock, ſo that it abides there, and fetcheth all its life from thence by cleaving to it; now it will grow and become a flouriſhing Branch. Now then the ſoul growes out of the Covenant, when the whole ſoul cleaves to the whole Covenant, for the whole benefit of it, and is fully ſatiſfied with it, 2 *Sam.*23.4,5. As take a ſoul that feels a want of all the benefits of the Covenant, pardon, peace, life, that the Spirit is ready oft to fail, and hath no aſſurance it ſhall have any part of that which is the Childrens portion; and looks upon his own unworthineſs, never to have any from the Lord, yet it looks up to the free mercy and Grace that made it to ſome, to make it good to me, and ſo pleads the promiſe, and ſo laies it ſelf there, and there reſts, and there looks, and here ſucks, and takes root, and the root ſpreads to every part of the Covenant. The Lord hath now rooted the ſoul in this Covenant, and it hath received life from hence, this is everlaſting, you ſhall continue. And when the ſoul eſpecially is like a bough blown by the wind, yet it ſtands faſt ſtill. If men have been in horrors and then fell to reformation, and there reſted, it will not laſt. If men have had ſome workings and actings of the Spirit upon them, and then ſay, God muſt do all, but they grow not into the Covenant, they will die; But here though God keeps thee ſhort and naked, and thou only pleadeſt the Covenant, thou ſhalt ſtand. If you plead for pardon, and ſome good, not the whole good of the Covenant, you ſhall die alſo. If you grow upon ſome diſtemper, and the whole heart grow not upon this, you will die alſo. Look as 'tis with a man that builds, he will make an end if the foundation be laid, but if not pull it down, ſo here.

3. If the power of Grace received and acted by the Spirit, hath riſen to the nature of fruits, and not leaves only, *John* 15.2. And that is, when the ſoul receives that Grace, as that in every thing its ſcope is to live to God, to give his heart

heart content. For fruit is the end of the trees growth, and leaves and fruit is not for the tree, but for the content of the owner of it. If so the Lord hath undertaken to purge thee, though there be much Self-seeking in thee, and he hath undertaken though little at present, to make thee bear more fruit. Many a man hath much affection and grace, but when he hath it, what is it but leaves to adorn and beautifie himself? But he lives not to the Lord; another man will live to the Lord in what he does, the Lord is so dear, and himself so vile, as that he doth thus.

4. If you pray for it in Chrifts Name. *Object.* Many pray. *Answ.* But when Christ and you pray together, you will speed; and then Christ praies, when his Spirit cries at the Throne of Mercy, then himself is at the Throne of Justice. And his Spirit cries, 1. Not for an unfit person, that hath some flight change, but for his Saints, whose hearts are endeared to him and his whole will. 2. Not for an evil or private end, but the Lords. 3. Not coldly, but with groans unutterable. Is it thus with thee? Oh then how canst thou fall? Doft fear Satan, *Mat.* 16.18. he shall not prevail against thee, but thou shalt give the last blow and wound. Doft fear the world, the deceits of it? *Mat.* 24.24. (*if possible the elect*) Doft fear the evil or good things of it, *John* 17.13. *though in the world, yet Christ prays you may be delivered from the evil of it.* Doft fear thy sin, that will separate? *Answ. Rom.* 6.2. *How can we that are dead live any longer therein?* Tis a strong, but a wounded, but a dying enemy. Doft fear the Lord, thou haft walked so unworthy of him? *He will not break the bruised reed till judgment come to victory,* though little, though weak. Oh therefore be comforted against this in these times, which are apostatical, declining, evil daies, and bless the Lord!

SECT. V.

Use 3.

HEnce we learn what verdict to pass and give in concerning those men that decay and fall off from the Lord. They never had Oyl in their Vessel, never had drawn of Grace in their heart, Thus, 1 *John* 2.19. *If they had been of us, they would doubtlesse have continued with us.* It seems they were such men which were so eminent and excellent, as that there were no brands nor marks upon them to give notice to the Churches that they were markt out for apostacy, but were only discovered to be unsound by their apostacy; and this was argument good enough. Hence Christ, when some of the *Jews* began to believe in him with a temporary Faith, *John* 8.31. *If my Word continue in you, ye are my Disciples;* as if he should say, your Faith is a Fancy, if it continue not. Look therefore as the Prophet said, *Zach.* 1.5. *Your Prophets, where are they? Your Fathers, where are they?* So say I to you; Your Tears, your Tenderness, your Groanings, your Heart-breaking, Prayers, *&c.* Where are they? Is it with them as with ships that are sunk and wrackt, some of the ribs remain, which gives you to see and say, there was a fair ship, but it's sunk, 1 *Tim.* 1.19. *Make shipwrack of Conscience,* and so lose their Faith also. Some men for a time seem to keep a whole Conscience, wind and water-tite, they can pass through many storms, yet at last it breaks, and when that is lost, their Faith is lost also. Their Faith before God, and Conscience before men, both of them break.

Now there are two sorts of Apostates: 1. Open in mens life, whose falls are like the falls of a mighty tree, it falls with noise, and breaks down all the under-wood : So their falls make a noise in all the Country where they lived, and by their falls some are sadded, others offended and damned. 2. Secret, when men are Apostates in heart, *Prov.* 14. 14. which have chosen some sinful ways, *Jer.* 3. When 'tis with men as it was with *Saul,* there is no commendation of him but this, that he was higher by the head and shoulders then any of

Israel :

Israel : So 'tis with these, in outward profession higher than others, but their oyle is spent.

But do not many of the Saints fall openly and secretly ?

True, they may and do fall exceeding greatly. But as *Moses* prophecying of the apostacy of *Israel* after his death, *Deut.* 32.29. yet 'tis said, 'tis not *the corruption, nor spot of his children*, Deut. 32.5. There is a great difference between an Hypocrites Apostacie from his grace, and Saints from theirs. Its one thing to fall from branch and root too, another thing only for the branches to be broken off and the root not pulled up, *Jude* 12. There are some apostacies that argue there was never a dram of grace in that soul. Saints fall down, but do not fall away : And of such Apostacies as argue want of grace, take the following Discoveries.

1. When a mans rising is the cause of his fall (or seals a man up in his fall) or at least the cause, through his corruption, *Ex.gr.* Time was a man lived a loose, careless, carnal life; by the Ministry of some Word, or reading of some Book, or speaking with some Friend, he comes to be convinced of his misery and woful condition, and sees no good, nor grace in himself, he hath been even hitherto deceived ; at last he comes to get some light, some taste, some sorrows, some heart to use the means, some comfort, and mercy, and hope of life : And when 'tis thus with him now he falls, he grows full and falls, and this rising is the cause of his fall, his light is darkness, and death to him, and grows to a form of knowledge : His rising makes him fall to formality, and then to prophaneness, and so his tasting satisfies him, his sorrows empty his heart of sorrow for sin, and his sorrows for his falls harden his heart in his falls, and all the means of recovering him harden him ; that now if men never had had means, even *Sodom,* they would have relented before now. This is a sad token of falling away, and having had only lighter work, it being a plain evidence that at their best they were filled with their lusts, because a little light and affection satisfied them, which is now turned by the power of their lust to harden them, *Isai.* 6. 9. This is given as one sure sign of a people forsaken of God, when *in seeing they see not, and hearing they hear not.* Look as it is in diseases, if the Physick and meat turns to be Poyson, then there is no hope of recovery, a man is sick to death now. The Saints little measure makes them forget what is behinde, *Prov.* 4.18. He shines *brighter and brighter till the perfect day.* So that let him fall he cannot be quiet there, but when he remembers from whom he is fallen, if once he tasted the Lord, this will fetch him again, and make him restless till he return. But if it be so as now it is with these, then the case is woful, when there is such a plague on men and they know it not.

When a man saith to himself, as the Glutton said to his soul, *Take thy rest, for thou hast goods laid up for many years,* so thou hast repentance, and grace, and peace enough for many years ; and hence the soul takes its rest, grows sluggish and negligent. Oh if you die in this case, this night thy soul shall be taken away to Hell.

2. If when men fall from the Lord, and they rise up only in Ordinances ; but fall down constantly out of Ordinances without feeling. A carnal heart falls, but he thinks himself is not therefore without all grace, because in an Ordinance his heart sometimes is affected, so they were *Ezek.*33. 31. The Prophets Ministry was sweet to them, *but their hearts went after their covetousness,* their Hogs, their houses, their lusts, their loss ; and they joy in the Prophet, but never mourn for that. A precious heart also falls out of Ordinances, but he feels his falls : Though he falls from the Benefit of his rising, yet not from the feeling of his fall, But to another man the sweet he finds in Ordinances, is but Musick to his meat, or as a man falls from Musick to his meat, *Mat.*7.26,27. *He that heareth my words and doth them not, that mans house is built upon a Sand, which falls,* and the cause of great falls is this : Look as 'tis with corn-ground, if rain falls upon that, though it be long before any ripe fruit comes ; yet it makes it at last come to some

H h   ripe-

ripeness: But if it falls on other ground, seed is sown there, but it brings forth Briars, though it drinks in rain, 'tis nigh to cursing, *Heb.6.7,8.* Look as it was with *Saul, God had forsaken him,* 1 *Sam.16.14,23.* and a Spirit of Satan came upon him, yet when *David* played with his Harp, it stilled the spirit in him, & affected him much; it did not cast out the spirit, for when he had done playing, *the evil spirit came again upon him.* So 'tis at this day, a man is forsaken of the *Spirit of God,* and I a inted with an evil spirit of pride, world, passion, lust, Libertinism; a man prays, hears, and is made much better; tis stilled, not cast out; for after this a man returns to his old spirit again, and in time he cannot be quieted with preaching, nor praying, no more then he could with his harping.

3. When a man is so fallen, as that he returns not in the season of rising: Look as 'tis with Trees in Winter-time, their leaves, their blowths, their fruit, their beauty is gone: Is it then dry and barren, and quite withered, and cursed? One would think so for the present, but 'tis not so, because the season of fruit and leaves is not now; if in Spring and Summer it should be so, then you might well suspect it. Thus *Jer.* 8. 5,7,8. yet they said they were wise, and they had Law and Ordinances among them: True, yet they did not know their season, hence fell with an everlasting backsliding. Hence *Psal.*1.3, 4,5. *They are like the tree planted by the rivers side which bears in season.*

Quest.
Answ.

What, and when is this season?

I cannot tell you the season of every man, but I will shew you the usual seasons of many men.

1. When Jesus Christ the Sun of righteousness draws exceeding neer unto the soul, and that to the reviving of others, *Isai.* 55.6. but thy heart never a whit the better, nor yet much troubled it is so bad. When *Peter* falls, a look recovers him; when *Ephesus* falls from her first love, to *remember from whence she is fallen,* is enough to restore her to her love again. When the Disciples fell after Christs death, yet when he arose and opened the Scripture, their hearts burned within them. But thou hast had Jesus Christ opening the riches of his grace from heaven, and thou hast heard a voice, but not seen the sight, the glory of the Lord in this thy day; and this thou hast done though the Sun hath come to his full height sometime: This is thy season; Gospel, and Christ, and promises, are grown common to you, &c. As it was with the possessed man, *Mat.*17.15. *The Devil takes him oft, and casts him into the water and fire,* but if when he come to Christ he have no help, the Lord be merciful to him then: So you have been possessed and fallen, but when the Lord Jesus comes he casts them out; but if the Lord speaks, enlightens, and cometh saying, Remember me whom thou hast abused, my wet locks, my watery eyes, and my sorrowful heart which thou hast broken, here is all my love, and this prevails not, but thou neither risest nor desirest the Lord to raise thee: This is sad. In the day of Jubilee, be a servant then for ever, if your old matter still pleaseth you; especially when all means are used; when the last of a course of Physick is taken, and is ineffectual.

2. When the Lord is ready to depart from the soul. Sometime Saints do not melt at love, but the Lord departs, now this recovers them. As a man that hath a friend, though they grow weary of their company, and they begin to carry away divers things, yet when they come to take their leave indeed, now they recover, and they cannot part now. Like *Joseph* and his Brethren, they can neither of them part. *Nicodemus* and *Joseph* cannot contain, but cleave to Christ, when most forsaken. *David,* when God *hides his face, is troubled,* Psal.30.7. 'Tis with Saints as with sick folks, when their sickness and sores come to their height, now they break and recover, *Hos.5.15.* But if Gods departing from thee makes thee more vile, it makes thee apostatize from him. 'Tis certain thou hadst never life then. This is a *Sauls* brand, 1 *Sam.*28. He forsakes the Lord, and goes to a Witch. Never saw you yet a Gracious heart, but the Lord made extremity fetch

fetch him in. And no surer sign of an ungracious heart, than to have this blast him and drive him from the Lord, *Mal.*3.14. A man hath Gods Ordinances, he finds no profit, no God, no Christ, his affection is lost, and now he forsakes the Lord. Oh when Christ is a rock of offence, wo, wo, wo to that soul! Now thou hast neither Summer nor Winter-fruit. Oh look to thy fall here!

4. When men so fall from the Lord, as that their whole hearts make choice of, and are espoused to some lust, wedded to some distemper. For though the Saints may fall, yet never to another Lover; for they cannot fall into any sin that breaks Covenant between them and the Lord, *Hos.*2.19. When men make choice of any thing in the world to take content in more than in the Lord, or together with the Lord, and hence defend it as lawful, and are fully free in it. There was never Grace there. For if any thing doth give the Saints content, 'tis not their choice, but refusing: But you are wedded to your lust. *David* could say, *I have chosen thy Testimonies, oh forsake me not utterly!* Others chuse somwhat else, not thee, *Psal.*125.5. *Those that walk in crooked waies, the Lord shall lead them forth.* This is given as a black mark of men that are broken off from the Lord, *Rom.*11.9. *Let their Table become a snare.* When it may be no unlawful thing, but lawful is that which banes them, 2 *Pet.*2.22. Sheep may fall into the mire, but if they lie and wallow in it, it's a Swine; and all their excellencies are but Pearls in a Swines snout.

But when doth a man make choice of it?

1. When a mans heart is set upon a lust, and God blesseth and prospers him in it. When God fills the *back-slider in heart full of his own waies.* His heart is worldly, and he thrives in it; his heart is ambitious, and he hath his Honour. This the Lord gives not to his people, but some rod or other upon their backs, *Hos.*4.17. *Let him alone.*

2. When a man lies long in his Fall. Saints lie not long: I limit no time, but when day after day, a man lives in it, *Rom.*11.10. *Let their Backs be bowed down alway.* Oh when a mans heart and back is bowed down alway! Saints are under Christs care.

5. When the Cause of a mans withering is a withering root. Trees in winter cast their leaves, as withered trees, but others root is hurt. If the branches do wither, yet if the root remain, it will recover again. So the Saints cast their leaf, and their branches wither in desertions and temptations, but they preserve themselves at the root. But why do others wither? 'Tis because their Faith withers, *Heb.*10.39. & 3.12,14. Many a man withers because of his Faith. He feels many wants. Why lives he so? Why dies he in beggery? Why see, *Micah* 3.11. When a man *is twice dead and pulled up by the roots,* so that the root perisheth; *for him is reserved the blacknesse of darknesse for ever.* That the means and way of enriching Saints is a way of beggery, to these 'tis very fatal. There is some false Faith in Saints, but it is not wholly such.

Oh consider these things! No Grace, What no Grace? I say then no life, no God, no Spirit, no Christ, no Glory. Oh mourn here! See it now, that you may be humbled, and so saved. Else you will fall worse and worse still, *Jer.*3. 5,6.

Quest.
Answ.

SECT. VI.

HEnce see how far they fall short of saving Grace, that serve the Lord by fits and starts, and whose hearts follow after the Lord, and make much of the Lord only in good moods. Dying pangs are not eternal graces ; Withering Grace is flourishing and prosperous wickedness. If the Spirit of Grace in the Saints be of an eternal, constant nature ; that is not the Spirit of Grace which accompanies salvation, which is alive to day, but dead to morrow, which a man is full of to day, but quite empty of to morrow. Hence the Prophet cries out, *Hos.* 6.4,5. *Oh Ephraim what shall I do* ? What more means can I use for thy good ? Why, do we not get good by means ? Yes, but *thy goodnesse is like the morning dew*, soon lickt up by the Sun, *and like a cloud which passeth away*, which promiseth much, but is scattered again. The Lord knows not what to do with such men ; yet how many be there of such, that like *Jonas* Gourd, spring up for a time, and then die the next day, and they comfort themselves under the shadow thereof. That take them in their Moon, they are as good as you can wish, more than men, but out of it, they are bruit beasts, not men. Whatever is in a godly man, the likeness and similitude of it is for a time in an Hypocrite. Would you have earnest prayer for a blessing ? look upon *Esau*, he *seeks for it with tears*, and mourns for it for a time. Would you have following the means, and that the most powerful and searching, and joy in it also ? See *John* 5.35. *What went they out into the wildernesse to see* ? a Prophet, a burning and shining light, and rejoyced therein for a season. Would you have hazarding life for *Paul* and Ministry of the Gospel ? *Alexander* did thus for a time. Would you have people enter into Covenant with God ? Look upon the *Israelites, Deut.*29. with 31.16. *I know that after thy death this people will go a whoring*. Would you have thankfulnesse ? *Psal.* 106.13. *They sang his praise, they soon forgat the Lord.* And these Affections are for a time stronger than the Saints, like land-floods ; and because they be violent and strong, they last not long. But however, it argues a wretched false heart, *Psal.*78.37. *Their hearts were not right*, because *not stedfast in his Covenant.*

But what man is there but changeth ? What body so healthful, that is found alway in the same temper ? Do not the Saints find their hearts soon cold, their joy soon quencht, their affections soon spent ? This therefore will discourage them.

I answer to it two waies,

First, They sometimes deny the constancy of Grace, where constantly it is, (for the Spirit of Grace in us is like life, for 'tis eternal life. It's ever acting or remaining in the soul) and this they do by reason of many mistakes. As

1. They think the Grace of God in them perisheth, when the act ceaseth. Whereas a man may be weary of actions of life, where life remaineth, as in sick men. A man may have a rich treasure alway with him, yet not alway spend it. There is a gracious frame of heart which the Lord regards chiefly, which is before the act,& hence may be without it. The wheel doth not run that it may be round, but it is made round that it may run. Hence when the act of running ceaseth, the frame whereby its fit to run again, remaineth ; And this is *the Seed of God,* 1 John 3.9.

2. Many think the act of grace ceaseth, when it doth not act alway upon the same object ; as some think, because they have not the sence of Gods love alway, all grace is lost, when it may be there is sence of corruption at that time ; sometime God gives victory over temptation, it riseth again : Now the soul thinks the very act of grace ceaseth, when yet its now warring against the temptation ; sometime

time the Spirit of grace may lead a man to prayer and sadness, sometime to a mans calling and cheerfulness. The act of grace is small, its dominion large.

3. They think they are not constant, when they are not so at all times, as they are at some times: As a man thinks he is unconstant at prayer, because he is not all day upon his knees; not heavenly minded, because he is not all day long minding heavenly things: Whereas the Spirit should be ready so to do and be at all times, and in every worldly occasion to be sowing or reaping some spiritual good; yet 'tis not a season alway to be upon the Mount. Sometime *Moses* must come down to the camp. God requires every fit season for his special Worship, not every Particle of time.

4. Many think the power of Grace is ceased and taken away, when some special enlargements are: As a Christian shall find at some times, having special work to do, special miseries to go through, he hath special enlargements of the Spirit, of joy, courage, boldness with God, love and zeal. These lasting not, he thinks all is gone now. But look as it was with *Jonathan*, 1 Sam. 14.8. Then *he alone and his Armour-bearer went against an Host*, yet 1 Sam. 17.11. Against *Goliah* not a word. *Paul* to his death was a faithful and able Minister of the Gospel, though sometime his mouth stopped, and his heart straitned: The Ship may be going to the Harbour, though somtime greater, somtime lesser winds.

Secondly, But yet I confess there is much changeableness in the Saints, and unevenness in their course, and their Spirits are apt to grow weary and faint, otherwise they had no need to be exhorted not to be weary, and when they are lifted up, they soon sink down, *Heb.* 12.1. And hence question, Was there ever grace in this heart? But yet there is much difference between the unconstancy of the one and of the other, in three things:

1. An Hypocrites affections when they cease, they are raised in him again by some external Principles and Motives; but the Faithful when they have lost what they had, they recover it again by a new nature, an inward principle; which is an evidence there was the being of Grace all this while. Empty a Pond, it will never fill again till the Clouds above it poure down rain. Empty a Spring, though it sees no Clouds in the Heavens, yet it runs of it self, and will fill it self again. So when an Hypocrite is left dry and empty, if some clouds of displeasure, fears of death and hell come, he is filled; but a child of God when no fear of death or hell, yet many times somthing within begins to work, as in *David* Psal. 39.3. *While musing, the fire kindled*, the sence of sin, to lie out from God, to quench his Spirit, the Beauty of Grace, the Command of God, the honour of the Lord Jesus recovers him, *Heb.* 8.10. *Deut.* 5.29. They spake as largely as any could desire, yet their hearts were naught, because this came from no inward principle, but only from external fear. *When the Priests feet touch Jordan, the waters stand on heaps*; but *when they are passed through, they overflow all the Banks a*gain, according to their nature. So when the Word is preacht powerfully, and the Gospel with authority, and the Priests feet touch mens Consciences, and they come to make way for the Arke, for the Lord, men in fits fall down before the Lord against their natures; & for a Sabbath day men are as full of good purposes and hearts as may be, yet perish at last, *John* 8.30,31. *Many believed when they heard his Word*; but then *are you my Disciples, if you continue*. All Hypocrites pangs come from external principles; and hence take them away, their affections die. Sometime the novelty of a thing affects a man; the sight of shore is beautiful; at last when Manna proves dayly bread, 'tis loathed. At first Ministers feet are beautiful, they would pull out their right eyes for *Paul*, yet afterward cast him off. A *Pharaoh* in Thunder and fear of death, cries, *take away the Plague*. A man in affliction promiseth much; when 'tis past, his care to find out his sin, his seeking to be purged from his sin ceaseth. *Joash* is good while *Jehojada* lives. A

man is good in quickning company, but *when iniquity abounds, his love waxeth cold*; whereas when these fail, a holy heart grows better. That which makes the one to fall, makes the other to fear, and so to stand. A Conceit carries a man on, but when his Conceit is gone, he falls. Look as 'tis with dead men, they may have heat and colour, but 'tis from the fire; a living man may be cold, and his beauty gone, yet he comes to be hot again, not from external heat, but internal life within: He can get himself heat, as we say, so 'tis here. Or as 'tis with the Clock and the Sun, the one moves by Art, the other by nature.

2. Suppose there be some inward Spirit to raise their Affections, yet these graces arise in them without the destruction of the contrary Corruption. And so are like to *Moses* burning Bush, *the Bush burning, but yet not burnt.* And thus it was with *Balaam, suddenly the Spirit of God came upon him, and he saw the beauty of Jacobs Tents and blessed them* above all people in the world, yet his covetous, malicious heart against them was not consumed: We never read of *Balaams* mourning for want of the sight of their glory, and of love to their persons and posterity; but the graces of the Saints do arise from the dying of the contrary lust or corruption which they see and are sensible of; and hence the act of grace ceaseth sometimes, because 'tis opposed by corruption, yet the being of it remains in full power, though not in the exercise thereof, because 'tis in such a Subject where corruption is dying, not living; falling, not raigning. Christ dies, and so lives in his people; where Christ is indeed, there we are first buried with Christ, before we are raised by him. *Paul* could do great things for Christ, yet sometime is weak, because his strength arose from the sense of his own insufficiency to think a good thought. The Saints see great things but 'tis in such a way, as that they *that see not, might see,* Joh.9.39. *Paul* is sometime set at liberty from pricking temptations, yet he hath them sometimes that he may feel them, and so be raised again. Hence many people suddenly finde they love the people of God, and love the Lord, but never felt the contrary sin; suspect 'tis but a pang, as *Capernaum* was much affected, yet repented not.

3. The continuance of the risings of a Saint are life to him, they are his life; his coolings, and declinings, and decayings, death: But *è contra* to an Hypocrite, the continuance of his affections in Ordinances are deaths and burdens to him; the loss of them his liberty and life, wherein he allows himself.

As for example, Take an Hypocrite to prayer, he is affected for a time, but let him be long at it, he is like a Fish in a Feaver fit out of the water, *Mal.* 1.13. So for sanctifying the Sabbath, and being very strict, but stay long here 'tis death, 'tis burdensome to him; and hence we shall see his decays are his life, and that which makes him walk loosely is, sometime he repents and beleeves, and hath his Canonical set hours of prayer, and he thinks this is enough, and pleaseth himself with this, (who is constant?) But now take a childe of God when his heart is enlarged for the Lord, that is heaven; it is his food, and now he is in health, as *Paul* said, 1 Thes. 3.7, 8. *Now we live, if you continue stedfast*: So for others, so also with himself, *Prov.* 4. 22. and if it might be ever thus, then happy; and the thoughts of this sweetens heaven; but take away these, 'tis his death; and hence he groans to God for the removal of it, *Psal.* 119.4,5. What good doth Christ, mercies, Ordinances, heaven do me with such a heart? Be not discouraged you people of the Lord, nor encouraged you that are good only in your Moods, as the winde turns you; whatever love you have 'tis whorish, and whorish tears, if you follow the Lord and yet have your haunts, whatever service you do it is odious to God, to work all day for another Master, and twice a day come to the Lord for bread. Do you think the Lord likes this, to taste of his grace, and make a meal of your lusts?

SECT.

SECT. VII.

First, To them that are fallen to begin again, if God would but give you ears to hear, who like strange Eggs being put into the same nest where honest men have lived, there you have been hatcht up, and when you were young, there you kept your nest, and lived by crying and opening your mouth wide after the Lord, and the food of his Word. But now your wings are grown you have got some affections, some knowledge, some hope of mercy, and are hindred thereby to fly from God. Can that man be good whom Gods grace makes worse? And that flies from Gods Ordinances, and people, and private prayer ? Consider what thou hast done.

1. You bring an ill report and name upon God, *Jer.* 2. 5. *What iniquity have you found in me.* If a Country be well reported of, its no matter if some others bring an ill name on it, Wise men will not beleeve them : But for the searchers of *Canaan* to bring an ill report of *Canaan*, this is sad.

2. Thou hast lost all thy prayers, all thy profession, nay better never to have *known these wayes*, 2 *Pet.* 2. 21. then to forsake the Lord.

3. No mens misery is so great, *Jude* 13,14. *the blackness of darkness is for such.* Search your selves, you may secretly depart, when you are turning to the Lord; as a Snail round about the wheel, the wheel moves it, but it moves a contrary motion of its own from the wheel : Therefore begin again. Oh but will the Lord receive me? Who knows but he may ? And *heal your backslidings*, Hos. 14. Because fallen, return : I know not how. *Answ.* Take words : But the Lord may not regard us, *You shall grow like the Lilly, and be as firm as Lebanon.*

Let them that stand, take heed lest they fall, and you discover your hypocrisie to all the world, or be like the Hypocrites whose beauty soon fades. And here let me commend three things to you.

1. Take heed that there be not found in your hearts *a root of bitterness to grow up and choak you*, Hebr. 12.15. If your house be left empty, and yet one living lust left in it, seven Devils will enter again, *and your latter end will be worse then your beginning.* You do not know what hearts you have. Am I a dog, saith Hazael, ever to fall so ? Let there be a lust after any creature, you will finde the spirit of prayer die ; then to think them too long in the Word, then to forsake the assemblies of Saints, then when your lust is met with, to oppose men, Ministers, &c. One reigning lust will bring all into captivity to it self, it will slay some, and make others serviceable to defend it self, *Psal.* 106. 14,15.

2. Take heed of taking on you the profession of a Christian course without finding the rest, peace, joy, sweetness of such a course, *Prov.* 2. 10, 11. There is a satisfying pleasantness in promises, commands, Ordinances, you will never hold out else ; for where-ever the heart finds rest, there it will abide, and for want of that it dies. As in Creatures, if it had rest there, the soul would not be unquiet, if in God, it would never go to the creature. Some sweetness you may finde, but look to finde full rest ; as men do find some sweetness in creatures, and so in Ordinances ; yet being used to them, they grow weary of them, because they finde no God there, *no fulness of rest*, Hebr. 4. 11, 12. and go through all the world you shall never have it : Get all the terrors of Devils upon you, you will never stand by that ; consider therefore as 'tis in sin, there is the act, and there is the pleasure ; so in every Ordinance and Duty there is both. All Apostacy is from this, Ordinances are too burthensome unto men to be held unto.

3. Take heed you neglect not private prayer, build your houses fit for that purpose,

pose, though you sell some of your clothes ; you will for your Swine to lie in, and will you not to meet God in ? one hours meeting the Lord in private will quit your cost : And pray for this, do it least you do it in the woods, and desarts, and dens of the earth : So much strangeness from God, so much Apostacie ; Pray that you may hold out in this hour of Temptation, that you may with *David*, not *be forsaken, when gray-headed.*

Thus you see now the particular Difference between Wise and Foolish Virgins, and what is the ground of the acceptance of the one, and not of the other ? What then will be said ? Can it be, That there are no Graces in Saints : Or , That there is no Difference between the one , and the other ?

THE

THE
Second Part
OF THE
PARABLE.

CHAP. I.

Of Carnal Security in Virgin Churches.

Matth. 25. 5. *Whilst the Bridegroom tarried, they all slumbered and sleep.*

 N this Parable were noted two things;

First, The Churches preparation to meet Christ from verf. 1. to 5.

Secondly, The Bridegrooms coming out to meet them, from verf. 5. to 12.

In this second part, which now we are to open, three things are to be attended unto;

1. The delay of Chrifts coming, or the long-suffering of Christ before he come, verf. 5.

2. The preparation he makes for his coming, a little before it, from verfe 6. to verf. 10. by an awakening cry, which makes all the Virgins look about them.

3. The coming it self; where those that were ready, were with ioy let in; and those that were unready were with shame shut out.

1. *The*

1. *The delay of Christs coming.*

Whence note First, What happened in the interim of his delay, and that is *Carnal Security,* expressed and set out from the lowest and highest degree of it.
1. They *Slumbered ;* *i.e.* fell a nodding or winking, as the word most properly signifies. 2. They *Slept ;* *i.e.* now they were buried in their sleep, overcome by it.

Secondly, Upon whom these sleeps and slumbers fell ; and that is, *They All slumbered and slept ;* *i.e.* though for a time they were both awake, yet good and bad, wise and foolish fell into this senceless and stupid, dull and dead, sluggish and sleepy condition.

Observ. I. *That in the last days Carnal Security either is or will be the universal sin of Virgin Churches.*

Observ. II. *That Carnal Security falls by degrees upon the hearts of men.*

Observ. III. *That the spirit of sloath and security is the last sin that befals the people of God.*

Observ. IV. *That Christs tarrying from the Churches, is the general occasion of all security in the Churches ; or the not coming of the Bridegroom when the Saints expect him, is the general cause of that security which doth befall them.*

SECT. II.

Observ. I. **T**Hat in the last days Carnal Security either is or will be the universal sin of Virgin Churches : When the Churches are purged from the gross pollutions of the world , and Antichristian fornications and bondage, then either there is or will be general Security: For these Virgins , when they first made presession of their Virginity by their burning lamps, were for a time all awakened, but at last they all slumbered and slept : This is the temper of the body of the Churches.

Matth. 24. 38. *As it was in the days of Noah, so shall it be in the days of the coming of the Son of man.*

Luk. 18. 8. *When the Son of man cometh, shall he find faith in the earth ?* *i.e.* an awakening faith.

Hence the Lord forewarns his people of this, *Deut.* 6. 12. *When thou comest to such a land, beware lest thou forget the Lord thy God.*

Quest. *But what is this their general Security ?*

Answ. Look as it is in our ordinary sleep, so it is in this general Security : There are these six things in it.

1. A man forgets his business, his work he was about, or is to be exercised about ; so in a carnal security, men forget the Lord, his works, and his will ; that which we most think of while we be awake, we least think of indeed when we be asleep : Take a man awakened indeed, O then the worst remember the Lord and his Covenant, *Psal.* 78. 47. But when asleep, the Lord and his errand is least thought of ; and hence security is exprest by *forgetting God, Psal.* 50. 21. And hence *Jerusalems* security was in this, *they remembred not their latter end.*

2. A man in sleep fears no evill until it be upon him, awakening of him ; so this is another ingredient into carnal security, though sin lies upon them, they fear not till evil comes ; as *Josephs* brethren, though warning is given them, they fear not : Like them in the days of *Noah* and *Lot.* And hence *Job* 21. 9. *their houses are free from fear ;* the misery for the same sin is lighted upon another ; yet the secure soul fears not, as in *Belshazar, Dan.* 5. 22.

3. In sleep all the sences are bound up , the outward sences especially, the
eye

eye watcheth not, the ear hears not, the tongue tastes not, the body feels not; so this is an ingredient of carnal security, it binds up all the sences, as it did the Prophet *Jonah* his in the storm; when misery was upon him, he heard not, he saw not, he felt not; so when misery, outward or spiritual, is upon a man, he that had quick sences before, his eye sees not, watcheth not; Christians neglect their watchfulness for their friends, the Lord, and his Spirit, and coming, nor watch against their enemies that daily besiege them; the ear hears not the voice of the Ministry, the voyce of Providences, the voyce of the spirit within; the soul smels not, tastes not the sweet of any promise, any Ordinance, no nor of the grace of the Lord himself; hence it commends them nor; nay the soul feels nothing, no evil, no good the Lord doth him; that look as the Lord there said, *Isa.*29.9,10. *The Lord hath poured upon you a spirit of sleep, and hath closed your eyes*; so the Lord closeth up all the sences, that a man is now stupid, when he is fallen asleep in security.

4. In sleep there is a cessation from speaking and motion: there a man keeps silence and lies still; so in carnal security, the spirit of prayer is silent, *Isa* 64.7. *Psal.*32.1,2,3. *David* calls it a keeping of silence; *up, why sleepest thou? seek to thy God*, say the Mariners; indeed men may talk in their sleep, so men may pray in their deep security, yet not throughly awakened: And there is a lying still, no progress; so in carnal security the soul stands at a stay, goes not backward, grows not worse, but goes not forward; such a one is compared to the door on the hinge.

5. In sleep the sences being stupified, and motion ceased, a man falls a dreaming; some dreams he forgets, some he remembers, and in his sleep fully and firmly believes them; so in carnal security, now a mans mind dreams of that which is not, and of that which never shall be; a mans mind is grown vain, and full of fancies and dreams; those things which never entered into Gods thoughts, something a man dreams of the Lord that this is his will and mind, which is not; of the world, that it is a goodly thing; of things to come which shall never be.

6. In deep sleep, though a man be awakened, yet he presently is overcome by his sleep again; so that is another ingredient into spiritual slumber; sleepiness is predominant over his watchfulness; and thus it was with the Disciples in the garden, they slept; the Lord came once and twice, and awakens them, yet they slept till temptation surprized them; scarce any Christian so secure in the chambers of Christ, but he hath some knocks of conscience, some cries of the Ministry, some woundings from the Lord, and they do awake him, but yet he falls to sleep again.

SECT. III.

WE shall now shew the Reasons why Virgin Churches in the last days are or will be overcome by security.

First, Because that in Virgin Churches there are the strongest provocations to this sin: Which are chiefly three. *Reason.* 1.

1. Rest and places of peace, and freedom from hard bondage; *Jacob* may sleep with his stone under his head, but much more easily under his own Vine and Figtrees. A man may be secure in the times of trouble, but much more in times of peace, when we have our beds made soft for us, and easie pillows. Friends can boldly desire us to rest, where there is lodgings for us: The world thrusts us out of lodging: While the prick is at the breft the Nightingale awakes and sings, but when that is taken away it sleeps in the day. In times of

perfection

persecution *Paul* is preaching till midnight, and the Lord is remembred in the songs, and sighs, and prayers of the night-season; but in times of peace, peace like *Faets* milk and butter stupifies all the fences, though destruction be near; Hence *Deut.*6.12. *Then forget not the Lord.* Do you think that *Noah* in the Ark, when the waters swelled above the mountains, was secure? no, but when the waters ceased, and he had his Vineyard planted, now he sleeps in his drunkenness, because he knew not the strength of wine. In the Virgin-Church, where this sleep is, we suppose this freedom from evil.

2. Because there men are most free from inward pain; for where there is much grief and pain, there's no rest, though all the house about be still; but when the house is still, and the body well, now tis hard but there may be rest; Whiles the Christian doth live under Antichristian pollution, his Conscience hath no rest, and hence 'tis awake there; here (saith the soul) I want the Ordinances of God, Oh that I had them! Here I see sin and wickedness abounding, that my childe is like to be poisoned therewith; here are such and such superstitions that my Conscience cannot bear: Hence Conscience is kept waking. But in Virgin-Churches, where the house is swept of these, now Conscience is quiet and at rest; now I have got a Levite into my house, God is now blessing me, &c. Now Conscience hath laid down its burthen, it falls down to sleep; now they cry, *The Temple of the Lord,*&c.

3. Because in such Churches there is most aptitude in men to spiritual fulness, *viz.* plenty of the means; there is all the Ordinances; in this mountain, *Isa.*25.1. Gods feast is made, and fulness of spiritual gifts and graces, because they have now escaped the pollutions of the world, conquered the enmity of the world; now have come to a good measure of grace, and conquered the way of their enemies, got the better of them; hence, as the *Israelites* made peace with the *Canaanites,* not when they were too strong but too weak for them: So now the Soul comes to be at rest, to lay down its Warfare, and to yield to a truce, to a league to his lusts and distempers for a time. When men are kept short of food, now they awake; so when the Word of the Lord and his Ordinances be rare and precious, and hard to finde, now a Christian can trudge after them; but when men are full, now they desire rest; so 'tis here.

4. Because in Virgin-Churches, there men are most apt to be overtaken with weariness; A man that never walkt on in a holy way, may at first setting out delight in Christ; but after he hath done walking in it, now he is apt to faint; especially, if he sows much, and reaps for the present but little. And hence *Gal.* 6. 9. *You shall reap in due season, if you faint not:* Now in Virgin-Churches, these Virgins are such persons as have begun to make a profession, and have made a fair progress; O how difficult now is it not to be weary! it's strange to see what short spirits after the Lord, what large after the Creatures vve have.

Reason. 2. II. Because they are the more easily overcome by this sin, than by any other.

1. Because it's a sin which a man least foresees or fears: The Apostle saith, *They that are drunk, and that sleep, sleep in the nigh ;* andyet here men sleep in the open light; Why so? Men see it not, men know it not; sleep steals upon a man: It's lawful to sleep; carnal security arises chiefly from the use of lawful things, on which a mans heart and thoughts are spent; they eate, drank, gave in marriage, they could see no hurt therein. When a man is had before Councels, now a man fears to sin, he knows he shall be tempted unto sin; but when the Lord brings the shoulder from under such burdens, now to fear our Tables, our Beds, our Wives, our Children, our Callings, our Professions and the snares of these, Oh it is exceeding hard!

2. Because

2. Becaufe Security is fo fweet a fin ; O fleep is fweet ; meat is fweet, but men may be foon full of that ; but when fleep comes, many hours are little enough to entertain that : Some fins are fweet for a time, as a fhort meal and away ; but floth is a fweeter fin than any elfe befides. Let a Chriftian ask his heart, when he can take no content in Pots, or loofe company, or Queans, and can find none in the Lord, yet this will give him eafe, *viz.* his floth : When he is weary of the Wold, and of walking with God alfo, yet floth is his delight ; and hence he crys, *A little more flumbr and fleep, untill deftruction comes as an armed man :* When a man delights not in his Wife, Children, Riches, Honors, yet is he fometimes contentedly fwallowed up with his fleep and reft. Prov. 6. 9, 10

3. Becaufe Satan doth make his ftrongeft forces ready alway to bring a man firft into this fin ; becaufe this makes way for the entrance of all fin and mifery ; no people fo happy as the *Ifraelites,* while they were awakened and up with God ; no mifery could hurt them, *Jer.* 2.1, 2, 3. but when they forgot him, all mifery came in ; *While the ftrong man keeps the Palace, his goods be at peace ;* it's his care to keep men fecure and ftill.

SECT. IV.

Ufe. 1.

Et us therefore now examine whether this fin be not our fin in this Country, if it be not begun among us ; if we be not fleeping, yet are we not flumbering ? if we are not Virgin-Churches, why have we the name of it ? if we be Virgin-Churches, then make fearch if this be not our fin ; we have all our beds and lodgings provided, the Lord hath made them eafie to us ; We never looked for fuch days in *New-England,* the Lord hath freed us from the pain and anguifh of our Confciences ; we have Ordinances to the full, Sermons too long, and Lectures too many, and private meetings too frequent, a large profeffion many have made, but are you not yet weary ? if weary, not fleepy, not flumbering ? it may be on you before you are aware, and you not know it ; and when fo it is, it may be fo fweet that you may be loth to fee it, that fo you may forfake it. Let me knock again, is it not fo ? Let me come to every mans bed fide, and ask your confciences.

1. Have you not forgot your God, and forgot your work alfo ? the bufinefs for which you made this great undertaking ? *Pfal.* 106.12. When they were faved from the Sea they foon forgat the Lord : Hath not the Lord by a ftretched-out arm brought thee and thine through feas and dangers, and delivered you wonderfully ? are not all his kindneffes forgotten ? all your promifes forgotten ? When the Lord had brought the *Ifraelites* out of their captivity, and fome hopeful beginnings were, they came for the Temple ; the duft was precious, but Gods houfe did lie wafte, *Hag.* 1.5, 6. *Confider your ways ;* no man profpered fcarce in his eftate ; God did blow upon their corn becaufe they forgat their end. What was your end of coming hither ? the Ordinances of God, the prefence of God ; and oh one day there better than a thoufand elfewhere ; hath it been fo ? No, but as it is verf. 9. *Every man turns to his own houfe :* Every man for himfelf, to their own houfe, lot, accommodation, provifion for children ; and in the mean while the Lords houfe lies wafte, you build not up that, the Souls of thy Brethren in Church-fellowfhip, yea, of thy family are not built up ; the Lords houfe is defpifed now ; and it's like the Schools of the Prophets, and much more. Oh thought we, if we had fuch priviledges, how would we improve them ? but when we have them, have we the fame thoughts ? do we not forget them, like men that come to a place for gold, and find it not

wichout

without digging, they fall to lade their ship with wood or coal, that which it will bear.

2. Have we not shaken off all fear almost of sin and misery? *Go to the Ant thou sluggard, she fears and provides against a winter* : Do not men think that we have fled too far for the cross to finde us, or as if the Temple of the Lord was such a Den as no Foxes or Wolves could follow us into? especially when there are causes of fear, when War is proclaimed, and the causes known, and yet they are never feared : How many men have the hand-writing of death in their Consciences against them! this they confess is naught, they have lived careless, sluggish, and have had some sense of it, yet no awakening fear of the terror of the Lord; when a Prince is nigh us, now to commit a little lewdness is great wickedness: where is the man that trembles at the nearness of God to us? when a breach is made, then fear enemies. Divisions and breaches go before falls of Churches; where is that spirit of *Jehosaphat*, that feared and proclaimed a fast? When God hath begun to smite, what cause is there to fear! we have been hurt, and yet not laid it to heart; the Lion roars, shall not the people fear? I believe we should not have had those Pequot furies upon us, but God saw we began to sleep: Where is the man that, with *Paul*, knows the terror of the Lord, and hence perswades men? when the enemy is ever about us, there is always cause of fear, and yet we fear but now and then.

3. Are not our sences bound up? look upon men in their fields and conversings, buyings and sellings; where is a daily, weekly watchfulness over our thoughts and tongues? Look to mens closets, do men there call themselves to account? can they finde leisure or need of it? are not mens eyes closed up, that the glory of God in the Scripture is a sealed thing? Men have eyes but see not; are not mens ears sealed up? Some Sermons men can sleep them out; mans voyce is heard, but not the voyce of the Son of God: Oh how many men are there that become quite Sermon-proof now adays! Are not men blockish, dull, senceless, heavy under all means! they taste not, smell not, whereas elsewhere, O how lively and spiritual are they!

4. Is not the spirit of Prayer, that lamp going out in the Church of God? the blessedness of all flourishing Plantations in the world began by means of that, and shall not continue but as it continues; and if ever cause to seek for prosperity of Plantations, these have need. If God should take away this generation of Magistracy and Ministery, what would this despised Country do? and what would become of your children? then no Schools for them, when no Gospel left among them; then every mans sword shall be against his brother, and God spreading the place with darkness, which through his presence is made light; what little hope of a happy generation after us, when many among us scarce know how to teach their children manners? How apt are we, like to those *Asian* Churches, to fall into those very sins which overwhelmed them, and ruined them? how many fall off, and in time break forth, that it would make men sick to hear of their pranks? what place more open to temptations of persecution and worldly delusion? go up and down the Plantations, where is the man that lays things to heart? who hath the condition of the Country written upon his heart, and presenting it before the Lord, rather than his own good? Oh men are silent because asleep! How do sins run thorough men as water thorough a mill, and men regard it not? what means, what deliverances have we had! but oh what little thankfulness? 2. Do we make progress; nay, is not our shadow gone back? *I sleep, but my heart waketh*; it should be so, but it is not so indeed.

5. Have we not fallen a dreaming here? what meaneth else the delusions of mens brains? what a swarm of strange opinions, which (like flies) have
gone

gone to the fores of mens heads and hearts, and thefe are believed alfo? and more dreams men have that are never fpoken; every man hath fome drunken conceit that rocks him afleep; dreams are quite contrary to the truths. What meaneth thefe, if men are not fleeping? Firft, Drunken dreams of the world. Secondly, golden dreams of grace; that thefe things advance grace which indeed deftroy grace; that there is no grace in the Saints, no grace in Chrift, no humane Nature, no promife to evidence grace; no Law to be a Rule to them that have received grace: Who would think that ever any fhould fo fall by a fimple woman? But if this be not general; yet look how do men begin to dream concerning the world? fcarce a man but finds want, or is well; if he wants, Oh then, if I had fuch a lot about me, fuch an eftate, how well then were I? and *è contra*, They that have it, and now they take their reft: *Take heed*, faith the Lord, *your hearts be not overcome with cares*; So fay I to you.

6. Doth not the Lord oft awaken us, yet we fall to fleep again? the Lord awakened us by the Pequot Hornet, yet what ufe is there made of that? doth not the Lord oft meet us in an Ordinance, but he is foon loft and gone again? Is there a man that hath not had his crofs fince he came hither, as lofs in cattel and eftate, a dear Husband, Childe, Wife dead? a fore and fharp ficknefs, &c. he hath been exercifed with, &c. but do we not fleep ftill? if it be not thus, it will come; fear it for time to come; but if it be thus, then I fay no more, but know it, you are in your enemies hand; and in fuch an enemies hand, that if you mourn not under it, will open the door either to the entrance of fome grofs fin and temptation, or for fome heavy and fudden wrath. It's fufficient for me this day to fhew you where your hurt lyeth.

SECT. V.

HEnce fee the reafon why men are worfe in Virgin-Churches, than in polluted places, and why it is fo generally; Becaufe here are more temptations to make them all flumber and fleep; here their beds are made foft, here the ftorms are paft, here they are under the fhadow, and out of the fun, and fecurity opens the door for an enemy: No wonder if the City be taken though never fo ftrong, if it grow once fecure: no wonder if the world be entred, and men are grown more worldly; and if Satan be entred, and men grow more paffionate than ever before; no wonder a mans work be neglected, if he be afleep, Ordinances more flighted than ever before: Never fhall you fee Security fall upon a man alone, but it brings its train with it; when the Husbandmen fleep, tares will be fown, and when the Difciples fleep, temptations will enter; This is that which the Lord teftifies of his people, *Jer.2.2,3,4.* I remember what thou didft in times of ftreights, in a land not fown; every one that touched you did offend; but in the feventh and eighth verfes, when brought to a plentiful Country, they did not fo much as fay, Where is the Lord that hath done this for us? But yet the Lord queftions his people for this, *what iniquity have you found in me?* which queftion you cannot anfwer without grief here, or confufion another day. You that are the Lords, often have heard this complaint (for this may be your condition as well as *Noah's* and *Lot's*) but now fee the caufe of it, how hard to awake on hour? how hard to walk with God one day? fhort awakenings you have, but long fleeps (this may be your condition for a time) but you cannot continue fo for ever if you are the Lords. But if you do continue fo, efpecially without bemoaning this unto the Lord, 'tis a queftion whether ever there was that oyl in your

veffel

veſſel, which others have, when not only a mans acts grow worſe, but the very ſpirit of a man degenerates; when not only the leaves of the Vine fall, but the Vine it ſelf groweth degenerate, and hence continueth ſo; this is a ſore evidence of a woful ſtate; *Jer.2.20,21.When the yoke was upon thy neck, thou ſaidſt, Thou wolſt not tranſgreſs; but the Lord hath broken thy bands; and now thou art become a ſtrange Vine:* Remember, it will be an heavy indictment againſt thee, to be good in *Meſhech*, but baſe in *Sion*; to be then worſt when the Lord is beſt.

Uſe 3. Hence ſee one reaſon why the Lord purſueth many a Soul with inward terrors and outward ſorrows. Thoſe that are faſt aſleep, becauſe ſoft ſpeechs cannot awaken them, hence we lay our hands upon them, and ſometimes knock them, becauſe this is the way to awaken them, and then they hear; ſo the Word and Spirit ſpeak to a man, but ſuch ſoft ſtill winds rock them aſleep rather than awaken them; hence the Lord layeth his iron hands upon a man, and knocks by blows, and now when affliction is upon you, now you can hear; When as the winds and water were ready to tear the ſhip in pieces, now they enquire, Why were they ſent? *And the lot fell upon Jonah*, who was then ſleeping; it is eaſie to awaken out of natural ſleep, but very hard out of ſpiritual ſecurity: All the terrors of God on *Jonah* within and without are little enough; but at laſt he could hear, and run on his errand. *Pſal.30.6,7.* Why did God hide his face from *David*? *he ſaid in proſperity he ſhould not be moved*; this was the reaſon of it; the Lord ſees you have need of it; ſeldom ſhall one ſee an awakening Chriſtian without inward temptations and terrors, or outward ſorrows: Oh conſider then if the Lord do meet with thee! conſider thy own ſecurity thou haſt been in, or art apt to fall into! This is the ſin you muſt enquire after and finde out; and do not account it hard, though long, though bitter; for never greater miſery than for the Lord to ſay *Sleep on*; it is one of the heavieſt Judgements, for the Lord to let a man go on in a ſecure condition without blows; mark therefore unto the end of thoſe blows, to be throughly awakend by them: For ſometimes when the Lord ſends them, a man (if they be not very bitter, if he hath any reſt) lays them not to heart, *Iſa.42.25. Fire burnt about him*; and in this Country I know not what curſe befalls men; peace makes men ſecure, and ſorrow makes men diſcontented, and ſunk, and diſcouraged, which may be for a fit in a Saint; but to continue ſo, this is that *Ahab*: Oh when as thou feeleſt the blow, look now that thou doſt awaken, and be thankſull for it, that you met with that you did never reckon upon, *viz.* to be frighted out of ſecurity thereby.

SECT. VI.

Uſe 4.

Of *Exhortation*, TO watch over one another, by *exhorting one another while it is called to day*, Heb.3.13. Let both the Watchmen and Members of Churches do this; for this is one means appointed by the Lord to preſerve the ſoul from ſleeping, 1 *Theſ.5.1,5,6. Exhorting one another*; as it is in Cities, when the Watch is apt to ſleep, they have their companies that are paſſing up and down the walls the greateſt part of the night, and ſo they are kept waking; and we ſhall finde, that as it is in a Town where men are all aſleep, one Bell-man, one waking Chriſtian will keep life, and ſpirit, and the power of godlineſs in many; and when he ſleeps, all are faſt. Nothing in the world brings ſecurity ſooner upon men than ſleepy company: Officers of Churches watch not over members, nor they one over another, exhorting

and

and crying one unto another to their work, while it is called to day: Oh then let every man get up, and fall to this work of mutual exhorting! go and visit one another, go and speak oft to one another; and if thou be a childe of the light, see that thou endure not thy fellow servants to sleep in the open day in one duty or another. Know, if God stirs thee, thou wilt awaken others, 2 *Cor. 5. 10. We knowing the terrors of the Lord perswade men.*

2. Consider thy labor cannot be in vain here; the best mettalled horse needs spurs; others are asleep.

You will say if I knew such a sin I would speak, but I dare not.

Answ. It is the case of all the Virgins, they have need of it, *Jude* 23. *Some save with fear, pulling them out of the fire,* Matth. 3.

3. Consider this is one part of your Warfare, to keep your watch whereby you may be made conquerors; You complain you have many sins and temptations arising and prevailing; never do they usually prevail, but when you are secure; first the Watch is taken, and then the City is suddenly taken; now look as *Paul, 2 Tim. 4. 6, 7. he hath finished his course, and fought his fight, and now expects the crown;* how can you end your days in peace, that cannot in some measure finde and feel this: The Church is the City of the living God, this is taken, and every man in it, unless you be watchful, and *exhort one another daily, while it is called to day:* And that I may not speak in the clouds,

4. Their sin will be yours.

First, Labor to know the state of thy Brethren whom thou art to exhort; what their sleepy neglects be, and sins are; it may be thou hast known one hath been very humble, tender, affected under Ordinances, made many fair shews and promises of growing, and thriving, and sensibly complaining of his own vileness, and now he is in a silent sleep; Dost thou know this, and wilt not speak a word to awaken him, for whom Christ shed his blood, who it may be will do thee as good a turn, and make many a prayer for thee? *Barnabas when he saw the grace of God, exhorted them with full purpose of heart to cleave unto him;* much more should you when you see grace dying, 2 *Thess. 2. 11. Paul* heard that some were idle, them he exhorts to work; what good might one word do?   *Acts 11. 23.*

Secondly, if you do not know, enquire with a spirit of much love, how it is with them; as *David* of his Brethren when they were gone into the fields; do you not decline, do you not stand still? how have you found your heart since last Sermon, Sabbath, Fast, Affliction? have you got any ground against that sin you complained of last year? &c. Suppose you cannot do this to all, yet why not to some? Suppose you have no other place than when you meet them in the fields, do it there, *Jude* 20. *Build up your selves,* &c. Now here a man must know the height, how high they are built already, how can they lay their stones else? It is one of the heavey curses of God upon the Idol Shepherd, *He shall not visit the hidden, nor seek the young,* Zach. 11. 16.   *1 Sam. 17. 16.*
Christians are to give up accounts one to another of their gains and losses.

Thirdly, If thou knowest nothing from them, then relate thy own condition, this is a most lovely provocation, and exhortation unto another frame; for one great cause that hardeneth men in their security, is because they see no such living Christianity in the world: But when they do, *now* (Zach. 8.) *many shall take hold of the skirt of a Jew, for they shall say God is with you; Agrippa* was almost perswaded and awakened when he heard *Paul* relate his conversion; although there be many impostors in the world that do so. Tell me, are all things in peace with you? the Devil is in you then: What? hast no temptations? yet many; Dost not observe how they prevail? yes; dost never get strength against them? yes; hast no good days after them? yes, much peace and life, and presence of God! Hath the Lord given these talents to

thee

thee to be hid in a Napkin, this treasure to keep and not to spend? who knows but that the speaking of these may awaken others? these temptations, and this condition is mine, these sins I find he makes a great matter of them; Lord what will become of me that am hardned under them? this peace they finde, my Soul is a stranger to it; Conscience will work thus: Women should speak thus to women, and men to men; others were provoked by the example of the *Corinthians*, to help others; so there is a provoking power here.

Fourthly, If this prevail not, speak often to them, of the sins of others; in condemning others you condemn them; and this will make them look about them; view the fields, and shew them the tares that are grown up by security; and laying down these sins you strike at the root of theirs; It may be, you cannot tell certainly, *Acts* 2. 40. The Lord made this one means to awaken a *Belshazzar*, *Dan.*5.22. God turned thy Father into a beast, &c. to live in the woods, yet thou humbledst not thy self, &c. How many Professors doth God deal so withal?

Fifthly, Enter into Covenant and brotherly promise to exhort one another, as *David* and *Jonathan*; If any hurt be toward *David*, *Jonathan* will speak of it, 1 *Sam.*20. Some may in Church-fellowship be more nearly knit than others, to call one another to account, to tell one another their fears, to know of one another their progress. Canst not give an account to man? how wilt thou give an account to God of it? I am perswaded many a man lies smoothered to death by means of this. Canst not come to the light of a candle? Oh how then canst thou appear before the light of the Sun.

Sixthly, Provoke one another to frequency in Ordinances, *Heb.*10.23,24. and therein consider one another; dost see thy Brother in doubts or complaints? call him to pray with thee; dost see things go ill in Churches, and men bite the bit? call to fasting and prayer, three or four together, as *Paul*, when he saw the ship sinking, then he exhorted them, *Act.*27.22. Especially when you see danger near mens hearts, ready to be lost in the World: In these times suppose only two, or three, or four should go and pray one half hour together, and tell one another their wants, now help here; in our times it hath been so, one living Christian helps others dying.

But yet how is this neglected, as if men were resolved not only to dye sleeping themselves but to let others sleep also? No, you will say, not my self; yet it may be in your family it is so, and before the Lord.

What art alive to God and family, where thou canst do but little common good, and art dead to thy Brother? it is made a sad sign of a man forsaken of God, if when he thinks he shall sleep his last, and be damned himself, yet he would have others damned also. Tell me, would you have all *New England* lye in security as well as your selves? No! do you not desire it when you use not the means that prevent it; and that is mutual exhortation; Oh therefore do it; Ministers may preach, and every man sleep still, unless some awake and rouse up the rest (as some, when others are abed and fast asleep) that lye a dreaming: Some there be, that though Doomsday were to morrow, they would sleep; Oh therefore let me perswade some one or two to fall to his work, lest their security prove your undoing; therefore speak oft one to another, forsake not your assembling, visit one another, pray one for another, warning one another, that you may awake with the Lord one hour.

SECT.

SECT. VII.

Et every man not only exhort his brother, but fear this himfelf; You have a race to run, many enemies to conquer, fleep not left you fall fhort, fleep not left you be taken captive: left in exhorting others, your felves proves Reprobates: I will not tell you what I fear, but *Luk.* 21. take heed left your hearts be overcome; be not drunk with fome delight, be not filled with vain cares; Hence, prevent it, as *Noah moved with fear made an Ark.*

Firft, Set a high price upon thofe awakenings and revivings of heart that God fometimes giveth you; I am fure you finde thefe fometimes. A man that hath nothing to lofe, will fleep with his doors open in the night; when a man hath a treafure he will be watchful to keep it; all fecurity comes from an undervaluing of the Spirit of grace, and its prefence among us, *Prov.* 4. 13. keep her, for it is thy life; and when it is loft, what are you but dead?

Secondly, Confider thy continual danger; if enemies be at the gates, all the Town is watching; one would not think the depth of fecurity that is in a carelefs heart, *Pfal.* 30. 6. *I faid I fhould never be moved;* he had good days and a thankful heart; then God did hide his face: A man would think *Sampfon* fhould awake when the Philiftines are upon him; but here Devils be upon thee, 1 *Pet.* 5. 10. If all be well now, yet remember evil days; would you know when? even then when men fay peace.

Thirdly, Know the work you have to do, and make it your main bufinefs; when men have weighty bufinefs of the world in hand, they cannot fleep in their beds; and as the wicked, *Prov.* 4. 16. *They fleep not without doing mifchief;* and fo 'tis their main work.

Fourthly, Call thy felf to account daily, let not thy Soul long go on without reflecting, What do I do? Harts and Hawks kept from fleep lofe their wildenefs, but they muft be conftantly tended and kept watching: So confider the account you muft give to God, 2 *Cor.* 5. 9. with 11. Hence *Hag.* 1. 5. Sins were upon them, and they repented not; miferies, and thofe were not removed; becaufe they confidered not their ways, efpecially before the great Tribunal of God. I am perfwaded the reafon why men walk in their fleep, and go dreaming up and down the world, is this, they confider not, nor reflect upon themfelves to any purpofe; what do I? whether go I? no Sermons awaken, you confider not of them.

CHAP.

CHAP. II.

Carnal Security comes by Degrees.

SECT. I.

*Observati-
on 2.*

Hat *Carnal Security falls upon the hearts of all men by degrees*; for all the Virgins here firſt ſlumbered before they ſlept; they firſt fall a winking and nodding (as the word ſignifies) ſhort ſleeps, and then ſtartle, and awake again, before they fall aſleep for a longer time: a Chriſtian is a ſlumbering Chriſtian before he is a ſleeping Chriſtian.

The truth of this may be ſeen not only in theſe Virgins, but alſo in other Examples of ſecurity in the Scripture : As the old World, *Gen.6.2. They ſaw the Daughters of men,* they let their eyes wander, and their hearts luſt.

2. Then *they took them Wives* for to ſolace their hearts in, to pleaſe themſelves only, and not the Lord; *they ate, drank, gave in marriage*; they came not to that height of wickedneſs, to commit Adultery, or to live in Whoredom.

3. Then *they became fleſhly and ſenſual*; ſpiritual things are ſout of taſte and reliſh with them.

4. *Noah* Preacheth, and they ſlight him; he condemns them, and they regard not him.

5. Then God ſets a time; no ſtronger means to awaken than this; and yet they go on; and now they were come to their height.

Secondly, The *Iſraelites. Deut.8.12.* 1. They *ate and grew full*; here is firſt ſpiritual fulneſs. 2. *Bleſſing themſelves,* in their eſtates, herds, flocks. 3. Then *proud in heart*, verſ.14. 4. Then *they forget the Lord,* and all that ever he did for them, verſ.14. 5. Then men aſcribe all which they have to themſelves and creatures, verſ.17. though onely in their heart. 6. Then *cleave to other gods*, verſ.19. and here lye ſo faſt aſleep, till *plagues came down upon them.*

Solomon ſaw the ſluggards Garden over-grown; now as it is in fields, the weeds do not over-grow all the ground in one day, but they are a long time a growing, but by degrees they overgrow all, that when he awakes (all is ſo over-grown) he knows not where to begin : So it is here.

Be ſober, be vigilant; ſecurity is a kind of ſpiritual drunkenneſs; a man is not for that time his own man, not a ſober man; now this is by frequent and often ſipping; a man he is half gone firſt, and then he is wholly gone; he hath not preſently drunk out all his ſences, not dead drunk; So it is here.

SECT. II.

IN regard of the quickness and power of the life of Conscience; whether it be a natural Conscience awakened, or a spiritual Conscience awakened; it is with Conscience as it is with a prisoner in a house; though all in the house sleep, yet he is bound, he cannot, and hence he is speaking, and will awaken the house; so Conscience hath known, These sins I have watched against, and been humbled for, these duties I have done; but now, Now saith Conscience, you neglect them, now you are worse, now fallen; now a man startles, especially when one stands at the door, and calls to Conscience it will awaken; so when there is a word to call, Conscience will be crying ever and anon within, especially when any hope or leisure to speak with any as they pass by; so it will take men sometimes in their fields, and talk with them, and chide them: Security grows up easily, but the awakening light of conscience cannot be soon done out in any man; hence sometimes a man sleeps, and then awakens again; Hence *Rom.* 2.15. Though they had many sins, yet it would accuse and excuse; as those that are come out of their own Country to dwell in another, or from a great estate in a mean condition, they cannot easily forget their friends and relations, but in time it wears away, *Prov.* 20.27. Conscience is Gods candle, it will shine, and is not easily put out.

2. Because the Lord doth never depart from men but by degrees, and hence security falls upon men by degrees; when God is near unto men, then usually they be awakened, as the *Israelites* before the Mount. Now the Lord to shew the riches of his patience and long suffering, he will not depart suddenly, and leave the Soul in a dead and sluggish estate. And hence the Cherubims glory *Ezek.* 9. 10,11. departed by degrees. *Isa.* 29. 10. with 13. God doth not so deal, as presently to close their eyes quite up, but they are awakened to draw nigh to God with their lips, which is of God, and then the Lord closeth up their eyes; never can a man be cast into a deep sleep, till the Lord saith Sleep on, or till God close his eyes; and that he doth not presently; as to the Disciples he comes a second and third time.

3. Because this is the most ready way and method for sin and Satan to bring the Soul into a deep sleep, nay, to make them give themselves to sleep, which is that he aims at; look as it is with those that sell things, their scope is not to put off their commodities, but to put them off so as they may have money or moneys worth for them; so it is here, the scope of Satan is not only to bring men into security, to give them ease and peace, *Luk.* 11.21. but to have his money, that the Soul may give it self to it: Now as it is in buying of Fruits, Sugars, Wines or Strong-waters, they will not buy all presently, nor buy before they see and taste, they know not whether tis good or no, or whether they shall need it at all or no: So here, to lie in such a secure condition, as to neglect all means, to be hardned after all sins, this Satan will not offer, nor will men buy, or give themselves to this, they know not whether this be good or no, less will serve them; and hence taste first a little slumber and sleep, and so call for a little and a little more until a man is a beggar, *Prov.* 6. 10. as at first in Paradise; first look, then taste, then eat; so here.

SECT. III.

DO not think you are out of a state of carnal security, because you have many times some quickenings and revivings of heart, because they may
be

be onely awakenings between thy flumbers, which like flaſhes ſuddenly come and ſuddenly go again, which make thee ſtartle, and rub thy eyes, and ſtir up thy ſelf, but down you fall again; whereever life is in a Chriſtian, it is ever acting for ſpiritual ends; a man will awaken firſt with God in the morning, and go firſt to him in prayer (extraordinary occaſions not preventing) and he will go from his prayer to his work, not as doing his own work, but as doing the Lords work, howing, plowing, ſowing for him, &c. Now when the life of Chriſt doth not act in men, and act men, it is either becauſe there is no life at all, but onely the awakening of Conſcience which ſoon dieth, or elſe that living Chriſtian ſlumbereth at leaſt then; ſlumber is upon thee though ſleep is not; make it out elſe any other way.

Object. *If ſo (you will ſay) who is not then ſleeping?*

Anſw. Take *Lot* whilſt vexed with the *Sodomites*, he awakens; take *Paul* while toſſed up and down in diſgraces and reproaches, his inward man is renewed day by day, though the outward man die. The Saints have ſome kinde of ſleeps when they are at their beſt; but theſe are ſick ſleeps; but thine are ſweet ſleeps to thee. I know Chriſt may ſay to his Diſciples, *Watch and pray, temptations may be near*, but their eyes may be heavy; the Spirit may be willing, the fleſh weak; and that it is infinite mercy the Lord will awaken them, a firſt and a ſecond time it may be by Sabbath awakenings, &c. Many cannot tell what to make of themſelves, becauſe of their drowlineſs and Goſpel-ſlumber: Methinks this may break thy heart, Cannot you awaken one hour? know therefore your ſin; It is a hard thing to be fully awakened, to have all heavineſs to ſleep taken away; the Lord hath taken you here alone to himſelf, you do by fits watch and pray, but it is onely as men aſleep, not awake: The Son of man is betrayed, Chriſt, and Goſpel, and Ordinances; and can you find in your heart now to ſleep?

Uſe 2.

Oh therefore ſhake off your ſlumbers and ſhort ſleeps, leſt you fall to ſleep; and for ſleeping, be awakened by ſome direful blow; Look upon thoſe men *Iſa.29.10. God hath cloſed their eyes*, that is a fearful thing; look upon many profeſſors, all their ſavor, and heart, and life is gone almoſt, and they know not that they be aſleep, nor all means cannot awaken them, or unſeal their minds again; God knows how far you may fall, if you give way to a little; eſpecially if God takes away Miniſters from you, and that the Elders that have known the works of God be gathered to their Fathers; eſpecially if you know it, and yet go on in your ſlumbers; if you will not awaken when God crys and calls, you ſhall ſlumber and ſleep; like the Smiths dog, the harder the Maſter ſtrikes, the faſter the dog ſleeps, being uſed to it. I knew a man of great eſtate, oft quickned by the Word; but he loſt all life and heat again, and he prayed, and deſired the Lord to keep him, and yet decayed, but he could not tell the reaſon thereof; at laſt the Word began to grow common, and he ſlept there alſo; Conſcience told him there was ſome evil toward him which he feared, yet ſtill ſlept, and continued ſo; notwithſtanding his fears would thus awaken him oft; at laſt an affliction came, he regarded not that, but was impatient and froward under it, till at laſt all he had was gone, and then he looked about him; when his houſe was burnt, he was aſleep; he prayed, but loſt all by ſleeping when he ſhould watch; ſo ſecurity grew upon him; and hence, no wonder miſery met him: Oh! take heed therefore of giving way, liberty, or toleration to a ſleeping profeſſion, and your ſlumbering Religion: as men will not tolerate Ceremonies, becauſe they are the fruitful ſeed of the body of Popery; ſo here, &c.

SECT. IV.

SECT. IV.

Queſt. **W**Hat are the firſt degrees of this ſpiritual ſlumber?

Anſw. 1. When men have loſt the ſatisfying ſenſe of the bleſſed face and love of God; when hypocrites have loſt the imaginary ſight of it, and Saints the real enjoyment of it, *Pſal.* 17. *ult. I ſhall be ſatisfied when I awake with thine image*; ſleep firſt ſhews it ſelf in cloſing up of a mans eyes that he ſeeth not any thing about him; hence, ſomething elſe contents, and muſt do it when you feed not daily on the Lords love; and when that, then vain cares and thoughts (*Luk.* 21. 34.) overcome a man, and then he groweth a very worldling, as if he had hope of no other portion; hence no mind after ſpiritual good things; hence he ſleeps at Sermons, hence he falls out into paſſion, and diſcontent with his preſent condition, nay, with every other thing when any croſs comes: Becauſe theſe things are ſweet to you, and God is not, when diſcontented; the Lord keep my ſoul from entring into thy ſecrets; Oh conſider it if you have had ſence of the Lords love in Sacraments! and ſome new doubts ariſe, and you are not ſatisfied with it; now look to your ſelves; it is impoſſible a Chriſtian ſhould do any work without reſt. Now as bodily feeding cauſeth reſt, ſo doth ſpiritual feeding, ſpiritual reſt; feed and reſt here, and it will make you fall to your work; feed not here, reſt not here, and you will in ſomething elſe; and carnal reſt will bring carnal negleſt.

2. When men have loſt all fear of the wrath to come, and the terror of God another day; not always a fear that I ſhall bear, but a dreadful apprehenſion what it is. Many Chriſtians loſe the ſenſe of Gods love, yet the Lord keeps them in the ſenſe of his anger, and ſo they are awake; but when both are gone, or this is gone, then there is and cannot but be the firſt ſecurity. For as it is with children, when their eyes are open to ſee and conſider the things of the world, now they are begun to be awakned; I never look upon a Chriſtian fully awakened till now, that the Lord lets him ſee the things of another world; and when this is loſt he begins to ſleep, 2 *Cor.* 5. 9. with 11. 2 *Pet.* 3. 11, 12. Some ſecurelings thought all things were paſt; *No* (ſaith he) *there is a time a coming when all things ſhall be diſſolved; what manner of perſons then ſhould we be!* Hence this being loſt, men fear not ſin, men prize not mercy, men wonder not if ever they eſcape; hence men live and hang between doubt and fear, never make ſure, becauſe they know not what Gods wrath is: Nay, laſtly, hence nothing awakens them, that though they know their miſery, yet they will go on (the higheſt degree of ſpiritual ſecurity) Oh then keep theſe thoughts awake! what it is to be forſaken of God! what it is to grapple with him!

3. When men have loſt their foreſight, and hence provide not againſt an evil day; when Chriſtians keep their profeſſion, and go on ſweetly in their courſe, but to lay up for after-claps, that they do not, when Chriſtians like Graſshoppers ſing all the ſummer, but what have they to live upon in the winter time? the Ant can learn them that, *Prov.* 6. 6. *Go to the Ant thou ſluggard, that provideth her meat in the ſummer*; the Ant by a ſecret inſtinct (though ſimple and little) conſidereth there will be a winter, and that ſummer is her gathering time; ſo a Chriſtian, if awakned (though ſimple) will be taught to do ſomething which may ſerve him, not only now, but hereafter alſo: when men in times of peace and enjoyment of Ordinances never fear, muchleſs provide for that time, that all theſe treaſures ſhall be taken away and carried to the King of *Babel, Iſa.* 39. when men in their life time think not of

setting

setting the house and heart in order before the evil day, when men are not that now which they would wish themselves to be another day, when me lay not up treasures of tears and prayers in heaven, nor are provident for eternity, nor think this will be my peace, nay my glory another day, though I lose now; men will lay up treasures on earth, and provide for themselves and theirs; hence their hearts are lost here, and lay in nothing spiritual for the future, *Prov.*10.5. he that gathereth in harvest doth right (but a sluggard will not) his heart and mind is taken up to provide this and that for future; and hence 'tis that the Christian is full of sorrow and tears in times of peace; but when the day of trouble comes, he can lift up his head (now redemption draws nigh) when another in times of trouble hath most terrors, because the one was not laying up against another day, as the other did.

4. When men go to prayer without receiving any answer, now a man begins to slumber, *Prov.*13.4. men that are fast asleep speak not all, but when awake a little they speak a little, and then sleep, and then awake, and sleep again; so men pray and sleep again; it is a deep slumber also when men shall beg for bread and money, and then fall asleep constantly, and so lie down satisfied: Oh take heed of this! Hence comes

 First, Snarling at God.
 Secondly, Heartlesness to the duty.
 Thirdly, Formality in it.
 Fourthly, Prophaness of course at last.

5. When men do gain something from the Lord in the use of means, but now stand still they go no further; they lose not what they had, but they gain no more; they grow not, *Matth.*25,26. *Thou evil and slothful servant*; that hid his talent, and did not imploy it; and here is usually the beginning of a mans fall, when (like one in a journey) he goes not forward or backward, but stands still, and so falls, *Prov.*18.9.

6. When men do duties that are easie, but when any difficulty is in them, now they fall down asleep, *Prov.*20.4. and 12.27. and hence beg the sweet and gain of Christianity: it's sown in difficult duties; when the Soul denies it self most: But when men not breaking through the difficulty finde not the sweet of it, Lord! what a tattered profession is there, that men come to be the shame of Christ, not his glory! It's easie to pray, and outwardly to fast, but yet to have a whole heart in the work is hard: it is easie to cleave to the Lord when quickened; but when God forsakes you, now more than ever to cleave to him, is difficult.

7. When men fear not the danger of little sins; they are not asleep, yet so as not to fear great sins; but in a slumber; and hence however they fear not lesser sins, hence come to commit them, hence also to be hardned under them: Many complain of hard hearts, but consider, is not this the reason of it? you fear not sinful thoughts, nor carelesness in your Christian course; your slumber is now upon you; thy Conscience startles at Whoredom, but not at a wanton word; or playing upon the Sabbath, but unpreparedness for it that's nothing; sin in a manner with thee; the reason is, because spiritual slumber is upon thee.

8. When men are deceived and deluded by appearances, or colours, as the *Israelites* when the *Gibeonites* came to them; confident of themselves, but deceived as the men of *Ai* by stratagems; if ever your Souls be hurt, it will be by appearances; if ever this Country receive a blow, it will be by appearances; error will creep in by appearances; the most vile wickedness hath been found to be hatcht under fairest colours: If ever any shall come under an appearance of piety, and promise of protection, safety, liberty, onely your Government must be a little altered; slumber here, and you shall sleep in your enemies arms;

arms ; Grace, and the love of Christ and the Spirit (the fairest colours under the sun) may be pretended ; but if you shall receive under this appearance, that God witnesseth his love, first, by an absolute promise, where neither grace nor life is seen ; take heed there ; for under this appearance you may as well bring in immediate Revelations, and from thence come to forsake the Scriptures : and then no wonder if men fall to deny all foundations in Christianity, and Scripture also ; take heed of meer appearances of repentance in evil members, be not deceived there : Never was the world more full of craft ; be not laid asleep with appearances of truth : Thus you see the point opened. Stop security when it is risen to your anckles, lest you be drowned in it, and perish in it afterward.

CHAP. III.

Security the last Sin of good and bad.

SECT. I.

That carnal security is sometimes the last sin which doth surprise and overcome the hearts of good and bad, wise and foolish in Virgin-Churches.

That as it is said, *That the last enemy that shall be destroyed is death* ; so this death, like sleeping, is one of the last enemies that surpriseth the souls of the wise, but Christ doth destroy it ; and of the foolish, but it destroyeth them : Thus it was here with the Virgins ; what was their sin that were ready with their Lamps burning, waiting for the Bridegroom ? you see the wise polluted with no sin, till they fell down by Security (the foolish were wanting to get oyl in their vessels before) but this they fell last into : What into open prophaness, or other foul corruptions ? No, but *they all slumbered and slept*, and we read of no sin after till the Bridegroom came ; many sins indeed there be, which like branches bud from the root, but this is the main : And therefore look upon the next Parable, you shall see this again confirmed, to shew the certainty of this point ; the servant that hid his talent, *verf.26.* is called *an evil servant* ; why, what evil did he ? he did not lavish it (as the Prodigal) upon others, nor lose it ; but he did not use it , sluggishness was his sin ; hence (faith Christ) *thou evil and slothful servant.* And hence the thorny ground flourished and grew, and suffered ; all persecutions could not consume them ; what was their sin ? *Mark 4. 12.* compared with *Luk. 21. 34.* it was the cares of the world ; they began to dream (strange fancies came before sleeping) and the pillow of their security was some worldly content : And this is the reason why Christ and the Apostles are also exceeding pressing to watchfulness , because this is the sin that Saints are ready to fall into after they have seen Christs love and care ; and because this is the sin the wicked will fall into, and their last sin ; it will be just preceding

C c c   ceeding ceding their last plague ; and hence the Apostle exhorts, *Oh sleep not you*, &c. 1 *Thess.* 5. 1,2,5,6.

Let me open this thus :

SECT. II.

VVE must know that the Lord in subduing a sinner to the obedience of himself, it is with him as with an enemy in a City, there are many strong holds of sin, to which he retires and resists, 2 *Cor.*10.4,5. and when one is down he flieth for shelter into another, and maintains that as long as he can ; so it is with men : Or as it is with divers fruits, they have their several seasons of growing, and then of withering ; so it is here ; according to the several seasons of a mans life, so are his lusts growing and decaying ; there are the first and the last ripe fruits.

First, Take a man that is born and bred up to some years, man is a sociable creature, and it is a misery to live and be alone ; hence the first evil he usually chuseth is evil and loose company ; his lusts are grown up to some years, and now he desireth a match for them, and first he chuseth a companion ; and Satan hath a mighty hand in this ; because as the Lord when he first sends to do his work, he sends two by two to animate and strengthen one another in the work ; so Satan doth first joyn hand in hand together that men might corrupt one another, and harden one another in wickedness ; this (I say) is the first usually ; hence *Ephes.*2.2. and *Prov.* 2. 12. Wisdom first keeps from the evil man ; and this sin is for a time the dearest sin ; for here he meets with some pastimes, mirth, and so much love from them, that he loves this last more than all the friends he hath (though they dissuade him ;) more than all the Sabbaths of God, and hence he prophanes them ; more than Christ himself, and hence when he hath many times purposes of turning to God, his company with-holds him.

Secondly, Continuing long in this sin, at last he comes to fall into the sin of lust, and from men he looks to women, and this is as dear to him as his right eye ; it may be God keeps him from the act of Whoredom, but wanton looks, lascivious thoughts, speculative uncleanness, self-pollution (which he commits when the candles are out, and none but God sees) and yet God spares him ; and this follows him to the Church, to the streets, whiles he is awake, nay, when asleep, and thinks it is no sin for a time, or if he doth, Oh the horror that he hath sometimes for it ! Scholars of *Westminster* have been detected from twelve or fourteen years of age to live in this sin. This is the second : Hence *Prov.*2.16. first wisdom keepes from the evill man, next from evil women.

Thirdly, It may be a man marrieth, and then this sin is out of season ; now therefore another comes in its place, and that is, immoderate love of, and dropsie desires after the world, and the wealth of it, for now charge is like to encrease, and it is a shame to walk in rags ; and hence now a man begins to look upon the estates of others, and to admire at them, and then he looks upon what he hath, and what labor, care, and providence in a saving way may bring him unto ; and hence burieth himself alive in the earth, and feeds upon clods of earth, and uncertain hopes. And this is the next sin which grows up (though I know some men will not come to this) but I speak of them that go on in the fairest way ; hence *Heb.*13.4,5. *Whoremongers God will judge* ; then *let your conversation be without covetousness*, that follows.

Fourthly, It may be at last God terrifies this mans Conscience, and he begins

begins to see *what profiteth it me to win the whole world and to lose my own soul?* hence falls now to take up another profession, to hang out another flag, and to lead a new life; and now pride in spiritual excellencies is his sin; when glory in worldly wealth dyes, pride in spiritual glory lives: There were divers of the Heathen contemned the world, yet puft up with pride in their morality; hence *Chuse no novice Bishop, lest he be puffed up, and fall into the condemnation of the Devil.* Now Lets of mind come in when he performs duties publickly, openly; and now he hungers after the honor of men, and sets himself to sale for it: Oh, saith *Saul, honor me!* when he had confessed his coveting of the cattel; but pride stuck in him still: And when he doth duties privately, he rests in them, and accounts highly of himself for them, though they neither bring him to Christ, but estrange him from Christ. Hence Christ chargeth, *when you do alms, do not onely do it not to be seen of men, but let not thy left hand know what thy right hand doth*; take no delight in this: This was *Simons* sin, *Act.* 8. he seeing the gifts of the Apostles, would give any money for them; these gifts are sweeter now than money; hence such fall to some foul opinions and crotchets; they can interpret Revelations, and ascend to the Ministry, and be the forwardest in a Town, but when to do publick service, respect is gone, their love is gone.

Fifthly, When this is dying in the Saints, and fallen down in Hypocrites, now sloth is the last thing that takes hold upon them, and this is sweet; What is the honor of men? what is this base world? now sloth and sleep is sweet. Now a man first ceaseth acting, and this gives rest; and now being here, Secondly, it's death to come out of this sluggish estate; when the hand of God is upon men, and the spurs be at their side and in their heart, it may be it will be otherwise; but else not; they will not awaken, sloth is so sweet to them, though sins yet be to be subdued; time is short, Gods wrath is great; yet that, as it is said, *He that escapes the sword of Jehu shall Elisha slay*: so it is here, he that escapes one sin, another shall slay him; but at last sloth shall slay: Hence let a man look, what joyeth my heart? God doth not, wealth doth not; sloth doth.

SECT. III.

BEcause it is the best and most fit season for this sin to arise, when all the rest are fallen indeed in Saints, and seem to be fallen in Hypocrites; as the temptation is, so mens sin is; when there is the fittest temptation without, it broaches corruption within, and it runs not out before; for it is here as in War; when the enemy (never seen before) is seen in the field (very dangerous and very strong) is it now a season to sleep? no, Arm, arm now; but when he hath driven and routed an enemy, and is enriched with spoils, and laden with prey, now it's a season to rest. Hence the Poet notes, *When all the World could not conquer them, their peace after conquest hath*; now they have themselves (an enemy within) to conquer; So here. Hence if they should have desired the *Israelites* to be at peace with the *Canaanites*, when they first came in and had the land; No, they will cut out their throats in time; but when they had conquered them, now *Josh.*15.63. it is said, they could not do it; had they not had Gods promise for it? yes, and he could make it good, but they could not, because now they had no list to do it, they were slothful; *Exod.* 23.29.

Secondly, Because it is the strongest sin; No bonds so strong as the bonds of death; it is a kinde of spiritual death, *Ephes.*5.14. though in the Saints it is not death eternal. Now as it is with the Lord, he reserves the best mercy till the last, so Satan reserves the strongest temptation till the last; and in many men it is sloth: Now it receives a double strength:

1. From the strength of natural corruption which will remain when other sins dye, and in a great measure in the Saints, when the power of sin is taken from the Saints; for take the best man and this remains; it is the sickness of the Soul which will cleave to it : Hence as 'tis with sick men, when no mind to meat, yet oh a little rest ! it is greatest pain to walk, and hence the greatest pleasure to lie still : sickness binds a man to rest, makes him love his rest; so carnal corruption, to carnal rest.

2. The strength of pleasure in some lawful thing; for sloth and sleep's best pillow is ever some delight in lawful things, that's the shadow: hence, when a man delights not in gross evils, yet in health, and peace, and freedom from dangers ; and here he wallows, as *Issachar.*

Reason 3.

Thirdly, Because (not onely so, but) it is the least suspected sin. I have known them that have been gracious, and long it hath been before the Lord hath made them know that they have had this (much less loved this) sin.

For 1. It is but a neglect or cessation from act ; it is no sin that doth openly war against the soul, but lives within like a friend.

2. 'Tis a neglect which the best have ; an infirmity; *All slumbered and slept.*

Thirdly, The main work is wrought ; it is not therefore any dangerous infirmity, men think ; and hence the Apostle, *Rom.*13.11. would have them *awake*; why ? we shall be saved, might they say, and had peace long ago ; but (saith he) *because your salvation is nearer.*

4. Because he sees many difficulties before him to break thorow, which unless God gave him more strength, he doth not see that God calls him unto ; and hence saith, *that there are Lions in the way*; after a long time of profession, then God presents greatest difficulties ; and hence now sloth reigns in a special manner.

SECT. IV.

Use 1.

HEnce see the reason why many Christians at their first beginnings grow, and thrive, and abound in the fruits of Righteousness; but afterward so poor and ragged; Oh the two or three first years, how frequently in prayer, meditation ! Oh what sorrow and peace ! but after this, now they can find little good they can get ; little growth they make, unless it be downward ; little life they have, and what ado to keep it, or to get a good spiritual meals meat ! this is the reason of it ; when they first began, then the enemy was out, and they were up, and now they conquered and had the spoils; but since, they have grown secure, and loved to sleep, I say love to sleep ; and hence, little to be seen about them but rags; hence (*Prov.*6.11.) *lest thy poverty come as an armed man, Prov.*20.13.11. truly this is it, and hence no wonder you are ever so full of complaints in midst of means ; where God gives you matter of fulness, joy, peace, everlasting glory , yet you find nothing; so that sometimes you think there is no grace, or are almost of the mind that there is no grace to be looked for in us ; if not, yet finding so little, there's no evidence for it: Oh your sloth it is the cause; hence 'tis you marvel at the Lord he helps not; Oh you do not awake, to awaken the arm of the Lord; you shall know, if you follow on to know the Lord, but that you do not ; and hence the pricks and vexations you made your peace with, and are again vexed by them, this is the reason of it: Oh therefore go in secret and say, I complain of my sins; the Ordinances and God that I seek, and have not, when my heart should be otherwise; but oh it is not because I cannot, but because I care not; it is not because of the strength of my enemy without, but because of my neglect of watch and diligence within. I know it was a sin for *Pharaoh* to charge *Israel* with idleness, because he commanded work without means; But is the Lords work so? look up to him for strength, he gives it them that have none; put forth that strength thou hast, he will accept thy will, but will never allow thee in thy sloth, but you shall to beggery at the last. Hence men *roast not what they take in hunting*, (*Prov.*12.27.) after Ordinances; Oh there's world there; never shall you see a Soul careful, but he finds every Sabbath something.

Use 2.

Hence we may learn the reason why many Christians, when the Lord begins to work upon them, have many combats and sore conflicts with various temptations, and one corruption after another, and scarce any breathing time wherein they are freed from such; and then many strong crys, &c. but afterward they are freed from all, and even these also; and they find nothing either within or without that greatly troubles them; but they go on smoothly in a course of profession also, without very much ado with their own hearts; their Consciences are at peace, their distempers are at peace, and lye not heavy upon them; and they think God is at peace with them, and hence they are quiet; the reason is because they are quiet, and fall asleep, and let their sin and Satan alone, and hence they let them alone: A sluggard faith, *there is a Lion in the way, and it's a hedg of thorns*; many difficulties God sets before him; now if a man meets with no Lions, no thorns, pressed with no great difficulties in his course, it is certain sloth hath seised upon that Soul, and he is carried away captive by it, *Prov.* 22.13.   For

Look upon men, why should they be quiet? is it because sin and Satan are quite vanquished, that they have no agonies and wrestlings with them? the Apostle denies that, *Ephes.*6.12. Indeed while he keeps the Palace then he is all peace, and it is a sign he is entred again if you have this peace: But else *Paul* himself, and all that are in the field, are opposed, and will have fiery darts; and hence the Apostle exhorts to *put off the works of darkness, and put on the whole armor of light*; why not works of light? because then a Christian will find many assaults, *Rom.*13.12. Or it is because they are men of such a refined faith, and such pure mettal that there needs no knocking, nor melting, nor temptations? I confess the Lord doth not see at all times the like need, but gives his servants many sweet seasons; but yet 1 *Pet.*1.6,7,8. *they were begotten to a a lively hope, and they did rejoyce greatly in that hope*; yet they had their seasons of trials, *manifold temptations*, &c. It may be they thought, did the Lord ever love us, when such desertions, such fierce oppositions? &c. I know the Lord may leave *David* thus, *Psal.*30.6. but then God was angry, and he saw it before many days: No, no, there is both reason for it, and need of it; and why are you at peace now? it is because of your sloth, *Jer.*48.11. *Moab is at rest*; and hence setled on her Lees, that they neither feel nor know their sin, and their scent is in them, though none is smelt or runs out; hence never stirred by any word they hear, nor by any blow unless it be very heavy; they are now at peace with Sin, Death and Hell, and are at league with them, *Isa.*28.15. And hence as it is, where there be two Kingdoms met, what's the reason that there is no hurt that the one do to the other? the reason is, because there is a peace; why so? because War was so troublesom, and rest was good: So it is here; Why are men never troubled? but only because they are at peace with their sin; and why so? because rest is good: Oh they love to sleep; I shall never overcome it, or I have other work to follow, say men, and hence they spiritually war no more; and hence Satan and Sin are at peace: this is the guise of men, they think the main is sure: they maintain a name to live before men, keep duties upon the wheels before God, and have comfort often; and though a world of vanity is in their hearts, yet it never oppresseth them, because they oppose not it, and so are quiet.

SECT. V.

Object. *But is not Christ's yoke easie and his burden light, full of sweetness, &c?*

Answ. There is a life of faith, and a life of sloth; a rest which Faith gives, and Christ gives; and a rest which a mans own sloth and security gives: but there is a wide difference between them.

First, a believing heart cleaves to the Lord, and so findes rest in the Lord, and that with purpose and decree of heart, to cleave to him in one thing as well as in another; the heart is not at peace with Satan, and at war with God, but joyneth to the Lord, and stands armed with a strong resolution against every temptation; and hence peace with Christ is maintained, not with sloth: as *Barnabas*, *Acts* 11.23. *exhorted with full purpose of heart to cleave unto the Lord, when he saw the grace of God*; seeing you find such mercy from him, oh cleave unto him: But now a secure heart cleaves to the Lord in some desires; and if he be resolved of any thing, it is only of that which he can do with ease, and will not be what he would be; he would be better, and knew the Lord more, and this quiets him; but he will not be what he would be, because his compact and covenant of peace is made with another; he will be sluggish and secure, and not use the means; oh sleep is sweet, *Prov.* 12.27. *The sluggard roasts not what he took in hunting*; he will not roast it, there is trouble there.

Secondly, A believing heart, or Faith, finds and feels its rest by trouble. *Unto the righteous there ariseth light out of darkness*, Psal. 37. *After you have suffered, God settle you*, 1 Pet. 5.10. *Not as the world gives peace, give I it unto you*, Joh. 14.27. For the life of a Christian is a life of faith, which is a life contrary to sence and reason: When the Lord kills, what doth he intend then to save me? and when he blinds me, doth he intend to teach me? yes that he doth, and by their warfare they find peace. Hence *Paul* at the end of his life makes his triumph, *I have finished my course*, 2 Tim. 4.6,7,8. this makes promises precious; when, though a man feels the strength of sin, yet sees the Lord will subdue it; when a man findes guilt of sin, yet sees the Lord will pardon it for his own names sake: It's a strange place 2 Cor. 1.8,9. *We were oppressed without reason*, why? *that we might not trust in our selves*, (why, was there no way but this?) why, this is the life of faith, to find life in death, peace in sorrow: But a slothful heart finds not rest by denying it self, and walking through trouble; but by pleasing it self, and easing it self of trouble, because it is at league with it: One that hath broken league, finds peace by war, and then takes spoils; but another è contra, &c.

1. A man denies the power of godliness, that's a burden; his slothful heart will not bear that, that's too hot; for the world carries a condemned carriage of them; and hence he keeps a name to live, and thereby hath peace with the world.

2. He wrestles not against Satan, and his lusts, pursuing them daily, carries not the sence and feeling of them; and hence being luke-warm, he *thinks he is rich, and wants nothing, when poor, and blind, and naked.*

3. Hence

3. Hence, not wrestling against sin, he feels not sin, and so conscience is at peace with him ; *sin is alive without the Law.*

4. Keeping a constant course of private duties, he thinks God is at peace also, and so his peace gives him rest, and sloth makes him make a league, because he loves rest: and hence we finde, a Christian most oppressed in times of trouble, many times hath most peace; and *è contra:* Because as it was with *Gideon*, he had his peace by trouble, they had their peace by rest whose flesh he tore with thorns, *Judg.*8.7. oh therefore fear and tremble at their condition.

SECT. VI.

Use 3.

HEnce see the reason why many a Christian, after he hath seen and felt the work of Gods grace in his heart and soul, and hence hath been filled with peace and joy unspeakable, that yet after long profession loseth the sight of it, and knows not whether there be any dram of grace in his heart or no; and consequently hath no assurance: but ask him, have you not known it? yes; but 'tis a question whether ever it was immortal seed or no, for then it would not dye, as I see it hath; the reason of this is, a man falls to a secure condition, fast asleep, forgets God and himself; and hence though there be grace, yet it is not exercised, *Matth.*25.26. and hence not seen at all, *2 Pet.*1.8,9. and one grace to another, and then an open entrance is made; this makes calling sure; if this they do not, they will not see a far off; why? because they forget the Lord, which is one part of security: Hence we shall find in times of persecution, never such assurance as then, *Zach.*13.*ult.* because grace is never so exercised as then; and hence men much in prayer abound with much assurance (when Christ was in his agony he prays more fervently) because then a man is watchful, and grace most exercised; when a man dyes in prayer, and grows secure, and hath little exercise of grace, now it is a question whether there is grace at all or no; and hence when men come to Sacraments, how oft are they put to it whether the Lord be theirs or no! and hence when men come to the Word, they lose all comfort, because they know not whether these promises are theirs or no, because they are asleep, and not waking with the Lord. Oh therefore lay no blame upon the Lord, but thy self; I have had grace, but I have not exercised it; I have lived a life of sloth and security, had I lived a life of thankfulness, prayer, watchfulness, and been ever awake, I should have seen my own heart, and what the Lord hath done for my soul: Here, here lies the security of a Christian, not in losing all grace he had, but in losing the exercise of it.

SECT. VII.

Quest. HOw shall I do this?

Answ. 1. Look that your eye be single, that the Lord be your last end, and that with an infinite love you cleave to that, and then the whole body will be full of light; but if your eye be double, &c. *Matth.*6.24. A ship that hath but one place to go to, will get thitherward in open sea with every wind. Who is so great as the Lord? who minds thee but the Lord? doth he provide, protect and pity thee, when thou seekest thy self? will he not do it much more when thou art set for him?

2. Consider

2. Confider the fweetnefs of this life. 1. In this life, 1 *Cor.*1 5. *ult. be ever abounding* ; why ? oh you know *your labor fhall not be in vain.* And what will it be when you come to dye ? *Ifa.*38.1,2,3. *Remember I have walked with thee* : And 2. After death, *Rev.*14.13. it may be you account them nothing, but they fhall follow thee ; do you not find bitternefs in the end of another life ? you will find your pillow hard enough before you dye ; oh therefore get fomething to make it eafie.

3. Take heed of forgetfulnefs of the Lord, for this is the reafon why many a man is not ever up in walking with the Lord, becaufe he forgets the Lord ; It is not becaufe he will not, or becaufe he cannot, but he remembers not the Lords love, the glory of his ways, *what an evil thing and bitter it is to depart from the Lord,*Pfal.22.11. *They fhall remember and turn,* Jer.2.1,6. The Lord complains of Apoftacy, *they faid where is the Lord? I remember thee,&c.* So I fay to you, the Lord of glory remembers you, thou art written on the palms of his hand, and like fhew-bread before the Ark, fo thou doft ever ftand before the Lord ; hence every moment he is pardoning, purging, preferving and devifing how to do thee good ; nay he remembers thy love, prayers ,feekings after him, nay, thy houfe and walls of it where thou dwelleft : Oh therefore forget not the Lord, that fo you may be ever feeking after, and cleaving to the Lord.

SECT. VIII.

HEnce fee the reafon why men after long profeffion fall into many flothful opinions, becaufe their hearts are furprifed with this enemy of floth firft ; and it is Gods juft judgement upon men, that feing they love their fleep and lazinefs, they fhall be lazy by rule, and fo be for ever hardned in it.

Queft. What are thofe flothful opinions ?

Anfw. Firft, What is this but one, To make the Law no rule to a Chriftians life ? as though a Chriftian fhould be like a man at Sea, and carried by the wind, but he muft have no Compafs to fail by alfo : In thefe laft times Chrift's Kingly Office is chiefly oppofed ; men are glad of Chrifts righteoufnefs and death to fave them, but when he comes to plant his Laws (as all Conquerors do amongft men) they do then fhake them off, and under a colour of love to their Prince, make his Laws no bonds to binde them ; fo thefe think this is the liberty of a Chriftian, the liberty of a Prince to be lawlefs, 2 *Pet.*2.19.

Secondly, That there is no activity of Grace received, no power to ftir till ftirred ; and therefore leave all upon Chrift, they can do nothing ; if he gives nothing, they cannot help it ; if he doth, then all is well,&c. It is true, till the Lord doth help what can we do ? But there is an immutable affiftance of Spirit, whereby the Lord doth enable his to act more or lefs like himfelf, when ftirred up : And if you finde none, becaufe you fall fhort of Chrift, do not think that the Lord will be a cover to fuch a cap ; nor a pillow for a flothful heart ; there is a ficknefs in the beft, and muft be followed, elfe we dye.

Thirdly, That Minifters muft not exhort : Why ? what can men do ? If fervants cannot abide to be fpoken unto when there is need, from what can it come but idlenefs ? What can words make better ? yes, the Lords words have a power to help or ruine, when you fhall fay, oh the exhortations, oh the intreaties I have had, &c. one main means of reconciliation is now abolifhed, 2 *Cor.* 5. 20.

Fourthly, That Chriſtians muſt gather no evidence from Sanctification ; we ſhall finde the root of it to be difficulty, which is never ſloths bed-fellow.

1. It is difficult to be holy always, but there will be many weakneſſes and ſins, &c.

2. When we do ſo, it will be hard to diſcern what holineſs it is, whether counterfeit or not.

3. When we do ſo, 'tis hard to keep it, but you will loſe it again, and be put to farther ſearch, and ſo off and on : I believe Chriſtians make them more difficult than indeed they are ; but yet it is the Lords way ; Scripture is plain for it ; and if avoided becauſe difficult (which to many is ſweet) what is this but an invention of ſloth ?

Fifthly, That what a man cannot do, is always a weakneſs which the Lord will pardon : Sometimes it is ; but not hereſ; for a mans chief ſin may be kept unſubdued from this ground, which ſloth makes warrantable.

Sixthly, That if once the main be wrought, though he never grow better, yet he is to keep his peace and confidence ; Oh intreat the Lord to keep your heads ſound (though hearts be ſluggiſh) ſo as you may not love, and defend your ſecurity, and then go and leave Chriſt.

SECT. IX.

Uſe 5.

LEt this be a warning to all, that there is ſuch an enemy to be ſlain ; truly I had thought if I could have got my heart broken, if I could ſeek the Lord till I had gotten a promiſe, then I ſhould be well enough; Oh no, there is a ſlothful heart yet continueth ; and let it be encouragement to war againſt it ; oh 'tis the laſt enemy, and then comes your crown, and then your warfare is ended; and therefore do as *Sampſon*; *Lord, help this one time, that I may be avenged for my two eyes*; ſo, thou haſt been made a ſlave to it in private duties, and God Judg. 16.28. hath neglected thee ; In publick, at meetings you have been forced to ſleep, that an Indian it may be, if he had ſtood by would have jogged thee ; therefore pray, Oh help Lord this one time (though I dye) againſt this one enemy; Thus *Paul* 1 *Cor.9.ult.* Is an immortal crown nothing ? will it be no ſorrow to you when you awake, to loſe eternal reſt in God, for a little reſt in thy ſloth ? Oh therefore beat down thy body ; it is the laſt, hence the worſt enemy; ſay as *Judg.9.54.* What ſhall I fall by a woman ? ſhall I fall by the worſt ? why did I oppoſe luſt and pride ? oh, becauſe vile ; why, this is worſe ; it is the laſt, and hence Chriſt hates it moſt ; and hath he given ſtrength againſt any ſin, and will he not againſt this ? Oh therefore pray God that you fall not here.

CHAP.

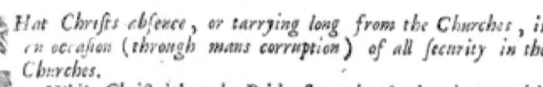

CHAP. IV.

Chrifts abfence the caufe of fecurity in his Churches.

SECT. I.

That Chrifts abfence, or tarrying long from the Churches, is an occafion (through mans corruption) of all fecurity in the Churches.

While Chrift delays the Bride fleepeth; look as it was with the Ifraelites, when Mofes went firft from them up to the mount, they had no fpeech of making a Calf; but when he ftaied long from them, now they make it, and make merry with it; fo it is here, *Exod.*32.1. The holy Apoftle notes this to be in the laft days, 2 *Pet.*3.3,4. *Men fhall fay Where is the promife of his coming? all things remain as they were;* and hence fcoffers (it may be with the tongue) at leaft in the heart, and fo *walking after their own lufts;* hence *Matth.*24.49. you fee an evil fervant fmite his fellow fervants (what is the reafons of divifions between men?) one fmites with the tongue, the other with the hand, and the other fuffers; *(and to eat and drink with the drunken)* it is a fign of a fecure man when (though he falls not into a pro-phane courfe, but) he can bear with it in others, to fit by and fee others fin with-out check; what is the caufe of this? *he faith* (not with his tongue, but) *in his heart, My Lord delays his coming:* The very fcope of the parable is to fhew the fin of men herein, and to prevent it by watchfulnefs.

SECT. II.

Queft. How and why doth this occafion and breed fecurity?

*Anfw.*1. In that Chrifts abfence from the world makes him to be much forgotten in the world (out of fight out of minde) efpecially at thofe times when men are ready to be overcome by floth; now forgetfulnefs of God is the beginning of all the deepeft fecurity that can fall upon men, *Deut.*32.18,19,20. whence the Lord faith, *I will hide my face from them, fo as they fhall not fee me, but I will fee them and what their end fhall be,* and hence this is made the begin-ning of returning to the Lord, *Pfa.*22.27,28. *All Nations fhall remember and turn, for the Kingdom is the Lords.*

Secondly, Becaufe the abfence of Chrift keeps thofe things from being feen which fhould awaken, and which fenfibly do awaken; that as it is within the night, when there is little noife, and darknefs over-fpreads all things, it is hard now to be kept from fleep, when the curtains are drawn; fo while Chrift is ab-fent, it is a kind of night (his coming is called *the day,* and *the day of the Lord*) becaufe the things of the Lord are hid from men: And thofe are thefe two chiefly.   1. The

1. The terror of the Lord and the wrath to come; why did men sleep all the Sermon long (which lasted one hundred and twenty years) when *Noah* preached? because they knew not of the flood; *so shall it be in the days of Christs coming*, men know not what wrath is; the thoughts of this kept *Pauls* eye waking, 2 *Cor.*5.9,10,11,12.

2. The exceeding riches and weight of glory that shall crown all the Saints; hence all the faithful have been abundant both in doing and suffering for the Lord; (2 *Cor.*4.) *It is not worthy the glory which shall be revealed:* Hence, *Heb.*10.34. *They took joyfully the spoiling of their goods*, because they had *in heaven a more abiding substance*; they overlooked all things here when they saw that. When these two things are seen (which are the last things that shall continue) it would awaken; but painted fire, and a painted Kingdom never draws a mans heart much; so neither do these work upon secure ings; or if they do see them, they soon are hid from them again, their light decaying, being not like the morning but declining Sun; and though the Saints do see them, yet they are very apt to lose (for a time) the sight of them, especially if the Lord tarrieth; and hence *Heb.*10. they had need of patience; but *when the day comes who can sleep?*

Thirdly, In regard of his absence, do the things of the world present and keep their glory before the eyes of men; for what is the reason that worldly things (which men in their judgements say are vain) yet they are of such price with men! It is with them as it is with Glow-worms and Stars that keep their shining, and are very glorious because the Sun is set; so Christ is hid in his glory, and whilst men are led more by sense than by faith, men doat upon these things; they know nothing more vain, yet nothing more glorious: When Christ comes a man shall see all the world, the honor, comforts, wealth, crowns, greatness of it buried before his eyes; and when an end of these things shall be seen, now the Lord will be precious; as doubtless when they saw the Ark floating upon the water, happy are they that are there might they say; and hence *Mal.*3. *ult.* those that said *the proud were happy*, what was the reason of it? but because of this, *The day of the Lord was not yet come to make up his Jewels?* Now when once the eye is bewitched with the glory of the world, nothing causeth security sooner; as strange fancies in the head work a man first asleep: *Psal.*73. When *David* beheld the prosperity of the wicked, he began to dislike all Religion, and to account it simplicity to be holy, until at last he saw the end of these things.

Fourthly, Because in Christs absence men feel not the evil of sin which doth befall them in their security, nor yet the evil of their own hearts; for if men should be presently punished, and smitten by some revenging invisible hand of God upon them after every sin, and as soon as first they begin to sleep, you should never see the heart secure; and hence the Devils live in horrors daily, in apprehension of the judgment of the great day; thus it will be at Christs coming, *then the secret things of darkness shall be brought to light*; but now is a time of forbearance, hence a carnal heart *is set to do wickedly*, and to go on securely, *Ecclef.*8.11.

Fifthly, Because while Christ is absent, conscience lyes still most commonly, and seldom is throughly awake, and hence a man sleeps; for conscience is the Lords witness, accuser, and notary; now the witness then speaks most fully and clearly when the Judge is come: Now however God doth awaken some mens consciences throughly in this life, yet it is not universal, but in few, to be thorowly awakened, and hence men are very secure, *Isa.*33.14. *Who shall dwell with everlasting burning, &c?*

SECT. III.

Use 1.

HEnce we see the vileness of the hearts of men, that Christ his absence(which time is given to us to make us watch)should make us secure;that men should turn day into night, a day of forbearance, into a night of forgetfulness; for if the Lord should not delay his coming, how many thousands would be swept away before any peace made with God, or before any work finished for God! now he in pitty gives such days, delays his coming for this end, and do we thus requite the Lord? 2 *Pet.*3.9. Christ himself doth his work while it is light; *the night cometh wherein no man can work*, *Joh.*12.35,36. Now what a crossing of the Lord is this? If he should come thou shouldst be consumed by him; and if he doth not come, you will grow secure before him.

Use 2.

Hence see the reason why the hearts of men are so secure in times of health and peace, but then cry out and look about them in times of sickness, and when the approach of death is near, because Christ now begins to come, and Christs presence is near in great terror, and severity, and glory; but be these are afar off; now the soul begins to see Christ, and how he must shortly stand naked alone (stript of all comforts and friends) before an all-seeing God; and now they look about for evidence; but before, the Lord would not come as yet, he delays his coming, I may live many years and provide thus and thus for my children, *&c.* Oh men complain of secure careless hearts, and the cause is this, they see not this day a coming.

Use 3.

Hence see one special way to prevent and remove security when it is fallen upon the hearts of any, and that is by daily setting before you the coming of the Lord; the Apostles penned this, and Saints believe this, 1 *Thess.*1.ult. I am perswaded some men have had in their dreams the visions of the Almighty, of which *Job* speaks, and have been awakened in terror and fear, even with the dream of it; but how would this awaken if seen and beheld whilst indeed you are awake! Many Monkish spirits have been much awakened in their superstitions way by this; but the spirit of a *Paul* will be much more; for by this means he awakened all the world to look about them, 2 *Cor.*5.11. And for himself, this did make him exercise himself, *Acts* 24.15,16. so it will be with you; you will not only be awake your selves, but keep all awake about you; and this is not legal neither thus to do. It is certain if you complain of security, I dare complain against you, that this is the cause; you look upon the coming of the Lord as a long time off, and see it not daily; it converted some in scoffing *Athens* to the Faith; much more (if converted) doth it awaken. Let us therefore commend Three things to you.

SECT. IV.

First, MAke the coming of the Lord real, see it real, and set it really (as it shall be) before your eyes: *Heb.*9.ult. *to them that look for him,* *&c.* Why do not men look for him? truly, very few do look for him really ; it is only a report, a noise with many men ; where there is the power of grace, it presents things as they are, which shall be so ; *Faith is the substance of things not seen,* it puts them in their being ; *it is the evidence of things not seen,* for

for otherwise it will never work upon you. Especially think on these Four things at that day.

1. The consuming of all things here in the world, which your hearts are so ready to doat upon, and of all carnal and fleshly excellencies which you trust unto, 2 *Pet.* 3.11. *Seeing these things shall be consumed, what manner of persons ought we to be!* If a man that is to make a sea voyage, did know that whatever he brought to shore beside Gold and Pearls, should be consumed as soon as he comes to shore, he would not fraught his ship with those things : if men were assured here is a house where you and yours shall be burnt, they would set it elsewhere ; men come from one Country to another, because sin will consume.

2. The amazing glory of Christ Jesus (when Christ shall come as a deliverer to refresh thy sad heart) and all his Saints at that day ; look upon Christ as sitting on the clouds of fire, raising the dead, then them that are alive changed in the twinckling of an eye, coming with all his Angels, Heaven left empty of them, and Saints sitting at his right hand shining like the Sun, so that all the word shall stand amazed at them, and then, when Judgement is done, up they go to Heaven (the third Heaven) with a shout, and so be ever with the Lord. And then

3. Consider the fierce wrath upon Reprobates, who shall rise like Toads coming out of their holes in winter time, standing before Christ's Tribunal, crying out of the day that ever they were born, and receiving their final doom ; imagine the silence while the Lord is pronouncing the sentence ; and when past, a cry ; and then Christ to depart, and shut up himself in Heaven with his Saints, the Reprobate never to see him nor his face any more ; are these things tales, fables, notions ? if they be, blot out the Scripture ; but if real, oh then who can but awake ! If God intends mercy to you, the thoughts of these things will awaken you ; you shall see them really, if not, they shall awaken you by feeling of them.

4. Consider how many will be found too light at that day.

Secondly, Make this day present : Optick glasses will take within them the present image of things afar off ; a Mud-wall cannot give the form of them ; so by Faith look at these things that be to come as near : for if we see really the Lords coming, but we look upon it as a thing that is afar off, it will not affect : Now a thing may be present to Faith which is not to sence ; it may be the last and great coming of the Lord is not very nigh (although we are doubtless in the last times) but the beginning of this, thy Petty-Sessions before that general Assize, may be nigh. Oh therefore make it present.

Quest. *How shall we make it present ?*

Answ. 1. By pondering that speech of Christ, spoken to that end, *Matth.* 24.44. *In an hour you think not of he comes* ; so that either thy time is, when thou thinkest it is nigh, and then you attain the thing ; or when far off, why then is the time, and that he will not come presently is more then you can say ; you see with wrong eyes, and wrong the Lords patience.

2. By comparing the present time with eternity to come ; for look as it is with base and little things, look upon them in themselves, they are not base, but compared with things excellent, as the Prophet sheweth, *Isa.* 40.17. so the time of this life, grant it be never so long, look upon it in self, it is long ; but compared with eternity, it is exceeding short : Set a prick alone and you may perceive it, but when made at the beginning of a line it is scarce perceptible ; this time of life upon which we sit is but a point of eternity : Oh eternity will amaze you, and make this time short, yea, nothing ; *Moses* hence forsook Pharoahs honor, because of the pleasures of sin for a season ; and *Paul* calls

calls *afflictions short,* when he saw *the eternal glory which should be revealed:* Oh that you could think this time to be as the delivery of a childe by many pangs into the world, so you by many sorrows are passing a short passage to eternity.

2. By making earthly things nothing, or not as great things: A mans friend is nigh to him, but there be trees and hills between them, and if these were down, or he could get above them, he would easily see and say, Oh I see him coming, he is even at the door, *James* 5.8. So Christ is nigh unto us, and we to him; but the things of the world, mountains, and hills, and cattel, and ground, this and that stands between us and our sight, that we cannot see the Lord; these things are so great, that the Lord is little, that though near, we cannot see him; now when God cuts down these things at sicknels, or when we can get above the world, now we can see them whiles we look at them as they are, 2 *Cor.* 4. *Prov.* 18.11. *The rich mans wealth is a tower in his conceit* (all things are swayed by conceit) pull down that, now you make all naked before you to see the Lord nigh.

Thirdly, Do thus daily; else you will grow secure by little and little: Oh that I could prevail with you to set before you once a day this time! how would it keep your hearts from dreaming and doating upon these things: When any sorrow, that day will refresh; 2. When any duty done, that day will recompence; 3. When in want, yet full at that day; 4. When in misery now, blessed then. When a man is ready with light and lamp at all watches of the night, oh blessed then! you can hardly keep from security and carelesness by this, how will you then do without it? you will die in security.

SECT. V.

LEt this be a warning to all those who have passed the first age of their Christian life, after you have waited long and tarried for the Bridegroom, take heed of security, and think this may occasion it, *viz.* The Bridegrooms delay: In the first heat of your youthful affections, there's not that danger then as now, lest you grow decrepit, passive and dull; and therefore think, Whatever else I do, I will be sure to keep this door, it shall not come in here; and yet do we not see men fall here! one would think it should not be so in these times, when God calls so many of his servants to Heaven to him, and is hacking at so many posts and pillars of this Tabernacle; especially considering withal that it is no time to seek great things to your selves: *Thou shalt have thy life for a prey* (as he said to *Baruch*) Who is it that thinks it long to death, that is within a days walk of his grave! Oh if you have your life, you are well; you may be glad of a place to die in.

VERSE

CHAP. V.

Of Chrifts awakning cry before his coming.

VERSE 6,7,8,9.

And at midnight there was a cry made, Behold the Bridegroom cometh, go ye forth to meet him.

Then all thofe Virgins arofe and trimmed their lamps.

And the foolifh faid unto the wife, Give us of your oyl, for our lamps are gone out.

But the wife anfwered faying, Not fo, left there be not enough for us and you, but go ye rather to them that fell, and buy for your felves.

SECT. I.

IN thefe words is fet down the preparation made fometime before the Bridegrooms coming, and that is by a *Cry* that *the Bridegroom cometh* ; and therefore the Churches fhould meet him : This is amplified from two things chiefly ;

Firft, The time when this Cry was made, and that was at *Midnight*.

Secondly, the effect that this Cry took upon the Virgins, from *verf.*8. to 10.

What fhould be meant by this Cry is difputed of by fome : Some think by it is meant the defcending of Chrift from Heaven with a fhout, the voyce of the Arch-Angel and Trump of God : 1 *Theff.*4.ult. which (as I do not wholly exclude) becaufe there fhall be fuch a clamor before the Lord comes, as at the giving of the Law ; fo at the time when the World fhall be judged by the Law : fo this circumftance is added (as *Pareus* and other interpret) in regard of the Parable, which fpeaks of Chrifts coming under the fimilitude of a Wedding folemnized in the night time, according to the cuftom of thofe times, who when they came forth out of their feveral houfes to meet one another, a cry and noife is made, *the Bridegroom cometh*. Now,

Queft. What is meant by the coming of the Lord, the Bridegroom ?

Anfw. The coming of Chrift principally here meant, is that coming of Chrift either to general or particular Judgement in the latter ages of the world. Then, for when, 2 *Theff.*2.1,2. they thought the coming of Chrift was near ; no faith he, not till Antichrift is revealed and deftroyed ; therefore when Antichrift is difcovered and deftroyed, and Churches upon this refined, now there remaining no more to be done in this world but Chrifts coming, all promifes being fulfilled except that, fo that they live in expectation of that ; Chrift ftaying and not coming fo foon, Churches grow fecure ; yet before the Lord comes

comes to either judgement he hath his cry : yet here is to be meant the coming of Christ at other times of the Church when they shall be Virgins, and hence a command to watch that concerns and bindes all to be ready against the coming of Christ, whether to general or particular Judgement at death, or any other coming of the Lord in this life, either in special mercy to his people, or in terror to Hypocrites, *Luk.*18. Christs coming to hear prayers, and to avenge himself of his Churches enemies, is a coming. When the Jews shall be called, and Antichrist destroyed, 2 *Theff.*2. it is called Christs coming : So the sum is this, look as before the Bridegroom meets the Bride, and cry is made to awaken them to come to meet him; so before Christ comes to his secure Churches to take his people to nearer fellowship with himself in this life, or at death, or at judgement, Christ hath his cry to awaken them.

SECT. II.

THat before Christs coming to his secure Churches, the Lord will send forth his cry to awaken these Churches, to give warning of, and to make them ready for his coming; his coming either at last day, or at death, or in this life, to take them into nearer fellowship with himself.

It is true, Christs coming is at midnight, at a time when one would think he would not come; but yet at midnight there is this cry, which prepares and goes before his coming.

Quest. *What is this cry?*

Answ. It is not a still voyce, but a loud cry, which hath its effect for which God sends it. Now we shall find in Scripture there are two ways by which God doth usually awaken a secure sinner.

First, The cry of the Word.

Secondly, The voyce or cry of the Rod. So this Cry of Christ is.

First, Sometimes the cry of the Word; for thus *John* (*Isa.*40.3.) is called a Crier, and *Prov.*1.24. *Zach.*7.7,13. And this is the first course God takes to awaken, by giving the first honor to the Word; this is his mercy to see if that will do it. Now it is not every word that will or can awaken; for many times it makes men more secure (as some can sleep best by the noise of many waters) *Isa.*6.9. When the Lord sent to fat them, he sent *Isaiah* to preach to them; however in it self it is a cry of Christ; and seldom doth he come but he gives warning by his Servants the Prophets : But when it doth awaken, there are these particulars in it that it may awaken.

1. It is a word of Majesty and glory in respect of those that bring it, *Judg.* 2.1. one that preached to them (he was no Angel from Heaven, for it is not said he came from Heaven, but from *Gilgal* to *Bochim*) why is he called an Angel? because of that Majesty wherewith God clothed him, when he came to awaken them; for they had made a league with the *Canaanites*, and they began to vex them it seems, and he comes to tell them they should do so still, and God set on this with majesty upon their hearts, and hence they fell to weeping : And this is usual with the Lord, wherein he hath a time when he will awaken men to purpose, he puts a spirit of glory and majesty upon his servants more than usually, that the most secure shall see more than a man, they shall see the spirit of glory sparkling, and shining thorow such Lanthorns; as when God intends to harden a man in security, or leave him for a time, then he shall despise the Messengers of God, and see no more but man, and shall have strange opinions of them; and hence *Rev.*11. when witnesses are raised up again to confound Antichristian Doctrines, the Spirit of life from God entred
into

into them, that great fear and aw fell upon all that saw them; such light shall shine through their curtains, that men shall not sleep.

Secondly, It is a word of discovery, and that of some secret hidden vein of sin, which men never knew before; for when a man is once grown secure, it is wonderful to see that torpour that lies upon a mans spirit, a most palpable and plain sin which may be smelt and felt, yet it is not felt by himself, like him that sleeps when the ship is sinking, he knows it not; now when the Lord doth awaken, he doth it by such a discovery, and this makes them look about them, *Hag.*1.6 7,8,9,12. *because of my house which is waste.*

Thirdly, It is a word of terror, that burns as well as shines, that so they may indeed be awakened; for though *Stephens* face shines like an Angel, and he singles them out, *Oh ye stiff-necked*; yet the terror of God not falling upon them, they are secure still: But now when the Lord makes his Word full of terror, it awakens them. 1 *Sam.* 12. They would have a King; they were told of their sorrows; and hence *they feared the Lord and Samuel*; and now were awakened to see that which they never saw; God helpt forward the terror of expecting of some outward misery.

Fourthly, A word of power to awaken some or other among the Churches, and this makes all the rest to look about them, as usually when the Word comes with never such terror and majesty, we shall see men fall asleep again, without they see the effect of it in some, and one or two will awaken all the rest; like some that are asleep, when they see others up, What do I here? *Isa.*40. The Lord shews how he comforts his people; First it is by the cryer; and then Verse 9.10. it is by *Jerusalem*: When *Samaria* generally received the Word, then *Simon* also believed; when the Jew begins to look toward the Lord, ten men shall take hold of their skirts, and say, *The Lord is with you, Zach.*8.23. Sometimes this is the cry before Christs coming, and yet men may shake off their fears, despise the light: Hence the Lord hath a second Cry, and that is

SECT. III.

Secondly, THE Cry of the Rod; for there is a loud voyce in every Rod, which many times those that are most secure, must and shall hear, *Psalm* 2.5. He *shall speak to them in his wrath, Micah* 6.9. Now what are these? (I speak not to secure persons alone, we know how the Lord doth exercise them, but how he speaks to secure Churches) sometimes he hath lesser blows; but he that is not awakened by the Word and the cry of that, is seldom awakened by the cry of smaller evils; he may be startled, but seeing his pillow is still soft, he must bear it, and cannot amend it, he sleeps again. Now the things whereby the Lord doth and will awaken are Two.

First, By bringing Churches into great extremities and distress, that they know not what to do, scattering them one from another in woods where they know not what to do for bread. *Judges* 6. the *Midianites* prevailed against them seven years, untill they fled to Dens like beasts hunted up and down, and at last they have no bread, but begged, and their cattel destroyed; Verse 6. Now they cry unto the Lord because of the *Midianites*, and he sent a Prophet to make them cry for their sin; for this is the nature of a secure heart, while it hath any thing to ease it, it will not be awakened throughly, if it be in a sleeping vain; and hence

the

the Lord distresseth them ; hence *Mat.*24.29,30.after Antichristian tribulation shall there be worse ? yes, after that *Sun and Moon shall be darkned, i.e.* there shall be a confusion of all things (for it is the language of the Eastern Countries so to express it,) *Dan.*12.1,2.

Secondly, By ruinating of Churches, breaking the Candlesticks, quenching the lights, delivering them to spoylers, until the Land be almost left without inhabitant, some slain, some carried into captivity ; and now conscience cryes, Word cryes, and Rod cryes aloud to awaken them, *Isa.*6.9. *Go and make this peoples heart fat* ; Lord how long? *until their house be desolate* ; and then you hear of the sparing of a little remnant whom the Lord awakens, *Amos* 6. you see them secure , Verse 7, 8, 9. there's captivitie and plagues to destroy families ; will the Lord deal so with *Jacob*, the most excellent people under Heaven ? yea, saith the Lord, I abhor them , and when you see them on the banks of *Babylon*, then they remember *Sion, Levit.* 26. 39,40.

SECT. IV.

Reason 1.

BEcause it is so difficult to awaken one throughly ; no bonds (next to death) so strong to keep men under as security ; and hence *Ephes.*5.14. sleeping and being among the dead are joyned together ; and hence the Lord will cry, and if the Word cannot, the cry of the Rod must and shall.

Reason 2.

In regard of the people of God, who are secure with them that are vile in secure Churches ; if the Lord had none among them , he would come without crying ; but because they are there among them, the Lord will awaken ; but if any do, it is chiefly for their sakes ; for though the Lord do pardon and wash away his peoples sins, yet they come not to the fruition of pardon without faith, and this faith is never severed from repentance ; and hence the Lord will not come upon them unawares before he hath broken their hearts (not from infirmities, for they will last till death, but) broken their hearts for and with their iniquity, their chief sin.

Reason 3.

In regard of Christ himself, that so he may be received with esteem, and attended upon with all respect ; for let the Lord shew never so much kindness to a secure sinner, he is not esteemed, he is forgotten, buried like a dead carkass (a dead Christ) out of doors ; as it is with men that sleep, let the King stand by them, provide never so much for them they regard it not ; so *Deut.*32.15. Therefore we shall finde the Lord never comes to his people, but he comes then when he is esteemed ; first the Lord works the esteem, and then comes, *Matth.*23.*ult.* Christ departs till men say, *Blessed be he that cometh in the name of the Lord.*

SECT. V.

Use 1.

HEnce we may see the dangerous condition of all those that fall into a secure condition, and so dye.

1. That have been once very forward, affectionate, strict, tender, &c. but now their lamp is out.

2. That have kept themselves and their hearts from soil, their lamps bright, but now though their hearts contract soil every day, they are settled upon the Lees, and their scent is in them, and their lamp never drest.

3. That

3. That did once delight in approaching nigh to Christ in his Ordinances, in going forth in them to meet the Bridegroom; but now they not onely neglect this, but take delight therein, and rest upon their neglect; as a sleepy man takes his delight, not in his work, but in the neglect of it; and though their hearts tell them of this, yet they go on their way, and dye so; what shall we think of them? I will not absolutely determine, but they give shrewd signs, that they are fallen into a dead sleep: For the Lord will awaken his Virgins before his coming; nay, he will awaken very many others for their sakes, rather than they shall be secure; Look as it was with Christ, the nearer he came to his end, the more enlarged, and heavenly, and spiritual; so it is with them that have the Spirit of Christ: Who are the Servants whom Christ shall bless at his coming? *Luke* 12.37. *Blessed are those that shall be found watching*; That look as there is no smaller evil, but usually before it, comes the Lord and gives warning; so the greatest and last evil Death, that so they may prepare for that; as *Paul*, 2 *Tim.* 4.5, 6, 7. *The time of my departing is at hand* (how could *Paul* tell that?) the Lord gave him secret hints of it, he could smell that state before he saw it or touched it; he could observe by the course and concurrence of providences; now my course is finished, the corn is gathered, all in *Asia* forsake me; so the Lord doth many times unto his people; however he doth keep them watchful: Oh consider it therefore, you that are secure, if the Word now doth not awaken, yet when thy sick bed comes, and death appears, remember this truth; But remember it now, I carry the brand of a Reprobate upon me.

Use 2.

Hence see what little cause any man hath to take pleasure in his security; no pleasure in any sin (especially to a holy heart) as of the sin of security; for if a man takes pleasure in his cups, or in his course company, or in dancing, as *Herod*, or in gaming, &c. conscience will give him knocks, to every bit he snatcheth here; there's honey, but then a sting in them also; But now when a mans carriage is fair, outward duties performed, conscience is quiet; when a man hath been at work, he thinks in conscience he may sleep; for deepest, sweetest security comes after most work we have done; it is but a neglect, a slip, which I hope to recover out of one day; it is not an unlawful thing, but a lawful that I quiet my heart upon: Now I have good company, freedom from dangers, Ordinances, curtains drawn about me, the best sleep with me; and what hurt is here? but see the little cause you have to sleep, especially in this Country.

First, It will not be your rest alwayes, for there must and will come a cry; *Moses* took but little delight in *Pharaoh's* pleasures, they were but for a season; and therefore as the Lord there said, *Micah* 2.10. *Depart, this is not your rest.*

Secondly, If the Word doth not awaken you out of it, your cold prayers, your heartless hearing, your careless walking with God, that your lamps be not burning (burning love to the Lord and his people, shining holiness, so as others may walk after your light, and be glad to follow you) that present pleasure you take is the rotten wood that breeds the worm of a gnawing conscience, when in the time of your trouble, it shall say, What hath your idleness gained to you? and it is the fore-runner of misery; that if lighter miseries will not do, the Lord will bring seven plagues more, and drive you into a wilderness, and there shall you be famished for want of bread; and if this will not do, God will send spoilers that shall sell you for slaves, and that shall carry you away captive, and then you shal remember *Sion*, and the days you slept over your time: Find any sin, but security in it will make a desolate Country and familes; if you sin and rest in it, (though not grofs) nay do but decay in what once you had; many fay it is more here than ever; I deny it utterly, unlefs it be to them that are fecure; and if it be fo, the lofs of your firft love (a fmall thing, *&c.*) will haften breaking. Let this truth therefore be a burning Beacon to awaken you; for God will make this word good, and not let one tittle of it fall to the ground. *Ezra* 10.3. them that trembled put away their ftrange wives, and wept fore for it; fo do you; you think you may have this and the Lord too; true, but the Lord will not long abide with you if fecure.

Ufe 3.
     Hence fee the reafon why the Word ftrikes deep, and is very fmart fometimes upon the confciences of men, that a man fpeaks as if he were in their very bofom, that a man faith, God is here, that the Lord leaves thee with fad qualms upon thy confcience, and no peace from all (it is oft fanctified unlefs no grace) nay, after all this affliction comes; if thou wert not fecure, why would the Lord cry, make his Word cry, and his Rod cry? *&c.* and therefore be not weary of either, but blefs the Lord for, and quietly bear both; unlefs I had thofe terrors within, and afflictions without, I had gone aftray, *Pfal.*32.4,5. *David* was fecure and kept filence, he confeffed, and the Lord pardoned; for this fhall every one that is godly feek; Oh fo do you! think then, am not I in the number? oh let me feek then and confefs my fin!

CHAP. VI.

Of the certainty of Chrifts coming.

SECT. I.

Obfervation 2.
     THat though the coming of Jefus Chrift to his Churches be late, yet it is certain.

For though it be midnight, yet he comes we fee: For this coming at midnight is not to be underftood of the laft day of Judgment which fhall be at midnight (as the Rabbins and Monks in their devotions conceive) for Chrift fpeaks here of his coming to particular judgement alfo, which is not always at midnight: The fcope of the Parable is to provoke to continual watchfulnefs; becaufe though the Lord doth not come in the beginning of the night (as was the cuftom of the Jewifh marriages) yet he will come late, even when you look not for him; even at midnight there is a cry. I confefs the Lord fpeaks principally of his coming to Judgment; yet it is true of any other coming of Chrift to his people in this life; and becaufe particular examples and inftances are the roots of general truths (as Circumcifion a feal, fo all Sacraments are fo; Chrift is a Saviour of his people; it is meant of great falvation at laft, yet is true of all falvation befide) therefore I fhall fpeak of the coming of Jefus Chrift to his Churches and Servants in the general; and fo involve the whole coming of Chrift, for the more ufe and comfort to us.

Now

Now we shall finde that the Scripture speaks of a sixfold coming of Christ, that as all our deliverances are but shadows of our great and last deliverance; so Christs coming now is but a shadow of his great and last coming.

First, Christ is said to come to his people, when he comes to hear their prayers, *Luk.*18.8. And the Lord argues strongly, Will an unjust Judge arise at night, to help a widow a stranger, when she is importunate? and will not the Lord hear his elect and chosen? *yet,when he comes, shall he finde faith?* i.e. such prayers of faith as shall continue; oh no! but soon apt to be weary before the time comes.

SECT. II.

Object. *Bu̇t if they cease, how do they pray night and day?*
*Answ.*1. Because they do so for a time.

2. When they cease, then they are ringing in Gods ears; so that let the prayers of the elect for any mercy be once offered and presented as incense before the Lord, the Lord will not be worse than an unjust Judge, never to come to his people.

Secondly, Christ is said to come to fulfil his promises; for sometimes the Lord keeps his people exceeding short, and gives his people answers to their Prayer in particular promises (you find it so) *Psal.*85.8,9. *I will hear what the Lord will say, for he will speak peace to his people,* that so they may live by faith, and glory more in the Lord than in themselves; yet he will come, though it be very long, *Heb.*10,36,36. *Ye have need of patience, that ye may receive the promise; for yet a little while, &c.* We think it long, yet it will be so.

Thirdly, Christ is said to come to his people when he speaks peace, and breaks the clouds of fears and troubles, and shines upon his people; for while the Lord is angry, and hides his face, that a man is beyond sight of the face and love of God, now God and Christ is said to be gone; so then, when he returns to speak peace, now he is said to come, as that Martyr said, He is come, *Zach.*1.16,17.*I am returned to Jerusalem, with my mercies, and the Lord will yet comfort Zion*; for when the Lord forsakes his people for seventy years,and takes away all his Ordinances,the external visible signs of his presence,one would think he would never come, yet the Lord will come and comfort his people, *Isa.*61.2. God hath sent and anointed him, and the Spirit hath filled him, and he is as willing himself to comfort them that mourn, nay when they have the spirit of heaviness; and when it is done, Christ is come; then that is a coming of Christ.

Fourthly, There is a coming of Christ when he comes in more full measure of his Spirit to his people,and that in his Ordinances; for there is a state and time of Christianity, wherein a man is carnal and blind, and the Image of Christ darkly stampt upon the soul, and is exceeding weak; now the Lord is said to come when he doth this, *Joh.*14.18. *I will see you again, and I will not leave you comfortless*, Orphans alone without any one to take care for you; now though it be long before the Lord do come here; yet come he will, when the soul thinks it impossible, and the thing incredible; *Behold thy God, thy King commeth*, *Isa.* 40. 9. with 23. *He shall come like the rain upon the fleece of wool.*

Fifthly, Christ is said to come when he comes to destroy and root out the enemies of his Church,whether outward enemies or inward enemies,*Isa.*26.21.

Now

Now grant it be long, the Lord doth suffer them to prevail, and to be pricking bryars to the hearts of Gods people, and to the heart of Gods Spirit in his people, yet he will come; and hence the Church pleads this with God as an usual thing with him, *Isa.*64.1,2,3. He comes when men look not for him, yea he came so here; and the name of God lyes upon it to make known his name to his adversaries, *Isa.*66.5. *Hear the word of the Lord, ye that tremble at his word; your brethren that hated you and cast you out said, Let the Lord be glorified, He shall appear to your joy, but they shall be ashamed.*

Sixthly, Christ is said to come to the soul, when he comes to it at death, to abolish all sin and sorrow, and to possess the soul of immediate fellowship with himself, and at Judgement when the great mariage day shall be, and the Bride made ready, and the Bridegroom in their perfect glory to the view of all the world, *Joh.*14.3. Oh many a one is troubled now the Lord is gone from it mediately to comfort it; *Let not your hearts be troubled,* you have a God in his Word to believe in, cleave to that, and me in it; but when death comes against me, and enemies come against me, and heart fails, and eyes fails, will the Lord come? Yes, I will come again, for I go but only to prepare a place for you, and make Heaven sweet and ready for you; some would have all Christs coming here, but there is some hereafter.

S E C T. III.

BEcause the love of Jesus Christ never fails his Churches and People; love will keep men from being ever absent from the thing they love: Now look as it was with *Lazarus* whom Christ loved, *John.*11.3. he heard that he was sick, he could have come then, but he lingers and stays until he be dead, (*behold Lazarus is dead*) yea, till he had been four days dead, and then awakens him again, and *Lazarus* must come forth of his grave, to shew forth the everlasting love of the Son of God, *verf.*4. For there are two things in Christ's love; first, it is pure independant, and dear, *Prov.*8.*penult.* hence he will not ever be absent; for 1. If it be dependant, then we might say (as we change he changeth) he was good, but we have provoked him since, &c. 2. If independant, yet 'tis apt to forget, he minds me not, nor my prayers, nor sorrows: Yes, it is exceeding dear, and assures us of all; if he in love came to suffer, what will he not come to do, and that when the Church is most withered, *Zach.*3.1,2,3. and hence faith the Lord, *why sayest thou, the Lord hath forsaken me and forgotten me, when written upon the palms of my hand?* Isa. 48.14.

Lest their spirit fail; Oh the Lord is very tender of that; he that bids parents not to be bitter to their children, lest their spirits fail and be provoked, will not do it himself, *Isa.*57.17. *he will not always contend, lest the spirit fail within him, and the souls that he hath made;* Oh remember this! now how apt is the spirit of a childe of God to fail upon this! what more bitter than Gods absence!

Because to come late, is many times the best time, for he comes ever in the fulness of time; if he should come sooner or latter, he should not come in season to his people.

Of unspeakable consolation to the people of God that lie under sad and heavy perplexities in respect of the Lords absence from them (as for you that can bear this, that say to God depart if he will, this concerns not you at all) and the Lord being gone, you lye under sad thoughts that he will never return

return again ; yes, you have now heard, he will come and return again, *Say unto Sion, behold your God cometh.*

Object. *But what ? when I have been secure and careless withal ?*

Answ. Yes, though the Virgins sleep, yet the Lord will come to them ; for if his love did depend upon your watchfulness, he might never return ; onely it may be longer as to these, and he will awaken you some time before he doth come ; and truly to mourn for his absence, is to awaken with him.

Object. *But it hath been thus long before the Lord come, and therefore he will never come.*

Answ. Though long, yet you see he comes at last to them ; first, the cry says so, and then he comes ; Ministers tell you so, and it is not long after ; nay, then is the very time, when so long as you look not for him, as here to these.

<hr>

SECT. IV.

Object. **B**Ut I know it not.

Answ. God keeps his best blessings (and perfumes them long in his own hand) from his own children ; as *Isaac, David, Abraham, Heman, Christ* ; but it is best you know it not.

Hast thou been seeking the Lord for his presence (that the Lord would but see and consider thee a little) until thine eyes fail thee ? and do you think the Lord will ever forget ? I tell thee if *Peter* were in Prison, prayers would deliver him, and fetch Angels from Heaven to him ; though the Church of God lay desolate, sins great, yet the prayer of *Daniel* shall bring down words of command to make all up again ; *If thou be in any want, be careful in nothing,* &c. *He asked thee life, thou gavest him long life for ever and ever* ; nay, when thou ceasest, thy prayers have their cry, when thy mouth, when thy heart speaks not ; for prayers are not dead things but living, begotten out of a living Spirit, from a living God, presented by a living Mediator, who takes them and presents them, *Heb.* 7. and though unclean, yet being laid on that Altar they become holy.

Object. *Oh, but I am fed with nothing but promises ; I cannot deny them, but I feel them not ; I think I shall never meet the Lord,* Isa. 55.10. *Look as the rain on the dry yeelds fruit, so my word shall give you joy and peace, and the desire of your heart,* &c. *Can a man live by promises ?*

Answ. Hezekiah faith, *by these things* (*i.e.* afflictions) *do men live* ; why not by promises ? the words Christ speaketh they are Spirit and life ; *David* did, 2 *Sam.*23.5. *Heb.*10. *The just shall live by his faith* ; and *if any man draw back, my soul shall have no pleasure in him, i.e.* wholly. It is admirable how the *Israelites* had a promise of the land, and many wars must they have, and yet *Josh.*23.14,15. *Not one thing hath failed of all that the Lord hath promised.* So say I to you.

Obj. *Oh but I have been long in trouble, and have had no peace ?*

Ans. Hast thou been longer than *David*, whose moysture was dryed up, who hath nothing to present before the Lord, *Psal.*6. but weakness, and bones vexed, *verse* 2. a soul vexed, *verse* 3. and that long weary with groaning, *vers.*6. tears in the night when others are at rest, his eyes consumed with grief, and yet *verse* 8,9. *The Lord hath heard the voyce of my weeping, and prayer too* : sorrows cry, and sins cry also ; and hence he faith, *Depart from me all ye workers of iniquity,* &c.

Object

Object. But I am so weak, my heart so streitned, so little light and life, and seeking I have been for more, and find it not.

Answ. If Christ's presence be sweet, and his absence bitter, that you seek not more for your lusts sake than the Lords sake, then know that the Lord will return again, as verily as he is gone ; *he will not leave thee comfortless* ; you shall have that is fit for you to keep you humble and faithful ; it may be one Sermon may do more good than twenty. *Joh.1.50. Dost believe because I saw thee under the figtree ? thou shalt see greater things than these ;* God hath greater things to shew thee, if the Lord hath *translated thee into the Kingdom of his dear son* ; hence it is said of the *encrease of his government and peace there shall be no end*, Isa.9.7.

Object. But enemies may oppose us ?

Answ. Let it be so ; but what if the Lord be with you ?

Object. But he is gone.

Answ. No, the Lord will either come before trouble to deliver you from it, as *Asa* when a troop came against him, 2 *Chron.*15.11. let not man prevail against thee ; *Asa* had wrapt God about him, cloathed himself with the majesty of God by faith, *Isa.*54.*penul*. They shall gather together, and shall come against thee, but they shall not prosper, because the Lord is come ; or if he doth stay, yet he will give them some blood, and come upon them for your blood ; *he that sheds mans blood, by man shall his blood be shed* ; but such as shed Churches blood, by God shall their blood be shed ; The souls under the Altar shall cry, and then comes wo ; he will do so in *Germany* if there have been Churches blood shed ; he is making way for glorious deliverance when God shall come, and the wicked shall melt away as wax : *Lucifer* must fall though lifted up with pride . *David* was troubled with a *Saul* and a *Doeg. Psal.*54. but God shall pull them up by the roots,&c. many of Gods Servants lye under reproaches and revilings (and the wicked boast of their sin) God shall pluck them up by the roots never to grow again : Hypocrites lie hid for a time, but all the Churches shall know that the Lord is a God that searcheth the hearts, *Luk.*12,1. *Psal.*12.5,2. No good man left, but some men of deceit and flattery, some Apostates, &c. We are in fear (in this Country) of enemies ; we came hither to shelter our selves under the wings of God ; left our comforts for it ; here we are at his posts, it is not honors we seek ; and now it may be enemies are plotting, or will be coming to take us unawares, when weak, and so run away with the spoil, unless we will be bond-men to our former yoke ; it may be the Lord will help then, *Ezek.*38. 10,20. to the end. If not, it may be the Lord will refine us more, and purge away our dross, and discover men that came hither for Ordinances and for peace sake, and betray the Ordinances ; yet the Lord will come, and his blow shall ruine them, especially if his awake not at his cry,*Isa.*25.9,10.it shall be said when the terrible ones are blasts , *Lo ! this is our God, and in this mount shall the hand of the Lord come.*

Object. But still my sin continues.

Answ. The Church in the *Revelations*, when they have all things, yet are absent from the Lord , and sin before the Lord makes them say , *On come Lord Jesus !* saith Christ, *Behold I come quickly* ! Christ will come at last and for ever comfort you, and be with you, and you ever with the Lord ; this coming to be sure shall be, and what then though you walk through the vail of the shadow of death ! the Lord is with you, and him that is the glory of Saints, the joy of Angels, the rest and delight of God, whom all ends of the earth have looked unto, shalt thou see with those eyes, and be with him for ever, and then shall he give thee double for all thy sorrows, sins, temptations, when every one else shall leave thee, and shall rejoyce and glory in thee, that ever he hath got

thee

thee, and (as he said) he will then serve thee, *Luk.*12. Oh his coming would swallow up all our sorrows; Christ tells them of nothing but this, *Joh.*14. I wonder at Christians that are sadded at losses and evils here; Why the Lord will come!

SECT. V.

Quest. **H**Ow shall I know whether the Lord will come or no?

Answ. 1. If the Lord ever hath or doth make this the rest and stay of thy heart, not only for righteousness, but for all fulness of comfort, and that not onely to thy conscience, but to thy heart and will: for many rest on Christ for righteousness; but what comforts their hearts? they joy in other things, and are greedy after things in the world, &c. Now as a man that rests on Christ for righteousness, he abhors all other righteousness; so if a Christian rest on Christ for consolation, you will deny all other things to comfort you also, *Jer.*17.5,6. *Cursed is the man that trusteth in man, he shall not see when good comes.* Psal.22.1. *Oh Lord, why hast thou forsaken me? I trust in thee; our fathers trusted in thee and were delivered:* Yes, but not you that are so poor and vile: True, I am so in the eyes of the world, but on God have I been cast; To trust to Christ for righteousness, but not for consolation, is to marry a man to pay debts, but not to live upon his house; try if it be so or no; thou feelest the Lord gone, yet thy faith is not gone from him.

2. If the Lord hath given thee a heart, whether the Lord comes or no, not to trouble thy self about success, and time of coming, as to minde the doing of his work against his coming, that thy heart is resolved and will live to him though he never comes to thee. *Joh.*2.5. When *Mary* said that wine was wanting, saith Christ, *it is not my hour;* then, *what ever he bids you do, do it ;* *Heb.*10.36. you have need of patience; for all impatience ariseth from minding inordinately the success, what the event will be, and distracting the mind there; but (as a poor servant) when a man thinks whether Christ come or not, these sins shall down; this argues love never to be forgotten; *Judges* 10.16. nothing grieves the Lord and makes the Lord absent, but because grieved with sin, misery comes; now sin is removed; it may be no assurance while thou diest or livest; yet if resolved my soul shall follow the Lord, now it is right, &c. But if while the Lord is now gone, your hearts are jolly, and loose every way, why desire you the day of the Lord? it is darkness to you.

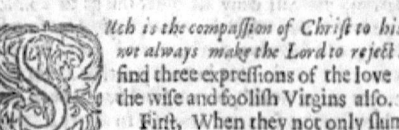

CHAP. VII.

Of Gods compassion towards wise and foolish Virgins.

SECT. I.

Uch is the compassion of Christ to his people, that deep security cannot always make the Lord to reject them; and therefore we shall
find three expressions of the love and kindness of the Lord to
the wise and foolish Virgins also.

First, When they not only slumber but sleep, and that long,
even to the coming of the Bridegroom almost, yet Christ
spares them, and doth not all this while cut them off, and bury them out of his
sight, as men that do forget him.

Secondly, He prevents them with awakening grace, and the Lord is up
when his servants be abed, and is awakened for their good when they are asleep
and regard not him; and first by his cry he awakens them before they shake up
themselves; when once the Churches fall asleep, they would sleep their long
sleep, and never awaken, if the Lord should not by some cry or other prevent
them.

Thirdly, He longs for their fellowship and company though secure; and
therefore it is not a cry of terror and wrath, the Bridegroom hath forsaken you,
for your secure careless course; but it is a cry of grace, *go forth to meet him*;
yet he iswilling to have communion with you, yet he desires that you would have
communion with him; oh come out to meet him; I shall wrap up all these
together, because I shall be brief. Wonderful was the grace of Christ toward the old world, when for the space of one hundred and twenty years he
waited for them, who after they had been an hundred and nineteen secure,
yet then the same spirit that waiteth for us in these days of the Gospel, preached
the Lord unto them.

Jeremiah was very long speaking to *Israel* (as the other Prophets) in so
much that the Lord professeth to send the King of *Babylon* against them, yet the
Lords heart melts, *cha.26.1,2,3. Speak unto them; it may be they will hearken, and
turn that I may repent*; So *Jer.3.* they had polluted the Law, *ver.2.* showres are
withheld (which is no great matter) small evils are arguments of hearts re-
volted from God; they did the Lord as much mischief as they could, and were
secure, *verse 3.* Yet mark, wilt thou not from this time cry My Father? meet
the Lord as thy Husband? will he keep his anger for ever? Nay, the Lord cast
off Adulterous *Israel*, and they knew the cause, yet went on securely in the same
sins; yet see, *verse 14. Turn oh back-sliding children*, Prov. 6. 5,6. *How
long, &c.*

SECT. II.

IN regard of the foolish, there is no reason, but the Lords pitty and compassion to a sinful people; he hath compassion on them because he will, for he doth not pity people only in respect of their miseries, but in respect of their sins, 2 *Chron. ult.* 16. he sent his Prophets among them (and they despised them) *because he had compassion on his people*; the cords of grace are let down to all sinners, Blasphemers, Opposers of God, &c.

In regard of the wise Virgins, because his Mariage-covenant with them is not suspended on any thing on his peoples part; for though there is a condition which the Lord doth require of his people in Mariage-covenant, yet the Lord so requires it, as that he intends to work it, and undertakes to maintain it; and there is no evil in them, but he promiseth in this Covenant to remove; he will heal them of it, but he will not cast them off for it; hence *Ephes.5.25.* Christ loves his Church; what, because it had loveliness? no, but that he might wash it; and if he loves it to this end, that he might wash it, then no pollution can make the Lord utterly to cast it off; if he loves because of deformities, that he might wash them away, then none can quench his love; hence no security, no carelesness, though deep, though long, so long as the Mariage-bond between man and wife continues, so long as no sin is committed that can break this Mariage-bond, so long infirmities or other distempers never separate. Now, no sin in them that are given to Christ can break the Mariage-bond, because it is wholly undertaken on the Lords part; women may commit Adultery, and break their Mariage-bond, because they are not kept by their Husband from that; but the Lord undertakes this for his people, *to put his fear in their heart, that they shall never depart from God. Hos.2.19,20. I will betroth thee unto me for ever, and you shall know the Lord*; hence the Lord may humble, but never utterly reject his, for security in a lust.

SECT. III.

OF Direction and thankfulness to the people of God; Oh! do not always fall to fits of doubts after security, though deep and long (as many Christians do) and so are ever laying and pulling up foundations; after most peace of conscience, most security, and then the Sea rageth again, and it is hard for any man to keep his peace; have you had such mercy, and love, and will you thus be careless and loose again? believe it, the Lord will break your bones if you love your beds, and not give you rest till you finde it on another pillow; but yet do not deny his love, though you have forgot it; do not say you are not Virgins, because fallen asleep; and that the Bridegroom will never come to meet you, because you have lingred in meeting him; for *behold he cometh*: I know there is a difference between the security of the wise and foolish; of which hereafter: The Disciples fall asleep in the garden after a trebble warning, yet it was against much reluctancy; hence Christ pitied them; *the Spirit is willing, but the flesh is weak*; and when they were awakened, their vessels were not found empty; *Peters* vessel was full of love to Christ before, and when the Lord awakens him, he tells the Lord he loved him; and his fall and security in it for a time made him more humble, and love the Lord with less self-confidence, and more purity: But oh, wonder at it, rejoyce in it, and be thankful for it! especially you that have fallen into any secure frame

since

since ye came into these Virgin-Churches; which you cannot but do, if you consider the greatness of this sin; to sin and be long secure, and fast asleep, is strange.

1. This is the great provoking sin; look throughout all the Book of God, let the sin be great, and immediately after conscience smitten, bones broken, and heart awakened, we shall never see the Lord but he is pacified, the Lord hears their groanings, and remembers his Covenant; but little sins fallen into, and by security continued in, the Lord visits for this, *Psal.*50. When a man shall not only sin, but take delight in it, as a man doth in his sleep.

2. This is a sin in places of liberty and Ordinances, whereas the Lord was never so good to thee, and thy heart never worse to him, never so secure, you thought and purposed never to be so watchful and tender as now; to be secure here, greatly aggravates such security.

3. This sin is a common sin; now this adds to a sin, when a man has a hand in a national sin, that runs in the blood of all the Churches; for so you see it is, all the Virgins secure: when all forget the Lord, as though there were not enough to lay more loab upon the Lord; what doth this but harden others in security; thy wives heart, thy brethrens heart, such a one is secure; as though it were not enough to fight against the Lord, but Giant-like to fall among the troops of them that securely dishonor the Lord: When the old world was secure we heard nothing of that; but when the Sons of God came to be secure, and all flesh corrupted their ways, the Lord falls a mourning, and repents that he had made man: When any sin groweth general in Churches, that sin is most grievous to God; Princes children when they sin alone it is grievous, but when they take part with all the mutinous crue against their Father, this strikes deep; Oh that ever mine eyes should see this evil.

4. It is a sin which is the last, and is the ruine of all the foolish Virgins, and perfects their perdition, as here it did; they slept till it was too late; oh that the Lord should not cast you off for this! admire at this; and let thy heart, and house, and work be filled with praise for this: You have complained long of a secure heart; see it humble thee that it continueth, but make thee wonder that the Lord will not cast thee off.

SECT. IV.

Use 2.

TO all those that have been long secure; let this compassion of the Lord awaken you, and draw you to him, and make you come out and meet him; and give entertainment to the Lord, who hath not yet cast you off from him, but yet crys, oh come and meet me: Methinks this should awaken you; what, hath not the Lord cast me off yet? no! but his cry this day is, Oh come out and meet me! The Lord might have cut thee off in thy security; this is his season to others, when men cry peace, peace; and he might have let thee slept and never awake more till past hope; yet here is his grace, oh come and meet him! and will you despise it and refuse the Lord?

Object.1. *I have no oyl in my vessel, no grace in my heart; what should I meet him for, or look for him! I am so vile and so secure, he cannot look upon me.*

Answ.1. You have the more need of receiving him as your Bridegroom, that so you may receive the eternal anointing of his Spirit of Grace and Life in your hearts.

2. Now you have time to get both.

Object. 2. *But it is long before the Bridegroom comes; there's time enough for this hereafter.*

Answ. 1.

Anfw. 1. Would you never look after the Lord, and being betrothed to him till the very time of his coming? will you despise Grace to the utmost, and weary out Grace to the last gaspe? behold the Lord shall come, and thy eye shall see him, and waile because of him; and the Lord will make thee cry out on thy death-bed, and warn others to take heed of trifling with the Lord long, who didst never take warning thy self.

2. You see when the Cry is made, the Bridegroom is not far behinde; now is his cry, and you see some that did awaken, and after the cry, had time too little to trim their lamps. It may be many cryes have been sounding in thy secure ears; and yet there's time, he is not come; grant it, and will you therefore despise this rich grace the more because of his goodness.

Obj. 3. *But I am well as I am without the Bridegroom.*

Anf. It may be sleep is sweet for the present; but if thou wert awakened, thou wouldst be of another minde; there are many here present that can say, they thought themselves well, &c. but now I see my error, &c. Oh Lord, what if I had been left to these thoughts; yet this is ever the frame of a secure heart (like swine) well when it is in the mire, basking in the Sun.

1. It is pleasure; but consider, it is but short; long security will end in hideous affrights, and doleful awakenings, for one days short sleep : I remember *Nineveh's* are set out by this, *Zeph.* 2. 15. *This is the rejoycing City, that dwelt carelesly*; painting out their misery for this sin above all the rest; so when plagues be upon you, God and Angels shall point at you, This is the secure sinner that lived loosly.

2. It deprives you of more rest and ease; carnal security keeps a man from knowing spiritual security; while your sin and sleep is sweet, the grace of Christ and the sense of his love shall be strangers to you, and to your hearts; Christ is anointed to preach to a weary, not to a sleepy sinner: *Isa.* 50. 4. There are seasons of refreshings and coolings, which such shall never know.

3. This which is thy pleasure, is the Lords sorrow and grief; look as when the sinner mourneth under his sin, the Lords heart is quieted, *Zeph.* 3. 17, 18. *I said I would confess, and thou forgavest*: So when a man delights in his sin, the Lords soul is then grieved; and the more delight, the more grief; Christ mourned for the hardness of their hearts, *Mark* 5. 3. Now grant that you have this pleasure, yet what joy is it to think, that while I have my ease and peace, the Lord hath his burden; my rest and peace is the Lords sorrow in Heaven; when the sons of God grow fleshly, the Lord repented that he had made man; Oh let the groanings of a compassionate God awaken you out of this security!

SECT. V.

Object. **B**ut there's none secure here.

Answ. It's hard for wise not to fall here; but for foolish not to fall to this sin, at least to be long preserved from it, will be miraculous; but for the most part of men not to be drowned in it.

1. Have not divers lived and never been awakened at all, not so much as to cry out, I am a damned man, what shall I do? thou never hadst a spark of eternal flames of wrath to kindle thy conscience, and that after an ignorant and prophane life.

2. If you have been troubled, have you not fallen asleep before ever you have gotten any settled peace and comfort in the blood of Christ, only hast got so much oyl as makes thy lamp burn, and gives thee a name to live, when thy vessel is empty, and heart is dead.

to

3. Have not many, nay most of thy days been spent without any sorrow for, or reckoning concerning thy sin? it may be you have a Lent and a cleansing week sometimes; but most commonly it is otherwise, that you never see sin, but sleep in it, and set your selves to go on, having found no hurt in such a course as yet.

4. How many use the Ordinances of God, come to them, but never gain good by them? What is there no gold in these mines? Yes, but a slothful, secure heart will not dig for them.

5. Nay do not Gods crys make the sleep thee faster? he taketh away a great part of thy estate from thee; and thou lookest upon the misery and shame of rags and poverty; and thy heart dyeth away with discontent, and grows more worldly. If light be darkness, if means of wakening be a means of sleeping, how great is that security? Oh therefore go out and meet the Bridegroom!

SECT. VI.

Quest. But how shall I receive the Lord as my Bridegroom and Husband?
Answ. 1. See what thy widowhood is, and forsaken condition, *Isa.*54.5,6. *When thou wast refused, the Lord loved thee*; what creature can help thee, when the Lord forsakes thee? what a misery is it to live out of a fathers house!

2. See his love that he makes to you, otherwise you will never conclude it, but sink, saying, *The Lord forgets me*: Oh see his love he makes to thee to receive him; and that thou wouldest give thy consent to have him, that thou mayst love him, *Isa.*56.6. A carnal heart, a whorish lover desires to close with Christ, that Christ may give gifts to it and love it; but a Virgin that she may love the Lord, and be wholly his; and this will answer all doubts; what have you to do with Christ, and all that mercy, grace and glory? Oh 'tis that I may love the Lord more.

Object. 'Tis presumption.
Answ. No, it is that I may love the Lord indeed; and now when the heart is drawn here, *Psal.*45.10. *Then shall the King have pleasure in thy beauty*; pleasure in thee, and all that thou dost: What, in me, that am weary of my self? Yes in thee. 1. When he forsakes others, he will meet thee. 2. Though he departs, and sorrows attend thee, yet thy sorrows shall be turned into joy, and he will see thee again, and never cease delighting in thee, but wrap thee up in everlasting embracings.

CHAP.

CHAP. VIII.

Of Christs coming, and his awakening sleepy Christians.

VERSE 7.

Then all the Virgins arose and trimmed, &c.

SECT. I.

IN these words to verf. 10. is set down the effect which the cry had upon the Virgins.

First, Upon all of them in general, in this seventh verse.

Secondly, Upon the foolish in particular, in the next verses.

First the effect it wrought upon all of them in general, both good and bad, is set down in two things. 1. They did all arise, *i. e.* they were throughly awakened out of their secure condition. 2. Being awakened they fell to their work, which was to trim their lamps, as to beautifie and adorn their lamps, which had now lost their light and beauty by soiling themselves, and all through neglect; now they trimmed them, when first, they wiped off the soil; secondly, made search for that which was necessary for the shining glory of them; Thus far the foolish trimmed their lamps, who yet did not find that oil in their vessels, which was the main thing to beautifie them indeed, which the wise had; so that they all trimmed their lamps; the wise trimmed theirs indeed; the foolish theirs, so well as they could.

That the serious real apprehension of the nearness of Christs coming, is e- Observa-
tion I. *nough to awaken throughly the most secure Virgins:* I say, if Virgins (especially that have been awakened to know any thing of the Lords coming) this will awaken them; for when the cry was made He cometh, now they all arose, whilst he did tarry as they thought, then they sleep; but when the cry comes, that he is near and coming, oh now they awake.

This coming is meant either of his coming to the last Judgement, or of his coming to particular Judgement immediately at and after death: I shall apply my self chiefly to the coming of Christ at death to his people, because this doth chiefly concern us; the near approach of this will awaken, when apprehended near.

*Rom.*13.11. When the Apostle would awaken them out of security, *Your salvation now is nearer than when you first believed, i. e.* that perfect salvation which is at that time; now if the apprehension that it is nearer than at first

awakens,

awakens, much more when it is apprehended so indeed. *Jam.5.8,9.* There was it seems divers that were oppressed, and they ready to faint, and forsake the Lord, and wait no more; what therefore doth he do? *the coming* (saith he) *of the Lord draweth nigh.*

1 *Sam.12.19.* When *Samuel* told them before that misery should come if they would have a King, they cared not; now when thunder came, that they saw death and the Lord near them, now they feared, and cryed, and repented; *Oh we dye,* say they, *pray for us:* It is with the Soul as it is with Sea-men, when they first set out in the Main, if the wind be good, and all things well, they take their rest and sleep, though going nearer every day than other; but when they apprehend they are near the shore, now they look out, though in the night; so here.

SECT. II.

Reason 1.

BEcause here a man sees an end of his sinful way, and of all his delights which have bound him up in the bonds of security; a soft bed, and an easie pillow, and much feeding in a place of rest, will procure much sleeping; the heart of a man would never be secure, if it had not some delight or other to quiet it self withal; now at Christs coming there is an end of it, then a man is stript naked of all his greatness and honor, friends, blessings; and when a man sees an end, and is come to an end of a sinful way, now all a mans delights and hopes perish; the beginning of a sinful course is sweet and beautiful (like pictures seen afar off beautiful) but the end is gal and woormwood; for every sinful secure course is sweet in appearance, or indeed; if only in hope, and conception (as in a dream) when the end comes, all a mans hopes perish. If indeed it hath been sweet, now there's the more grief; now my heart, my life, my blood must be taken from me, and what profit is there now in this my stubborn way! when a man is sinking, and the boat is breaking, what a miserable wretch now, Lord help! hence *Ezek.7.3,6.* when an end is come, now they fling their silver in the streets; Oh the stumbling-block of mine iniquity, verse 18, 19. now *they shall seek peace and shall not find it,* verse 25. now *they shall seek a vision of the Prophet*, verse 26. Like a man that is drawn into a fair way, and is out of that his way, when he comes to an end, and is forsaken of all and left in a wood, now what's the profit?

Reason 2.

Because at his coming there is the entrance and passage into eternity, and into an eternal state of weal or wo; now though the apprehension of the end of a secure sinful way, may and will awaken, yet when eternity is apprehended it will amaze; for this time is but a little spring or river which runs into eternity, and carries all men living down with it to eternity: Now when men see an end of time, and the beginning of eternity, and themselves posting thereto, it is as when a man sees himself floating upon the waters, where there's no bottom, and all stay gone, though he hath been long secure, now he will cry out if he sees it. It is with men now, as it is with those that are ready to be cast down from some Towr, it makes the heart tremble, oh! where shal I alight! oh it's impossible but if men do apprehend eternity, and that also near unto them, but it will awaken them; it will make a stout, stony-hearted *Saul* to run to *Urim*; it will make Kings and Princes run to Monasteries, and men to Cells and Deserts; It will make the proudest *Felix* tremble when *Paul* reasons of Judgement to come. It's usually the first thing that doth awaken the people of God; eternity doth amaze them, and them that have fallen to all lasciviousness. Oh eternity!

Reason 3.

Because of the terror at the coming of the Lord; *Revel.6.ult.* to them
that

that be unprovided and unprepared; hence it is, and will be, when an evil is near, fear will flie out: Men as men will do it, unless they be walking blocks and bruits. **For,**

1. Then they are to stand naked before the Lord so great and holy.

2. Then they shall have all their sins set in order, *Psal.* 50. 21. and especially those secret sins which they never saw, and whereby they did perfect their own perdition.

3. Then the final sentence past, never to be recalled again, and they shall know it; for if there might be a day to repent, then some hope; but if not, oh this awakens.

4. Then to be surrendred up into the hands of Devils, to be kept by that Jaylor in Prison, 1 *Pet.* 3. 19. *until the coming of the great day*; and so to be kept in their custody, and to be in their fellowship, looking back, and mourning for time mis-spent, looking to time to come, shortly to meet my body, and then to be parted for ever from the Lord! oh when this evil is apprehended, it will awaken a man to search and look about him.

SECT. III.

Use 1.

HEnce see a great cause of the deep and long security of many a man, and that in Virgin-Churches under all awakening means, Ordinances and Providences of God; men put far from them this day of death, and time of Christs coming, they think seldom of it, come not near to it, nor make it near to them; sometime they complain of a dead sluggish spirit, secure heart, and yet remain so, and wonder sometime at the reason of it why it should be so; why? this is one reason of it, either you think not of this coming of the Lord, or see it not near, even at the door, but number many days to your selves, and this is the cause of it, you do not lodge in, nay look to your Coffins, and walk to your graves side often, and so stand there and hear the cry, and see the Lord a coming; there will be more in what I say than what you see at first blush of this truth; but this I know, and the Word proves it, universal security ariseth from hence. As for instance.

1. Why do men minde the things of the world so much? that there is such care for them, such eager desire after them, that many times prayer is neglected, Sabbaths neglected, when will they be at an end? God neglected, Souls of wife, children servants, a mans own soul neglected and overgrown with nettles; that there is such an high opinion, dreams of worldly goods, and when a man hath them, then at rest; because, with the glutton, they think they have goods for many a year; and hence we shall see when a man waketh, death is near to him, and when it is near to a man, now he thinks he hath been deceived in all the things of the world, that they are not good for him, 1 *Cor.* 7. 29. *The time is short, and the fashion of the world passeth away:* Nothing makes these things so sought after and good but only esteem; now this is because men look only to things present.

2. Why do mens hearts sink with the meanness of their outward condition, and the troubles of it? (for this is security) it is because of this, they do not remember the nearness of the coming of the Lord; it is but a little while longer, and then the God I have chosen will alone be sweet, and he will make me amends for all my troubles, and therefore let me bear up my head a little while. *Psal.* 39. when *David*s heart began to be troubled by seeing others prosperity, his own misery, Lord (saith he) *make me to know my end, and the measure of my days, mine age is as an hand breadth*; hence ver. 7. *Lord what hope I for? truly my hope is in thee.*

Ggg   3. Why

3. Why are men puft up with their own excellencies, and filled with such pride and high conceits of themselves, sometimes of their beauty, sometimes of their apparel, sometime their friends, sometime their esteem, and they value themselves much by this? men consider not the coming of the Lord, which shall stain the pride of all glory, *Isa.*23.8. and that this time is near.

4. Why do people complain they cannot prize the Lord or his Ordinances as they could? why do men on their death-beds then prize it, then pray, then hear? then oh a little mercy, then send for *Moses*, then the Lord is righteous; and if he shew mercy, never such a pattern as I, because now death and Christs coming is near: you do therefore undervalue the gain of Ordinances, because of this; if you did, you would glory in nothing but the Lord, *Jer.* 9. 21, 23.

Jer. 9. 20, 23.

5. Why do men go up and down without any assurance of the Lords love, or the truth of any grace, and that after conviction? why do men upon their death-beds seek for it, and then fall a searching, and then open their estates, and then desire peace? because the coming of the Lord is near; you put the day of the Lord far from you; if you saw it near, you would get on your armor in readiness against the day of battel; if your Husband be at door, you would get on your apparel, *Psal.* 89. 46,47,49.

6. Why is so much time spent unfruitfully, that a Christian is not abundant in doing and receiving good? who is the better for thy speeches, for thy prayers, for thy example? when *Moses Psal.* 90. had numbered mens days, then v.17. *stablish thou the work of our hands upon us*; Look upon a Christian at first conversion, he thinks he shall not live long; it's strange to see what prayers, what tears; how fruitful, how diligent he is; Oh therefore see your sore this day! 'tis nigh almost, O therefore up and be doing.

SECT. IV.

Use 2.

OH therefore, if ever you would be freed from this infectious, this damning sin and plague of security, make the coming of the Lord near unto you, and come you near unto it, be ever near it; number your days, they are soon told over, and often think of your latter end when the Bridegroom comes; for this will awaken you out of your secure fits, and make you fall hard to your work.

First, This will make you do much work for the Lord in a little time; when *Moses* was to be gathered to his Fathers, now he provides for the Church, now he instructs the people more than ever concerning their estates, &c.

Secondly, It will be very sweet; it is but a very little while though it be bitter, and it will put strength to do it; work is wearisom for want of strength; so Christ's work is wearisom, because we want strength; now this doth put strength into the soul, *Jam.* 5.8,9.

Thirdly, It will be very glorious; works even of dying men are very glorious and successful: Speeches of living (yet dying Christians) sink deep; for then God is near unto us when we are near unto him, and see things as they are; and hence such speeches are commonly blest to men; the speeches and works and carriages of Christ were never so glorious, as when most near his end.

SECT. V.

SECT. V.

Object. But should a Christian in Christ use this as a motive to stir up his heart, or no? this is mockery, this Philosophy sends men to; doth Divinity do so? a Christian must be acted by love, not fear.

Answ. 1. That which God hath sanctified for this end we may make use of for the attainment of it; now God hath sanctified afflictions, death, and the fear of them for this end, to awaken the secure sinner; *Jehosaphat* fears and proclaimeth a fast; *Noah* feared and built an Ark; Christ himself to the Church of *Sardis* (to awaken her) professeth *he will come as a thief in the night suddenly,* 2 Pet.3. *If the heavens shall be dissolved, what manner of persons should we be:* It is true, it is hypocrisie for a man to be led only by fear; but it is prophaness (the original of the Sadduces) not to be terrified at all; it is not hypocrisie to be awakened partly by fear to the apprehension of these things; for God hath sanctified them for this end, and though these do not work grace (where there was none before) barely, yet the awakening of conscience, is that whereby the Lord prepares for grace; and this is good in its kinde; and it stirs up grace where it was before, as here this cry makes the Virgins to kindle their oyl, and set that a burning.

Objection 2. *But the time is not near; Should I apprehend an untruth?*

Answ. It may be 'tis near; the apprehension of this is not false, and this the Lord gives verse 13. as the ground of constant watch, *for you know not when he comes;* now if men love their goods, they will watch.

2. It is near; if you had but wisdom to see into eternity, and the nature of time, you would say so also, *Psal.*90.4. *A thousand years are but as yesterday, and as a watch in the night.* Verf.5. our time is as a sleep, short and vain. Ver.6. it is but as a flower of one days glory; nay, it is but as a thought, verf.9. It is so when you see things as they are, and you will account it so. Oh therefore let me beg this of you, make Christs coming, and death near to you, that you may be delivered from your dead palsies, deep slumbers, and dying sick sleeps; especially seeing the signs of the Lords coming to reckon with you, do you think to escape? Masters that betrust Servants with most, will they call others to account, to whom they have betrusted less, and not you? what people under heaven be trusted with more mercies and liberties than we! and do you think he is gone to a far Country, and will never return? He let *Palatine* and other Churches enjoy the means long, he summons them to an account by famine, sword, and pestilence, wilde beasts, and cruel Souldiers; and shall he never ride in his circuit this way? yes verily: Do you boast in the goodly stones of this Temple? If the Lord by your security be despised, and his Messengers, and Ordinances, and Kingdom, he will not leave one stone upon another: When will this be? not yet: that's true; yet awake at the signs of it, *Mat.*24. *Wars, rumors of wars, famine, aerthquakes, deceivers that come in the name of Christ, Apostacy of Professors, whence many come to be offended, Divisions and scatterings of one Brother against another, Iniquity abounding in the World, and Love growing cold in Churches;* If these be not amongst us now, we have the less cause to fear; if so, have we not cause to awake one hour considering our time is nigh! if not, yet Christs time is nigh of coming to particular persons.

SECT. VI.

Quest. HOw shall I make it near?

Answ. Truly till the Lord teach us the number of our days, we can never do it: yet three things do;

First, Convince thy soul of the sin and evil of looking after to morrow, and reaching after that time which is to come, *Prov.*27.1. 1. It is none of thine. 2. Nothing draws the heart so much from God. 3. You will never find what you expect hence; these are lying vanities, therefore come not to these wells.

Secondly, Either thou wantest assurance, then fear his coming, for fear will make misery present, and so awaken; and hope (*è contra*) good present: Or thou hast assurance; then love his coming, see all thy good wrapt up there; and love will make things absent beloved, and present comfort in the thoughts of them; as wicked men that love the things of this life, and are in certain hopes to have them, they oft rejoyce in the hopes; because the good is present, they reckon upon it as theirs already.

Thirdly, See how near you are unto the Lord Jesus: 1. That you are made for the Lord, not to enjoy these things; they are made for you, and not you to serve them; because God hath called you out of this world, from the grave, hell, sin, to life; now the next is glory, 2 *Cor.*5.3,4,5.

2. That now there's nothing but thy breath, thy body between thee and Jesus Christ; when this shell is broken, thou art with the Lord, and shalt see him with open face; this will make you look for the day of delivery.

CHAP. IX.

Of Christians, trimming their Lamps; *and how holiness is the Christians glory.*

SECT. I.

And trimmed their Lamps.

 HE word (*ἐκόσμησαν*) signifies adorned, beautified their lamps, made clean or cleansed; It is the same word which is used 1 *Tim.*2.9. *Womens adorning let it not be with pearls, but good works.*

Quest. What is the glory of the Lamp?

Answ. First, When the filth is wiped away, which did defile it.

Secondly, When oyl is gotten, and the lamp is lighted; now its in its full trim as it was at first when they went out; whilst they were sleeping, their lamps not being looked into, began to lose their shining glory; now they recover them. Object.

Object. *But how came the foolish to trim their Lamps?*

Answ. They did endeavor it, and did something that way, as is apparent from the context, and so they trimmed them so far as they could reach; but the compleat and full adorning of them was this of the wise. And therefore look as by oyl in the vessel is meant the eternal anointing of the Spirit of grace within, so by shining is meant the glorious profession arising from it, as the adorning of women, 1 *Tim.2.9.* is their holy conversation.

That the Spirit of holiness abiding in the hearts, and shining in the lives of Saints, it is their excellency, ornament and glory: This adorns the Virgins lamps; through security they began to lose their glory; Now when they prepare their lamps, they adorn their lamps; and this is their glory.————   *Observation 2.*

2 *Cor.3.ult. We are changed into the same image from glory to glory;* grace and holiness is glory. *Ephes.5.27.* Christ presents a glorious Church; wherein? *without spot or wrinckle, and holy before the Lord.* 1 *Thess.4.4.* Sanctification and honor are joyned together.

SECT. II.

Quest. WHat *Spirit of holiness is it which is a Christians glory?*
    *Answ.*It is not every patcht profession of holiness which is a Christians true glory; for by what means is the name of God more blasphemed by the wicked of the world, than by those that profess holiness, yet break out into scandalous sins! *Rom.2.14.* it is a wonder if a prophane man be good a little; but it is a greater wonder and scandal if a professor be bad a little. Neither is it a most glorious appearance of holiness; this is deceit, craft, and hypocrisie, not a glory: A Stage-player that acts the part of a King, wants the glory of a King; and hence *Paul* opposeth himself to these, 2 *Cor.5.12.* But when there is first an exemplary holiness, arising secondly, from the fulness of the Spirit of grace within, as here in the Virgins, a shining profession from an inward Spirit, when Christ hath attained the end of offering up himself, *that men are a peculiar people, zealous of good works:* Suppose the lamp doth burn, yet if not for the end it was made, so that a man can scarcely see his way, nor others by it, its glory is much lost: Now the end of the Spirit of holiness is this, the end of Christ's death and ministery is this; *Phil.2.13,14.* and though they may speak evil, yet 1 *Pet.2.12.* they may glorifie God in that day; when it is with men as it is with those, *Zach.8.ult. We have seen God is in you,* when a man maintains a sleepy careless profession and name, the lamp now wants its trim; when lamps are put under bushels, they lose their glory.

Quest. 2. *Before whom is this their glory?*
*Answ.*1. Before the eyes of God the Father, *Joh.12.26. He that shall serve me, him shall my Father honor;* and though the world honor them not, yet they shall be spectators of it.

2. Before Jesus Christ his eyes, *Psal.45.11. Forget thy country, and thy fathers house, so the King shall take pleasure in thy beauty.*

3. Before all the people of God themselves, 2 *Thess.1.4,5. So that we glory of you among all the Churches;* every one will be speaking of such; oh there's one of a thousand; hardly shall you go into his company but you shall get some good, and life, and heat from him.

4. Before Hypocrites many times, who of all others are the greatest haters of the ways of holiness and the power of godliness; hence *Herod, Mar.6.20,* loved *John,* because a holy man, not because a deep Scholler, or a great man; hence

hence, while *Joshua* and the Elders live, the people serve the Lord; and while *Jehoiada* lives, *Joash* is forward; the greatest Monarchs fall down here.

5. In the eyes of bad men, and hence *Deut.*4.6,7. when they kept the Statutes of the Lord, what nation so great, as hath such Laws, and so wise also! this is their glory before all the world, at least in the consciences of all men, which is their better part, 2 *Cor.*5.11. *we are manifest in their consciences*; and hence the worst say often, if all were such as they are, &c.

Quest.3.*When is it their glory?*

*Answ.*1. In this life (as hath been already shewed) in midst of reproaches, the Spirit of glory, 1 *Pet.*4.14. in midst of weaknesses, *Davids* heart was perfect.

2. At the great and last day; let a man by his wisdom, conquests, excellencies get himself a name, yet when death comes, his glory perisheth; if it doth last, yet not long; the greatest Monarchs have been like a mighty wind, filled the world with a noise for a time, and then down; but at the last day, then Oh their shame, what everlasting contempt shall they arise unto! But this shall be our glory at the last day, 1 *Pet.* 1. 5,6,7. *which shall be to glory and praise at the comming of our Lord*; and it is said, *then shall the righteous shine as the Sun*; and then *all the world shall stand and admire, and wonder at them.* And

3. Throughout all eternity this shall be their glory, even *an everlasting name unto them, better than the name of Sons and Daughters*; when the wicked shall see them all at the right hand of God, and gnash their teeth, that themselves are shut out, when the Lord and his Saints shall take infinite delight one in another, *Luk.* 12.37.

Jer. 33. 9.

Isa. 56. 5.

SECT. III.

Quest.4. WHy is this a Christians glory, excellency, and honor?

    *Answ.*1. In regard of the baseness of other things wherein men do use to glory; the wise man in his wisdom, the strong man in his strength, the rich man in his wealth: There are Three things which make these base.

First, These things make a man not the more to be accepted of God; the Lord respects not, values not the worth of any man by these things; and to make all the world know this, *he staineth the pride of all glory*, and *chuseth the poor and foolish things of the world to confound the wise*; a wise man will never respect the horse the more because it carries store of rich treasures, he will not fall down and reverence it for this; hang Swine about with pearls, who honors them the more? and will a wise God respect a man the more for these things? 1 *Pet.*3.5. What is that that is of great price with God? Holiness is of great price with God: And what though all the world honor a man, and a man honoreth himself, while this is wanting?

Secondly, All these things leave a man dead under the reign of Satan, power of his sin and dominion of death; and hence *Jer.*9.24. *Let no man glory in his wisdom,&c.* Death is entred into your windows; take any bondman bound with fetters (though golden) doth any man account him the more glorious? a Prince that is made a vassal and slave to every base fellow, is he the more glorious? no: So whiles men lye under the reign of death; stick a man that is dead with flowers, what is he the more glorious? alas no! his life is gone; now the Spirit of holiness is called the Spirit of life, even of the

life

life that never shall dye, *Rom.* 8. And therefore as it is said of a Flye, there is more excellency in a Gnat than in a Cedar, than in the glorious heaven, because it hath life, which the other hath not; so though men wonder at the goodly trappings of wicked men, yet the poorest and most despised Christian, that hath the Spirit of life, is more glorious.

Thirdly, Because these things only purchase the more credit and honor in the eyes of men, and that of wicked men; for 1 *Cor.* 5. 10. *We know no man after the flesh*; if they do, it is that which they account themselves beasts and fools for, as *David* did, *Psal.* 73. And what is the honor of man? it is the basest thing that is; for it is that which is without a man, it is no excellency within the man; it is but the thoughts of a mans head and heart, than which, what more vain, what more mutable? nay, 'tis but the dreams of a mans head, for they are mistakes: If all the town should dream another was a King, who yet were indeed a Beggar (which when they awake they see) what were he the better for this? *Paul*, 2 *Cor.* 11. 23. how he doth glory in priviledges, which were better and more goodly hangings than these! *this* (saith he) *I speak as a fool*; and what be these a Christians glory? no surely.

Answ. 2. Because that is a Christians glory which is Christs glory.

First, It is that glory wherein the glory of Christ consists, *Psal.* 45. 2. *Thou art fairer than the children of men, full of grace is thy lips*; and 2 *Cor.* 3. ult. *into the same image from glory to glory*: Indeed Christ's greatness in governing the world is his glory, but it is because it is mixt with such holiness, *Isa.* 6. 1, 2, 3. *Phil.* 2. 8, 9. *he humbled himself*, and this hath given him a name, and shall be his name for ever; this is that which makes the Lord Jesus lovely and amiable in the eyes of all his people, *Rev.* 15. 4. *Who would not fear thee, for thou onely art holy!* and so he is, for all the stars receive their light and shine with it, by this Sun only; and so the more a Christian excels in this, the more like he is to Jesus Christ, and so more glorious and lovely.

Secondly, This is that which gives him glory, *i.e.* so far as creatures can, which is to manifest it, and hence 2 *Cor.* 8. 23. which is the glory of Christ; and hence *Isa.* 46. 13. *Israel* is called *the glory of the Lord*; *Isa.* 62. 2, 3. the righteous is called *the glory, and crown, and diadem in the hand of the Lord*; and as God is better than the Soul, so this, *viz.* to glorifie the Lord, is better than to be glorified by the Lord.

SECT. IV.

HEnce see one reason why men lose their honor, their love and respect in the eyes of God and men; their judgements are not reverenced, their persons not accepted, their names and practises despised; this is one reason among the rest, a decay in holiness; the lamp is defiled, the light and lustre of it going out, and who will reverence it then? 'tis admirable to see the complaints abroad.

First, Look but into Families, what is the reason there is so much discontent there, that Servants are weary of their Masters, Masters of their Servants; and there is such complaints one of another, little respect one of another? it is for want of holiness, power, and life of godliness; the Master saith, the Servant is unruly, froward, surly, slothful, unfaithful, untrusty, and must not be spoken to; the Servant saith, his Master is passionate, unkinde, wants pity to his body, and sometimes strikes him without cause, and much more careless of his soul, never instructs him, but is eaten up with the world, &c. truly this is the cause. It seems the Lord wrought upon divers in Primitive times, and the

the 1.

the Apostle gives Servants an item, *that they may glorifie God, and adorn the Gospel of the Lord Jesus*; how came *Joseph* into *Potiphar's* books? oh, he was very holy, and very prudent; and Ile warrant did his Masters work better when his Master was absent than before, and prayed for success in his business, as *Abraham's* Servant. Look but upon Husband and Wife, it is strange to see what divisions and jars there; and what's the cause of it, Wife doth not honor Husband, nor Husband honor Wife? how comes this? oh, there is little holiness seen in their private walking one with another; the woman thought the man godly; had I known this, I would have seen you a hundred miles off, &c. the man also he complains of his wife, I see now I am like to be troubled with a continual dropping, a very fury of hell, so impatient, (and the next neighbor hears of it) nothing can please her; what's the reason of this? your sin makes your shame, and there's the want of holiness, 1 *Pet.* 3.3. man might be converted by the Wife, and the Wife by the Husband; not that it is always so, but usually so.

Secondly, Look into Churches, what is the reason people lose their honor much in the hearts of Ministers? he respects others, but not me; and somtimes they think; now he strikes at me, and meaneth me, and then the heart swells, &c. what's the reason that *Paul* professeth he will come with a rod among the *Corinthians*? *they were babes, and carnal, and contentious, and puft up, little love and life*; and what's the reason he sets out the *Thessalonians* so? 1 *Thess.* 1.5. because of this they did abound, and hence commended of all Saints; hence want of growth and holiness; they travel in birth till Christ be formed, and when they cannot see that, hence they are in throws for you; what's the reason Ministers lose their glory among people? I confess 'tis not always for decay here; for *John* in prison did not lose his holiness; and hence, when they despised him, Christ commended him, and his reward was with the Lord; it was not a testimony of his unholiness, but a fore-runner of the end of his days, as well as of the end of his work; and hence when all *Asia* forsook *Paul*, 2 *Tim.* 4.16. *it was the time of his departing now at hand*. But that which is the cause of it many times, is want of holiness within; and hence though men see not, yet the Lord will not give a false testimony, nor let men do so; hence neither judgements nor their speeches reverenced; or because men see not the ancient Spirit of holiness, hence no mourning for them in secret, no holiness in speeches, they smell of the field, not walking as patterns before them, *Mal.* 2.8, 9. *not caring for the flock which Christ hath purchased with his own blood*. What's the reason there is that complaint of want of love one man to another, one member to another, who are bound by covenant to it, such jars, divisions? &c. Truly nothing makes so firm an union between man and man as holiness and grace, this tieth the knot; and it is not holiness hid, but now seen; it not being seen, hence comes all your breaches, its impossible else such small things should make it: Oh a tender heart and the life of Christ is not indeed seen; a holy man exact shall never want love, that in every company scatters something, that like Christ, goes up and down doing good, healing the diseases of mens hearts; there's a man I could dye with him in my very bosom: I am perswaded the decay of holiness in the lives of men, is the cause why Sanctification is questioned as an evidence of Justification; and hence division.

Thirdly, Look abroad into the world, what is the reason the Churches lye among the pots, and are soiled with so many disgraces, that though we be the people of the Lord, yet we are not called so? why, jars, divisions, earthliness, want of love and mercy, murmurings, loss of former life. When Jews are shining with the glory of God, Kings and all Nations shall bring in their glory to them: Oh consider this! sin doth make you vile in Gods eyes and

mans

mans eyes: Many complain they cannot be respected, nor received; this is the cause of it, you excell not here; others take notice of your unrighteousness, unholiness of life; there's some evil in their bargaining and buying, and ill language from the people of God. Oh therefore go home and lament this, as she, *The glory of God is departed from Israel*; so do you here.

SECT. V.

HEnce see when the Lord doth honor us to do his work, what little cause there is to seek honor of men (nay though all the worlds glory be taken from you) because it is honor enough to do the Lords work; would you have more honor than Christ? this was his beauty, glory, and honor; God hath an everlasting name for you, though you have disgrace by it, nay though no success, yet *Isa.49.5. glorious in the Lords eye*: Oh it was a sweet course of *Barak*, *Judg.4.9. thou shalt lose honor*; that's all one, said she, *Let me do the Lords work*, though it be in a difficult work of pursuing the Lords enemies; what profit have you on the other side, when you seek it in your pitchers? what company? &c. this was *Sauls* sin, 1 *Sam.* 15.30. Oh *worship and honor me nevertheless this time before the people*; it's his reward, and it's the Devils sin to be puft up; this pull'd down *Nebuchadnezar*; *Herod* was smote with worms, *because he gave not glory to God*, but took it to himself; it was a heavy speech to *Eli*, 1 *Sam.*2.29. *Because thou honrest thy sons above me*, this and that I will do unto thee. Nay though men are so holy as to honor God with their lips, yet God will blast the wisdom of the wise for it: Oh therefore let this be enough, and then you will not hunger after other honor; for this is glory and honor enough, and you have thought so, when your selves, Oh if I may but honor the Lord, it is enough.

Hence see what little cause any wicked man hath to lift up his head with any glory he hath, *because the spirit of holiness, beauty and glory is departed from them*; as when the Soul is departed from the body its glory and beauty is departed from them, it's withered; and therefore we shall read in Scripture what names the Lord gives them, as *Dogs*, *Swine*, *Serpents*, *a generation of vipers*, *painted Sepulchres*, *Devils* in the time of the greatest profession, as *Judas*, *Joh.6. Wilde beasts*, and that in the greatest outward glory; and hence the four

Monarchies of the world are resembled to such beasts, *Bears*, *Leopards*, &c. Thus for their persons: And as for their actions, all they do is unclean, and ignoble and hence compared to *Thistles*, that cannot bring forth Figs or Grapes; and hence *Solomon* compares them, *As jewels in a Swines snout, so is a parable in the mouth of a fool*, it becomes them not, it's abomination in the sight of God all that which they do, though glorious before men; and at last day they *shall rise up to everlasting contempt*; and it is said *Isa.66.ult. their*

worm shall never dye, and they shall be an abhorring to all flesh, though they may carry it out fair for a time; the fairest professors that by their Sorceries and enchantments deceive the people shall be filled with shame, and as the Magicians were smitten with sores they could not stand before *Moses* (being smitten

with sores) so you shall not be able to stand before the Lord at the last day; and look as it is with Christ and his people, their cross and shame here, it is but their preparation to their crown; and hence, when Christ was put to the most open shame, then was the day-break of his glory; so all that you glory in, which God gives, 'tis but a solemn preparation for your shame: And hence, when *Nebuchadnezar* is at his highest pitch and thoughts of glory, then is his down-fall;

fal ; if a man should have a crown upon his head, all honor given him, and it should be whispered to him, This is but a preparation to your execution, what little glory could he take in that ? but rather fall a weeping as *Paul, Phil.* 3. 18,19.when he saw some *that made their belly their God, and boasted of the things of the earth, whose glory is their shame* ; and he speaks of them weeping : And therefore you that can sit in a chimney-corner, when you meet with your companions, hang, draw, and quarter within your selves, and censure all Churches, Ministers and Christians of a Town and Country, and if you see any sores, like flyes, go and suck them and make them worse ; or if not, you can make them and imagine them, and scoff at holiness secretly ; and though your consciences condemn you of wickedness, yet lift up your selves with something that you have ; Oh know it, your beauty is gone ; never a man but glorieth in something ; so much estate, so much esteem, so much wisdom, and gifts, birth, and beauty ; and now as proud as Satan, but yet a stranger to the life of God, your conversation is not above : Oh poor creature ! happy were it for thee if thou wert no man, (dying so) but the most despised of all Gods creatures, who art now abhorred of God, and shalt be the shame of all creatures another day.

SECT. VI.

Use 4.

HEnce if any man hath lost his glory and esteem in the consciences of the people of God, see how to recover it ; the Country is full of complaints and murmurings ; among the rest this is one of the sorest that many complain of ' They are not respected, they are no body ; they had this and that esteem in their own Country of such Ministers, Christians, and were of this esteem ; now the market is fallen here, and hence offended at every one, and cannot pass for members in many Churches ; and hereupon bear a private grudge against the Church, and all Ordinances in it, and flie Towns, or sit still, and comfort themselves their conscience is clear, &c. It is with many as it is with *Bristow*-stones, they are like pearls, and so they go till they come to the Jewellers ; and then when tried not worth two pence ; so many men never came to the trial, as here Gods providences try some men more than ever losses, sorrows ; Gods Ordinances try men, and thus they are found too light, would you now recover it ? Oh get a Spirit of holiness ! and think, Oh I have had a high esteem of my self, but I fall short of that brokenness for my vileness, and want that esteem of, and acquaintance with the Lord Jesus, that the glory of the Lord is not to this day risen upon me ; Oh then make after, and merchandise for this, *Prov.* 3. 14, 15, 16. Sometimes a godly man loseth this ; is there not inwardly a decay of holiness ? and hence God hath forsaken, and suffered to fall into some sin, so as man hath seen it ; do you think the Lord will honor you in the hearts of his people, while you dishonor him ? when you live in a vain dead-hearted condition, and disguise your selves, or in impenitency for open offences either of opinion or practice ; *Be it far from me,* saith the Lord, 1 *Sam.*2.30. *them that dishonor me shall be lightly esteemed* ; and hence God will cut off *Eli's* children ; you know what a sad letter *Paul* wrote to the *Corinthians* ; but when they saw the spiritual meaning, 2 *Cor.*7. 14,15. *Paul* boasts of them ; *Titus* his affection was abundant toward them ; if not abundant confession and giving glory to God, how should you look that God should else give glory to you ? it's wonderful to see, how men that have been convinced of sin, and yet would hide it, how the Lord in his jealousie hath discovered them in his time ; the sin hath been committed by them, and enquiry

hath

hath been made, and some conviction, and yet they have wound off, and cried out of wrong; the Lord hath left them to worse evils; And so the Lord will deal with men; and so I say, hide your sin, it shall be your shame at last, and the Lord will never honor you in the consciences of his people till you out with it, and confess it; *Jannes* and *Jambres*, their madness shall be made known at last; I speak not this that men should make holiness a bridge to their own honor, and so to stand upon Christs shoulders; but that this is the way to regain such a blessing, which an humble heart knows how to want, as well as to have.

use 5.

Oh then place your glory in this; of all things in the world, a man desires nothing more than honor; it's dearer than life, and it is that which every one doth desire; Oh beloved, hunt not after shadows, feed not your hearts with dreams; make not your Garlands of withered flowers, but in this which is your glory before God and men. *Jer.9.24. Let not rich men glory in riches, but in this, that he knoweth me;* It was the heavy complaint the Lord took up against his people, *Jer.2.11. That they did change their glory;* the Lord himself is the glory of his people, as shining in them by his Spirit; it was the great sin of the Gentiles, *Rom.1.23. that they changed the glory of the incorruptible God, into an image of corruptible men and beasts;* so you know this is your glory; and oh now to change this glory for an image of glory! and hence given up to vile affections, to a corruptible minde; and therefore *Prov.8.4,8. Exalt her, she shall promote thee;* admire at this! a man excels in nothing but what he admires at, or seeks not to excel in any thing but what he wonders at; you will never place your glory in holiness, nor excel in it, unless you admire at it, and it will then exalt you, and bring you to honor, because indeed it is your honor: Oh that God would work this, men would not be so greedy after the world, nor praise of men.

SECT. VII.

Quest. But how shall we come to this?

Answ. 1. Consider the example of Christ, and all the people of Christ at all times, who did not place their glory in these things, but in things above: If a man is to lay much out upon somthing in the market, if he be wise he will enquire of prudent men that know things, the worth of them, and then it fals out sometimes those things he esteems highly are of no value; so here, look upon *Paul, Gal.6.14. God forbid I should glory in any thing but the cross of Christ;* 1 *Cor.4.13.* When the *Corinthians* were puffed up with greatness, to pull them down from this, he professeth he and others *were the off-scouring of the world;* and this was their glory, *verse 16.* Look upon Christ himself, he had as much excellency as could be, yet he cast it off, *despised all the glory of the world, was a worm and no man;* he professeth *he sought no honor of men, but the will of him that sent him;* this was his glory.

2. Look upon the excellency of your estate in Christ, 1 *Cor.3.21. Glory not in men, for all things are yours;* take any Prince that hath a Kingdom, will he house in a cottage, or spend his time and care to thatch and repair that? no, all the Kingdom is mine; and hence he will have Kingly thoughts and Kingly aims, and ends, and acts that ennoble him indeed: So here, 2 *Cor.5.9. Knowing we have a house above,* that there is but a breath between us and glory, *we labor* (are ambitious) *that whether absent or present to be accepted of him.* The very reason why the hearts, minds, lives of men are so debased, as to seek their

glory

glory in that which is their shame, is this, they know no better estate in greater glory; the God of glory, and Kingdom of glory, and promise of glory, and Ark, and Cherubims, and Oracles of glory in Christ have been to this day hid from their eyes; hence *Heb.* 12.2. *Christ for the joy set before him despised the shame.*

3. Make the Lord present with you, and see him shine about you in his glory; when poor men come to the Court and see no King there, they bow down to his Chair; whereas if he was seen he should have all the honor then; so when men see creatures, but see them like empty chairs, the God of glory not filling of them, we bow down to creatures; but when God is seen, now the soul gives all glory to him; a man that lives without any in his house as chief, all servants attend on him; but when the Prince comes with his train, now all his Servants with himself are too little to attend on the Prince; so here, when men come to pray, or preach, or speak, Oh how doth a wicked heart seek it self? but when the Lord is seen, now all attend on him; hence when God sends his people to honor him, he first appears to them in his glory, and it never is long out of their minds; hence *Abraham* forsook his own Country, *Acts* 7. *Moses* forsook *Egypt*, he saw God invisible, *Heb.* 11.26,27. *Psal.* 22.ult. *All nations shall remember and turn to the Lord*; when the Lord is seen, all our glory is shame, *Isa.* 6. and now glory in that, and make him as present as at the last day, then all shall fall down before him.

4. See how every service you perform unto him, every act of holiness, quickned by the Spirit of life is pleasing to him; if a Prince be with a man, and cannot be pleased, nothing can content him, or we hear not one word from him whether we please him or not, we shall grow weary of him at last; but to consider this, *he that serves me, him will my father honor,* that *every cup of cold water, shall have a Disciples reward,* that *every groan shall be heard,* that *what you do to one of these little ones, you do it to Christ,* and Christ takes it as kindly as done to himself, that *the Lord remembers the love of your espousals, Jer.* 2. when you follow him in a land not sown, that the comfort of all your labors, tears, sufferings, shall follow you to heaven, and for ever lodge in that blessed brest of thine; Oh *Brethren,* saith *Paul, always abound,* and spend your time here, *knowing your labor is not in vain in the Lord;* why do men seek to please men, and place their glory there? because men see and approve them; Oh what is this to the approbation of a God?

SECT. VIII.

Use 6.

OH then preserve this your glory; when men have any thing in the world that is their glory, their Crown their Treasure, Oh they will keep that especially; rather lose life than lose their names, and glory in the world; Oh preserve the spirit of holiness, especially in these places; this hath been, this only shall be our glory; and that not in name, and yet dead, but in deed and in power we have had our Christian conversation, and that not by contenting our selves with a little, but to be exactly holy; a little spot is soon seen in your coat; you shall observe it.

1. When the Jews shall be made the glory of all the earth, their glory shall not consist then in immediate Revelations, but in Sanctification; there shall be holiness and sanctification; there shall be holiness on pots and horse bridles.

2. When the Lord will be a defence to his people, and a shadow from heat, and from the Sun; it shall be when the Lord hath purged away the filth of men by a spirit of burning; not which burns up all holiness, but filthiness and self-confidence

confidence in any holiness, and hypocrisie, and so they shall be holy, *Isa.*3,4.

3. How many men stumble by opinions, divisions, &c. (the fruits of a corrupt head, and streams of a dunghil heart) that had rather live in sorrows among e-nemies, than divisions among friends! Oh the spirit of people, as soon as any new Calf is made, fall down and worship it, and break the antient Land-marks which the Word hath set, and then make prognostications of all ill weather, to arise from opposing their opinion; never shall our glory be recovered till these evils are confessed and lamented, and the sin of the heart, which begat them.

4. I have wondred why so few be converted (though blessed be God, some the Lord doth pick out, a few Servants, Children and Natives) is it not because either this exemplary holiness, which is our glory, is not, or not so shining, but our lamps are dim? Ministers preach, and hearers are troubled, but they then look upon scan-dals and offences from others, and so are beaten off again, *Zach.*8.20,21,22,23. Oh therefore preserve it.

5. How will all the world abhor the ways we walk in, if we miscarry?

6. God will have holy Churches, he is refining the whole world now for that end, and will do so more and more, and go on.

SECT. IX.

Quest. **H**ow shall we preserve it?

*Answ.*1. Take heed of harboring an ill opinion of holiness, for then if your judgements dislike it, your tongues and your lives shall disgrace it: Take heed of imagining that First, there is no grace in Saints, only immediate actings of the Spirit; this is no spirit of holiness, no more than in *Balaams* Ass, through which God spake to him.

Secondly, That these graces are only common; who will seek much after that, or esteem that which is but common? this is to despise the Spirit, to con-temn the blood of the Covenant, whereby the Church is sanctified.

Thirdly, That grace is so dark and obscure a thing always as no evidence can be had by it, though it be peculiar grace: this is a high degree of disgrace to the Spi-rit of Grace; if one should say here is a man, but believes not his testimony, 'tis doubtful and very questionable what ever he saith, it is a dishonor to him, take heed of this: When the Spirit of Holiness comes to us in form, it comes thus, with little peace; but when in power, with much assurance, 1 *Thess.* 1.5. It is a sad thing, if that which was the complaint of the Prophet, shall be the complaint of the Spirit, *Who hath believed our report, and to whom is the arm of the Lord revealed*!

2. Take heed of decaying in a spirit of bounty and love, and in largeness of heart to all the people of God, nay, to all men, so far as you have time and strength; let a man be never so great a Prince, if he once lose his boun-ty, he loseth his glory; so here *Isa.* 58.8. *Give bread to the hungry, then shall thy light break out of obscurity*: Many complain that *New-England* hath so little love, Non-members not visited, not regarded (though many times unjustly) Oh they thought to see so much love, and care, and pity; but here they may live and never be spoken to, never visited; Oh take heed of this; Nothing beautifies a Christian in the eyes of others more than much love, (hypocrisie is naught) Oh excel here; visit poor families, sit one half hour and speak to discouraged hearts, shew kindness to strangers, such you were; Ile warrant God will bless you, this was the glory of Christ, full of grace and truth.

3. Be very careful in receiving in of Members into Churches; one ill man

man will be a spot and pollution to all the rest, *Jude* 12. *spots in your feasts*; you know how many come over, how it begins to be pleaded for, What, not baptifed, and Profeffors? and yet how many are disfigured? therefore try them well ; take heed of thinking Elders or Churches are too strict.

Fourthly be much in prayer for the Churches, *Ifa.*62.7. *Give the Lord no rest till he make Jerufalem the praife of the whole earth,* that's the way ; do you see any fins in the Country, go and stand in the gap with *Mofes,* and though the Lord offer to do good to you, yet turn him not off so, till he promife to relieve his poor Churches also ; beg and this will do it ; be much in fasting ; it is a fhame for us (who are laying the foundations of many generations) not to be much with God in prayer and fasting ; and that when in other places there is fo much sowing of this feed.

CHAP. X.

Shewing that counterfeit Grace is not lasting.

Verse 8,9.

And the foolish faid unto the wife, Give us of your oyl, for our lamps are going out.

But the wife answered faying, Not fo, left there be not enough for us and you; but go you rather to them that fell, and buy for your felves.

SECT. I.

IN thefe words is fet down the effect which this awakening cry took in the foolish Virgins only :

First, They come to feel, and so to complain of the want of oyl.

Secondly, They petition the wife, that they would give them of their oyl ; which latter is amplified in verf.9. from the anfwer the wife made unto them.

We shall open the words as we come to obferve any thing from them ; and begin now with the complaint [*Our lamps are gone out*] or *going out,* it is all one ; The wife Virgins lamps did grow dim, but yet their oyl was not fpent ; but here their oyl was fpent, and hence their Lamps were going out.

Obferva-tion I.   *That counterfeit and common grace of foolish Virgins, after fome time of glorious profeffion, will certainly go out, and be quite fpent*: It confumes in the ufing, and shining and burning. *Luke* 8.18. *To him that hath shall be given, but*

but he that hath not, shall be taken from him that which he hath. Joh.15.2,6. *Every branch in me that beareth not fruit it withers,* then it is taken away, and so it is consumed, and in time burned; and hence, *many that are first, are in time last,* Matth.9.20. *and many that are last first :* Men that have been most forward, decay; their gifts decay, life decays, and these *are last: and last are first ;* many newly brought home to Christ, excel them, and live so, and die so, that one would think should never hold out. I need not speak more, Scripture is so abundant: I say it is after some time of profession ; for at first it rather grows than decays and withers ; but afterward they have enough of it, it withers and dies: And look as it is with some bodies when they are healthful, they grow by all means ; but when once Nature is spent, and now declining, nothing recovers them, though they may be kept at a stay for a time, but dye they will with their best cordials in their mouths ; so it is here.

For Explication of this Point, we are to attend how and why this is thus ; and that not in the worst, but in the best of the foolish Virgins.

First, The Spirit of God comes upon many hypocrites in abundant and plentiful measure of awakening grace; I say it comes upon them as it did upon *Balaam,* Numb.24.2. And as it is in overflowing waters, which spread far, and grow very deep, and fill many empty places, they fall upon the ground, they come not from any spring within the ground ; and hence though they last not always, yet they last some good time ; so it is here, the Grace and Spirit of God comes suddenly and plentifully upon many a man, which gives them a time of flourishing, it comes not from imitation, or education, or moral perswasion only, but physically from the Spirit of God, 1 Sam.10.12. when they wondred that *Saul* was among the Prophets, one answered, *who is their father ?* who gave them this gift of prophecy ? is it not the Lord ? so the same Lord is rich to *Saul* also: And I say it is only awakening grace ; for renewing grace, savingly to change their nature, is not given, but awakening grace, which works upon conscience, and conscience upon the whole man ; and thus it was here with these Virgins, they had wonderful light, and a spirit of illumination to see the Lord Jesus, and hence to look for him with much affection and forwardness, as well as the wise, and to keep them company in Church-fellowship, and though they were secure, to complain of their decays, and desire the spirit of grace which they saw in the wise.

Secondly, Though it doth come upon them thus, yet it doth never rest within, so as to dwell there, to take up an eternal mansion for himself, Isa.11.10. *his rest shall be glorious,* Isa.57.15. This is a favor the Lord shews only to the contrite above all people in the world besides. Rom.8.11. *If the Spirit which raised up Jesus Christ from the dead dwell in you, it shall quicken you, and seat you up to be Sons,* as it is there expressed.

Thirdly, Hence it doth decay by little and little ; as a man that dwels not, but sojourneth for a little time in a house, he removes by little and little, till at last he is quite gone ; as ponds filled with rain water, which comes upon them, not spring water that riseth up within them, it dries up by little and little until quite dry ; as it is with light, after the Sun is declining and setting, it decreaseth by little and little, until it be turned into darkness ; so it is here ; and as it was in the Cherubims, where the glory of God was, and the Lord departed by little and little ; as in *Saul,* first he neglects the command of the Lord in one thing, then in another, then the *Spirit of God departed, and an evil spirit of sadness came upon him ;* and then he threatens *David,* then kills the Priests of the Lord, then goes to a Witch, and at last kills himself ; and I say this is because the Lord dwels not there ; and hence *Joh.*15.because the branch is not engraffed into the stock ; and this is usually at the very height of affection

on and profession ; as the ftony ground fprang up ; when did it wither ? when it came to its height ; as flowers that come to wither when they are come to their height of growth ; and hence alfo men when they have moft, and beft means, and affect , and love them , yet then they dye and wither. And it decays by Four means.

SECT. II.

Firft THrough want of daily nourifhment and fupply from the Lord Jefus ; for look as it is with many bodies, fuppofe they have life, yet if there be not daily nourifhment for it, and wholfom alfo, it will dye ere long, and confume ; fo it is here, there is a kinde of life which hypocrites have from Chrift, and it may be fed, and fo they live for a time ; but this the Lord never doth for them, they are not always fed, and hence die, as it is *John* 6. fome were quickened to follow after Chrift in the wildernefs for loaves, fome for better ends (as his Difciples) but the Lord knew their want, *labor not for the meat that perifheth, but for that which gives everlafting life,* which Chrift will give you ; and hence the whole Chapter is fpent upon this, to feed upon himfelf, whence the beft were offended : Let a man partake of all Ordinances, Priviledges, he fhall finde nothing elfe but decay unlefs the Lord be in them all to give daily nourifhment, *Ephef.4.16.* daily, I mean, as there is decreafe of that tafte they have had of the Lord.

Secondly, Through the emptinefs of a form ; for when the Spirit of God dwells not, but only comes upon a man, it is not long but it corrupts into a form ever after ; a man at firft knows many truths, and at firft is affected with them, he doth not prefently forget them, or fhut his eyes againft them, but after he hath known them a little while, at laft the fweetnefs of that knowledge is loft ; and fo he hath a form of knowledge, like leffons which a man hath been much affected with, but having plaied or heard them oft, he hears and knows them, but is not affected with them, *Ezek.* 33.*ult.* So at firft a man doth many duties with delight ; ftay a while, and he keeps the duty, but the delight is gone in it, and fo hath an empty form ; now where the power of godlinefs and the eternal life of Chrift is not, it degenerates firftly ufually into this form, and this is all that is left ; and the form being empty, hence firft, A man comes to loath the truth, and profeffion of the ways of God which once he loved, and fo in time to fall and decay without as well as within ; as drink or milk at firft are fweet, but ftay a while and (the fpirits not preferving themfelves) then it grows dead, and fowre, and faplefs, and fo it is here. *Capernaumites* at firft be affected, then they fall to a form, then hard to be wrought upon, their hearts fat under all means ; *if thy light be darknefs, how great is that darknefs !*

Thirdly, Through the power of luft ; for where the Lord dwells not, there fin reigns, and it will get head where it hath had any affront, and fo choak the power of all means, and hence a man withers, as in the thorny ground, it grew up and choaked the word.

Fourthly, Through the fitnefs of external temptation, which muft and will prevail, when the Lord is not within to keep the Palace ; it is ftronger than all common graces in the world, and will draw away the heart and life, *Rev.3.10.* there is an hour of temptation which tries men , which will difcover men indeed ; now thofe temptations are ever fuitable to places and perfons.

SECT. III.

SECT. III.

First, SOmetime the temptation is extream want, as it was with the *Israelites*; when they were under the oppressions of *Pharoah*; Oh to sacrifice to the Lord in a wilderness, and to enjoy the land of *Canaan*, where they should have Ordinances, Oh they are much taken with this! and many prayers and groans to be delivered out of their oppressions; but when they came to the wilderness, and there did want bread, and then water, now they murmur; which murmuring God remembers, and casts them off for: Had they not *Moses*, and the cloud, and God's promise, and experience, why did they complain? Oh to bear want, they could not! extream want is like extream sickness, it makes all sweet things bitter; some wants men can bear, but not extremity; this saddle doth pinch so hard; so the young man, *forsake all for me*, saith Christ, but he could not; God and Creatures are enough, but not God alone; so it is with many a man, he can be content to lose something, but when brought very low, cares and fears grow up and choak all.

Secondly, Sometimes the want of spiritual supply; a man looked for much from the Ordinances, and finds it not; not because the Lords heart is streitned, but because theirs are not enlarged; and hence they have enough of God, and all his Ordinances; they have had the heart of them, and now let them lie fallow, *Zach.11.* my soul loathed them, and theirs me.

Thirdly, sometimes abundance of outward blessings, peace, liberty, plenty here; now these things, like ground in Summer, 'tis strange to see what lusty weeds now there be, that did appear dead in time of winter, *Deut.8.11.* Oh then take heed thou forget not the Lord thy God; now proud and secure, and forsake all.

Fourthly, Sometimes persecutions from men: if hot and total ruine be threatned, this scares from God.

Fifthly, Sometimes corrupt Teachers and delusions among them.

Sixthly, Increase of iniquity in good and bad, in the place where men live; hence love waxeth cold: All which are *Matth.24.*

I will name no more, but thus mens common grace comes to wither, and dye in them; and the Reasons are these.

SECT. IV.

HEnce do not trust men too far, nor boast of any man too much, especially in regard of his glorious profession and affections at the first; God sends divers of his faithful servants to a place, and many at first hearing are wrought upon, battered down, convinced, mourning after peace, going to Ministers, delight in Ordinances; now many Ministers bless God for their conversion, and many a Christian is put out of doubt of it, parents of their children, and children of their parents, one brother of another, and one Christian neighbor of another; whom he got out once to hear, and once hearing overcame; and for a time there is no other: Oh take heed of boasting too much, it may be they may and will fall (before they have lived many years) down, when at their height: what man was ever sought unto more than *John*? all *Judea* came unto him, yet at last they forsake him, rejoyced but a season in that light; they went also from him to Christ, *Joh.7.26,32.* yet *John* complains, none received

Use 1.

I i i   ceived

ceived his testimony; Christ himself preached in *Capernaum*, and never exalting a man, they boasted in him; yet onely a few Babes which the Lord wrought upon; the *Galathians* would lose their eyes for *Paul*, yet afterward they slight him, and join with false teachers against him: Oh therefore pray for them, and weep for them, but do not trust them too far; neither trust your selves too much; *Joh.8.31. Then are ye my disciples if you continue*; *Demas* forsakes *Paul*, all in *Asia* forsake me.

SECT. V.

Use 2.

HEnce be not offended if we see many apostatize, and fall from their most eminent profession; the Lord hath here foretold that after some profession their lamps will go out; we do not wonder if ponds full in winter are dry in summer, because it is the time and season of it, and they want springs to feed them; and never was there any time since the world began that there were such Apostacies as now.

First, One man after much profession intends to follow the Lord, conscience is troubled at humane inventions; Oh, saith he, if delivered, well enough, though I lose never so much! well, he lays out all, and is delivered; but that which quiets conscience, doth not quiet his heart and affections; but his very loss for conscience makes his lusts and desires after other things break out more eagerly, and men cannot now live upon Gospel only, with bread and water; no, no, you are deceived; as it is with sick men, they let go all their estate for recovery; but when recovered, they must get up their estate again, this will not satisfie: And thus some fall spiritually.

Secondly, Others they sought for much in Ordinances, but finding not what they looked for, Ordinances are but as pictures fair a far off; but when men come near them, Word, and Fellowship, and people of God, then they despise them, because they find not a living God there.

Thirdly, While God keeps men under sad temptations, wants and afflictions; Oh then they are humble, and pray; but when blest with ease, and peace, and plenty, and honor, then how lofty and secure? this is better than the Lord: Never such a decay of the spirit of prayer; never was there such a confusion in the world, such burning of Cities, slaying of men, rents of Churches, God minding to stain the pride of all glory; and yet never such hearts.

Object. But to stand so long, and yet to fall, seems strange?

Answ. If soon it is a wonder, but if long it is no wonder; if once past growing, you do not wonder if an oak be now decaying.

Obj. But they keep their profession still, only in one thing vile, the error is only in their minds; a spirit of discention from the people of God.

Ans. Scarce shall you see one man in a hundred that is vile in every thing, that falls totally; the foolish Virgins did not so, yet their oyl was spent, and their lamps going out; there was a man that was slain suddenly, and his blood in his face was fresh, his beauty glorious, and many weeks continued without putrefaction, yet life within was gone; so 'tis the condition of many a man by one wound or sin: And hence a Physitian at *Wittenberg* writes of the cause of it; be not therefore offended at them, but wonder at the Lord that he keeps thee; I know there are decaying Saints, but they recover again here.

SECT. VI.

SECT. VI.

OH therefore labor for the grace that may laſt, the bread that may laſt to everlaſting life; in all bargains and buildings men will have a ſpecial eye to that which will laſt; if it be rotten, let whoſoever will take it; and be ſure it is ſo; for when God doth fully awaken you, you will ſee it is not right; the fooliſh Virgins they thought they were well before; but now after ſome time, and awakened, they ſee it will not hold nor continue. For the Lords ſake be ſuſpicious here; fear leſt a promiſe being left, any fall ſhort of it; other things will not laſt, neither Creatures, nor the Lord to do you good, unleſs you have everlaſting grace. It is a time the Lord is ſtripping the world of all ornaments, your Wives, Children, Churches; God will take your Husbands, Parents, Members, Miniſters from you; yet if a heart to cloſe with the Lord, Oh this is right.

Queſt. *How?*

Anſw. 1. Take heed of any affection, without firſt ſubduing the contrary luſt; for if you mingle them, the one will choak the other; this is ſowing among thorns, *Jer.* 4. 3, 4.

2. Maintain it upon an everlaſting root; if the Lord gives you grace, and you ſet it in your own garden, it will dye; no, let it receive life from the promiſe, that unchangeable love, and grace, and faithfulneſs; ſay, if that ſupports not I fall, 1 *Sam.* 23. 5. *Iſa.* 46. from gray hairs, I will carry thee; *Pſa.* 23. 2, 3. the Lord leads to waters, he feeds: But I decay? yet he reſtores my ſoul: Oh but he afflicts much? yet his rod and ſtaff comfort me; I ſhall dwell in the houſe of God for ever. Be more empty as the Lord fills you. But oh the ſin of this world, all the creatures in the world cannot content, but grace doth, and hence men regard not the Lord; and hence you periſh, and your grace ſhall periſh alſo.

CHAP. XI.

Unregenerate perſons may have a ſence of their want of Grace.

SECT. I.

Our Lamps are out.

THat fooliſh Virgins, or unregenerate perſons may ſee and ſo complain of an utter want of all ſaving grace.

Look but upon this pattern, they thought they were rich; and had ſomething, but now they ſee they have nothing; and hence when they ſearch their lives, our lamps are out; when they ſearch their hearts, is there any Grace, or Spirit of Chriſt, or Chriſt by his Spirit there? no, our oyl is ſpent, and hence *give us of your oyl*; they ſaw nothing

now.

now.   The same persons that are sometimes so puft up, that they think they are rich and stand in need of nothing, may be basely dejected, and so feel a want of all things.

Quest. *How may this appear?*

Answ. First, Because this is no more than what the Devils have; if this be Sanctification, to see, I have no Sanctification; if this be Humility, to see, I have no humility; if this be cleanness, to see, I have nothing but uncleanness; the Devils then are sanctified and cleansed; who as they are unclean spirts, and accursed of God, and set apart to all evil and sin, and bound up in the chains of darkness, so they know it; they believe the Word, and they know they have no Christ, no Grace, no love of God, never shall see mercy, comfort, &c. and tremble at this, *with whom there is nothing but a fearful looking for of Judgement.*

Secondly, Because this is no more than what the Law may bring a man unto, *For by the Law* Rom.3.20. *is the knowledge of sin*; i. e. not only of gross sins but also of secret sins; for Conscience which is in every mans heart will discover the first, men that live under the Law see more; and hence *Paul* speaks of himself, *so far forth as under the Law,* Rom.7.7,8,9,10,11. Now that which may be wrought in a man meerly by the Law, may be wrought in a man under the Law; a man under the Law, is under the reign of the Law, which is to convince of pollution universal, and so to curse; *The Law is not the ministration of life to any man,* 2 Cor.3.7. Gal.3.24. and if the Law may convince of sin thus, this sight of sin and vileness is no part of eternal life; and therefore foolish Virgins may well come thus far; and this will especially be found among them where there is a searching Ministery, that there is scarce any close conveyance but the Word discovers them: *Gehazi* cannot carry it so closely, nor *Ananias* so cunningly, but *Elisha* and *Peter* will find it out; Heb. 4.12. *The Word is quick and powerful, and searcheth,* which is but a common work; and hence when *Peter* had told *Simon Magus, Thou art in the gall of bitterness,* he denieth it not, but saith, *Oh pray for me*; indeed if the Word discovers the strong-holds, and high forts, and secret lusts and imaginations, and beats them down, and so brings the Soul in subjection to Christ, and into captivity, that is it which is the power of the Gospel, and love of Christ peculiar to his peoples works; but to let a man see he hath nothing but filth, and to be a little affected with it, this is no more than what is wrought in a deceitful hearer, *Jam.*1. 23,24. The Law or Word lets a graceless heart (a forgetful hearer) see himself; and what can it truly discover to him but his vileness? this glass will discover their smallest spots; this Sun will let you see motes; you know and see, and that's all.

Thirdly, Because this is no more than the awakening of sleepy Conscience, which the worst man, and closest hypocrite may in time have; *Cain's* conscience while it is secure, thinks his offering as good as his Brothers; but when awakened, now *my sin is greater than I can bear*; *Saul* goes on in persecuting *David,* and thinks God will help; and hence 2 Sam.28. 5. goes to Urim, &c. but God answers him not; now he sees his condition, and makes a doleful complaint of it, That God was departed, and no answer: This is usual; Psal. 9.20. *Put them in fear, O God, that they may know themselves to be but men,* weak, sinful, vile men: When the Lord sets up his Judgement Seat in a mans conscience, not only gross evils, but the secrets of all hearts, all mens hypocrisies are then opened to themselves, as at last day to all the world; and hence as hypocrites consciences shall be broken open at the last day, so now also in this life, they may see their profession to be but paint; hence Isa.33.14. Hypocrites are afraid when God appears in anger; *Oh who shall dwell with God?* they are sometimes so confounded with the holiness of God, and the terror

of

of God from thence againſt ſin, that who ſhall dwel with God? are there any in the world that can ſtand before him? now all is paint, and vile before him.

Fourthly, Becauſe Hypocrites may have experience of a great change wrought in them, which decaying and corrupting, they may ſenſibly finde a want of what once they had; which though they thought it had been ſaving grace, or that which would commend them to God; now they ſee they have no grace at all, hence are left as theſe Virgins; if a man never was rich, he cannot be ſenſible of being a Bankrupt, a Beggar; Look as it was with *Adam*, he was in a happy eſtate, in the image of God; now when loſt, he ſaw himſelf naked, and was aſhamed, and was this ſaving grace? no: So though Hypocrites attain not to that righteouſneſs, yet they may attain to many ſpiritual excellencies, which they may prize exceedingly, as thoſe that commend them before God and men; but theſe corrupting, they may now eaſily ſee their nakedneſs, and vileneſs, and want of all: *Saul* had the Spirit of God we know; but 1 *Sam*.16.14. *an evil ſpirit came, and Gods Spirit departed*; did not *Saul* know this? the having of Gods Spirit made him more ſenſible of the evil ſpirit; ſo it is with many a man; the Spirit of God doth depart, and he cannot pray nor prophecy, nor ſpeak, nor think, not do, as he did; nay he may find an evil ſpirit upon him; and is this unknown? may not fooliſh Virgins know this? as *Sampſon* when ſhaved.

Fifthly, Becauſe that which is ſometimes a juſt judgement of God upon a carnal heart, that they may ſee and feel; but many times (I ſay not always, becauſe the Lord doth uſe this to prepare for mercy) it is ſo that men that have deſpiſed grace, and Chriſt, men that have coloured it over with God, and thought highly of themſelves for what they had; they ſhall ſee all their profeſſion is but paint, and all their Gold, Tin and Copper: *Joh.*8.21. *You ſhall ſeek me, and ſhall not finde me, but ſhall dye in your ſins*; ſeeking ever preſuppoſeth a want; ſo that you ſhall finde a want of me; and if of me, of all life, of all grace, of all comfort and good; and this loſs the Lord makes a puniſhment which they ſhall bring upon themſelves by contempt of him.

SECT. II.

Ence we may ſee the woful condition of thoſe. *viz.* Firſt, Conſider how far from eternal life thoſe are that never knew their fall; the fooliſh Virgins knew their want of oyl and ſhining, and yet were fooliſh, and yet were ſhut out; how great is their fall then, and how great their miſery, that have had burning lamps, but now know it not? this is the ſtate of many a profeſſor, many a man who is fallen from the Lord, and the affections once he had, but he knows it not; God did enlighten him, but now he is blinding of him; he did affect him, but he is now benumming of him; he did make him render, but not he is making his heart fat; he did make him low in his own eyes (as *Saul*, but when a King then puft up) ſo God is ſwelling of him; but this is moſt grievous, he knows it not, *Iſa.*6. If a man did know his lamp were going out, he might ſeek, as theſe, for it, and poſſibly find it; but now no hope unleſs the Lord help; as we ſee men wounded and falling, they are aſtoniſhed at the blow, that they know it not, and may die, unleſs thoſe about them dreſs them, and ſend to and fro for help for them; ſo it is with many; men are ſo ſtupified with ſome blows of their luſts, that unleſs Chriſtian friends exhort, admoniſh and ſend their prayers and tears to heaven to the Lord, no hope of recovery again; and whether the Lord will be entreated is hard to ſay; ſurely it is rare, and yet

thus

Uſe 1.

thus it is 1 *Joh.* 5. sometimes, if it be not a sin unto death; but in a Brother, grace will fetch help; but if the man never had grace, and now fell without feeling, there's little hope; if a man can feel no sun rising upon him, nor yet how the day goes away, whether the Sun be setting or no, it argues miserable carelesness, or miserable blindness, and that the man is in darkness; so here.

Secondly, What will become of them that were never cast down so low as these, that never came to be so good as Hypocrites,

For 1. You were born and have lived not only in a sinful estate, but in a Christless estate; dead without all life, every part of thee polluted.

2. If the Lord doth draw any out of this estate, he will make you know what poor creatures you be, that you shall say, I thought I had been thus and thus, but I see I am wretched; I thought I should be saved, but now I am condemned, so that your mouth shall be stopped, *Rom.* 3. 21. else you would never come to the Lord, to your Fathers house, and prize the grace of God, if any husks to live upon now.

3. You never knew this; never came to complain to any Christian, Oh my oyl is spent, my lamp is out; Christ and Spirit, and all good is gone; no, you think your selves rich and want nothing; you have some knowledge, restraint of good affections, and full of these, *The Lord will spue you out his mouth*, if it is thus with you: Nay, although you have means and hear of it, yet all the world cannot make you know your nakedness, misery, sin and emptiness; Well, if the Lord doth not set up a Judgement-Seat now, you shall be called before it one day, and then your secrets shall be made manifest before all the world; and because you say you see, *therefore your sin remains*; so say I to you: You never did contemn God, nor hate God, &c. therefore your contempt remains; if it be, there Christ will discover it, and so remove it; but is it not so? therefore your sin remains.

Jer. 9. 4.

SECT. III.

Use 2.

HEnce see the deceit of that sinful opinion, That true Sanctification is to see I have no Sanctification; and cleanness of heart to see nothing but uncleanness; and that this is poverty of Spirit, to see no grace in a mans self, nor no Christ there; and this not only hath been, but it seems is scattered still; which as it is pleasing to many a graceless heart, and suitable to his lust, so it carries a fair cloak of Humility and Self-denial in it, and makes way for such an Evidence which the Scripture did never yet declare.

Poverty of Spirit is a Grace peculiar to them that shall have the Kingdom of Heaven; But to see no Grace is common to those that shall be shut out of the Kingdom of heaven; none but those that are justified can be savingly sanctified; many that shall be condemned, may see, do see that they have no Sanctification: And therefore this is no Sanctification.

1. If this be Poverty of Spirit to see no Grace, then Common-grace is Special-grace, peculiar to the Elect, as true Poverty is.

2. Then it is a grace of the Spirit of God to maintain an untruth, and to give the holy Ghost the lye; for where there is Poverty, there is Grace and Christ.

3. Then the Grace of Poverty of Spirit, should be quite contrary to the Spirit of Grace, *which makes us know the things given us of God*; but this poverty of Spirit makes us not to know them at all.

Yet

Yet many will profess this true Poverty of spirit, and this is true Sanctification indeed.

First, It is true, where there was never any of the Grace of Christ, but men have run upon Reformation without Christ, and affection, &c. there men are bound to see their black feet, and happy is the heart that can pull off every feather from such crests; but where it is, and the Lord hath given evidence thereby according to his Word; now to deny it is devilish, for it was he that said *Job did not serve God for nought*, and is a lye, of which he was the Father; and is great unthankfulness to the Spirit for what he hath done.

Secondly, If there be no Grace in a Christian nor Spirit, but all in Christ, then say it upon the house tops, and be not ashamed of it; men must see nothing, because they have nothing; otherwise let this delusion rot, and never find acceptance in holy hearts; and yet how many still describe an Hypocrite by all the Graces of the Spirit, Faith, receiving Christ as King, Priest, and Prophet, &c. and so are clean creatures and upright men, by seeing nothing in themselves, contrary to Christ, *Joh.* 13. *Ton are clean, but not all.*

Thirdly, It is true, a gracious heart is apt to deny all the Lord hath done for him; yet the Lord likes not this; as *Calvin* thinks *Peter* did, Lord, hands, and feet, and all; no, saith the Lord, thou art clean in head, and all but thy feet; and hence needs no washing but in that: And what more frequent than this sin? but to make what is sinful a duty, this is to turn day into night, and night into day, to call evil good, and bitter sweet.

SECT. IV.

Quest. 1. *BUt doth not the Lord bring every man to see nothing in himself?*

Answ. Yes, that the Lord doth in preparing him for Christ, or in drawing him toward Christ, but it is where there is nothing, neither poverty or any other grace.

Quest. 2. *But is not this poverty of spirit, or do not those that are poor in spirit see nothing?*

Answ. 1. In regard of their unregenerate part, which the longer they live, the more they feel of the evil of it, and so the more poor they grow; they see no good there, and so account themselves the most miserable men, mourning more under it than ever; yet to see no good at all in themselves, this, if their eyes be open, they are not to say, *I delight in the Law in the inner man*; and hence a regenerate Christian is vile in his own eyes after all duties and enlargements, he sees how all is defiled with a filthy heart, and hence *Prov.* 30. 4. *I am brutish*; and he speaks of his natural estate, and in that part, for else it is cross to 1 *Cor.* 2. 10.

2. They see nothing in themselves to commend them to God in point of Justification; here all *Paul*'s past and present righteousness is accounted dung.

Quest. 3. *If an Hypocrite sees and feels nothing, and those that are poor in spirit do so? what is the difference?*

Ans. The differences are many. 1. He that is truly poor, sees so much vileness, as that he loaths himself, *Ezek.* 6. But the Hypocrite if he hath any excellency, remains full of it, proud with it; if it be gone, he seeks himself again, and loaths not himself.

2. True poverty of spirit drives a man out of himself, and all carnal contents;

tents, as well as graces, to mercy, to live there, and cleave there, as in the Prodigal, he did not only see a want, but feel a need of bread; I die without it, *Psa.*40.9,10. But another that sees no good, either is not driven out of his contents, but when he sees nothing, as *Cain,* builds Cities, or if he see's some good in himself, then he is not driven out of himself.

SECT. V.

Use 3. HEnce see which is the surest and safest way of evidencing our good estate, for here men now are perplexed, either 'tis by seeing no grace, and so expecting the witness of the Spirit, or by seeing some saving work of grace, and so looking to the witness of the Word, and waiting for the confirmation of the Spirit; for seals do but confirm the Promise and Covenant; if it be by seeing no grace, then either by seeing no grace, without having the being of it, and now wait for a revelation, and then 'tis a delusion, for he is under the condemnation of the Word, and therefore far from consolation of the Spirit; or by seeing no grace without seeing the being of it : If so, then a man must seek for a witness of the Spirit, without understanding the meaning of the Spirit, or of the witness of it ; and so a man must shut his eyes against part of the truth, that he may see another part ; a man must see that he is beloved, but not thou believer, or thou called, art loved or justified. Oh then take heed of this way of evidence ; or else by now seeing grace, and waiting for a witness ; now this is safest ; for when ever the witness comes it is certainly right now, not a delusion : Hereby we shall see the full meaning of the witness and compass of the Lords love. And therefore take heed of denying all grace, and seeing nothing, and then wait for a Revelation, and if it comes now 'tis right ; no such matter ; you may see nothing, and to hell, and no consolation to them that see nothing ; think not that this is poverty ; it may be a seal to a blank, to such a one as the Lord never intended mercy unto ; that which God promiseth pray for, *Zach.* 13.*ult.* first, to say It is my people, and then the Lord is my God ; find that the Lord makes you his people, and then say so. Let all know this is never questioned, whether the Spirit be the cause of witness, and clearing our estate ; but whether by seeing nothing, or shewing something ; here's the mystery of it : Oh that God would make you hear, that are called away from the simplicity of the Gospel of Christ : These foolish Virgins were wiser than many now adays in this particular, they cried for oyl in their lamps, or they knew they could not be accepted of the Bridegroom.

Use 4. Oh search and try your selves throughly, for you may come in time to see all your paint fall off, all your guilt discovered, *&c.*

CHAP.

CHAP. XII.

Of the desire of Grace that may be in Hypocrites.

SECT. I.

Give us of your Oyl, &c.

*Observa-
tion* 3.

Hat foolish *Virgins* may, and seriously do desire, not only *Sal-
vation,* but *Grace is self.* For these *Virgins* did not only de-
sire the Lord to open to them, but *give us of your oyl;* and
this they do not desire in shew, but seriously, for they felt a
want of it ; our lamps are out, our oyl is spent, our misery is
great ; Oh now help us with your grace: This may appear in
these particulars.

First, They may feel a loss and a want of it, and having some hope in this
life to gain it, hence may seek it ; thus not only the Virgins, but *Simon Magus
Acts* 8.24. when he was convinced he was in the gall of bitterness ; he doth
not only content himself with his own, but doth commend himself to the desires of the Church, and Apostles, *Oh pray for me, that none of these things
may come upon me,* but that I may be brought into another estate, whereby I
may escape all this, *Amos* 8.11,12. *I will bring a famine, not of bread, but of
hearing the Word, i.e.* you shall feel a woful want of that, and of the consolation,
life, and spirit of that, and you shall go from sea to sea to find it, and shall not:
Oh that I had taken my time, will the careless ones say !

Secondly, They may have a high opinion of it, and see a marvellous excellency in it, and hence may be drawn to desire it, *Joh.*6.33,34. *My father
gives you bread from heaven, which Moses gave not, and such bread as gives
life unto the world;* then said they, *Lord, ever give us of this bread,* and yet
they were carnal, and desires carnal, arising from the sight of the excellency
of it ; that Scribe *Math.*12.33,34. *To love the Lord thy God with all thy heart
is better than all burnt offerings and sacrifices;* Oh that's admirable, the Ordinances are good, and Creatures are good, but this is better: As a man when
he admires the world, he ever desires the world, though he never hath it ; so
here, as in *Balaam*: Not only Word and Spirit may commend it, and so
they may desire it, but the excellency of it in the lives of the Saints will commend it, so as carnal hearts may desire the company and love of such men a-
bove all in the world, *Rev.*2.8. *Gen.*26.28. *We saw God was with thee, and that
thou wert blessed of the Lord;* and hence there are some desires after it, 2 *Pet.*
2.19. Men escape pollutions by Christ.

Thirdly, They have a taste of the sweetness of it, and hence may desire it,
Heb 6. *John* was a burning light, and they rejoyced in him, and all *Judea* and
Jerusalem flocked to his Ministery, and came into the wilderness after him ;

the

the favor of the grace of Chrift may wonderfully draw defires after it, they may find fuch a fweetnefs in it, *Luk.*13.26. *Many fhall fay, Lord, have not we eat and drank in thy prefence?* that is, they find much fweetnefs there; the Lord taught among them; they defired him, and thought he was their own, yet fhut out; and hence verfe 24. *Many fhall feek to enter in, and fhall not be able.*

Fourthly, They may and do grow up in a glorious profeffion in the ways of grace, and fuch a profeffion as to ftand it out againft perfecution, as the thorny ground did, and may have fome growth toward it, which cannot be without fome defires and fpringings of heart after it.

SECT. II.

Ufe 1.

HEnce let this be an item to all the people of God, to preferve with all care, and not to lofe, but to make much of the Spirit of Grace inherent in them; for look as the Lord Jefus, when he would make his Difciples wonder at their bleffednefs, and make much of him, and his love, faith he, *Many Kings and Prophets have defired to fee thefe days, and have not feen them*; fo many profeffors of great parts and gifts fhall defire to have that Spirit of Grace and Peace which you have, and fhall never fee it, never fhall have it: When *Davids* heart began to be drawn away by the evils of the world, and then beheld the vanity of that, his defires are now turned another way, *Oh it is good for me to draw nigh to God*, that's good: As if he had faid, though it be good to have the things themfelves; yet it is not good for me to draw too nigh in my defires and efteem of them, but *good for me to draw nigh to him.* It may be fometimes your hearts are taken off from efteeming your condition, and what the Lord hath done for you; and hence no defire after the Lord or his Grace, but the lawful comforts of the world, not inordinately, but if I had fo much, or as good as others, then well. *Pfal.*141.4. *David* entreats the Lord not to encline his heart after any evil thing, no not after the wickeds good things, *Let me not eat of their dainties*; for grant that thou lofeft all thefe things, which others have, the time will come when the greateft Prince, and thofe that have their defires filled here, fhall fay, Oh that I was in that mans eftate! Let the Lord therefore exercife you with many wants and forrows; remember this, your end will be peace, which the worft would give a world for another day.

Ufe 2.

What then will become of them that never defired grace at all, becaufe they are well enough without it! a man cannot live (fay they) by praying, and hearing of Sermons; fuch duties are troublefom; hinderances, not defirable helps; and when any Ordinance comes, when will Sabbaths be ended? and as for the people of God themfelves they can fee no difference between them and other men, nay, they think them worfe; if this be your Religion, God keep me from your Religion. Nay, they can fee no beauty in Chrift to defire him; they can defire that they were not kept info much on the Sabbaths, nor fo much pains taken with them to inftruct them; it may be thefe may defire that their hands be kept from ftealing, their tongues from curfing, and their feet from runing to fhed blood; but the life of Grace, and power of it, they defire not that, nor never did: I remember when *David* was in extremity, Lord, faith he, *my groanings are not hid from thee*; this was his comfort when he could not pray, *Pfal.*38.9. But here it is otherwife: Canft thou if extremity fhould come upon thee, fay, Now I am not able to fpeak, Oh remember my clofet tears,

my

my midnight groans, and daylight complaints, and those daily sighings after thee which have arisen from this sorrowful heart? did the Lord never work this in thee? if extremity comes, and thou hast no such thing to witness for thee, do you think that you shall meet the Bridegroom in peace? Oh no! go home, and make thy moan over thy own Soul; the Lord is far from me; if *many seek to enter and shall never be able*, what will become of me?

Hence see how many people deceive themselves in their evidencing of a good estate, who because they see no oyl in their vessel, nor see no shining in their lives, yet because they desire it, they think hereupon the Lord accepts them and their desires, and therefore the Lord will fulfill them; this very conceit keeps thousands in their sins and miseries, and that under conviction of them; yet I desire it were better with me; and they think Hypocrites make shews of this and that, yet they have not unfeigned desires; and here thousands rest, and this slays them, as *Prov.*27.5. *The desires of the sluggard kills him.*

SECT. III.

Quest. But doth not the Lord respect the groanings of his people? doth not Christ say, *Joh.* 4.10. if thou hadst asked, &c. doth not the Lord look upon the inner man, the very frame, nay, desires that have been past?

Answ. Yes, there be some desires which are evidences; some which are not; I shall discover them that be unsound in the particular example of these foolish Virgins, &c.

First, Those are unsound desires, which arise in the soul easily, without feeling a need of the Lords almighty power and Spirit of life to work them at first; we shall finde that the desires of regenerate Christians do not come easily, but they finde a need of the Lord to draw them. *Jer.*31.10. *Lam.*5.21. but the desires of others spring up easily and quickly; as these foolish Virgins, they wanted oyl, they could quickly desire it; and they go to their fellow-brethren for help, *Oh give us of your oyl.* Look as it is with wilde Rye and Pease, they will come up at the season of the year in abundance, without sowing or plowing, the ground bears them naturally; but other corn and grain will not come so easily; your ground will not bear it till plowed and digged, and then the hand of man must set it, and dye it must, before it can live again; so here, if desires come and spring up easily, it is a sign they are wilde; the Lord must break the heart, and then sow these; and plant these from heaven, and you must fetch it out of heaven, else it is naught; for when the Lord works saving desires indeed, he ever sows them in a broken heart, which is throughly broken indeed; when God sets the smoaking flax on fire (which are desires) he first bruiseth the reed it self.

Secondly, The subject in which these desires are; a man hath a Son and a Servant; the Son hath all his desires granted him, because he hath a sonly spirit; all the Father hath is for him, that may be good for him; a Servant desires importunately, but he prays from the spirit of a Servant, and all that his Master hath is not for him; and therefore if he pray for the inheritance or a part of it, of the portion of the Son, shall he have it? no, he shall have what is fit for a Servant; so it is here, the Lord hath some Sons in his Churches; these praying and desiring from a son-like spirit, all that God hath being theirs, they

shall

shall have it; and hence *Psal.*145.18,19,20. He will fulfil the desires of them that fear him, will love him, and delight themselves in him; for that is the son-like disposition; when he is cut short of all comfort in the world, nay, when he may have his fill of them, yet he delights in his Fathers face, love, and grace, and fellowship, and house, *Psal.*27.4. *For they are heirs and coheirs with Christ, being Sons*; but now there are Servants in the house of God; shall they have their wills and lusts? no; thus it was with these foolish Virgins; they were only Servants in the house, no true Spouse or Sons, and were foolish at best, and had not the spirits of Sons, but had their lusts; never were espoused savingly to the Lord Jesus himself, nor laid up all their hope in him, but were foolish and that is the ground why others desires are heard, not theirs.

Thirdly, Unsound desires make after a certain measure only, whereas the desires of Saints seek after this Grace without measure; and thus the foolish Virgins fell short of the wise; all that they could get was little enough for themselves; but the foolish look after some of their oyl, as many a man looks upon the gifts and parts of another; Oh, saith he, if I was as honest, as humble a man as such a one! and many a man sets up such a measure, and if he hath that, is well, while he wants that miserably: Look wisely upon the foolish Virgins, they did content themselves with a measure, and now they are in want of it, seek for it; at first a little did content them, and now when it is spent, a little will serve them again: And what is their measure?

1. So much as will beautifie and adorn them before men, *our Lamp is out.*

2. So much as will comfort them against the coming of Christ; for now they were troubled that their oyl was spent, whereby they might meet the Bridegroom: he that desires it for a little measure of it, his desires are certainly unsound; so much as will serve his turn (he cuts his coat according to his cloth) but he that desires it without measure, *è contra,* as *Paul, Phil,* 3.12. *That I may apprehend by any means, that for which I am apprehended:* As *Chrysostom* calls *Paul* that *insatiabilis Dei cultor*; for he makes it his last end; as he that desires wealth without measure, though he gets not all the wealth of the world, yet the more he hath, the more he craves; this his fleshly lust is his last end.

Obj. But he may desire it without measure for his own ends.

Ans. I confess 'tis true; for men may desire honor and no honor but by gifts, and no gifts but by grace; and hence may desire infinitely, but yet it is but a measure, *viz.* to serve his own ends, but not the Lords ends; to set up himself; true desire of grace, is for that which may pull down self, and make God all, *Psal.*119.455.

Fourthly, It is not their only desire, or the only thing they desire, *viz.* the good Spirit of the Lord, and that they might not live or any thing else in them, but that the Lord may live, and his Grace and Kingdom may prevail in their hearts; the desires of Saints are only after this; or if their desires are after other things, the Spirit lusts against them, 2 *Sam.*23.5. As carnal desires are after life, so the comforts of it, so spiritual desires are after the life of Christ in them, and the comforts of the Lord thereby, *Psal.* 27.3,4. *One thing I have desired, and that I will seek for*; what was it? a Crown, a Kingdom? no, *but that I may dwell in the Lords house for ever, and visit his Temple:* Notable is that example of *Abraham, Heb.*11. Two things he met with that might draw down his desires.

1. He came to a land which God promised to give him, where he lives among enemies and in fears.

2. He might have returned to another Country, and now have been better.

3. *God bleſſed him,&c.* but it was nothing he deſired, only another above; hence God is not aſhamed to be called his God: but the fooliſh Virgins fell ſhort of this, and hence they now ſeek only in times of extremity: And this is the frame of many graceleſs hearts in time of extremity. 1. When all grace is gone. 2. When death is come, then they ſeek earneſtly after the Lord, and Grace; Oh their ſin lies heavy! Oh then an humble heart is ſweet! but before their hearts were overcome with luſts after other things; and this double heart every carnal heart hath, *Epheſ.2.3, fulfilling the luſts of the mind,* i.e. Diabolical luſts, *and luſts of the fleſh,* i.e. ſenſual and beaſtly luſts, it's the ſtate of all men; and hence promiſes are not made ſimply to mens ſeeking the Lord, for they may miſs, but to them that do it with their whole heart *Pſal.* 119.2. *ſer.* 29.13. this they never do; and hence men pray daily, and live in their luſting all the day after; men long in miſery, but are cool in peace.

SECT. IV.

Queſt. BUt ſeeing there is in Saints two Natures, fleſh luſting againſt the Spirit, and ſpirit againſt fleſh, and a double heart in a Reprobate, whereby he deſires grace and other things, how ſhall we diſtinguiſh them?

Anſw. 1. The luſts after grace and worldly things in an Hypocrite agree together in the ſame heart; but thoſe luſts which are after the fleſh and ſpirit in a regenerate heart are contrary one to another, and like fire and water one ſeeking to deſtroy the whole being of the other. *Exem. gr.* A man wants the things of this world, he ſeeks and deſires after them, riches, honor, reſt, and peace; but thinks he, if I have no more but this, I may to hell; if no Grace; hence he deſires that, and ſo doing now he hath peace, and all is quiet with him, and goes on ſweetly in a way of profeſſion and prayer; and a gracious heart is ready thus to do, and to make his head lye ſoft with two pillows, but yet the Spirit riſeth up againſt this, that the ſoul thinks, I ſhall fall by this heart; Lord, how apt to reſt in theſe lees! luſts in Hypocrites are like brethren, that help one another to this end to get peace; but here as enemies to deſtroy ſuch a curſed peace as that is in the Godly.

2. In a falſe heart, luſts and deſires after theſe things are dear to them, like their limbs or beſt members, they cannot be nor cannot do without them; but in Saints they are ſores and blains, and ſo hated of them; *ex. gr.* Let a man have a full table, and fair eſtate, and outward bleſſings, promiſing much, and the Ordinances of God, and a heart to follow God there; now ſee him lively in the ſervice of God; but let him be brought to extremities, and want of all this, and fears of poverty, eſtate waſteth, poverty appears, many rates come in, and the wife crys out; now he falls down to the earth in diſcontent or worldlineſs, and his life and affection to Ordinances, or the ſervants of God is now gone; as it is with a bird, when ſhe hath two wings ſhe can flye, but when ſhe hath only one, then ſhe falls, and the fowler takes her, becauſe it was a limb precious to her; ſo here: Thus it was with *Davids* ſervants at *Ziglag, 1 Sam.* 30.4. *all wept till they could weep no more;* but here it was otherwiſe with *David,* he could flye to God without thoſe wings; ſo when God gives a man a condition not ſo great as he would, and the heart luſts after ſo much, and God croſſeth; he cannot be content with a little, or with a mean eſtate, becauſe his luſt is his limb, he cannot ſuffer it to be cut off, or be pared; if a man hath a wooden leg, he can cut it anſwerable to his ſhoo, but if

Gal. 5.1.

but

but a limb, he must have his shooe cut answerable to his leg; because it is his limb, no cutting of that less; oh it is dear: So it is with a man that hath a lust after any thing, it is dear, and hence he is said to live in them, and to be in the flesh; but the desires after these things in a gracious heart, they are blains, they can be without them; Oh never such a happiness if the Lord would dead them to me, *Gal.* 5.24. *they that are in Christ have crucified the flesh, with the affections and lusts thereof.*

3. The lusts and desires in a false heart are reigning lusts, and make the lusts after grace and holiness serve them; but *è contra* in a holy heart. *Ex. gr.* A man prays for the love of God, and the Spirit of grace, and 'tis affectionate, but yet 'tis ever for some lust: *Jam.* 4.3. a man desires grace to perfect his gifts, and gifts to deck him, and purchase him honor before men; a man desires grace to quiet his conscience in assurance of Gods love, and pardon of sin, that he may live the more peaceably with his sin, *Isa.* 58.3,4. Now in a gracious heart, the desires of these things serve the desires after grace; for he desires the things of this world to be the more holy, *Prov.* 30.7,8. *Feed me with food convenient, that I may not tempt thee;* he desires and hath them for *Israels* sake, 2 *Sam.* 5.12. Like a Tradesman, he buys and sells, but it is for gain, *Phil.* 1.20. Oh consider of these things, and if your hearts have had only such false desires as these, know it, that as verily as these Virgins were shut out, so shall you another day.

CHAP. XIII.

The desires and endeavors of Hypocrites after Grace are not lasting.

SECT. I.

THe foolish Virgins in their first endeavors after the Spirit of Grace, usually cease from seeking farther, before they have got that measure and fulness of it which will continue to the last. Or,

That there is ever a cessation in the first endeavors of carnal professors from seeking after that measure of grace which will indeed last and continue until their meeting with, and appearing before the Lord Jesus Christ.

For these Virgins here did seek after the Lord Jesus Christ, and the Spirit of Christ, and hence did get that measure which lighted their lamps for a good season; and they contented themselves with this, and gave over seeking untill it is too late; and therefore now they say, *Give us of your oyl, our Lamps are out:* These foolish Virgins when they had got somewhat, they are carried with abundance of affection and profession, they think themselves as good as the best, and what need they seek for more! and then grow secure and fall asleep untill all

all is spent. The Scripture is pregnant every where for this. But let us look and see the causes of this.

First, Sometime it is because they know not what that measure is which doth accompany salvation; but they set up an imagination of their own heads, which is a false image of Saving-grace, and when they have that, now they think all is well, and they go no further. *Judg.*2.11,12. People that know not the Lord, not the power of his grace, *will set up other gods, and serve them,* and there rest; until it is with them, as it was with those, when *the anger of the Lord waxeth hot, and spoilers come,* now they cry unto the Lord; What is the reason why many a man falls short of the righteousness which is of God, *viz.* of Faith? Because he sets up in his head a righteousness of his own; and if I get that, then I hope the Lord will accept me, and forgive me: and hence *Rom.*9.31,32. why did they miss of it? Because they sought it by a righteousness which is of their own; so why do many miss of Faith? because they think it is an assurance; or when a man rests upon Christ, not considering the need of an Almighty power; and hence the Apostle prays for this, *Ephes.*1.19. So for Repentance, why do men fall short of it? they think it is when Gods anger is exprest, the soul then comes to seek the Lord, and findes some comfort *Psal.* 78. *Matth.* 3. and so runs away with it: So for Holiness, they think it is to be like others; and then well, they think these are the men that shall live, and are happy; and look as it is like it was at *Babel,* when head and tongues were confounded, one calls for a Brick, the other brings him a Trowel, Hammer or Tile, because he did but imagine what he spake, and so understood not his language; So 'tis here; men read and hear God speak, and Ministers call for Faith, and knowledge of God; but earthly minds cannot understand heavenly language; and hence they imagine that is Faith and Repentance which indeed is not, and so miss of that which indeed else would continue; and this is the misery of many thousands that in seeing see not. The experience of the work of grace, makes men savingly to know what Grace is, *John* 5.37,38. Now men graceless never felt it in the life and power of it, and therefore cannot tell it.

Secondly, From the nature of Common-grace; the nature of which is as the Apostle speaks of lifeless knowledge, 1 *Cor.*8.1. *to puff up;* it never leaves the soul more sensible of his vileness, as Saving-grace doth, *Ezek.* 16.*ult.* and so makes a man never rest in seeking after the Lord; but makes the soul feel himself full, and hence the stomack is gone from seeking after more, as *Rev.* 3.17. *She thought she was rich,* &*c.* The Spirit of Grace which is but common, that heals a vile, proud heart, it easeth him, it quiets him, in healing some sin, which lies sore on the conscience, it heals and quiets the man, so he is well, needs no repentance; but the Spirit of life indeed destroyeth the man, and slays corruption, and hence he resists; and now saith the soul, I never felt my heart so vile as now; and hence, saith *Paul, Sin revived, and led me captive, Oh wretched man!* as it is with a Prince, if any great ones come and serve him, he likes them, this gives him rest, settles him in his Throne; but if any one come to reign over him, now he gathers all his strength to oppose: So Common grace it ever comes as a servant to corrupt; and hence take a man of best wit and parts, he turns them against the Lord, and makes them serve himself.

Thirdly, From an apprehension of this difficulty, and an unwillingness in the heart to break thorow the difficulty of seeking after the Lord; many a man sees (as *Dives* in hell, *Abraham afar off*) Grace, and God, and Christ afar off; but there is a great gulf between them and Grace; now to be watching, fasting, seeking the Lord diligently, to follow the Lord hard, *Psal.* 63. to keep the heart lamenting till the Lord comes, this is hard, as *Heb.*2.

'tis

'tis faid, *They could not enter in becaufe of unbelief.* 1. They thought they could never overcome. 2. They thought the Lord did therefore hate them, *Deut.* 1.27. They did not regard the ftrength of God ; *they fhall be but bread for us faith Caleb* ; they could not believe that to be bread that is fo hazzardful. So 'tis with many a man ; and hence he fits down with defires and hopes, and fo perifheth ; *the fluggards defires flay him* ; hence many complain of difficulty, but never break difficulties, and fo perifh ; and fo not like to the Merchant that goes far for pearl. It is his bufinefs, and no ftorms nor ill weather drive him to defire the fmoak of his chimney, till he hath got them, he hath now refolved to venture all for, *Prov.2.5. if thou dig for filver,&c.* many prize Chrift and Grace, Oh that I had it, but are loth to dig for it, they love their eafe fo well, and hence reft in their defire after it ; but indeed mifs it ; and hence many can come to, and follow God in outward Ordinances, but never find fruit and comfort in any of them, becaufe of difficulty, yet fit down content becaufe they feek for Ordinances, as *Prov. 12.27. The fluggard roafts not what he had took in hunting ;* there is a very great delight in coming to Ordinances, as travellers under the fhadow, but then to climb the tree that is hard, and hence lofe the fruit ; and hence God feeing a man love his floth, and hath that bafe efteem of his Grace, as that he will not follow fo hard after it as he hath done after his lufts, let's loofe Satan, and he comes and ftakes down a finner in this, God muft do all, and there he refts, and fo he falls fhort ; like one that comes to Husbandmen, and tells them they have taken much pains and care to get their ground good to bring forth much, but for time to come their ground fhall bring forth fruit without planting or fowing, only reap you the fruit, it would be good news to them, and they believe it, and then when the year comes about, they are to feek for corn ; fo this affects, and here they reft, and by this means want.

Fourthly, From feeling the unprofitablenefs of feeking the Lord through difficulties, and hence they give over but a little before they finde that that will continue.

1. Some follow the Lord for carnal ends, as *Judas* did, but he finding the purfe grow lank, and the bag empty, he forfakes the Lord.

2. Some for comfort, and hence pray and mourn ; and hence *Mal.3.14.* what profit is there that we have walked fo ? as it was with *Naomi,* when fhe returned home, both her daughters accompany her fome part of her,way, *Return again,*faith fhe,*to your friends, here is no Husband for you where I go ;* the one would not be beaten off, it is not a Husband I came for, but a God ; *thy God fhall be my God,* the other hearing her fpeeches, and loving her Fathers houfe, and Country, goes back, not without fome affection ; fo it is here ; whereas Faith will cry the more.

Fifthly, From the offences which ufually Satan cafts in when they are in the heat of their firft endeavours ; as the ftony ground being offended fell away. As,

1. Perfecution, and hence they fall ; a childe begins to look towards God ; the Father, Mother, Friends fcoff and reproach.

2. Corrupt Teachers, *Matth.24.* that like falfe Chrifts deceive, and put a world of fcruples into mens heads, and then lead them away ; as the *Galatians* that would pull out their eyes for *Paul,* yet by love and fmooth carriage of falfe Teachers fo plaufible, they fell off ftrangely.

3. Corrupt company, women or men ; many ftrong men have fallen by the one, and *men alfo who having a form of godlinefs, yet denying the power of it,* their hearts be taken in thefe fnares.

4. Some hard point of doctrine, *Joh.6.60,66.* fomething is preacht that is crofs to our apprehenfions ; He never believe it, fay they ; and away they fall.

Sixthly, Becaufe of falfe comforts which ufually men meet with before they get that which will abide in them, in their woful hours; and this quiets all.

1. From themfelves; A man fees Chrift only can redeem him by price, but he feels no need of Chrift to redeem him by power; and now feeing what a miferable creature he is, ftays himfelf upon the Lord, and that it may be by fome word which he hears. *John* 8.30, 31. *when they heard that, they believed*; yet the Lord tells them, they are not free, but were yet captive to their fin, which they need the Son himfelf to dye to fave them from; and fo many a one comforts himfelf, and ftayes here, though he have no other affurance.

2. The approbation and comfort of others, *Ezek* 13.3, 4.

3. Strange extafies of joy which many a man meets with fuddenly; they have eaten and drunk in Chrifts prefence, and have been comforted at fuch and fuch a time in fuch a manner; this, we fhall finde it, perfwades men that God is theirs, without revealing the fubject, *viz.* we be his people, and that change which God hath made.

SECT. II.

Queft. WWHat is that meafure which will laft, and throughout continue?

Anfw. I have fpoken of this at large; but he that loves the truth as his daily bread, will feed upon it, when ever it is fet before him: Now there is one thing (this is different) and I fhall exprefs my felf in one thing only, *viz.* *They give over before they have tafted and drunk the fatisfying fweetnefs of the grace of Chrift, and the prefence of his grace in their fouls:* That look as it was with *Ifrael*, they came out of *Egypt*, and faw the wonders of God in the wildernefs, and had his fiery Law, and glorious Tabernacle among them, yet they never came to the land of reft; fo it is at this day with many, they have fome glimpfes of the excellency of Chrift, and his grace, and fome defires after it, and fome taftes of it; they are pulled out of their woful bondage, and feeing words of God, are oft affected, yet their carkaffes muft fall in the wilnefs, becaufe they never come to reft; they fall off from God becaufe they never knew what this reft meaneth, *Heb.* 4.11.

Hypocrites have awakening grace, and are much troubled; they have enlightning grace, and know more than many Chriftians; they have affecting grace, and are wonderfully taken with the glad tidings of the Gofpel; but fatisfying grace, or that grace which brings them to full reft, and fatisfying fweetnefs in God, not only to their confciences but to their hearts; not carnal, but fpiritual, this they never came to, *Joh.* 4.14. *he that drinks the water I give, fhall never thirft again*; *Joh.* 6.54. *If ye eat my flefh and drink my blood, there is life*, if not, no life; eating and drinking, is not fipping and tafting; many may eat and drink in his prefence, as thofe *Exod.* 24.11. but yet not feed at all on his perfon; this makes the foul hold out, *Prov.* 2.10, 11. *Pfal.* 90.14. this makes the foul glad in God, and in all the days of his life; where any creature is at reft, there it is in the proper place; it is a token the Lord is the proper place of the foul, (not fin, nor hell, which was *Judas* proper place) when it is at reft there; and this is the laft end, and fruit of the redemption of Chrift, *Jer.* 31.11, 14. *i.e.* not having fo much of God as to be a God-glutted Chriftian (as he faid) but fo fatiate as not to defire other things, but there to ftay, though the heart doth oft feel not the fame fweetnefs.

SECT. III.

NOw there be four things which do concur to this fulness of satisfying sweetness.

First, Manifestation of the Lord Jesus in his full proportion, and in all the dimensions of his goodness to the soul; the soul of man is made for, and so desires an infinite eternal good; whiles this good is not known to be such a one, it never satisfies; and hence let a man look upon any one creature, there is much sweetness in it, but not all; hence it satisfies not; there's sweetness in honor and wealth, but if sick, a miserable man; there is sweetness in health, but if poor and naked, a desolate man; and if one creature had all in it, yet when one thinks this must be taken from me, it is like *Jonah's* gourd, it never satisfies:

Now the Grace which satisfies must first, Manifest the fulness of infinite goodness suitable to me in the Lord; if that now do I want any outward blessing it is in Christ, for he is Heir not only of heaven, but of all the world.

2. Do I want spiritual blessings? *Ephes.*3. there is all in him, life, and peace and glory.

3. Have I nothing to move the Lord to do any of these to me? yet there is fulness of tender mercy, and pity in him, *Ephes.*1.17. and 3.18.

Secondly, Possession of this good as mine; let a poor man see heaps of gold before him, it satisfies not him, because it is none of his; let a Christian hear of Kingdoms, peace, glory, in and with Christ, yet it satisfies not him; it troubles him the more, if Christ forsake him, and grow strange to him; but to be sure that Christ is mine, this makes the soul do, nay suffer the utmost for Christ, and to know that nothing can separate, &c. as a man that knows he shall kill, and not lose his life, will venture like *Sampson* upon an hoast of men; they may wound me, they cannot bind nor slay me, *Rom.*8.*ult.* there is joy and some satisfaction in finding the pearl of great price, what joy when it is possessed!

Thirdly, Communication of this good to the soul; let a man have meat and drink, but he cannot come at it when he hath need of it, will this satisfie if it be lockt up? let a man have real possession of never so many lands, yet if he hath not the benefit sure to him, as well as the thing, he will never hold out; what am I the better? so that grace satisfies that brings the soul to fruition of the good, that it is now in respect of the benefit of it conveyed to the soul, *Psal.*16.4,5. *the Lord is the portion of my lot and cup,* and he maintains both; and hence *Jer.*14.9. *Why art thou like a man astonished, yet in the midst of us!* if a man have meat and clothes, and the one never feeds, the other never warms, would this satisfie? no, unless that he may feel them, nay he would think this a curse; so let Saints have God in his Ordinances, the best in the world there is, if not fed thereby, Lord! what a misery is this? especially if the Lord helps not in time of need.

Fourthly, Reflexion of good again to the good which doth refresh us, else it never satisfies; if a man have meat dealt out, and it is very sweet, yet if it gives him no strength to perform acts of life; if a man have a friend, and he cannot love again, nor shew testimony of love, it will not satisfie him; so that grace satisfies which makes the soul reflect the love of God to God again; *shall I serve the Lord,* said *David, of that which cost me nothing?* you know the Vine and Olive, *Judg.*9. were quietted by this, *that they did rejoyce the heart of God and man;* what do you tell me of bonds? *I account not my life dear to finish my course,* saith *Paul.*

Now a carnal heart gives over before he fees or poffeffeth or enjoy-eth the Lord, or found the fweetnefs of a holy life in walking with God. Hence,

1. He loaths and is weary of all his profeffion and truth he knows, and the God he talks of.

2. Hence they break out to fome lufts or others; which becaufe if not fatisfied here, they muft fatisfie themfelves fome other way, either in vain conceits or opinions, or lufts of the world.

3. Hence, defperate doubts, Is the Lord mine? whereas if it were other-wife, then as it is with a man, ask him, how do you know you eat and drink? it fatisfies me, faith he, it puts ftrength, I fhould die daily elfe.

SECT. IV.

OF Examination, Inftruction, and Exhortation to all thofe who have reft content with that meafure of the Spirit which will never laft, to begin a-gain, and lay a better foundation, left it befall you as it did thefe Virgins, or as the finner in *Prov.*5.11,12,13. *you mourn when you,not your flesh, but foul is con-fumed*; Oh how have I *defpifed inftruction*! left wrath break out which cannot be quenched, for dealing flightly with God and your own fouls; how many Chriftians take that for grace, which when it comes to tryal will be found too light, and know it not, and regard it not, *till the hand-witing of God is upon their confciences!*

If therefore you have not found the fatisfying fweetnefs of the Spirit of Gods grace, that water which quencheth all your inordinate thirft, that bread which feeds you to life, be fure your oyl will be fpent, and your light will go out before you dye.

SECT. V.

Queft. HOw fhould I know that fatisfying fweetnefs?

Anfw. Ah methinks you fhould fay, Oh that I did know it! yet wary I would be of giving any juft occafion to break off what the Lord in his grace hath wrought; yet you may know fomething of it by this.

1. When the Spirit of Gods grace difpenfed in his Ordinances doth glut you and flay you, and make you worfe; here is not the grace of Chrift which doth fatisfie you; if the more knowledge you have of the truth, the lefs glory you fee in the truth, and the lefs you love the truth; if the more comfort you have found by it, the lefs you now defire after it; if the more abilities you have re-ceived by it, the more proud you grow, and high-minded; if having come for to feek the Ordinances of God, the lefs good you find by them, the more weary you grow of them, and the more you defpife them; it is certain, the fatisfying grace of Chrift is not here, when the bread to feed, is poifon to flay; is not this the condition of many? what is the caufe they are growing worfe, that they are worfe in their latter end and middle of their Chriftian profeffion, than the begining, becaufe they are grown full by Gods Ordinances, and fo worfe; what is the caufe in places of perfecution the Lords Ordinances were precious, not when they come to them? Gods Ordinances plenty makes them to under-value them through their fin; that look as it is with men in confumptions, whofe life is going out, they think they can eat, yet when it is before them,

loath the smell of it, or a little serves them; whereas another finds it otherwise; not but that Saints may think thus, but they with *Hezekiah* mourn under it, 2 *Chron.* 32. *Hof.* 6.5. *I have hewen and flain,* what is the cause? *because your goodness is like a morning dew, which soon vanisheth, therefore have I flain them.* Oh God loves us, and we are the best people in the world, because we have Ordinances; no, but because you be shallow, hence you shall have Prophets to slay you.

Secondly, If any man maintains any living lust in himself in the midst of his profession, and hungers after it, and the life of it; for when a man hath better food to feed upon, he will neglect his own at home, as Christ said to them when they asked him, why he did not eat; how many be there which have strange gifts, and have had marvellous ebbings and flowings of the Spirit of Life and Peace, and yet one sin have they lived in, and would not, could not live without it. Look as it was in the wilderness, they were for a time pretty well content with their allowance and wilderness-walks and provisions, but they could not stay long, *They asked meat for their lusts, but he sent leanness into their souls, Psal.* 106.14,15. So that there it is, if lust be stirring, the Lord either denies it his own people, because he will starve the lust, that the soul may grow, or if he gives it, slays the lust by it, gluts it, makes the soul grow weary of it, and prize his first Husband more; as *Solomon* by his experimental discovery of the creature: Many men confess and pray against their sins, but by their sorrows and desires, they do maintain the life of their sin, fall to it as the dog to the vomit; you will be cast away at last, 1 *Cor.* 9. *ult. I beat not the air, lest I become a cast-away;* whereas a gracious heart doth not maintain, but waste and consume his lust. His life is to live to God.

Thirdly, If a mans heart and affections reach not the people of God with the dearest embracings, nor yet mourn for the want of such a heart; for sometimes there are some drops of the Lords goodness falling into the heart, whereby the soul cleaves unto the Lord, and is moved and ravished, and bears much love, as it thinks, towards him; but look to their love to the people of God, there they fall short; because *the love of Christ is not shed abroad abundantly into their hearts, filling and satisfying of them;* and hence have none to poure out upon the souls of their neighbors, 1 *John* 4. 20, 21. In our own Country, what was the accusation of Saints? *viz.* They are Hypocrites before God; What did you think of those men that said so? *Answ.* Surely they were enemies to the Lord, and that never loved him; for then they would love his people. But what is the occasion here? Now they say they come far for Ordinances; but they are unjust oppressors, cruel; poor men may starve before regarded by them; and so they cast reproach not only upon some few, but all the people of God, and Church of God; If that it be so, their accusation is Gods accusation; if not (as generally it is) for many, though unable to do much, yet if called to it, would lay down their estates and lives for others; then know thou never hadst Christ's love shed in thy heart (which will continue) but drops of it only; because thy love cannot reach to these. Beloved, what is the end of your coming over hither? is it not to enjoy first Christ, and nextly his People, so his Ordinances? because next to fellowship of Christ, the Saints company is most precious; and do you here bite, and censure, and devoure, and neglect, and reproach one another, and upon any conceived injury stumble? are poor men neglected? It is a sad sign the love of Christ in not in power, *Heb.* 6.9,10.

Fourthly, If there have been abundance of sweet affections and sweet refreshings, thereby rising up within the soul, without the death, and killing, and removal of the contrary lusts and sins; it is certain this soul was never truly filled nor satisfied with the Spirit of Gods grace; for as it is with vessels, while they be filled

with

with lime or chaff, they cannot be filled with wheat or with water; so while the heart is filled with some noisom distempers, it cannot be filled or satisfied with the Lord; look but abroad in the Churches; how many be there that say and think they hate their sin as the only evil, they close with the Lord Jesus, they love the people of God all of them, they seek the glory of God, and yet they do but think so! for though they hate sin, yet it is unsoundly, because they see not how closely their hands are knit to their sin; they never did believe, because they never felt their unwilling heart to close with Christ; they never loved the Saints, because they never felt their contempt of Saints; never sought Gods glory, because they never mourned under that which did stain it; they never make work with their own hearts; the stony and thorny ground withered because their soil was naught; a heart filled with sweet affections, which never felt the strength of contrary corruptions lying underneath, it is an ill soil, and where those affections will never prosper, nor prove right; and hence, 2 *Tim.* 2. 20, 21. he that purgeth himself from these things shall be a vessell of honor, ever preserved, never broken. Do not put it to a venture, it may be I may have grace, and so put your salvation on the hazard of such hopes; but the Lord that hath come to thee knocking, open the door that he may come in and feast; cry for infinite creating power and mercy to make haste and come and help thee; what have you to do else but to get your old lusts purged away? what do you labor for else? if you have children to bring up, if you have any love to them, nay if swine or cattel, meat you will have to feed them, and satisfie them if possible; and yet behold thy soul perishing for want of true spiritual refreshings!

SECT. VI.

Use 2.

OF Exhortation to all young beginners, and so to all others; Take heed you chop not at your comfort too soon; take heed you do not perish in the way, that whiles seeking after the Lord and rest, you fall from the Lord by security and scandal, and so you perish, but labor for that which will continue and last.

1. Mariners when they go a voyage, they will trim their vessel, and search if there be not something amiss which may sink the ship at last; if once out at sea, they may dye before they come home; and hence at first setting out are careful; so do you.

2. You will meet with trials enough to exercise all your grace, that you will find all little enough in the issue.

3. This will be your comfort at death, that though it be difficult, yet if you have fought a good fight, and run a good race, there is now a crown, this will make you to go out of the world wondering, and go up to eternity in your triumphant Chariot of glory, when you shall see on the one side, here a *Demas* forsaking, there a *Judas* betraying; here one Christian withered, there another scandalised and offended, and yet the Lord hath upheld thee (in thy integrity) a poor creature, that thoughtst thou shouldst never have held out at all.

That you may do thus, two things are to be done.

First, Be sure your wound at first for sin be deep enough; for all the error in a mans Faith and Sanctification it springs from that first error of his Humiliation; if a mans Humiliation be false, and weak, and little, his Faith is light, and his Sanctification counterfeit, as may be seen in the stony and thorny soil; if a mans wound be right, and Humiliation deep enough, that mans

Faith

Faith is right, and his Sanctification is glorious ; for Christ cannot be exceeding sweet and satisfactory to the soul, unless sin be first exceeding bitter; and this is the reason why Christ is not sweet nor precious at first nor afterward, because sin is not so bitter to them, especially heart sins ; Christians shall find it, the esteem and price of Christ falls, whiles sin lies light and is not bitter.

SECT. VII.

Quest. How *bitter must it be?*

Answ. So bitter as that nothing contents your heart, whiles sin is with you, and the Lord is gone from you, *Lam.*3.49. *Mine eye ceaseth not mourning, till the Lord look down from heaven*; as a man that looks for a Prince to come and live with him, he prepares rooms for all his attendants, but he reserves the best lodgings for the Prince himself, and they are kept empty whiles he comes : So the soul entertains Creatures, and Ordinances, and Saints of God, but yet the heart is not content, but sits empty, desolate whiles the Lord is gone ; for whiles the heart is delighted with somewhat else beside the Lord (that if the Lord comes, it is well, if not, it is merry and jolly) see what the Lord there speaks, *Jam.*4.8,9,10. *Cleanse your hearts and he will draw nigh unto you*; turn laughter to mourning, else you are not humbled. Let Gods own people do so, it stops up the fountain of Gods love, and sweetness of mercy, *Psal.* 30.7. *When carnally confident, I was troubled*; as it is in marriage, if a man knows there is familiarity between the woman and another Lover he will have none of her ; but when sin is thus bitter, the Lord hath the garments of joy to give for the spirit of heaviness, *Isa.*61.1,2. Oh therefore, though it be cross to have limbs cut off, and breasts seared, bones broken, &c. yet part with all for life, even this life of Christ in you, which will give you full content.

SECT. VIII.

Quest. How *shall I do this, my heart will be wanton and carnal?*

Answ.1. Set this down for a conclusion, I shall never be comforted by the Lord, whiles any thing else comforts my heart, *i. e.* for it self, as hath been proved ; and if this was well thought of, this would make a man above all other things detest his carnal content, because this indeed keeps the Lord from him.

2. Keep the remembrance of the bitterness of your sin and evil in it ; thus *David, Psal.*51.3. set it ever before him ; for all the sweet of sin comes into the heart by a delusion first begot in the mind, of some present good in it, which the soul not attending to is drawn away by it, *Jam.*1.14. *drawn away and enticed* ; hence fortifie here. Three things in sin, which if remembred, would make it bitter.

1. Sentence of condemnation past upon thee by the Law of God for it, which may make a soul to mourn : Little content do men take in their Prison-bolts.

2. The death, and agonies, and sorrows of the Lord Jesus, to acquit the soul from this condemnation ; this is that which may work *bitterness as for a first born, Zach.*12.10,11.

3. Crossing the will, and so grieving the heart of Christ now in glory ; as
when

when the old world grew senfual it grieved God to the heart ; keep thefe in remembrance ; what pleafure canft thou take in that which makes the Lord figh ? *The end will be bitternefs*, Pfal. 73. 17.

Secondly, Take heed you mifs not of that Faith which will bring in fupply, Heb. 4. 1, 2. Take heed left a promife being left, any fall fhort of that reft which comes by the promife, by an unbelieving heart ; for many defire the Lord, and reft upon the Lord, and they are fatisfied with their hunger, and with their reft on him, without receiving life from him ; truly you will fall from the Lord then : for if the Lord doth not daily drop life into your hearts, you will grow weary of him ; and Ordinances they are empty wells, and Promifes they are dry breafts : if you have bread, but it feed you not, you will not care for it.

SECT. IX.

Queft. **H**Ow fhall I get this Faith ?

Anfw. 1. Honor and advance the Lord's rich grace in thy heart, before thou goeft to him for the Spirit of life ; thus that poor woman, *If I can but touch his skirt, I shall be whole*, if I can come to him, I fhall have help ; many can think before they go to Chrift, I fhall never fpeed, I fhall never overcome thefe evils ; and hence the *Ifraelites* are excluded *Canaan*: though I know the Lord doth pity his poor people when they believe, though not thus far ; as it is with men, if you would get their hearts from them, commend them ; fo here ; and though this doth not move the Lord, yet it is an Ordinance ; 'tis a way of God, *Micah* 7. 17, 18.

2. Take up a firm refolution never to let thy heart go from feeking the Lord till this is wrought, Pfal. 27. 4. *this I will seek after* ; fee that thou muft needs have this ; and hence do not fay, I have defired and gone to the Lord, and no help comes, and now fit down ; no, but take advantage hereupon to defire the more, and to make the Lord's denials or delays the ground of thy crys ; as the *Canaanitifh* woman, crums ; as *Jacob* by wreftling againft the Angel, he had the bleffing at laft ; Say, as it hath been long, fo therefore Lord help becaufe of that. But fins are many, and the heart is worfe : Oh the more need of Grace ; *Mofes* Exod. 33. 18. *If thou wilt not go with us, carry us not up hence*.

3. Wait for the Lord quietly, and look out when will it be better. Ifa. 64. 4. *eye hath not feen* ; and wait for him firft ; and fo for other things, Ifa. 30. 18. *Bleffed are they that wait for him*.

4. If the Lord gives not ; yet feek to give him content, though he doth not content thee ; as *Mary*, Joh. 2. when they wanted wine, 1 Joh. 3. 22. we do what pleafeth him ; and hence have our anfwer ; this will fetch it.

CHAP.

CHAP. XIV.

Shews that the Grace of one person will not advantage another that wants Grace himself; and that the best Christians cannot dispense Grace to those that want it.

VERSE 9.

But the wise answered, saying, Not so, lest there be not enough for us and you; but go ye rather to them that sell, and buy for your selves.

SECT. I.

Erein is set down the Answer of the wise to the Request of the foolish Virgins.

This Answer of the wise Virgins contains two things.

First, A denial, together with the reason of it, which is a check to their folly.

Secondly Their counsel and advice directing them to the remedy, if there be any which might supply them with oyl; *Go to them that sell and buy for your selves.* The Spirit of Grace comes not so lightly by: You would have it given; no, you must buy it; you would have us help you; no, there are others appointed for to sell it you; away to them before the Bridegroom comes.

1. *Not so*] They are words inserted in the English Text, not so in the original; but yet they are safely put in, partly because they are intended directly in the strength of their reason, and involved therein, implied thereby; partly because they do more clearly express the meaning of the words, and give their sense more distinctly.

2. *Lest there be not enough for us and for you*] What did the foolish now look to works of supererogation and prayers of Saints, and the treasury of the Churches holiness and Indulgencies ? surely no, for these were Virgins, had escaped the pollution of Antichrist, and they go for this not to Popish Treasurers, but unto them that are wise ; neither is it likely that Christ's coming could awaken them out of their security to fall to gross Popery so suddenly, whiles they were the Companions and Imitators of the wise, and therefore this is not the meaning, as some have wrested the words, and so make the Answer of the wise to be a Protestant Answer to a Popish Petition, and therefore bid them

go

go to Shavelings that will for money sell Pardons, and Indulgencies, and Prayers, and Merits.

SECT. II.

Queſt. **W**Hat then are the wiſe unwilling to communicate of the Graces they have? what Chriſtian but is willing?

Anſw. Firſt, We are not to adhere to words in opening Parables, but the ſcope; now their ſcope was hereby, Firſt to ſink and humble the hearts of the fooliſh, and to let them know that all that which they had in time of extremity, was little enough for themſelves at this ſeaſon.

Secondly, This anſwer is made anſwerable to the ground of their requeſt; you know how Hypocrites in Churches reſt in outward priviledges, and how they are carried unto Ordinances, but not above Ordinances indeed to Chriſt; and though they have ſome knowledge of, and lookings above them unto Chriſt, yet miſſing him, like men ſinking catch hold upon that which is next, and ſo look for help thence; ſo theſe being in the fellowſhip of the wiſe, and admirers of them, and having got good by them, and imitated them, hence they relye too much upon them for it; and hence they anſwer, We have but our meaſure, and therefore it is not in our hands to diſpenſe grace in times of extremity; that muſt come from him that hath received the Spirit without meaſure; ſo that this anſwer doth not imply unwillingneſs to communicate, but to let the others ſee that they were not the firſt that could communicate.

Thirdly, You are to conſider that God had now broken open the conſciences of the fooliſh, that they profeſſed they had no oyl; hereupon the wiſe Virgins are not unwilling to communicate altogether; but conſidering other means are ſanctified to beget Grace where it never was, or rather of greater efficacy and power; hence they ſend them to other means, to them that ſell, profeſſing this for their ground, that they had little enough for themſelves; and it was not in their power now to convey any: This I conceive is the direct ſcope of the Parable in this Verſe: Hence three Notes.

SECT. III.

THat the Grace of Gods Spirit in other wiſe-hearted Chriſtians, will do no good to fooliſh Virgins, and ſlothful Chriſtians in the days of their extremity. Ezek. 14. 20. Though Job and Daniel ſtood before me, they ſhall but deliver their own ſouls; gracious holy men, if not only in miſery but ſin 1 Joh. 5. 16. they ſhall recover; not others, Jr. 4. 4. leſt my wrath break out like fire. Oh therefore dally not under Ordinances; to have them, but no gain of them; to have Vines planted, but not to eat fruit of them, and all by reaſon of a ſlothful heart, is a dangerous thing; as many a man hath a rich ſtock, and a good trade, and yet thrives not; Oh he is not careful to keep, nor diligent to improve, but is idle; ſo here

Oh conſider the wrath of God! In extremity uſually the Lord hears and helps his poor people; but it ſhall be far from the Lord, when others ſhall ſay Lord help; no, let others tears and prayers be regarded; no, what Lord, not in extremity? no, not in extremity.

Obſerva-tion 1.

SECT. IV.

Observa-
tion 2.

THat it is not in the hand of the most eminent Christians to dispence the Grace of Christ to whom, and when, and where they will: Not in all separably, nor in all joyntly; it is not in all the wise Virgins hands together: It is not in the hands of a whole Church, or all Churches to do this. These poor foolish Virgins it may be they did not in their judgments think thus; however in their practice they now trust to this. But these answer, It is not in us.

It is not in *Moses* to give his spirit to whom he would, but the Lord, *Numb.*11.17.

It is not in *Paul* nor *Apollos,* the one deep in wisdom, the other admirable in expression, but in God, who gives the commission to fetch the whole world in, 1 *Cor.*3.5,6.

It is not in Christ as Man, to give to one to sit at his right hand or left.

It is not in the hands of the best Parents; It is not in the wills of all men living, *Joh.*1.13.

SECT. V.

Reason 1.

BEcause they have but their measure received wholly, and dependent wholly from another, answerable to their own necessities; therefore it is not in their freedom, but in the hands of him who hath received it without measure, *John* 3.34,35. *but the Father hath put all things into his hands;* as it is in stars, one star doth not give light to another, but the Sun to all, having received it without measure comparatively; so one Spring doth not beget another, but it is in the Sea, which hath water without measure, from whence they come and return again.

Reason 2.

Because all the Saints, and all the fellowship of God's people, it is but a means, or they are but instruments in the hands of Christ to convey Grace; now you know all instruments act and work according to the will of the principal agent; as it is not in the axes hand to cut down one tree for fuel, another for building; but in the agents hand, especially if the instrument be weak and powerless, and such are the people of God; 1 *Cor.*1.29. *they are poor things, and weak things, and nothings, things that are not;* 2 *Cor.*3.5.*not so much as to think any thing of themselves:* It is not in the people of God as it is in salves, that there is an inherent vertue abiding alway to heal, and that in any man which is cureable; but there is only an adherent vertue which doth not alway abide; and when it is there, works not upon all, but only at the pleasure of the principal Agent the Lord Jesus; those means which providence hath put an inherent vertue into, cannot bless, but as the Lord will: meat cannot nourish sometimes, muchless can these without the will of another; hence *Ephes.*4.16. the Saints are edified by this, but from Christ still.

Reason 3.

In regard of the greatness of the power and honor that is required to dispence the Grace of God, and the Spirit of Grace, which the Church is not capable of.

First, Knowledge of the Elect; the Spirit of Grace which accompanies Salvation, shall never be given to any but to them, *Rom.*11.7. *the election have obtained it;* hence they must be known first to them that have power to dispence

pence it ; now that they cannot tell ; indeed *Paul* by seeing the power put forth, knew the election of the *Theffalonians*, 1 *Theff.* 1. 4. but not before ; he could not say This man I will give grace unto, and not to that ; a Minifter, as *Paul*, *Acts* 18.10. may in general know that there is fome people in fuch a place, at leaft probably, but who they be he knows not, no more than *Samuel*, who knew one of *Feffes* Sons was to be King, but not one whom he liked, but whom the Lord did chufe ; and hence a Minifter calls all, becaufe he knows not who they be : only fome are called, becaufe Chrift knew, and therefore in his hand it is.

Secondly, The power muft be omnipotent, both to lay the foundation, and to go on with the building ; now that cannot be put forth by a poor finite crea-ture, when it will, but when the Lord will ; a Minifter may preach and quicken, a Chriftian may exhort and comfort, and yet they may hear and meet again twenty times and never find the like day, becaufe their weapons are only mighty through God, 2 *Cor.*10.4.5.

Thirdly, Shedding of blood, dying and bearing wrath, to purchafe and fo to have the Spirit to fend ; for the Spirit of Grace could never be given, nor en-creafed, nor continued in any, had not blood firft purchafed this ; our fins are faid to be healed by blood, and we cleanfed from them by it, *i.e.* by the Spirit purchafed by it, *Heb.*9.14. *Blood fprinkled purifies your confcience with blood*, *i.e.* the vertue of blood applied by the Spirit : If any of the Saints fhed blood for the Church to redeem it, then they have power to convey the Spi-rit of Grace to the Church ; and it is as hard to convey one dram of Grace as to dye.

SECT. VII.

Use 1.

HEnce we may fee the glory and excellency of the Lord Jefus above all men ; nay, above all the beft men and beft Churches living ; ask *David* whom he loves and honors moft, he will tell you, *Pfal.* 15.4. *He defpifeth a vile perfon, and honors them that fear the Lord* ; and that Chriftian that is moft excellent had all his heart ; ask any Chriftian, to what men his heart is moft knit, and whom he doth moft of all honor, if he fees one man in forty moft holy moft humble, moft like to God, moft acquainted with God, and the mind of God ; a *Paul* for wifdom, a *David* for brokennefs of fpirit, an *Abraham* for Faith, a *Steven* for courage and zeal, &c. their very feet are beautiful, their very names are an alablafter-box broken up. And why doth he thus ? Becaufe he fees they are holy, and like to God ; Oh but confider they cannot make thee holy, it is not in their liberty ; though they fhould like thee, they cannot teach thee one truth favingly; thon haft a rugged heart, they cannot polifh thee ; and wilde, they cannot tame it ; they cannot convey one dram, or tafte, or favor of the life of Grace to thee : Oh if thefe be lovely who only have oyl in their veffels, though they can give none for thee : What is the Lord Jefus then ? who is not only holy, fairer than the children of men, having all without meafure ; but can alfo make thee holy, which none of the Saints can ; who not only is good and holy, but doth good, and makes holy. Thou lookeft fometimes upon Saints, and feeft their grace and life, and mourneft for want of it, keepeft company with them, and withal thou hadft their oyl, but they cannot help thee to it : Oh look up to the Lord : If thou loveft and prizeft them, oh prize and love the Lord much more who hath it in his hands to give it unto thee : who like a Spring fends not forth its ftreams to refrefh it felf, but the weary, but the faint, *Ifa.*50.4. who like the Sun sends not his beams out to enlighten it self, but *that those which fit in darkness might fee*, and blind might know, Joh.9.49. Joh.17. *for their fakes I fanctifie my felf*, he hath an humble, meek fpirit to give to thee that art proud and flurdy ; he can make a Lion a Lamb, who hath a wife and heavenly Spirit to teach thee that art fimple, and thee that art earthly, if his good pleafure will.

SECT. VII.

DO not fay I have found good from them, as well as feen Grace in them, that I bleffed God that ever I faw or fpake with them, or ever faw their examples, &c. I anfwer, Know it that they were but powerlefs inftruments in the hand of a merciful, yet powerful Chrift, otherwife thou hadft never received good from any Chriftian, any Minifter, any Sermon ; the Lord Jefus could as well have ufed them as means to have condemned thee, as he did *Noahs* Miniftry, and *Noahs* example, by which he condemned the world, as well as to have called thee, or done the leaft good to thee ; therefore this ftill puts a beauty upon Chrift above all others in the world ; all the Saints and Minifters in the world could not have changed one hair from being black to white, nor by all their cares for thee added one cubit to thy ftature ; Oh it was the Lord Jefus : if they have any pity, the Lord put it in them ; if they ever fpake one word, or made one prayer, the Lord put it in them ; if bleffed, it is by him.

Now doft thou honor and love them, becaufe they have done thy foul good, elfe thou hadft been in hell ? Oh admire the Lord much more, for they were but fet on work by him ; and now they have done thee good, there is a ftop, they can go no further you think ; I did receive good by a little, while being with fuch Chriftians, but now when thou comeft hither again, thou think-eft (it may be) thou fhalt receive much more ; no, their hands and feet may be bound, thofe Conduit-cocks cannot turn themfelves. Oh but Jefus Chrift he can go on, nay, he will go until he hath made thee like unto his own felf ; and hence 1 Joh.3.2. *then we fhall be like him, now we be fons* ; children though born of poor men, yet love their poor father that begat them : Who gave you your being ? who begat you to God, and fo made you fons of God ? Oh me-thinks the Lord that d'd this fhould be precious and lovely ! that you fhould call the world to wonder at it, that the Lord hath made an incarnate Devil a bleffed Angel : But thou haft a vile heart ftill ; Oh but you fhall be like him ; he will make you like himfelf at the laft day, who is brighter than Angels, and whofe face is fairer than the children of men ; only he will do it by little and little here, rather by caufing thee to feel thy vilenefs, than removing it wholly.

Therefore, as the Apoftle *Gal.4,9.* when they were turned from the Gofpel to Mofaical obfervances, he calls them *weak and beggarly rudiments*, which had no power of themfelves to convey Grace, nor at beft in that abundance which the Gofpel did ; fo fay I, do you now know the Lord, who did not once know him ; and do you now admire and love Chriftians and others, if they do good efpecially to you ; and do you refufe to honor the Lord, but look only upon beggarly, weak means and Chriftians ? God forbid ; it is the Lord only that can enrich you, &c.

2 *Cor.3. If the miniftration of condemnation was glorious, oh what is the miniftration of the Spirit* ; if thofe which have the Spirit be glorious, what is the Lord that not only hath it, but can alfo give it, *and make you like unto him in glory, and that by the very beholding of him !* verf.ult. If a man had fuch a glafs which

not

not only gave him the sight of some dear friend always, but as oft as he looked in it, makes him like unto him, how would he prize this glass, but especially the image of his friend in it! so Christ is not only glorious, but he thereby makes himself glorious.

SECT. VIII.

Object. DO not say the Lord can do this, but he will not; Saints would if they could.

Answ. 1. You do not know but that he will do it; when Christ was here on earth, and men were sick, though their friends willed their good; yet I doubt not but Christ was most glorious, because though they knew not that he would, yet they knew that he might heal and pity, and if it were for his honor he would.

2. Pray to him for it, and do it; *he will pour water on the thirsty, and give the Spirit and water of life to them that ask;* Do not think you seek in vain, especially if your cryes arise from a sick heart, that sin is thy disease not torment onely; it is not thy delight, you need a Physitian, he will not heal you, if it is not your temper, your food, &c. If a man hath a mind to a thing, and another denies him, he will not see less beauty then, than he did before; if you have a mind, Christ hath a mind also.

Obj. But I do not feel the Lord giving me the Spirit.

Answ. Yet if you prize it, and reach after it, the Lord hath done this for you.

SECT. IX.

TO all the Servants of the Lord, if ever you did any good to any, Oh boast not of your selves, but carry the glory of it to the Lord Jesus, as he said the Lord doth good by me, but I know no reason why: So add also, but I wonder at the manner how a poor, weak, dead nothing, whose unclean heart and lips might have made others worse, not better, as infection sticking to the best garments, *Act.*3.12,13.*Why stand ye looking on us? be it known to you, byt he name of Jesus it is that which is done;* when Christ was known to heal all diseases, all the Country round about by this fame of him came to him, and so he healed them; this will bring in customers to Christ. Some Christians are very forward to speak to others, to let in some new notion, or to convert, that they may make an *Absoloms* pillar afterward, and that they might report I did this; some take content in speaking of conversion of others, that I did this. *Let your works praise you,* but let your tongue praise Christ; it was the Lord that did this. If bread could speak it would say, it is not I that feed; and fire, not I that warm: You can speak, tell others so; you would fain be accounted some body, and therefore will devise new Gospels, and mint new notions; that not only Christ may be pleased, but men may say, this I received of such a one, that their names might be spoken of. The Theif takes the sheep for himself, a good Shepheard carries it home to his owner.

SECT.

SECT. X.

Use 3.

OH then do not rest in this, that you have now got to partake of the fellowship of Gods people; I confess next to fellowship with God, their fellowship is best and most sweet, 1 *Joh.*1.3,4. and nothing more powerful to preserve and keep Gods people from Apostacy than this, *Col.*2.5. order and stedfastness in faith are coupled; they that be planted in the Courts of the Lord shall flourish here, nothing encreasing Grace more, *Col.*2.19. when many eyes to see by, many hands to help work by: When a man sinned, if one or two men only took up stones to stone the sinner, it may be they might miss, or the man live; but when there be many it is strange if it doth not kill; so out of fellowship of the people of God, one may admonish then another, and it may be he can shift, but here there be many, &c. 2 *Cor.*2.7. When a mans life is going away in a swoon, if one or two be there present only, he may never recover; but when one rubs, another chafes, another holds him, another runs and setches hot water for him, it is a hundred to one but he escapes. But yet as the best means, if neglected or trusted to, will make men worse, as *Capernaum* was worse for Christ's preaching, which they boasted of; so the best means if not trusted to, will make men better; as it is with some Extracts, and Spirits, they will make quick work one way or other.

1. If ever you see or receive any good, look to the Lord in them, 1 *Sam.* 10.11,12. who is their father.

2. If ever you look to receive any, look to the Lord that by them he may convey help and succor in his time.

SECT. XI.

Quest. HOw *shall I get that good?*
   *Ans.*1. Feel your need of their fellowship, and their help, you will then be getting good by every example, every prayer, 1 *Cor.*12. *the eye cannot say to the hand I have no need of thee:* Oh be not full, for God hath not made you so full, but if you be an eye, you need the foot, &c. *David* knew more than the Levites did, yet how did he long to see God, and the goings of God in the Sanctuary!

   Paul did need the mutual comfort of Christians; it was a strange thing in *Paul* when he was to carry money to others, yet he beseecheth them, Oh *pray for me,* Rom.15.30,31. Do not say only, I feel a need of Sacraments or Ministry, but I need the prayers, the counsel, the examples, the exhortation of the meanest Christian.

   Secondly, Be sure you joyn your selves to living Christians, that is, not only such as have Grace, but such as are lively in the use and exercise of it; for those God sanctifies especially to communicate Grace to you; if a living hand be knit to a dead arm, sure little good will it receive from it, Rom.1.12. a lively believing Christian will comfort *Paul*, and an humble Christian will humble.

1 Joh. 1.3.

   This is the very reason why Christians do not get good, because their hearts are dead, and their fellowship with God little; and hence others despise them, and withdraw from them.

   Thirdly, Love them dearly; a man will never get good from any Christian that he despiseth, or slighteth, as it is with a man, if his hand would have
                                                                                    life

life from the head, set it in his place, and let not it be tied outwardly, but united as a member, and then it receives it ; and hence it edifies it self in love ; so by love are men edified.

CHAP. XV.

Of the plentiful dispensing of Grace in the Gospel Ministry.

SECT. I.

Now follows secondly, their Counsel and Advice, [*Go to them that sell and buy,* &c.

Hem that sell] Some there be that make this an Irony, or a plain mock of the foolish Virgins for their folly ; as if they should say, You have lived like Hypocrites hitherto before the Lord among us, and deceived us and your own souls ; now you would have our Grace to help you ; no, get you gone to Mass-Priests, and Pardon-sellers, and Merit-mongers, and buy for your selves, they have merit enough, &c. But this meaning as it cannot be evinced necessarily from the words ; so such an answer cannot stand with that sad and gracious compassionate spirit which is in every holy Virgin ; for suppose God should break open the conscience of any in these days, and they opening their hearts to others, they should receive this answer [*Nay seeing you have neglected your season so long, get you gone to Mass-Priests, let them help you* ;] would any of common honesty in like manner mock ? much less a gracious heart ; no, but if any have a true sence of their misery for sleeping out their season of Grace, their bowels will melt over them.

Those that sell] These are the Ministers of the Lord Jesus.

For 1. 'Tis manifest it is not a mock.

And 2. Those that sell are not ordinary Christians ; though they may and do convey the Spirit, yet not in this case so powerfully ; and hence they do send them from themselves.

3. They do send them to those means which do most abundantly convey the Spirit ; now the Word and the Spirit are united, as shall be proved ; the cheif dispensers of which word, are the Ministers of the Gospel.

4. Because Ministers are called such as sell, *Prov.* 23.22. *Buy the truth and sell it not* ; now where is the truth cheifly sold, but by the prime publishers of it ? *Mal.*2.6,7. Not that the Holy Ghost is to be sold for money; but to buy it there, as it is to be sold without money, *If.*55.1,2,3. *Come and buy wine and milk*, that is in the ministry of the Gospel, which calls all that thirst to come, *Rev.*3.18. not that they should fix their eyes upon them, as upon the cheif means to convey

vey it, for the Lord Jesus sells, and we are to buy of him; only these are servants under him, and appointed as an Ordinance of his for this end; the Apostle conveys his ministry, *2 Cor. 2. ult.* sincerely and gloriously.

Buy for your selves] that is, seek for it there, though you lay out never so much of your money, your time, and thoughts, and affections for it, and receive it there when it is offered upon any terms, though you part with all you have, that so you may make it your own, and so have of your own, and so may with comfort meet the Lord; and this suits with the custom of the Saints, to send them there where they got theirs.

SECT. II.

Observation 3.

THat the *Spirit of Grace is principally and most abundantly dispensed in the ministry of the Gospel by the Ministers thereof*; That is, they are those that sell; this is their business, and trade, and work, like the Olive-tree to the Candlestick, *Zach. 4. 5, 6.* which take rooting in the Courts of God to this end, to drop in their golden oyl; but still observe it is as servants under the Lord Jesus, who gives what and when he will by them.

You know the famous expressions of the Apostle, *How can they hear unless they have a preacher? Rom. 10. 14.*

2 Cor. 3. 7. The Gospel is called *The ministration of the Spirit in the mouthes of the Apostles and their Successors*; *by which it is made more glorious than the Law delivered in tables of stone, though less outward glory, for we have it but in earthen vessels.*

Gal. 3. 2. By whom received you the Spirit? by hearing of the Law? no, but by the hearing of Faith; thereby is the Spirit revealed and dispensed.

SECT. III.

Reason 1.

BEcause they are set apart principally by the Lord for this end; for Gods separation of any thing for an end, though the thing be unlike to bring that end about, yet by this it hath a strange power accompanying it; as the Brazen serpent, how comes it to heal? It was set a part for that end, and sanctified of God; and hence God setting apart an Ordinance, is present with his Ordinance; as *Aaron* and his Sons were sanctified for the service of the Tabernacle: and this is done two ways.

First, By the Church, according to the will of God, they are set apart from all other employments, unless those which other relations bind them too, that so they may dedicate their time, their strength, their private studies, their selves, their prayers, and tears, and all for them; and this ought so to be unless necessity compels, *Act. 6. 4.* The Disciples would give themselves to the word and prayer, and would not be cumbred about the Deacons office; and so their studies; *Paul* exhorts *Timothy* to give himself to reading, to think on these things, *1 Tim. 4. 13, 15.*

Secondly, By the Lord himself, *Gal. 2. 15, 16.* What is true of Gods separating *Paul* to an extraordinary, is true in a measure of all his servants set apart for ordinary work, *Mal. 2. 7.* For the Church sometimes may not set a man apart, yet the Lord may and doth; and hence (by these sometimes he sends to call a Church before there is a Church to call) and how is such a one set

apart?

apart ? not as an ordinary Christian, but as an extraordinary Ambassador, as it were in the room of the Lord Jesus himself ; For Christ being Mediator of his Church, two things are required to make peace. 1. To speak to God for us. 2. To speak from God to us ; the first he doth by his intercession. But we hear not from him ? Yes, for he sets these in his room, and by them he speaks as Mediator to our ears and hearts, 2 *Cor.*5.20. so that if Christ was here present to speak, we would look for the Spirit by him and his Ministry ; Now all Messengers of the Lord Jesus are in the room of the Lord Jesus, &c. Nay, if Christ was here, the Spirit would not come but by this means ; and hence Christ converts not so many as the Apostles by their Ministry within *Judea.*

Because the Lord hath furnished them with special abilities to dispense the Grace of Christ for the Churches sake ; 2 *Cor.*3.6. *Christ ascended on high to give gifts for edifying the body* ; if a man should have an Apprentice set apart to sell, but his shop is not furnished, how could he then sell, and how should men in wisdom expect to buy ? I will not speak of what is required to make men able ; Christ not only as a free agent sets them apart, but as a wise agent furnisheth them with abilities for that end. There must be that knowledge which may make the man of God wise to salvation from the Scriptures, which cannot be without knowledge of Tongues and Arts in some competency and study about both.

Reason 2.

1. They cannot think a thought ; Christ furnisheth them with thoughts ; the Minister knows not what to say, yet his thoughts are from him.

2. They cannot speak ; hence *Ephes.*6.19. the Lord opens their mouth ; *Ezekiel* must be dumb for a time.

3. Have they therefore any knowledge of the mysteries of Christ ? it is to teach the Church, 2 *Cor.*4.5,6. all their gifts and spiritual abilities, though never so great, and peculiarly sanctified, but it is for them, 2 *Cor.*2.*ult.* have they any temptations, tribulations, and gain by them, *viz.* spiritual consolations? it is for them that are sad, that want it, 2 *Cor.*1.4,5. (and though it is true, there is in other Christians Christian abilities to help and comfort others, yet not ministerial in every Christian (the whole body is not an eye) nor which hath a special presence of the Spirit of God in it and with it) which they should never have received but for the necessities of some in the Church ; there is good to be had by watering-pots, when grass and herbs are dying ; but yet sometimes the rain falls, and that hath a peculiar vertue in it, as being fitted for that end ; and hence Ministers are compared to clouds ; and hence men will pray especially when many clouds are, the Lord grant these bottles may drop ; so hither you are to look ; dish-milk and flit-milk may convey some nourishment, but brest-milk hath spirit going with it ; good books may be blest, but there is not that spirit in them as in lively dispensations of the Gospel by Ministers themselves.

Because the Lord hath given them hearts enlarged to dispense the Gospel, that so the Spirit may be conveyed ; *we preach not our selves, but the Lord Jesus, and our selves your servants, &c.* 2 *Cor.*4.5. 1 *Thess.*2.8. If one be appointed and furnished but hath no mind to sell, they have other trades to follow, little help is to be expected there ; take a Minister of large abilities, if once he comes to have some other penny in his eye, besides the souls of people, seldom shall it be seen that the Lord is present there ; Satan doth not cast out Satan, neither is his Kingdom divided ; when *Peter* fisheth for himself, all night he catcheth nothing, but when the Lord comes, and for his sake he casts out the net, then the net is full ; and for to be a means to convey the spirit to any, it is their life ; as in others, when gain comes in, they could not live without it ; *Now we live, saith Paul, if you stand,* 1 *Thess.*3.8. This is their glory, *You are our*

Reason 3.

N n n

our joy and glory, 1 *Theff.* 2.20. this is their gain though it be by loss of all; life is not dear to finish their Ministry, *I suffer all things for the elects sake,* they are willing to spend and to be spent, 2 *Cor.*12.15. *Paul* wisheth himself *anathema, amor divinus est exstaticus,* it carries out of self, *Rom.*9.1,2,3. though it is true the Ministry was not blest to all, yet the election obtained it, *Rom.*11.7. hence the ministry is from men not Angels, that there might be the more pity, and so the more help, *Heb.*4.2.

SECT. IV.

Reason 1.

2. **B**Ut *why by the Ministry of the Gospel?*
Because the *Law cannot give life, Gal.*3.21. Now the Lord cannot make him that hath sinned not to have sinned, that would be a contradiction; *and he that hath sinned must dye,* and hence there is no possibility for the Spirit to give life here; hence the Spirit takes another instrument, the Gospel can persuade to believe, and bring to Christ, where life is seated.

Reason 2.

Because there is more of Christs blood here, and hence more Spirit; for they are all one to be cleansed with Blood and Spirit; for the Lord Jesus did not by his blood purchase the unsealing of the Law; but the Gospel is a secret, and not known but by this means; it is the New Testament which ariseth from the death of the Testator, to have the news of the Gospel printed, it is by means of Christ's blood; but to have men sent to open it, there is more of his blood therein; and hence more Spirit.

Reason 3.

Because there is more of Christ's love in the Gospel; and where most of his love goes, there his Spirit goes most; it is love to make us know the Law, though it be a hand-writing against us; but now (when we see death) to bring the Gospel and therein to entreat and wait, there is great love; and hence it is called *the Ministry of Reconciliation.* Oh it is infinite pity to offer to take a dead carrion up under his wings; here he longs for the salvation of a sinner most: if we were fallen Angels, he would never send the Ministry of the Gospel to us; but so it is now, that he hath taken the seed of *Abraham.*

SECT. V.

Use.

OF Instruction. 1. Hence we may see the glory of the Gospel, in that it is the Ministry of the Spirit of God; this the Apostle professeth *it exceeds in glory;* glorious light it scatters, *that which hath been hid from the wise,* nay, *from Prophets, and Abrahams who desired to see this day, and saw it but afar off;* hence it is called marvellous light, which brings the soul to the light of that blessed face of Jesus, and his glorious love, which never shal be sounded to the bottom of it, which damps the glory of all other things; and although many great and wise despise it, yet if they did know they would not despise the Lord of glory, nor crucifie him; but their eyes shall never see those glorious consolations and comforts promised to the people of God; *I will send the Comforter,* saith Christ, *which never can be taken away* from Beleivers, which in midst of all miserie comforts; it is a great mercy when a man sees his sin, else he would never seek for remedy; but the Law cannot do any thing but arrest, and imprison; it cannot get sin removed; yet the Gospel can set at liberty, *which preaches deliverance to prisoners;* Joh.8.32. *You shall know the truth, and*

that

that shall make you free. I can through Christ, &c. Phil.4.13. It is a marvellous mercy to tremble before God, and see, and know, and be affected with Gods wrath; but yet if this be all, the heart will sink and flye from God; now the Gospel reveals Christ, and so *Joh.10.16. his sheep hear and follow him;* and the Gospel comes to hell with the Spirit, to a poor sinner when he is blind, captive, broken, mourning, never so miserable; now the Gospel penetrates thus low, and brings the Spirit with it; it makes the soul not only to see Christ, but gives it him, and now it is safe. Oh *(beloved!)* if the Spirit be glorious, then is the Gospel glorious; if the Ministry of men could bring in, and draw with them the Princes of this world, and all their wealth to serve you, Angels and their Ministry, nay, bring Christ himself bodily to you, how glorious were this? but what is this to bring the Spirit into a Sty, into thy Soul! Oh therefore take heed of a light esteem of the Gospel, as those *Matth.22.3.* which were shut out: Men must speak something; take heed you that have once esteemed it, of accounting it a common thing (it is next to the unpardonable sin) of accounting the Gospel, Ministers, Truths, Justification by Faith, &c. common things; but see them glorious; the greatest glory that ever was in the world, did once lye hid under the meanest outside, *viz.* Jesus Christ, and yet the Apostles beheld his glory; so the Gospel is most glorious now, as being his glass, and this notwithstanding is most mean in the account of many; *Paul* is in the eyes of the *Corinthian* Doctors a mean man, his presence was contemptible, his words mean also; men despised them.

Secondly, hence see what cause they have to sit, and go home to their houses lamenting, that never found the Spirit conveyed by the ministry of the Gospel in life and power. *Lam.1.16. Oh the comforter that should refresh my soul is far from me;* if there be any hope of help, it is by the Spirit; and if the Spirit, it is by the Ministry where the Gospel is published and the Spirit conveyed: Oh thinks many a one in himself, I find no such good! thus long have I heard, and thus oft do I hear, but I come, and go away as I came, my heart never shaken, my soul never broken, my spirit never humbled, nor comforted, &c. and therefore what care I for Ministers or Gospel? it is true, *it is hid, 2 Cor.4.3.* but then it is *from them that be lost* only, whom Satan hath blinded; it may be the last medicine is now using; as it is with many that have the last remedy applied when they be sick to death; truly so it is here.

Heb.6.8. The tree or ground that brings forth bryars, is nigh to cursing; the condition is sad, as it is there exprest, *it shall never see good when good comes, Jer.17.6.* Oh it was a sad complaint of *Saul, Oh the Lord answers me not!* and of the people of God, *We see no vision;* but you have none, and lament it not; if men in the old Law did not meet with the Lord in their Tent doors, it was no wonder, it was not usual so to do; but when at the Tabernacle, if they met not there with him, it was sad then; so here; if you meet not the Lord there where he dwells, it is strange; not but that Saints may find the Lord absent; but I speak to them that find it not, and mourn not for it; others shall rejoyce when they mourn for the absence of the Lord.

SECT. VI.

Use 2.

OF Confutation of those that think there is not that necessity of the Ministry to convey the Spirit;

But First, think good Books may do the deed, and hence can profit as much at home as thereby; but these Virgins are not directed to books, but

persons,

persons, (though there is a good use of Books also) Books are but a carkass of the living Word.

Secondly, They that would have it by immediate revelation, by elevations of the Soul to God, a Familistical principle collected from the Apocrypha speculations of devout Monks, received in *Germany* when the Gospel was preached to overthrow it, and entertained by the deceitful experiences of some (as in *London*, &c.) she that was converted by dreams, &c. indeed we are to look for the Spirit; but to look for it without the Word is vile; if the Apostles were living, these would overthrow their doctrine.

Object. What can man do? (say many) you must look for the living voice of Christ; the Word is but a dead letter, and will only make you a Jew in letter.

Answ. If indeed we had only souls, and no bodies, then we might lay aside our Bibles; but seeing it is not so, look to the Word thus dispensed; hence the Lord saith, *Hear and your souls shall live*; these say, Hear not, &c.

SECT. VII.

OF Terror to all them that oppose the Ministry of the Lord Jesus, and resist it; the Holy Ghost being in it, you resist the Holy Ghost himself, and that not only where he is dropt, but most abundantly poured out, *Acts* 7. 51, 52. How did they resist the Holy Ghost? they did but resist men; No, it was the Holy Ghost there, for so he spake those words, and the Spirit had some operation upon their hearts by those words, *Zach.* 7. 12. *Neh.* 9. 30.

Sometimes the Spirit puts forth its prerogative power; then it is not overcome; sometimes words without power, and then men resist and overcome it, (for that is the meaning, because all men resist, more or less) and this is enmity against the Spirit, *Act.* 5. 39. *Fighters against God*, which is a most sad and heavy evil, for to be left to that evil to overcome the Comforter himself; as he said, *Is it not enough to grieve man, but you must grieve my God also?* Isa. 7. 13.

SECT. VIII.

Quest. BUt who doth resist thus?

Answ. 1. Some do it by silencing and persecuting of the Ministry of the Spirit, which is most grievous: When *Amos* preached against *Bethel*, up steps *Amaziah* the Priest of *Bethel*, *Amos* 7. 10. and first makes complaint of him to the King; First, that he was factious, and conspired against the King: And secondly, That the Land was not able to bear his words; that he troubled the Country and Kingdom with his Doctrine, *viz.* That we shall all dye if we receive not his Doctrine; and hence he commands him to depart and flee from thence, and prophesie no more there; but you see what he answers, *I was a Herdsman, and the Lord called me*; think not that you oppose a private spirit, but the Lord's that called me: And hence see because he did but say so, what his sentence is, upon his Wife, Children, himself and upon all *Israel*: Are there not many *Amaziah's* in these days? do they not take the same course? is not the same spirit working against the Spirit of God now? what will their end be? Let a man be never so peaceable in his place, blessed

in

in his work, if he doth but reach *Bethel*, nay, if only the judgements of them, the Altars there, and Idols there; *Amos* may prophesie in another Land, but no more there; but what will be the end of this? see verf.17. it is a sad speech 1 *Thess.* 2.16. *Forbiding us to preach to the Gentiles that they may be saved; for the wrath of God is come upon them to the utmost:* You know the Jews raised up persecution against them where ever they came, but *wrath is upon them for it even to the utmost*; why, look as it is in hell, to resist the Gospel ones self is heavy; but when in hell there they wish that no others might receive it, or that it might not be preached to any other, that none might ever know the Lord: So it is here, it is greater wrath to oppose God in hell, than to be opposed of God; and the first they are come to: Oh but they garnish the Sepulchres of the Prophets, and beautifie their Temples, and if they had lived in the days of the Prophets, they would never oppose them.

Object. *But these are other kind of Hot-spurs, and Novices.*

Answ. Matth.23.30,35. *You shall have Scribes and Wise men, and you shall kill them, that upon you may come all the blood that ever was spilt*; and blood they must have who are the open persecutors of the Prophets and Saints of God first or last; certainly God is remembring the tears and troubles of his banished distressed Seers.

2. Some others by reviling and reproaching of the Ministry; for Satan in the hearts of the wicked, if he cannot hurt it with his teeth, he will seek to destroy it by his tongue; how was *Paul* censured by a company of proud *Corinthians*, that when they had nothing against him almost, yet they censure him for his manner of speaking and carriage! 2 *Cor.*10.10. *His letters are mighty, but his presence base*; how was *John*, though for a time, flock'd after! and Christ Jesus himself was thus evilly reputed; this was that which brought the total ruine of the Jews, *viz.* mocking at the messengers of God, 2 *Chron.ult.*16. When *Paul* had persuaded *Sergius Paulus*, and *Elymas* gainsaid, saith *Paul Acts* 13.10. *Oh full of subtilty, and child of the devil, enemy to all righteousness* (why to all? because all Grace comes to be wrought here by the Word) *thou shalt be blind.*

How have the Messengers and Ministers in this Country been trampled upon by some, who though they have not yet been able to reach them by their power, yet by vile reproaches so pursuing most of them, that one would stand and wonder at the blindness and boldness, not of moral men, but Church-members and Professors, and at the wrath of God upon them, that ever they should be left to be scorners of them, of whom the consciences of the vilest cannot but sometime say, *verily God is with you!* Yea, Grace it self hath been pretended to be the weapon, by which the Ministers of the Gospel of Christ have been fought against; and indeed the vilest opinions usually have been sheltered under Grace; that hath been the Kings colours, which the enemies of the Kingdom of Christ have lifted up to deceive; for in places of profession, not merit and works, old shooes, &c. but Grace and Christ, *Matth.*24.24. are most fit to deceive.

And hence if Ministers have persuaded men to believe, and receive the Gospel, what can we do (say many?) God must do all; if evidences and signs of a good estate be called for out of the Word; it is a way of works, almost flat Popery in their books: If Ministers have had the Spirit burning within them, seeing people led from the truth, and so speak against them that deceive them, 'tis passion and bitterness; if they have sought to keep the hearts of Gods people close one to another, the strong man then keeps the palace: What should I name all?

Quest. *But for what is it that they are thus scandalized?*

Ans.1. For preaching that we are justified by Faith, and that Faith is required

to

to the entertainment of Chrift as a condition of the Gofpel ; here is not bread (fay men.)

2. For preaching that Sanctification is an evidence of Juftification ; and though it be granted the Lord never juftified any without a work of vocation at leaft, and this is not againft Gods Grace to juftifie by Faith ; yet it is againft Grace, and 'tis a way of works, fay fome, to fee my felf juftified by Faith. If the Word did reveal a fecond Juftification by Faith, and a firft Juftification without Faith, then our firft evidence might be without fight of Faith, becaufe there is fome word which reveals our being Juftified without it ; But the Word reveals all our Juftification to be by Faith ; and thus for preaching the Gofpel of Chrift have the Servants of the Lord been reproached. And though they keep it in, yet how many are there whofe hearts go after thefe deteftable things !

3. Some refift the Spirit by defpifing inwardly, and fo cafting off the Word of the Lord, *Heb.* 2. 2, 3. *if we neglect or flight fo great falvation* ; and when was the Gofpel more flighted by many ? every thing we fay is dear but Gofpel, which fhould make us mourn that ever it fhould be faid fo in this Country ; you defpife the Spirit of God ; a man of greatnefs fuffers by nothing fo much as by contempt ; fo it is with the Spirit of Grace : And it is a thoufand to one but that there will be fomething to make them defpife at laft the Lord himfelf : But the Word comes thus to be defpifed and caft off

SECT. IX.

Firft, **P**Artly by the falfe reports of others, as if they were factious difturbers of peace, men under a Covenant of Works, &c. It is the Jefuites policy to raife up lyes ; and though all will not beleive them, yet fome will ftick.

Secondly, Partly by covetoufnefs ; the glory of the things of this world is greater than the glory of the Gofpel ; tell them of living by Faith and Promifes, they deride you in their hearts ; tell them of a Kingdom, and the excellency of holinefs, they flight them ; to be fo rich and honored, it is glorious indeed , *Luke* 16. 14. The Pharifees fcorned him becaufe they were covetous.

Thirdly, Sometime becaufe Minifters and Miniftry are Bills of charges to a congregation, and are too coftly inhabitants among them.

Fourthly, Partly becaufe of ignorance of the truth ; why was *Paul's* Miniftry foolifhnefs? it was a myftery ; fo many come and underftand not the truths preached ; they be too high points for them to conceive of ; let truth be never fo precious, they efteem it not, becaufe they know it not.

Fifthly, Partly becaufe they have known all that our Minifters do preach before, which is now like flowers and rofes withering, which were flourifhing heretofore ; *Capernaum* defpifeth that which *Sodom* would not, and *Tyre* and *Sidon* would have repented at ; and fay, They can do as well themfelves as this, and better.

Sixthly, Partly becaufe Minifters are fo long at it ; and that may be delivered in one hour which is ftood upon an hour and half ; and they wonder men preach fo little, and yet fo long ; which argues contempt, and that every truth is not precious. Men cry not out of men when they are telling money to them many hours ; and yet this is more precious ; *Eutychus* grows fleepy ; thank *Paul* for preaching fo long ; and falls down ; thank long Sermons for that : This is the finful language of fome.

Seventhly,

Seventhly; Because they cannot profit by them; hence when they should mourn for themselves they despise the truth of the Lord, *Mic.*2.7. *are not my words good to him that walks uprightly.*

Eighthly, Because some have weaker gifts than others: And thus I say, the Ministry of the Lord and his Spirit is despised, *Mat.*18.8. *Take heed you despise not little ones, for Angels behold them:* Oh what is it then to despise the Spirit himself? And thus I say the Spirit of God is resisted; go home therefore and mourn, and consider, 1. The time is already set; *the Spirit will not alway strive;* and time may come that it will go from you and never return to you more. 2. Fire will come out of their mouthes, *Rev.*11.5. 3. The Ministry shall be taken from you and your children, *Act.*13.46. 4. The Spirit it self shall torment you, *Isa.*63.10.

SECT. X.

Use 4.

OF Exhortation; Oh therefore if ever you would have the Spirit dispensed to you, wait here upon the Ministry of the Gospel for it; neglect not private helps, books and meditations, &c. but know if ever you have it dispensed, here it is chiefly to be had; buy at this shop.

Do you not find parched, dryed up hearts? the Spirit of God is gone from men; and this verily is the cause of it; what consolations, what peace, what glory from the Spirit of all comfort, of peace and glory might men have, but for this?

Obj. *But I may never get this Spirit!*

Ans. Yes, *Hear and your souls shall live, Isa.*55.3. (for to reprobates the Lord never gives an ear) what a comfort is this? you cannot help your selves to look to Christ, to come to Christ, hear him then when he is come to thee, *Rom.*11.7,8. he hath given them ears not to hear; and usually the first work of the Spirit in the soul is to give an ear; the Lord awakens that to listen, that never regarded any thing before; and then something enters first or last.

SECT. XI.

Quest. HOw shall I so hear as to receive the Spirit?

Answ.1. Get a deep sence of your wants particularly and distinctly before you come; if a man comes to the Market, and knows not what his Family wants, he will never come and buy of them that sell; a poor man if he comes into a rich shop, hath a mind to buy all the commodities he sees if he had money; but if it may be had without money he will take them gladly, *Matth.*11. *The poor receive the Gospel;* I am perswaded that this is the great cause why scarce any buy here; they know not their need of every truth; hence *Isa.*50.4. *He hath given me the tongue of the learned to preach a Word in season to the weary;* the Lord will do it in season; when the heart is weary of its own deceit and ignorance, and all carnal contents, and blessings, and sins, now the Lord Jesus must speak at last; let a people be more weary of outward miseries than of inward, *they will not regard Moses by reason of anguish of spirit;* this keeps off many a man; either he feels only outward miseries, his mind is broken with cares, how shall I live? with losses and crosses, Family is sick, Cattel die, Servants are untoward and unfaithful; his drink is turned to water, and the English flower is gone, his Friends respect him not, his acquaintance grow strange; these things lie more heavy than sin.

2. Pray

2. Pray before you come ; for as it is in men that trade, their Servants are ready to let out their commodities, but ask the Master first whether he will sell them or no to you ; so ask the Lord first. Ministers are but Servants under the Lord, it is not as they will, but as the Lord will difpence, *Matth.11.25. I thank thee that thou haft hid the e things from the wife and prudent,* though Christ himfelf preached : Oh therefore look up to the Lord ; Oh Lord let not thy Gofpel be a hidden thing from mine eyes. I am perfwaded you should fee strange things, and grow up more and more if thus you did : When Christ told them that the Spirit should come, he bids them wait for it, *and they continued inftant in prayer, Act.1.4. and then the Spirit of God came upon them,* though extraordinarily, yet here ordinarily ; *Pfal.51. Lord caufe me to hear the voyce of joy and gladnefs, that the bones which thou haft broken may rejoyce ;* and hence the Lord complains, *Ifa.50.3. Why, when I came, was their no interceffor ?* as if he should fay, he would have given them help elfe ; Oh therefore before you come, and when you come, pray , Lord fpeak ; pray all the week long that there may be fome Sabbath mercies for you.

3. Give the Lord the price of his Gofpel ; men that come to buy muft give the price, *Zach.11.12.* And God will not let you have any thing without price ; give away all thou haft (when thou comeft to hear) to the Lord, let him pluck or take any thing from thee, only let him not take away himfelf, and his Spirit ; prize the leaft truth above all the world, as indeed it is better, the Lord may elfe deny thefe pearls to you, *Heb. 4.2. The word did not profit becaufe not mixt with faith ;* and what is the property of that ? *vide 1 Pet.2.5,6.To him that believes the Lord is precious ;* it makes Christ precious,and every truth precious ; and when the Lord himfelf is precious, *the Spirit is fent,* Joh.14.17. *whom the world cannot receive, becaufe they know him not.* Oh he is not fweet nor precious to them.

Three things are here to be laid out and given to God at the hearing of the Word :

1. Thy Thoughts ; let a man have never fo much meat, if he feed not upon it, never will he have fpirits thereby ; therefore while hearing time lafts, be taken up with thofe things you hear ; be in them, *that your profiting may appear to all ;* you know not fo much, but that there is more yet to be known.

2. Thy Heart ; Love it ; Chrifts love was fo great as to fhed his blood, that he might purchafe this Word of his Gofpel for thee ; and wilt not thou let thy love out of thy heart to it , when it is for thee ?

3. Labor ; labor for the Spirit here, *as for the meat that endures for ever, Joh.6.27.* Chrift will give it you, fpare no pains and labor upon it, to enjoy, and be eternally advantaged by it.

CHAP.

Thus much of the Second thing, in this Second Part of the Parable; Now the Third follows, *viz. The Coming of Chrift himself.*

CHAP. XVI.

Concerning Chrifts Coming.

SECT. I.

OW this coming of Chrift is fet forth and amplified from two things.

1. From the time of his coming; While the foolifh went to buy, he came.

2. From his different entertainment of the Virgins, and carriage towards them being come.

Firft; The wife they went in with him to the Mariage.

Secondly, The foolifh were fhut out, &c.

By this coming of the Lord is (as hath been oft faid) meant the coming of Chrift to Death or Judgement; but efpecially and principally his coming to Judgement, as may appear by the whole feries of this Chapter and the next, wherein the Lord anfwers to the fecond queftion of the Difciples, *viz.* the figns and time of his coming; *i.e.* his fecond coming, which is called his coming to judge the world, &c.

That there is and fhall certainly be a Second coming of Chrift to Judgement.

This truth the Prophets have foretold; *Enoch, Jud.* 14. *Solomon, Ecclef.* 12. *ult. Rom.* 14. 11. with *Ifa.* 45. 23. The Apoftles have preached thus, as 2 *Cor.* 5. 10, and it was ever in their eye, and the main part of their Miniftry when they preffed people to believe in Chrift as a King; where is he? He fhall come, they tell the unbelieving world; Angels alfo have publifhed this, *Act.* 1. 11 and Devils believe this, who are in their chains bound over to that day; and all the Saints have looked for this, 1 *Theff.* 1. *ult.* and hence promifes of mercy at that time are made to fuch, *Heb.* 9. *ult.* And laftly, the confciences of many wicked people have confeffed this; *Paul preacheth of Judgement to come, and*

O o o

Felix

Obferva-tion 2.

Felix trembles, and *Heb.* 6. 5. divers felt *the powers of the world to come,* and by judgements on them have been made to know that he is the Lord.

SECT. II.

Quest.1. **B**ut when shall the Lord Jesus come?

Ans. In general, when all the Elect are gathered under the wings of Christ; hence *Matth.* 24.22. *For the elects sake those days, shall be shortned, i.e.* an utter ruine of all had then come but for them ; and therefore when they are once collected, the Lord will come ; and hence in particular Judgements the Lord doth thus ; only a few Elect keep a whole land from being utterly wasted, *Isa.* 6. *ult.* 1 *Cor.* 15.23,24. *first Christ is quickned, i.e.* in soul and body raised, *then those that are Christs at his coming, and then comes the end* ; and hence the tares are spared, lest in pulling up them, the wheat also be plucked up.

Now as for setting down the particular time, the Lord Jesus doth it not in this Chapter; onely gives some signs of it, by which we may give certain credit that it is not far off (as of the death of a crazy man) and there are two that are not yet accomplished.

1. The destroying of *Antichrist*, at least in the principal power of it, and throne of it.

2. The calling of the Jews, *Rom.* 11. who must have a great day of it again : which dry bones shall live ; and their restoring a kinde of resurrection and life from the dead : Some have thought two thousand years before the Law, and under the Law, and under Christ ; and then when these six days of a thousand years a piece are ended, comes the great Sabbath ; this is already proved to be false in the second two thousand years. In the Primitive times and Churches the Apostles, especially *James* and *Peter*, spake of the end of all things to be at hand, who writing to the scattered Jews had good reason to tell them of it, *viz.* the end of the Temple. Though *Baronius* to weaken the Authority of Scripture, thinks they spake only their own apprehensions ; divers Christians thought then it was nigh ; and hence *Paul* intreats them to beware of those thoughts, seeing much danger in them , 2 *Thess.* 2.1,2. And in succeeding ages, *Tertullian* expresseth the affection of the Christians to the *Roman* State, that they sought not the ruine of it, but prayed *pro morâ finis,* as fearing it was then coming upon the world for sin ; and so many Saints seeing wickedness abound, have thought that time is not far off ; but yet the times and seasons are not in our hands to know, *Act.* 1.7. and that must quiet us, that come he will.

Isa. 65. 8.

SECT. III.

Quest.2. **W**Here will he come to judge?

Answ. Into this visible world again ; for if it should be in heaven, as no unclean thing shall come there , so we should then rather come to Christ to be judged, than for him to come to Judgement : No, there is a second coming ; that as his first was into this visible world, so shall his second, *Act.* 3.21. *Whom the heavens must contain until the time of the restitution of all things* ; and then shall he break out of heaven again for this work ; Now to what particular place in the world he shall come to judge is disputed on by many, especially some of the Schoolmen: Some think that it shall be in Mount *Calvary*, where he was crucified; some in Mount *Olivet*, where he ascended; others in the Valley of *Jehosaphat*, *Joel* 3.2. which as it cannot contain all people that ever were, so the place only speaks of the terror of God against the enemies of his scattered Jews at their conversion; I would not be wise above what is written, all that I read most plainly of, is, 1 *Thess.* 4. 17,18. *That then we shall meet the Lord in the air*; now how high, or where the Lords Throne shall be set, those things are not for us to enquire after, but so the Lord will order it, as that all Nations, *all the dead, small and great shall stand before him* and see him in one place; which shall not be very low; where men have sinned, there they shall be judged; and hence as Judges have their Circuits; so men having sinned in this world, shall be judged here.

SECT. IV.

Quest. 4. *HOw will he come to judge?*

Answ. He shall come in power and great glory, *Matth.* 24.20. As first, The glory of the Father, *Matth.* 16.27. the brightness of his Diety, his infinite wisdom was hid in the dark lanthorn of his humanity, but then he shall appear, as 'tis said, *Rom.* 1.4. manifested to be the Son of God by his Resurrection, so then much more when he comes to raise the world, all the world shall see his power, wisdom, greatness then.

Secondly, All his mighty Angels with him, *Matth.* 16.27. all shall be there, so that heaven shall be left empty; *a thousand times ten thousand shall then minister unto him*; and you know how gloriously the Lord made the Angels shine at Christs Resurrection.

Thirdly, With the voyce of the Arch-Angel and the trump of God, and with a shout, 1 *Thess.* 4. 16. *He shall descend with a shout*, i. e. of joy to the Saints, as in the day of victory and triumph of God; as at giving the Law the Trumpet did blow to work dread and terror then, so now.

Fourthly, With burning and consuming of the world, 2 *Pet.* 3. 7. 2 *Thess.* 1.

Fifthly, Raising and calling all the dead before him, small and great, good and bad, in earth and sea, and that in a moment it shall not be a long work, 1 *Cor.* 15.52. and thus the Lord shall appear at this day, that as he came before with baseness, so he shall now come in glory, and nothing then shall have any glory but himself, and those that are his, because he will damp all the glory of the world; and thus sitting in the clouds in a Throne of glory, he shall judge, i.e. examine, convince, and condemn; examine all secrets, and convict men of their evils, and then condemn them and pass sentence upon the wicked, and grace to his Saints; the Saints examinations, and all their duties and actings for God opened, and that all the world that censured them may see then the infinite wisdom and love of God in his people, in making and keeping them sincere.

SECT. V.

Quest.4. WHy will he come?

*Answ.*1. If it was only for his peoples sake, for their perfect redemption, and refreshing, there were reason enough for it; hence it is called a *day of redemption*, and *a time of refreshing*; here they are captived under miseries, and sadded by them under sin, Satan, world, but then they shall be redeemed: Now that it shall be so;

First, He hath come already to redeem his people from sin, which is the greatest evil, and which redemption was performed by his blood; now if he hath redeemed from the greatest evil, *viz.* Sin; then from Corruption, then from Death, and Satan, *&c.* If he once came by blood and basenefs, then he will come in glory and greatnefs; if he came through fire to them, then he will come through fair ways to them; if by death to them, then by life to them; and hence *Joh.5.24. all judgement is committed to him, because he is the Son of Man.* And though it be long, yet surely he will, he must come, especially seeing himself hath perfectly redeemed his people, and is now himself exalted above all: A man that hath been in prison himself, with his poor brethren that are left there still, the price of their redemption being paid, and there being nothing for their deliverance wanting, but one to fetch them, if none help, he will do it alone: So here.

Secondly, in regard of the Justice of God, that that may be cleared before the eyes of all the world; men sin now, and are not punished; but flourish, and the Saints are grieved; every man sees patience, bounty, long-fufferance exercised; but the wrath of God against the least sins is not yet made known; there must therefore be a day to declare it, and the equity of it.

Thirdly, In regard of the Wisdom of God: Look in all Commonwealths well governed in the world, and we shall not finde any but they have Court days, and their Petty Sessions, and great Assizes, as in *Israel*; for to what extremity of wickness would places come to else? so here; Shall the wise Governour of the world never have a day of hearing and trying causes? hath he no care? others are but in his room under him till that time: neither is it enough to say that there is Judgement of death. *Answ.* That is only Christs judging the soul in private either to his shame or glory before Christ; but the body is to be judged as well as the soul, to shame before men, or glory before all the world.

Fourthly, In regard of Christ's soveraignty and excellency; the coming of Christ is called his Kingdom, 2 *Tim.*4.1. Why, doth not Christ rule now in the world? Yes, but it is in the midst of his enemies; his enemies rule and he rules also; but there must a time come that no enemies must rule, but Christ alone: and this is his kingdom in a most illustrious manner; for the things of Christ are said to be with us, when they do in a special manner appear; as the coming of his Spirit, and his love, so his Kingdom; now Christ must reign till all his enemies are put under foot; for it is not fit he should lose his Kingdom; hath the Lord suffered others to reign and rule, and himself to be hid, and his glory lost, and that so long? and will he never return to his Kingdom to be glorious, there to reap all his glory that he hath lost by all his enemies in the world? Was there ever King that would ever endure one generation of Rebels after another, and never make himself sole Sovereign? however Man may suffer it, yet the Lord will not, he must reign. And wherefore doth Christ reign? It is to trample enemies under foot, his and his peoples enemies;

Christ

Chrift fets death his enemy, to deftroy his enemies, and keep them as in a Goal; but afterward Chrift will call them forth, and pafs an irreverfible doom upon them.

SECT. VI.

Ufe 1.

SEE therefore and believe the truth of this Point as well as hear it : At the firft coming of Chrift, *Heb.* 11.13. they did thus, faw the Promifes afar off, and embraced them; fo fee it afar off : There be divers people that profefs this truth that do not fully believe it ; for if they did, they would never live as they do : That look as men that know the Judge rides Circuit within half a year, dare not commit any open fins ; fo if you believed this, you would make confcience of fecret fins which this Judge fhall judge.

Others there be that do believe it as they do reports that every man faith, but they do not fee that really to be true indeed, which their hearts literally believe; and hence mens hearts are not a whit moved with grief, or forrow, or joy, or fear at the remembrance of this day. For as it is with us in reports of news out of *Germany*, many hear things, but are not affected with their mifery, becaufe they do not fee it acted before their eyes; God prefents not their forrows; and hence they are not moved; but when they do fee them acted, then they are moved much ; fo here. Look as it is with a man awake and in fleep ; a man awake believes the day of Judgement, and never ftirs ; but when afleep he dreams of it, and is much affected with that becaufe he fees it acted before his eyes; much more when men have not dreams but real vifions or fight of it, it will affect : And hence fet painted fire before a Malefactor, it affects not, but fhew him really it wherein he muft be burnt, now it amazeth him ; and hence 2 *Pet.*2.11,12,14. *looking for* ; and hence *Peter* faith, *what manner of perfons ought we to be ?* and wherefoever there is Faith, thus it will be; *Heb.*11.1. *it makes things abfent prefent, and things unfeen evident.*

Oh that God would fhew you this truth, you young men, *Ecclef.*11.9. you would not fpend time vainly, but know God : You aged men whofe hearts are rooted in this world, Oh know that God will come and burn up your delights; will you never fee this day and fear it before you fee it, and mourn becaufe of it !

Ufe 2.

Oh take heed of rafh judging and condemning, and fufpecting, and cenfuring other men: In *Pauls* time *Rom.*14.10. one Brother in a Church there judged another about indifferent things in a Chrift-like manner, as if he had no Grace, &c. *You fhall ftand before Chrifts Judgement Seat,* faith *Paul*; and hence *Paul*, 1 *Cor.* 4.3, 4, 5. accounts little of mans Judgement, and bids them judge nothing, &c. What if Chrift find that to be a lye which thou judgeft to be true.

Many of Gods Servants lie under hard thoughts and fpeeches in private, not only from Enemies abroad, but from Inhabitants at home; men out of the Church cenfuring and judging of Members; men in the Church, one of another, efpecially if they take to a fide; The Lord will difcover hard fpeeches, and an edition of all your hard thoughts put out in print at the laft day : This breaks love, this breaks Church-fellowfhip, and is the caufe of breaches in this Country.

Oh

Use 3.   Oh take heed of an hypocritical heart; if the Lord should come to judge according to the seeing of the eyes of the outward man, then well were it with many; but when the secrets of the hearts shall be judged it will be terrible; if there should never be a calling over of things again, happy were it for many, but 'tis otherwise, 2 *Cor.*5.10. *Paul* sought only to please the Lord, *for we must all appear,&c.* Civil men if they can carry it so as men may not say hurt of them, they think 'tis well; Hypocrites if they can maintain a name of Religion, so as they may maintain their interest in good mens hearts, it is well; if they get some enlargement in duties, that they are commended of them, well; if they can get so much mercy as to get the Lord to accept of Christs righteousness for them, it is well; but saith *Paul, We labor to be accepted of him.* I am perswaded godly men do not think of this; we think the wicked shall have all their secrets laid open, but the Saints come not into condemnation; 'tis true not of wrath, but of trial, so as that their righteousness shall be laid open to all, to their glory at the great day, 1 *Pet.*1.6,7. And therefore get that life which Christ himself may commend; that as Christ said, *I have not found such faith in Israel*: So here, when thou hast spoken a good word, repeated a Sermon, spent a Sabbath, ask thy heart, is this worth shewing to all the world? that though it be vile, yet Christ himself will commend this? Oh you will finde only acting for him will commend the act, *Mat.*25.40. there is that needlework, and golden Arras of Holiness which is lapt up in the Saints, that Christ will open before all the world another day.

Use 4.   Oh therefore repent, *Act.* 17.31. *Paul* tells them times past were spent in ignorance without God, time to come was a time of Judgement and wrath of God against all sin; Oh then repent: Mourn for all wrongs done against Christ: You will wail then, if you take not your season now; mourn therefore for time past, and for time to come agree with him; now he sits on a throne of Mercy in Heaven if thou wouldst not be put to shame; then, Oh be ashamed for all sins now; if not judged then, then condemn and judge thy self now; the Lord looks for no more; Oh welcome him as King into thy heart as his Kingdom.

CHAP. XVII.

Of Christs coming as a Bridegroom to his own.

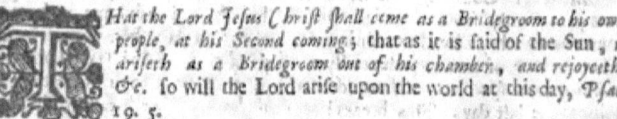

SECT. I.

Observation 2.   *That the Lord Jesus Christ shall come as a Bridegroom to his own people, at his Second coming; that as it is said of the Sun, it ariseth as a Bridegroom out of his chamber, and rejoyceth &c. so will the Lord arise upon the world at this day, Psal. 19. 5.*

This Point will be cleared and proved by opening the several degrees wherein

in he will manifest himself to be a Bridegroom then to his people; not but that Christ is a Bridegroom to his people now, but then he shall be so also in a more eminent manner, and then the perfect accomplishment of all.

First then, there shall be a personal meeting between his Spouse and himself, as it is in mariage; before the mariage is consummated, there are the friends of the Bridegroom and Spokesmen, and he sends letters and tokens, but then he comes himself; so here Christ sends his Spokesmen, 2 *Cor.* 11.2. and his word and spiritual refreshings; but when this time comes, he appears himself in person, and both meet in person; 1 *Th. ff.*4.16, 17. here we meet the Lord spiritually in his Ordinances, but then visibly in the clouds; while we live in this world, it is a time of parting, 2 *Cor.*5.8. and when we come to dye, in respect of the whole man, it is so also; but then the whole man shall meet him; these eyes shall see him, and those arms shall imbrace him; you are left as Orphans here in this world alone; it will not alway be thus, for there is a time of meeting.

Secondly, Then all deformities shall be taken away from his people, and he shall adorn his Bride in perfect beauty; for this is one part of Christs conjugal love to his Spouse and People, *Ephes.*5.25. different from other Husbands, who finde but do not make them beautiful; for if the Lord should meet his people, and they him with their deformities, they would do it unwillingly and with shame: as in this life why are Saints unwilling yet to be with the Lord? *viz.* because there be so many deformities and spots abiding on the Spouse; sometimes the soul would not have Christ, and such a heart too, though he offers himself to it; *Lord depart, I am a sinful man, Luk.* 5.8. Oh but then all deformities shall be removed; *Phil.*3. *ult. Who shall change our vile bodies*, not destroy them; *and make them like his glorious body*, which shines brighter than the Sun: *Matth.* 13.43. *Then shall the righteous shine like the Sun*; is there any beauty like that of Christs? *then shall they be like unto him*; 1 *Joh.* 3.2. it is a dishonor for a mighty Prince on the day of mariage to let his Queen go in rags; they shall be Christs then; And look as it was with *Joseph*, all his shame, baseness, imprisoments, did but make way for his glory; and hence he was delivered out of prison by the Kings command; now his apparel, and countenance, and name, and estate, and all is changed; so here, all your shame, imprisonment in the grave-chains of sins, that enter into your soul, doth but make way for this certain glory; As it was with *Jehosuah*, Satan stood at his right hand to accuse him, he only stands before the Lord, at last the Lord saith, *Take off these filthy garments*; is not this a brand? So Satan and Conscience accuse often here, but then it shall be so that all thy filthy garments shall be taken away.

Thirdly, Then there shall be an open manifestation, and glorious declaration of the dearest love of the Lord toward them; before the great day of mariage comes, there is love expressed, concluded between the parties, and it may be some few know of it, as Friends, and some of the Family; but the open declaration is at the day of mariage; so Christ loves his people now, *&c.* and will not only love them then, but openly declare his love before all the world; *Come ye blessed*; he shall declare then his own love, *Matth.* 10.22. *Luke* 12,8. He that hath made it his glory to confess Christ in a holy life, Christ will confess him before God and before Angels; and so before all the world: Men in great place will not know their poor friends, especially in open places; but the Lord Jesus will, and he will divulge the Fathers love to them also, *Act.*3.19. *You blessed of the Father, Joh.* 17. 22,23,24. *I have given them that glory, united them and made them flesh of my flesh, that the world may know thou hast loved them as thou hast loved me.* Here the Lord doth love his people dearly, but it is not so known; the Sun shines on good and

and bad; the world hates and persecutes them as Hypocrites; civil men think them like themselves; worldlings think them as little loved as any, their estates thrive not; Hypocrites bear a base esteem of them; and if they love them, 'tis because they love them; Saints themselves many times suspect them; or if not, yet they judge as well of others as them; nay it may be they are so disfigured sometimes by those sores that break out of them, that they know not themselves; but now the Lord will openly declare his love to them, and to all the world besides; These are the men which I have born on my brest, and carried on my shoulders; for whom I have built and planted Churches, and destroyed enemies, and trod the wine-press alone, and prefered above mine own life, and blood and glory; whose hairs have been numbred by me, whose walls have been continually before me. No greater misery to a holy heart than this: *Psal.*42.10. *Where is now thy God?* So when conscience saith, and men say it here: Oh what a mercy is it that then it shall be heard, I am now come to comfort thee!

Fourthly, Then they shall be brought into actual possession and fruition of all the glory promised unto them, of all their inheritance and portion: Before mariage there be promises made of such an estate; but when the day is come, then they come to actual and full possession of it, and become equal possessors of the estate; so much in this life the Lord doth promise to possess his people of; there be promises of peace, redemption, victory, and triumph over all enemies, fellowship with God, and all the Saints and Angels together, an incorruptible inheritance, and now they shall enter into possession of all these; nay, all that Christ hath, signified by that word *Kingdom*, *Matth.* 25. *Come and take the kingdom prepared for you;* 1 *Cor.* 15. 54. *Then shall be brought to pass the saying written, O death where is thy sting, &c.* Isa.25.7,8. So that reckon what Christ hath, you shall have it then. Much mercy the Lord shews to his people now, but *Psal.*31.19. *how great is that which is laid up* | then it shall be brought forth; now you shall have an end of all your desires, prayers, faith to feel that which you have believed, &c. as it was with *Joshua* 23. *ult. Not one thing whereof God hath failed.* Here the poor hardly get bread; here many prayers get nothing, &c. but there, 2 *Thess.* 1. 9, 10. God doth then what he can for them, and gives what he can give to them, then all treasures are broken open.

Fifthly, Then there shall ever be cohabitation and living with him, never to be any more parted from him, or he from them; for while any is a Suitor to one in a far Country, he comes and goes away again; but when mariage comes, then he carries her to his own house, and now live they must together; so the Lord in this life is sometime with his people, sometime absent from his people, but then they must cohabite together, and shall; 1 *Thess.* 4. *ult. And then we shall ever be with the Lord.* If the Lord should do all the former, and not this, it would be a bitter cut: When the Disciples had Christs presence for a time, it was sweet; but when parting came, that was bitter; but here is no more parting with the Lord; to be in a Kings dominion where peace rules, when other places are slaughter-houses, and Golgotha's, tis good; but to be with the King, and ever with him, and to follow him where ever he goes, and to be familiar with him, this is wonderful; Husbands depart either because not pleased at home, or because of business abroad; all such motion arguing imperfection; but now there shall be nothing in the Saints to displease; and Christ's business shall then be done, he shall have no more to do but only to give up the Kingdom to God the Father; that is the last work of Christ in this world: To see the Lord in his beauty of grace and love, will be wonderful; but for dust and worms to be with him for ever; the poor things of the world to be with him, when thousands are cast by! we say that's the beauty of a thing which no picture can express; now to see that beauty in Christ is marvellous ; but to be in the bosom of one so amiable, how great is this ?

Sixthly, Then shall the Lord rejoyce over his people, and they in him ; Mariage day is the great day of joy, they long for it before ; and when it comes, the longer it hath been deferred, the more fears of parting, the more are they affected with joy then ; so here, the soul hath desired the Lord in grace first, and then in glory, *Rev.22.* Christ hath been desiring after them in glory, *John* 17.24. now their desires being fulfilled, all his scattered lost Elect gathered, now he rejoyceth with exceeding joy ; and the longer lost, and meeting deferred, the greater joy now ; hence *Zeph.3.11. he shall rejoyce over thee with joy,&c.* Look as the Lord when they were but converted to him, poor, and miserable, and sinful, and some of them but very babes, *Luk.10.21.* yet he rejoyced in Spirit, and falls admiring of the Father ; so here much more when they shall become glorious and perfect, and altogether at this day. If the Lord, *Isa.40.1,2.* would have his Prophets speak to the heart of *Jerusalem,* when it had but Seventy years captivity, much more will the Lord himself then do it at that day ; and look as it was with them, *Rev.* 19.1. to 6. Allelujah for the destruction of Antichrist, and that Christ reigneth, Oh let us rejoyce ; so shall all Saints meet him with joy, being delivered out of the hands of all their enemies ; they shall cry Allelujah with joy to see them destroyed, and the Lord reigning ; and then shall they up to heaven in a shout of joy with Allelujah, &c.

SECT. II.

Use 1.

Hence see how ill the sin of worldliness or any sinful lust suits with a gracious godly man : Shall the Lord come as a Bridegroom to you, and will you run a whoring from him in this day ? A man can bear it when others that he never set his heart upon, depart from him ; but these to do it, it is a sin against his kindness, against his person most immediately, and against his name and honor. *As a vertuous woman is a crown to her husband ;* so here. Covetousness is a vile sin in any, but especially in these ; and hence *Jer.3.4,5.Wilt thou not from this time cry my Father.* When *Baruch* sought great things, *Wilt thou seek great things when God came to destroy all?* so will you keep great things here when the Lord is destroying all, when your Husband will be all in all ? when a woman knows that a great Prince loves her, she scorns all other Suitors,&c. So should you be content, though poor, though sinful, &c. *Col.3.4.5.* as long as Christ loves thee.

*Jer.*45.5.

Hence see what a great sin it is not to receive evidence of mercy and comfort from any promise of Christ wherein he reveals his love to his Spouse ; if Christ shall come as a Bridegroom to you, by what promise soever (therefore) he shall manifest his love to you, receive it ; some would not have Christians to receive evidence of Christ's love by any conditional promise ; but remember this, that if Christ doth not speak them, if they be not the Bridegrooms voyce, or if not true, then do not receive them, or any evidence from them ; nay if he doth not by his own Spirit clear them, and apply them ; but if they be the voyce of the Bridegroom, if you be friends, or shew your selves friends, rejoyce at it, *Joh.3.29.* As for that immediate revelation of his love, expect it at his meeting when you shall see him face to face ; in the mean while if he by his letter reveals his love, Oh make much of it because it is your Bridegrooms ; if the day of Judgement be come, and Resurrection past, and

Use 2.

Christ

Chrift feen immediately, then look not for your evidence from fuch Scriptures; but if otherwife, then own his love here if he fpeaks. It is true, it would be a fweet thing if that day would come; yet as Chrift faid to *Thomas* fo fay I to you, *Bleſſed are they which have not feen and yet believed*: and therefore when ever the Lord doth this, firft or laſt; hear his voyce, and believe his word. Do not fay you fee nothing in your felves: fuppofe a woman ſhould make a match by love and confent, though hardly; ſhe did with him, but he was fo mighty as to prevail for her goodwill, and now ſhe is comforted; and another ſhould come and fay to her, How do you know this? Why thus he fought me, thus I concluded with him, and fo far: 'Tis no match; Why? You muſt fee no confent, no love no imbracings, *&c.* would not fuch a one be counted a deceiver? 2 *Tim.* 4. 8.

     Of Terror; What will become of you that refuſe the Lords kindneſs now, that regard not the Bridegrooms voyce, that refuſe to beſtow your hearts upon the Lord! he ſhall never be a Bridegroom to you at this day, when others meet him in the clouds, *&c,* Now you fee Saints abſent from the Lord, poor and mean, and queſtion the Lords love to them; but then all ſhall be feen, and all this you ſhall loſe, *Joh.* 3. 32. *No man receiveth his teſtimony, &c.* you that never mourned as widows without him, never felt need of his love, what will become of you at this day!

     Of Conſolation to all thoſe that be eſpouſed, and contracted to the Lord, who have **chofe him**, who have given themſelves to him, who look now no further but **content** themſelves in him, or have a frame of heart ſo to do, though fears keep them from poſſeſſion of him; Oh Chriſt ſhall come as thy Husband at that day. Many Chriſtians fear this day, and hence do not ſenſibly love, nor long for this day, being under the whip continually of fears, and queſtioning their eſtate; but why do you *fear*, when *the Lord ſhall come as a Bridegroom*! Iſa. 54. 4, 5. why *doſt fear*, himſelf the Judge *ſo holy*, when he is thy *Husband*! thy chains and debts, and fins, when the Judge is thy *Husband*! thy accuſers or enemies, when *the Lord is thy Husband*! You ſhould rather long for this day, and rejoyce in it, becauſe now comes your full Redemption from all finnes, all ſorrows; the coming of a *Husband* is ſweet.

     Firſt, Though the people of God have weakneſſes and wants, the Lord hath none.

     Secondly, Though they muſt part for a little while, the Lord is ever with thee.

     Thirdly, Though they cannot help out of all evil, yet the Lord Jeſus will. Oh they ſhould rejoyce, that when he comes like a Judge, and all the wicked ſhall melt like wax before his preſence, and burn up before him, Oh yet a *Husband* to thee!

SECT. III.

Object. IF I knew this!

     Anſw. Yes, you know it; but there be ſome things that are falſe Objections againſt it: as,

     Object. 1. *Becauſe the Lord is fuch a Stranger, and the Lord abſents himſelf ſo much.*

                          Anſw. Is

Answ. Is that a good Argument for a Woman? *Isa.* 54. 6, 7, 8.
It is not the time of being ever with the Lord in his time of wooing;
John 16. 20. *I will depart, and you shall mourn, the world will not, and your*
heart shall rejoyce.

Object. 2. *Because my heart goes so soon, so oft a whoring from him.*

Answ. It may be that you are sorely tempted, and thy heart may begin to be
taken, &c. but yet if you cannot yield to lie in your falls, this is not an evidence
of a breach of the match. *Psal.* 73. he was almost gone, yet the Lord recovers
him, and faith he, *the Lord is with me*; therefore as it was with Christ, it
was not possible that the bonds of death should hold him; so here shall it be
with the poor doubting believer.

Object. 3. *Because my heart cannot love him.*

Answ. Why do you then sigh under captivity and bondage of your love? you cannot love him, other things do keep you under; oh but can she say she loves not
her husband, that doth sigh in bondage to be with him? Consider how it is at Christs
absenting himself from thee (as thou thinkest) at any time; for then love is
seen, especially at the time of parting.

Object. 4. *Because he is so unkinde to me, he hears not all my*
prayers.

Answ. This is a great Objection; if Christ would give them all their portion together which he promiseth them freely in his time, then they think he
is kind, not else.

First, Though he doth not hear all prayers at once, yet he hath given thee
that which is better than all prayers; (*viz.*) himself, and a pledge of all the | 1 *Sam.* 1. 8.
rest, and this is better than ten sons.

Secondly, It would do you hurt; oh therefore rejoyce in this day, whatever
thy condition be now: Give some women their will, and you give them your
lives, and losse of all; so here, and therefore faith Christ, *I will be Lord in*
my house.

SECT. IV.

OF *Exhortation:* To those that are out of Christ, or do not know that | *Use* 5.
they be in Christ, to labour to get your souls espoused, and match't to
the Lord Jesus; it is a laudable custome grounded on Scripture, that before
marriage there is the time of espousals or contract; and such may know though
there be absence for a time, yet that when he faith he will return to marriage,
he will come as a husband, though others in the family cannot look for any
such thing; so here the great work of the Ministery is to espouse people to
Christ; now that they may be presented chaste Virgins unto the Lord Jesus,
2 *Cor.* 11. 2. you may look then that he *shall come as a Bridegroome to com-*
fort you; others cannot look for any such presence of Christ, to them that
are not espoused to him now; —— Now Christ is gone up to his Kingdom,
but let base dust, and vile man hearken, the time is coming, that he shall come in
glory to the amazement of the World; before whom all the wicked shall melt,
but the Saints shall live in glory, caught up in the clouds of heaven; Christ infinitely rejoycing in them, and they in Christ. Would you have him come thus
to you, or as a revenging Judge, and consuming fire for your contempt? if
so, then get your souls espoused to him now.

SECT. V.

Object. Alas! What can I do? the Lord must do it.

Answ. True, but he doth it by means; the Ministry of the Gospel; else what need there be any Scripture writ, or Gospel preached? use you the means, and wait on the Lord thereby, for the effecting of this.

Quest. What should I do?

Answ. Look as it is in marriage here, or espousals here; there be but two things that make up the match.

1. Earnest suit on the one side.

And 2. Consent on the other; and therefore if any thing hinder, it ever lies either on the one side, the man is unwilling, he desires it not; or on the other side, if he be desirous, she is unwilling; but both these finish the business; if therefore you would be ever espoused to the Lord Jesus, look to these two things.

First, See evidently that earnest suit the Lord makes unto thee for thy consent, for thy good will; and this will appear by his own speeches, and this is a sufficient testimony; by what speeches? by his voice in these Scriptures; for is this the Bridegrooms voice or no? if not, away with it; if it be, and that they do breath the Holy Ghost, then know it, it is as if he spake from heaven to thee now.

Object. But he doth not speak to me there by name particularly; he speaks to others, not to me.

Answ. 1. The Lord when he calls any to himself, he doth not in his ordinary Call speak to them by name, and yet they have so received the Lord in the Word, as if he had called them by name; for look, as when the Law saith All that sin shall dye, the Lord speaks to all by name; and if conscience be awake, it will apply it, This sentence is against me; so when the Lord saith, *All that will receive the Lord, shall live before the Lord*; and therefore receive him; if conscience be awake, it will apply: As in the three thousand that were converted, *What shall we do?* they were not called by name; but when they heard that they that repented should live, because the promise was to all, they gladly received the Word; so here it should be so; and therefore we see when the Spirit makes particular application to a man, he so sets on a truth, as if the Lord spake to the soul particularly; and therefore if you do not, it is because you are left of the Spirit of God, and the power of the Word; for it is your duty so to do.

2. Though your names are not set down in the words of the promise, yet your names are wrapt up in the meaning and sense of the promise; and this is as good as that; for though the Lord doth not desire every man to keep the Sabbath by name, yet he means every man, and there your names are; so when the Lord Jesus makes suit to a wretched heart to receive him, he meaneth every man, as if he had named them; that which is set down in Scripture, and written to others, God means not them alone, but all others in like case; — as *Jer.* 3. 12. *What the Lord spake to Israel to return*, he meant especially *Judah*; so *Esay* 2. *ver.* 1. *to* 5. There is a Prophesie of the *Gentiles to flow to the Mount of the Lord*; what means the Lord by that? the Lord meant hereby to stir up the Jews, and therefore he saith, *Oh come house of Israel*, &c. And hence *Rom.* 15. 4. *What is written, it is for our learning, that we might have hope*; i. e. God meaneth us therein also, so that when you see

the

the Lord calling the wretched Jews in his Word, the Lord calls thee; and when the Lord in his Ministery comes to them, he comes to you; and to have thy name in the sense of the Scripture, is most for the glory of the Spirit, and suiting best with the work of faith, and most sure, and most sweet to you; but especially I say, when the Messengers of God come to you, they make things particularly clear; which were but generally set down. O consider therefore the Lord is earnest in his suit to have thee receive him.

SECT. VI.

1. IT breaks the heart of the Lord Jesus to see thee depart away, and go a who-ring from him; when a man is so set in his desires that when he is crossed of his hopes in marriage, it makes him sick and pine away with grief, because he is very earnest for the match; so it is here, *Ezek.* 6.9. And therefore we shall see *Mark* 8.12. the Pharisees who had seen all his works, yet an adulterous generation sought after a sign, it is said Christ sighed deeply in spirit for this; nothing grieves the Lord so much as this; to despise any part of his will, or poorest member of his, grieves him; but to despise himself, this much more; as we shall not find any joy in Scripture like this, when the Lord hath overcome the unkinde heart of a rebellious sinner; and hence heaven and earth and deserts are commanded to rejoyce at this; devise to grieve him, and you cannot do it so much as by refusing him. [margin: Isa. 35. 1.]

2. The Lord is so desirous of it, that he will pass by all thy former lewdness, if now thou wilt receive him, *Jer.* 3.1 with 4. men will not do so, yet the Lord will; what, when so many vanities are loved more than the Lord, can the jealousie of Christ receive me? Yes that he can.

3. When the Lord hath cast off a poor creature for refusing him, yet then his heart yearns and his soul longs for it (many times) again, *Isa.* 54.5, 5. the Lord hath called thee as a wife of youth when refused; i.e. when God did appear to them, to refuse them; Oh wonderful! that when the soul hath refused the Lord, and the Lord it, and all creatures refuse to love it, yet these the Lord calls again; and hence the Lord comes upon his people *Isa.* 50. that complained, *God had utterly rejected them,* and all the fault is in him; so their sins had done it; but then he blames them that when he came, no man answered, *&c.*

4. All the anger of Christ, especially his greatest anger is expressed against a soul for want of this being willing to receive him; when you say How doth the Lord regard or desire me, when he fights against me?

First, Is there an evil not inflicted, but devised against thee? (as many a one fears what is not yet made known) this is *to make you returne*, *Jer.* 18. 11.

Secondly, Are there any sorrows upon thy conscience, upon thy outward man, *that God takes all comfort from thee?* Hos. 2.9. 14. 16.

Thirdly, Are there any evils inflicted upon others in this life, especially whole Churches, their Ordinances broken, Temples consumed, and laid into dung-heaps? it is to *get thy good will,* Jer. 2. 8.

Fourthly, Are there any gone down to Hell, who did once flourish here, that you have even seen the flames and tears before you of crying Ghosts: if so, then know it, *it is that thou mightest draw near the Lord,* Psalme 73. 26, 27.

5. The Lord professeth that he will give the choicest of all blessings to them that

that receive him ; and this argues strong desire, *Pfal.* 81.11,12,13. *Honey out of the rock.*

1. Thou shalt have himself taking infinite delight in thee ; because he will make thee beautiful with his own beauty, and cloath thee with it, *Pfa.* 45. 12.

2. All creatures shall be servants to thee throughout the world, *Hof.* 2.*ult.* As when one is married, all the servants in the Family are to serve her or him, so here it is in regard of the faithful : Oh that you could hear the voyce of the Lord Jesus, and his earnest suit to you herein. This you see is clear.

There now wants nothing but for you to give your consent unto him, and therefore this is that which the Lord lays to the charge of men , *viz.* their breaking off the match ; and so *Rev.* 22.17.*Whoever will, let him come and take* ; *Prov.* 1.29, *0:hey did not chuse the Lord, nor would none of the Lords counfel;* and this made the Lord cast them off ; so that now there is nothing but thy wil : Shall the Lord desire it, and wilt not thou be glad of it ? there is no beauty in thee, why he should do this to thee : there is in him beauty and excellency ; Oh shall not this love win thee ? Shall it be said another day, Wherefore is all this evil come upon such a one ? had he not means ? had he not offers ? But this shall come against thee , *You would not* , Oh you would not.

SECT. IV.

ONly take these four Cautions concerning your consent.

Take heed that your consent arise not only from fear of misery, for this is a forced consent, and is ever naught, and it appears so when the misery is past ; many do thus in fears of death, or times of calamity ; Oh then the Lord, *Hof.* 8.1,2,3. *Pfal.* 78.34,35.

Secondly, Take heed it be not a conceit of your own making in days of peace ; for that which you make from your selves, you will break also ; but that it arise from the sence of thine own insufficiency to give consent, and the Lords Almighty power and infinite grace to work it, and then no powers of any creature can untie that knot.

Many hearing of this, Will you have Christ ? Oh yes, withal my heart, and force a consent by their own labor ; this is naught ; and hence *Ezek.* 16.60,61. The Lord will receive that harlot but not by her covenant, *i.e.* which she undertook in her own name ; no, the Lord must work it, *Jer.* 3. 19. *How shall I do this for thee, &c. Hof.* 2. 19. *I will* ʃ *etroth her :* For no creature can incline the heart to another but the Lord ; there is a natural antipathy between Christ and the Soul ; and hence we see it in many a Christian, ask him, Why cannot you love the Lord, nor cleave to him ? Oh because I know not why ; I cannot , I have no heart ; the truth is, you have hearts that do loath him ; unless the Lord overcome you, you can never submit indeed unto the Lord.

Thirdly, Look that your consent be not made according to your own terms and conditions ; for look as it is with a woman, if she shall say she is content to love such a man ; but if she keeps an open Inn to entertain all strangers, and love all commers, or if there is one she is in league with ; there can be no mariage ; so therefore the conditions are so, Receive the Lord, and give your consent to love him only, *Prov.* 8. 17. *I love them that love me,* otherwise the match will never be made, *Ifa.* 50. 1. if you keep your wretched,
untruly,

unruly, stubborn w lis still, never hadst thou, or shalt thou have the Lord; Let thy sin be never so little, so close, as (it may be) sloth, it is death to pray; it may be 'tis pride; or whatever else it be, you must have your hearts first divorced from them, or thou canst not have Christ.

Fourthly, Take heed then that sence of want of dowry, beauty, portion in or from your selves, doth not hinder you from consent; for the Lord requires no such thing of you; hence *Matth.*22.4. All things are ready in Christ to receive from him, *Ephes.* 5. 25. 'Tis not for you to make ready to bring to him; only come; and the Lord doth bring his people to sence of vileness, that they may do thus, know that it is his Grace that makes the Lord close there.

SECT. VIII.

NOW will you refuse, and not let the Lord have your hearts this day?

First, is there any thing in the Lord that should keep thee from consenting? what good is there else but in him? what want of perfection there? his love is better than life; if there be any thing in the world that can be better to thee, or do greater things for thee, make thy match; but who can pay thy debts? who can fetch thee out of prison? who can put beauty on thee? who ever did thee good but the Lord? therefore there is none like him; he will cloth thee, possess thee, &c.

Secondly, is there any thing in thy self that keeps thee from consenting; hast thou no need of him, or consenting to him? you may, it is true, have other creatures to adorn you; as they *Ezek.*16.37,38. But *the Lord will gather your lovers together, and give you blood and fury in his jealousie* : I mean, when the Lord shall come at this day, to embrace, comfort, glorifie others; thou shalt not have a smile from him; Oh men now despise the Lord, and his Grace and Patience; tell them of a match with the Son of God, they regard it not, no more than a tale that is told; well, the Lord will bring you into horrors, wherein you shall prize and be glad of this, before you die, even one glimpse of his love.

Post tenebras lucem spero.
After my sickness *December* 12. 1639.

CHAP. XVIII.

Shews that Christ will not tarry when once his time is come; and the folly of such whose work is then to do; and that the blessedness of Saints consists in immediate communion with Christ.

SECT. I.

He coming of Christ, we have heard is set forth first from the time of it, *viz.* just then when the foolish went to buy: Could not the Lord so patient and long suffering, tarry a little while longer for them? especially seeing they went not about any sinful work, but were using the means to get that grace now which their vessels were empty of before? No, but the Lord deals with all men, especially that live under the means, as he did with these foolish Virgins.

Observation.   That as God is long-suffering towards men, whiles through ignorance of their spiritual wants and security of heart they have no hearts to use the means for supply. So if once his time of forbearance be slept out, he will not tarry one moment longer; even when men are most diligent in the use of means for spiritual supplies; when Christ hath a heart to help, many people have none either to see their wants, or seek for help; when men have hearts thus to do, then Christ hath none, because his time of tarrying is out; when men are worst and most secure, Christs door is open to them many times; when men are best and indeed awakened, Christs heart and door is shut against them, as it was here; for what are the best endeavors of foolish Virgins? what excellency is there in them, that the Lord of glory should stay their leisure, after long neglect of himself, and loss of precious time?

SECT. II.

Use   BE sure you sleep not out the day time of Grace; especially you.
1. That know you want oyl in your vessels, and Grace in your hearts, and mercy to your souls, and think I would not die yet for a world.
2. You that being asleep with these foolish Virgins, dream you are rich,

and

and want nothing, and would be half offended with them that should tell you to your face, or but think in their hearts that you have no grace, when indeed you are poor and empty, and naked; —— Take heed you give not that answer to ti ne that tarries for you, and unto Christ that waits upon you, as *Felix* to *Paul, when his heart trembled to hear of judgement to come; I will speak with you at a more convenient season;* The Lord hath not left Churches without examples of the terrour of Christs patience in this kind, who upon their beds of distresse have lamented before men; Oh my time is out, Call time again, call time again; and who have besought it of God with tears, as he did the blessing, and cryed out, *What Lord, wilt not give me one houre', one day more!* and so like men sinking have catch'd hold on any thing to save them, whiles others have stood upon the shoar lamenting of them, the Lord be merciful to them; this may be your case, that neither your tears nor blood can purchase a moments time.

Look to it that your vessel be not found empty at the coming of the Lord; it is a dying time in this Countrey, and the Lord hath taken away some, and those that were ready are gone into the Marriage. Consider of it that saith, that grace which you think you have now, may prove but chaffe and stubble when it comes to be tryed in the fire of the Lords coming; the best man will finde all little enough; then be sure you misse not of it now: Do not think I will pray, and seek then, and I hope to finde, though thou art secure now; think of this point, When did Christ come and shut the door, but when the Virgins went out to buy? but woe, woe to thy dead heart; some here present shall seek Christ, and not finde him, but shall dye in their sins; till arrows are in your hearts, you will not cry.

SECT. III.

THat after long profession of godlinesse, it is a piece of foolishnesse to have any thing then to do but to dye, and so to give welcome to the Lord Jesus: These Virgins when they were to dye, were then to buy; when they were to receive Christ, were then to seek for oyle in their Vessels, that so they might be ready to receive Christ; but of this hereafter. *Observ.* 2.

Oh their sad condition that have all to seek yet! *Use* 1.

Be not ever seeking, never finding; but so seeking, as that when you dye, you may say, *Come Lord, I am ready!* *Use* 2.

SECT. IV.

2ly. THis Coming of Christ is set forth from the different entertainment of the Virgins, and Christs different carriage toward them.
1. *For his entertainment to the wise Virgins*; that is set down to be an entring or admittance into marriage, fellowship, communion and joy with the Lord Jesus; which is amplified
First, From the Antecedent (not cause) of it, and that is their readinesse.
Secondly, The Consequent of this their Communion, the Door was shut.

That

That the laſt end, and full bleſſedneſſe of all the Elect eſpouſed here to Chriſt, it conſiſts in immediate communion with Jeſus Chriſt alone.

What becomes of theſe *Wiſe Virgins* ? they enter into near communion and fellowſhip with the Bridegroom Jeſus Chriſt. What becomes of the ſouls of all the Elect when they are ſeparated from the body, and from this World ? the ſpirit returns to God that gave it ; ſo the ſoul returns to Chriſt that bought it. When this World ſhall be burnt up, what will become of the ſouls and bodies of the Elect, when there ſhall be no more Sun to ſhine, nor Kingdom to rule, nor Creatures to comfort ? they ſhall aſcend from the clouds up into the marriage-chamber of the Son of God, and be for ever with the Lord, and the Lord alone; and this is their bleſſedneſſe, &c. Bleſſedneſſe, yea, the laſt and only bleſſedneſſe, even of heaven it ſelf.

John 17. 23. There are variety of creatures here, and in every one there is drop't ſome ſweet; but *the Lords end is to make his people perfect in one*, how is that ? God in Chriſt communicating all his goodneſſe to his Son, and ſo living in him, then Chriſt communicates all his own and Fathers love and goodneſſe unto them, and ſo lives in them, and now they are in him, and ſo *made perfect in one*; as thoſe that are thirſty for a time, are refreſhed with ſome drops, or waters running in their Channels, at laſt they come to the well-head, where they partake of all together.

1 *Theſ.* 5. 10. *This is the end of Chriſts death, that we might live together with him*; not *live only from him*, but *live with him*, and together *with him*; in beginnings here, hereafter fully.

SECT. V.

BEcauſe God the Father hath laid up all his glory moſt abundantly in *Chriſt*. Col. 2. 3. *Treaſures of wiſdome; it ſhines in the face of Chriſt.* 2 Cor. 4. 5, 6. *and all our glory alſo.* Luk. 2. 32. *Glory of his people Iſrael.* Pſal. 29. 19. *In his Temple he uttereth all his glory*; in the world, there it ſparkles in every creature, and the heavens declare it ; but there is but ſome, and that common to all tongues and languages; but in this *Temple*, the Lord Jeſus eſpecially, there all the Fathers glory is uttered, and himſelf doth utter it. Treaſures are ſuch things where there are

1. *Precious things.*
2. *Abundance of them.*
3. *Hidden, not open to all.*
4. *They are ſure and ſafe* there, for their owners to take and enrich themſelves withall ; ſo it is in Chriſt, there is firſt, *precious things*; all Gods preciouſneſſe, and all our precious things ; our life, our peace, our joy, our ſtrength, &c. and ſecondly, *abundance of them*; thirdly, *hid from the world*, and unknown in part to the Saints ; fourthly, but *ſure* there for their owners, and Chriſt is the treaſure of all theſe treaſures, which are infinite as God himſelf is ; now if all our glory, and the glory of God be in Chriſt; then as privation of, and ſeparation from this glory is the laſt and only miſery; ſo conjunction to, and communion with, and fruition of this glory, muſt be the laſt and great happineſſe of the Elect. I would convince any carnal heart by this Argument; Didſt ever finde any comfort from any creature ? that comfort is not from it, but from the Lord by it ; for creatures are but as cold water, all their warmth is from the fire ; now there is but a little of the ſweetneſſe of God, becauſe creatures can hold but little, it is ſo narrow a veſſel ; but in the Lord Jeſus all the goodneſſe of God is gathered together there,

there, which is scattered in several creatures here; nay, not finite, but infinite goodnesse and glory; therefore this is our blessednesse.

In regard of God the Fathers exceeding great love, and the purpose of God to manifest it to the sons of men; this is the nature of love, when one is in a blessed condition himself, he will labour to bring those it loves to that condition; now the blessednesse of God lies in fellowship with his son, *Prov.* 8. 30. Now God the Father loves them dearly, and would have all the world to know that he doth so, and hence brings them at last into the same fellowship with himself in his son; *John* 17. 22. *That the world may know thou hast loved me*; the Father out of his infinite love communicates himself to Christ, and his fellowship is with the Father; all know this is a dear love; in mean while love to his Saints is unknown; they and the wicked share all alike; and the Saints have the least portion and worst part many times; so that men cannot see by any outward thing any more love to them, than unto others; the time will come that they shall be made perfect in one, as near the Lord as can be, that the world may know this love, &c.

When *Absolom* had slain his brother, and fled from his father, it is said, 2 *Sam.* 13. 39. that *the soul of David longed, or was consumed to go forth to him*; *David* might have said, I will never look after him more; so might the Lord have said to us; or if he loved, he might never have manifested it (as *David*) but the Lord must shew his love, &c.

Because this is the end of all the prayers and endeavours, and all the workings of the Saints in this World: Suppose all glory be in Christ; let a thing be never so good, but if a man hath no desires after it, hath no mind to it, it would not be blessednesse to him; but this is the end of all the prayers, duties of the Saints, if at last *they may be with the Lord*, Phil. 3. 8, 9. Joh. 4. 14. *He shall never thirst*, their desires are taken off from other things, but only their hearts are to this. If there be any pillow the Lord lets them sleep upon in this world, they shall finde it hard at last, and arise with a Kings head and heart, and say, Oh here is not my rest; the best entertainment this world can give, hath ever somewhat mixt with it, that makes the people of God say, *Oh that I might be with the Lord!*

SECT. VI.

Quest. SHall not the happinesse of the Saints partly lie in fellowship with the Saints?

Answ. 1. True, but this is but a consequent to the former; as separation from God is the substance of misery in hell, but other things follow upon it; *viz.* communion with Reprobates and Divels; so here we have first communion with Christ, here is the substance of our blessednesse; then this is accidental, and follows upon that; *viz.* the communion with the Saints, which is exceeding sweet.

2. That good we shall have in communion with Saints, is not from themselves, but Christ in them; as 2 Thess. I. 10. *Christ shall be admired in all his Saints*; so Christ shall then in his Saints and Angels; it is the light of the Sun that shines in the Stars, and they shall do nothing but set out the praises of Christ.

Quest. But what blessednesse is there in this, seeing it is in one thing only? when a man is sick or poor, can grace refresh him, can he live by that? (*thus many carnal hearts think.*)

Answ I.

Answ. 1. The Lord shall then take away all fleshly appetites or desires; for then our bodies shall be spiritual bodies; in this life sometimes God takes away the stomack, when he takes away food. Christ forgot his wearinesse, because he had other bread to eat.

2. It is therefore blessednesse, because it is in one; there is

First, Trouble in seeking and fetching our comfort out of many things.

2. Unsatisfiednesse, because one thing can give no more than it hath; now all things in this one thing are there together; the sweet of all creatures, all Ordinances, nay, *variety of unknown mercies,* (Prov.8.21.) shall center here in Christ Jesus.

SECT. VII.

Use 1.

OF *marvellous Consolation to the Saints of God*: Now you have many wants, many sorrows, many temptations, many sins, many cares and fears of livelihood; but the time will shortly come when you shall be with the Lord alone in communion with him, and so out of the crowd and presse of troubles, and temptations, and sins, and evils in this world; that as himself is above all these, so shall you. *John* 14.1, 2, 3. Their hearts were grieved for the losse of Christ; *I will come to you, and take you to my self, that where I am, there you may be also*; sometimes outward losses and fears trouble thee; sometimes absence of Christ from thee troubles thee; hear what the Lord saith, *Let not your hearts be troubled*; for the Lord will take you to himself again, John 16.22. Christ tells them, *I will see you again,* and *your hearts shall rejoyce*; what if he had said, I will come down from heaven to you again? I tell you the Lord will do so to you, but that he is in a better place preparing it for you, and doing better things for you; but he sees you for the present, and you shall be with him at last.

The Apostle prays that they might know *what is the inheritance of the Saints*; so I desire of the Lord for you, that you may know what it is to have communion with Christ alone; oh see your blessednesse, &c.

SECT. VIII.

1. **T**his *Communion it shall be by sight, not chiefly by faith, as it is in this world:* Many go many Miles to the supposed Sepulchre of Christ, and account their time, though superstitiously, yet happily spent; oh but what will it be to see the Lord himself, not as he was here in his abasement, but in all his glory, brighter than ten thousand Suns! now we see, 1 *Cor.* 13. *as in a glasse* where we see the glory of God in the face of Christ; but then we shall know as we are known; as a childe knows not the father, but at ripe years doth; but as *Philip* said to *Nathanael,* who said, *Can any good come out of Nazareth?* so can any such mercy come from heaven? come and see him of whom all the Prophets have spoken of; so then the Father and Spirit, and Saints and Angels will say, oh come in and see him of whom all the Prophets have written; come and behold him that hath shed his dearest blood for thee, that hath taken thought and care for thee night and day; that hath been all thy life interceding for thee; *Revel.* 22.4. *There you shall see his face.*

2. *This communion it shall be spiritual and inward with the soul and conscience;* suppose the soul should be with Christ, and not have spiritual communion with him, what were it the better! as many had when Christ was here in this world, that eat and drank in his presence, and yet are now shut out: Oh no! the glory, beauty, goodness of Christ is not to be seen with bodily eyes, nor tasted, nor handled with our carkasses; and hence Angels though in heaven with Christ's person, yet look to the Gospel, to hear, see, and enjoy the spiritual excellencies of the Lord; hence *Simeon* when he had Christ in his arms, yet now desires to depart, because he should then come near him into his spiritual communion; Oh this the soul shall have, inward light, love, peace, &c. it is Christ's great love to live with the soul; but so to live with them that are his own, as to live in them; Oh this is exceeding love, for Christ to live in one that was a dunghil: It comforted the Disciples when he went away, *I will send you the comforter;* Oh but what a blessedness will this be, to be with him, and the comforter in us also?

3. *It shall be a full and perfect communion,* communicating himself out to the *utmost extent of the capacities of his people;* for here we have spiritual communion, but we see but little and know little, and receive but little, the first fruits and tastes of what we shall drink; but there fully. 2 *Thess.* 1. 9. *They shall be separate from the Lord and glory of his power,* i.e. as much as ever the Lord is able to fill or load the soul withal, a crown of glory as weighty as ever it can bear, it wraps up the heart sometimes; the soul lies down confounded before the Lord; Oh that ever the Lord should here look upon such a one so vile! much more then shall there be wonderment; he will set open all his treasury; *Oh come take thy fill of love!* there he shall poure out all his heart, &c.

4. *It shall be an exceeding familiar communion:* When Christ was here on the earth, we know how familiar he was with his poor Disciples; how one leaned on his brest, could come to him, speak to him, &c. (Oh brethren) much more shall it be then, *Joh.* 21. 17. *touch me not for I am not ascended;* as if he should say, Oh then there shall be sweet embracings, as *Joseph that wept over the neck of Benjamin;* Oh the spiritual embracings there! the Lord and Christ will say, *I love thee dearly.*

5. *It shall be an everlasting uninterrupted communion;* We have here communion with other creatures, but they as passengers will leave us; we have also communion with Christ, but it is interrupted; many clouds come between us and him; but then it shall be everlasting without any interruption. 1 *Thess.* 4. *ult. We shall ever be with the Lord;* hence comes comfort; infinite is the glory of the Lord, we cannot see it nor enjoy it in a short time, we have no leisure here, nor time enough to see it; hence we shall be to all eternity beholding and enjoying of it.

6. *A joyful and most sweet communion,* Psa. 16. ult. *filling the heart with unspeakable peace; believing ye rejoyce with joy full of glory;* much more than feeling. And Three things make it so.

SECT. IX.

First, *IT will be after many troubles, labors, and conflicts here in this world;* there's not a godly heart but hath his burden, if not of misery, yet of sin; if not from flesh and blood, yet from hell; and he fears also (it may be) that he shall never come to heaven; now hence this communion must be the more joyful, as *Jacob* that thought he should never see *Joseph;* and as *Isa.* 9. 2, 3.

Those

those that divide the spoils, and reap the harvest; then there shall be an answer to all thy doubts, &c.

Secondly, *It will be thus because this communion shall be chiefly in sucking out the sweet of all Gods love, past, present, and to come,* Eph.5.4.9. Psal.24.6. Love from a friend is sweet, but from a God sweeter; it doth us good to think of their love, their honor and respect to us, much more the Lords; Oh this *will like wine, chear the heart,* that as the damned shall suck the fierce wrath of God, Oh it shall sting them; so this *è contra,* we shall see all his bowels open.

Thirdly, *The Lord Christ himself shall rejoyce over the soul, and so all Saints with him,* Luk. 10.21. And the soul shall see this, and all Saints rejoyce in its communion. Oh consider this and comfort your hearts with this all ye people of the Lord! I only say as *Joseph* dying, *God will surely visit you when I am dead,* Gen. ult.24. So when thou art dying the Lord will surely visit thee with his presence, and you shall surely be with him : You have been praying for this, and hearing, and now and then you taste a little, but think it is too good to be true ; yet if Christ be blessed, thou shalt at last, thou shalt not miss (though thou finde but little of him here, and walk in the dark) of being with him for ever ; God hides his face from some of you, and you mourn, though the world rejoyceth ; but happy art thou, for *thy mourning shall be turned into joy.*

SECT. X.

TO mourn for our *strangeness now to Jesus Christ, and our distances from the Lord Jesus,* may not the Lord take up that speech as to *Philip, Have I been so long with thee, and hast thou not known me?* So hath Christ been so long with thee, and shalt thou be for ever with him, and yet dost not know him?

There are five things that are ever conjoyned with a neat communion with Christ.

First, *Knowledge of him* ; Alas, how little do we conceive of the Lord?

Secondly, *Perswasion of his love and faithfulness* ; Alas, we have little assurance of him, Psal. 9.

Thirdly, *Love to his fellowship* ; and the more in it the soul is, the more desirous it is of it : Oh but the weariness of being with him that we have! no oftner are we with him now than needs must ; but hereafter it shall be otherwise.

Fourthly, *Likeness to him in his vertues,* as *Moses* comes shining down ; a man imitates them whose fellowship he loves in all their imitable excellencies. Alas, how unlike to him now are we, to what shall be?

Fifthly, *A daily opening of, and bemoaning daily evils to him* ; Oh it easeth the heart ; if a man is gone from his friend, yet troubles will fetch him in again ; but we pour not out our souls thus to him ; hence he poures not out his blood into our souls to heal us ; Oh may not we take up that complaint of *Agur,* Prov.30. that *we are more foolish than any man!* speaking of Christ ; Oh therefore mourn for it ; *David, when God hid his face for a little time, was troubled.*

It was the complaint of the Prophet of evil men, *That in their eyes, he was rejected and despised, and we hid our faces from him.* Let the world do so, will you do so also? it should not trouble so much that he hides his face from you, as that you have from him.

When *David* turned aside to *Bathsheba*, the Prophet comes and tells him, *I anointed thee King, and delivered thee out of the hands of Saul, and gave thee thy Masters Wives, and more also; now wherefore hast thou despised the Lord? the sword shall not depart;* Oh (saith he) *I have sinned against the Lord;* so say I to you: if the Lord had never made known himself to thee, it had been another matter; but *the Lord hath delivered thy soul from hell, thy eyes from tears;* the Lord hath anointed thee to partake of the glory of Christ, the Lord hath given himself to thee, and saith Suck my blood, take my life, and more I would have given; and hast thou looked after *Bathsheba, other lovers,* and *despise the Lord?* Oh say *I have sinned,* and mourn for it, 2 *Sam.* 12. 9.

There are two evils in this. 1. *Forsaking thy own good,* nay *blessedness, Jonah* 2. 8. own mercies.

2. *It is despising the Lord and his fellowship for other things,* base things; that whereas you shall be for ever beholding of him hereafter, yet you should proclaim him not to be worth looking on now.

Object. But *I would have fellowship with the Lord, and he will not.*

Answ. First, Never did any desire thy fellowship so much as the Lord when he wants it.

Secondly, Nor love it, and glad of it when he had it.

Thirdly, Nor mourn and lament more when he wants it, as *Jer.* 2. 2, 5. God pleads for it.

Fourthly, he calls to the heavens, 2 *Jer.* 10, 11. *Did ever nation deal thus with Idols!* If this will not break thine heart for strangeness, I know not what will do it: It is your sin that breaks off communion, not the Lords unwillingness.

SECT. XI.

Hence see the exceeding great worth and excellency of *Jesus Christ*; and learn hence to esteem a sight of him; there is no blessedness in the fruition of all the creatures together; good there is, but not blessedness; or if there were, yet it lies in many things; no one thing, nor twenty blessings can make blessed; and it is but a broken blessedness in divers pieces; or if there were a kind of blessedness to be found in one, yet it is not a lasting blessedness, it is so but for a time, and so the loss of it at last will trouble us more than the having of it for a time.

But as he saith, *In him is light and no darkness;* blessedness, and no misery; peace, and no trouble; fulness and no want; beauty, glory, and no blemish; life, and no death; pure, dear, infinite love, and no anger; and it is in him alone, *Psal.* 148. 13. *His name alone is excellent;* all our glory and the glory of God also is met together in him, all things in one thing; whatever good there is in other things, it is borrowed from him; base, beggarly things; but the fulness and plenty of all is in the Lord, so that we shall not need to cumber our selves about unnecessary things; we need not a candle when the sun shines: and our last blessedness is here; when every thing else will make them wings to hasten from us, this will continue and last; when all our vessels we are tossed in here are sunk, and where our entertainment hath been very good, yet the shore sinks not, it is above over-whelmings; here alone we are safe.

However the world sees not this, because their blessedness lies in preserving themselves by creatures, from feeling that misery which lies upon them now, as also because they shall never share in it; yet the Saints have been exceedingly

Use 3.

ceedingly taken with this that *David accounted them blessed that might dwell in his Courts* in this world; *Solomon* was blessed that *might but wait at wisdoms gates*, and so be ready to be received when they be opened; *Abraham rejoyced to see Chrst's day afar off*; *Moses esteemd the reproach of Christ great riches*; what did he then esteem of the presence of Christ here! but what in glory!

Think of this, you that say you cannot finde in your hearts to esteem of the Lord Jesus; especially let him be precious to you, you espoused of the Lord; for others may say he is precious, but I shall never enter into this fellowship: No, no, but you shall, but he will take you to fellowship with himself: It was a great favor to *Moses*, *Exod.* 24. 1, 2. when others might come towards the Lord, yet *Moses* alone might only come near; *and he was in the Mount alone with God*; so that the Lord should let others come towards him; but that you alone above many thousands in the world may be suffered to draw near to him, this should make the Lord precious to you at least. *Lev.* 13. 46. *The Leper was to dwell alone without*; the Lord might have dealt so with thee; but when thou wert vile indeed, and most vile, nay when thou didst separate thy self from thy self, then for the Lord to come near thee, and (as if thou couldst never be near enough) to manifest himself to thee for ever in glory! When *David* found out *Mephibosheth* (saith he) *what am I a dead dog that I should sit at the Kings table*! 2 *Sam.* 9. 7, 8. It was a great favor to Christ himself, that when rejected of men, yet that he was chosen of God and precious, and taken up to him; it may be thou thinkest thy self unworthy of fellowship of any man, and men do, or men man reject thee; yet for the Lord now to receive thee, it is much; but whereas thou wert not only rejected of men, but of God also, *Isa.* 54. 6. now for Christ to take thee to him; that as he lies in the Fathers bosom, because thou couldst not for sin immediately lye there, he should lay thee in his bosom, and say, *Father love this soul as thou hast loved me*: Besides, the Father took Christ because he had worth; but for Christ to take thee when thou hadst no worthiness! for one to take dross and prize it when others cast it away, it is much; it is no wonder if pearls be so esteemed of, but for dirt to be prized! Oh therefore let the Lord be precious, and his fellowship precious to thee, seeing thou and thy fellowship is so to him.

Object. *But I cannot believe it, why should the Lord do so?*

Answ. It is hard to believe it when we look upon our own vileness; but consider the reason why the Lord doth this; it is not because he loves any for fleshly respects as we do; but

First, Because of his own grace and glory; the Believer is infinitely beloved of him, without moving him thereunto; and hence if his grace be exceeding dear, and his glory dear to him, thou art so to him.

Secondly, Christ loves not first because men are holy, but that he may make them so.

Thirdly, He loves because the father loves them.

SECT. XII.

HEnce learn to be content with the Lord alone, *Heb.* 4. 9. *there is a rest*; hence labor to enter into it; so if he will have rest and blessedness hereafter, that you shall be content and for ever glad in him and with him alone; Oh labor to possess this blessedness now. You are in your worst condition now, your best is behind; shall the blessedness of thy best condition, not be blessedness in thy worst condition unto thee? shall that which satisfies thy soul in

heaven

heaven, not satisfie thy soul here. *Moses*, *Deut.* 32.10. reckons this as the happiness of *Israel*, (viz.) *That God alone did lead them when they were in a wilderneß*, a land of drought, and pits, and wants, and the shadow of death; so Christ now.

Solomon reckons it as one part of his folly, madness and vanity, when he forsook the Lord in his degenerate condition, *Ecclef.* 2. 3. that he *gave up his heart to vanity, and to wifdom alfo*; as if that was not sufficient alone.

Men are not contented with the Lord alone; *Solomon* as you heard, was gone, whom God appeared twice unto; *Davids* heart was sorely assaulted, *Pfal.*73. until he went into the fanctuary of God, and then, faith he, *whom have I in earth but thee?* but as for others they are far from this; and hence come the many murmurings and finkings of heart; why do not men fink and drown? because they are not in the ark or ship, and ftay there alone; fo it is here, *Pf. l.* 16.4. *their forrows are multiplied*, &c.

SECT. XIII.

LAbor for this contentedneß in fpirit, in four cafes efpecially, wherein the heart is apt to withdraw from the Lord;

First, In cafe the Lord takes away the dearest, nay, all outward bleffings from us; men can rub it out with quietneß of fpirit, when fome of their money loofe in their pockets is loft; but when their jewels are loft, their deareft bleffings fingled out, Wife, Husband, Children, then as *Jonah*, the foul is almoft angry with God, *when his gourd is fmitten*: 1 Thef. 4.13. *without hopes*; again fome can rub this out till they come to part with all; when fome of our boughs are cut and branches lopt, we can be content; but to have our top boughs cut off, and to ftrike at the root too, that we fhould remain as withered dry trees, this can hardly be born: Men can be content to follow Chrift, if they may carry fomething on their backs befide the crofs; fome can endure any thing but poverty, becaufe covetous; others any thing but difgrace, becaufe proud; if fome thing or many things be caft over-board in a ftorm, men can be fometimes contented therewith, if fomething efcapes; but when there is a wrack of all, now to be content is as hard as to walk upon the waters; *Ifrael* when they be fed and led by God, all was ftill; but when they want bread and water, then they murmure, and alfo question, *Exod.*17.7. *Is God among us now?* And truly it would break ones heart to fee what finkings of heart there be amongus (the fruits of extream pride and Chriftlefneß) and what vexations men are to themfelves, that men are become devils to themfelves, their own tormentors; what cares, fears, griefs, loffes, decays, that their heads are dawled, and their memories loft, and their hearts funk, and their countenances altered, and the Ordinances comfortlefs, and themfelves heartlefs, and pining away in their iniquities, becaufe of outward forrows: Oh confider, either thou fhalt fhortly be with the Lord, or not; if not, there is caufe of mourning: Oh to go home and fee *Abraham, Ifaac*, and *Jacob* in Gods Kingdom, and thy felf fhut out, it were a lamentable thing indeed; but if it be otherwife with thee, Oh confider thou fhalt be happy enough without thefe things in heaven; and therefore though thefe things be loft, thou fhalt not lofe one jot of thy happineß: A man that is bleffed with bleffedneß it felf, and yet funk, either fhould fay Chrift is not bleffedneß, or elfe recover.

Obiect.

Object. Oh but though I have loft my eftate, yet that doth not fo much trouble me, as to have loft friends and their love!

Anfw. And what if thou hadft loft thy life, and thy body were rent from thy foul, if that goes to the Lord! *Heb.* 11. *They were fawn efunder.* It may be thy heart hath gone from Chrift; Oh therefore return! for it may be this is Gods end; and methinks this fhould make you content with any crofs, thou art not near enough to the Lord; Oh therefore you poor Saints, be not in heavinefs by many temptations; the Lord doth it to try your faith; can you be content with him alone? It was *Juftin Martyrs* fpeech, *Nothing elfe to care for.*

Secondly, In cafe the Lord makes outward peace and bleffings to abound upon you, fet not now your hearts upon thefe things; fometimes when miferies abound, and there is wracks of all, now the foul is glad to ftand upon the rock to fave its life, *Pfal.* 78. 35. *When he fmote them, they then remembred God was their rock*; but when the Lord begins to fill the foul with outward bleffings, it is then exceeding hard not to lodge them in the Lords own room and habitation for himfelf, and *the Lord is forgotten and forfaken alfo*, *Jer.* 2. 1,2,4,5.

But when thefe things are removed, or with you continued, yet let your hearts ftill be kept for the Lord; for if thefe things were neceffary, you fhould have them in heaven; but there is no need of them there, but only of the Lord. *Pfal.*17. *ult.* It was *Davids* prayer that *he might be delivered from the men who had their portion in this world*; *but I fhall behold thy face, and therewith be fatisfied when I awake*; *i.e.* Some outward troubles now made him heavy, that he flept the fleep of death, faith *Calvin*, but then he fhould be fatisfied; it was *Davids* argument to prove his faith, *Pfal.*16. *The Lord is the portion of my lot and cup*; not his crown nor kingdom; 1 *Cor.*7.30. *Paul* mixes this with his counfels, *ufe the world as if you ufed it not, poffefs as if you poffeffed not, for the fafhion of it paffeth away.* The love of Chrift fweetens thefe things; nay, the fweet of them is Chrifts; he lets into them his love and his fweetnefs, &c. Oh the peace that comes by this means, when no outward evil detracts, and no outward good thing adds to your bleffednefs! It is fo in it felf; Oh that it were fo indeed unto you, *Pfal.* 23.

Thirdly, In cafe the foul comforts it felf in hopes and defires after good things to come in this world; for fometimes that which fills the heart, is not things prefent; a man findes a bottom here, but he looks for things to come, and fo lancheth out his heart in the deep, lets the rains of his heart go ftrongly after things to come, and fo the Lord alone doth not quiet him; many mens bleffednefs here is imaginary, and chiefly becaufe of that which is to come.

Oh confider when it will be found to be bleffednefs to enjoy the Lord alone, without hope or defire of any good elfe to come; thy foul fhall fay, *Let me ever fee and love this God, and none elfe.* It was the fweet affection of *Paul, I defire much to be with Chrift*; he did not defire thefe things, no not body nor life; nothing elfe but to be with him; and that not faintly but earneftly, 2 *Cor.*5.1. becaufe *he was now abfent from the Lord*; Oh the finful lufts of men! men think themfelves miferable if they be not fatisfied; and they are not fatisfied becaufe Chrift is not enough alone. Oh but know it, he will be fo fhortly, foul-fatisfying bleffednefs to his people: And this I add, the way to have all defires fatisfied, is, to joy in Chrift alone, *Pfal.* 37. 5.

Fourthly, In cafe of all fpiritual wants; for this troubles the heart above any other thing; thou fayft thou haft fuch wants and fuch fins; Oh but remember

member this, thou shalt have thy fill of him hereafter; he is absent now, but thou shalt be with him; he hides his face now, but he will arise upon thee and never set more, and will supply all thy wants. Thus the Apostle perswades to love the Scriptures, though they gave but a little light, and they were in darkness, until this day-star arose; so then all darkness shall be abolished; so the Saints complain, If a Son, why so unlike Christ? yet remember *When he appears we shall be like him*, 1 *John* 3, 2. Col. 1. 3.

Object. *But these things are to come, how can I be content now?*

Answ. 1. Carnal hearts feed themselves chiefly with hopes, and false hopes of base things to come, why will not you now with this? *Rom.* 5. 2, 3. *we rejoyce in hope, and live by hope.*

2. Faith makes things absent present, *Heb.* 11. 13. *They saw the promises afar off, and were perswaded and embraced them*; so do you, and the Lord in them here, but the fruition and possession of those things promised is more.

3. Though there is not perfect and full fruition of the Lord here, yet it is in part here, which gives unknown sweetness, *Revel.* 21. 23. *They need not the Sun, but the Lamb is the light of that Temple*, Psal. 23. ult.

4. What though the Lord keeps thee short, yet for his sake be content whiles he keeps thee in want; there is not a cross but the Lord saith, For my sake bear it; nor a denial of any mercy, nor a putting by any prayer, but Christ saith, For my sake be content with it, as they *Psal.* 44. 22. and be content a little while; glory is not yet ready for thee, nor thou for it; now let this prevail with you; be content to be afflicted, buffetted, forsaken; quieting the heart with this, *I shall one day be with the Lord*; Christ was thus for thee.

And as for you that never had heart to receive Christ yet; oh that this thing might make your hearts come off from all creatures to him; *Isa.* 55. 3. *Why spend you your mony for no bread, and for that which satisfies not*, and for that which continues not; what though thou lose by parting with thy lusts, all comforts, friends, favor of men, gain? thou shalt find all these in him; lose him, and thou canst not finde these in them: Oh but this you will not come to; but yet remember, *Psal.* 81. 11. *Heb.* 5. 9. and therefore is there any soul here that as *Hannah* was praying for a Child, so you for Christ alone? I offer thee Christ; in the name of the Lord take him; thou canst not exalt Christ more by any act than by taking him; and therefore, as hers, so let thy heart go home quietted, mourn no more, and let it ever bear up thy heart, as the ark above all waters, that thou art shipt safe in him.

SECT. XIV.

OH therefore be as near the Lord Jesus now as you can be in this world; be as much alone with him as you can; there will be a very near conjunction and communion between you and Christ another day; and herein alone lyes your blessedness; you are yet in your race, and absent from home; yet be as near home, and *reaching after the price of your high calling*; when *David* could not come to the Temple, yet his heart was as near it as it could; he would be coming after it, and accounting them happy that might be near, even the very Swallows. That is the nature of love, Where it cannot go, it will creep; it will be as near the thing beloved as it can: So here.

The Saints when they were cast from the Temple, when they could not go to it, yet they would look towards, and pray towards it; *Daniel* did it though

he

Use 5.

he died for it; *Jonah*, though discouraged, and thought he should never come there, but be cast out of Gods sight.

Jacob and *Joseph*, though they might have had honorable burial elsewhere, yet such was not only their faith in the promise, but their love to the Land of promise, where they knew God intended his presence, that their very bones must lie there, *Heb.*11.22. when they could not live there, their very carkasses shall lie there.

This was the power of the timorous faith of *Joseph* and *Nicodemus* (when they had lost the life of Christ, and Christ was departed) yet they loved and begged the dead body of Jesus; so though you have neglected the Lord, yet now be as near the Lord as you can; Christ himself when he was to depart from his people, yet he would be as near to his as he could; hence he sends the Comforter; Oh so be you towards him! I know his love to us exceeds ours to him; but there is no reason why it should, for we are vile; there is reason ours should exceed, for he is worthy; this is the honor of the Saints, *To be a people near to him*; as it is the curse, and shame, and misery of all the world to be far from him.

Mens hearts lie further out from Christ than we are aware of; some stars seem to be within a hands breadth of the moon, when they are indeed far off, because of our weaknes not able to judge of things at that distance; so it is with many; niy many of Gods own people are far off, or not near enough to the Lord: And hence come

First, All afflictions for the most part; why are they sent but to fetch you in from your strayings? hence *Psal.* 23.4. *the rod of God comforted David.*

Secondly, Hence comes your sleeping in your strayings from God; as *Jonah* that went away from the presence of the Lord, and the Lord let him alone for a time; I know there are daily strayings; but to lie and live in them not lamented, this argues your hearts are gone, and lie out from the Lord, at least, for a time.

SECT. XV.

Quest. HOw *should we be near unto the Lord?*
    Answ. In Four particulars.

First, *Be near to him in his Providences*; the Lord is exceeding near to all men thus, *Act.* 17.27,28. *in him we live and move*, as the beam is in the Sun, so as he may be felt; it is wonderful to think how near the Lord is to men, not only by the immediatenes of his vertue, but of his person; yet they are far from the Lord, and men are to seek for him; hence verf.30.31. he perswades unto that, especially to be near God, not only as a Creator, but as a Mediator, by whom the affairs of all the family in heaven and earth are ordered.

Oh therefore seek him till you come so near as to see him and find him here; *David* saw this really, and that in times of peace, when he had fat pastures and full cups, *Psal.*23. he saw the Lord as his Shepherd; *Joh.*10.1. who is known of his, feeding, leading, restoring, comforting by rods, adhering to him *in the valley of the shadow of death*; and then for outward things, furnishing his table, annointing his head, giving necessities and superfluities; he looked not only on second causes, but saw God as really doing all these, as carnal men see second causes doing these: Nay, he so sees the Lord, as that he falls a wondering; and indeed the Lord is never seen in his Providences till then; as

Manoah

Manoah saw the Angel do wondrously, Judg. 13. 19. Psal. 139. 14. *Marvellous are thy works*, verf. 17, 18. *How precious are thy thoughts!* he saw from the Lords works, and gathered an idea of the thoughts of God; so should we; and hence when he did awake he was still with the Lord; the first thing that appeared was the Lord, *Psal.* 73. 23, 24, 25.

To the beasts the Lord is near, but they cannot reflect upon their own actions, much less upon the Lord; The Heathens may see we are Gods off-spring, and see God as a Creator at some times; but let them that profess Christ, see and finde out Christ as Mediator; as *Moses* that desired to see the Lord passing by him, whom he had seen a little before; truly the Lord not only passeth by you, but is with you proclaiming his name by the voyce of his Providence toward you, patience, pity, love, truth, wisdom; and yet truly this is very difficult and hard to see.

SECT. XVI.

MEN see not Jesus Christ, First, Because second causes seem to work all; This estate my friends gave me, or my labor got me; this house the Carpenter built for me, these provisions my money bought for me; and so the creatures like broad leaves hide the boughs of the glory of God in Christ on which they grow, and are opake and dense, and not transparent, through which the soul may see the glory of God abroad.

Secondly, Because men have so many businesses and cares that they cannot have leasure really to see the Lord.

Thirdly, Because there is a malice in all mens hearts naturally which suffocates all that which may be known of him, *Rom.* 1. 28. *They delighted not to retain God in their knowledge*; the works of God grow vile and sordid through their commonness to them.

Fourthly, Because men can live well enough without him; hence like a childe at nurse, that forgets friends and home, because it is well enough without them; thus mens minds are not fed with the thoughts of him, *Jer.* 2. 6.

Fifthly, Because Nature never heard of a Mediator governing all their lives, and comforts, and all; they see not all given them by the Almighty hand of Christ, *who hath all power given him in heaven and earth*, and who must reign not only over friends till they are gathered, but over his enemies also till they are subdued, and to question this is to question Christ's sitting at Gods right hand. He is owner of all, and disposer of all to the least growth of thy stature, and the most careless fall of the least hair; to do not only the greatest, but the meanest offices of love for thee.

You say indeed you believe all is from Christ; oh but you see it not; come near therefore and see the Lord, *Deut.* 8, 9. they were forty years a learning that Man lives not by bread, nor is warmed by cloaths, &c. and though they had marvellous wondrous works, yet *Deut.* 29. *To this day the Lord hath not given you eyes to see.*

Oh therefore labor to see who it is that nurses you, guides you, tends you, leads you, teacheth you, lays you down, and takes you up, and let the works of Christ raise up your minds to the thoughts of Christ in heaven, remembring thee in his Kingdom of glory, who might forget thee; and the poorer and smaller the mercy is, the more do thou wonder that he should therein be a servant unto thee; see all blessings growing upon this tree, seated in the midst of Gods Paradise, *Rev.* 22. 2, 4. though thou liest thy head with *Jacob* upon stones, and sorrows, yet see this ladder of the Lords providence

dence towards thee ; common blessings sometimes descending, sometimes taken out of thy hand and ascending, and the Angels of God with thee, ministring to thee ; but the Lord at the top of them ; the Lord his care, his love, in all ; and let not this be a dream, but a reality to you. It is a wonderful sin to be thus unmindful of Christ.

1. Because hence all whoring from Christ ariseth, *Hof.*2.8. *Judg.*2.12. especially in times of peace.

2. Hence the Lord is forced to hedge your way with thorns, and to bring you to extremity of troubles that you may see the Lord, *Isa.*41.17,18. nay sometime to bring ruine, *Isa.*5.12,13.

And truly as it is a great sin, so it is a very great shame, *Isa.*1.2. *The ox knows his owner* ; is the Lord the owner of you, and do you not know him ? when he comes by you, and to you, provides for you ? *It is a worse thing,* saith *Chysostom, to be compar:d to a beast than to be so.* To let many days and streams of goodness pass by you, and yet not to take any notice, and still to be so far from the Lord : I know in heaven this is perfected, and then comes acknowledgement of the Son of God ; but here you may be near him ; I think unless the Lord did descend in cloudy pillars, and of fire, some men would never see him.

SECT. XVII.

Secondly, **B**E near him in his promises ; for Christ is near to us here also, *Rom.* 10.8. *the word of faith is nigh thee ; so that you need not ascend to bring Christ down from heaven,* &c. When Parents are dead and gone, children will then search out their last Will and Testament, and preserve that, and keep that near them.

Christ draws near to his people, 1. In his Promises, according to his thoughts of them.

2. In his performances, joyning the soul immediately to himself, and filling it with himself ; this we cannot enjoy yet, the Lord laies it up in his promise, which they have in lieu of the performance : Oh draw near not to words and syllables, but to the Lord there, apprehend him there ; as it is with the Attributes of God, his Glory cannot be comprehended by us ; hence he manifests himself there according to our capacity, God manifesting himself severally ; so in promises we cannot comprehend Christ as yet ; hence Christ manifests himself in his glory, in several promises ; Oh embrace him there ; *Heb.*11.9. 'Tis not said that *Abraham and Jacob were heirs of Canaan,* but *heirs of the promise,* and *Sarah first received her son in the promise ;* so do you embrace Christ in the womb and bowels of the promises ; we live by faith in this life ; and hence all our enjoyment of Christ is first in the promise.

First, Labour to draw near unto, and enjoy the Lord Jesus by the Promise.

Secondly, Labour to enjoy him in the Promise.

First, By the promise or by means of it ; all that which the Lord conveys to his, is not by meer providence but by promise, *Psal.* 25.10. He was free before their calling, but now he hath bound himself by an eternal covenant, to be all, and do all for them, *Gen.*17.1. So that the Saints may and should bring all their empty pitchers to the wells of the promise, *Isa.*12.2. *and draw out of those breasts,* , and get Christ Jesus Spirit in your hearts by them ; now some think the Promise is not theirs, hence they go not thither for spiritual refreshments,

ments, or at least, they let other things come by providence, especially common blessings, without going to the promise for their daily bread, or looking to the promise out of whose bowels they are begot, *Heb.*13.5,6. the Apostle there sends them to the promise. Or else they use not the means, or faint in the use of it; whereby they come to enjoy the Lord by his promise, and that is restless wrestling with Christ by prayer for it, *Gen.*32.12. *Thou saidst I will surely do thee good*; He might have said, *I have a promise, what need I pray?* or he might have said, *I had a promise of safe convoy, but now I see the Lord is coming out to break it*; and so he might have perished; yet he prays, and wrestles, acknowledging himself unworthy of all the truth, &c. So *Neh.*1.8. Men have so little of Christ because so little of the Spirit of Prayer, pressing Gods promise; thou hast a barren, empty, weak heart, because the promise is not improved as it should be.

Secondly, Labour to enjoy him in the Promise; sometimes the soul hath a Promise fair, and seeks and finds not; now the heart goes on to seek, but is exceeding unbelieving, or sad and troubled whiles it doth not feel; and unthankful also, and accounts it self miserable whiles it wants, and so doth not glory in the Lord, and his fulness, which is his in the Promise, unless he feels the good come from the promise; like a man that doth not account himself rich while he hath it in his treasure, a most safe and sure place where it is kept for him, unless he gets a little out of it into his pockets; and fears he shall be slain with thirst, though he stands by the Spring and that be full, if his dish be empty; oh this is vile, *Heb.* 11.13. *These received not the promise, i.e.* things promised, yet saw them, believed, and embraced them *i.e.* in the promise. You say you are sinful and born down by your distempers, and base, and poor; I say you have power, victory over all sin and misery, and have eternal glory already in the promise; only here is thy wound, you think you want it because you have it not out of the promise, though you have it in the swadling clouts of the promise lapt up there; and by means of this sinful distemper of heart you partake not of Christ, because you apprehend not your exceeding great riches in the promise, 2 *Pet.* 1.2. 2 *Sam.*23.4. *God made an everlasting Covenant*, this is all his desire; sweet was *Davids* spirit. 2 *Sam.*7.22. *Who is like to thee*, when he had no accomplishment of the promise; Oh so do you say. *Heb.*6.17. *The Lord hath appointed we should have strong consolation by promise and oath, not by dreams*; it was the complaint of Christ, *unless you see signs and wonders you will not believe*; so you call in question, like *Thomas*, unless you feel; Oh close with the Promise, keep it as most precious; and then *Psal.*25.10. He saith not to them that keep their covenants or their feelings, but *his covenant as their portion*, and get the Lord to undertake to keep it for them, and so make sure.

SECT. XVIII.

3. **L**Abor to be near the Lord in all his Ordinances also, both privately and publickly, for there is his presence, *Ezek. ult. ult.* *Psal.* 26.8. he not only loved Christ's presence, but the place where it was; it was an argument of his integrity. *Psal.*102.13. *They did love the dust of Sion*; never think there is a time of mercy till then.

First, Be with him in secret as oft as you can, prayer, meditation, daily calling your hearts to an account; time hath been that you have been so, when in affliction, or at first conversion; but now twenty hindrances; and now you cannot only neglect, but think you have reason so to do; there have
been

been tears, and prayers, and thoughts, and preffings hard after the Lord, but now no words, nor groans; you women have children to fuck, and families to tend; you fervants love your fleep rather than the bofom of Chrift; and though Confcience cry out againft you for it, yet you hope to be better one day, and fo you grow ftrangers to Chrift, and no publick Ordinances profit, becaufe private duties are neglected, and thy heart like the fluggards garden is undreffed; is this to be as near the Lord as you can? no, if the Lord oves you, look for the death of thy Husband, Wife or Childe fhortly; look for terrors, and then you fhall account it an honor, if you may but once more fpeak to the Lord.

Secondly, Be with him, and as near him as you can in all publick Ordinances, and not only to have them (which fome care not greatly for, becaufe they fee no glory in them, unlefs glorified fouls fhould come out of heaven to be members, and *Mofes* and *Elias* to build tabernacles here, and fo be Elders) but come through them, look beyond them to the Lord; look at them as empty and weak, unlefs the Lord fill, and be powerful in them; *David* did enjoy God fecretly, yet there was more in publick; hence *Pfal.*63.2. The Saints are a generation of Seekers, *Pfal.*63. *My foul followeth hard afteh thee; mercy and truth follows you* many times when you forfake it, *Pfal.* 23.*ult.* much more when you cleave to it: *Hezekiah's* frame of heart, *Ifa.* 38.*ult.* is imitable; *Act.*1. *Chrift promifed to fend the Comforter; wait at Jerufalem,* as there they did in prayer, and at laft the Lord came.

You have forfaken all for Ordinances; and now you have them, you defpife them; I confefs they are meer outfides, yet the Lord is there; there is a glory which wife men can fee in Chrift in the manger.

SECT. XIX.

Fourthly, **L**Abor *by thy defires to be near him,* *Rev.* 22.20. So defire *as to wait for thy change all thy life,* look for it, 1 *Theff.* 1.*ult.*

1. Chrift's defire is that thou wert with him, when thou art ready, and when thy work is done; Oh let this make thee to defire it alfo.

2. If you cannot keep your hearts from vain hopes, and foolifh and noyfom lufts, without defiring him, do not then defire to be with him; for you may defire communion with lufts and Chrift.

Object. *But death is terrible, and feparation from him bitter?*

Anfw. Long for him therefore to come and then take thee, and fee thou defire nothing but him; rebuke thy unwillingnefs of not being with him. If Chrift was on earth, you would hazard your lives to get unto him; much more herein.

Obj. *But what will become of Gods name?*

Anfw. Let the Lord alone for that; whiles thou liveft endeavour to the utmoft; but its appointed for thee a little feafon only to be here, and be willing the Lord fhould honor himfelf alfo by others as well as by thee.

Object. *What will become of my wife and children?*

Anfw. Who regarded thee in thy blood? when thou liveft, they are thine; but then the Lords.

Defire to be with him, this will fupport your hearts in all your changes of this life.

SECT. XX.

Use 6. YOU *that never received Christ, now do it.*

Object. Yes, I have.

Answ. No, you have not so received him, as to let all go for him. Why so ? because he alone will be blessedness , but he is not so to thee ; Oh therefore let all go now ; you must part with Christ, or all these things. Which will you do ? If with Christ, you cannot finde him in these things, but if you part with these things , then you shall finde them all in him.

Object. But he will have none of me ?

Answ. 1. He cries down thy laying out money for what is not Bread.

2. He promises to give thee to drink, now, and hereafter.

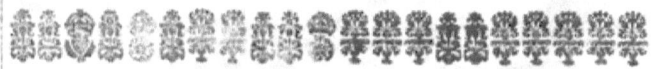

CHAP. XIX.

Shewing, that none shall enjoy Christ hereafter, but those that are prepar'd here.

VERSE 10.

They that were ready , ἕτοιμοι*, prepared.*

SECT. I.

THose only who are ready and prepared in this life for Christ, *Observ.* 2. shall enjoy eternal and immediate communion with Christ ; those only who are now fitted for his fellowship , shall partake of his fellowship ; for of all these Virgins (though many of them were otherwise very well qualified) only those which were ready, did enter in with the Bridegroom ; which readiness in these wise Virgins, was not, nor is not any Popish preparation , either meritorious , or congruous , or wrought by the power of corrupted or adorned nature ; but Divine and glorious, wrought by the power of Christ, out of his eternal love to the Vessels of glory, as an Antecedent , not moving cause of this eternal fellowship ; it is the first degree of our Resurrection with Christ. *Rom.* 9. 23. *Vessels of glory prepared unto glory* ; the same

same word which is used here, there are two ends God hath appointed all men to; either to be Vessels of wrath; who are those? *Ve se* 22. *Those that are fitted for destruction*; others of glory; who are those? *prepared unto glory.* 2 *Cor.* 5. 5. with 8. How comes *Paul*, and all the Saints, to know, and groan for to be out of the body, and to break the Cage, and to be with the Lord? one reason is, they are wrought, and moulded, and fashioned for that condition by the hand of a merciful God, even as one may know what Vessels are for special use, by their mettal, and curious engravings upon them.

SECT. II.

Reas. 1. BEcause all mens souls are *naturally unfit*, *and unprepared to enjoy communion with Christ*, it is said, *Rev.* 21. *ult. Nothing enters into the new Jerusalem on earth, which is uncleane, and defileth*; and *Hib.* 12. 14. *Without holiness no man shall see God.* Now naturally all men are defiled, and unclean Vessels, and under the power of their sins, loathing Angels food, the grace of Christ, and weary of the fellowship of Christ; and therefore they must be prepared for the Lord first; this is one reason, why preparation to every holy duty is needful, and so needful, that let men performe any holy duty, wherein they draw neat to Christ without a heart prepared, *Psal.* 10. 17. their performances are rejected, or not blessed; and hence *Rehoboam*, though he did maintaine the worship of God at *Jerusalem*, yet he prepared not his heart, 2 Chron. 12. 14. and hence *Hezekiah* mournes, and begs pardon for this, *That he is not so purified according to the purification of the Sanctuary.* Now if to a holy duty, and communion with Christ here, this is needful; much more to eternal fellowship with him; sore eyes cannot behold the Sun without grief; sick bodies loath the best food; if the Lord should let a carnal heart into heaven with that heart he hath, and not change his nature, he would not stay there if he could escape; but having his swinish nature, he would be in his mire againe; and the Government of Christ being a bondage to him, he would break bonds, and break his Prison, if he knew where to fly from the presence of the Lord; And hence no work so wearysome as Christs now, no time so uncomfortable and tedious as abiding under Christs wings in his Ordinances now. 1 *Cor.* 15. 50. *If flesh and blood cannot enter into the Kingdom of heaven, much lesse corruption.*

Reas. 2. *In regard of the rich grace and wisdom of his love towards his people*; for who sees not, but that it is a curse to be unready as these foolish Virgins, who were therefore shut out! Oh therefore it is grace and mercy to make ready, and indeed an answer to prayers, and a comfort against all feares of the Saints, who are then desirous to be with the Lord when they are indeed ready; readiness for Christ doth not destroy grace, but being a fruit of Gods grace, advanceth it. *Rom.* 9. 23. the Apostle makes it the first fruit of glory, that the Saints are *prepared unto glory*; glory of mercy is the end, preparedness thereto is the meanes, or way leading to that end; if God appoints the end, his wisdom also leads first to the meanes which lead at last to that end; if out of his rich grace he appoints the end, out of the same grace by this other, he leads to this end; and though you think it not now grace, you shall say it is so another day, when with these

foolish

foolish Virgins, you shall say, *Oh that I were ready!* I know not almost which is greatest love, to prepare for glory, or to bring into the possession of it; to make a Vessel of poysonous dross a Vessel of gold, or when it is so, to fill it; for the Lord to look upon a man when he is in his blood, and then to wash him; when a man is as water spilt upon the ground, and a broken Vessel of no use, now for the Lord to pity, and fit for use, it is exceeding rich grace.

Reas. 3. *In regard of the honour of the Lord Jesus*; it was one part of the honour of Christ, to have *John* go before him; and *Luke* 1. 17. *to prepare a people ready for the Lord*: As it is part of a Princes honour, to have his Bride ready, and attired to welcome and entertaine him, when he shall returne to her, she owes this honour to him, and he expects this honour from her; So the Lord Jesus deserves this honour from all his people to be in a readiness for him. Suppose these Virgins had turned Harlots, and gone a whoring from him till his very coming, and then had been taken in, what might the world think? doth he love the fellowship of Harlots? for a mans heart to go a whoring from the Lord, after the world, or lusts, to die so, is to disgrace the Lord Jesus; And hence, *Phil.* 3. 17. to the end, there are two sorts of men professing godliness; some minde *earthly things*, others look and minde *a Saviour from heaven*; the one disgrace Christ, and are enemies to him; and hence *Paul* weeps for them; the other are his friends; And are Princes so far respected as all things are ready for them? and is the Lord worthy of no such respect, so as that his People then should be unready? No, know it, as he said, *Mal.* 1. *He is a great King.*

The particulars wherein this readiness consists, I have spoken of in the first Part of the Parable, and shall now only speak of them in the subsequent Uses.

SECT. III.

Use 1. OF *terror and astonishment of heart, to all those that are wholly unready, that have no readinesse at all to meet, or to have fellowship with the Lord Jesus; if those that are ready be received in, then those that be unready, shall be shut out.*

There is a number among us, young and old, of all sorts almost among us, that swarme up and down Townes, and Woods, and Fields, whose care and work hitherto hath been like bees, only to get honey to their own Hive, only to live here comfortably with their houses, and lots, and Victuals, and fine cloaths, &c. but not to live hereafter eternally. Suppose the Lord should stop thy breath, and cut thee off, what would become of thee? I trust to Gods mercy, I hope I should go to Christ, though I am not assured; but are you ready for Christ? yes, I hope I am; Oh poor wretch, why dost hope so, if thou never hadst one houres serious thoughts, What will become of me? or how shall I be ready? feeling thy unreadiness and unfitness thereunto. Or if thou hast had any thoughts, never wast possessed with any strong feares of eternity, and separation from the Lord Jesus, which hath dampt thy mirth, and sunk thy heart, and perplexed thy thoughts, and made thee think with terror upon thy conscience, What will become of me? nor made thee desirous to ask others that question, as it is commonly one of the first, though but a common work, to think of dying presently,

sently, I have lived long without God and Christ in the world, and dye I must shortly, and what will become of me then?

But you have slept quietly enough in the night, and sung care away, and cast feare away in the day, and thy heart never had one houres fit of shaking and trembling at eternity to come, when it is the nature of true fear, even to have the eye upon what it feares, till it is taken away; and if difficulty attend the same, to remove it; it cannot be quiet, but will cry for help, if possibly help may be had; this you never did: No, thou never hadst so much as these foolish Virgins, *viz.* to be awakened at all, but a spirit of slumber hath been upon thee; God hath given thee eyes, but thou canst not see; eares, and thou canst not here; Thou sayst (it may be)that thou dost hope thou art prepared; alas, thou hast not a Virgins name, much less nature, nor dost not deserve it neither; thou hast not forsaken thy loose company, nor yet come to the company of the wise, neither dost thou desire it, or think thy self unworthy of it; thy Lamp is out; nay, thou never hadst any light at all; never mad'st profession at all, as of one ready for Christ; but O poore wretch, all is yet to do with thee! if so, then remember that if thou diest now, thou shalt never have communion with Jesus Christ in glory.

SECT. IV.

Object. **W**Hat if I have not?

Answ. I know it is the misery of men; they can make nothing of this till they feele it: But two things I will say.

1. Do but consider what if thou shouldst be deprived of the light of the Sun; nay, only of bread, only that one creature, and have cloaths, Sun, Friends, all other blessings but that; would it not be a wo with a witness, would it not cut a mans heart to heare him cry, Bread, bread, a little bread for the Lords sake, to save my life! there is but a drop of the sweetness of Christ in that. Oh what a misery will it be to pine away, and famish under wrath in chaines of darkness, and to cry, Oh a little refreshing from the presence of Christ, and canst not get it, but to live ever tormented without that, when thy soul shall cry, Lord, thus long have I been tormented without thee, till my spirits are weary, and my heart faint; Now, O now a little mercy, ——— Oh no.

2. That though thou seest it no great matter to be separated from Christ now, yet when the heavens shall be in a flaming fire, and the earth shall give up the dead that be in it, and Christ shall appeare in infinite glory, admired of Angels, blessed of Saints, Crowned of God, comforting his Elect, *Come, oh come ye blessed*; then you shall think this separation something. Oh that you would now go home and mourn, and look up to the Lord, that he would make thee ready a Vessel of honour, and acknowledge it's righteous with him, if he should never do it.

SECT.

SECT. V.

Use 2. IT is of examination to all the Virgins; *Would you know whe-ther the Lord will bring you to eternal fellowship with him? are you ready for him, made fit to live with him or no ? for here only those which are ready, are received in;* the foolish Virgins did lie so long asleep, that little did they think they were unready, untill the Bridegroome came, and it was too late. It is the condition of many at this day, that little dream of their separation from Christ, and yet shall be when he comes; but they have some hopes and assurance; they look to meet the Bridegroome when he shall come, and so fall into a sweet sleep; a comfortable conditi-on, untill the Lords coming, puts them upon more narrow searching than ever before; that which many think gold now, shall be found hay, and stubble, and consumed to nothing at the coming of Christ; therefore search now.

I know there is many a gracious soul that is ready, feares to slip in at the passage over that narrow bridge, between life and death, this end of time, and beginning of eternity, and loth I am to sad any; but, heare what I shall now say in feare; when there are these three things in the soul, then it is ready; whiles any are wanting, it is unready; And by these try your selves.

SECT. VI.

1. WHen the soul, the Spouse of Christ is made lovely by its Wed-ding Garment, the Royal Robe of his own righteousnes in the eyes of Christ; for this Bridegroom, though he findes his Spouse filthy, yet he being glorious and lovely himself, makes it lovely and glorious, *Eph.* 5. 25, 26. A Queen fit for the fellowship of this King of Kings, and thorow this righteousnes (though otherwise weak and vile, yet) the object of his, and the Fathers infinite and endless delight in heavenly Glory; now it is fit, *Zach.* 3. 1, 2, 3, 4, 5. 2 *Cor.* 5. 2, 3. Without this righteousnes, there is nothing but shameful nakednes in the best; so as the soul with *A-dam*, will rather seek bottomes of Mountaines to hide it from Christ, than to appeare before him. Now examine you Saints; time was, that sinne was no shame to thee, though thou didst wallow in that Vomit, and livedst in it, and livedst by it as by thy Trade; or if the Lord did keep and cleanse you from foule sins, and that you could pray, and sorrow, and know and remem-ber what you heard, and had some good affections, now you were some bo-dy in your own eyes, and it may be you thought if you died then, you should to heaven, and Christ must needs save you; who should he save else ? but now the Lord hath made thee poor in spirit, and ashamed; nay, the Lord hath made thee lie down confounded, because of all thy shame before him; and the Lord hath made thee see a glory, a rising Sun in Christs righteous-nes which the Gospel hath brought to light; though thou wert a poor, naked, condemned, vile creature; yet the Lord hath made thee seek for it, so as to esteem all things loss to be found there, and now here is all thou hast to glory in, as that which may make thee lovely in the Fathers sight; and here the Lord hath quieted thy conscience, and heart also; be not discouraged,

couraged, nor afraid to stand before the Lord, if he should send for thee this night; for though thou art vile in thine own eyes, yet the Lord looks upon thee as lovely.

The Apostle makes a question, why the Gentiles are justified, and not the Jewes, *Rom.* 9. 30, 31. he answers it, *verse* 32. viz. *they sought it by the works of the Law*; but if it be otherwise with thee, that in Christ thy righteousness and strength is, then thou mayst glory; so that now thou shalt have peace againe, against all the condemning of conscience, Satan, and God himself.

But have you seen your nakedness, known, and stood convinced of your vileness, and have heard the voyce of God condemning thee for thy sinful, though civil life, and been afraid, and hereupon you have reformed your life, lamented your course, set upon some duties, gone to Christ for strength against some corruptions, and you have had it, and you have looked about you, and have been ready to say, If the Lord saves not me, who should he? and so have sowen these leaves and skinnes together to cover your shame; and now you are well, being strangers to this true righteousness, you shall never see the Lord in peace, if you die thus. Or if thus, you see not Christ to be all, sin is not your shame, but you lie in it, and holiness is not your glory; and hence you esteem it not, but it's a common thing to you, if that was, then it would be your glory to be like Christ, and to live to him: Know it thou art not yet ready, for thou only seest the Garment, and you catch at it, but the Lord helps you not by faith to put it on.

SECT. VII.

2. VVHen the soul is filled with the Spirit of Christ; when there is not only some of the workings of the Spirit in the soul, but the soul is filled with the Spirit; for this was the wound of the foolish Virgins, they had Lamps, outward Profession, and glorious, which was a work of the Spirit, and some dipping of their week in the oyle, some lighter superficial changes, and works of grace in their hearts; but they had not oyle in their Vessel, they had not plenty and fulness of the Spirit; some unripe eares there were, but not full; and hence they were to buy when the Lord Jesus came; but the wise had.

The blood and righteousness of Christ, ever brings the plenty of the Spirit of Christ; hence 2 *Cor.* 5. 5. *earnest of the Spirit.*

I speak not now of extraordinary fulness, which Prophets and Apostles had, nor of that fulness which is in glory, as if we must have that here, but of that which the Saints attaine to in this life, every one according to his need and measure of capableness of the same; the Spirit of love is not dropt, but shed into the heart; the Spirit of God in them, is not a Spirit of some light affection, dying affection, but of *eternal life*, *Rom.* 8. 2, 3. The spirit of mourning doth not only drip upon them, but *it's powred down upon them*, *Zach.* 12. 10. the spirit of wisdome doth not only give them light and knowledge, *but Marvellous Light*, 1 Pet. 2. 9.

I have opened this at large; only three signes now I shall give you to discerne this Spirit by.

SECT.

SECT. VIII.

1. *THis Spirit and fulnesse of it, the Saints not only pray for, but they follow their prayers to Christ, untill th ir souls are sweetly satisfied with it, and so it abides daily satisfying their hearts.* John 4. 14. *The wa-ter I shall give, shall be a spring, so as the soul shall not thirst after more grace;* i. e. with a tormenting thirst; nor after the world, the grace of God, and the Spirit of God in the heart is so sweet, that the soule faith, Oh it is enough, oh if my soul might ever be thus near the Lord, indeared to him, walking thus humbly, thankfully, cheerfully with him, this should be all my desire; and hence, *John* 14. 16. it is called *the Com or-ter*, which dwells in them, and is known by them, the world knows it not. Now here is the wound of others, they have the Spirit convincing them of emptiness, misery, nakedness, and they lie so, and they desire; but as *So-lomon* faith, *Prov*. 13. 4. *They are forsaken of the Spirit, before they finde him to be a Comforter quenching their thirsty desires, making them to feele the sweetness of his Presence, of his Grace.* Isa. 58. 11. There were divers that did pray, fast, draw near to God, and did delight in it, but they felt not what they desired at all; there were some lusts, their souls were leane, and like parched desarts; but when the heart is indeed humbled, the spirit comes in, and makes the bones fat, and like a watered garden; Oh there-fore take heed you give not over, till the Lord pour out in thy empty heart, of the fulnes of his grace.

2. *This Spirit ever keeps a man poor and vile in his own eyes, and em-pty.* Take a man that hath no knowledge, nor taste of Gods grace, whiles he findes ignorance, he may pray, and be diligent in use of means, and full of life; but when he hath got some knowledge, and can discourse pretty well, and hath some tastes of the Heavenly Gift, some sweet elapses of grace, and so his conscience is pretty well quieted, and if he hath got some answer to his prayers, and hath sweet affections, he grows full, and having ease to his conscience, casts off sence, and daily groaning under sin; And hence the Spirit of Prayer dies, he loses his esteeme of Gods Ordi-nances, feeles not such need of them, or gets no good, feeles no life and power by them; and whereas before he could catch at every word, and mourn when he found the Lord passed by him, and speak never a good word to him: now no such trouble, because he is full. This is the woful condition of some, but yet they know it not; but now he that is filled with the Spirit, the Lord empties him, and the longer he lives, so that others think he needs not much grace, yet he accounts himself the poorest, and feels a need of every truth of God, and Ordinance of God; his sin ('tis true) continues, 'tis not quite abolished, and his sighing within himself continues also to his grave. *Isa.* 57. 15. *poure*, and yet the Lord dwells there; how can these stand together? very well in those who are the Lords.

3. *This Spirit comes in that fulness, as that it so purifies the heart of sin and self, as that it makes the soul see it self for God, as his last end and happinesse, and so as that the work of Christ is his blessednesse.* 2 Tim. 2. 20, 21. *He that purgeth himself from these things, is a Vessel of honour, and fit for his Masters use.* It is with some souls, as it is with some drossy Vessels, they are put out of the fire, and they are taken out before their dross is removed, or they melted, or if melted, yet not fashioned for use, even

even to every good work; so some have great troubles without and within; now the fire goes out, or they get out of the fire; *viz.* the trouble, before their dross is removed, or their sinful natures be changed; or if they be melted, yet they are not fashioned, and framed for their Matters use only; they are for their own use, and their lusts use, and seek themselves in all they do, but not for the Lords use; it is not their life to live to God. Promises are sweet, and Christ is sweet, and Heaven is sweet; but the work of Christ to be of use for Christ, this is not their bliss: I know Saints fall short here much, and seek themselves; but yet their hearts are prepared, fashioned, set for this end, and they through the help of the Spirit, refine themselves for the Lord; that when sin desires them to serve it, No (their answer is) I am no debtor, nor servant to you; I have lived too long to you already, I am now the Lords, and for the Lord; Oh that I might have that honour as to be employed for him; I say unto you, the Lord hath here filled you, and fitted you for his use, and you may be comforted.

SECT. IX.

3. WHen the soul is recovered out of that security, which usually befalls men after some time of first affection and profession, in that measure, as that now it lives unto the Lord in a daily waiting for him, and longing for him, when the Lord sees it meet to come and take him to himself. For all these Virgins fell asleep, after they came out to meet the Bridegroom with their burning Lamps; and not only the foolish, but the wise also slept. Now I ask you, Do you think they were ready then for the Lord? No, not untill they were awakened againe, and the wise had got their Lamps burning againe, and waiting for him; but yet the foolish had got not only no light to their Lamps, but Oyle was wanting also to their Vessels; So it is here.

Time hath been, that the Lord hath awakened you with feares and terrors about your estate, and you have got into the assemblings of the Saints together, and kept company with them, and you have escaped the outward pollutions of the world, and defilements of Gods worship and services, and you have seen the insufficiency of all duties, and it is Christ you have look't after, and prayed for, and got some peace and comfort that he is yours, and have look't to meet him, hoped if you die, that you should be saved; but have you not faln into a secure frame againe, both wise and foolish? have you not turned Prodigals, and spent, and lost all, after you have had your portions? if not, thank God, be not high-minded, but feare; for very few, but after fulness fall asleep; and after they have had some peace of conscience, but they fall to enter into some peace, if not with some foul open sins, yet some truce with some lesser secret sins; and if their oyle be not spent, their sorrows spent in sorrowing, their trouble spent in trouble, their desires spent in desiring (as water spends away it self in running out of a Cisterne, not out of a Spring) yet their light hath gone out; the beauty of thy profession is (it may be) lost, that heat and life is gone which others saw, and you saw much more: are you ready now? and though you may have some awakenings, yet are they so far as to cause you to get up, and kindle your Lamps, and waite for the Bridegroome? If it be so that still you keep sleeping, and have not your Lamps

ready

ready trimm'd , then you are just as all the foolish Virgins were, before the cry came.

SECT. X.

Quest. BUT may not a godly man die in a declining, decaying, secure frame?

Answ. 1. He may die in an uncomfortable frame, without great peace of conscience; for sometimes a mans Lamp may shine brightest, when his peace is least; but the more prayer, the more searchings and washing of heart is then to be attended; a godly man may die mourning for ought I know, and the Lord give him his garment of gladness in Heaven, for the spirit of heaviness here on earth; because though he loseth the comfort of his estate , yet not the safety of it, because he dyes under the wings of a Promise ; So that though he dyes uncomfortably , yet not securely.

2. He may die to his feeling in such a frame, poor, and contrite ; for growing in the sence of emptiness, is not decaying in the being or power of holiness; the Lord is now preparing of him to honour his grace, when he doth not help him to honour his Will in that inlargedness of heart to it as he would, so that this soul is not decaying.

3. But yet I do not know that the Lord lets his people die ordinarily in a withering condition; especially if it appear so to others of his discerning servants; the Lord will send some cry to awaken his servants before he comes to them, or they enter into the Marriage with him : I will allow some unusual exceptions against general rules, and put in *Asa* for one, and leave secrets with God; but ordinarily the Lord doth not let his deare Servants dye in a sottish secure estate : When *Sampsons* locks are cut , and his strength lost, he shall lie in the Mill untill they be grown againe before he dies ; and *Solomon* may run ryot, but he shall proclaim his folly to all ages in the world for it, in *Eccles.* before he dies. *Ephes.* 5. 26, 27. *Christ presents his Church without wrinckle*; you are to be presented by Christ to the Father, and to be set before Christ without wrinckle, without witherings, and decayes; if he loves you, he will wash you , that it may be so.

SECT. II.

Quest. BUT must they be so farre awakened, as to wait for the Lord, and desire to be with him, having got Vessels full, and Lamps burning?

Answ. Yes, in some measure at least; for there are awakenings to the life of glory in another world, and awakenings to the life of duties in this world; by the one the soul is raised out of this world to the Lord in Glory; by the other the soul is raised up to duties in this world; if the Lord awakens not his Saints to the first, either they are not awakened truly, or not throughly and effectually; for till then the soul is not ready, *Luke* 12. 40. with 35. As it is with a man who is sent for to enjoy favour and fellowship of the King, he is not ready for it, untill he stands waiting at the door, and that it

Ttt

it is his busineſs; the patternes of mercy, and Veſſels of glory, are ever ſet out in the New Teſtament, by this, *Heb.* 9. *ult. Tit.* 2. 12, 13.

Look as it was with *Simeon*, *Luk.* 2. 25. He had a promiſe he ſhould ſee Chriſt before he died; hence he waited for the conſolation of *Iſrael*; ſo the ſoul having a promiſe of ſeeing Chriſt when he is dead, it makes him wait for this time; and when he wants a promiſe ſealed, though he waites not nextly, yet he waites remotely, that the Lord would cauſe him to believe it, that ſo he might wait for it; that is his end, this is the meanes; he knows it is beſt to be with the Lord, where is no ſin, but holineſs; he hath found him ſweet in his looks, in his words, in his works, in his hopes, his firſt fruits, but to be with him is beſt.

This is not ſuch an high pitch which Saints come not to, it is indeed ſuch which Hypocrites come not to; the Hypocrites end is to eſcape miſery; hence they deſire comfort by duties, that they ſhall be freed from it, but not to enjoy Chriſt; the Lord never died in their ſouls ſuch a knot of faith and love which works this.

For 1. Security of Saints, 'tis not the privation of life (that is death) but a ſuſpenſion of the acts of a heavenly life; there is in them love to Chriſt, delight in him, happineſs in living to him, pleaſing of him; but it is ſuſpended by cares or contents of the world, and love of eaſe; hence a Chriſtian is never throughly awakened, till he comes to that life againe; his heart is with Chriſt in heaven; and becauſe he cannot be there, hence he ſtayes awhile, and looks, and waits for it; anothers ſecurity is the privation of life, of empty duties ariſing from ſome vaniſhing affections, as in the fooliſh Virgins which were to quiet conſcience only; Hence their awakening are only to that life againe at the beſt, if ever God do awaken them, unleſs the Lord indeed convert them.

2. Every thing will mightily tend to that to which its nature bends and inclines it; as a ſtone if thrown upward, will mightily tend downward. Some ſay there is an Element of fire above, becauſe this here endeavours to aſcend, as being out of its place; he that is of the earth, he will be tending to it, though awakened, though lifted up; Saints will be tending upward, becauſe their nature is heavenly, loving, looking, waiting, longing, 2 *Cor.* 5. 3, 4. with 1. as Angels here be willing to ſtay to do the work, but yet they long to be before the face of God againe, becauſe their natures are heavenly, and there their proper place is.

Now for the Lord Jeſus ſake examine your ſelves here. I hope ſome are awakened, the Word hath done it; cry of afflictions, inward temptations have made you look about you, and you are wearied out with your own wayes; but are you not ſince grown ſecure? time was the feet of the Meſſengers of peace were glorious, but now their Meſſage is meane; Sabbaths longed for, now you are weary of them, heartleſs in them, ſleep with the ſpoon in your mouths; private duties were ſeaſons of breaking the heart, refreſhing and comforting from the Lord, but now you neglect them, ſleight them, and the Lord in them, and are not much troubled at it, becauſe you have ſome excuſe or other for it; thy mouth was full of good queſtions, now thou thinkeſt thy ſelf more fit to teach than learn; thy ſociety was ſweet as the Roſe in Spring, now the ſweet odour of it is loſt; time was thou wert exceeding tender of the leaſt ſinne, and not a day paſt, but thy cheeks were wet in ſecret before the Lord; now thou art grown blinde and bold, and you can defile your ſelf in all your wayes, and your faith in Chriſt keeps you from repentance for ſin; time was, the truth was glorious, and you could make uſe of your Notes many a day after, when you did not finde good in publick; but now pen and Ink is left at home, you caſt your bread into

cor-

corners, and feed not your hearts therewith? Time was, you could take a rebuke kindly, when you were little in your own eyes; but now if you think a reproof is meant of you, your hearts can swell, nay, now your judgement decayes; What warrant for private prayers twice a day? what warrant for weekly Sermons, when we have six dayes to labour, and one to rest in? you were formerly more exact, but now wifer, and thus you lie, and as if you were come to the end of your race already, and reach not after things before you, you have enough grace, hence you think you sha'l be saved, and so sit still, and now play the good Husband: Oh the Covenants you have had, if ever you came hither what you would do! oh the esteem of the Lord afar off! but now you are broken by your Voyage, and your Vessel is crackt, and oyle is run out, and Lamp is out, will you dye so? if you say yes, I profess you are not ready; it is a question if ever you had grace, if it be so; and therefore bless God, the Lord gives you warning this day; but I feare many will not stir till Christ comes; I say as she to *Sampson*, *Up, for the Philistins are upon thee*; so I say, Security is upon thee, and wrath is now gone out to awaken thee, if the word doth not.

SECT. XII.

Use 3. OF Exhortation. *Labour to be in a readinesse, awaken out of sleep, and get your Garments on, your loynes girt, your Vessels full, your Lamps burning, that you may be indeed ready, and the Lord may finde you so, as well as men think you so;* It is Christs Exhortation, *Luke* 12. 40. whereupon *Peter* askt, Did he speak that Parable onely to the Disciples, or of all? *Verse* 41. he answers all, especially them that know the Lords minde herein, and do it not, *Verse* 47. So you may ask me, Whom do I press to make ready? I answer all. Two sorts I shall therefore name.

1. Those who are yet unready, either in whole or part.
2. Those who are ready, but not so ready as those should be who stand before the Lord, and as themselves will wish another day they had been; the wise as well as foolish, may be sleepy, and so unready for a time; but O awake.

First, Those who are unready and unprepared for the Lord and his coming; are there any such? Yes, very many; some there be who know they are unready, and will not yet buy, and yet prepare not for it, because they are young enough yet, or have time enough to provide for that hereafter. Some others, because they cry, Lord, Lord, and look to Christ, and are well thought of by the wife, that think they are ready; but know it, all your thoughts, and cares, and prayers, and endeavours, are little enough for it, even all your life; and yet to prepare for this, hath been the least part of many a mans life; and such is the security of some, that till Christ come, they will not Gird up themselves to this Work.

SECT. XIII.

Motive 1.

COnfider the *lamentable end of one who dies unready* ; fome (not all) the Lord leaves for terrours to the fecure world, who are as good as men rifen from the dead, to tell men of the vanity of their finful courfes, who looking upon time paft, they fee that it is irrecoverably loft, and paft away as a dreame, and loft as a fhadow; look upon time prefent, they feel their fouls left naked, their accounts not made, an end come to all their hopes and comforts here, their body fick, their confcience trembling, if not tearing, their hearts hard, God departed, the grave opened for their filthy carkaffes, and Devils waiting for their fecure foules ; And now fay fuch, What profit have I for all my anity under the Sun ? Look to time to come, there they fee the Throne fet, the Lord Jefus on it, their foules ftanding naked before him, whofe grace was great toward them whiles they lived, but whofe face now is a confuming fire ; and they behold eternity, even that eternal black Gulf between them and the Lord; and here they lie wifhing they had taken their time, profeffing now their time is loft, befeeching others to take warning by them, defiring the prayers of others; but yet thinking though *Noah* and *Samuel* fhould ftand before the Lord for them, there is no hope. Come and tell them, Do not caft away mercy, caft not away that blood, which is worthy to be gathered up by bleffed Angels in V ffels of gold, lament, and returne, and the Lord will, to you; what tell you me of repenting and believing? is a fick time, a fit time to repent in ? but the Lord hath done great things for you, you have thought fo, but there were fuch fins, or fuch a fin, I knew, you knew not ; I knew it, yet I loved it, I had indeed fome lazy purpofes to forfake it, but the Lord hath taken me in my feemings ; but mercy is infinite, oh it's my torment ; I have feen an end of my finnes, and now I feel the beginning of my torment; happy are they that die in the Lord, and thrice happy that make ready for the Lord.

Motive 2.

Confider thou haft but a fhort time to prepare in, and the time will be then, when thou doft leaft think of it, Luke 12. 46. The Lords Arrows are now flying abroad; if you did think you fhould be next fmitten down dead, you would prepare ; but you think the Lord delayes his coming ; Oh Remember, that time thou do'ft leaft think of, Chrift will come.

Motive 3.

If unready now, you will be much more unready next day, grant thy time to be long ; you will be the more unfit the longer you delay; thou haft hinderances now, the longer thou fiveft, thou wilt have more and more; hy heart will be harder every day than other.

SECT. XIV.

Meanes 1.

PRay *unto the Lord that he would prepare you, and fit you, give this Chrift, and fulnefs of his Spirit unto you,* which you know the Lord will give to them that ask ; for man like the Potters clay, is no more able to prepare himfelf for glory, than to appoint and elect himfelf thereunto. Hence Pfal.

19.

10. 17. *Rom.* 9. 23. *prepared to glory* ; therefore pray, not that prayer can move the Lord to it, but because it is a means appointed of God to execute his eternal purposes of grace unto the Vessels of grace, *Acts* 9. 9, 11. *Paul* was three dayes mourning, and he did not eat and drink, and yet was not discouraged, but kept on praying, and ceaseth not, till the Lord sends *Ananias* that he might receive the Spirit, *Verse* 17. So say I to you, Time hath been thou hast not prayed, mornings, evenings, your sleep would not suffer you, or if so, yet it hath been without mourning for living without Christ, abusing of Christ, and the sin of your nature ; or if so, it hath been on y by fits, and you could hold up your head again, before God sends *Ananias* with a Message of peace, or that Message without the Spirit of grace ; Are you now prepared ? Oh no ! oh therefore now begin this work ; say, I am thy clay, Lord, and have been a broken unclean Vessel, unfit for any use, to hold any grace ; if mercies come, I forget thee, and grow worse ; if sickness, I am blockish ; if Ordinances, I despise them ; if thou forsakest me, I forsake thee ; if thou drawest neare to me, I resist thee ; if Christ be offered, I reject him ; if not, I presume, and turn his grace to wantonness ; now Lord gather a broken Vessel ; if I live, I shall still sin ; if I die, I shall blaspheme ; if I forsake acts of sin, yet lusts of sin remaine ; if they be quenched, yet my polluted nature remaines not cleansed ; and the guilt cries ; Now Lord undertake for me, begin thou the work, and take the glory ; and here mourn till the Lord comes ; know the worth, and prize the presence of the Spirit, and then *pray*, *John* 14. 16. The world cannot receive it, because they know it not, with *John* 4. 10. Sacrifice is unfit to be offered, till by shedding blood, life is taken away.

Be very watchful over your hearts, that they grow not too gentle, and handle tenderly sinnes arising after faith, and profession of your interest in Jesus Christ, sins of the second growth ; some sins grow up before profession, as all manner of ignorance, and hardness, and lasciviousness, and vanity ; now many grow terrified for these, and comforted by the Gospel against these, and now peace is made ; Oh but there are some mens natures like some fields, which when they are mowen and weeded, yet they have a second growth ; it may be as with other kinde of Weeds, you may never fall to those sins you lived in once ; but other sins more close, more spiritual ; like the *House Luke* 11. 24. swept and emptied, but *seven other spirits worse than the former, may at last enter in* ; Oh take heed of these, for they will make your latter end miserable ; you know habitations of Satan, are not fit mansions for the Spirit of Christ ; you know Vessels not only of Wood, but of Gold, if filthy and poysoned, are unfit for Princes use till cleansed ; and look through all the Scriptures on the faces of the best hypocrites, you shall finde some filth growing up after their Profession, or together with it, like blood and sacrifice mixt together, *Matth.* 7. 23. *Luke* 13. 27. Not those that have iniquity, but those that work it ; not those that work against it, and are destroyers of it by little and little, but workers of it.

If you ask me, what these sins be ? I answer, These tares, and choaking Thornes, as they are sown, and grown whiles you be asleep, so they may be seen when they are grown up, if you walk in your fields, and meditate on your hearts. I'le only name some.

1. Pride, affecting some excellency above others, and thinking your self some body.

2. Spiritual

2. Spiritual fulnefs, and fecret loathing of Ordinances, when men are clogged with them.

3. Defpifing known truths (which like flowers, were notwithftanding fweet at firft gathering) either concerning your mifery, or Chrift: if the Gofpel were preacht to the ignorant, they would take heaven with violence; but thy foul now is not moved, and the meffengers of God that bring them, defpifed, as *Galatia* and *Corinth* did *Paul.*

4. A fpirit of contention with good people. Now you cannot bear unkindneffes, and they offend you, &c. *Alexander* at firft ftood for *Paul,* and he oppofeth *Paul* to his face at laft.

5. Boldnefs to fin in fmall matters commonly without forrow, begot by counterfeit affurance of Gods love.

6. Seeking of God in Ordinances, and working of iniquity out of them; fits men have of good affections, but healthful conftitutions of bad ones.

7. Thinking you are indeed what you would be, and yet indeed would not be: There be other fins, but thefe are fome of the moft fpecial which I fhall now mention; take heed of letting thefe grow, or dealing gently with them; for Saints may feel thefe, but they put their hook to the roots of thefe Weeds, and would faine pull them quite up; but if you deal gently, (as *David* with the young *Abfolom*) and think God muft do all, I cannot part with them; and hence you give way to them; and though there be thefe fins, yet I have many good fignes and promifes too I fhall be faved; and fo long as they cannot deftroy my foule, what though they grow in my foul? You perifh (1 *Cor.* 9. 26, 27.) if thus it be with you.

Meanes 3.

Take heed you do not run away with fuch comforts arifing from your feeding upon the promife and perfon of Chrift, without refrefhing the foule alfo with the good Will and Commands of Chrift; do not think your felves ready to enjoy Chrift, when his promife, perfon, and love is fweet, (which is good) but his will is bitter, and a burden to thy foul, even thy whole foul, (I know 'tis fo to the unregenerate part of godly men) for fuch men there be, 1 *John* 1. 6. To the Saints, Chrifts love is fweet, and promife fweet, and therefore his Will, his Work. *John* 4. 34. —— Bread you know not of, *to do the Will of him that fent me, and to finifh it*; fo it is their food to do the Will of him that loves them, and to finifh it; If a man is to remove from one Countrey to another, and he cannot live upon the Bread of the Countrey, nor water where he goes, he is then unfit for fuch a Journey, becaufe he cannot live upon the bread of it. Now what is that which feeds the life of Saints in glory? not only Chrift, but living unto Chrift, to be perfected under the Government and Kingdom of Chrift; can you live upon this now in part, and the firft fruits of it? if you can, know it is then prepared for thee, and thou for it; if not, but you live (as you fay) upon the prefent fweet of the promife; nay, it may be upon the thoughts of old comforts; but to do the Will of Chrift, is death, not life to you; and it is meerly your task for wages, to do his Will, not part of your Inheritance, you are unfit to be with Chrift; *Acts* 21. 13. *Why break you my heart?* (faith *Paul*) *I am ready to die for the fake of Chrift,* and to do much more; So think thus, Was *Paul* ready to die, and I not ready to do? my heart loaths thy Commands Lord; but what the Law makes heavy, the Gofpel makes fweet; for thy fake, Lord, I love thy will; pray, Oh thy love is fweet, but let thy will be fo alfo.

Labour to grow poor in spirit, that when you cannot honour the Lords Will, yet you may be gathering something out of all sinnes and weaknesses, to honour Gods grace; the glory of grace is the last end; those that be prepared for it, shall enjoy it; Who are those? The poore, who when they see they have lost their lives, their soules, their comforts, in not doing his Will, which is bitter to them, yet the Lord shall not lose the honour of his grace, *Psalme* 74. 21. The poor will be thankfull; What doth *Paul*, that Vessel of grace, Persecutor, Blasphemer, but a Saint, now say? Oh but the least of them; but he was an Apostle; but I deserve not that name; but yet he is received to mercy; 'tis very true, yet never such an example, as he thinks; and therefore saith he To the King immutable, &c. when *Jacob* had seen the Lord, *Gen.* 26. *ult.* if he shall give me food and rayment, he shall be my God (*i. e.* I shall then magnifie him, he having said he would be so before, and he had it in plenty; So say, If the Lord shall pity, pardon, I shall then give all to him, if I had a thousand hearts, tongues; truly as *Psalme* 40. *ult. The Lord now thinketh on you*; When a Servant hath spent and lost his Masters estate, and he is to give up an Account, truly then he may give it with comfort, when as he gaines one way abundantly, though he loseth another, and makes the best gaines; so here.

SECT. XV.

2. **T**O those who are ready, but yet not so ready as is meet.

The Lord hath given you warning to prepare, by some sharp afflictions on thy self, or by the death of thy friends, or by secret feares of thine own heart, thy time is not many hands breadth longer; and it may be this shall be the Funeral Sermon of some of you; you have been flying like Bees abroad in the world to gather your honey, and the Lord hath been smoaking of you, and that in your own Hive; you have thought to dwell long in Tabernacles; the Lord hath let it fall to decayes, and repaires it not again.

If you live unready, it may be the Lord will try you with some sore conflict, with fears of death, and terrors of darkness; and all your preparation is too little for your combate then.

The place of glory is made ready for you; how shall I so unholy, see God? Christ is there *John* 14. 3. waiting for thee, longing after thee.

Thou art it may be yet in many respects unready. As

1. Not yet planted in the House and Church of God, not yet gathered to communion of Christ in his Saints on earth. I know men may have just reasons to deferre; but if they have none, I would be loth to die in their room; *Hezekiah, Isa.* 38. *ult. Psalme* 26. 8. *I have loved the habitation of thy House; Oh gather not my soule with the wicked.* I am perswaded, some deare to Christ linger here, and you cannot finde this nor that saving good in your selves, you say; I had rather hear one mourn for emptinesse, than boast of his grace.

2. There are many sinnes not yet mourned sufficiently for, in dayes
of

of youth, and in a secure condition; in heaven is no mourning; oh therefore take time now, for want of this grace is not so sweet.

3. It may be some main duty is neglected to the souls of them, whom thou hast a charge of, as not Catechising thy family, children not careful for their souls.

4. It may be thou hast been little in prayer for the Churches (though for thy family and children) which is usually the last work of the Saints; there's no praying for them in Heaven; as Christ at the end of his life like a Priest shed blood, and prayed for them, so Saints are made Priests to God and Christ.

5. It may be thy house is not yet set in order, nor thy Will made, Reckonings between men not yet set right and even, and then there is Quarrels when thou art Dead, and trouble when you dye.

6. It may be thou art grown secure, and art lost, and driven away, and many wrinckles be on thy face and heart, &c. you cannot say with *Paul*, 2 *Tim.* 4. *That you have fought, &c.* but are rather at truce with sin; you run not, but have slipt, and fallen down, and so lost all.

SECT. XVI.

THerefore to help here in this readiness, *Get a heart more loosned and weaned from the world.* *Solomon* he did launch out his heart herein too far; not in Epicurisme, but *Eccles.* 2. 3. *applying his heart to wisdome* all this time; so may you, and be unready; How? I cannot, but God will teach it you by affliction. *Psalme* 39. 6, 7. You are Sojourners here with God, as all your Fathers; there's nothing proper, nothing long to be enjoyed.

Own the Lord Jesus; he is yours, but you own him not; as *Simeon* came to the Temple and there found him, and there blest God; *and now* (saith he) *let me depart in peace;* hath the Lord stirred up unutterable sighings, and groanings, and mournings, (you think (it may be) if Christ was present, you would not doubt of answer) and they continue still, and do you think Christ is hard-hearted? hath the Lord come to thee in the Temple, and manifested his love by his own promise, sure, and faithful, and wilt thou not yet own him? hast had, and hast now the first fruition of the Spirit, and wilt not yet own him? and art afraid to go to him, when others are in glory that trod in thy steps? Oh be humbled for it; I know there is nothing which makes thee feare it, but a Rebellious vile heart, and nature; and can the Lord love such a one? Yes, such a one, if he mournes under it, *Rom.* 7. 24. *Isa.* 57. 18, 19. *The Lord will create peace; he hath seen thy wayes, and he will heale them;* And when you have him thus, own him daily, keep your peace, do nothing which may make you lose boldness in prayer, and therefore reckon daily with him; and Remember, the promise stands, when feelings are lost.

Object. *But I can do but little for him.*

Answ. True, *Isa.* 64. 6. Thou the Lords clay, his Vessel, though of little publique use, yet in thy place do what thou canst for Christ Jesus. Servants, Masters, Members, Rich, Poore, be-

beftirre your felves for Chrift , you fhall lofe nothing by it , &c.

VERSE 10.

The Door was fhut.

IN thefe words is fet down the confequent of that which immediately followed the Wife Virgins gracious entertainment with Chrift ; *the door was fhut*, by which is fignified the exclufion of the foolifh from the fellowfhip of Chrift ; as alfo the greatnefs of Chrifts love to the wife , opening the door of glory unto them ; and when they are gathered , fhutting the door againft every one elfe.

Hence Obferve,

That the endeared love of Chrift to his Elect, doth much appear in this, In opening the door of glory unto them , and fhutting it againft others of great efteem and name in the Church of God; for this is one Scope of the words, Gen. 7. 16. | Obferv. 1.

To open the Kingdome of Heaven to all the world, and fave all, would be great love in the eyes of the Saints; but to fave them, and condemne others ; to receive them, and exclude others, and that of great name and efteem, Virgins, this fets out the Lords love exceedingly; Chrifts diftinguifhing, feparating love, is his great love, *Mat.* 11. 25.

If we confider the multitude of the one, and fewnefs of the other ; not only in regard of the world, but in regard of others in Churches , Luke 13. 24. *Many fhall feek , and many that are firft , fhall be laft , Matthew* 19. 30. | Reafon 1.

If we confider that there is as much reafon appearing outwardly, that the Lord fhould choofe thee one as well as the other; what difference is appearing outwardly between thefe Virgins ? I'le warrant you the wife did think the foolifh as good, and it may be far better than themfelves. *Judges* 6. 15. Saith *Gideon, How wilt thou fave Ifrael by me ? I am the leaft in my Fathers houfe*; yet faith the Lord , *I will be with thee* ; fo the Saints may fay, and do fay , Why Lord, wilt thou fave me, I am the leaft and pooreft of all others. | Reafon 2.

If we confider the reafon why the Lord doth this, and that is becaufe of nothing but the Will of God, his good pleafure; *Matth.* 11. 25. For why fhould their Veffels be filled; they received, and not others only the Will of God ; *I know not you*, &c. Of which hereafter. | Reaf. 3.

If we confider the intolerable torment of thofe who go farre , and yet are excluded. Mat. 8. 11, 12. *Children of the Kingdome caft out, there fhall be weeping*; the higher a man is rifen, the greater is his fall, and his bruifes at the bottome ; fo when one hath been raifed up to great hopes, profeffion, affection, yet now to fall, to lofe all, to fee he hath been fpinning Cobwebs all his life ! when *Ifrael* were near to *Canaan*, now to be fhut out! Now they wept. | Reaf. 4.

Uuu

We

Use 1.

Use 1. We may see hence, what little cause any have to boast only in outward priviledges, or common gifts, graces, excellencies. I confess it is great mercy for the Lord to call a man out of his prophaneness, and separate him from the world, bringing him to the fellowship of Saints; and give him that which makes him reputed well of by others; but boast not only of this, as if the Lord did therefore highly favour you; for the Lord Jesus may shew (for all this) his love to his own, and his terrour to thee, and may shut the door of glory at last upon thee. 1 *Cor.* 1. 27, 28, 29. *The Lord chooses things that are not, to bring to nought and to staine other glory.* Rom. 11. 17. The *Gentiles* boasted themselves, that they were *graffed in*; oh saith the Apostle (seeing this spirit apt to rise) *boast not*, be not high-minded, do not grow secure, but feare; common graces ever make men proud, as others make men humble; they despise not others, they magnifie God, if the Lord hath made a difference; see the goodness of God, *verse* 22. but boast not therein; therefore do not content thy self with a name to live, and having some cankered hopes, some shining excellencies; for the Lord may do this to shew others his love, and yet staine thy glory; as one that hath great hopes of preferment, many Friends to commend and speak for him, if one tells him, You shall certainly lose all your labour, he will mourn more than another that had no hopes, nor helps at all of rising; he will not glory in any thing he hath, but will take some sure and safer way; So I say to you, If there be the least Grace and Favour, blesse God for that, but do not boast of any thing else.

Use 2.

Use 2. Hence the Saints may learne how to affect their hearts with the Lords love to them (for there is such a poysonful disposition in them, that though they have it, yet they cannot be affected sometimes with it: *Up Deborah, Awake Lute and Harpe*) and 'tis this; Do not only Remember, and think on the Lords love saving thee, calling, humbling, &c. but so as to call thee, and leave others; to quicken thee, and leave others dead; to open the door of glory to thee, and exclude others; to call thee out of the Kingdome of the world, to look upon thee in a sinful Town, to awaken thee, and leave others (so many) secure, to call thee out of thy sinful company, some of which like brands, are now smoaking in this world, others burning in another; to call thee out of a sinful, ignorant family, thou the least, the worst of them, and to leave the rest, this is much!

But when thou art brought into the Kingdome of Heaven, Fellowship of Saints, for the Lord to love thee, set his heart upon thee, when he forsakes others of thy own company, of great parts and abilities, whom thou thinkest better of than thy self, at least as well; to pull down these Princes to the dunghill, and to exalt thy horn; to cut down these Cedars, and to preserve a Shrub; to tread upon the greatest glory of man, and to pity a worm, for so thou art in thine own eyes; Oh let this fire warme thy heart, though thou hast been affected with it before, especially considering no reason for it, but only the good pleasure of God; this affected Christ himself, *Mat.* 11, 25. 'Tis true, you do not see this done, but you shall one day behold it with your eyes; only let this love kindle love, thankfulness, humility in thine heart againe.

And hence, if the Lord hath put a difference between thee and others, do not deny, do not doubt of, do not despise his grace; that if thou hast lost thy first love, this may recover it; if all his love makes thee more humble, and thankful, *you stand*, Rom. 11. 20. *Isa.* 65. 16. Do not feare

thy

thy estate, becaufe the Lord cuts off the natural branches, that therefore thou mayft be one; but befeatful of the leaft fin, and wrong to Chrift, that hath loved thee, efpecially of pride, and unthankfulnefs the root of that; and Remember, that the poor things are chofen to confound the Mighty.

That the door of grace and glory fhall be fhut against all wicked men living, at the coming of the Lord to death or judgement; there is a time that the door is open unto men, in regard of Minifterial difpenfations (for fecrets of election we are not to minde) *Ifa.* 55. 6, 7. This time is in this life; but when death comes, then it is fhut; when Angels finned, the Lord immediately fhut the door againft them; but through Chrift the door is open for term of life to men.

Obferv. 2.

Becaufe after death there is no meanes of grace or glory left, which is the Miniftry of the Word and Prayer; for that is the chief key of opening the door, even when the doores of heart and heaven are fhut, Mat. 16. 19. and hence, 2 *Cor.* 6. 2. Now is the time of prayers and preaching, and fo to be helped; but after death there are no Minifters, they are at reft from their labours; and the Miniftry of men is for men, not for naked foules. *Lazarus* muft not give a drop of cold water then to cool the tongue, much lefs Minifters to comfort or convert their hearts; 'tis true, the Lord can work extraordinarily; but do you think he will do it for one that hath defpifed grace all his life?

Reafon 1.

Becaufe it's impoffible they fhould repent after death, by any other means (if meanes were afforded) as by feeing their finne, and feeling their punifhment. John 9. 4. The night cometh wherein no man can work; becaufe after death, comes judgement of wrath to the wicked, *Heb.* 9. *ult.* all patience, and pity have forfaken them, and fo wrath lies upon them, that they can do nothing but bear it; as one under a great load, or burning in the fire, all his thoughts, and affections, and fpirits, are taken up with that, and that is all he can do, *Heb.* 10. 27. So here.

Reafon 2.

Ufe 1. Of Confutation of a viperous, fatanical, fecret opinion, which like a ghoft haunts the mindes of fome people, (*viz.*) that think and conclude even in time of health, in midft of faving healing meanes, that their time of grace is paft, and door is fhut to them, before Chrift comes againft them at death or judgement; which though God many times turnes for good, to humble a bold heart which will burne Gods day-light out, and linger in its finnes, yet it doth fometimes dead the heart from all effectual endeavours, and difcourage the heart from all duties, makes all the Gofpel the Miniftry of blood and death, and a hand-writing againft it; and when it concludes God hath fhut the door againft it, it fhuts God, and Chrift, and all his Promifes out of its heart.

Ufe. 1.

1. Some think they having finned againft light, have had fome blafphemous thoughts, that they have committed the unpardonable fin, &c.

2. Some others think not fo, but yet they heare that fome mens time is out before death; they think theirs is alfo, having fought fo long, they are even fealed up by God to hardnefs of heart; and thus fome feemingly coming to Chrift, are indeed kept off from him.

3. Others of the Saints meeting with many fore troubles and tryals, and that for fome fins; and one deep calling to another, they think with *David*,

God hath forgot, hath ſhut up his mercies, will remember no more to be gracious; and though he hath been ſo, yet becauſe he hath been ſo abuſed by them, that therefore now he will not be merciful again; and thus their hearts ſink.

Oh Remember, the Gate of Gods Grace is not ſhut up before death, then is the time for it to be ſhut. I confeſs indeed there is a time in this life, the Lord doth ceaſe to ſtrive, and doth forſake the ſoul; and we may ſay of them, as Chriſt, *Oh that thou hadſt known ! but now they are hid from thine eyes;* ——— But yet this is a ſecret, which as a ſecure deſpiſer of grace ſhould tremble at; ſo thoſe that are awakened, and ſet in their way to Chriſt, ſhould not trouble themſelves about it.

Object. *But oh that I did know, whether it be paſt or no!*

Anſw. I ſhall rather give to theſe people ſome good counſel, for 'tis not for you to know theſe times and ſeaſons; though this I would ſay, if the impardonable ſin be not committed.

1. This time of the doores being ſhut, is not in time of health and peace, but in time of extream trouble, wherein trouble doth affect them more than the ſin; as *Prov.* 1. and as many when a ſick bed is come, and in *Noahs* Flood, 1 *Pet.*3.20.

2. Or if it be in time of health, this is ever the companion of it, (viz.) hatred, and oppoſing Saints ſecretly or opening, becauſe Chriſt having quite forſaken him, his heart ſwells againſt the Saints; hence *Saul* envied *David,* *Eſau* hated *Jacob* Murmurers againſt God; were in the Wilderneſs, and againſt *Moſes*; But I come to counſel; for God lets looſe Satan full of malice, upon a poor creature, ſometimes to vex and trouble.

Firſt, *Conſider the root of this diſtemper,* (viz.) either great pride, or deſpiſing of the riches of Gods grace.

1. Pride, for (this we ſhall finde) ſuch ſpirits, becauſe they have not peace ſealed, ſtrength againſt ſin granted unto them, and that which they would have, (if diſcouraged, and not quickened by this) they regard not life, meanes, offers of grace; What is all this, if God hath forſaken me? What is it? Yes, that 'tis; as might at large be ſhewed.

2. Deſpiſing of grace; if I had not committed ſuch ſins, I could then think for mercy; but ſuch evils, ſuch miſeries, cannot be remedied. Truly, as it is a deſpiſing of a Phyſician, to think, If I was not ſo ſick, he would be tender, and helpful; but not now, being ſo exceedingly diſeaſed; So it is here, &c.

Secondly, *Conſider,* Suppoſe the time be paſt, yet remember thou art worthy to be forſaken of God even from thy birth, not worthy of thy daily bread, much leſs to taſte of Gods Supper; the Lord was loth to ſhut the door; Hence *he wept on Jeruſalem;* and *Pſalme* 81. 12. cryed out, *Oh that my people had walked in my wayes !* thy ſinnes provoked the Lord unto it, if he hath in juſtice caſt thee off; therefore though it be paſt, be not diſcouraged, but lie down humbled, as *Judges* 10. 14, 15. and as *David,* *Pſal.* 42. 3. *My teares are my meat, whiles they ſay ſo, Where is your God ?* So tell the Lord, Satan ſaith, and feeling faith, and feares ſay, Where is my God? Lord pity! And if thy heart be ſick, tell the Lord of it, *Verſe* 6. I am perſwaded many ſhould quickly feele an Anſwer to this Queſtion, by taking this courſe; but they miſs at leaſt of the comfort of Grace and Mercy, becauſe they will be Diſpoſers of the Lords Grace and Time.

Thirdly, *Conſider,* it may be that time is not paſt, it is a ſecret only known to God; the door of grace may only ſeem to be ſhut; why doth Chriſt bid knock elſe? When the *Ninevites* heard that they ſhould dye within fourty dayes,

dayes, *Jonah* 3. 9. say they, *Who can tell but the Lord may repent?* you say the Decree is past, and spoken; and as *Spira* said, I have that Witnessed. I say againe, Who can tell, but (if God had said so, but) that he may repent? therefore be not discouraged, or faint because of this. Nay, 'tis most probable time is not past.

1. Because the things of thy peace, the discovery of the vileness of thine own heart, the glory of Christ, is not hid from thine eyes.

2. God calls thee now to returne; When *Judah* had banisht *David*, and they might think He will not receive us; yet when *David* sent by his Messengers, *Why do you not bring the King back? I am flesh of your flesh*; then they all were encouraged to hope for favour, 2 *Sam.* 19. 12, 14. So,

4. *Consider*, if thou dost return, the time of love is so farre from being past, as that it is then come indeed unto thy soul.

Object. But my sin is great!

Answ. Suppose it be lasphemy of Christ, nay, murder of the Sonne of God; yet *Acts* 2. 38. when *Peter* preached *Repentance to life*, they that gladly received that word, who might be instrumental to crucifie Christ, were received. Oh but my heart is hard! *Hosea* 10. 12. break up your fallow ground, &c. 'Tis time, saith he, &c.

Object. But I have refused to returne, and have not been ashamed!

Answ. Yet, *Jer.* 3. 3, 4, 5. *Wilt thou not from this time cry to me? &c.*

Object. But I may returne to the Lord, and he refuse to returne to me.

Answ. No, *Jer.* 8. 7. *Shall he fall, and not arise? shall the Lord turn away, and not return?* why then is he fallen perpetually, the reason is given, *No man said, What have I done, how have I despised God; grace? the Stork knows her season*; but, &c. the Lord keep you from dashing your selves in pieces here, and make this a Word of Christs Encouragement to thee.

Use 2. Of Exhortation *unto all men, not to delay your making peace with God*; for when you are dead, the gate is shut; and if Angels should cry to have it opened, they shall not be heard.

You that are young, take warning this day, do not think there is time enough hereafter: You that are old, do not think it too late, or that it would be a shame for you to begin now, who have propt up your hearts with base comforts; you that have been stirred, but are now faln asleep, beware of dying in your ditches, and pits, wherein you are faln; you must stand before God shortly. Though you never repented yet, &c. never was in bitterness, never had any great mourning, &c. never knew the life of Christ, peace of conscience, never felt the Kingdome, and mighty power of Christ, yet despaire not, for yet there is hope; but if once death comes, then thou art gone; it is day yet, and Christ holds open his wings yet; but if death comes, his time is our.

Object. But I have a faire time yet before me.

Answ. 1. It may be not, for thou art condemned already.

2. If you have, yet wilt abuse patience, and forbearance of God? wilt despise what leads thee to repentance! as a man sinking, spits in the face of him that holds up his Head; wilt thou be worse than a devil?

Objection. But a little repentance will serve the turne, 'tis quickly done?

Answer. Oh no! as *Paul* said, *I have fought a good fight*; thou hast

sins

sins as dear as thy life to forsake ; thou hast Devils, World to wrestle with ; nay , God himself to wrestle with ; you cannot runne your Race in a day.

Object. *What if I be shut out ?*

Answ. I say no more but only what *Solomon* said , *Prov.* 5. 11, 12, 13. *O how have I hated reproof* ! that shall be thy woful dirge another day, when shut out ; oh never to have one look, one word from Christ, but to see him afar off , this shall be thy fearful portion hereafter. Truly we may take up that complaint of Christ, You can discerne the times of the Weather, not Christs coming.

VERSE 11, 12.

Afterward came also the other Virgins , saying , Lord , Lord , open un-to us.

But he answered , and said , Verily I say unto you, I know you not.

IN these two Verses, is set down the entertainment Christ gives unto the foolish Virgins , and his behaviour toward them ; and that is, he did not own them as his, but saith, *I know you not.* Their miserable rejection is aggravated from these particulars, shewing their misery.

1. The note of certainty of this, *Verily, &c.*

2. Though they came afterward to the Lord, (it is not said, with their Oyle in their Vessels, &c.)

3. Though they prayed to the Lord to open when they came.

4. Though they prayed earnestly, *Lord, Lord.*

5. Though they sought thus with Arguments , *Lord, Lord* , as if they should say , Thou art our Lord and Saviour, we look for life from none but thee.

Oserv. 1.

That after the coming of Christ to death or judgement , then shall those who are most secretly wicked , know certainly that the gate is shut, and their exclusion, and final separation from the face of Christ.

These foolish Virgins had some hopes and assurances of mercy, whiles the Bridegroom was absent in their life ; so men have in this world such hopes ; but when Christ came, and shut the door upon them , then they knew their miserable condition.

This life is compared unto a sleep, and dreame, *Psa'me* 90. 5. wherein men understand and conceive of things with false shapes ; so here ; but when they awaken , then they appeare otherwise ; after death men are awakened, and then they see things as they are ; the Parable of the rich man , *Luke* 16. proves this.

Reason 1.

Because then God lets in a new light, most full and cleare , to see and know things as they are , and so to know themselves and their estates ; it is an Atheists speech, *Eccles.* 9. 5, 7, 10. *That the dead know not any thing* ; and hence , be as merry as you can , eat thy bread with joy, &c. No, now they do know, &c. as the Saints know their eternal acceptation, by a most glorious light ; God walks darkly here, but then this full light shall come in; As it is with a man that is to be condemned , before he be cast, the Judge
brings

brings in full evidence; so *Heb.* 9. *ult.* *After death cometh judgement*; there is full evidence; when *Adam* stood before God, the Lord fully convinced him; when death comes, then there is an end of mens *Stewardships*, *Luke* 16. 2. and when an end comes to that, what comes then? Come give up thy account; now those whose reckonings are naught, must either deceive and blinde the all-searching eyes of God, and so not be found out, or they shall see wherein they have been faithless and false. What is spoken of the general Judgement, is true also of this particular; it is the day of Revelation; God himself will now cleare up matters as Christ here doth, *Verily, I know you not.*

Reas. 2.

Because then the soul will desire to know, and have leisure to see and know it self; as these foolish Virgins, their souls were looking (in a sort) in their life-time for Christ, but now they look and see indeed; some know not themselves, though having light; nor their present misery, because they desire not to know; and hence reflect not upon themselves according to light now; or if they desire so to do, yet they have not leisure; the noise and multitude of cares, keeps them from a cleare knowing of their estates: but now men shall be brought to the Land of solitariness, and shall have leisure to see, having Gods light let in to see by; there shall then be no business, but only to consider, Who am I? and what have I done? men shall have no Cities to build, nor business to do, as *Falix* then, and hence put out the light.

Reas. 3.

Because then conscience is throughly awakened, because it is a time of judgement now; and if so, then the witnesses must appeare; though they have been silent long before, they shall be forced to speak. Now it is wonderful to see what conscience will speak when God awakens it; men many times will not see the evil which they have done; but conscience will make them see it, nay, confess it, when 'tis awakened. Three things conscience will do, when it is awakened.

1. It will shew a man his chief sins, which he defended, which he extenuated, which he never suspected; *These things hast thou done.*

2. It can bring fresh to memory sins forgotten, sleighted, dead and buried, a great number, all of them as if new done. *John* 4. 29. *all things that ever I did.*

3. It can, and will aggravate all these things and sins, and present them in the greatness of them, that mens mouths shall pass their own Sentence upon them, as *Cain* did; that let all the world perswade them their case is good, they cannot believe it; now this we see in this life in some; but when life is ended, then these things shall be acted much more lively, *Psal.* 50. 21. *I will reprove thee;* even of what they thought God did approve, *and I will set them in order,* in their number and greatness before thy eyes; *i. e.* of conscience; all falshoods, deceits, loathsome tricks, &c. I did this and that, but I had these ends in them, and I harboured these sins by them, will conscience make men say.

Reas. 4.

Because now Satan, to whose custody the soul is committed, appears to the soul, and it sees it self in his hands. The best Hypocrite is never delivered out of the hands of Satan and his power; he will either keep constant possession; or if not, yet he will returne againe; now he will not appear in this time of peace to the soul, because there is yet hope; but after death, then hope is past, and therefore then he appeares; for as the souls of the Elect are carryed to Heaven by Angels, and blessed among them; so *è contra,* trà, the souls of the wicked are in the hands of Devils; 1 *Pet.* 3. 19. *He preacht to the spirits now in Prison*; Theeves, so long as they are not known, or if known, not apprehended, they fear not death; but when taken, and laid up in prison, there they know their death , and there they see their Jaylour; so here; and as Satan did condemne , and sad the heart of the humbled out-cast, 2 *Cor.* 2. 11. so much more these, when cast out from the presence of God. A Captive when taken by him that hath overcome him , the Conquerour appeares, and sets his foot upon him, especially if one eminent whom Satan hath conquered.

Reason 5. Because of the intolerable and heavy wrath of God , which then doth seize upon the soul. *Luke* 16. *I am tormented*: In this life, though God be lost, yet mens hearts are comforted with creatures , and patience, and common bounty; as it is with skall'd legs, eased in the water; but now when men are dead, then there is no creature to enjoy, to ease the heart ; the body is dead , and what are these things to the soul; now hence the soule feels God is gone, and for ever gone ; and now when he hath most need, in great torment gone, the soul feels this, I say; and feeling this woe , it knows it indeed; the beasts know their misery, when they feel the Knife in their hearts. Let men deceive themselves never so deeply with false imaginations, yet when they feel it otherwise , it shall confute them , as the Generations of men in the dayes of *Noah* ; men will have some hope while patience lasts, but when that's gone , then their hopes and hearts sink also; whiles men be in the Vessel , they hope to live , but if that sink , and they can see no plank, nor shore, but see waves, and men crying, &c. now their hearts must needs fail them.

Use 1. *Of terrour to them who upon cleare conviction from the Word, will not believe their doom, their misery now.* Sometime the Word comes so near men, and the very sin they live and lie in, is pointed at, found out , and words, and thoughts opened , as if some body had told the Minister of the man; and they think He speaks against me, but they will not believe that sin is so black, or God so angry, but hope well; but if they do sleight, and regard not these convictions , yet oh remember the time is drawing on , and it is not farre of , but therein you shall know, the word of the Lord is more precious to him than to you; you let it fall, but the Lord will not; 1 *Sam.* 3. 19. The Old World would not believe *Noah*, the Lord therefore made their experience convince them of it. I know men may be deceived; but as he said in another case, The word is not bound; so the word which like God, searcheth the secrets of thy heart, and thy Hypocrisie, that is not deceitful; thy Scepter, O Lord, is a right Scepter, and it cannot be crook't and bent. And if man doth condemn thee, know it, God is greater then man, and it is his glory to confirm the words of his Servants , that are not Diviners, South-sayers, and uncertaine Prognosticators of mens destinies, *Isa.* 44. 26. but having their warrant from the Word, it shall be confirmed by God himself; nay, that very Word shall arise, though it sleeps now; the Word is only left as a *Witnesse*, *Matth.* 24. 14. and do you think it shall not be so? if Christ lives, he will confirm it. Is it not better to know your condition now, and be humbled for it, seeing else you must know it, when it is too late to know it? If two have a Quarrel against each other, and the one who hath the better side entreats to agree with him, to acknowledge his fault, be humbled, he will forgive him, before he comes to higher Courts where it will be tried, and himself cast , and such a Fine, and damages be set upon his head, as will utterly undo him; is it not a misery for such an one so brought under, to feed himself with hopes, and not to listen, till he hath spent all, and is utterly undone, and beggar'd; truly thus 'tis here; And so I end, with reminding you of the speech of God to *Elies* Sons, 1 *Sam.* 2. 25. *They heard not their father, because God would slay them;* so here you will not hear Ministers condemne you, because God will do it.

Use 2.

See the great folly of those, who having got some false comforts, and are loth to know the worst of their estates now; *Isa.* 30. 10. that say to the Prophets, *Prophesie deceits;* or if not, they will not come to the light; *John* 3. 20. or if light come to them, *they hate it,* and put it out, choak it, if they do not also hate the man. Shall you know your estates hereafter, and will you not see them now? what comfort will this be to you? There is a Beast, when it is hunted, and weary, runnes its head into the ground or bushes, and thinks it self then safe, though its body be all seen, and that the Hunter doth not see it, nor the Hounds, because it sees not them; So it is here; What will it profit you to hide your eyes from the Almighties search, who cannot hide your selves? It's true, if there was no hope now, then men might comfort themselves, and not dye with thoughts and fears of it, till they come to dye; but there is hope; —— Oh folly not to see it now! and truly this is mens frame.

1. Because some think it a shame to begin now, after they have been so well thought of, now to strip themselves.

2. Because of trouble, men naturally will avoid it, and hence skin their sores over superficially.

3. Because they think it impossible, or very difficult to be saved now, if all should be naught that they have done already; and hence, rather hazard all, and put it to the venture.

4. Because they must maintaine their innocency and confidence. What? must I not believe, nor hope well?

5. Because when they have done their best, they can do no more than what they do now, *viz.* trust to Gods mercy.

But more particularly this appeares

First, When men will not see, nor desire the Lord to reveal their sinne and deceits, *Psalme* 36. 3. That's one part of heart-flattery, not to see to do good; a gracious heart is broken off from flattery; he knows it, and hence will to the Lord; when he knows not himself, and his estate, Lord teach me; the damning sin, is some dear sin; a sin which the soul allowes habitation, and house-roome, and heart-roome unto; and hence it will not see it, because it would not part with it; and hence it saith, It cannot see it, because it will not, it's in love with the flattery of it; and hence 'tis strange to see some that live in oppression by unlawful prizes, and exacting immoderate wages, cannot see their sin, though privately, and publickly spoken of, because they will not; cannot see it, because they will not; 'tis strange to see how time-servers will defend their Fashions; and they cannot see it, because the heart is secretly in love with such vanities; and 'tis just, seeing they love not the truth, they should be deceived by errors; Two wayes men have to hide their sins from God himself.

1. By covering them with reason; A man that is ashamed of his na-kednesse or sore, he will get a covering for it; hereby one may know what a mans chief sin is; *viz.* by his reasonings for it; as one may know where the eggs be, by the Hens sitting upon them, and truly, a little reason will blinde the eyes many times; nay, though God and Scripture be brought in; *Balaam* would fain finde out some light from God to curse, and from Altar

X x x

to

to Altar he went , &c. but found nothing ; Thus here , &c.

2. By covering them with duties and sorrows, and yet keeping them ; for when men do see their sin , and 'tis great , what do they therefore ? they wash it with teares ; they confess it as those, *Isa.* 58. 5, 6. they fast for strife or debate ; they would be vexed with enraged consciences but for these duties ; and this makes them hope well ; and here come in those distinctions , I have sins as others, but I mourn under them ! oh but Remember, those sorrows destroy sin by little and little , and do not feed sin ; but these ease thee in thy sin ; *Hosea* 10. 4. *Hemlock growes up in the Furrows* ; *you speak words* , saith the Lord , &c. So here, &c.

Secondly, When men are willing the Lord should let them see their sin, but unwilling to attend him in the use of all meanes for that end ; especially these two.

1. Diligent watch over the heart daily , by frequent reflecting upon its own acts ; it's strange to see what discoveries might be made by observing ends, aimes, motives of workings ; Hence Christ beats much upon this.

2. Daily Meditation in some solemn manner. 2 *Tim.* 2. 7. *Consider what I say* ; *and the Lord shall give thee understanding* ; 'Tis a thousand to one if men do not lose themselves, and souls in neglect of this. *Hag.* 1. 5, 7. *David* said, *I considered my wayes* , *and turned.* Now to say, Let the Lord search me, but not to use means, is to shut your eyes against the book, and say , Now Lord teach me.

Use 3.

Of Exhortation ; Oh therefore know the worst of your own hearts now. *Phil.* 2. 12. *Work out your salvation with feare* : Saints with a feare of careful search , but you much more. *Gen.* 27. 11, 12. When *Rebeccah* would have *Jacob* go to *Isaac* , saith *Jacob* , *What if my Father feel me* ! *I may get a curse then.* So the Lord Jesus (believe it) will feel thee ; he will see who thou art , before he let thee into Heaven ; if thou art a stranger to thy sin , and Christ, and his grace, thou shalt see the gate shut upon thee hereafter ; therefore know it now how 'tis with thee ; nothing will be such a cut to thy heart as this , *viz.* when 'tis too late to see the sin which ruined ; oh this will torment ! as it doth Politicians, when they see, There I forsook a Rule of Policy , there I was mistaken ; if I had carried the business otherwise there, then I had got this ; oh it troubles them ; so it will do you , when you shall see your Projects and Hopes dasht.

Quest. How shall I know this ?

Answ. 1. Mark what others, godly, and discerning, speak, or fear concerning thee ; for though God reveals not a Hypocrite to all, yet 'tis seldom but it is to some or other. 1 *Tim.* 5. 25. not speak against, yet not give a full Testimony.

2. Mark what conscience speaks, or feares thee with in cool blood , without getting those feares quencht by fresh Application of Christs blood ; it's said, The feares of the wicked shall come upon him ; there are some hot pangs which men have , and then think well of themselves, but generally live out from God and Christ. Mark which way the scale turnes , when you are still; the worme that is not killed, will gnaw for ever , if it bites now.

3. Mark what troubled thee when afflictions were upon thee ; then God many times convinceth men of folly ; when *Benjamins* sack had the Cup , *The Lord hath found out our iniquity* , said they, *Gen.* 44. 16. So some

evils

evils may be falsely imputed, but then you shall see some other sin (it may be) for which the Lord may have had long, a Controversie with you.

4. Mark what thou art when crossed; many a one is good, while men and God please him; but when reproof comes, or he is crost, then he is mad, hair-brain'd, hateful, scornful, wilful, *Ecclef.* 10. 11. for men may be crost of their will, but their own ends they will not be crost in; Mark how you deny your own ends in what you do, then you may appeale to God indeed.

5. Mark your temptations, and corruptions, with opposition; if all be quiet, either there is a truce for a time, or else there is peace between you and sinne, and Satan, and so Warre between God and you.

6. Mark thy Opinions; Sometimes, faith *Solomon*, a fool is not known till then, *Prov.* 17. 28. for they arise (unless some in simplicity) from some corruption.

Queſtion 2. *How may the Saints come to be fetled, that they may know this?*

Anſwer 1. Beware of contenting your self with any measure; but with *Paul*, *reach after things before*, &c. for hence the foolish Virgins were deceived; but after all fillings be ever empty, hungry, and feeling need, and praying for more, setting thy self against all sin; say with *David*, *Cleanſe me from ſecret ſins.*

2. Strike at the root of all sin, (*viz.*) your evil natures, mourn daily under it, and the activity of it; and though some sins be unknown, yet when the root dyes, they shall dye. *Iſa.* 57. 18. When you mourn for this, God will speak peace.

3. Be sure your end be right, that having received Chriſt, and doing duties, you do them before him, and for his sake; for here Hypocrites fail; and this makes *Paul* to appeale to Chriſt, 2 *Cor.* 5. *Depart you workers of iniquity*, will Chriſt say hereafter; You have fought your selves in all this: Though the duty is hard, and thy heart loth to come to it, yet say, *For thy ſake, Lord, I love it.*

The earneſt cryes and prayers of unregenerate men at death or judgement, are then too late to procure mercy from the hands of Chriſt. If there be any means in time of diſtreſs to have help, it is by prayer; it helps the Saints out of deep pits, dark dungeons, *Lam.* 3. and Iron Furnaces, bitter agonies, intolerable preſſures; but this meanes, though they ſhall uſe it then, becauſe their torment is great, and their ſelf-love remaines, as theſe Virgins did, yet it comes too late then; I know their prayers differ; but of that I ſhall ſpeak hereafter. *Obſerv.* 2.

If in this life sometimes they come too late, much more after this; but ſo it is sometimes; *Prov.* 1. 28. *Pſal.* 18. 41. *Prov.* 15. 1. even unto the Lord. The Lord sees it meet to give a taſte of his ſeverity after life, and in this life, that men may fear, and the terrour may fall upon many. *Reaſon* 1.

Becauſe then Chriſt ſits upon the Throne of judgement, and ſo no Mediatour to help them, as hath been proved; and if it be ſo, *how ſhall they ſtand?* *Pſalme* 130. 3. In this life mercy waits, and patience bears, till it can bear no longer, and then doth eaſe it ſelf, *Ezekiel* 5. 13. and cries to juſtice, &c. And therefore the prayers and howlings of the wicked are to no more purpoſe than of a Malefactor before the Judge condemned for Treaſon. *Reaſon* 2.

Reaf. 1.

Because their cryes are but only *Howlings*, *Hosea* 7. 14. only rising from their own torment, because the Spirit of God is quite gone; and if the Lord should heare, they would be as bad againe as ever before; if mercy should save these Thieves from this Gallows, they would cut the Throat, and Stab the heart of mercy afterward; as all such persons do, who are carried from that principle in their prayers; and therefore let them never look to be heard now.

Use 1.

Hence see the exceeding greatnesse of the wrath of Christ, to them that die without him, Psalm 18. 41. Many times the Lord hides his face from his people for a time; but then they pray, and seek his face again, and the Lord heares them, and shines upon them again; when his Spirit in them speaks to him, his Son in his Covenant speaks unto them; and the Lord hears the cry of their weeping, as well as their praying, *Psalme* 6. 8. But if when they pray earnestly, and the Lord hears not then, but is angry with their prayers, oh this is bitter to them, *Psal.* 80. 4, 5. *Lem.* 3. 44. 'tis that which Christ typically complaines of, *Psal.* 22. 1, 2, 4, 5. There is no wrath like this; for a God so pitiful, as many times to help without cryes, more than a Mother with tender bowels, and not to regard cryes, as if he had cast off his nature; this makes wrath and sin bitter to the people of God; and indeed this is the reason why the Lord gives his people mercy; but 'tis by means of prayer usually, that they might see in what favour they are in his sight above others, that when he seems to be averse from hearing, yet prayer will turn the wheele, and *Jacob* prevailes over God, and hence *Psalme* 2. *Christ shall have all Nations for his possessions;* but yet Ask of me; as *Herod* said, when he said, *Ask of me,* to half of the Kingdome, &c. And hence exceeding wrath is shewn, in denying for a time, to hear prayer many times: Now look upon the condition of poore sinners dying without Christ; they shall then cry, and cry earnestly, and yet not prevail; if the wrath of God did break out at this time, and lie heavy, and the Lord say, Now cry, and I'le deliver; it was no such sorrow, though bitter enough to lie under wrath one moment; but to cry, and cry vehemently, Lord, Lord, and never to be heard, oh who can beare this! their torments are intolerable; hath the Lord no pity? their cries are many, and hearts are faint; hath Christ no bowels? hath this Lamb no more meeknesse, gentlenesse? yes, that there is; but such is his terrour now, they are shut up from you; and so shall ever be, though you shall cry, and weep as many teares, and more too than the Sea hath drops; and when you cannot come before his face, the Gate being shut, you shall cry, That the Rocks and Mountaines may fall upon you to hide you from this wrath of the Lamb; and you shall then cry, Behold, and see, if ever sorrow were like mine! but all shall be in vain.

Oh therefore see the greatnesse of this wrath, so as to see the bitternesse of any one sin, which stands yet between thee and Christ; which though it be sweet under thy tongue now, yet when the day of thy anguish shall come, it shall shut up Christs heart from hearing all cryes.

Use 2.

Of Exhortation, *To perswade all men to take their season of praying now.* Isa. 55. 1. with 6. when the Lord cryed, *Come to the waters, &c.* and because they might plead, *Hereafter;* oh saith he, *Call upon him whiles he is neare;* there will be a great Gulf between you and Christ, when you are dead; now therefore when the Lord comes in his Word especially, cry unto him for help and pity.

You

You will fay, There is no great need, thanks be to God, of prelling men to prayer here; Who is fo prophane but doth? he is not worthy to live, or to enjoy the benefit of the Sun, nor fit to live among the fociety of men, who dares not do thus, but to live among Bears and Wolves, and Beafts in the Wildernefs. I would to God there was no need to prefs this point; but truly, the Countrey being a place filled with difcontents, which ever keeps from prayer, becaufe the Devil is in them: and alfo of great peace and reft; hence, here men are more apt to fleep, and grow fecure, than in any other place of the world; and the Spirit of prayer is ready to dye, even in Gods own; and hard 'tis for this Incenfe to be fweet, without fome fire, fome affliction thereunto.

1. Some there be, that do not fo much as feel their mifery at all, neither fin nor wrath; and hence they cannot pray at all; they are not in fo good a cafe to pray, as the damned who feel their mifery, and cry out under it; thefe caft out of Gods fight, yet having hope, and fo fhould pray the more, and fo cry out under it, yet cannot; though the earth groanes under their fins, yet their hearts are hard, and they cannot feel them, and fo cannot pray; and they quiet themfelves with fome formes, and their Coleworts twice fodd, and fome cold prayers morning and evening, and hope that thefe will ferve the turn, and here is all the comfort they have; nay, not only fo, but if others that know their hearts better, and fo pray longer, reprove them for it, they finfully reply, What? you are like the Pharifees, that think to be heard for their long prayers. Oh the Lord gives many up to this fpirit of flumber, their hearts are heavy, and can no more lift them up than a ftone.

2. Some there be who feel their mifery, and go unto the Lord with many cries and prayers, but yet herein behave themfelves like *Saul*, when God anfwered him not, then they forfake him; and like them, *Mal.* 3. 14. *What profits us that we have walked mournfully?* and thinking they fhall not finde, they build their Cities as *Caine* did, and eafe themfelves that way.

3. Some there be that do not give over, becaufe they think they fhall not find, but eafe themfelves by their very prayers, pray out their prayers, and confefs out their confeffions, and mourn out their forrows; and are compared to the Dog, who eafeth himfelf by his vomit; they are troubled, and their prayer eafeth them; and when a little eafe, then prayer is done, as *Pfal.* 78. 35, 38.

4. Some that have no eafe, yet have no leifure, nor time; as many fervants, and men greedy of the world rife betimes, and work hard, fleepy at night, that they cannot have leifure; and when confcience asks, Why do you not take time? this is their excufe. Oh but cannot you take it out of your fleep, and lofe your life, rather than lofe your feafons of prayer? they hope hereafter fo to do.

5. Some that have leifure, yet their hearts are dead; they can pray, and ftand convinced of mifery; but I fay their hearts are dead. *Ifa.* 64. 7. *None ftirreth up himfelf;* nay, fometimes as a man afleep, when the fire burns round about him, yet he feels it not. *Ifa.* 42. *ult.* They can vex, and be difcontent when croffes and afflictions come, but no heart to pray, or lay their condition to heart: Oh this is fad and fearful.

I Befeech you therefore take your time now; you muft and fhall pray.

1. Do you think ever to have mercy without feeking it, and praying hard for it? No, if ever God intend good to thee, if an Elect Veffel, thou muft pray; yea, and glad you may have fuch an unvaluable priviledge, and that

that you are alive to do it. I know the Lord is found of them that seek him not; but he will make you seek, that so he may be found; seek therefore in time now, before it is too late.

2. Do not say the Gate is shut; no, 'tis yet open, and that by the blood of a Mediatour, *Heb.* 10. 19, 20. So that when you object God hears not sinners, yet *Zach.* 13. 1. *there is yet a fountain opened, for to wash in for sin and uncleannesse;* all thy sins cannot shut it, because 'tis opened to wash away sin.

3. Do not say, If I had a part in Christ, I could then be encouraged to ask. I pray what think you of that Woman of *Samaria*, when Christ spake, *If thou didst know and ask, he would give thee living waters;* What did the poor Woman of *Canaan* do, when Christ himself told her, She was a Dog, and had nothing to do with Childrens bread; when you have no Promise to assure you the Lord will give; yet the glorious bounty, and riches of grace, may encourage you sufficiently to seek.

4. Do not say, But it may be I shall be denied, let me pray never so long; I know you are worthy to be denied, and as you have cried the Lord should not heare, and as you have abused grace, it should cry against you, why should you Quarrel? the Lord owes thee not strawes; but yet Remember the Parable of the unjust Judge, who heard a woman, a stranger when importunate; and this is found a sure truth; 'tis with all men praying, as 'tis with women in travailing, either their pangs will deliver them of their burden, and so they live, or else they will be their death; if they cease, and give over, then they die. Prayer will deliver you of your sinnes, unbelief, or whatever stands between Christ and you; or if not, they shall die, and perish. Sow your seed of Prayer, it will multiply if it be the right seed, untill your Harvest be great, and your gain unknown; security will fall on a Hypocrite, before he gets the blessing, and the cares of the world will choak his prayers.

5. Oh therefore follow the Lord; *Hosea* 6. 3, 4. *You shall know him, if you follow on to know him;* especially if you be truly wounded, though he hath been as a Lion to you; Is Christ so glorious, his presence so sweet, his Kingdome so great, his mercy so rich, his Inheritance so full, and wilt not thou pray, awake one houre? hath Christ bought mercy with his blood, and wilt not thou spill thy blood? nay, not spare and spend thy poor prayers to beg it, (it may be praying time is declining apace) and so get it; and by that meanes hear Christ Jesus say, Come, oh come thou blest, that hast been praying, weeping, following me, and take thy Crown, and sit down on my Throne; oh it will be a cut to think, Had I sought it, I had had it! *Psal.* 24.

Use 3.   Of Thankfulness to the Saints, *that the Lord hath given them hearts to seek the Lord in a finding time,* Psal. 32. 5, 6. Time was thou couldst not pray; but the Lord hath found thee out, and stirred up unutterable groanes here, and all thy groanings have not been hid from the Lord.

Object. *But many pray and finde not; how shall I know I have found?*

Answ. When the spirit of prayer, not the gift of prayer hath carried thee, *Rom.* 8. 27.

Quest. *How shall I know that?*

Answer, 1. It is not fervency. 2. Nor looking to Christ and his Mercy. 3. Nor Arguments that are evidences of this Spirit; for these

thefe the foolifh Virgins had. But I fhall fhew it in three Degrees.

Firft, Obferve what is the utmoft end in prayer, and fo hath been in all
thy prayers; it is certain all the prayers of unregenerate men, though en-
livened with fome common gift of the Spirit, are ever for themfelves; if
any outward calamity befalls them, they then pray, *Pfal.* 78. But it is as
Pharaoh, for themfelves, becaufe the plague is upon them; if the Word
meets with them, and troubles them, their prayers (if fervent) are only
for eafe, when their bones are broke, 'tis for peace and comfort; and if
they defire grace, 'tis for peace-fake; if they have peace for the prefent,
and feel blindnefs, hardnefs of heart, they think thefe will damn them; and
hence falvation and deliverance from mifery, is the utmoft end they aim at;
and fo in all their prayers; let men ftudy their hearts, and they fhall fee
themfelves the mark they fhoot at, and the God they ferve, and Idol they
worfhip in all their prayers; and do you think thefe fhall be heard? No,
no; but Saints they look not at thefe things chiefly, but their utmoft end is
another thing; at firft converfion it is much felf, but it turnes in time to
higher ends, &c. and that is, what though I have peace, falvation, thefe
loaves, but yet mifs of Chrift himfelf, and the life of Chrift, to live by
him, and live to him, which is our laft end! 2 *Cor.* 5. 15. And here all
his prayers end, though crooked many wayes; elfe thefe are the prayers of
that Spirit of life, which is ever heard; and hence *James* 5. 3. *Ye ask and
have not, becaufe ye ask to fpend it on your lufts.* Ifa. 58. 5. though they
fafted and prayed, yet it was for ftrife and debate; the Saints do it to deftroy their lufts; and hence, though all fervent prayers are not of the Spirit, yet all prayers of the Spirit are ever fervent, though expreft with chat-
terings, mournings as Doves, becaufe the laft end hath a mighty force with
it; and hence waiting on God in all meanes for Anfwers, follows; and
hence, prayers of the Saints are endlefs, *Appetitus finis eft infinitus*; hence
Rom. 8. 23. *life in heaven* is his Scope, and he is longing for it, glad of
that time (for all prayers of Hypocrites are but iffues of felf-love) and
all occafions do but quicken up that principle; fo all the prayers of the
Saints rife from the fpirit of love to God, and faith in him, *Rom.* 8. 27,
28. The Sonlike Spirit, or Spirit of Adoption, not fervile, is in
them.

Secondly, If the foul receive any thing from the Lord thus praying, 'tis
exceeding thankful; the Spirit of Chrift, wherever it is, glorifies Chrift,
John 16. and *Pfal.* 116. 1. and that in time of peace; hence *Pfalme* 50.
14, 15. *Offer to God thanksgiving, and pay thy vowes, and then call though
in time of trouble, and I will heare.* For the Lord to begin to do the foul
any good, and fhew it its mifery, the worth of the Lord Jefus, to give him
any heart to feek, to give him any hope, to give him the leaft hint by any
word of mercy, oh its heart melts (it fhould be thus) and wonders but to
think, nay, to fee the Lord hath anfwered him ! oh this fwallows him up,
makes him give all to the Lord, as *Hannah* did, when fhe had her Childe,
1 *Sam.* 2. 1, 2. *Efau* loft the bleffing, though he begged it with tears; he
had a prophane heart that did not efteem it indeed, and fo would never have
been thankful for it; poor *Jacob* gets it, though he had but a ftaff to hold
him up.

Thirdly, If it receive not anfwer, it mournes, and loaths it felf, juftifies
God, gives all to him; prayers from felf-loathing, are not prayers which
come from felf-love, *Pfal.* 22. 2, 3, 4. Zach. 12. 10. *Pfal.* 72. 12.
There the Spirit dwells in the poor and contrite, and their cries are heard;
when men pray, and want, and are quiet without wifhing they could lament,

ment, 'tis not from the Spirit; oh therefore try here if 'tis thus; as he said to *Hezekiah*, *The Lord hath heard thy cries, and seen thy teares*; and oh wonder at the Lord, that he should give thee a heart to cry now.

Use 4.

Reproof to Saints, Who though received and heard, yet think the Lord regards them not; and as *David*, think his mercy is shut up.

1. Remember former times, *Psal.* 77. 7. Your experiences of the Lords pitying thee in thy blood, and he will not cast thee off now.

2. Consider the Riches of grace; when you cannot find any thing past, but what might cause him to loath thee, yet the Lord may then love, when thou art lamenting thy vileness, *Isa.* 63. 15, 16.

3. Consider the Lord doth purposely seem to dis-regard thee sometimes; not to shut out prayers, but to make you pray better; not that you should not pray at all, *Judg.* 16. 10. but to make you seek, and follow him, though in the dark. *Lam.* 3. 45. with 55. *in a land of pits, eye hath not seen what God hath laid up for you.*

4. Consider there is as much in the Lord to move him in thy worst estate to help thee, as in the best, (*viz.*) *his mercy, Psal.* 6. 4. You say, If my heart was not so vile, if I had not committed such sins, the Lord might! this is as if you said, The Lord shews not pity only for his mercy, &c.

VERSE 12.

I know you not.

WOrds of sence in Hebrew, beare and signifie affection also; The principal affections, are Love, and Hatred. 1. Love, *Psal.* 1. *ult. John* 10. 14. 2. Hatred, *Hosea* 7. 2. *Revel.* 8. 12. In this place such knowledge is meant, which hath the affection of love joyned with it; so that 'tis as if Christ should say, I love you not, I delight not in you, my heart is not toward you, whatever good words you give me, and how ever your heart is toward me, or you have thoughts of me; And this is the great misery of foolish Virgins.

Observ. 3.

That it is a most heavy and dreadful misery not to be beloved, not to be known of Jesus Christ; for now when the Tables are turned, and the Stage is pull'd down, and the Foolish shut out, and when Christ himself would give them a doleful Answer, express in words their woe, he coucheth it under these, *I know you not.* I do not say that men do feel it so, but it is so, and at last it will be found so.

This may appear, if we consider these particulars.

Consider at. 1.

If you consider the exceeding greatness, and glory of his place, and person; He is exalted, and set at the right hand of God, upon the Throne of his Father, and his Dominions reach from sea to sea; he is King of Kings, and Lord of Hoasts of Angels, &c. *Phil.* 2. 9. *A Name above every Name* he hath, and God hath sworne, *To him shall every one bow.* Now being thus great, and not to be beloved of such a one, is heavy; if we want the love of poor men, and base ignoble spirits, it is no such matter; but to lose great ones favour, especially if we depend upon them in life and

goods,

goods, peace and honour, this is bitter; hence 2 *Thef.* 1. 9. *from the glory of his power.*

2. *Confiderat.*

If you confider the terrour of the wrath of God for time to come. If a man be abroad in the Fields from home, and no ftormes, nor colds, nor heats arife to hurt him, a fhelter would not be fo much prized, nor the lofs of it great; but if there be fuch, and then to want it, and to lie open to the injury of all Weathers; now it is a woe to want it: So I fay to you, men that are abroad in the wide Fields of this world, and gone from home, if there fhould never be mifery, but you might eat your bread, and drink your Wine with a merry heart, and rejoyce in your Wives, and there then fhould be no knowledge of any thing after death, as thofe Epicures fpake, *Ecclf.* 9. the Love of Chrift would not be fo fweet; but there will be ftormes, fcorching heats that fhall burn, and never be quenched, there will be colds which fhall blaft all your budds, and bloflomes, and beauty, &c. Now to have no love of Chrift to take your felf to, as to a fhelter in thefe times, is very heavy; hence *Ifa.* 32. 2. Chrift typified by *Hezekiah*, fhall be a fhadow in a weary Land, which is fpoken to fhew the fweetnefs of his love, and their bleffednefs that have him to fly to; and hence their woe who want him. It is faid, *Gen.* 6. 8. *Noah found grace in Gods eyes*; not in the eyes of men; for before the Flood came, they did not fee it fuch a favour, for to have an Ark; but when that came, and they fled from Houfes to Trees, from Trees to Mountaines, and waters beneath, and above prevailed; now they faw it fomething to finde favour in the eyes of God, and their woe to want it. *Mofes* dies, wondering at the happinefs of the Saints, in regard of this, *Deut.* 33. 26. and *ult.* The eternal God is thy refuge; he fore-fees ftormes, he preferves from miferies above head, fo as they cannot touch the heads of the Saints; if fo be they do fall, yet they cannot fall fo low, but underneath are his armes; As a Child which ftands alone, if it be in danger to fall, and others cry out, Pray take heed, I have my armes fay they, under it; hence *Mofes* dyeth with this word, *Oh Ifrael who is like unto thee? happy art thou!* then wo to thofe who want this; there is not one man living, but he fhall meet with extremities, which fhall make heart and fpirits to faile, and the powers of heaven fhall be fhaken; every thing may forfake you, but Chrifts love; but if that alfo doth, wo then to you.

3. *Confiderat.*

If you confider the power which this privation of love hath to damp all joy and mirth in all things prefent; it invenomes, and puts a fting and poyfon in all bleffings, and makes comforts torments; to have all bleffings, and all priviledges, and not to have Chrifts love with them, is to have a fnare, a trap, a ftumbling block, and a Recompence, &c. *Rom.* 11. 9. Men regard not wrath to come; but confider of this, thy bleffings are woes, curfes; and you fhall one day cry, Wo is me that ever I was, or that ever I had any bleffing! Suppofe a man fhould be enriched with bags of Diamonds, hung with chaines of gold, fare delicioufly, but condemned to die, this would damp all. *Pharaoh* had a ftout will, *Mofes* tells him, *Exod.* 9. 16. *For this caufe God had raifed him up to fhew his power upon him*; one would have thought it fhould have pull'd him from his Throne, and made him lie in the duft; it did not, becaufe God had hardened his heart; fo would this, if the Lord had not hardened yours.

Hence we fhall fee Saints, when they lie under falfe feares, only of lofs of love; thofe very things which are moft fweet, are made moft bitter. *Pfal.* 77. 3. *I remembred God, and was troubled*; but what think you of thofe that be not indeed loved, it is enough to bring down the moft mer-

merry heart , and highest looks for the present ; what are my friends , mine enemies? is there none to comfort me of all my Lovers ?

Considerat. 4. If you consider the sweetness of this Love of Christ. I'le instance only in one particular ; *Psal.* 63. 3. *Cant.* 1. 3. The Elect, when they are glorified, and with Christ, what shall be most ravishing in their eyes ? what shall swallow up their thoughts most ? oh the love of Christ, his free love ! why should I be accepted, beloved ! oh that ever the Lord should cast his eyes , and set his heart upon such an out-cast ! Hence, praise of the Riches of Grace , *Ephes.* 1. is *the work of Heaven.* Now to be cast out of this love, will, must be exceeding bitter to the soul ; hence *Mat.* 7. 23. *I never knew you*, will be daggers at the heart, or the stone upon the graves mouth, which shall torment for ever.

Considerat. 5. If you consider the nature of this want, or negation of Christs love, what it is.

1. Degree, Is for Christ not to have so much as one purpose, or thought of peace and good to them , not to put the least Character of their names in the Book of life ; that is the first degree and fountain of all other ; *Gods love, Jer.* 29. 9.

2. Degree, Is not to speak one word of peace and love to a man, no absolute promise of life to them ; *Psalme* 50. 16. They have nothing to do *to take Gods Covenant into their mouths* ; those promises which comfort and support the hearts of the Saints against all sins, all miseries , belong not unto them.

3. Degree , Not to suffer for them , not to shed one drop of blood for their lives, *Joh.* 17. 9. so that all their sins must lie upon them , to bear and answer for.

4. Degree, Not to do the least good for them ; good things they have , but through their sins , and Christs ordering of it, are not good for them , but they are thereby fitted by patience for destruction.

5. Degree, Not to accept any thing which they do to him ; their sacrifices and prayers are sins , *Mal.* 1. *I have no pleasure in you.*

6. Degree, Not to pity them in time of their trouble , but to laugh at their Calamity , and to rejoyce in their Ruine , and eternal overthrow ; Christ shall get glory from them then , whom they despised so long before.

Use 1. This may let us see , what cause all the people of God have to be abundantly satisfied with the love of Christ; the heart of man is naturally like the raging sea, never quiet, if the least windes do but arise ; the Saints may have unmortified affections , and are very apt upon troublesome temptations to be disquieted ; the Saints are compared to the Apple of Gods eye ; and we know little things will trouble much there ; it's because in losses and sorrows which befall themselves , and in beholding the madness and folly of others, they are very apt to look upon the anger of the Lord in them for their sin, which others usually do not. Oh consider, is it such a misery to lose Christs love ? and have you a share in it ? oh then be thankful for it , and contented with it. When Christ was to depart from his Disciples , *Joh.* 16. 22. *you shall sorrow* ; but what doth he leave with them to quiet them ? *I will see you againe*, that mourn now for loss of my presence ; What else ? doth he promise them nothing else ? truly that is enough. When *David* looked upon the prosperity of the wicked , and that they should *never see light* ? Psal. 49. 15. with 19. *But God will redeem my soul from the grave*, not from troubles, *and he will receive me* ; Some read it , *For he hath received me* ; both may stand together, and this was enough to him.

If

If a Traveller have lost his way, and not come home to his journeys end, he may be very well unquiet; but when he is come to the end of his journey, and can go no further, then he sits down, and lives there, and would not go back againe, especially if he considers how many are out of doors, and under tempests, he may now bless God, they have a shelter; So if the Lord had never revealed his grace to you in the Gospel, and you were not yet drawn by it, nor drawn to it, but were lost in your sins, or selves, or world, and had miseries upon you, then you might be unquiet; but now when laid in the bosome of Christ, when sucking the breasts of the grace of Christ, when you can go no further though thou wert in Heaven, for there's no other happiness there; Now sit still contented, and be glad of this, as under thy Vine and shadow; especially considering the woes of them, that are yet farre from this grace and mercy in Jesus Christ, and under Clouds of blood. Men that saile upon the Sea, if they see nothing but waves, and vast raging of waters about them, they keep themselves close in their Ship, though their Cabbins be but little; tell me one thing that is good, where Christs love is not; shew me any thing but misery, death, and eternal sorrows out of it; oh therefore sit still, quietly, meekly, contentedly, though you be tossed as high as Heaven, and go down as deep as Hell again.

You are troubled sometimes with losses of outward things, Cattel dye, and *Rachels* Children and Husband are not, increase little, decayes many, and *Jobs* wife bids him bless God (and give glory to him, by confessing he is an Hypocrite, because so much afflicted) and dye; and *David* sees the ungodly flourish, and he thinks he hath washt his hands in vain, and 'tis good to fare and live here as they live; Oh consider, supppose the Lord should give thee these things as he doth to others, to be snares, and at last say, *I know you not*, when thy soul shall come trembling out of a sick and weary body, before the Tribunal of God Almighty, as these, was that portion then so good ? Oh therefore take your portion, and be thankful for it! Oh therefore be glad in this, and say, I have these miseries, but Christs love to sweeten them ! these sorrows, but Christs love to sanctifie them ! I see Floods of Fire arising, but oh here's this shelter to be a Refuge to me !

You have heard what it is not to be beloved, what a misery it is; by that contrary, see th's, *viz.*

1. For the Lord to have thoughts of peace to thee, when thou wert nothing but death and misery before his eyes, to bear thee in his heart ever since he was God.

2. For the Lord to speak to thee, and make an eternal Covenant, and every promise thine. *Davids* dying words, are, *This was enough*, even all his desire; and not one tittle but shall be accomplished one day.

3. For the Lord to shed his blood, beare thy sins, curse, and tread down death and sin, and teare away the hand-writing of the Law against thee, rather than the least evil befall thee.

4. For the Lord to be working for thee by all good things, all evil things, all providences, all Ordinances, night and day, and you may find it in part, and shall find it hereafter.

5. For the Lord to accept all thy poor endeavours, desires, prayers, *Isaiah* 56.

6. For the Lord to pity thee in all thy misery, and worst times ! then to shew his greatest love, when death, and powers of darkness put forth their greatest malice ! truly thus it is; Oh let this love be enough, considering especially the woful condition of them that want it, who shall cry for one smile,

smile, and cannot get it! See this love, and doubt not of it; how could you love him, if he did not love you first? especially if you have been satiated with it? *pray for it*, Pfalme 90.14. I speak this the rather, becaufe of the fad miferies which make men lame in their Chriftian courfe, that they are ready to lie down difconfolate, becaufe they Remember not this; Do not alwayes doubt, but once at laft get through the Crowde to this Love.

Ufe 2. Let thofe who want this love, mourn for it, though the Lord gives you, and doth for you never fo much in regard of other things. Suppofe he doth not fmite thy body with ficknefs, thy name with difgrace, thy eftate with loffes; yet if he doth not love thee, this is woe enough. It was the mifery of *Ifrael*, Jer. 15. 1. with 5. *My minde is not to this people, caft them out*; and as the Lord there faid, fo I fay; If the Lord deal thus, who fhall pity thee, or bemoane thee, or ask how thou doft? *Joel* 1. 8, 9, 10. They lament when the Fig-tree was wafted; much more now the Lords love is not towards thee. *Lam.* 1.16. The Church there laments, that the Comforter which fhould refresh was farre off.

Queft. *How fhall I know that?*

Anfw. If he never did affect thy heart with lofs, and want of his love, and abufing of it, but hath let you go on in peace all your life; you were borne out of his love, caft out to the loathing of thy perfon, and have lived fo, though he hath been pitiful to thee; now if you were never troubled with lofs of this, and wrongs done againft this, you are as yet out of love. Look as it is with a Father, if he hath a Childe froward, and cannot reftraine him, he lets him alone, he loves him not, elfe he would chaftife and correct him, and make him fhake at his frownes; fo here, as it is *Heb.* 12. 8. *If no correction, you are Baftards*; So here you have gone on, and never have been yet troubled in minde with the frowns of Chrift, never lamented your wrongs done to Chrift; are you loved? I know the Lord may let you go Prodigals for a time, but he will bring you back, if he loves you. I never knew any whom the Lord brought home, but this broke their hearts. O that the Lord was fo patient, and I all my life abufed him! nay, he would oft have gathered me! he did oft ftrive, and I was *like a Bullock unaccuftomed to the yoke*, Jer. 31. 18. and he might have cut me off, or given me up to my ftubborn heart. Many are troubled for want of memory, ignorance, and want of power to pray, or fome fin, and then God is merciful to them, and this eafes them againe; but this is nothing, till you come to this, *viz.* feares of the eternal lofs of this love, and this lies heavy. If this be thy condition, that for the prefent thou art not loved of the Lord, tell me but one thing which thou haft to comfort thee; thou haft friends, peace, health, but they are all without love; if without love, then thou haft them with a curfe, and wrath of God. Suppofe thou wert dying, and the Lord fhould fay to thee, when thou cryeft, I know thee not; would it not be fad! Lie upon thy Pillow, and fleep quietly if thou canft; for ought I know, there was never drop of blood fhed for thee, never thought of peace in Chrifts Breafts to thee; a vile wretch that never lamented the lofs of his love, nor contempt of it to this day!

Obj. *But I care not fo long as I have been well without it, fo I hope I fhall do ftill, I will not believe I am out of his love.*

Anfw. Yea, this is the mifery of men, as it was of thefe Virgins; but time fhall come, when you fhall fee him fit upon his Throne, brighter than a Thoufand Suns, in the glory of his Father, a fire burning round about

bout him , and the Kings of the earth trembling at his prefence , and his
Saints in his bofome like unto him , then you fhall wifh you had his love ,
and lament, Rev. 1. and waile, becaufe of him. Oh fecure world , will
you fit ftill in your finnes, and lie in your unbelief, till the fire burnes a-
bout you, and there be no efcape ! Oh that the Lord would pity you, many
of you that have yet lived with dry eyes, and merry hearts, and yet have no
love from Jefus Chrift.

Ufe 3.

Learn hence not to defpife or refufe the love of Chrift when it is offered to you, and propounded to you in the Gofpel ; we can be content to
want the love of fome men , becaufe we can live well enough without them,
and their love ; their love loft hurts not us ; but if the lofs of their love
may be the lofs of our goods and lives , then (if it may be had) men will
feek for, and long for it, though it fhould not be offered ; but if offered , it
is gladly accepted : So if you could live without the love of Chrift , you
might content your felves ; but the lofs of it is more bitter than ten thoufand deaths; and therefore refufe it not when it is offered ; but as they,
Acts 2. 39, 41. when they faw how they had imbrued their hands in the
blood of Chrift, and yet faw grace offered, it is faid, *They gladly received the
Word of the Lord.*

The Law is a word of condemnation ; but that is not the laft word the
Lord hath fpoken , then I fhould fpend time in vaine now ; the Gofpel ,
even the whole Gofpel is a word of love and Reconciliation ; 2 *Cor.* 5. 19, 20.
wherein the Lord doth *befeech men to be reconciled* ; i. e. to accept of Gods
love offered therein.

The Lord knows full well that mens hearts are fo full of enmity , that
they will never feek for Reconciliation firft , though they have good caufe ,
becaufe they have offered the wrong ; and therefore he ftands not upon
termes, but offers love firft , without which he knows they are for ever undone ! Oh therefore receive it, accept of it when it is offered to you ; and
lofe thy life, rather than lofe his love.

For the further opening of this Point , I fhall fhew three things.

{ 1. That Chrift doth offer his love in the Gofpel, and how.
2. Upon what termes.
3. Motives to accept it, and anfwer Objections againft accepting
of it.

Firft, That the Lord doth offer, and how he doth offer his love in the Gofpel ; and this I fhall cleare , becaufe nothing can draw the foul to accept of
love but this. For the better underftanding of which, you muft conceive
that the love of Chrift in the Gofpel, is diverfly manifefted unto men ; either to men after they be in Chrift, and are brought home by it , and this is
a love of delight in them. *Pfalm* 45. 10, 11. Or it is a love of good
will to men not brought home ; as it is in Husbands, before their affections
be fet upon any, they make love, as it is 2 *Theff.* 2. 10. *They received
not the love of the truth, becaufe the truth made love to them.* Luke 2. 14.
Good will towards men; and this love, I fay is offered ; this love the Lord
makes unto you ; ftand amazed at it , that after all your finnes, wrongs done
him, nothing but love is offered , even his deareft love ; for though there is
patience, power to help, wifdome to guide ; though there is terrour in
him, yet , *Take my love*, faith he , *John* 3. 17. And hence , *Heb.* 2. 2.
it is called *Great falvation, or love*: 'tis offered ; elfe how could men be faid
to reject it, or neglect it , which he warnes them of ? A man may as well
que-

question whether there be a Gospel, as whether love be offered there ; for as the Law is nothing but the manifestation of sin, the hand-writing of death and wrath against all men, writ with the Finger of God ; the Gospel is the manifestation of grace, the hand-writing of grace and peace to all men, written with the blood of God ; and hence the Gospel is that which brings *life and immortality to light*, 2 Tim. 1. 10. Not that there is life absolutely for all, but there 'tis for all that shall by faith accept of it. More particularly,

First, It is offered Universally to all wherever it comes, and therefore personally to every man ; the words are plaine, *Mark* 16. 15. *Preach the Gospel to every creature*; and not only to them that do belong to Christ, and shall believe; for though it be offered with the power of it effectually to these, yet offered it is also unto those that never shall have God, nor portion in the Son of God, and hence, *Luke* 14. The Lord of the Feast invited those that never came in ; and Christ himself, 1 *John* 11. *He came to his own, and they received him not*; *he would have gathered them under his wings, and they would not*; not only to them that be humbled (though none will care for Gospel but such) but to them that be unhumbled, *Revel.* 3. 18, 20. doth this Gospel come. There be many object, Yes, the Lord offers love to them that are his, but not to me ? yes, to thee; there is not a man here, that can exempt himself. And I would make no doubt to go to every man particularly, and say, The Lord intreats thee to be Reconciled; nay, if there be one man worse than another, though his hands have been imbrued in the blood of the Prophets, and his soul stained with the crying guilt of the most hydeous sinnes that ever the earth bore, or Sun saw, yet the Lord makes love to him ; the price is paid for him, if he will accept of it, and that the Lord would have him so to do ; neither doth this Universal offer inferre an Universal Redemption ; for the Gospel in the offer of it, doth not speak absolutely that Christ hath dyed for all, and therefore for thee, as the *Arminians* maintain ; but it speaks conditionally, 'Tis for thee, if ever the Lord gives thee a heart to receive that grace there ; therefore consider of it, there is not one here present, but the Lord would have you receive his love ; and consider this one reason, Thou shalt be condemned for refusing it; Hence 'tis Gods command, and Christs desire you should receive it, *John* 3. 19. If not thy duty to receive it, 'tis not thy sin to refuse it; but 'tis such a sin, that all men that perish under the found of the Gospel, are principally condemned for.

Secondly, 'Tis offered really; I put in this, because men cannot see the reality of this; because not Christ, but Ministers (they think) only make it, and so the offer is only external and Ministerial; the Lord himself they think is not of that mind.

Answ. 1. What any Minister according to the Gospel doth, that Christ would do if he was here present ; hence 2 *Cor.* 5. 20. *We beseech you in his stead*; as Embassadours speak what the King himself would do, and no more, and himself would speak what they do if he was present ; and hence Christ did not only preach the Gospel to his Elect, that should receive him, but to them who did reject him also, which made his blessed heart and eyes also break forth into teares, *Oh that thou hadst known, &c.*

2. 'Tis Christ in them which doth speak, *Heb.* 12. 25. *Him that speaks from heaven*; and hence *Ephes.* 2. 17. *He came and preached peace*, when he was gone up to Heaven ; and hence receiving of these Ministers and Embassadours of Christ, is receiving of Christ; despising of them, is despising
of

of Chrift ; and look, as the bowels of God the Fathers love are opened to Chrift, fo the bowels of Chrifts love are opened in thofe whom he fends. Never didft thou fee any Minifter pity thy condition, and offer peace to thee, but becaufe Chrift put it in his heart ; and as in rejecting the Gofpel, you fhall not fad their fpirits fo much as Chrifts Spirit in them, fo in accepting, e contrà.

3. Your life and falvation, and certainty of mercy from Chrift, hangs upon your receiving their Word ; for men will fay, If Chrift were here, I durft believe his Word ; I tell you, the Lord hangs thy life upon believing their Word fpoken according to him, *John* 17. 20. *I pray for them that shall believe in me through their word*; Why not through my word? *Anfw.* Thefe may ftand well together ; my word as the foundation, their word as building upon it : their word in the external adminiftration and view of man, but my word indeed ; my word in their mouths, and fo their word as inftruments under that principal agent ; fo that if an Angel, or one fhould rife from the dead, I fhould not look for more certainty of life by believing thefe, than them. Chrift will fpeak no more, till he fhakes down heaven and earth with his voice ; but their word he honours, and faith, Believe it ; their word is not, Chrift hath loved thee ; but Believe, that thou mayft be beloved of Chrift.

4. The Lord is fo real here, that he punifheth men more for this, than if he was prefent. Chrift lived among the Jewes, and preached, they crucified him, and rejected him in his perfon ; yet this caft them not off, till *Luke* 13. 45. they put away the offers of grace by the Servants of Chrift from them, and now the Apoftles are to fhake off the duft of their feet againft fuch as thofe.

Thirdly, It is offered with vehement defires to accept of it, 2 *Cor.* 6. 1. *Pfal.* 81. 11. *We befeech you receive not Gods grace in vaine*; for you may fay There is fome offer, but the Lord defires it not in good earneft ; never did man defire to get the affection of another moft beautiful, as the Lord doth thee that haft none ; we ufe to judge of the affection of another to a thing, by what he is willing to part with for it ; As he that fold all for the pearle, and bought it ; So the Lord is content to part with all he hath to thee ; the deareft thing he hath, is his precious blood, and all fruits and benefits of it ; his Spirit to comfort, himfelf to dwell with thee, his Father to love thee, his Kingdome to receive thee, his fweeteft promifes to affure and ftablifh thee ; all things, except his glory ; it is not fit that you fhould receive that, but for him to receive it from thee ; and giving it to him, is better than having of it to thy felf. To thee I fay, that art like an incarnate Devil, Dead, and Damned, and undone for ever, unlefs thou accept of this Grace, is all this Mercy of the Gofpel tendered.

Fourthly, It is offered freely, *Ifa.* 55. 1, 2. For this makes many ftand and wonder, Why fhould the Lord make love to me fo vile, fo unworthy, good for nothing but to fin ! dry bones ! or what need hath the Lord of me ? what can I do for him ? what can I add to him ? why goeth he not into the Palaces of Princes to call in them ? but that he fhould deale thus with me that have finned worfe than *Paul* before converfion ! not ignorantly ; I have known the grace of Chrift, yet rejected it ; and have gone on defperately, have been mad in following my lovers, forfaking the Lord ; True, I know no caufe, but only his free love, becaufe he hath compaffion on thee, and becaufe 'tis for his grace fake ; hence he defires it vehemently, for that is worthy to be honoured, received, embraced of thee. Methinks it is in this cafe, as 'tis with poor Marines, whofe fhip is wrackt,

many

many drowned, and they cast upon the shore, one comes to them, and offers them house, and meat, and home, they tell him We are poor men, have nothing to pay; true, I know that, but I have compassion upon you, because I see you are distressed men; so 'tis here with the Lord Jesus, I know thou hast nothing to requite me, but I have compassion upon thee, accept my grace, take it, live upon it, because thou art a distressed soul; God hath shewn wondrous mercy in giving life, now I offer more, one would think; now surely men should be glad to accept of this grace.

Quest. *Upon what termes is this offer of love made?*

Answ. There is nothing required, but only and meerly receiving of it; *John 1. 12.* Under the Law it was, *Do all this*; but the Gospel saith not so, but *Receive me who have done all, and suffered also*, with thy whole heart; as it was in the Land of promise, nothing required, but going up, and possess it; here it's no more. *Prov. 4. 8. She shall bring thee to honour when thou dost embrace her.* The offer of love, is like the offer of a rich portion, nothing required but receiving it thankfully, and so living upon it; so *Psal. 16. 5, 6, 7. I thank the Lord that gave me counsel, &c.* Or as it is in the offer of a Prince to a Traitour, he offers life to him; Upon what termes? I could crush thee as a fly between my fingers, but I desire nothing, only accept my favour, come and embrace me, and then live under my Government in my Kingdome, because that I love thy company, and because here is my honour, and thy safety; so doth the Lord in the Gospel, the Lord professeth he had rather a soul should return, and live upon his love, and under the Government of his love, than dye; *Come under my wings*; saith Christ, *Matthew 23. you may all.* I would have you safe, and near unto me, that you may feel the warmth and life of my love; this is all the Lord looks for; and who would not accept of love upon these termes?

Thirdly, Motives to accept of it. Why should I name any more than what the Text mentions? no woe like this to lose it! and though it may be now you may esteem it nothing while 'tis faire weather, and whiles it is a day of patience, yet when the depths of anger are broken up, then you shall see, and say, No people like unto those that have it, when you shall see Christ on his Throne with ravishing beauty, and see him tread the Wine-press of wrath alone, and his garments dipt in the blood of his enemies; then you shall say, The want of this love is bitter; and hence if it be offered, take it now gladly, thankfully, joyfully.

Obj. *But I am but one, will the Lord receive me?*

Ans. I have been stirred up to preach the Gospel for the sake of that One, and *Jer. 3. 14. I will take one of a Tribe.* Though all else be rejected, the Lord minds thee.

2. Object. *But Christ is in Heaven, how can I receive him, and his love?*

Answ. A mighty Prince is absent from a Traytour, he sends his Herauld with a Letter of love, he gives it him to read; how can he now receive the love of the Prince when absent? Answ. He sees his love in his Letter, knows it came from him, and so at a distance closeth with him by this meanes; So here, he that was dead, but now is alive, writes, sends to thee, Oh receive his love here in his Word; this is receiving *him by faith*, *Acts 2. 37, 38.*

3. Object. *But I am not elected, nor redeemed; if I knew that, I durst receive the Lord and his love.*

Answ. What have you to do with Gods secret Decree of Election? 'tis your duty to look to the Gospel, which is the Will of Gods command; there

there is a Will of Gods Decree, and a man may fulfill this Will and sin; as *Jeroboam* in revolting according to the Prophesie of the Prophet; and to submit to this, is not moral obedience, though moved thereto by a Divine instinct, as in *Cyrus*; but there is a Will of Gods Command, and this you are to look to; obedience to this, never wants its recompence; You say you are not Redeemed. *Answ.* True; but it may be thou art Redeemed; and therefore do not crucifie Christ a second time; receive this love, and 'tis certain 'tis for thee.

4. Obj. *But I am no: humbled sufficiently?*

Answ. I know no man can receive Christ, till the Lord hath humbled and broken him down; but know, there is no more humiliation required, than that which brings thee to receive the Lord Jesus Christ. Many have a spirit of cleaving to, and receiving of Christ, as hath been opened, but are kept off, because they feare they are not humbled; but methinks the very order of Christ to one condemned and lost for ever, who must else lie to all eternity mourning (methinks this) should break thy heart, if it be not a Stone, and a Rock, as it did *Pauls*; indeed you must be more and more humbled all your life; but this is a consequent required of those who are in Christ.

5. Object. *But I cannot believe, why presse you me to it?*

Answ. 1. The Lord doth not presse you to believe, because you should believe from your selves; but that feeling your own inability, you might suffer him to make you believe.

2. The Lord by words of Exhortation doth work Faith; there goes a power with it; as *Acts* 2. *Repent*; they gladly received the Word; and whose heart may it not draw and compell, especially if there be any spark of God in any soule? and therefore pray give the Lord leave to speak, whose Word can quicken the dead, though the dead can neither stir nor heare.

3. There be many of you that say You cannot believe; but this Gospel drawes out a power; *The way of the Lord, is strength to the upright*, Prov. 10. 29. Will you? can you despise or refuse his grace? No, it should constrain.

6. Object. *But I have received him, and I feel no vertue from him.*

Answ. 1. I know many do receive him, and feel not the vertue of Christ; but because Saints may be kept poor in Spirit, possesse all things in Christ, and yet receive little from Christ, I shall only ask two Questions.

1. How dost thou esteem of, and desire that blessing of Christ? Dost esteem of nothing so precious, desire nothing more, and followest the Lord on with prayer for it? it is in Christ for thee; what thou wantest, thou shalt have it, *John* 4. 10. *Phil.* 2. 9, 10. No false heart but undervalues these things; and the Lord will fulfill all thy desires; in heaven thou shalt have all thy sins subdued and trodden to death.

2. How is thy heart for thy general frame, affected with the absence of the good thou feelest not from the Lord? dost mourn bitterly for this? look as the Disciples that mourned for Christs bodily absence, the Lord tells them, *They should rejoyce*; so here; a carnal heart is indifferent, though he lose Christs vertue. And therefore accept the Lords love, you poor mourning souls; the most stony heart I speak to; but much more unto the weary, and them that have been seeking after the Lord, behold salvation is come to thy heart this day, only let it in; do not reject it, because thy sinnes are great, thy unworthinesse great; the Lord knows them, yet he offers;

fers; some of you have had some hopes or assurance Christ is yours, yet he may be thine; Suppose he was never thine yet, now stretch out thy shaking hand, receive him who is this day crucified before thy eyes, his head hanging down, his blood gushing out, beseeching thee to accept of that which is shed for thee. I remember a godly man receiving Apples from a poor Woman, he took them thankfully, but said withal, This came from the Spirit of God; so doth this offer much more, and therefore take it: But I know this love will be despised by some of you; some not knowing your woe, some not feeling it, being without Christ; some under terrours, but shut up under unbelief. If I did think the Lord had no purpose to do thee good, and I knew thee, I would read thy doom; but the Lord may pity; and therefore I'le go and mourn, and pray that the Lord would not lay your sins to your charge; your base lusts are better than Christ to you; O therefore mourne for this; you that know him not, prize him not; but carry this *Acts* 13.41. about with thee, *viz. hear you despisers, and wonder,* &c.

Observ. 4.

That many men may, and do apprehend Christ by a seeming Faith, whom yet Christ Jesus apprehends not by his dearest love.

For here were Virgins many of them, who cryed, *Lord, Lord,* only looking for salvation from him, hanging upon grace, clasping about his feet (as it were) and who in their life-time went out to meet the Bridegrom, expecting love from him; and yet Christ here professeth, I know not you, I love you not.

I say, this is by a seeming faith; for no man apprehends Christ by a lively Faith, but is apprehended of Christ, *John* 1. 12. But if it be by a seeming Faith, *i. e.* which seemes to be Faith in the judgement and opinion of others, and also which seemes only to be so to their own apprehension, as it did unto these Virgins, the Lord doth not apprehend such by his dearest love; and that is I say, with his dearest love; with common love he may, but with deare and eternal love, never.

The Faith of some men, is like the casting of some Anchor at Sea; it sometimes falls upon a Rock, or light sand, it toucheth the ground, but the Rock holds not it; and hence the Ship is ever driven before the winde, or carried away with the ebbings and flowings of the water; So it is here; and hence men are tossed to and fro with lusts and temptations, and driven before strong windes. Or as it was of *Saul* to *Samuel*, he apprehended *Samuel*, but *Samuel* departed from him, saw him no more untill the day of his death; So here, the Kingdome and Love of Christ is rent from you. *John* 2. 24. *ult. But he committed not himself to them.* Luke 13. 26,27. *Have not we eat and drunk in thy presence?* and yet Christ will say, *I know you not*; and this is the case of many. *Job* 8. 13, 14. *When an Hypocrite dyes, his hope perisheth;* if the Lord had apprehended him with his dearest love, it could not be so.

For Explication of this Point, three things are to be opened.

$\left\{\begin{array}{l}\text{1. How one may be said to apprehend Christ Jesus by a seeming}\\ \quad\text{Faith.}\\ \text{2. How Christ is said not to apprehend such.}\\ \text{3. Why he doth not.}\end{array}\right.$

Quest. First, How may one be said to apprehend Christ by a seeming faith? *Answ.* Five wayes usually.

1. When men are forced to fly to Christ meerly out of extremity and pressures

preſſures of miſery, the ſtroaks, and dry blowes of Divine Vengeance light upon them, and now they cry, Lord, pity us; it may be, in time of peace, while conſcience and Divine Vengeance were aſleep, they regarded not Faith, nor Prayer, nor Chriſt, nor any thing elſe, notwithſtanding all the heart-breaking cryes, and loud calls of God, but were merry and light, and licentious, &c. but in extremity then they will cry, and prize mercy above a thouſand worlds, *Prov.* 1. 28. One would think their mouths ſhould be ſtopped then: ſome think thoſe words are an alluſion to the Ark in *Noahs* time, *Hoſea* 8. 1, 2, 3. *When the Eagle ſhall come againſt Gods people,* Pſal. 78. 35. *they ſhall cry, My God, we know thee;* No ſaith the Lord, *The enemy ſhall apprehend them,* I will not; this is not faith, but only ſelf-love; when as men are naught before, and their hearts ſitting looſe from God continualy, having no daily embracements of him, and would be worſe after Gods afflicting hand, if he ſhould help them; but ſo it is, that they cry out to God for help, meerly becauſe of torment, &c. This is like that cry of our *Indians* to the Devil, who worſhip, and cleave to him, becauſe he plagues them. True, in times of extremity, the faith of the Saints may be awakened which was aſleep before; and when God hedgeth their way with Thornes, they may then returne to their firſt Husband, becauſe it was better; but when extremity begets it, it begins and ends with it, lives and dyes with it; here ſuch may feare that then Chriſt apprehends them not. *Pſalme* 66. 3. *Becauſe of thy power, thy enemies ſhall flatter, and ſubmit.* A proud Rebellious Wretch in times of peace, ſwells bigger than God, and is above God; the Lord Jeſus hath his times wherein he grapples with them when no Miniſters can, and flings them down with his Sword at their heart, and his hand at their Throat, and terrours in their conſciences; and now they yield; Chriſt may hence take theſe as common Subjects; but never as ſpecial favourites to ſtand before him; and this is the caſe of thouſands, who fly to Chriſt meerly for extremities. Thus the caſe ſtood with old *Joab*; he ſhould have dyed before; 1 *Kings* 2. 30. but at laſt he neglects his charge, he runnes to the Altar only out of ſelf-ove, and there he will dye; one would think a man that had been ſo uſeful, flying to the Altar in his old age, might be pitied; No, the Altar which ſecures others, ſecures not him; juſtice may be ſhewn to him that will abuſe favour long; ſo 'tis here.

2. When men fly to Chriſt in times of peace, that ſo they may preſerve their ſins with greater peace of conſcience; ſo that ſin makes them flie to Chriſt, as well as miſery; not that they may deſtroy and aboliſh ſin, but that they may be preſerved in their ſins with peace. For this is the frame of all men living; ſin before it is commited (not all ſin, but what is ſuitable ro mens conſtitutions, corruptions, places, temptations) is very ſweet; and if conſcience be awake, it's after the commiſſion bitter; ſweet in the mouth, bitter in the belly; or elſe they know it will be bitter another day; *Prov.* 23. 32. *ſtings like a Cockatrice;* and what profit in inheriting lyes? Now becauſe men have not other good to live upon, or delight in, for God they have not; hence many an heart ſecretly ſaith this, If I can have my ſin, and peace, and conſcience quiet for the preſent, and God merciful to pardon it afterward, then all is well; hereupon hearing thoſe that put their truſt in Chriſt ſhall be pardoned for preſent, and ſaved afterward, hence he doth relie (as he ſaith) only on the mery of God in Chriſt; and now this hardens and blindes him, and makes him ſecure, and his Faith is Sermonproof, nothing ſtirres him, &c. and were it not for their faith, they ſhould deſpaire, but this keeps them up; and now they think, if they have any trouble of minde, the Devil troubles them; and ſo make Chriſt and Faith

pro-

protectors of sin, not purifiers from sin (which is most dreadful) turning grace to wantonness, as they did sacrifice; so these would sin under the shadow of Christ, because the shadow is good and sweet, *Micah* 3. 11. they had subtle slye ends in good duties, for therein may lie a mans sin; yet they lean upon the Lord, &c. *Matthew* 3. 7, 8. The Scribes came in peace to *Johns* Ministry, which was to awaken men to believe in the Messiah, *Oh generation of Vipers, who hath forewarned you to flee from wrath to come!* hence saith he, *Bring forth fruits*; as if he should say, You would have the blessing of the warme Sun still, but you care not to have your viperous nature changed, you will bring forth the old bitter fruits, &c. when Mony-changers came into the Temple, you have made it a Den of Thieves; Thieves when hunted, fly to their Den, or Cave, and there they are secure against all searchers, and hue-and-cryes; so here, but Christ whipped them out; so when men are pursued with cryes and feares of conscience, away to Christ they go, as to their Den; not as Saints, to pray and lament out the life of their sin there, but to preserve their sin; this is vile; will the Lord receive such?

I am perswaded, many a mans heart is kept from breaking and mourning, because of this; he saith (it may be) that he is a vile sinner, but I trust in Christ, &c. If they do go to Christ to destroy their sin, this makes them more secure in their sin; for (say they) I cannot help it; and the thing I would not do, that do I, and Christ must do all; whereas faith makes the soul mourn after the Lord the more, as *Paul* did; yet do you think they that believed said, *Let us sin*, *that Grace may abound*? No, No.

3. By seeing some glory, and tasting some sweet in the Gospel, and Christ manifested and arising therein; hence some men may apprehend Christ neither out of feare of misery, nor only to preserve some sin; but God lets in light and hear of the blessed beames of the glorious Gospel of the Son of God, and therefore there is mercy Rich, Free, Sweet, for damned, great vile sinners; Good Lord (saith the soul) what a sweet Ministry, Word, God, and Gospel is this? and there rests; this was the frame of the stony ground, *which heard the Word, and received it with joy, and for a time believed*, Luke 8. 13. And this is the case of thousands that are much affected with the promise and mercy of Christ, and hang upon free-grace for a time; but as 'tis with sweet smells in a Room, they continue not long; or as flowers, they grow old and withered, and then fall; in time of temptation, lust, and world, and sloth is more sweet than Christ and all his Gospel is; 'tis in this case with the soule, as it was with *Mary*, who applyed the Spikenard only to the feet of Christ, but all the Room was filled with the sweetness of it; so in the Gospel, the sweet odour of it is scattered to all; and the Apostle *Paul* saith, *We are a sweet savour of God to them that perish*; but Christ only applyes it unto the heart of a wounded, poor, humbled sinner; and though smells and odours refresh, yet men cannot live by the smell; so 'tis here; such is the rich grace of Christ, that the worst shall know and say, He is good; As the King passeth by, many come to see him; but doth he take all up to the Chariot with him? No, but they go home to their several houses againe; and then they commune, and speak of what they saw; so Christ accepts only of, and apprehends none but those that have forsaken all at his call, and so live upon his favour; so here, as *Psal.* 45. all his Garments smell of myrrh, yet only the Queen which heares, considers, and forgets her Fathers house, stands at his right hand.

4. When the soul is perswaded to close with the Lord Jesus Christ by the
power

power of immediate Revelation, without the *medium* of the Word; the Word they grant hath its use, and 'tis good to attend to it, as to a light in a dark place, but stay till the day-starre arise; the Word is obscure, and may deceive, but this cannot; and they think Christ never apprehends them, till this doth; and this some feel, and rest upon, as upon a light and comfort in sickness, and leave others to the Word; some feel and hold no other evidence but this; some hold it, but never felt it, but live in admiring of it, and 'tis a prety new thing, &c.

I confess the Spirit must reveale the meaning of the Word, before ever it can draw any to believe, and it must mightily, immediately apply the Word; but for Christ to reveale himself without a Word, and a Word of promise in the Gospel truly understood, is a delusion, especially if the evidence of the Word be herein despised. *Rom.* 15. 4. *Paul* had Revelations; so may a godly man have more than common manifestations of favour at some times; but *Paul* speaks not of these, *Heb.* 6. 17. *that we might have strong consolation*, &c. All the Heires of the promises, as Heires that have Legacies left them, they go to the Will of the deceased Father, and that comforts that they hold to; that is sure, such a one shall have it, if his name be there; but if one shall say, Such a one hath promised me such lands, is it in the Will? No; but since he dyed, as I was taking a Pipe, he came to me; oh be not deceived! but say some, I hold to the Will; let us see, where is it? I love such and such, saith the Lord; true, but whom? 'tis Children believing, broken, poor, humbled. Now if you say, No, I regard no such Will, then you regard not the Lord; so 'tis here, *Ephes.* 2. 20. *Built upon the foundation of the Apostles*; i. e. upon the Word, and Christ in it, &c. Hence, if you build without the Word, you build without a Foundation, and you will fall; and do you hold to that comfort that the Word never gave you? Christ is not the object of Faith, but as revealed; *John* 6. 45. *He that hath seen*, &c. Christ is not revealed, but in his Word of the Gospel preached; all your conceptions without it, are idolatrous and monstrous; you neither see nor apprehend Christ, nor Christ you.

5. By closing with Christ upon false signes of grace; there is a company of people, if they have but some pangs, and some Reformations now and then, they are presently Christs, they hope, and if they be like unto all other good people, and do as they do, now all is well. Thus these foolish Virgins did deceive and delude themselves; they were Virgins, they were like others, and they thought well of them, and hence they fell to have hopes, out of some sleighty work of the Spirit of the Lord Jesus; but they are in the interim, strangers to the life of God, and Christ, and Grace; these should have looked to have oyle in their Vessels before now.

Secondly, What is it for Christ not to apprehend such, and to withdraw from such?

Answ. You may know this by the Affirmative. What is it for Christ Jesus to apprehend? Consider a soul drawn home to the Lord Christ to believe; there are two things he doth apprehend his people by. As,

First, By an eternal Covenant of grace which the Lord makes and enters into with a poor sinner, whereby he bindes himself for ever to be his, a God unto him; we cannot make the Lord apprehend us. (as in 2 *Sam.* 5. 1, 2, 3.) But by his Covenant, he bindes himself unto the souls of his people; *Isa.* 55. 2, 3. which is a mighty strong Covenant, as strong as Gods purpose is; for 'tis nothing but Gods purpose revealed. Now this the Lord reveals usual'y two wayes.

1. In the Word, without the conscience knowing it, so as that

a man hath not affurance of Gods Good-will to him. And

2. To Confcience ; and this two wayes.

1. By prayer, the foul being inftant with God to reveale his good-will, the Lord doth it. *Ezekiel* 36. 37. *I will yet be enquired of for this*, &c. *Zach.* 13. 9. Hence the Lord asks the poor heart, Will nothing content thee but the Lord? I wil fulfill thy defires then, the Lord hath heard thy cryes; all thy finnes fhall be pardoned, all thofe corruptions fubdued, &c.

2. By the Miniftry of the Word, when the foul hath been froward in feeking the Lord, but now mournes under it, that it cannot finde the Lord; the Lord profeffeth, I'le create the fruit of the lips, peace. *Pfal.* 25. 14. *He will fhew them his Covenant*, &c. So that the foul is for a time, ftablifhed and fupported by thefe and the like bleffed words of Grace from the Lord.

Secondly, By an eternal Spirit of life, which (as from Chrift the Head) comes into every member, and is in them, and fhall be in them, never forfaking them, though it be grieved a thoufand times in a day by them; this Spirit fets on the Covenant, and gives the firft fruits of glory, &c. *Ifaiah* 59. *ult. This is my Covenant, my Spirit fhall never depart*, &c.

Thus Chrift apprehends his; herein differing from *Adam*, he was next to God, and was apprehended by God. But 1. It was by a Covenant of works. 2. As a firft caufe upholding, and preferving, and governing the fecond; but this Spirit which fhould never forfake, this he had not; now when by Faith we are turned unto Chrift, Chrift apprehends us with both thefe armes. Now *è contrà*, you may fee what is it not to be apprehended by Chrift.

Reafon 1.   Becaufe they were never given unto Chrift in Vocation by the Fathers drawing, *John* 6. 65. And Chrift takes hold on none but them; they are apprehended for the Givers fake, though they be worthlefs in themfelves; All lawful Marriage, is by the Parents confent; fo here.

Reaf. 2.   Becaufe he knows the vilenefs of fuch mens hearts, lying in their fin, the falfenefs, deceits of them, *Joh.* 2. *ult.* As we ufe to fay, Such a one! No, I know him well enough.

Ufe 1.   Of fad *Reproof* to thofe who never trouble themfelves with any thoughts whether Chrift hath apprehended them; if they have once apprehended Jefus Chrift, they never queftion whether their Faith fo apprehend Chrift, as that Chrift apprehends it. Oh confider! thefe Virgins they did thus after a fort apprehend Chrift all their life, but now they know Chrift never loved them, becaufe they never favingly apprehended him. I remember *Ifa.* 4. 1. *Seven women fhall take hold of one man, and fhall fay, We will be called by thy Name, to take away our reproach, but we will eat our own bread*; So many take hold upon Chrift, Lord, let us be call'd by thy Name, to take away our reproach; when as they care for no part, nor portion in Chrift, but they will eat their own bread, live upon their own lufts. It was Chrifts fpeech unto divers that faw him, and followed him, *John* 6. as to his Difciples alfo, *Except you eat my flefh, you have no life in you*. What doth a man aim at in eating? not only that he may have Bread in his hand, but he examines, What vertue hath it? His end is, that it may grow one with him, and be turned into the fame flefh with him; and fo, that there may be a moft near union that can be; fo fhould all Chriftians ftudy that, and aim at that, that the Lord may be nearly united to them, and grow one with them; a gracious heart prayes and mournes for want of this.

Oh

Oh there be many that profess, What should I trouble my self with this and that grace? when I have done all, I can but look up to Christ! True; but will you not yet try whether you so look to Christ, as that he looks towards you? *John* 10. 10. *I know mine, and am known of mine*; there is a world of false faith in the world. *Jer.* 7. 8. When they cryed the Temple of the Lord, saith he, *Do you sweare, &c?* So I may say, Are you slothful in carriage, discontent in families, live in secret adultery, and your eyes and thoughts are full of it? do you break your promises, and Covenant with God and men, and forget the Lord in a Land of Peace, care for little but that your Plough may speed, and your names may rise? and do you cry, Christ, Christ? go to *Shiloh*, go to the *Palatinate, Bohemia,* and see what God hath done; Oh but I am better! oh but go to these foolish Virgins, let their dead ghosts affright thee, if the Lords Word cannot make thee search here.

A man drowning, all his care will be for a hand to take him; so would you if all were right; but you will not so.

Of Examination, Whether ever the Lord Jesus hath apprehended you with his dearest love, as well as you have apprehended him? 2 *Cor.* 13. 5. In all Covenants among men, whereby they are to binde themselves one to another, men will make it sure on both sides; Christ will make you sure to him; do you see that he be also made sure, and fast bound and united unto you. | *Use* 2.

Methinks the consideration of the example of the Virgins, might awaken every one unto it; for if this was the frame only of some rude, prophane Rout of carnal Protestants, professing Christ with their lips, but denying him in their lives, it might be excusable for us; but when Virgins, and so many, and that in these times of Christs coming, to faile here, this may strike a holy awfulness even in the best; and with much feare and trembling to search themselves, as it did the Disciples of Christ, when they heard not many, but one only should betray him; for there is this union on both parts, *John* 10. 14.

2 But though there is cause to search, I confess 'tis very hard to finde out this blessed Love-knot, the union between Christ and the soul being so mystical, and secret, and spiritual a work, especially in this life; wherein the Lord Jesus ariseth in the souls of his people, not in his perfect fulness, but only as the day-starre, at which time there is much darkness before the rising Sun; and hence the Apostle, *Gal.* 4. 9. *You have known God, or rather are known of him, &c.*

3. But yet it may be known, the many examples I might alledge, might prove it; and the promise of Christ to his Disciples doth evince it, *John* 14. 20. They were weak for a time, and Christ forsook them, and left them very sorrowful for a time, but saith he, *I will come to you again*; yea, and they might be never awhit the wiser for that; Nay, (saith he) *At that day you shall know I am in you, and you in me*; As a childe cannot tell how his soul comes into it, nor it may be, when, but afterwards it sees and feels that life: So that he were as bad as a Beast, that should deny an immortal soul; and 'tis an Article of our Faith; so here, &c.

4. And truly when it is known, 'tis exceeding useful, if a man was never apprehended by Christ, that now before he be cast out of sight, and reach of Christ, he may (if possible) get the Lord to apprehend him; and if he hath been apprehended, he may be supported in sad combates, and comforted against all feares of Apostacy from the Lord, but may know he stands as fast as Mount *Sion* that never can be removed; for times of spiritual

ritual assaults are to destroy faith. *Pfal.* 22. 8. *He trusted in God, let him deliver him;* and therefore you had need make sure of this; time may come, that to sence and feeling, hope and heart may faile; What supports now? yet Christ doth not, Christ will not, Christ cannot.

Quest. *How may this apprehending love on Christs part be known?*

Answ. In these five Degrees of it; it manifests it self; for it is unknown in it self; but in the manifestation of it, there is seen of us.

1. Degree, When the love of Christ apprehends the soul effectually, it overcomes the soul by sence of love, and thereby draws the soul from the strong holds and bondage of sinne to Christ; wherever there is exceeding deare love of the one unto the other, it is winning, it's of an overcoming nature; and though Christ doth threaten, or terrifie his people sometimes, yet the end is love; the love of Christ is of a winning, overcoming vertue; and he overcomes by love; and where he sets his heart on any, he will sooner or later overcome by love (if he can) the hearts of his, to forsake all other Lovers, and cleave unto him. *Jer.* 31. 3. *I have loved thee with an everlasting love;* What follows? hence, *I have drawn thee;* How? *by loving-kindness.* Cant. 1. 4. *Draw me, and I will follow thee;* this is the prayer of all those whom the Lord espouseth to himself; and 'tis as if they should say, I have neither strength, nor heart, to come nor follow; my iniquities clog me, and my feares discourage me, &c. but yet Lord draw me.

Let a man believe in Christ, and accept the offer of Christ when he can; but he can never do it, untill his heart averse to Christ, and unbelieving, be drawn to the Lord Jesus; and that not violently only by terrour, but by stronger cords, even the cords of Love, which perswades mightily the soul of unwilling to become willing; the Lord revealing the glorious grace and righteousness of Jesus Christ, and all the benefits of him, and therefore he offers this to it, and requires nothing but faith to receive it; this which stirs not the heart of another, overcomes the hearts of the Lords own, even with an holy admiration at this grace? What, Lord, am I! so vile I am, and filthy, and hellish, after so long abusing God and Grace, now to reveale, offer on such termes, Christ and Grace to me! Oh Lord, I am swallowed up with this kindness! how canst thou think such thoughts of love! yet I see it. *Rom.* 1. 17. *The Gospel is the power of God to salvation; for therein is righteousness revealed from faith to faith.* And mark, 'tis such a drawing of love, as pulls the soul from all the strong holds of sinne, to Christ; for that which the Prophet complaines of people in his time, is true of ours, *Jer.* 8. 5. *They took fast hold of deceit, and refused to return;* they hold it as their life, and it holds them as fast as spiritual bonds of death; either the pleasure of sinne holds them, or the power of unbelief in refusing grace, attended with sinkings, and sadness of heart, or objecting against grace through pride of heart, when the Lord comes to apprehend it; hereupon the Lord Jesus Christ, *uno & eodem actu & ictu,* in drawing the soul to himself, draws it from the captivity of sinne; thus, *Acts* 26. 18. *from darkness to light.* 1 *Thes.* 1. 9. and the soul saith as they, *Jer.* 3. 22, 24, &c. The Lord Jesus doth not so draw it to himself, as that at the same time it abides in sinne; nor so from sinne, as that it abides without Christ; but *uno,* &c.

For I observe a double errour in mens drawing to Christ.

First, Either they come only from misery (I say, Only) and so are rather driven, than drawn to Christ; they rather come themselves on the legs of

of their self-love, than on the feet of Faith. Now when Christ doth effectually draw, he doth it by love; Oh this me ts, this draws, this breaks,
this overcomes; and now as we say in Warre, It is better to Reconcile an
Enemy, than to Conquer him by force; because the one overcomes his
power only, but the other overcomes his will; so Christ could crush (and
he doth bruise his peoples souls with miseries, they would never else be suit-
ably affected with the bruises of his soul) but this makes way for love; he
overcomes the will by love.

Secondly, Or else if love doth meet, affect, and draw them, yet it
doth not overcome them, or draw them from the hold of sinne, but as Ivy
clasps about the Tree with a root of its own. I have known some that have
been melted, affected with the patience and goodness of God towards them;
that have been almost perswaded, and yet have turned almost Devils afterward; the Reason hath been, because they were never quite taken off their
own bottomes. Now a soul whom Christ draws, the Lord in drawing him
to himself, pulls him from his sinne, so that he is weary of it; the light
of Chrsts grace, oh this draws indeed! that now not only it dare not, will
not, but cannot live in sinne. *Rom.* 6, 2. *Titus* 2, 11, 12. *Grace appeares to all; but it teacheth us (saith the Apostle) to deny ungodlinesse;*
ungodliness will be suing and seeking for love, but they deny it; the soul
thus comes not unto Christ, without feeling of sinne in it, but that the Lord
would take away all iniquity from it. *Jer.* 3. 22. And because it feares
there may be some secret evil; its care therefore is, that the Lord would
strike the root of all, and make it more bitter than death, to its grave.
The greatest evil of all, is sinne; 'tis greater than Death, Grave, Hell; hence
Chrsts greatest love is in Redeeming first from sinne; And as if there had
never been sinne, grave, nor death should never hold; so when he breaks
the power of sinne, no power of Satan, World, Death, shall hold thee
from Christ; and 'tis never overcome by love till now. Let a man be in
never such feares and troubles of minde, and sinkings of heart, and soon
after he pretends to great joyes, and assurance, but sin is not overcome,
though it be snibbed and hid, yet it will overcome you at last, and would
pull thee down from heaven, if ever thou wert there; As if one that makes
suit to another, and she is forced to give consent, but she hath her heart still
to another Lover, he will never have her; Not that the Saints are really
free from all sins, and weaknesses, but they are free from peace with sin,
though not free from War with sin till death; as when two Lovers are faln out,
it's enough if the League be broken.

2. *Degree.* The apprehending love of Christ; it satiates, fills, and feeds
the soul with the sweetness of its self, now the soul being come to Christ,
and seeing the heighth and depth of the love and pity of Christ. *Psal.* 65.
2, 3, 4. *Blessed is the man whom thou choosest, he shall be satisfied;* the
stony ground received the Word with joy, was affected with the grace of
Christ; as one that stands by where smells are (but smells do not feed) (or
they may taste, but tastes do not feed nor satisfie) So 'tis here. You know
we feed on our meat, that we may be strengthened thereby, and it may be
turned to nourishment, and good blood, and flesh, and be made one with
us; so Christ gives himself to be spiritually eaten by Faith, out of an earnest
desire, that he may have a neare, a very near union to him, and he to us.
Now the maine end of eating, is satisfying; and if a man be satiated with it,
though he think it will never prove nourishment, yet it doth; So, where life
is, &c. *Joh.* 6, 56. *He dwells in me, and I in him.*

If a man tastes not a greater good in Christ, than in his lusts, he will
fall to them againe from Christ; but if he feeds on Christ, and is satiate with

Aaaa   him,

him, never can he hunger againe; otherwise the foul will say, It was better with me once, than now it is; *Solomon*, though he tasted all good of the creatures after he knew God, and God had appeared twice to him, yet he felt them fall short of what he once found, and at last he remembred his rest. When *Abram* gave his children gifts, he did not lay hold on them with special love, but to him to whom he gave his Inheritance; So the Lord may take hold on a man, and give him many abilities, but when he gives himself as an Inheritance and portion, this is special love; and when is that known? (*viz.*) when the soul is fully satiated with it, *Psalme* 16. 2, 3, 4. And hence the Prodigal he did not know he should be received; but when he came, *Make me a servant, if not a Son* (saith he) *and his Father hung about his neck*, &c. So here. *Exodus* 6. 3. God hath two wayes to satisfie his people.

1. By fulfilling his promises.

2. By manifesting himself, and that to their satisfying, as sufficient to do all what he hath promised.

Oh Consider of this, you that have seen mercy, but it hath not satiated you, nor doth yet! but you have other bread to feed on; the Lord never took hold on you.

3. *Degree.* This apprehending love of Christ, having thus satiated the soule, it constraines the soule to live and act for Christ. Now, what shall I do for the Lord, and the poor soule begins to lament dayes past of folly; and secretly desires of the Lord, it might rather not live, than not live to him; and though happily it often serves sin and self, yet the soul accounts that life death, and so laments it before the Lord, 2 *Cor.* 5. 15, 16. *That they that live, might live to him.* John 6. 57. *He that believeth in me, shall live by me;* i. e. both by me, and for me; and Christ apprehends the soul fast now; for Christ must rather lose his life, than lose this soul. Look as 'tis with a Graft, put the science close by the stock, tye it fast, if there it withers, and rather loseth life than gets it, we say, Surely it's not put in right; for if it were, the living Stock would convey sap and nourishment to it. So 'tis here; some herbs are very precious, but for ornament, rather than use; so Christ is deare, but what use do you make of Christ? what life do you fetch from Christ? the least joynt in a mans finger united to the soul, hath life of it; but Signets though near to the finger, yet they have no life, and hence no union, and hence no members; so the Saints have life, though weak; but unregenerate men (as Signets) may be near life, and near the true Members of Christ that be quickened, but receive no Life.

Gluttons will feed, that they may go to sleeping; others, that they may fall a working; So, many take Christ, and get some peace, and then turn Grace into wantonness, and so sleep in their sloth; but a gracious heart, all his prayers and feeding, is, that he might have strength, and heart, to live and work for Christ; Hath the Lord pitied, pardoned? how Lord shall I now live in my Calling? now his friends are by him pityed; now he is fruitful, and mourns, when others be not so.

4. *Degree.* This apprehending love of Christ having thus constrained the soul, it ever follows it, *and dwells in it, Joh.* 14. 17. For after Christ hath apprehended the soul, so as that the soul thinks it shall never be as it hath been before; yet oh the lamentable decayes and losses that it feels! it loseth favour and life too afterward, and lives against Christ sometimes (a thing never to be lamented enough) but mark, if Christ hath apprehended, he will not forsake the soul, though it hath forsaken him; and hence the Lord by his constant assistance of the Spirit, recovers it again, brings it

back

back again, and that after questionings sometimes, if ever there was grace indeed in it; yea, if not, yet oh that it should thus forsake the Lord! nay, the Lord sometime preventing before it was seeking.

Judas falls, the Lord never looks after him; *Peter* falls, Christ looks after him, and recovers him; all the Disciples denied Christ, and fled after promise never to do so; yet, saith he, *Mark* 14. 28, 16, 7. *I'le go before you to Galilee; my Sp.rit is in you, and shall be in you, though you grieve it, and sad it.* *Adam* falls, and one sin cut him from Gods hold of him; hence he dasheth quite to pieces; but now Christ upholding on other termes, hence, though his people forsake him, yet he holds them still fast and sure, and keeps them from breaking utterly to pieces; nay, if they be as water spilt on the ground, he will gather them up againe; he deals not so with others, *John* 6. 66. Many forsake him, being never given indeed to him, he lets them go; but Christ speaks to his Disciples, *Will you go?* So if a man hath a stranger in his House, he will let him go, and enquire not after him; he came to me for a time; but if he hath a Son, and he is gone, he will finde him out; and there he wonders at a Fathers love, to see his Spirit; So here; and hence come the Saints to wonder at the Lord so much, *What is not the Lord yet gone?*

I speak this partly to terrifie those that go, and never return again, and to answer Objections of Saints; the Lord hath hid himself from me, and I have forsaken him; yet mark, he will bring thee back again to himself lamenting, &c.

5. *Degree*, This apprehending love of Christ, it now witnesseth love to the soul most clearly and fully; the Question is, Doth Christ apprehend any but those to whom he witnesseth love? No, for he doth witness to all in some measure; but here comes the cleare manifestation of it; When I was dead he quickned me, and since that I have lost the Lord, and he me, yet he hath found me out; and hence now the soul concludes, the Lord loves it. *Gal.* 2. 20. *Who loved me, and gave himself for me.* Psalme 23. *Ult. The Lord restoreth my Soule, surely mercy shall follow me.*

Now try if the Lord never dealt thus with thee.

Use 3.
As this may serve to discourage, or terrifie those that never did, so it may encourage those to preserve their faith who so apprehend Christ, as that they are apprehended of him; If a Woman was never Married to such a man, for her to call him, or speak of him, or think of him to be her Husband, 'tis presumption; but when he hath given himself to her, then let her own her priviledge, and maintaine her claime against all Law, and wranglers, and preserve her interest; So those that never were given to Christ, let them know their faith is but smoke and vanity; but let *Job* say, *Though he kill me, yet I'le trust him.* David Psal. 42. 3. had that temptation, *Where is now thy God?* that his teares were his meat, and drink, and was much shaken, and cast down by it; but what, Doth he lie still? No, he stirs up himself, and chides himself, *Why art thou cast down? Ver.* 5. 11. *He is my God.* 1 Tim. 6. 12. *Fight a good fight of faith, and lay hold of eternal life whereunto thou art called.*

'Tis very unsafe for any Christian to lay by Faith, and cast off the exercise of it, because 'tis Christs apprehending of us which doth preserve us; True, but 'tis by faith, which may not be at all times seen, as neither the other can; and therefore take heed you make not this use of Doctrine here, because many may apprehend Christ, whom Christ never apprehended; therefore what have I to do to close with Christ? To be kept from putting out

faith

faith either in your judgement and practice, or practice only? I would but only ask of such these Questions.

First, If we were only to look to Christs apprehending us without the other, why doth the Apostle put such a weight upon Faith, as that all the benefits of Christ are communicated by it? *Heb.* 3. 14. *We partake of Christ, if we hold the beginning of our confidence stedfast*; and *Heb.* 10. 38. *The just lives by it*, not from it.

Secondly, If so, why doth Satan so much strike at faith? when *Peter* fell, what did he strike at? what did he winnow him for? To shake out his faith; and hence Christ prayes *that it faile not*; When Satan comes to Christ, the first thing which made way for all his temptations, was, *If thou beest the Son*, &c. Our blessed fellowship with Christ, he sees consists of two things; Faith on our part, and the Spirit on Christs; and Satan strikes at the weakest first.

Thirdly, If so, Why doth the Lord Jesus so carefully seek to preserve it? both mediately by all meanes and Ministries, Word, Sacraments, which are to feed Faith; and hence *Paul*, 1 *Thess.* 3. 2. *To establish you in faith.* And ver. 5. he hence *rejoyced*; and ver. 10. *We would be yours to perfect your Faith.* And also immediately; *Peter* falls, Christ prayes *his faith faile not*; his grace should not; And 1 *Pet.* 1. 2, 3. *Preserved by faith to Salvation.*

Object. But I cannot believe?

Answ. Before faith you cannot; and after you do believe, the Acts of faith, and lively working of faith, may be many times in desertions of the soul from God, or God from the soul, hindered; and when he hath those lively workings of it, it's from the power of Christ, that it is acted, as well as preserved; but yet if Christ hath once given power to believe, he maintaines it constantly, and increaseth it; and therefore you have no cause to plead, I cannot; so that you cannot sin, and live in it, especially in unbelief, and lie there, you cannot draw back to perdition, but believe to the salvation of your souls; *the just lives by faith*; we say we must live, Faith will be stirring, when no other grace can be so; it Victuals the whole Camp, Relieves the besieged; and it's most strong, when man is most weak. 'Tis true indeed, there may be many acts of presumption for one act of faith; take heed of that; That faith is not presumption, which the more it works, the more humble it makes the soul to be, and vile in his own eyes; because as Faith ever fetcheth of Christs fulnes to the soule, so it ever is attended with sence of emptines in the soule naturally, and then it's right.

Use 4.　Oh resist not the Lord Jesus, when he comes to apprehend you by his Almighty Arme! In a shipwrack, if a man sees many drowning, and perishing, never a hand to take hold of them, when one is reached out to him, will he resist it? Oh no! I know indeed when the time of love comes, there is no power of overcoming and frustrating the grace of God, but yet there is a power of resisting, which the Lord complaines of in them, *Acts* 7. and which he makes his people to complaine with bitternes of in his bosome when his time comes. *Isaiah* 50. 2. The Lord cryes out of his people when they had sold themselves into the hand of their enemies, and were apt to lay the fault on the Lord, as men do. Now the Lord gives not me a heart to believe; Saith he, *Wherefore when I came, was there none to answer? Object.* You can never pardon such sinners, help against such sinnes, mercy cannot reach us? *Is my hand shortned?* No such matter. I do not press you now to apprehend Christ, but resist not the Lord when he hath

・his

his hand upon thy heart or conscience to apprehend thee. Is the Lord at work with none of you ? art forsaken of Christ altogether ? There are many wayes of Resisting Christ thus ; I'le only name these two.

First, When the soul will not suffer the Lord Jesus to bruise , or cross its will , that so he may prevaile over the resistancy of it. A strong arme , a strong man when his arme is bruised, or broken, or wounded , takes away the act of resistance; as taking away the very life from it , takes away the very power of resistance ; so Christ would unite himself to the soul ; there can be no constant union , where there is constant resistance. Christ comes to take away that ; hence bruises and wounds the soul ; outwardly sometime in name, estate; inwardly in conscience , in heart. Now here is mens folly, That they will not be humbled , when they heare of their estate in the Word; they will not believe 'tis so, though they stand all the while convinced therein, as if they had been named ; nay, they will not think of it ; if it begins to trouble them , or if they do begin, they think it is the temptation of the Devil; and if their estates or names begin to dye , they will not be poor nor despised ; they had rather dye , or live in vexing and fretting, rather than yield ; they will have Gods Will bowed to theirs , not theirs to the Lord , nor yield themselves Captives to his mercy, let him do with them what he will , who owes them nothing. Thus it was with *Ephraim*; *Capernaum* heard, admired, embraced Christ , but yet repented not ; that was to live in the smoke and fire ; Wo to you , saith he , for it. *Jer.* 6. 7, 8. *Be instructed* ; He saith not , Instruct thy self , but *be instructed* , be convinced , be humbled for thy sin , *lest my soul depart* ; I am with thee yet to pardon it, yet to take it away.

Secondly , When they will not be gathered to Christ, nor come to him, nor receive his love when it comes to them , but put it farre from them as much as in them lies. The Disciples told *Thomas* Christ was risen , but he would not believe he saw him ; nay, unless he felt ; nay, unless he felt his very wounds ; Christ pities , and beares with the weaknes of Faith ; But (saith he) *be no more faithless, but faithful* ; and hence saith he , *Blessed are they which have not seen, and yet believed*; this , Christ complaines of in the Jewes , *He would have gathered them , and they would not* !

Now here resistance is made two wayes.

1. By the will ; when the soul sees the offer of love faire and full , but will not be drawn to close with it , because it knows whether to go , and live, and be yet well enough without it. *John* 6. 68. *Whether shall I go* ? It hath some other Lovers to give it content ; but loss of Christs love, is not for the present as bitter as death to him ; because having of it , is not life to him , because something else is his life ; this is enmity of heart ; and indeed the root is worse (if worse may be) you can finde some pillow to ease you , when you refuse Christs love to help you.

2. By the minde ; the soul knows not whether to go, and yet the minde doth not , nor will meditate with fixed meditations on the grace of Christ, whereby it might be drawn to Christ ; but pores upon its sinnes , and unbelief, and feares, and objects strongly, and continually against the Lord. *Isaiah* 40. 27, 28. *Hast not seen, &c.* (Beloved) Tis with the minde , as it is with burning glasses , hold them to the Sun , and you gather and unite the beames ; that they burn ; So the soule by musing on Christs Love.

Object. *Many say, I cannot believe though I see a command for it ; and God will not help me.*

Ans.

Answer. The fault is not here , but in this , You will not use this means in musing on the gracious freeness , riches and need of his love , *Psal.* 6 : . 6,7. but on the earth.

1. Object. *You will say, I cannot but resist.*

Answer, Yet I pray give us leave to exhort you to believe ; give *Peter* leave to perswade ; *Acts* 3. 19. *Repent and be converted* ; the Lord requires that only ; it may be the Lord may go away from thy soul , and take his leave of thee for ever ; and if you did know, you would not crucifie, nor resist the Lord of glory ; if you would consider, you would know.

2. Object. *I finde my heart much affected and drawn , but then I am afraid of presuming ; how shall I know when I may close with the Lord ?*

Answ. 1. When the Merchant hath sold all, let him take the Pearl , and enrich himself with it ; the Devil may grudge thee it, but the Lord doth not , will not.

2. When the Lord comes to draw indeed , you cannot but accept ; your need will be so great , the offer so faire , love so abundant , and like the honey comb dropping into thy heart before thou suckest it ; and Christ so dear, that thou canst not tread upon him whom God hath smitten for thee. *Mary Joh.* 20. 15, 16, 17. *stands weeping* ; at last Christ appeares , *Woman, why weepest thou ? whom seekest thou ?* she knew him not ; hence her heart stirres not ; but at last he calls her by her name , and then she knew him , and saw him present ; *Rabboni* , saith she ; and now had she the best apprehend ? Yea , she cannot but embrace him ; *Oh touch me not as yet* saith he, &c.

Of Exhortation , To labour that the Lord Jesus may apprehend you : I know it's nothing but his mercy can move him to it , even to take away that resistance of your hearts ; but yet heare his voice , as well as know his power , and harden not your hearts whiles it is called to day, in use of means for this end, *Psal.*61.7.

1. Consider your need of this. *Isa.* 42. 1. *Behold my servant whom I uphold* ; Did Christ need ? Yes, Christ himself must be supported by the power of the Lord ; *Psal.* 40. 11, 12. *Let thy mercy and truth continually preserve me* ; and this was not only when sinnes swallowed him up, but when he had been preserved, *Psalme* 17. 5,6. *Hold up my goings* ; You are gone in a moment , if the Lord lets his hold go ; you are kept in strong holds, in Iron bolts, in invisible, everlasting chaines, in the Dungeon where no water is, unless the arme of Christ help.

2. Consider the benefit of it. *Acts* 2. 24, 25. It was impossible Christ should be held under paines of death , because of his Princely Spirit exalting him ; so here , Christ is and will be with you , and when once he hath apprehended you , none can pull you out of his hands, no not the Fathers hand that was angry ; and he will never cast away his (*Joh.*10.29.) *when they come to him.*

3. Consider how few finde this. *Isa.* 53. 1. *To whom is the arme of the Lord revealed , and who hath believed our report ?* both joyned together , the arme is Christ , and the power of Christ by his Spirit in the hearts of his Elect ; but for want of this, it is that one lives loosely , and another falls foulely , and never riseth ; another falls secretly, and is never known, and dyes in a dreame, &c. and that there is such miserable scrambling for promises ; and that men are so worshipping whom they know not.

4. Consider the misery of the want of this.

But further,

Be careful to get satisfaction by blood , before Application by the Spirit ;

if ever you look for the latter, be careful to get the former; God is full of Spirit; why sends he it not? sinne is not satisfied for, first get that done therefore. *John* 6. 53. *Except ye eat my flesh, and drink my blood, &c.* God could not send the Spirit nor Word but for this to thee; a man feeles the strength of sinne, and prayes, Lord, subdue it; oh but look to pay thy Ransome. If a man be in chaines for debt, and gets out without satisfaction for the debt or wrong, he will be taken againe; but if it be satisfied for, though he be taken by the Jaylour, and ill-intreated, yet he shall be set free againe; and therefore do as those, *Levit.* 3. 3, 4. You are freely to go to Sacrifice; and it's said, *it shall be accepted to make Atonement.*

If the Lord with-hold his Spirit, mourn for the want of it; as *Psal.* 41. 3. *My tears are my meat.* *Meanes* 2.

If the Lord gives any thing, be thankful for any little; see it, and make much of it, for it is from Christ, the least thought or knowledge of thy misery; *John* 14. 17. *The world cannot receive it, because it knows him not; i.e.* so as to prize it, love it, bless, and wonder at the Lord for it. *Thy Spirit is good, Lord let it lead me,* saith David. *Meenes* 3.

Quest. *What if I finde not these things in my soul?*

Answ. Mourn then.

Object. *What if I cannot?*

Answ. Then muse on thy misery.

Object. *But I cannot?*

Answ. Then hear what the Lord will speak.

Quest. *What if he helps not?*

Answ. Thou art unworthy, thou art his clay, he may and will do what he will.

Of thankfulness to the Saints who are apprehended of the Lord Jesus; you know him, and he knows you; you come to him, and he takes you; you give up your selves to him, and he gives himself to you; you make him your God and Head, and he makes you his people and Members, &c. *Use* 6.

Oh be thankful for this; 'tis a choice and peculiar mercy, denied to many, and given unto you. *Psalme* 73. 23, 24, 25, 26. *Thou art continually with me when falling from thee;* What is the use that David makes? *Thou wilt guide;* and hence, *Whom have I in heaven but thee?* I might be broken, and like water spilt on the ground every moment, but thou keepest me

Object. *But I finde the Lord methinks sometime utterly gone from me; and I fear he will faile.*

Answ. True; and hence *Jeremiah* asks, *Jer.*15.18. *Wilt thou be unto me as a lyar, and as waters that faile? shall thy truth and mercy be spent?* No, once apprehended, he will not lose thee.

Quest. *How shall I know that?*

Answer. Something I have spoken, and three things more I shall add now.

Fir̄ſt. You may know it by time present; There are two things which seldome fail in deepest desertions.

1. The soul forsakes not the Lord by unutterable groanes, when the Lord seems to forsake it, *Psal.* 22. 2, 3. and it presseth hard after the Lord, *Psalme* 63. 8. and doth not as the Philistines, 2 *Sam.* 5. 21. forsake their gods, when they forsake them.

2. If this faires, it grows poor in spirit, and vile, and loaths it self, as worthy the Lord should never regard it, *Isaiah* 57. 15. and so magnifies
grace

grace moſt , when the Lord makes it leaſt ; and when the Lord makes it nothing, it makes God all things to it.

Secondly, If neither of theſe will ſerve , yet you may remember dayes of
old; as *David* , *Pſal.* 77. 10. *Pſal.* 71. 6 , 9 , 11. Some ſaid, *God had
forſaken him* , but yet now he remembers Ancient mercies.

Third'y , Then ſtay awhile longer in waiting for the Lord ; what the Lord
doth now, you know not, but you ſhall know afterward; *Iſa.*64. 4. *that which
eye hath not ſeen, hath God prepared.*

1. You that are young men , hath the Lord pluck't you out of your *Sodom*
ſin , when you lingred in it , when you reſiſted the Lord in the heat of your
youth? &c.

2. You old men; how many temptations, corruptions, back-ſlidings ,
pollutions ? beating out (as it were) the breath of the Spirit ? yet from
the belly to gray haires the Lord hath carried thee , kept thee ; Oh thy foot
had ſaln, if the Lord had not kept !

3. You that have been once ſinful , vile creatures, yet hath the Lord loved you for all this ! what if the Lord take away comforts from you , and
afflict ? yet hath he not taken loving-kindneſs, nor mercy from you ,
but done good to you by your ſorrowes , when others go by Droves
before his Door , and takes none, &c. O what cauſe have you to mag-
niſie mercy !

Obſerv. 5.

*That the Lord Jeſus at his coming to death or judgement , will make a per-
fect ſeparation between the wiſe and fooliſh Virgins.*

For the Virgins were all one together till Chriſt comes, and now the
one ſort is received to Chriſt, the other ſeparated from Chriſt ; nay , not ſo
much as known of Chriſt. There are not , have not been any Churches in
this life , but there will be wiſe and fooliſh , Tares and Wheat grow up together ; not Virgins and Harlots , not openly prophane (it may be) or
wicked and godly ; No, but when all are Virgins in outward Profeſſion, and
Converſation , yet then ſome will be wiſe, and ſome fooliſh in the ſight of
Chriſt, (though not in the ſight of man) and between theſe the Lord Jeſus
will make a ſeparation at his coming. *Matth.* 25. 31. *He ſhall ſet Sheep
and Goats at his right and left hand.* Mat. 3. 12. *He ſhall thorowly purge
his floore , and ſeparate chaffe and wheat.* 2 Theſ. 1. 9. *puniſhed with eternal deſtruction from the preſence of the Lord.* The Son of the bond-woman,
muſt not be Heir together with the Son of the free-woman, and therefore caſt
him out ; they muſt part companies.

Queſt. 1. *Whether ſhall they be ſeparated?*

Anſw. 1. At particular judgement; what became of the ſoul of *Lazarus?*
It was carried by the Angels to *Abrahams* boſome ; *i. e.* to the Third Heavens where *Abraham* was , and to fellowſhip with him, dearly loved of him;
What then becomes of the ſouls of others? they being ſentenced by God,
are dragg'd down to hell by evil Angels, and are reſerved; Where? they are
reſerved in the Elements.

2. At general judgement; the Elect ſhall be called to come and inherit
their Kingdome ; and hence others ſhall be caſt with the Devil and his Angels, to eternal fire , which is there where the Third Heaven is not ; and
here ſhall they be parted , and never joyned together more , which is
fearful.

Queſt. 2. *Why will there be ſuch a ſeparation?*

Anſw. 1. *Reaſon.* Becauſe at Chriſts coming they ſhall be immediately
judged, and examined by Chriſt; he ſhall then make ſtrict and immediate
trial of them ; Why do theſe fooliſh Virgins creep in now? is not Chriſt
preſent

present with his people, ruling and judging among his people? Yes, but Christ judgeth now mediately by meanes of his servants; and hence he not giving, and they not having perfect knowledge of the secrets of mens hearts, nor having perfect hatred of the evil and hypocrisie of mens hearts; hence they are not separated now, nor cannot be (though the Servants of God should be very watchful) so long as they cannot see nor convince men of all their Hypocrisie; some light and life he gives them to see beyond their own natural abilities, but it is not perfected; and hence his work is (as the instruments are) imperfect; but now when Christ himself comes immediately to judge, and they fall into his hands, he can perfectly see all their secret evils; he hath his eyes like a flaming fire, and themselves shall know, and all Churches shall know; nay, all the world shall know *that he is a God searching the hearts and reines*, 1 Sam. 16. 7. and he perfectly hates Hypocrisie; he regards not any mans person, or parts, or profession, or kindnesses, or relations, (which move us many times to accept whom he refuseth against some light) but as 'tis, *Isa.* 61. 8. *He hates robbery in burnt offerings, and loves judgement*; and hence, the more present Christ is with his people, the more able are they to discerne, as *Peter*, the secrets of *Ananias* in the Primitive times, or the Lord discernes for them, and by some unexpected way or other little thought of to themselves, discovers them by their own mouths, or base actions; by their fruits you shall know them; *Matthew* 22. 12. when the King came, he was *speechless*, whom the Guests could not discerne; So here, men have many things to say for themselves, who when they come before Christ, will be struck dumb. A wise Prince when he judgeth by inferiour Officers, they may discern of some cases; but if a King (as *Solomon*) was present, secrets which they see not, would be found out; so here.

Reas. 2. Because this is part of the Curse upon Hypocrites, To be cast out of the fellowship of the Elect; secret sinnes do not only separate us from Christ, but from all our fellowship with the Saints, which next to separation from Christ, is the greatest evil in the world; It comforts the hearts of Hypocrites, they are loved of good people, and liked of good people; and though privy to a world of filth, which a gracious heart is ashamed of, and loaths himself for, and thinks himself not worthy of a look of love from any of the least; yet Hypocrites quiet themselves, if they can cover it from the eyes of Gods people, *Matth.* 24. 40. but now they shall no longer rejoyce under the shadow of these Vines; No, the Lord will separate them to evil, *Deut.* 29. 21. which is partly begun now, and perfected afterward; *Mat.* 8. 11, 12. they shall see *Abraham* and *Isaac* in Gods Kingdome, and mourn when themselves are cast out.

Reas. 3. For the joy and comfort of the Saints; for it's a wonderful joy to the heart to enjoy fellowship of Saints alone; when in a Sacrament we see prophane people approach to it, it troubles us, grieves us; when we come to a place where we may be perswaded of the uprightness of all, it's very sweet; but now there is some feare, and hence less joy; but when we shall see the Saints together, and say, These are they who are eternally beloved of Christ, deare to him, and to be with them, and be alone, this is very sweet; those that love together only, rejoyce to be alone together; so Saints, so Christ himself, 1 *Thes.* 4. *ult.* *Rev.* 22. 14. *Blessed are they that keep his commands, and may go to the City; for without are dogs, and those who make lyes, &c.*

Reason 4. In regard of the Glory of Christ, and Honour of Christ.

First, Hereby Christs infinite wisdome searching the secrets of all hearts, shall be seen, and that before all the World.   1 *Cor.* 14. 25. 'tis said when the secrets of mens hearts are discovered, they shall fall down and say, Verily *God is in you.* Rev. 2. 23. *All Churches shall know, &c.* Why? are Churches so ignorant of that? Yes, they believe it in the general; but they shall see it in the example, as well as in the rule, more fully afterward. We think he searcheth all hearts, but are there no hypocrites to be found in such and such Churches? Yes, he shews some even in such; and the more secret and subtle any thing hath been, the more openly will the Lord Reveale it, because this makes the more for Him.

2. Hereby Christ shews his exceeding great love to his people, in parting them and others; *John* 17. 23. *I in them, that the world may know, &c.* Gen. 6. 8. *Noah found favour*; Wherein was that shewn? *Verse* 7. *I'le destroy man and beast*; but *Noah* found favour; and *ver.* 13. *Make an Ark, &c.*

3. Hereby he sheweth his acceptance of the uprightness of the hearts and wayes of his servants, which it may be are poor and mean in their own eyes, but precious in the sight of the Lord, above all the pompous furniture and pithless profession of Hypocrites, *Mal.* 3. 16, 18. hence *Mat.* 25. *Come take the Kingdome for you, &c.* What is glorious in the worlds, is vile in the Lords eyes.

Use 1.

Let none be then offended at the Apostacy of men (eminent in profession) from the wayes of God, in the purest and most reformed Churches; What are these people (say some scorners) better than others? some of these make a greater shew than others, and yet they fall; What are these Churches better than others, where there is no such examination, nor trial? and these be your Church-members, and your holy people, and your Covenanters, and thus men stumble. Oh consider, in the purest Churches there be many foolish whom Christ will separate one from another; and therefore if Christ doth give a taste of this before hand, and those that are vile before him, he makes them vile before others, that all *Israel* may see and feare, do not wonder at it. *Isa.* 32. 5, 6. *The Churle shall be no more called liberal, for he will speak, and think, and work so.* Luke 12. 2. *Nothing secret, but it shall be revealed* (many secret evils are hid) but it shall be put in part here. Christ saw his Disciples apt to be offended at the fall of *Judas.* Did not he know him? then he was not the Son of God; or if he did, why did he suffer him? Saith he, *John* 13. 18. *He that eats bread, shall lift up his heel against me, that the Scripture may be fulfilled*; and 'tis the portion of the Churches and people of God, to be troubled with such as these, that the Scriptures may be fulfilled; therefore be not offended; it ever hath been so in the Primitive times, as well as in Christs Family; *Paul* foretells of Wolves devouring the Flock, arising out of themselves; and 2 *Pet.* 2. 1,2. as there were, so there shall be false Prophets; and *Paul* (though discerning) reckons his danger in regard of false Brethren; and it is a heavy judgement of God, that that which should make a man adore the depth of Christs Wisdome, Holiness, Presence in his Church, and fear his own heart and Spirit, should offend men in the least measure; for surely these are warnings to all the Churches, and all men, and examples before our doors, as those are, 1 *Cor.* 10. A man that is prescribing Rules of Art, he gives one or two examples, he could give twenty, but that is enough to make *the wise understand*, Hos. 14. 9.

Use 2.

Hence see the fearful and sad condition of those who shall voluntarily separate

parate themselves (and are glad of it) from the fellowship of the faithful; nay, the Churches of Christ, they do but execute the divine sentence of Christ upon themselves in this life, which shall be past upon them at the great day; they shall then be parted, and cast out of the family of God, the Church of the first-born, of which the Churches on earth in their purity are a resemblance.

Look as it is in sinning, a man departs from God, and executes upon himself that which shall be (though now 'tis not felt) his greatest doom; so it is in parting from the Saints; they do but execute their sentence upon themselves; and hence, 1 *John* 2. 19. *They went out from us, that it might be made manifest they were not all of us*; if ever they had portion in the Saints, they would never have parted; not but that one may separate from the incurable corruptions of a true Church, and not but that one may remove from one Church to another, provided it be with love, and utmost care for the good of that where he was; and also, not but that one may be forced upon some special cause to dwell in *Meshech*, and be forced to forsake Sacrificing, to shew mercy; but I speak of such forsaking wherein men voluntarily separate themselves from all the Churches of God at least, though not the people of God, out of a base esteem of their fellowship, and a high esteem of something else which they shall have without it; they regard not Communion of Saints, no further than it may serve their turne; and when it will not serve their turne, then they forsake it.

This separation it commonly ariseth from certain preparations to it, which are the loosenings of a mans heart from Gods people; Like the Apple, before it falls, it begins to grow loose from that which holds it. I shall briefly shew how this is, that you may be watchful; many not yet fallen, but their hearts sit loose from Churches, and fellowship of Saints, and people of God, even when they think their hearts sit close to Christ; and I will not name all; for particular men have their particular temptations; but what is most common, and this is one secret sin, and plague of men in these Churches, and there will be rendings; Christs work is to gather, and Satans ever quite contrary, to scatter; and it is a Rule, What is Christs greatest work, the contrary is Satans chiefest; as when Christ is humbling, he is hardning; when drawing to believe, he to unbelief; when Christs work is to gather and unite, his is to scatter, loosen, and divide; with that foot Christ treads on Satan most, there he bites most.

1. The Lord withdraws that honour and love from a man, which either he looks for, or thinks he deserves from the hands and hearts of Gods people; either they are not lovely, or not loving to others; when they have either no personal worth to purchase love, or they have nothing to give of love in exchange for love, or else (to try them) the Lord for a time leaves his people to a blockishness of spirit; their love waxeth cold, or they think they are not honoured, or have not enough; and so (if men do not make) Satan will make them scandals to themselves through their pride of spirit. 1 *Sam.* 15. 35. *Saul* desired, *Honour me before the peop'e*, but *Samuel* came not to *Saul*; hence what did *Saul* do? you never read that he came to, or made use of *Samuel* again. We are united to Christ by faith, but to the Saints by love, and mutual love, *Ephes.* 4. 16. Take away this mutual love, that you love not others, or they love not you, unless you have Christs Spirit which was in *Paul*, and all the faithful, 2 *Cor.* 11. 16. you will fall secretly; and hence *Hebrews* 10. 24, 25. *Provoke one another to love and good works*; say to one another, Pray Brother tell me of my faults, and your feares; I'le tell you my heart againe, &c.

Tru-

Truly here is the temptation of some, if not of most, to Apostacy from the Lord and his Servants; and this is the guise of Hypocrites, let any godly not honour them, they despise them; let any ungodly honour them, if they be not extreamly vile, they love them and their fellowship, and are ready to think them as honest as the best, because they make themselves their own gods, those that honour them, are their good Angels, and *è contrà*.

2. They begin to feel by woful experience, no spiritual good, or power of the Spirit and Presence of the holy Ghost in their fellowship, or in these Ordinances in it; they have them, but not the use nor comfort of them, and this sets them going, and ripens, and rots them for a fall; for as want of love made them sit loose from the persons, so this makes them sit loose from the Ordinances; and a man thinks now, What am I the better for the purity of Ordinances? and so hence, when he should loath his heart, he loaths the truth, and wayes he seems to approve, and hence falls. For this is a standing Rule, Let a man have Ordinances, and not know how to use them, or not indeed make spiritual use of them, if he knows it, but he will sit loose from them. *Mal.* 3. 14. *Zach.* 11. 8. *My soul abhorred them, and they abhorred me*; not their own hearts, as it is with the soul and body, they are not knit one to the other immediately, but by spirits, which if they be extinct, then they fall asunder. Let a man have meat, and it not feed him, cloaths that cannot warme him, physick that cannot purge him, a Vineyard planted that never hath fruit on it, he will cast them off, and despise them; and this is the second step, the heaviest judgement of God on men for not loving the truth, but taking pleasure in unrighteousness; and this works thus especially, if they have had some trial of the people of God sometime, and after great expectations of receiving good from them, meet with but little; the Word, Sacraments, Fastings, hence come to be stones, not bread; the heaven of promises is Iron, and there is no raine falls on them; and hence they, 1. Carelesly refuse at sometimes to come to the fellowship of the Saints. 2. Hence if they do come, they come late. 3. If timely, yet without prayer, or prizing of them; they have felt no good, and now they expect little. 4. If conscience force to duties, yet they think them too tedious, or too frequent. *Ezekiel* 11. 21. they are losing, and dying, no man will tell you so particularly, but the Lord tells thee so now.

3. The Lord visits them with many sad and outward evils, and strange unexpected Trials, which they thought they could beare, but indeed cannot, puts them upon great losses, and leaves them to sad wants, their estates decay, they run into debt, and provisions are scarce, &c. and now they secretly repent themselves of the fellowship of Gods people, but accout their course and hazards they have run, either madness or rashness. *Moses Heb.* 11. 25. *did choose affliction and suffering*, that he lotted upon, and upon nothing else; hence forsook honour and preferments, and *pleasures*; men not doing thus, hence choose the world, and forsake the wayes of God; the *Israelites* brought to the Wilderness, they would go back; why? they questioned whether God was with them; why? because they wanted water, bread, and variety of blessings, *Numb.* 16. 13, 14. And this sets them off; as a man that loves his friend very well, but when he puts him to so much cost, and is so costly by his company, let him then even go; so do many men, the Lord and his Ordinances.

4. Hereupon they come to call all into question again, which were without question before, the wayes and Ordinances of God; What warrant now say they, have you for Covenant, such constitution of Churches, of

Saints,

Saints, strict examining of members? and why not a forme of Prayer? and why not a Ceremony lawful? and now they want but a temptation, and then they fall. 2 *Theſſ.* 2. 10. *They receive not the truth in love;* Why not? becauſe they feel loſs by the truth, or feel not the ſpiritual good of the truth, and hence are given up to believe *lyes*; the firſt beginning of which is to queſtion the Truth, not from tenderneſs of conſcience, though that be pretended, but from carnal luſt; and hence, *Ezekiel* 11. 24. whoſe heart goes after that deteſtable thing, and this they are hardned in; if any good men by violence of temptation fall therein. Thus men fall from fellowſhip, and ſit looſe; you will fall, if you look not to it (which I ſay is fearful) And as Chriſt ſaid, *By this ſhall all know you are my Diſciples, if you love*; ſo all men ſhall know you are none of Chriſts, if you fall here, if you ſit looſe, &c. I have been ſearching and diſcovering that which is working in ſundry, and lies as leaven, caſt it out of your doores.

Uſe 3.

We may ſee hence one juſt ground of that diligent and narrow ſearch and trial, Churches here do or ſhould make of all thoſe whom they receive to be fellow-members with them; the Lord Jeſus will make a very ſtrict ſearch and examination of wiſe and fooliſh, when he comes, and will put a difference between them then; may not men, not Churches imitate the Lord Jeſus according to their light now? If indeed all the Congregation of the baptized were holy, then as *Korah* ſaid, *They take too much upon them*; if Chriſt at his coming, would make neither examination, nor ſeparation, not only of people baptized at large, but of profeſſours, and glorious profeſſours of his Truth and Name; if Churches were not ſet to diſcerne between Harlots and Virgins, fooliſh Virgins and wiſe, as much as in them lies, that ſo ſome of the glory of Chriſt may be ſeen in his Churches here, as well as at the laſt day; then the gate might be opened wide, and flung off the hinges too for all comers; and you might call the Churches of Chriſt, the Inn and Tavern of Chriſt to receive all ſtrangers, if they will pay for what they call for, and beare ſcot and lot in the Town, and not the houſe and Temple of Chriſt only to entertaine his Friends. But (Beloved) the Church hath the keyes of the Kingdome of Heaven; and what they binde and looſe, following the example and rule of Chriſt is bound and looſed in Heaven, and they judge in the room of Chriſt. 1 *Cor.* 5. 4, 5. 2 *Cor.* 2. 10. Whom the Church caſts out, and bids depart to Satan, Chriſt doth; whom the Church receives to it ſelf, Chriſt doth; we ſhould receive in none but ſuch as have viſible right to Chriſt, and Communion of Saints. None have right to Chriſt in his Ordinances, but ſuch as ſhall have Communion with Chriſt at his coming to judge the World; hence if we could be ſo Eagle-eyed, as to diſcern them now that are Hypocrites, we ſhould exclude them now, as Chriſt will, becauſe they have no right; but that we cannot do, the Lord will therefore do it for his Churches; yet let the Churches learn from this, to do what they can for the Lord now.

There is a foure-fold Glory of Chriſt ſhining in his ſeparating fooliſh and wiſe at the laſt day; which when Churches imitate now, they hold out now.

Firſt, Hereby he ſhews his wiſdome, in diſcovering the ſecrets of darkneſs, and all the wily knots men have tyed, to hamper themſelves in their own miſeries; ſo Churches ſhew forth this wiſdome, not only in diſcovering ſuch whom you may feel to be hairy, rough *Eſaus* with Mittons on, but ſuch as have *Jacobs* voice, and are very wily when the ſecrets of his ſpirit

rit are dicovered, they will fay, if not proud and paffionate, God is in you; hence the wifdome of Chrift, *Rev. 2. 2.*

Secondly, Hereby the Lord Jefus fhews his holinefs, who withdrawes himfelf from thofe that are foolifh, though outwardly moft glorious; for he will be fanctified; fo the Churches fhadow out the holinefs of Chrift herein, who are bound to be holy as he is holy.

Thirdly, Hereby the Lord keeps the Communion of his Saints pure; this is a wonderful glory in Heaven, that only the Elect and faithful of God fhall lie down together; and is the laft and greateft glory that ever fhall be feen in this world, *Revelations 21. 27.* One man or woman fecretly vile, which the Church hath not ufed all means to difcover, may defile a whole Church, and bring it under wrath, as *Achan*, and make work and forrow enough for many a day and year after, and bring that blemifh and fcandal as will not eafily be worn off again, and then men will wifh that they had kept their communion pure.

Fourthly, Hereby the Lord abundantly vouchfafes his prefence to his people in Heaven, when the Goats are feparated; now come and take your fill of love, and poffefs your Kingdome; fo the Church hereby gaines more of the prefence of Chrift Jefus in publick and private; when *Judas* is gone out, now Chrift comforts the hearts of his Difciples; when the Lord hath his Spoufe alone, then he fports himfelf with her. *Ifaiah 4. 4. 5.* When all in *Jerufalem* are holy, there fhall be a Cloud and Pillar of fmoak on all their Habitations. And therefore not only the Churches fhould do thus, but a godly holy heart will defire it; it's the end of his coming that he may be fearched; better had men be tried and examined now, than by Chrift another day.

Objection 1. *But we muft look not to what may be done, but to what muft be done; Churches have power to caft out them that be bad, but what power to keep out them that be Baptized, and have a name to be good?*

Anfwer 1. Chrift doth not only fhut out Harlots, but profeffing Virgins; which example is to be imitated now fo farre as we can; for on the fame ground Chrift excludes, we have the fame if we know them.

2. The Apoftle is punctual for it, *2 Tim. 3. 5.* fpeaking of the laft dayes, *Having a forme of godlineß, turn away from fuch;* He faith not, Let them in, and turn to them; and if they prove evil members, cut them off, and turn them from you; but turn away from them; He faith not, If they be prophane, or not baptized, and cannot fay, I was humbled, and now I believe; but which is more, if they have a forme, under whofe garments of profeffion you will ever fee fome of thofe fores, *Pfal. 2. 3.*

3. *Rev. 2. 2.* It was accounted part of the wifdome and power of grace of the *Ephefine* Church which tried them which faid *They were Apoftles, and had found them lyars;* they could not creep in there, but they were found out.

4. In the *Jerufalem* come down from Heaven; it's part of the glory of it to caft out the unclean; but *Rev. 21. 27. nothing enters therein which is unclean;* and are not they to be imitated now in their glory, who are fet out for that end?

5. To omit all other proofs, fee *Ezekiel 44. 8, 9.* The Apoftle gives a fad charge, *Hebr. 12. 15. Look diligently, left a root of bitterneß grow up;* the Apoftle doth not fay, 'Tis no matter what roots you fet in Chrifts Garden; only when they fpring up, and begin to feed and infect others, then have a care of them; but look there be not a root there; truly fo we do

do; for they tell us they believe and repent, and we believe them, other strict inquiry we make not; Oh but faith he, *Look diligently to it*; it's ill counsel to the Gardner to say, have a care to weed your Garden; but 'tis no matter, God looks not that you should be careful of your seed, so long as it be seed; nay, the Lord that forbids me to suffer weeds to grow, forbids my carelessness in sowing what seeds I please.

It is the judgement of some Divines, That the first sin of *Adam* and his Wife, was in suffering the Serpent to enter into the Garden uncall'd for; the ruine of a Church may be the letting in of some ill member.

Objection 2. *But they that are innocent, and say they believe, are in the least degree of probability converted; and the best, we are but certain of their conversion in the highest degree of probability; and therefore may both sorts be admitted?*

Answer, No; *Paul* may feare with a godly jealousie some of the *Corinthian* Church, 2 *Cor.* 12. 20, 21. and may know some to be childish, and carnal, and weak, yet children; yet he calls them all Saints, and dares not mince his speeches with such notions of probability; and *Heb.* 6. 9. *We are perswaded better things of you*; A moral certainty a man may have, and should have of all Church-members; a certainty of faith, conditional, though not absolute; as if it be thus as they say, and I cannot, ought not to say otherwise of them, 'tis well with them.

Objection 3. *But the Primitive Church never received in any with such strict confessions, and large examinations; three thousand in a day were admitted.*

Answer, I remember a godly Divine in answering an Objection of late repentance from the example of the Thief; having whipt it with many other Rods, at last lasheth it with this, it's an extraordinary case; and hence not to be brought in for an ordinary example; hence he speaks thus, When therefore the time comes that Christ shall come and be crucified again, and thou one of the Thieves to be crucified with him, and it fall out that thou be the best of the two, then shalt thou be saved by Christ; that despising Christ now, puts off thy repentance till then; So I say here, there is somewhat imitable and ordinary in the Apostles example, in admitting three thousand in a day, but something unusual, and farre different from our condition now; and therefore this I would say when the time comes, that the Spirit is poured out on all flesh; and that time is known to be the Spring-tide, and large measure of the Spirit, when Ministers are so honoured as to convert many thousands at a Sermon; and so God and reason call for quickness; when Elders of Churches are as sharp-sighted as the Apostles; when the conversion of men also shall be most eminent, and that in such places where 'tis death, or half hanging, to profess the Lord Jesus, as that they shall be prickt at their hearts, gladly receive the Word, lay down their necks on the block, cast down all their estates at the Churches feet, out of love to Gods Ordinances; when men shall not have Christian education, the example and crowd of Christians from the teeth outwardly to press them to the door of the Church, as those times had not; then for my part, if three hundred thousand were converted, I should receive them as gladly and as manifestly as they receive Christ; but truly, there is such little takings now, that we have leisure enough to look upon our money, and the Hypocrisie of the world gives us good reason to stay and see; yet we grant *Simon* believes also; and if he doth deceive the Apostles eyes for a time, let him come in, and tell him of his gall of bitterness afterward; and if he be not obstinate, but intreats Prayers, Charity hopes the best, and lets him stay in, *Matthew* 3. 7.

Obj. 4. *But you may in weeding out the Tares, pull up the Wheat, and keep out the godly in such strict searchings.*

Answ. 1. Tis true; and the want of tenderness and love to them that be Christs Lambs and Babes, having much ignorance, and carnalness, out of zeal in some, not guided aright; and pride in others, despising those that are of meaner gifts than themselves; or because of some weaknesses, which if they were convinced of, would soon lament and amend; and to be so rigorous toward them, will not be suffered by Jesus Christ, if continued in by Churches; Hence Churches must be Watchful against this: And then

2. If they follow the light, are weak with them that are weak, and strong with them that be strong, and are all things to all men, and gain all to Christ; look as the receiving of ill members shall not be laid to their charge to hurt them, so not the excluding of some that are good. And this I'le add, The Lord may see in some good people that are : bout to joyn themselves to the Church, that which makes them fit to destroy a Church; not to build up a Church, as in case of some secret sin not sufficiently repented of, and some decay of the first love, *Rev.* 2. 5. and the Lord by this means may recover them by Word or Rod under witness of the Church against them; and hence many say, If I had then come in, I should have been proud and vile.

Obj. 5. *But there are many odd confessions by those that are received, and extravagant enlarged discourses of the set time of their conversion, and their Revelations, and ill Application of Scripture which makes such long doings, and are wearisome and uncomely.*

Answ. So I would say, There may be many weaknesses in an Ordinance, shall I therefore despise or cast off an Ordinance? I could then cast away all, and my own life, and soul too, when I had done; No, lament them, and heale them. I confess it is not fit that so holy and solemn an Assembly as a Church is, should be held long with Relations of this odd thing and tother, nor hear of Revelations and groundless joyes, nor gather together the heap, and heap up all the particular passages of their lives, wherein they have got any good; nor Scriptures and Sermons, but such as may be of special use unto the people of God, such things as tend to shew, Thus I was humbled, then thus I was called, then thus I have walked, though with many weaknesses since, and such special providences of God I have seen, temptations gone through, and thus the Lord hath delivered me, blessed be his Name, &c.

I have done; let all Gods people, Watchmen on Gods walls, still be watchful and careful; there be temptations enough to make men fill and pester Gods House with Swine; one hath his friend, and his affection leads him; another he is a man of estate, and his money is in the mouth of his Sack; another thinks there is one bad enough, but we shall do well enough with them; Oh take heed of these things! methinks a godly man should abhor the opinion, at least, if it was but for this reason; *viz.* it is so suitable First, To a proud man; shall I stoop to Churches, and give an account of my heart and course to them? I am as good as they. Secondly, To Apostates from Churches; who when they are gone, then they give way to these conceits, You are too strict, and are loth to confess their falls afterward. Thirdly, And Libertines, who cry out, Why shut you your Gates so close, that Swine and Sheep, Sheep and Goats, and all their Herds and Herdsmen come not in? No, the Lord will separate one day; do what you can therefore, you that are in Christs stead now.

Boast not of Church-priviledges only, I am a Church-member, and now all is well; say not, *We have Abram to our Father*; cry not the Temple of the Lord, and all the Christians in the Church think well of me; for Christ Jesus will make a separation one day (all is not Fish that comes to the Net) and then better never have known what Church fellowship means, and yet be all the while a stranger to Christ; thou thinkest all have given their approbation of thee; so in charity they may; but yet it may be some have had secret feares, and doleful thoughts of thy estate; and what have they done? Even as we do with those we cannot cast by any inferiour Courts, we put them over to be tried by the Highest Court of the Kingdome; and that is very dreadful, if their case be bad; so here, one thinks it a shame to live out, and hence for to serve his honour, sets himself up there; another wants Marriage, and that's the way to it; another thinks of his gaine in a Town, in Fields, or in shop, hence desires it; anothers conscience is only troubled for want of a Sacrament, hence would come in, and there they sit still; oh take heed of this.

Hence see there is need of conversion in some Church-members; Did you ever see a Church-member converted? said one, as if then the bitterness of death was past, when once in the Church; some should look about them herein; I'le only give this Rule, Be alway converting, and be alway converted; turn us again O Lord; When a man thinks, I was humbled and comforted, I'le not lay all by, and so live on old Scraps; Oh beware of that frame! not that a Christian should be alwayes pulling up foundations, and ever doubting; but to make sure, be alway converting, more humble, more sensible of sinne, more near to Christ Jesus, and then you that are sure, may be more sure; and you that are not, may be sure indeed.

Of thankfulness to all Gods people called to Christ, that he should make a separation between you and others; this is the wonder and Diamond of Gods Ring of love compassing all the Saints, in separating them from others. *Mal.* 1. 1, 2, 3. *Was not Esau Jacobs brother?* yet I loved one, and hated the other. Psal. 78. 67, 68. *He chose not the Tribe of Ephraim, but Judah*; and there was *Sion*, and there *David*; so for the Lord to choose thee, and leave so many thousands in the World, is mercy; but to choose thee, and leave many of the Town where thou livest, that's more; that had some meanes, and were better in birth, place, and parts, than thee; but to choose thee from thy friends, two grinding in a Mill, and lying in a bed, one taken, tother left, is more; but of professors, and glorious ones too, whom thou dost highly esteem, to choose thee, and leave them; to open to thee, and shut the door against them, this is indeed wonderful! if thou art one of these, he hath made thee thankful for it; Oh this the mark and Crown of glory, and fruit of the Lords old love, for his opening of thy eyes, and changing thy heart, and giving thee rest and peace on his Son.

VERSE 13. *Watch.*

THat all the Churches of God are bound to be very watchful, by considering the Parable of these foolish Virgins.
Quest. 1. *Against what shall they watch?*
Answ. 1. Against security, and dead-heartedness.

Cccc

2. Against sleightness and shallowness of the work of grace in them.

Quest. 2. *For what should they watch?*

Answ. For the blessed appearing, and glorious coming of Christ Jesus. at his first coming, 1 *Pet.* 1. 10, 11, 12. they searched after, and waited for his coming, and rejoyced to see that day; so should we now for his second.

Use. Of exhortation to these Churches in *N. E.* Oh be watchful,

First, Against security. Motives.

1. Because 'tis the last sin as you have heard, which surprizeth Saints; a Christian at first conversion, strives and gets mastery over many sins, but some are very hard, that he cannot overcome them ; and because he cannot, hence like the *Israelites*, he is ready to think the worst is past, and I cannot be better; and hence lies secure, and makes truce with sin.

2. 'Tis a very dangerous sin ; What temptation may not a man fall into, and be overcome with, when he is sleepy and secure ? A strong man that is asleep, may not a childe, any weak enemy cut his Throat, or pick his Pockets ? it may be when awakened he may recover his losses, but it is sad for the present with him ; so here.

3. It is a most bewitching sin ; because nothing is so sweet as sleep, and the sweeter, the stronger, and the worse.

4. 'Tis the temptation of this place. 1. Because when Churches grow secure, then all begin to slumber; else one might awaken all. 2. Because here's peace ; we have our ease, and our pillows, and feather-beds, and are out of the noise of persecution ; and hence sleep, and watch not ; are secure and dead-hearted, and pray not ; our hearts dye, and prayers dye by this means. 3. Because of many sad wearisome Trials, and heavy loads ; 'tis hard to live for some, and their bodies are weak, and cares, and distractions many, and griefs from servants rudeness, &c. exceeding ; and debts come upon men ; sorrow made the Disciples eyes heavy, *Luke* 22. 45. The poor loaden horse when spur-gall'd, and the Load heavy, and Legs weary, he will lie down in the high way, till rest and provender be given him.

5. Oh therefore blessed are ye if you endure temptation, and watch one hour in this place and time. I tell you the Lord will set thee down, and serve thee, and give thee what thou callest for.

Secondly, Against sleightness, and an hoverly work ; Motives.

1. Many looking after Christ, deceive themselves here; here is their wound; they have some taste of sins bitterness, and some taste of Christ, and some affections; but the life of Christ they want ; not that all must have the same measure ; but consider of what hath been opened to you ; Oh these colours, formes, and figures, and images, and pageants, and pictures, and names, and paints, and gildings, are the undoing of many.

2. Consider the example of *David*, who though a Prophet, yet desires, *O that I might see the Lord in his house*! *Paul* reached after more and more ; as for his prize, he made work of it.

3. Christ is full, and hath enough Spirit ; oh therefore seek for more ! if you know this gift, and ask, he will give Rivers of waters ; Young Christians, look to your selves as you wax old ; what is become of your gold ? why doth Copper appear now, in comparison of what it hath been (it may be) formerly?

Thirdly, For Christs coming ; Motives.

1. This is the beginning of glory ; *Adam* looked only for his happiness in an earthly Paradise, but you are heirs of an heavenly, *Tit.* 2. 13.

2. You have nothing else to look for ; if only of the things of this world you might look for your portion here, it were another matter ; but now when

called

called, juftified, fanctified, fin warring againft thee, and nothing but thy body and breath between thee and Chrift ; oh look after it.

3. Sorrows in the Country cry for it ; we think within few years the Land will be out of heart , and want of cloaths , or not money to buy , or pay debts, and this and t'other evil will enfue ; fo for particular perfons , What fhall I do hereafter ? &c. True, but glory will pay for all at Chrifts coming.

4. All Saints ever looked for this long ago ; the *Corinthians* , 1 *Cor.* I. 7. and the *Theffalonians*, 1 *Thef.* 1. *ult.* and the *Philippians*, *Phil.* 3. 20, 21. grace teacheth men fo to do , *Tit.* 2. 13. and promife of mercy is made to fuch only , *Heb.* 9. *ult.* and hence *Rev.* 22. the Church cryes out , *Come Lord, come quickly* ; Oh wait for this time when he fhall Redeem , comfort, glorifie, free from all fnares and fins ; if no hope in this life, of all men moft miferable ; fome young ones think 'tis too foon ; old men that are near do it ; many have bufineffes, and cannot ; cannot you carry it to the fields, and rejoyce in expectations of this , but muft be alwayes caft down ? &c. O teach it your Children ; fpeak of it one Brother to another ; fome of you are poor and mourning, oh be comforted , 'tis for your fake Chrift will come, and refrefh, and wipe away your tears.

Thus I have finifhed this Parable ; there are divers and many Interpretations hereof given by fome , but I fpeak what I believe ; I differ in nothing but ever gave reafon.

And verily if you regard not, the Lord fhall bring all thefe things as Witneffes againft you another day; I believe it fhall not be without fome fruit ; give him the glory that gives it.

FINIS.

AN ALPHABETICAL TABLE,

Shewing the chief Heads contained in this TREATISE.

An Alphabetical Table.

An Alphabetical Table.

An Alphabetical Table.

FINIS.